Contemporary Kazakh Literature
Prose Anthology

RÝHANI
JAŃǴYRÝ

The project
«Modern Kazakh Culture in the Global World»
has been realised upon the initiative of the First President of
the Republic of Kazakhstan – Elbasy (Leader of the Nation)
Nursultan Nazarbayev within the framework of the State Programme
Rýhani Jańǵyrý (Spiritual Rebirth – Modernisation of
Kazakhstan's Identity)

Contemporary
Kazakh
Literature | Prose

This book is commissioned by the Ministry of Culture and Sport of the Republic of Kazakhstan

©Ұлттық Аударма Бюросы (National Bureau of Translations) 2019

18 Dostyk Street, Office 25, Nur-Sultan, Esil District, The Republic of Kazakhstan

https://100kitap.kz/kz

This book is published by 'Ұлттық Аударма Бюросы' қоғамдық қоры (Public Foundation National Bureau of Translations) working in partnership with Cambridge University Press.

The publishers would like to acknowledge the support of the Chairman of Rýhani Jańgyrý National Commission Marat Tazhin, the Secretary of the National Commission Aida Balayeva, and the assistance of the following individuals: Khaliolla Baimen, Dauren Boranbaev, Assiya Issemberdiyeva, Aigul Kemelbayeva, Rauan Kenzhekhanuly, Gaukhar Khalyk, Timur Muktarov, Zira Nauryzbayeva, Umit Tazhken, Zhibek Tileshova, Roman Tokbergenov, Aknur Toleubayeva, Alikhan Tuiebay, Murat Yergaliyev, Zemfira Yerzhan.

First published in 2019

Printed in the United Kingdom by Latimer Trend

ISBN 978-601-7943-60-8

**NATIONAL
BUREAU
OF TRANSLATIONS**

If we want to be a nation with a unique place on the global map of the 21st century, we should implement one more project – Modern Kazakh Culture in the Global World. We need the world to know about us not only because of oil resources and major foreign policy initiatives, but because of our cultural achievements as well. First, we need a targeted approach in order to make our domestic culture better known in the six UN languages: English, Russian, Chinese, Spanish, Arabic, and French.

For the first time our culture will be known in all continents and in all main languages.

First President of the Republic of Kazakhstan – Elbasy
Nursultan Nazarbayev

CONTENTS

CONTENTS

A NOTE ON TRANSLITERATION

The international *ISO 9 standard of Romanizing the Cyrillic Characters* has been applied while transliterating the Kazakh terms, geographical and personal names. The fact that this norm has been developed by the International Organization for Standardization and adopted by a number of countries in Europe and Asia as a main tool in transliterating the Cyrillic characters into Latin characters has been taken into consideration. Moreover, the Euro-Asian Council for Standardization, Metrology and Certification of 9 CIS countries adopted *The System of Standards on Information, Librarianship and Publishing Rules of Transliteration of Cyrillic Script by Latin Alphabet* in 2000, authentic to the ISO 9 standard.

The Kazakh government has been developing a Latin alphabet for the Kazakh language which, it is planned, will replace the current Cyrillic script in 2025. Although the new version of the alphabet was published in 2018, the grammar is yet to be developed. The current standard of transliteration of Kazakh terms is used in order to avoid any misspellings and discrepancies in the future.

However, while transliterating the names of contemporary Kazakh authors, their own preferred spellings through which they are recognised internationally have been applied.

Russian terms, geographical and personal names have been transliterated according to the *BGN/PCGN Romanization System for Russian* widely used elsewhere.

FOREWORD

I am delighted that this exceptional anthology of Kazakh prose is being published in English for the first time. Kazakhstan has an incredibly rich and deep literary heritage, from folktales of the steppe to epic poems and from *ajtys* narrative singing to modernist short stories and novels. But until now, readers in English have been denied the opportunity to access the great trove of Kazakh literature, as it remained largely untranslated.

As such, this anthology represents a new epoch, in which a range of Kazakh literary voices from the twentieth century can be discovered and appreciated by readers the world over. It is one of the many exciting products of President Nazarbayev's 'Rýhani Jańgyrý' initiative, an ambitious programme to revive, modernise and internationalise the Kazakh cultural sector, while burnishing the best of Kazakh heritage and national identity.

These short stories and novellas vividly conjure life in the *auyls* – the famous Kazakh steppe villages – with tales of tribal rifts, hardships and migrations, filial separation and reunion. But they also chart the impact of modernisation and geo-politics, with stories of life under Soviet rule, militarisation, nuclear contamination, and the draw of late-twentieth century urbanisation. Above all, these are stories of fortitude, wit and ingenuity in the face of adversity, laced with folk wisdom; indeed, the anthology is an indispensable repository of Kazakh aphorisms and there are helpful footnotes providing historical and cultural context.

I am thrilled that the authors within these pages are taking their rightful place in the pantheon of world literature. A nation's literature gives voice to its people. It transcends time, summoning the past to life before our eyes. It flies across borders, piercing the hearts of readers in distant lands. In this way, this wonderful anthology brings us closer together, cultivating friendly knowledge and understanding between the people of Kazakhstan and the rest of the world. As such, it is to be hoped that this anthology is not a destination, but a vital first step on a journey for English-speaking readers into Kazakh literature, a tantalising glimpse of what is to come.

Sir Ciarán Devane, FRSA
Chief Executive of the British Council

SHERKHAN MURTAZA
(28.09.1932 – 8.10.2018)

Sherkhan Murtaza was a Soviet Kazakh writer, politician and public figure. He studied journalism at Lomonosov Moscow State University and graduated in 1955. He began his career as a literary critic and newspaper correspondent (1955–62). Subsequently, he was editor-in-chief of the Žalyn almanac (1971–72), secretary of the Writers' Union of the Kazakh SSR, and editor-in-chief of the *Žuldyz* journal (1973–80) as well as *Ķazaķ ădebieti* (1980–89) and *Socialistik Ķazaķstan* (now *Egemen Ķazaķstan*: 1989–92) newspapers. He was also chairman of the State Committee for Television and Radio Broadcasting (1992–94). Murtaza was a People's Deputy of the Kazakh Soviet Socialist Republic (1990–94), member of the Supreme Soviet of the Republic of Kazakhstan (1994–95), deputy of Măžilis (Mazhilis), the lower house of the Parliament of Kazakhstan, and chairman of the Committee for Culture, Literature and Art (1999–2004).

His first book, *Ķurylysšy Dăku* (Dăku the Builder), was released in 1958, followed by *Tabylġan teņiz* (The Sea Discovered, 1963), *Bultsyz kùngi najzaġaj* (Lightning in the Clear Sky, 1965), *Belgisiz soldattyņ balasy* (The Unknown Soldier's Son, 1967), *Myltyķsyz majdan* (The War Without Weapons, 1969), *Ķyryķ birinši žylġy kelinšek* (The Woman of '41, 1972), *Ahmetžannyņ anty* (Ahmetžan's Vow, 1973), *Internat nany* (The Boarding School, 1974), among others. His novel *Ķara maržan* (Black Pearl, 1976) won the State Prize of the Kazakh SSR in 1978 and his epic novel *Ķyzyl žebe* (The Red Arrow) was published to wide acclaim (1980–84).

He was designated a People's Writer of Kazakhstan (1992), a People's Writer of the Kyrgyz Republic and an Honoured Worker of Culture of the Kazakh SSR (1984). He was awarded the Ķurmet and Otan orders (1999), as well as the Independent Tarlan Award (2000).

Bojtůmar

How sweet it is to sleep at sunrise! At first, I tell myself: 'Just a bit longer, just a little bit more', and carry on lying there. But still, somewhere deep inside, piercing through the thick, drowsy layer of sleep, something keeps on nagging at me: 'Get up, you'll be late for work, get up'. But I think: 'Just a bit longer, just a little bit more.'

The red bull calf is licking my hair again. 'Go to hell, damn you', I mutter, not completely awake yet, 'I could just cut out that scratchy tongue of yours...' I finally lose patience and, still lying there with my eyes closed, I free my hand from under the blanket and fling it upwards really, really hard...

'Oho, just look at this bold horseman's fancy capers!' I hear a familiar voice say. And only then do I open my eyes – there, kneeling down beside me, is one-armed Siâķůl. His beautiful, slightly watery eyes, the colour of bird cherries, are narrowed in a smile. His little goatee beard is trembling, clearly in laughter, and he is stroking my hair with his only hand. This time the red bull calf had nothing to do with it.

It was the hour when the first pale light of dawn in the east has just lit up the peak of Manas with its rose-pink rays. The day has not yet begun in earnest, but the very first thing the Sun's rays do is light up Manas. In these parts there is no summit higher than this peak among the Celestial Mountains.[1] It greets the Sun's rays earlier than all the other peaks and is the very last of all to bid them farewell.

Although the time of year was late July to early August, the heat had not abated as yet. That was why we slept outside, laying out our mattresses in the courtyard. Completely awake now, I looked around. Ajša had already milked the cow and tethered the red bull calf firmly to the stake. The red cow was already plodding off in the direction of the pasture.

'Hey, foreman, is it really a good idea to send a feather-headed young lad on a long journey? Can't anyone else be found in this *auyl*?'[2] asked Ajša, starting

---

[1] Aspantau or Tăņirtau, as Tien Shan is known in Kazakh. Manas – a 4482-metre high peak of Tien Shan. [Ed.]

[2] *Auyl* – socio-economic formation considered to constitute the heartland of the nation and a basis for an ethnic and cultural union of the nomadic community. Consisting of 50–70 yurts in the eighteenth century, it developed into its current permanent state of 'rural settlement' (of a minimum of 100 dwellers) when Kazakhs adopted a settled mode of life in the nineteenth and twentieth centuries. *Auyl* can also be used as a synonym for 'native land' and 'homeland', concepts revered by the Kazakhs.

up her old song again. She had driven the cow out past the edge of the *auyl* and was already walking back. Now she would take a hasty gulp of tea from her tea bowl and set out for the beetroot field.

When Ajša said 'on a long journey', I gave a start and instantly jumped to my feet. 'A long journey' was my dearest dream. What could be tougher than working on the threshing floor – heaping up the stones and unloading the wheat,[3] spinning round and round like an ass who turns the water wheel from morning till evening in the sultry heat? If they let me go off on 'a long journey', I would take wing like a bird.

Seeing me leap off my bed in confusion, one-armed Siâk̦ùl brightened up and his moist eyes narrowed in a smile again.

'Oh, my bold horseman! My intrepid tiger! Now there's a truly dashing hero! Who but this bold tiger would dare set out for Tobyšak̦ty with his Atalyk̦ *ata*?'[4]

'Let his own child go!' Ajša objected shrewishly, wrapping a bottle of *šalap*[5] and a thin bread cake in a towel made of unbleached linen. 'His son's the same age as this boy here.'

'Oh, *žeņeše*,[6] why say that, when you already know?' the foreman asked, shaking his head mournfully on his matchstick-thin neck. 'Atalyk̦'s son Sùlejmen is really sick.'

Ajša fell silent. That was probably a way of conceding defeat in an argument. A habit of women in wartime: first, they would start arguing fiercely with the foreman to vent their exasperation, and then they would give way and go off to carry out their instructions.

A stripped bullock cart with its shelter removed was standing beside Atalyk̦ house and a pair of piebald bullocks, regarded as the strongest in the collective farm, had been harnessed to it. When he saw me standing there with one-armed Siâk̦ùl, Atalyk̦ sagged downwards, as if trying to stretch his back, then lifted his chest up slightly and then hunched over again, trembling in silent laughter and wiping his half-closed eyes with his sleeve.

When Atalyk̦ *ata* stretched up to his full height, he stood as tall as two metres. But fate, evidently having guessed that he would not be able to walk in and out of the low doorways of the squat houses in Myņbùlak̦, had made him stooped over and bent like a question mark. And indeed, perhaps fate really had created him as a question to which no answer could be found. But how could I have known that?

'Well then, you misbegotten youngster, so you've shown up then?'

---

[3] This refers to a traditional method of threshing: horses dragging large stones walk in circles on the grain laid out on a hard surface.

[4] *Ata* – lit. 'grandfather'; respectful form of address to an older man.

[5] *Šalap* – a drink, *ajran* (sour drink made of cow, sheep or goat milk fermented with lactic bacteria) diluted with water.

[6] *Žeņeše* – form of address to an older sister-in-law or, generally, an older married woman.

3

'There, uncle, no better travelling companion could possibly be found for you than Baryshan here', said one-armed Siâḳûl, boasting to his uncle as if he had performed some heroic feat the day before.

We walked out into the road. Sùlejmen, a boy the same age as me, was standing there near the house, haggard and exhausted, leaning his thin shoulder against the fence and coughing as he sadly watched us go. And he waved his hand as if he was seeing us off to the front line.

The bullocks were moving at an agonisingly slow pace. Ataly*ḳ ata* had said that we would cover a fair distance in the coolness of the morning, but we were still making our way out of the *auyl* and the Sun had already managed to creep up to ten o'clock and started warming the tops of our heads. As if sensing that its end was near, the summer exhaled a final breath of scorching heat. The winding country road kept climbing uphill, on and on. The rear left wheel of the bullock cart screeched like a painful tooth and then started squeaking. I remember the landscape I saw when I looked around – there were five or six houses hidden along each ravine and hollow of Myŋbùlaḳ, but the *auyl* itself had remained somewhere down below. That was how high we had climbed. A flock of blue-grey pigeons that had made the ascent with us, seemingly unable to bear the snail's pace any longer, easily outpaced us and settled on the greyish hills, soaring back up into the air when we approached and flying on along the road without turning, as if this was a race, galvanising the trudging bullocks and urging them on: hurry up, hurry up!

Suddenly, there appeared before us a ravine with shallow inner slopes and edges that reared up sharply. Surrendering to the steep gradient, the cart started picking up speed of its own accord, so that the yoke rammed hard against the horns of the bullocks, threatening to send them tumbling down and forcing the slouches to pick up their pace. The bottom of the ravine was broad, and its bed was entirely covered with immense boulders. These rocks had evidently come tumbling to this place in mudslides. Running along the bottom of the ravine, glittering like silver, was a pristine stream. Without pausing for thought, the bullocks immediately lowered their heads and started straining water in through their teeth, carrying on like that for a long time. The old man and I got off the cart. We sat down on a little meadow of fragrant mint and trees with dense foliage, and set about our meal. For lack of anything else to do, I started looking around at the dense thickets of meadowsweet on the slopes of the ravine; suddenly, red marmots appeared before my eyes and I jumped to my feet like a scalded cat.

'What do you see over there?' asked the *ata*, alarmed by my sudden movement.

'Marmots, *ata*, red marmots!'

'Where?' he asked again, shielding his watery eyes with his open hand.

'There's one, standing to attention on that rock over there. The others have divided into pairs, and they're wrestling with each other.'

'I see something misbegotten flickering about in front of my eyes', Atalyķ *ata* replied and laughed.

Then, after thinking for a while, he added:

'The marmots have put on fat now. Eh, if I could just catch one, its meat would make genuine medicine for my Sùlejmen ...'

Sùlejmen's gaunt face rose up in my mind's eye: I saw this boy who was my own age hobbling towards me, barely able to stay on his feet, waving his hand in farewell. He was gasping for breath, coughing violently and streaming with sweat for no reason at all. He watched, sad and curious, as his father took me instead of him on this long journey.

'You were born within a week of each other', the *ata* said, recalling the event of thirteen years before. 'I think Sùlejmen is a day or two older than you, or maybe you were born first? I don't know for sure, I only remember that it happened in September, when we all went out to harvest the millet. Well then, my misbegotten small-fry, so now you two have passed the first threshold of your life at twelve years. You'll be grown-up men soon enough, God willing... Listen, at thirteen your father became master of hearth and home', he suddenly exclaimed, switching to a playful tone, and a rush of blood reddened his face. 'What if we help you find your feet and marry you off, eh? Why couldn't we come back from Tobyšaķty with a girl you take a liking to?'

'No need for that', I blurted out, looking in the direction of the marmots.

'What does that mean, no need?' the old man exclaimed, laughing his soundless laugh and wiping away the tears that had sprung to his eyes. 'Oh, you fool, what does that mean, no need, eh?'

Hoping to distract him from his guileless joke, uttered without any ulterior motive whatsoever, I suggested:

'*Ata*, why don't we shoot some marmots? Then there'd be something to bring back to Sùlejmen ...'

At that, the old man really did forget his joke in an instant.

'My eyes have grown weak. Make sure you don't shoot someone by accident. Don't bring down misfortune on yourself. Stay well clear of disaster.'

'Oi, *ata*, Tarbaķbaj *aġa*[7] taught us how to fire a rifle at school...'

'What's he doing teaching you that? Are they really teaching children to shoot now?'

'But we have to be able to shoot! If the war goes on, we'll be called up into the army, too. So, they teach us.'

'What are you blathering about? If they call all of you up, who'll be left? What then, will that be the end of our bloodline? Bite your tongue for saying that, don't go babbling anything that comes into your head!'

Atalyķ *ata* was furiously angry. But even so, he hobbled across, hunched over, to the front of the bullock cart and pulled the old, black Berdan rifle that

---

[7] *Aġa* – respectful form of address to an older man, which can be translated as 'brother', 'uncle'.

one-armed Siâkul had given him before we started out from its secure hiding place under the heaped-up hay, where I would never have found it. 'Be careful it doesn't go off by accident.'

When the gun was already in my hands and I had composed myself, I felt really cocksure, fancying that I was an important man. I wanted to prove to everyone that Tarbakbaj *aga's* lessons had not been a total waste of time. Jerking the breechblock open with a clatter, I glanced into the chamber. I knew that on the end of the cartridge there was a tiny little cap the size of a lentil, called the percussion cap. Moving the breechblock back into place, I glanced towards the marmots – the lookout was still jutting up on the grey boulder. It looked as if he had grown used to the sight of us and wasn't afraid. As if checking whether there was any danger from a different direction, he was now standing sideways to us, frozen to the spot like a sentry...

If I had tried to sneak up, they would get suspicious and dive into their burrows. And anyway, the distance seemed a bit too far for that. Trusting my luck, under the cover of the bullock cart, I trained the rifle on the lookout marmot, aiming below his belly button. That was the way Tarbakbaj *aga* had taught us to do it in our shooting lessons, saying that the semicircle of the sight should always be lined up with the lower edge of the target.

The crash of the shot seemed to set all of the Celestial Mountains tottering. At first, I couldn't make anything out because of the pall of blue smoke emitted by the rifle. Atalyk *ata* stood there, rooted to the spot and pressing his palm against his ear, which had been half-deaf for a long time anyway, repeating over and over again: '*Bismillah, bismillah*'.[8] Looking towards the grey boulder, I saw a dark stain on its edge. All the other marmots had instantly dived into their burrows and disappeared.

Taking hold of the back legs of the red marmot, which was the size of a small dog, I dragged it back to the bullock cart and dropped it in front of Atalyk *ata*.

'Before we go, I'll bag you another one', I blurted out, unable to resist indulging the pride that was brimming over inside me.

Instead of rejoicing, the *ata* seemed at a loss.

'Ah, that's a pity, we shouldn't have done that', he said, turning the limp marmot over this way and that, running his palm remorsefully over its glittering sides, its gilded belly and bluish-red fur, and then he added: 'It turns out that she's a mother.'

'Then her cubs have grown up.'

'Darling boy, they say that this animal originated from man in ancient times. God's curse fell on him, and he became a little gnawing beast. You saw for yourself, the cubs are just like human children, you saw the amusing way they were straining so hard, fighting with each other. Maybe everything does

---

[8] *Bismillah* – the first word in Qur'an; it means 'In the name of Allah'.

flicker in front of my eyes, but even I spotted that. I hope no curse comes of it. I shouldn't have allowed you to shoot, oh, that was wrong of me...'

'*Ata*, that's not right...' I said, gasping for breath. 'I read somewhere in a book that in the far north, where the sledges are pulled by dogs, the Yakut-*sakha* first shoot a deer and then, when they're butchering the carcass, they say: "Forgive us, deer, it wasn't us who shot you, it was the Tungus people, and we just found you." So why don't we say: "Forgive us, red marmot, it wasn't us who shot you, it was Žoldashan, and we found you on the road."'

Atalyķ *ata* chuckled with his soundless laugh.

'So, my misbegotten friend, you want to dump the blame on Žoldashan, do you? The two of you and Sùlejmen are *ķirdases*.[9] And just look at the airs they put on over how to be a proper *ķirdas*! But that book of yours was printed in the language of infidels. There are no such words in the Qur'an.'

'Don't say that, *ata*. Last year, before you slaughtered your only lamb for Sùlejmen, you announced: "It's not your fault, little sheep, the children have nothing to eat."'

'Oh, my extraordinary counsellor, may the evil eye and malicious tongue never do you harm. If you live, you will achieve a great deal. May God protect you from defamation and slander, and from the horrors of war. May good fortune smile on my Sùlejmen, and may that be his healing', said Atalyķ *ata*, carefully placing the marmot beside the rifle under the hay on the cart.

We crossed the stream and made our way up the opposite slope of the ravine. And now the road wound its way between the sides of hills, inclining in a westerly direction. In the distance we could see a blackish forest.

'*Ata*, is it still a long way to Tobyšaķty?'

'Don't you see the forest?'

'I see it, in the distance.'

'Then that means there's not far left to go. God willing, we'll get there shortly past noon.'

The old man started humming to himself, or rather, purring under his breath, with his eyes screwed up tight. He was holding a whip alright, but he didn't lash the bullocks even once. And as for the bullocks – beat them or not, they still wouldn't quicken their pace. Their measured, unhurried pace. The bushes of dark-red or rusty-brown meadowsweet growing along the sides of the road had been left behind us now. Red summer cypresses rose up to meet us, blazing like burning coal. The mulleins and desert candles had dropped their flowers long ago and their stiff upright forms displayed their thorns. Marjoram and dodartia, which bloomed so exuberantly in the spring, had faded now and were in the same unenviable condition as the feather grass. But the chicory flowers, scattered around on all sides, as blue as the azure of the

---

[9] *Ķirdas* – term for people of the same age or contemporaries. In Kazakh culture, relations between *ķirdases* are affectionate, allowing the taking of liberties and undue familiarity, and often accompanied with poking fun at each other.

heavens, inspired a feeling of joy. Here and there we came across lilies with white flowers the size of a hand that shimmered like ingots of silver. And larks sat on the tops of these plants, warbling their rippling melodies.

Remembering something important, Atalyķ shook off his drowsiness and said: 'If they send you off to the army, it means there are good grounds for doing it. You fired that rifle like a real expert – it was terrifying! Well, I never, though, are they really taking you? If they're taking boys – they'll take you. If this war doesn't end, they're bound to take you. It's been going on for more than three years, which makes this the fourth year already! Mm-yes, so it turns out they're ready to fight such long, bloody battles. A long, long time ago, I was the same age as you are now, and at that time there was the so-called Kokand War.[10] I think our Bajzaķ Datķa[11] went off to fight with that Kokand. Not even a week had gone by, when everyone started suing for a peaceful settlement, in a word, they all calmed down. To cap it all, Kokand killed Bajzaķ Datķa and they called it a day after that... But this war is just sheer horror. There hasn't been any word from our Ķajyp for a lo-ong, lo-ong time now. Look, I've got his latest letter in here. And by the way, instead of just sitting here idly, why don't we do something to while away the time? Come on, read it one more time.'

Unbuttoning his worn, black velvet *bešpet*[12] on his chest, Atalyķ *ata* thrust his hand under his greyish shirt, darkened with sweat, reached as far as the inside pocket sewn on under his left armpit, and pulled out his prayer beads. I was astounded that the old man hid his prayer beads away in a sack so deep that it could only be compared with a *ķyluet*.[13] The string of black and coloured beads was secured with a triangular leather *bojtümar*.[14] Clutching the beads and the *bojtümar* in his hand, Atalyķ *ata* pressed them to his forehead and then, unfastening the clasp of the *bojtümar*, with his finger and thumb pulled out a

---

[10] The khanate of Kokand was a Central Asian state in the Fergana Valley that existed from 1709 till 1876 on the territory of modern Kyrgyzstan, eastern Uzbekistan and Tajikistan and south-eastern Kazakhstan. (Source: *Aibyn encyclopedia*, ed. by B. Jaqyp, Almaty: Ķazaķ enciklopediasy, 2011; text transl. by the National Bureau of Translations.)

[11] Bajzaķ Mămbetùly, also referred to as Bajzaķ Datķa (1789–1864), is the hero of the national liberation struggle against the Kokand Khanate and the Russian Empire. (Source: Aibyn encyclopedia, ed. by B. Jaqyp, Almaty: Ķazaķ encyklopediasy, 2011; text transl. by the National Bureau of Translations.)

[12] *Bešpet* – light, embroidered, knee length outerwear worn over dress or t-shirt.

[13] *Ķyluet* – a secluded place, typically underground, for spiritual retreat and devotion oneself to Allah of a Sufi. There is only one known *ķyluet* in Kazakhstan, a hidden place under the mausoleum of Ahmed Âssaui (Akhmed Yassawi) in Tùrkistan.

[14] *Bojtümar* – talisman or amulet of a triangle or tubular form worn around the neck. It is a revered item which typically contains a paper with Qur'an verses wrapped in leather or fabric to ward troubles and misfortune off the wearer.

folded piece of paper. He unfolded the triangular letter, applied it to his lips and in his slightly trembling hands held it out to me.

'Here, read it again.'

The old man handed me that piece of paper with such great trepidation and apprehension (as if I was intending to tear it up, and the wild wind was intending to toss it away) that my fingers started quivering too. The letter had really and truly started coming apart at the folds. If it wasn't held with extreme caution, then Atalyk̦'s apprehensions could easily be proven correct. Carefully smoothing out the crumbling letter, I sat a bit further back in order not to fall off the cart, and had just prepared myself to read it, when the clattering and jolting of the damned wheels set the words in the letter skipping about, and my eyes couldn't keep track of them. The pause dragged out. At the thought that Atalyk̦ *ata* might take me for an illiterate oaf, perspiration sprang out on my little snub nose.

'A letter with wishes of good health', I shouted. Otherwise he wouldn't have heard.

More precious than gold, purer than silver, my worthy parents, my beloved little brother Sùlejmen and little sister Hanzada! I expect that in our native land you are successfully carrying out the tasks set by the party and the government, living in good health and in harmony... If you were to ask about my life, I would tell you that I am honourably fulfilling my duty to my Motherland, with my rifle gripped firmly in my hands, preparing a just retribution for the villainous enemy. After having emerged safe and sound from the bloody battle of Kursk, we are driving the cursed fascists farther back. It is true what they say: Fight for forty years, if you wish, in war the one who dies is the one whose death is preordained. At Kursk many of our young lads laid down their lives. And it seems to me that now, after miraculously escaping death in that massacre, I shall never die. Time does not allow me to write a lot. Please accept this brief message, written before the next attack, during the few short minutes of a brief lull. If God continues to preserve me from here on, then, after carrying out Comrade Stalin's order and crushing the enemy... If I get a chance after all this, I'll write a more heartfelt letter, more detailed than this one. May the Creator preserve you, until we meet in happiness again. Live in good health, my dear ones!

Written in a trench –
Guardsman K̦ajyp Ataly̦kov, 17 August 1943

Why doesn't he say anything? I thought, glancing at Atalyk̦ *ata*: he was weeping silently, taking no notice of the tears coursing down his beard. I folded up the letter and held it out to his hands. He briefly caressed the paper and sat there without speaking for a while, then hid it away in his concealed pocket.

9

After a while he asked:

'It's August already, but what date is it today?'

'The fifteenth.'

'Oi-ei-ei-ei, good grief, so this letter is already a year old! Eh?'

Not knowing what answer to give to that, I lowered my head. If no news had arrived for a whole year, then of course there was a good reason for that.

Narrowing his eyes, Atalyḳ *ata* turned his gaze towards the mountains.

'A man should never speak arrogantly. What was the poor soul trying to say when he declared "now I shall never die?" Those words were definitely given to him by Satan the Tempter. Ah, what kind of fool are you, if you have dared to go against the will of the almighty Creator? Ḳaj-y-yp!' he gasped with a sigh that rose to a scream.

The old man's bellow into the distant expanses of the steppe made me feel uneasy, setting tremors running across my body. Why had he shouted out so loudly, as if Ḳajyp could shout back from the remote distance?

It was getting close to midday. The Sun was shining with blinding brightness, piling on the heat. Even the roller bird sitting on the wall of an abandoned cattle pen was breathing heavily, with its beak open.

'Ah?!' – it was as if an immense flame had burst out of Atalyḳ. Even the roller bird, which had flown a good distance from the road, fluttered in alarm and went rushing away for dear life.

Not just an ordinary 'a' sound, but 'Ah?!' It wasn't a moan of grief, but a kind of question that was incandescent with wrath, a kind of command that was crushing in its fierce determination.

Now, I wanted only one thing – for him not to declaim another 'Ah?!' like that. I started feeling a bit scared.

There were only the steppe buzzards soaring above the ravine, where luscious wild alfalfa and clover grew, interspersed with foxtails and couch grass. Unable to lift anything bigger than a quail, the buzzards have a hard time surviving here. The flourishing of their wings and their soaring motion exuded an elusive flavour of sorrow, homelessness and orphanhood.

Everything around me suddenly became veiled in a shroud of sadness and the world hid its sunken eyes in weariness. Steppes withered by thirst, buzzards roaming in search of something to eat. An immature juvenile, a stooped old man. Only the Celestial Mountains were still and as sublime as ever. One glance at them uplifts your spirits. The Celestial Mountains can uplift you without words. Atalyḳ *ata* had never in his life been able to straighten up, but when he looked at the mountains and trumpeted out that 'Ah?!' of his, his hunched back seemed to grow stronger.

Then Atalyḳ *ata* started singing in a low voice. It was either in the Kazakh or the Kyrgyz language – I couldn't make that out:

If in dreams you melt away,
Only scales will show your weight.

10

If your youth is on the wane,
Do not repine at bitter fate.

You will suffer and repent,
Where now are joy and sweet delight?
If youth's days have all been spent,
Can borrowing more set things right?[15]

'Did you understand, eh, my misbegotten friend?' he said. Having noticed that I was sitting there completely at a loss, he asked this to feel out my mood a little.

Atalyķ *ata* cast a warm glance towards me, smiling benignly and warmheartedly, which also improved my mood somewhat. Everything around me no longer seemed so very melancholy and lachrymose. And even a buzzard, after first performing a couple of fine aerial somersaults, seemed to me to be gambolling in joy. Even the grasshoppers were not chirping quite so very tediously in the space they had occupied between the grey, salty soil and the withered saltbushes among the ruins of old houses, although they kept churning out exactly the same chirping sound. The swallows, who had gathered in a single colony on the top of the crooked clay wall, sat there for a while, then raised a deafening pandemonium and started soaring upwards chaotically, swooping down and circling round my head. Probably they were preparing to migrate.

The swallow is one of the blessed birds: it is willing to sacrifice itself for the love of its homeland. The fledglings born this year would devote all their strength to returning to their native parts next year. Many of them, exhausted by flying over the boundless ocean, would fail to reach their homeland, and perish. But those who did reach their native land would twitter their songs and whistle their virtuoso *kùjs*.[16]

If they were not sent plunging down into the watery abyss by savage exhaustion, they probably would reach their goal. But sometimes, entirely out of the blue, I am transfixed by sudden dread at Atalyķ *ata*'s cry of 'Ah?!' rising up in my soul.

***

Immediately after midday, we reached the dense forests of Tobyšaķty. A man, evidently the chairman of the forestry *auyl*, came out to greet us: his right eye goggled resolutely, his cheeks were red and his beard was streaked with grey. Foppishly flaunting his black velvet breeches, he courted Atalyķ *ata*'s attention

---

[15] From the poem 'Kim biler kimniṇ armanyn' ('Who Will Know Others' Dreams') by the Kazakh poet Tùtķabaj Imanbekov (1937–95), translated by NBT.

[16] *Kùj* – musical piece for traditional instruments.

11

zealously, bustling obsequiously and gushing profuse courtesies, uttering wishes for good health and spreading himself out like a pillow under his guest's head and a blanket under his guest's back. Only then was it revealed to me just how highly esteemed Atalyk̦ *ata* was. Recalling how we had sometimes interrupted him without listening – 'Ah, the deaf, old hunchback' – I felt my face blazing bright-red in shame.

After restoring his strength by regaling himself with tea, Atalyk̦ *ata* shouted, in the manner of old men who are hard of hearing:

'Hey, Saġymbek, it's time we were getting on our way. You get that blasted timber loaded up now.'

'Oi, Ateke,[17] the Sun is declining towards the end of day. While you are wending your way back at a snail's pace with those bullocks, night will fall. Stay for the night, and you can set off early in the morning', old Saġymbek rattled off in a loud shout, well aware of Atalyk̦ *ata*'s irascibility and deafness.

Atalyk̦ *ata* remained true to his habit, laughing soundlessly. In his heart he was clearly certain that he was producing loud sounds: soundless laughter is said to arise from a desire to suppress the shrill or peevish notes in one's voice, but who can tell? ...

'Hey, kinsman given to me by God, what is all this about staying for the night? Those two wretched bullocks bear all the burdens of the collective farm. If I don't get back today, then tomorrow, dear man, the work will come to a halt. And these logs of yours... If I don't get them there in time, they probably won't get our collapsed school finished on schedule. And the children's classes are only just around the corner. If the teaching year begins, and the school is still lying on its side, there'll be no hiding from shame. It will be like death.[18] Surely, to goodness, we can create the right conditions for the little kids whose fathers and older brothers are at the front? Eh? The school that those front-line soldiers had built with their own hands is in a state of ruin now! That's a bad sign.'

I just couldn't understand these grown-ups. I'm talking about one-armed Siâk̦ŭl now. He couldn't just simply explain at the beginning where I was going and what for. And now I saw that this journey of mine was directly concerned with our school. In the spring of that year heavy deluges of rain mixed with snow had lashed down for two or three days at a stretch, following which the roof of the school had collapsed, crashing down right in the middle of the classroom. God spared us and the collapse happened at night; if it had happened during the day, we would all have been caught under it. Then I would not have set out together with Atalyk̦ *ata* or arrived at Tobyšak̦ty. How bitterly miserable Ajša would have wept then! She didn't usually mince her words; I only had to slip away for a game of sheep's knucklebones, *asyk̦*, for her to grab a ladle and start chasing after me and swearing at the top of her voice: 'May

---

[17] Ateke – respectful form of address to someone called Atalyk̦.

[18] Referring to a Kazakh saying, 'shame is more powerful than death'.

you rot, blast and damn you!' – 'May Mother Earth take you for her own!' – 'May you be cursed, you good-for-nothing brat!' – 'You'll come to grief with those knucklebones, you'll get what you deserve!' and so on. But if I had been buried under the ruins of the school, if I had been left, as she put it herself 'before the age of thirteen, buried under thirteen rocks…' then I'd like to have seen how Ajša howled and wailed. Oi, what a foolish thing for me to say: how could I have seen it if I had died under the rocks? Do the dead feel how the living weep? If they do, then why don't they come back to life out of pity? And wouldn't Ḳajyp have come flying from afar if he had heard Atalyḳ's fatherly bawling? Stop now, don't just babble whatever comes into your head, who told you Ḳajyp has been killed?

I was completely beside myself, thinking that Atalyḳ *ata* could somehow intuitively have guessed these despicable thoughts of mine. But evidently he hadn't guessed; thrusting his stick behind his hunched back and squeezing it with both elbows, he stood there, casting occasional sideways glances at Saġymbek, who had hooked on his glasses. He was waiting for a reply.

'All right, Ateke, have it your own way. It's just that you got here a bit late, an infirm old man and an inexperienced youngster, so I thought you would have a really hard time of it at night. I'll get everyone together right away, old and young, I'll draft in everyone to load up the timber.'

***

Now it seemed that our aching tooth – the rear left wheel of the bullock cart – wasn't just squealing, but had started groaning quietly and interminably. It was a heavy load, thirty or forty trees had been piled on. And although they couldn't match the pine trees in thickness, the trunks that were conspicuously longer than the others drooped drown from the rear of the cart like naked legs, tracing out fanciful lines on the ground. Both beasts marched along like the collective farm's most precious assets, as if they were afraid of disgracing themselves in front of people, striding solemnly and maintaining their dignity until we had travelled a respectable distance from Tobyšaḳty.

Ah, the hardy, triple-strength bullocks of wartime! These days even in the countryside the young guys don't really know what a bullock is. But in the days of our childhood a bullock was a reality as significant as a K-700 tractor is for people today.

When the edge of the vast region of Aḳsu Žabaġly – the forest expanse of Tobyšaḳty – had been left behind us like a black mass in the distance, the Sun descended into its bosom; blood-red haze veiled the entire western world like a blanket and tinted the snowy peaks of the Celestial Mountains in warm tones. The black cloud above Tobyšaḳty, like a large felt mat that has caught fire when a yurt is being assembled, was completely covered in red hues. However, this reddish-pink world immediately dimmed as the black cloud from the west lowered, thickened and advanced against the projection of the eastern celestial

13

bastion. Before we realised what was happening, everything had been plunged into darkness, and the Celestial Mountains that we revered as sacred became invisible...

When the first drops of rain fell on the nape of my neck, the rain that we had been waiting for all summer, exhausted by drought, I fell face down, tucking my head under my shoulder, and lay quiet. The greyish contours of the road had been visible from a distance, stretching out drearily towards the east, but suddenly for no apparent reason the road became hummocky and potholed. The piebald bullocks, twitching their ears as if they were flicking away tiresome flies, continued hauling laboriously. After a while the rich soil on the road became as slippery as soap and turned into slush. And that was when the wheel started groaning in earnest.

I wouldn't call Atalyk *ata* insatiably greedy. But when the logs were being loaded, it was this genial man who had admonished Saġymbek in these terms:

'Pile it on, pile it on! We don't want to be left without material when we're covering the roof of the school. If there's some left over, so be it, it's worse if we don't take enough, then we'll have to come all this way to see you again', he said, and made them load on another ten trees. Those piebald bullocks may have been as strong as elephants, but once they started panting, they couldn't get their breath back. The crippled cart started squeaking even more desperately now, and the groaning wheel's cracking became deafening.

Atalyk *ata* didn't say anything. He seemed to regret now having loaded on too many logs, but who could tell; he kept turning towards the back of the bullock cart and examining it. And behind us the long tree trunks smeared the mud about, still tracing out their convoluted patterns on the road. Eventually, after resting for a while, we reached the ravine where the marmot had been shot.

'Right then, my little misbegotten friend', said Atalyk *ata*, prodding me in the side with his finger. 'If, with the help of God and the spirits of our ancestors, the *aruaķs*, we manage to cross this ravine, the road will start running downhill. The going will get easier, and we'll get there without any worries. Bow down to God, Baryshan! Bow down to the spirits of our ancestors. Get off the cart and take the reins, and when we start climbing up the bluff on the other side, tell yourself: forward, only forward – and that will give you strength. I'll work away with the whip, and if fortune smiles on us, we'll pull it off. And by the way, Baryshan, here, please take this and hang it round your neck, I'm afraid of losing it in the confusion', he added, taking out the prayer beads and the triangular *bojtūmar* from inside his *bešpet* and holding them out to me after I had already got off the cart onto the ground.

'Make sure you don't lose it! And by the way, don't forget to take the marmot that you shot to Sùlejmen.'

'But you'll give it to him yourself.'

'Eh, dear boy what kind of memory have I got left now? Reason has abandoned your *ata*. Just remember this: if my Sùlejmen could become as healthy as you, I would surrender my soul to God right now – I'd slip away without any regrets, a miserable wretch that I am. And that's the way of it...'

As we went down the slope into the ravine, I stood in front of the bullocks, repeating 'easy, easy', as if I was pressing on the brake. But the cart carried on rolling down the slope and despite the desperate efforts of the bullocks, the yoke instantly slipped down and wedged itself against their immensely broad horns, threatening to tear the poor animals' heads off. At risk of falling under the hooves, I fussed about witlessly and floundered blindly, and didn't even realise how I had managed to ford the deep stream. Now we had to jump out without losing any momentum and climb up the other side. A moment ago, I had been restraining the bullocks, but now I had to give them their head, haul harder on the reins and strain to clamber up the other side of the ravine. I hauled and strained in earnest, like a genuine strongman inspired by the confidence that it is no problem for him to tug out the bullocks and the huge cart with a single jerk. My bare feet skidded on the slushy road as if it had been smeared with soap; there wasn't a single bump to brace myself against.

'Ah? Ah! Oh my God, oh spirits of my ancestors!' Atalyḵ *ata* bellowed, giving the bullocks a lashing with the whip. When we got exactly halfway up the slope of the ravine, our bullocks, straining as taut as a bowstring, suddenly froze, caught in that pose of intense effort. From the continuous traction of the rein, my feet slipped and I went tumbling under the bullocks' feet. And – woe is me – as soon as that happened the cart shifted and started rolling back downhill. I don't even know how the old man managed to leap out of it... He immediately started straining all his might to stop the cart, moving in from the left and attempting to slow down its movement with his shoulder. But then the moment came when a loud crack rang out, the bullock cart lurched over to one side, the hemp rope restraining the load snapped and the logs started slithering and rustling down onto the ground one after another.

I heard Atalyḵ *ata*'s hoarse, strained cry:

'Pull the couplings out of the yoke!'

Moving with frantic speed, I managed to pull the iron couplings out. If I hadn't done that, the overturned cart would have snapped the bullocks' necks. I had saved them. But where was Atalyḵ *ata*?

'*Ata*! *Ata*!'

No answer. As they tumbled out, the logs had gone flying in all directions and the wheels of the cart had been hoisted up towards the sky. The left rear wheel had lost its rim and its spokes, and I could only see the central boss. That troublemaker had finally been smashed completely.

'*Ata*! *Ata*!'

Fussing anxiously and stumbling in my haste, I kept running around the dumped heap of wood. The darkness was pitch black and the rain kept lashing down with no reprieve. I was covered from head to toe in sticky mud and couldn't feel if I was wearing any clothes or not. I started sorting through the tree trunks one by one. The logs, which even two men had struggled to lift during loading, were too heavy. I recognised my *ata*, lying face down and badly battered, by feeling his head and shoulder blades.

'*Ata*, dearest man, hold on. I'm here, I'll roll them all off you in a moment', I said, laboriously taking hold of the thick ends of the logs and dragging them off to the side.

'*Ataj*! *Ata*!'[19]

He was groaning very faintly and the lower part of his midriff was still covered by the timber. His face was smeared with mud and so, after adjusting his head, I tried to wipe it with the edge of my soaked shirt.

'*Ataj*! *Ata*!'

If I had a voice as resounding as a colt's, it would have burst out with a force great enough to rupture the eardrums of the Lord God himself. How can a man hear what God does not hear? And yet from somewhere behind me I seemed to hear the tramping clatter of galloping hooves. And indeed, hastening towards us down the opposite side of the ravine, splashing through the mud on the road, there was a rider on a horse.

'Oi, you poor souls, now see, you have been struck by a real catastrophe. I seemed to sense in my innards that some such disaster had befallen you and I couldn't stay sitting at home, so I came hurrying after you', said old Saġymbek, jumping off his horse.

Working as fast as we could, we first cleared away all the wooden litter sticking to Atalyk *ata*. He was lying face down, and when we turned him over onto his back, he asked with a great struggle: 'Ah?!' It seemed to me that he had stretched out and grown taller. Believe it or not, as you wish, but his hump seemed to have disappeared completely.

***

Joining forces, Saġymbek and I heaved the overturned cart to and fro, and finally set it back on its wheels, then harnessed up the bullocks again and led them out to the edge of the ravine. We lifted up the central boss of the broken wheel, attached the very slimmest log to it and made a runner. Then we dragged the logs up onto the cart one by one. But lifting up Atalyk *ata* was far harder than dragging the logs. At the slightest movement he would groan quietly; he was in terrible pain. But although we could barely stay on our feet from exhaustion, we lifted up the paralysed body and gently laid it on the logs.

The road began running downhill and the bullocks strode along freely, without straining. Saġymbek rode his horse and I settled myself on the logs. The heavy downpour began subsiding, the heavens cleared and the radiant moon and the stars, winking to each other, started glimmering up above us. The lines of the country road were clearly visible now and it was impossible for us to lose our way.

---

[19] *Ataj* – term of endearment when addressing a grandfather (*ata*).

The prayer beads and the black *bojtümar* were dangling round my neck like a necklace and the shot marmot was lying in front of me. I was going to give it to Sùlejmen. But if Atalyķ *ata* didn't recover, who could I give the black *bojtümar* to? I had no idea. I glanced again and again at Atalyķ *ata*, but couldn't bring myself to ask about that. And he lay there, like a log set out on show, stretched out to his full height. And perhaps that was why it seemed to me that he would be set on the roof of our school along with the other logs, propping up some extremely important part of it.

The tall, three-wheeled bullock cart trundled sluggishly towards the *auyl*, where the school would definitely be restored. My soul was filled with lament and my throat was filled with bitterness, but there were no tears in my eyes. I seemed to have frozen, glowering with hostility at someone or other, like a shell-shocked man who has returned from the front line...

Translated by Andrew Bromfield

AKIM TARAZI
(b. 9.09.1933)

Akim Tarazi is a writer, screenwriter and playwright. He graduated from Kazakh State Pedagogical Institute (now Abaj [Abai] Kazakh National Pedagogical University), Faculty of Philology, in 1955 before going on to study screenwriting in Moscow (1960–62). From 1957 to 1959, he taught Russian language and literature to high-school students. He was a correspondent of the *Literaturnaya Gazeta* in Kazakhstan (1962–64), managing editor at Ķazaķfil'm (Kazakhfilm) studios (1964–70), First Secretary of the Union of Cinematographers of the Kazakh SSR (1970–80), Secretary of the Writers' Union of the Kazakh SSR (1986–90), adviser to the Ministry of Culture (1991–94) and a lecturer at the Žùrgenov (Zhurgenov) Academy of Arts (1994–2004). Since 2009, Tarazi has been a professor at the Kazakh National University of Arts in Astana (now Nur-Sultan).

He is the author of several novels, including *Ķorķau žùldyz* (Into the Abyss), *Žaza* (Retribution), *Măskeu – Balasaz* (Moscow – Balasaz), and numerous plays, such as *Kùlkisiz komediâ* (A Non-humorous Comedy), *Žaķsy adam* (A Good Person), *Šer* (Grief), *Mùstafa Šoķaj* (about a Kazakh scholar and political figure known as Mustafa Chokai who fought for the liberation of the Turkic nations from the Soviet Union), *Mahambet* (about a poet, a hero of the Kazakh upheaval against the Russian Empire in the nineteenth century Mahambet Ôtemisùly), *Tăž* (Crown) and *Žaņbyrly tùnde* (On a Rainy Night). He is credited with scripting a number of films, including Măžit Begalin's *Sledy Uhodyat v Gorizont* (Traces Go to the Horizon, 1964), Bolat Shamshiyev's *Ķaraš-ķaraš oķiġasy* (A Shot on the Karash Pass, 1968) and lastly, Satybaldy Narymbetov's *Lăjlanyņ namazy* (Leyla's Prayer, 2002) and *Mùstafa Šoķaj* (Mustafa Chokai, 2008).

He was awarded the State Prize of Kazakhstan (2002) and the title of an Honoured Worker of the Republic of Kazakhstan (1999), as well as the Orders of Ķùrmet (1999) and Otan (2015).

Retribution

Whirling and twirling, blue ball in the sky,
Whirling and twirling, up ever so high,
Whirling and twirling, blue ball wants to fall...
Ball wants to fall... ball wants to fall...

– Old marching song[1]

The name of this short work in Kazakh is *Žaza*, which means 'retribution'. In writing it, I was directly influenced by the December 1986 student riots in Almaty. I wrote it hot on the heels, as you might say, of those troubles. However, in order to avoid the habitual fate of writers in those days, namely being misunderstood, I was forced to provide a preface to it in which I assured our vigilant censors (and not only them, I might say) that it was a translation of a Japanese tale. Thank the Lord, that time has passed, and I can now dare to restore my name to it. I hope, forever. Amen!

Early one morning, when the whole city was still asleep, an ear-shredding scream rang out in the vicinity of State Nursery Number Two in District Number One. It was as if a sadly inept opera singer had leapt out onto the stage and decided, taking advantage of the absence of any government officials, to demonstrate to the whole world the immensity of his talent – only to find that no matter how hard he tried, his croaky voice let him down. Let him down? Shamed him, even, shamed the man who had in his grasp such a rare opportunity, namely to perform to a wide audience of pensioners, who had stuck their venerable silver-grey heads out of all the windows of the five-storey cardboard and reed houses. That great creative force, curiosity, now took possession of all the venerable silver-grey heads, and it was the pensioners who were the first to leave their stuffy little rooms and hurry silently in their twos and threes towards the ill-fated State Nursery Number Two.

Someone tumbled to the need to call the police. The night duty officer at the department, half-asleep, remembered that when someone called, he was obliged by law to pick up the phone, although he was mightily disappointed that the call had interrupted his sweet dream in which girls of easy virtue (who happened to be in his charge) played key roles. The officer deputed to respond to the call, puffing and muttering to himself, managed to get his decrepit UAZ started, and, weaving his way along the dark streets of his beat, made his way

---

[1] Translated by Richard Coombes. [Ed.]

20

to State Nursery Number Two. While all this was going on, the ear-shredding scream weakened noticeably, and turned into an inconsolable sobbing.

The above-mentioned deputed officer arrived and saw with his own, official, sharp-sighted eyes the full horror of the terrible tableau created by the unknown villain. He managed to figure out what he was supposed to do at such a scene, and notified the appropriate authority. The appropriate authority, whose job was to know and decide everything, pressed ahead with knowing and deciding everything, and a platoon of law enforcement officers threw a tight cordon around State Nursery Number Two. All this went on before the pitiless southern July sun showed any inclination to make his solemn ascent and disperse all the curious.

The curious, though, already knew everything. Not only the curious, either, but the whole of District Number One knew by lunchtime precisely what had happened to the leadership team of State Nursery Number Two. Someone had cut off their heads, with a remarkable lack of spurting blood, and then laid the bodies out very neatly side by side on the yellowish carpet. Moreover, the heads of all three were turned, as if on someone's command, to the right.

The word soon went round that the heads so neatly left on the carpet belonged to the director of State Nursery Number Two, Anna Andreyevna Petrenko, the bursar of this same State Institution, Nŭrdin Saidov, and to the head of the District Education Department, Bajbak̦ Malšybaev.

By evening, all the town's pensioners knew that our redoubtable Soviet detectives had quickly found and arrested the brutal murderer. He was the dear husband of Anna Andreyevna, the low-life and hardened old drunkard, Styopa. They had found him in the cramped nursery store-cupboard, fast asleep as if nothing at all had happened. On him they also found the murder weapon – a black-handled axe covered in blood, and in the blood, there were poor Styopa's fingerprints, clear for all to see.

***

His heart was whining wearisomely. No; not whining wearisomely – it was crying. A question flashed through his mind: can a heart really cry? Still delirious, he asked himself another question: can a man really engage in deep thought while he's asleep? I must be still alive!

'There he is! Scoundrel, up to no good, skulking down here. Get up!'

That's Kano's voice. Real name K̦uantaj. He's usually as cowardly as a hare. Look at him now! Got some pluck from somewhere. Listen to how he's talking to me.

'Get up! Huh. Pretending to be asleep.' This is the smoke-raddled, wheezing voice of that butch lard-arse Mila. Milana, she likes to call herself. Putting on airs.

'Come on, look lively. You're in big trouble. Poor sod.'

Not only have these cowardly rabbits plucked up some courage, they've also allowed themselves to insult me. Me! Abo, a veteran of the war in Afghanistan.

Abo, from sheer habit, turned himself in a tenth of a second into a super-elastic steel spring. He leapt straight from his recumbent position, landed on his feet and stood to attention. Also from force of habit, he lifted his chin slightly, and in a clear, rich voice reported, 'I serve the Soviet Union!'

Abo resolved not to recognise his own colleagues, and act as if someone had taken over from them during the night. He decided not to acknowledge Ķuantaj (whom Abo privately called the Wax Weakling), nor Milana (whom Abo privately called the Tin Soldier, after her crisp steps so characteristic of retired commissioned officers). Now the right thing was simply not to show any recognition. Ķuantaj walked – or rather, marched crisply – in front. Abo noticed that the battered holster housing Sergeant Ķuantaj's service revolver was hanging carelessly open (Abo had time to compare it in his mind to the 'toothless mouth of an antediluvian old crone'). 'And that means', thought Abo, 'that he's shoved his revolver into the pocket of his old-fashioned riding breeches, just in case. And that means...' Abo shot a quick glance at the lardy Milana, marching behind him with crisp steps, and saw that his civilian co-worker was holding her left hand as if she were cradling a rifle, and the index finger of her right hand was bent, as if ready to pull the trigger of her imaginary rifle.

Abo also had time to notice Ķuantaj's dishevelled hair, looking like an old haystack forgetfully left in the field at harvest by a careless farmer.

Abo could hear the ladybug Milana hissing through her rotting teeth, 'You sssssnake! You animal!' He realised, with some surprise, that she was referring to him.

'You sssssnake!'

He even had time to notice that Ķuantaj's legs were scarily crooked and thin, like bicycle wheels.

'Hey! Are you deaf or what?' snapped Ķuantaj sourly. 'Whaddid I say to you? Din' catch it, uuh?'

'Uuh?' Abo repeated the question in the style of Ķuantaj.

'Whaddid I ask yer?' Ķuantaj waved his right hand towards the neatly laid out corpses. 'Whass this, then?'

'This then', said Abo, mimicking Ķuantaj, 'this then is the work of a master. A master!'

Kano (real name Ķuantaj) flared up with such anger that he staggered and almost fell over. 'Whaddid he say? Whaddid he say? Master? The work of a master? You off your chump?'

'Sssssnake!' Milana's little right fist all but clocked Abo on the nose. 'Sssnake!'

Abo instinctively struck Milana's outstretched arm; he did it so quickly that he hardly knew he'd moved. He scared himself; he was afraid that he had broken the hapless lard-arse's right arm. 'I could so easily break this poor woman's arm in two', he thought to himself.

The poor woman was seriously frightened. Abo saw that she had instantly turned pale, her narrow eyes widening and becoming unnaturally round. 'Please, my dear fellow', she begged, 'My dear chap, spare me, don't kill me. I'm nothing. Good for nothing!'

A thought flashed through Abo's head like a flicker of dry summer lightning. 'Why should I kill this woman? Am I even capable of killing a living being? No! And what is it in the first place to kill a real human being?'

The offended look Abo gave Milana and Ķuantaj as he asked himself this question seriously discomfited them, and they withdrew from the office of the murdered director, Anna Andreyevna, even though they had only just escorted him there under civilian arrest. Abo followed them out into the spacious corridor. There he saw neither Ķuantaj nor Milana – they had both vanished. He stopped and stood there for a long time, rooted to the spot, painfully thinking some distressing thought of his own.

'What did I find to think about just now?' He seemed to have forgotten already. He went down to the ground floor, where right by the exit was his little cubbyhole of an office. A similar little cubbyhole was to be found on the opposite side of the spacious corridor. This cubbyhole housed old man Styopa, the lawful husband of the late Anna Andreyevna. Abo wanted to look in on his co-worker, but something held him back.

Abo, standing motionless in the middle of the wide corridor, thought, 'He did me a good turn yesterday. He stayed on duty instead of handing over to me. He even gave me a written note that said he had stayed on and done the night shift on his own initiative. At the bottom of the certificate, he wrote in his own hand, "Agreed with the Director Anna Andreyevna Smirnova." He…'

He cut off his musings abruptly. 'What are you doing, Abo?' he chided himself. 'Looking for ways to explain yourself? What a worm you are, Abo! Have you… Have you become a coward? Have you become a louse?'

Abo stepped outside, and found himself stopping again, and staring. Pitch darkness had descended on the whole city and its million inhabitants, and was pressing down on it like heavy lead. It was very stuffy. Really stuffy. Abo recalled how this short time just before dawn was called the 'black darkness' in the language of his people. He knew that at this very moment, the Whole Wide World would stop for a second, in order to take a little break. He knew that he, too, needed only to wait a moment, and the entire universe would suddenly be lit up, as if illuminated by the smile of a sinless baby. He remembered his own children: six-year-old Ajna and four-year-old Bolo. Abo was about to give himself over to a father's oh-so-sweet feelings when the Whole Wide World, which was recklessly racing through Infinity and Eternity, shuddered sharply, and the sky gradually began to brighten. At this same moment, Abo saw Kano and also suddenly shuddered. Afterwards he would often recall with great shame that moment when he, Reinforced Concrete Abo, as he was known to a narrow circle of military specialists, had allowed himself to shudder.

Abo, calling himself a wimp for shuddering, walked resolutely over to where Ķuantaj was waiting for him under the nursery awning. Abo was in a heightened state of awareness and could feel how frightened Ķuantaj was. The man was ready to run, as the saying goes, over the hills and far away. He might even have done so, but at that very moment four sirens rang out, all at the same time but not exactly together, and four cars, accelerating sharply, appeared seconds later at the high gates of State Nursery Number Two. Ķuantaj, who had seemed about ready to dash off over the hills and far away, was instantly transformed and rushed to the gates to meet the guests. Abo knew that Ķuantaj was the maestro of bootlicking. The thought flashed through his mind, 'Each of us has his own specialism'.

Abo paid no attention to the top brass now clambering out of one limousine and three UAZ. He walked off slowly, entered the two-storey building, turned into his cubbyhole, and lay down at once on his iron cot. In keeping with long habit, he gave himself an order: 'Sleep until eleven!' and instantly fell asleep.

***

In the spacious grounds of State Nursery Number Two, there were several groups of painted wooden horses. Abo sat on one of them, and, spreading his strong legs wide apart, began to rock. Ķuantaj made his way out of the building, smiling to himself. It was indeed Ķuantaj, Sergeant Ķuantaj, but he was unrecognisable. Abo saw that his colleague was wearing an expression of triumph. The lowly sergeant Ķuantaj, smiling insolently, insolently beckoned Abo to him with his index finger. 'Well, look at him', thought Abo, but dutifully came down from his horse, and equally dutifully went over to his colleague. Over the five hours which Abo had permitted himself to sleep, Ķuantaj had changed beyond all recognition. 'Has he got younger, or what?' wondered Abo.

When Abo came up to the sergeant, Ķuantaj triumphantly, and with undisguised pride, declared, 'You are one lucky son of a gun, pal. You were born under a lucky star!'

Then, still in triumphant mode but frankly not making much sense, Ķuantaj talked at length about some colonel or other, then some major, some prosecutor, about poor Styopa, about an axe with a black handle with traces of blood on it, and then, with a sly wink, abruptly ended his tirade with a massive bellow: 'Riiiiiight then! You may now go home. IN PEACE!'

So he did. Abo went home in peace. 'What else would I do?' he thought, as he strolled his normal route home through the narrow streets of District Number One. 'What else would I do?'

It was all quite routine. He walked unhurriedly and peacefully to his stop, taking two hours to get there, waited for his bus, which took up exactly three more hours, zigzagged peacefully (not cursing, as the other passengers did) along the route taken by the bus number 526, and peacefully got off at his stop.

For some reason, his stop was called The Last, although it was the last but one.

When he reached his hut, which he rented for thirty roubles (on a salary of sixty), he stopped uncertainly, and stood there for a long time, wondering whether or not to go in. He looked at his watch. At any moment his hell might begin. He cursed himself for being a coward, and made his way back towards The Last stop. And then ... on to the heights which Abo himself called the Camel's Hump.

***

Now... and now... by some sort of intuition, Abo understood that he was still standing on Camel's Hump, and all around him was pitch darkness, and his favourite rider of the skies, the Great Bear, had made it as far as the Arctic Ocean. 'That makes it one a.m.', he thought.

The Great Bear (also known locally as Aḳbozat, the White Horse), leaning firmly on its two hind legs on the Yamal Peninsula and reaching its two front legs high over the Arctic Ocean, was about to speed like a flying bullet into the blue yonder of Infinity and Eternity. The disposition of the stars told Abo that it was already two in the morning. 'How long have I been standing here?' he asked himself. 'What am I doing here? Why am I even here at all?'

Abo recalled how, when he was called up to join the Soviet Army, his 100-year-old great-grandfather Ḳara-Aspan, who by that time had irrevocably renounced all worldly things and gone off to the mountains to live as a hermit in the cave of Tùjyḳ, made a special trip down from the mountains to say just one thing to his great-grandson. 'Don't be afraid of the enemy. Be afraid of lies, great-grandson of mine.' With that, he trotted smartly back to the mountains on his donkey.

There on the carpet lie the Troika, inseparable even in death. They were: the director of State Special Children's Nursery Number Two, Anna Andreyevna Petrenko, the bursar of this same government agency, Nùrdin Saidov, and the head of the District Education Department, Bajbaḳ Malšybaev. Just lying there. So quietly. Only... all three heads are turned slightly to the right, as if at someone's terrible command. On the necks of all three, almost identical, barely visible, are red scars. The open eyes of all three, though, are muddy in different ways, differently dirty. Their tongues, all similarly swollen and similarly bluish, have popped out under some unknown pressure. Only now did Abo remember how the day before, when he had first seen that horrific tableau, he had expressed his stupid admiration with the words, 'The work of a master!'

He felt an unfathomable satisfaction in his soul. 'It's OK to go home now', he said to himself. Arriving back at his hut, Abo turned round and worked out that it was by now four o'clock in the morning.

In that very instant, he felt something like a physical blow. Again it hit him. 'This is it!' he thought. 'I wasn't wrong to wait until now. I just need to get through it this time as well. Oh Lord, my Creator! Grant that I may survive this time as well. Let me survive... let me... survive....'

He fell, but did not hit the ground at once. He fell for a long, long time, painfully swaying, the way a slender poplar falls when it is unexpectedly battered by a ruthless steppe whirlwind. But he lifted himself back up at once, realising by sheer willpower alone that his wife and children must not, must NOT see him in this position – his beloved, precious Ajna, Bolo and Zara, for whose sake he, Abo, endured and would continue to endure everything.

For whose sake... for whose sake... he remembered what they had dubbed him there, in Afghanistan, that small but elite group of the elect. Abo the Immortal. He, Abo, irrevocably made up his mind... but then he did fall; he crashed to the ground, but felt no pain. He was still there, still in Afghanistan, where he had attained that high level of mastery over pain. He felt no pain. He was still a master.

A master. He was proud of it. Even Ivasi recognised this – Ivasi, the Divine Magician (in everyday life known as Lance Corporal Ivan), before whose command 'Attention!' generals and their superior officers froze. Yes, back then Abo had reached that level of mastery, but the question now was, would he be able to reach the deep gully, at the bottom of which, he encouraged himself, he had three times survived unbelievable torments so as to save Ajna and Bolo. 'Oh my Lord, my Creator! Give me another chance to save them...' By some inner intuition, he realised that he had reached the coveted hollow, where he had a straw mat. Exhausted, he fell to the ground.

'It would be good to forget, it would be good to for... for...' He automatically tried to control himself, so as not to lose consciousness. 'Give me strength, Lord! Just one more day. Save me from disgrace.' It seemed to Abo that he could embrace the Whole Wide World, and he felt that someone was giving him a cue: 'Give us "The Whole Wide World".' He wanted to answer this someone, 'Ah, yes!' but at that very moment an itch started up in his brain. Hundreds and thousands of ants started to dance on the soft membrane of his brain. They danced their way right inside that mish-mash that people for some reason call the brain.

'You wretched ants', he said. 'I can beat anyone and everyone, oh yes I can. But you... before you creatures I am powerless. Powerless. Oh, Lord, help me for the sake of my children. They are angels. Angels. My Ajna. My Bolo. For the sake of my children.' He knew that he was losing consciousness. That would be the end; he would never reach his Great Goal. 'How, and as whom, would I then stand before you, my Lord, my maker? How? How?' He knew that those wretched ants were mocking him to their hearts' content – him, Abo! They would migrate to his throat, to his guts, and a fearful cold would grip all of his insides. His teeth would begin to dance nervously to the tune of the permafrost. His teeth. Abo's teeth. His big, strong, white teeth, like those of

26

the famous Afghan horses on which he had so often raced. Abo, that dashing *shuravi*, as the Soviet forces in Afghanistan were called, who was known and revered in all the border villages of the Pashtuns, Uzbeks, Kyrgyz, Turkmens and Kazakhs. Known and revered. And now this swashbuckling young soldier was lying here, lying doubled up at the bottom of a dry irrigation ditch. In his inhuman agony, he dug his teeth into his left forearm to try to alleviate his suffering. Oh, for some relief, even a little, just so that he did not start bawling from this hellish pain and wake his wife and children.

Abo knew what was going on. He was waiting for the representatives of the permafrost, as he thought of them, to start on his legs. First, the official delegates of the permafrost would start to twist both his legs, twisting them the way the women on the banks of the quiet river behind the village twist the one shirt owned by their husbands so that it dries more quickly while he is still asleep. Twisting it and then beating it without mercy on great big stones or the powerful trunks of the ageless trees growing along the riverbank. Bash, bash, bash. They would beat him until he was raving. Until he lost consciousness. Bash, bash.

Abo knew that in a while they would lay off a little, ease up a bit, as it were – but that's the game. That's the game of an out and out sadist. A sadist – the Great Sadist – apparently derives great pleasure from it.

Next the Great Sadist would move the site of this hellish torture game from his legs back to his head. Millions of tiny iron ants would once more leap across to his brain, and there throw a wild, hellish party. This torture was beyond the endurance of any living being. Enduring it would be beyond even a dead donkey. Im-poss-ible! But Abo had to hold out, had to, so as to save his innocent angels, to save them and take them away with him. Take them away? Where? Where? How? What for? Save them? Who from? Abo realised that the finale was coming, and that he should pronounce the words appropriate for this moment, namely, 'Oh, my Lord, my Creator'. He could scarcely get the words out. He immediately wanted to utter the words, 'Forgive me', but at that moment, with a superhuman effort, he managed to bring up onto the muddy screen of his befogged brain the sad, pleading little faces of Ajna and Bolo. Out of his mouth burst the words, 'Save them, oh my Lord, my Creator.'

***

The only weakness that Zara allowed herself was sleep – sweet, early morning sleep. Yesterday morning on his way out to work, Abo had warned her that he might swap shifts with Styopa, and that would mean that he would not be home for the next two nights. 'So what?' she thought. 'Just be alive and healthy, my falcon!' Like most Kazakh women, Zara only ever called her husband 'my falcon'. She knew that Abo was not beside her, but from habit, and still half-asleep, she sent her right hand searching for the hairs on the burning hot chest of her beloved husband.

'Abo!' she muttered. 'Abo, save them!' She jumped awake with a feeling of anxiety, and a sense that Abo was somewhere nearby. 'How? How can he be nearby?' she asked herself. She got up, and, following a sudden instinct, rushed straight out in her silk nightdress. She ran at full tilt towards the deep ditch. And found him. She found him.

Abo was lying in a strange, unnatural posture. For Zara, the daughter of a famous *bùrkitši,*[2] the scene was reminiscent of when the Lord of the Skies[3] – a broad-winged falcon – had crushed a helpless rabbit against the ground.

Zara knew not to wake her husband by speaking loudly or moving suddenly, so she sat down on the straw next to him, and patiently waited for him to wake up.

Zara did not know how to cry. All she could do was allow her heart to whimper. She would make little whimpering noises, but her eyes remained dry the whole time. At such times, she either turned herself into a stone idol, or, if her soul was in very great torment, her whole appearance would resemble a trembling arrow which had just that moment embedded itself in its enemy's hauberk. At the same time, she would tirelessly repeat: 'O my Lord, my Creator, how have we sinned before you? Have mercy on us! Have mercy!'

Zara noticed that Abo seemed to be angry at someone in his sleep. 'How else can I explain the way he is so viciously grinding his wolfish teeth?' she asked herself. The thought scared her. 'Is he really having another of those terrible fits?'

Only now did Zara see her husband's badly bitten forearms, and as clearly as if it were on a screen, she saw it all again... that moment from the most terrible hell...

On the clear screen of her consciousness, Zara saw how a striped viper silently but with an odd kind of beauty slithers up to a dove's nest, finds there four chicks not yet fledged, and prepares to gulp them down... and they can do nothing to defend themselves.

Zara instinctively threw herself on her sleeping husband and embraced him, as if her embraces would be enough to rescue him from the fit. Abo, as if he could sense it, sighed a deep sigh of relief.

Zara readied herself once again to turn into a statue and wait patiently until Abo, her Abo, woke up.

Zara did not know how to cry. All her tears had dried up long ago, when her husband was drafted into the Red Army and sent to Afghanistan; then she had wept all her tears. All cried out. Now she was stone, an idol. Nothing more.

An idol has no concept of time. None at all.

---

[2] *Bùrkitši* – eagle handler, trainer and hunter.

[3] The name given by Kazakhs to birds of prey.

Nevertheless, the Sun was already up. It was already up and shining. The height of an *arḳan*,[4] as Zara's kinsmen would say. The height of an *arḳan*. The Sun was baking everything, baking, baking. Zara was like a sliver of ice left out in the full glare of the Sun. The sliver of ice was melting away, but Zara did not feel it. She was an idol.

For Zara, no world existed besides Abo, Ajna and Bolo. No, there could be no other world, no other planet. Everything else was false.

Everything else was a lie, falsehood, deception, cunning, corruption; everything else was just, in a word, politics. Everything else was hostile. That was all there was to it.

***

At midnight, two militia men arrived in a car and took Abo away.

At five o'clock in the morning they brought him back home. The police very politely said goodbye; one of them even put on an ingratiating tone, fawning for some reason, and apologised to Abo for something. Zara felt very flattered. She gave an involuntary smile and, when the men had gone, with undisguised pride asked, 'Who were they?'

There was something holier-than-thou in Abo's smile as he replied, 'Ah, yes. At work. Styopa – you know, he shares the shifts with me. They found some kind of black axe on him.'

'Ahh… Praise the Lord, my Creator! OK, have a cup of tea and get some sleep.'

Abo took a sip of tea, lay down and fell asleep at once.

Abo may have dropped off to sleep, but Zara… Zara… Ajna and Bolo's sheets had slipped off, and Zara covered the children back up, then fell to thinking. She fell deep into thought, which meant that she turned back into an idol, stone, immutable. When she came round, it was already eight in the morning. 'I'm late for work', she said to herself. 'Well, it's OK. There are other folk on the shift. I'll make it up later.' Holding her breath, and as quiet as a cat on its guard, she went out into the yard, looked quickly around, and then went into a narrow, cramped closet. Inside, she froze in indecision. She felt like a thief.

It was dark in the cramped closet, and Zara knew that she had to wait a while, to let her eyes adjust to the darkness. She would then be able to see all the cluttered corners of the pantry, as the mistress of the house liked to call this poky little room.

Carefully going through various things quite obviously of no use to anyone, Zara quickly found what she was looking for. She was looking for a bundle of plain canvas.

---

[4] The sunbeam on the height of *arḳan* (rope) – ancient measure of time, indicating from 8 to 10am.

She stood for a long, long time, unable to make up her mind whether to undo the bundle or not. Then she decided. Undo it! Undo it!

Very carefully, she undid the bundle. There she saw an object she knew very well indeed. She managed to stop herself from crying out. Hidden in the canvas was a black axe with a white handle.

Zara then very, very carefully, with her index finger, tested the shining blade of the black axe with the white handle.

Only then was she convinced that her Abo... was above even the slightest suspicion. No! No! No! Her Abo would never bring himself to do such a thing. 'He would not!' she said to herself.

Then, and only then, Zara sighed with relief. But her sigh seemed to her to be somewhat strange; not so much a sigh as a natural explosion.

***

There would be another natural explosion later. Later. Meanwhile, on this very day, in the evening, or more precisely, just on midnight, two policemen would knock roughly on Abo and Zara's hut and then, with exaggerated politeness, ask Abo to go with them. They would take him away in a UAZ with red stripes on it.

Everything was done with exaggerated correctness and without natural explosions. Abo was brought to a branch of the Ministry of Internal Affairs, escorted into a spacious office – an office with no windows, he noticed at once – and asked to wait a little. The policemen went off somewhere. Vanished completely. An hour passed. Another hour passed. Three hours passed. Abo, though, despite sensing from the very first minute that someone was keeping a very close eye on him, to his own surprise, remained perfectly calm.

After three and a half hours, a man came in. Although were it not for the military uniform and major's stripes, you could not have said that it was a human being.

The thing that came in resembled an orangutan. Those same long, long forelimbs, hanging to his knees, and – particularly noticeable – the fist.

Abo himself well knew that in circumstances such as these, a fist is crucial. A fist.

Following his old habit, Abo closed his eyes for a second and silently invoked the name of his Lord, his Creator. He was ready.

But no crushing blow to the groin followed. At the vital moment, Abo looked boldly into the man's eyes – completely empty, unreadable eyes – and saw the soul of this professional butcher tremble. It trembled.

This was when the next natural explosion occurred. A crushing blow to the groin was delivered, but the recipient was the orangutan, of the rank of major. Abo carefully measured his blow so as to leave the man alive. 'What a naive sucker!' thought Abo. The naive sucker was still alive when the two police officers who had escorted Abo into this august institution came back into the office with no windows. One of them turned to Abo and again with exaggerated politeness said, 'Come on, bro, let's go. We've been told to take you straight home. Right into the arms of your young wife! You lucky devil. You were born under a lucky star!'

Abo was surprised – amazed, even – to catch in the policeman's voice a clear note of jealousy. Jealousy. 'What does that mean?' he asked himself.

When the police car had vanished off into the maze of crooked streets, Abo stood looking at his own hut. It was not clear what was going through his mind. Then, smiling to himself, he marched on in a northerly direction. In the north... well, in the north, he witnessed a little miracle. His very own personal seven-star constellation, the Great Bear, was dipping its neck down towards the Arctic Ocean, indulging itself with a drink. 'I am the only one enjoying this sacred moment', thought Abo. 'No one else in the Whole Wide World knows about it. Only me.'

Abo was surprised – amazed, even – to see that he was on Camel's Hump. 'How and when did you get here, Abo?' he asked himself. 'You didn't notice where you were going? That means your pot is overflowing with junk. You need to clear your head. Otherwise, you won't achieve your Great Goal. Abo! Don't act like a worm. Abo, you are not a reptile. Remember that. Your Great Teacher, Ivasi, he of the red nose, told you this over and over.' The Great Teacher sometimes, in moments of enthusiasm, begged Abo to call him Lance Corporal Ivan.

Abo knew full well, though, that this was just a sly trick used by the *shuravi*. In the first weeks of the course, Lance Corporal Ivan had even dared to insult Abo, hissing angrily through his teeth, 'You, Cadet Kara-Aspanov, are a diehard infidel! Let me tell you in clear Russian – you have the brains of a donkey.'

The next second of Abo's life seemed to last a very long time, but he got through it by listening to the unhurried, soothing voice of his great-grandfather Kara-Aspan. 'You will not best a fool by being foolish, Abo. Stupidity is powerless before good sense.'

Thus Abo's great-grandfather Kara-Aspan saved him from being dismissed from TSTS-17 (which stands for Top Secret Training Sarytau-17).

In this way, Abo survived being the target of mockery, and quickly became the Great Master Ivasi's favourite pupil.

So it was that Abo, a simple guy from Kegesi, managed in some three months to master all of the three hundred and sixty-five secret ways in which one man can kill another.

Abo collected his surging thoughts together and looked around. He was astonished to find that he, Abo, the most organised graduate of the famous TSTS-17, had somehow unbeknown to himself left the Camel's Hump and come to the end of Snake Street. 'How did that happen?' he wondered. 'When did I get here? Have I really...?'

Looking at the time, Abo was astonished all over again. His watch was showing seven o'clock in the morning. 'How? When? I've… I've gone ma-' The word was too awful: he did not dare finish it.

Abo immediately plunged into a new, more alarming slough. He knew that the very end of Snake Street marked the start of the city's rubbish dump. The dumping ground. 'How did I get here?' he asked himself. 'Why did I come here? What for? My head is full of garbage even without the dump. Garbage! The Whole Wide World is cluttered with every sort of garbage. Poor world, I am so-o-o-o-o sorry for you. Very sorry. Still, you can clear garbage from the streets. You can take away the town's garbage, clean the town up, but who can clean up the garbage in my head? And how? How can you sweep away the garbage in a human head? It's utterly cluttered. The human brain is frightfully cluttered. Oh, my Lord, my Creator! He-e-e-e-lp!'

Just then, a very strange thing happened. Someone came sprinting out of the last hut on Snake Street, and, as if chasing after the runaway, a thin, shrill female voice rang out, 'Stop! Come back! Or I'll kill you! You and your six pups!'

A very odd-looking man rushed straight past Abo. Meanwhile, a beautiful female head appeared at a squat window in the hut. The owner of the beautiful female head knocked the glass out of the window with a sharp blow. Abo waited, gaping, for the woman with the beautiful head to stick her beautiful head out of the broken window, but she ran out of the house herself, out of the door, most likely, and chased after the runaway.

Events became no more comprehensible. The man, hobbling strangely, started running around Abo, followed by the woman.

'Who are you leaving your six little ones for?' she wailed; it sounded like something she'd learnt. 'Who?'

The husband just went on running and running, as if taking part in some silly game. His running was reminiscent of a children's game of tag.

At that moment, Abo, not even aware himself of how he did it, leapt like a panther in full flow towards the woman, and managed to grab the shining, curved dagger from her right hand.

The man and the woman suddenly stopped dead as if by mutual agreement, looked in embarrassment at Abo, and both began to beg. 'Forgive me, please. Please forgive me. Please forgive me!'

Only now did Abo take a proper look at these two strange creatures who were making no sense at all. He noted that the husband was an ugly freak, with all the distinctive features appropriate to such a categorisation, and the wife, as they say, was drop-dead gorgeous: young, slender, with large, black, bright eyes and a fantastically elegant, miniature figure.

Abo found himself looking at the eyes of the freakish husband, and what he saw made him shudder. Cold, sharp needles pierced his heart. These were not eyes, as people usually understand the term; they were… space, the cosmos

– only it was space with no stars. This was not the night sky; this was Eternity and Infinity themselves.

The freak stopped abruptly and, looking right into Abo's face out of the blue cosmos of his eyes, said very clearly, 'Come into my hut, and I'll tell you everything. I will. I'll tell you everything. Let's go! Come in!'

Later, Abo would let himself feel his surprise. Later, he would try more than once to delve into the meaning of this strange situation in which he, a cold-blooded Soviet *shuravi*, as the Mujahideen called him, had suddenly found himself. For now, he dutifully went into the pitiful little hut, and could do no more than marvel at the poverty of his surroundings. He was even more taken aback, though, to see the frightened eyes of the six little boys tucked away in a corner of the room. 'The oldest is maybe ten, the youngest two', he figured.

Standing in the middle of his home, the wretched father of six boys gave vent to a fiery tirade, the like of which, presumably, had caused the woman to chase after him with a small but sharp dagger in her hands.

The wretched man, fixing his glorious, pure, cosmic eyes on the cold-blooded but dumbfounded veteran of Afghanistan, said, 'All over the world, appalling outrages are being perpetrated. Our own beloved Soviet authorities have dug the Warehouse of Hell deep beneath our very land, from the Aral Sea to the Caspian Sea, and stored there thousands and thousands of hydrogen and neutron bombs, ready to go off at zero hour. How can a man sleep in peace? I have decided to go to Ùstirt,[5] to force the Soviet authorities to dismantle the Warehouse of Hell, where resides the capability to blow the Whole Wide World to smithereens. The only inhabited planet in the entire Universe! Do you understand, young man? Support me and convince my foolish wife to let me go without scandal. So that I can save our blue planet! Persuade her! Convince her! I'm a top-quality bomb disposal expert. That's my specialty.'

Abo, dragged from the world he was used to, did not know how to react to this madcap situation into which he had unintentionally stumbled. He looked helplessly at the pretty young woman, frozen in anticipation of his verdict, or rather, frozen in anticipation of hearing him seal the fate of her six helpless sons, huddled in the corner of the tiny room. He realised that on him and him alone rested the resolution of the question – was the Whole Wide World to be or not to be? (He had a jocular way of pronouncing the words, 'the Whole Wide World').

Abo, dragged from the world he was used to, said decisively, 'Go, Teacher, go to Ùstirt! Save mankind, Teacher, from the dark designs of stupid politicians!'

With that, Abo left. He left without looking back.

***

---

[5]   Ùstirt (Ustyurt) – plateau between the Caspian Sea and the Aral Sea.

Abo came into his hut in a jolly mood. He even felt himself smiling. Zara saw him, and jumped up off the felt rug, radiating joy and well-being with her whole self. The children, Ajna and Bolo, saw their mother's joy, and immediately began to racket about and giggle for no reason.

Going into his little hut in a jolly mood, Abo started up their usual family game of 'jump on the camel', which basically came down to Ajna and Bolo taking turns to sit on their father's back, while the father-camel desperately tried (or sort of tried) to throw the rider from his 'hump'. The child who succeeded in staying on the back of the raging bull the longest received a prize, in the form of sweets and other goodies.

Having conclusively 'lost' to his children, the father, once again a mild, gentle soul, took them to the nearest 'wild market', as folk called the impromptu stalls at crossroads in places out in the sticks where people bought and sold second-hand stuff.

Evening was coming when Abo arrived back home with his contented, happy children. Of a sudden, he remembered his strange adventure with the freak and the freak's wife and children, in which he, a usually serious, one might even say, gloomy man, had felt compelled to cry out, 'Go, Teacher! Go to Ustirt. Save mankind! Save us!'

'What nonsense is this?' Abo thought to himself. 'What heresy? How can one man, even one blessed with the wisdom of Solomon – how can one man save the whole of humanity? How can that feeble specimen, a chap who looks like a hoopoe, save anyone? And why me... I (who do I think I am) called him 'Plato' – the Plato. I called him Teacher. Why on earth did I do that? I should have called him Hoopoe!' Abo chuckled. 'You found yourself a teacher, Abo. You, Abo, famous throughout Afghanistan as a Master – the title your true Teacher, the virtuoso Ivasi himself, gave you. How could you?'

No answer came. Dejected and irritated by his inability to find an answer to such a seemingly simple question, Abo did not sit down to eat at the *dastarhan*[6], but said that he was already late, and hurried off to work.

***

At eight o'clock in the evening he took over care of State Nursery Number Two from Sergeant Milana. Abo knew that Milana was *really* really flattered when her colleagues addressed her in a military style, calling her 'Comrade Sergeant.' She straightaway became all courteous and good-natured, and before your very eyes, the lard-arse would start to glow. Even a glowing Milana, though, did not stop being vigilant. A Soviet sergeant can't be an airhead, and that's that.

---

[6] *Dastarhan* – traditional concept concerning all the dining-and-hosting- related practices and etiquette norms. Asking to a *dastarhan* is hosting according to all the norms of hospitality. More specifically, *dastarhan* is a synonym for dining table or table cloth.

About an hour was spent on the handover – a purely formal routine. Milana Petrovna, who liked to call herself a 'representative of the authorities', opened up a bulky and filthy journal and took the night watchman (which was how Abo was described on the staff roster) on a round of the whole place – out into the spacious courtyard, into the classrooms. She read out the name of each item as it appeared in the register in a loud, clear voice, like so: 'chair', 'mat', 'desk', along with the quantity of each, then placed a tick against each entry and told Abo to countersign.

The Government Representative herself, it has to be said, never once countersigned a single item of 'state property'. This was her established procedure, and that is how it went today. With only one minor difference.

When the handover ceremony had been successfully completed, and Milana Petrovna had been prattling on for a whole hour about whatever came into her head – though not about the one thing that poor Abo had, with good reason, been so painfully pondering for the past three days – he, poor Abo, cried out from his very soul, 'Oh my Lord, my Creator, why this echoing emptiness?'

When at last the handover ceremony was finished, and Milana's husband had whisked his smiling, happy wife away in their old Moskvich, Abo felt a sudden sense of relief. Hoopoe came back into his mind. 'Why?' he started up again. 'Why did I call him a teacher? What kind of teacher did I think he was, that Hoopoe?'

His relief, so suddenly acquired, gave way just as suddenly to disappointment. 'What kind of man are you, Abo? Have you forgotten those six little sprats, the children of the man you called your Teacher? Have you sentenced those children to death by starvation? And how could you forget those eighteen lads that the Greedy Troika sold to those foreign scoundrels? How?'

Abo had been in such a state of confusion that during the handover with Milana Petrovna, they had not got round to counting in those twelve kids who…

In his confusion, Abo did not notice how, marching vigorously, he had made his way up to the top floor and wrenched open the heavy iron door of the famous Class Thirteen.

Class Thirteen housed the thirty boys who one month previously had been collected and brought here by the bursar of State Nursery Number Two, Nùrdin Saidov. Saidov had explained his actions as those of a humanitarian. The day the boys arrived, the Troika had convened a general staff meeting and explained that… crying shame… orphan children and all that… so they, the Troika, had decided to accommodate orphan children. In a word, the Troika…

…So why, then, on that very same day, during Abo's night shift, had Nùrdin Saidov, Anna Andreyevna's right hand man, taken eighteen of those thirty kids to an unknown destination in a blacked-out car? Abo was starting to ask himself a lot of questions. Because…

…Because, one month prior to that, again while Abo was on duty, Nùrdin Saidov had taken away, in that same windowless car, and again for what he said

35

were humane reasons, forty little children collected from the poorest *auyls*.[7] On that occasion, Abo had asked, 'You say "the poorest *auyls*", Nùrdin, but does Kazakhstan actually have any really rich *auyls*?'

Nùrdin had answered with a very loud – one might even say a booming – laugh. Then he patted Abo on the back, abruptly cut off his booming laugh, and said, 'You're a very clever chap, Abo. You're very bright. Do you know where being very bright gets you?'

'Where?' asked Abo.

Nùrdin grinned unpleasantly. 'To hell, my dear Abo', he said. 'To hell.'

Oh my Lord, my Creator, thought Abo to himself. This nonentity is threatening me. Me! Of course, how could a chancer like Nùrdin know that the real hell is waiting not for me, but for him?

Then, following a long-standing habit of his, he had started to question his foresight. Three days previously, Abo recalls, he had scolded himself. 'Abo! You need to know your place. The only one who can know this sort of thing is the Creator of Eternity and Infinity.'

***

'This sort of thing' started later. Two hours later.

First, Abo had a shower. It was a blessing that today was Sunday. He was the only person in the whole institution at this time, and he spent a long time taking pleasure in being alone. He took a cold shower in the legendary cold mountain water of Almaty.

Then, feeling blessed, he went into his office and lay down on his narrow iron bed. This was his territory. He must have dozed off, because he found himself being woken up by a vague, disturbing thought. He looked at his watch. Exactly ten o'clock.

He was remembering how that dimwit Nùrdin had smiled his insolent smile and said, 'To hell, my dear Abo. To hell.'

He said that to *me*! Abo thought. Where is he now, the slimy dimwit? Where? In hell, of course. In hell. Immediately he scolded himself. 'Abo, Abo! Fired from the super elite unit. No one needs Major Abo now, admit it. Reduced to the ranks.'

The word 'hell' prompted Abo to think of 'purgatory'. This exotic word drew him in its turn towards another picture – a 'class'. From there he came to 'Class Thirteen is the gateway to Hell.' And that became the name that Abo gave to Class Thirteen.

---

[7] *Auyl* – socio-economic formation considered to constitute the heartland of the nation and a basis for an ethnic and cultural union of the nomadic community. Consisting of 50–70 yurts in the eighteenth century, it developed into its current permanent state of 'rural settlement' (of a minimum of 100 dwellers) when Kazakhs adopted a settled mode of life in the nineteenth and twentieth centuries. *Auyl* can also be used as a synonym for 'native land' and 'homeland', concepts revered by the Kazakhs.

For some reason, Abo next remembered an expression of his own, 'a construct of meat and bone.' Why did I say that?' he wondered. 'Who was I talking about. Ah yes – the late—'

Then he remembered that he and Milana Petrovna at their handover had not counted in the twelve little chaps who had still been there when *that* trouble happened.

Abo went up to the top floor. He opened the heavy wrought-iron door of the ill-fated Class Thirteen and froze in astonishment. The ill-fated Thirteen was empty. 'So', he thought, 'the Troika have heirs – and they are active. Hmmmmm…'

Following another of his numerous long-standing habits, Abo remained unmoving on the spot. A loud, imperious ringing from the tall double gate to the street brought him round, and he automatically looked at the watch on his wrist. Two p.m.

***

Abo was most certainly not expecting the guests who descended on him at that moment.

'Visitors for you, bro!' said one of them. Abo recognised him as a colonel, who back then had called himself Zăŋgiev. The second was a major who back then had called himself Yevstigneyev. It was Abo's guess, though, that they were both using aliases. Just as he had back then, Abo now pretended to be an idiot. When the need arose, he was well able to turn himself into a moron. It had helped him out more than once in Afghanistan.

'Visitors for you, bro!' repeated the colonel (who was now in civilian clothing) as they entered Class Thirteen. 'Today's Sunday, and there's nowhere for us to get ourselves sorted. You popped into our heads. After all, we once spent a whole night in friendly conversation. Give us somewhere to hole up for a bit, will you? You know how it is – men like us can't just show up in a liquor den – but we have to mark the occasion. No choice but to mark it. My friend here – you know him too – was awarded another star yesterday! Meaning what? Meaning we need to pop a cork or two. He's now a lieutenant colonel.' And the self-styled 'bro' burst into wild laughter.

The self-styled bro then pulled two bottles of white vodka and some nibbles out of the pockets of his wide trousers.

The bro politely, s-o-o-o-o very politely asked their host to bring out whatever crockery he happened to have around the place, and Abo fetched some thick glass tumblers. Then began a long process of cajoling Abo to share a *dastarhan* with them, which meant to drink vodka with them. Abo could not stand even the smell of alcohol. The guests, convinced that Abo was a 'worthless creature', which was the name they gave to teetotallers, waved their hands dismissively and started to rinse the lieutenant colonel's new star, as the ceremony was called. Every toast, basically, was made by the bro, while the lieutenant colonel, basically, nodded.

Once or twice, Abo tried to slip away, but was unsuccessful each time. The bro, intoxicated, grabbed him by the scruff of his neck and hugged him round the waist with both arms. Giving Abo a look like that of a hungry dog, he repeated over and over, 'Don't leave us, bro. Don't leave us. Don't leave us!'

The lieutenant colonel now surprised everyone by leaping up in the air and crying out in a reedy voice, 'Why are you bullying him like that? We should be praying for him!'

The bro gave the lieutenant colonel a bewildered look, then straightened up and asked, 'Us? Should be what? Praying? For him? Why?'

'Because he's an Afghan.'

'Who is? He is? An Afghan?'

'Yes. Yes! Him!'

The bro had apparently not been expecting this news, because he bellowed in a thunderous voice, 'Me! I'm an Afghan! Understood? And you're a land rabbit! Understood?'

'I'm a rabbit?' The puny guy calling himself the lieutenant colonel flushed crimson, sprang up, and grabbed the bro by the collar.

They went at it good and proper. This was a real fight, with the occasional short break.

When both these cockerels (which was how Abo saw them) had got their breath back a little, they rushed at each other once more, managing the while to exchange abusive remarks, such as, 'You scumbag!' or, 'You dirty rat!'

During one of the breaks, the bro angrily looked right into his colleague's face and blurted out, 'You snotty-nosed git! You don't know, you can't possibly know, who I was in Afghanistan! You have no idea! I made everyone tremble. Even the generals! Because I was the favourite pupil of the great Corporal Ivasi! I was the best graduate in TSTS-17! You don't know that! You can't possibly know that! You know why?'

'Why?' asked the lieutenant colonel, breathing hard.

'Because you're a jerk!'

That was enough. Abo once more froze. Turned into a lump of rock. For one second, one second only, he was dumbfounded, as if he had been struck by lightning. Then, as always in critical moments, almost automatically and lightning-fast, he managed to get a grip on himself. All without moving a muscle.

'That means... that means they're both...' His thoughts were spinning like flapping pieces of torn cinema film. 'They're *arandators*.' In his mind, he mixed the Kazakh and Russian words meaning 'agent provocateur'.

The two *arandators*, meanwhile, went back to tearing at each other like wild animals. 'This is not a show', concluded Abo. 'This is an outburst of pent-up hostility.'

Abo noticed that it was getting late.

A little later, he noticed that it was already night. He had got up from the sofa and turned on the light without being aware of doing so. His unruly guests were sleeping in awkward positions on two camp beds.

Abo saw that his guests had once again opened bottles of vodka. 'Where from?' he wondered. 'When?' Then he remembered how his only commanding officer, the great Lance Corporal Ivasi, sometimes when he was feeling pleased, or rather, well-pleased, with 'tricks', as they used to call their work, would enthusiastically clap him on the shoulder and say, 'Good work, my worthy pupil!'

The business in which the forty-nine apprentices of the Great Corporal were engaged was codenamed 365. Abo scratched his head. 'Do you suppose this lousy colonel, this *arandator* knows about all that?'

***

Abo knew how to be patient. For this reason, even the great Lance Corporal did not hide from the other forty-eight chaps under his command his special respect for Abo. He always held Abo up as an example. And when the top brass came from Moscow, he always presented Abo last of all, as 'dessert', as the great Lance Corporal liked to put it.

Abo knew how to be patient. And today, from noon to midnight, he remained silent, almost invisible, while the colonel and the major who had allegedly received one more little star carried on with their unbridled booze-up. 'Naive *arandators*', thought Abo. 'These ordinary dime-a-dozen officers can't possibly know who they're dealing with.'

Abo knew how to be patient. He was patient now. He remained patient. Finally, at about midnight, when the drunken fights of the 'big shots', as they fancied themselves, turned really nasty, he very calmly stood up, took both brawlers by the scruff of the neck, hauled them down to the ground floor, and threw them out into the street. He aimed his throw in such a way that both officers found themselves in the muddy, dirty water of the irrigation ditch.

Abo knew how to be patient. He did not have the slightest doubt about the fairness of his action. Throwing the two presumptuous Sherlock Holmeses into the dirty ditch had even brightened him up somewhat, and he had also saved himself from criticism. 'Tomorrow or more likely the day after', he said to himself, 'they'll come crawling back to me asking for forgiveness and begging me to let "this matter" remain strictly between us. They'll even try to buy me off. After all, they measure everyone by reference to their own stunted personalities.'

Abo felt a sense of relief. For some reason he wanted to sing, although he had not been able to sing a note his whole life long. Not even when he was marching and obliged by the regulations, as were all soldiers, to give out at least some kind of cacophonous bawling.

Abo felt a sense of relief. For the first time in his life, he even allowed himself several times to swagger along the long corridor of the ground floor, there and back. Then he turned into his kennel and told himself, 'Till seven!' and went to bed.

He slept until seven, then went into his own morning exercise regime. He sat cross-legged on the floor Kazakh-style, closed his eyes, and 'withdrew into himself', as he put it. He turned into a *balbal*, a stone statue. He called these his 'inner gymnastics'. He opened his eyes and stood up when he felt energy flowing into him in full force.

Former Sergeant Milana Petrovna tended to arrive at work very late. Everyone forgave her, though – they knew that she had to change twice on the way. Today she appeared just before ten o'clock. She took over from the night watchman with her usual meticulousness, but did not go into Class Thirteen to count the twelve lads in there. She did not go in. Did not demand the handover of those 'temporary' (as she called them) kids who had been brought in from distant Kazakh *auyls*. 'That means', thought Abo, 'that this loyal servant of the party and the government is in the loop. In the loop! She's in on it.' Then he immediately checked himself. 'I don't care', he told himself. 'As the song goes, "We're Tatars, it's all the same to us".'

An unusually playful mood seized him, and he allowed himself to lark about. 'Yes Ma'am!' he cried with a wide grin, 'Aye aye, Comrade of the Guard, Staff Sergeant Milana Petrovna!' He deliberately gave her a promotion.

Abo saw that his unaccustomed flattery pleased the bursar of State Nursery Number Two. That was enough to lift his mood.

Abo returned home in high spirits. He knew only one song of his people, and he started to sing it now. Well, he knew its name, 'Bindweed', but not all the words. How did it go? 'Treacherous fate… by a thread I'm dangling… treacherous fate, creeping and strangling…' It was said that the song had been written by the great composer and singer Aķan Seri. It was also said that the song could not be sung in public. 'Interesting', thought Abo. 'Why's that? How can singing a song you like in public be forbidden? That's absurd.'

'This is also absurd', Abo continued, when he saw the long queue at the bus stop. 'Can nothing be done about this?'

'This is absurd, too', Abo thought again, when he saw a group of five strapping young lads brazenly jostling the old men and women, forcing their way onto the already crowded bus. 'Why is this allowed?'

'Absurd again', thought Abo, when the bus on which he had ridden as far as his stop did a lap of honour and left without picking up any of the passengers who were standing, weary from waiting, at the stop.

He remembered the proverb, 'It's a careless owner whose dog has diarrhoea'. His mood had changed. He was upset. He walked past his own hut. He felt that he had to. He had to. A sixth sense was nagging him, saying, 'You can't go in there now.' 'There?' he asked himself. 'I can't go in there?'

Abo walked past his hut. 'What's happening to me?' he asked himself. 'It's like someone is stopping me from going in to my own wife and children. Who? Poor Zara, how will you live without us when the three of us have gone away? Wait. Gone away? Where? And what does "when we go away" even mean? Who are "we"? Why should Zara be left alone?'

Abo was surprised to find himself on Camel's Hump. 'When and why did I come here?' he asked. 'Have I gone completely mad?'

He had a sudden urge to find the shack where Hoopoe lived. He chuckled to himself. 'Why did I call him Hoopoe? He's a perfectly normal guy, right? And what he wants is perfectly clear.'

Then it dawned on him. He was afraid of himself. 'That's it', he said. 'You're a coward, Abo. A coward!'

He could not understand the state he was in, but he finally mastered himself and made up his mind to go home. At that very moment, though, his whole body shuddered as if struck by a huge bolt of electricity. His intuition was telling him that Ajna, his beloved daughter, his golden Ajna was suffering. 'It's begun', he found himself thinking. 'That accursed, unbearable pain. This attack from hell...'

Abo felt in every fibre of his soul that his Ajna, his beloved Ajna, his clever Ajna, had just felt the first treacherous blow. He felt it strike her brain, so soft and vulnerable, and knew that an inhuman pain was contorting her. He knew that she, his ever-patient daughter, had let herself fall onto the soft felt, so that her mother, the kindest of all mothers in the world, would not realise that her beloved daughter had suddenly fallen victim to 'that fit from deepest hell', as the family had come to call the sickness that Abo, the children's father, had brought home to them from Afghanistan.

Abo the father froze at the very top of the hill called by the locals the Camel's Hump. The humpbacked hill.

Abo's heart began to ache. No. Abo's heart was crying. Abo's heart was crying floods of tears. 'How can this be?' he sobbed. 'Three – three! – attacks in just one month. It means... it means that I must... Oh, must I? Yes. I must. I must!'

Abo knew that his usually calm, sensible, Ajna, clever beyond her years, would now be stopping herself from crying out, from frightening her delicate mother, by starting to bite her arms, first one, then the other. Until they bled. Tearing them to shreds.

Abo knew this because he, his children's father, was battle-hardened, a specialist in this matter. So he knew. He knew that now it would be as if barbed wire were tearing the living tissue of his five-year-old daughter into still-living strips, and slowly, slowly making its way to her very insides, her lungs, her guts. It would start to turn them and twist them, as if some evil Žalmauyz Kempir[8]

---

[8] Žalmauyz Kempir – mythological character, often introduced as an old and fearsome woman, similar to Baba Yaga in Slavic cultures.

were wringing out a sheet on the bank of the river behind the *auyl*, to dry it. Once the sheet was wrung out, Žalmauyz Kempir would start to beat it with all her might against the trunk of a one-hundred-year old oak tree, to speed up the drying process.

Try to endure it… Oh, my Lord, my Creator! When and how did mankind get under your skin? Oh, Lord, the Almighty…

Abo could feel that he was drenched with sweat. 'Me, sweating!' he thought. 'What does it take to make me sweat? Me – purified through fire and water… I do not sweat. Me, Abo, purified on the hot griddles of Afghanistan. Me, the famous Abo, second only to Master Ivasi… it would need all the devils of hell to come down on me at once! Maybe then I'd be sweating. I'm covered in sweat, though, drenched beyond belief. That means that Ajna is really ill.'

Oh, Ajna… Now Abo suddenly sensed that something was not right with his younger one, Bolo, just four years old. He wanted to run home, but something held him back. Somewhere there, in the depths of his consciousness, an explosion went off, an explosion of thought. 'I must not… What I planned to do… I must not do it with Zara there… their mother… I must not!'

Abo's head was beginning to spin. He had no idea what was going on. That ridiculous remark flashed into his mind: What will happen to poor Zara when the three of us are gone?

***

When, at seven in the morning, Abo returned to his hut, he was greeted by the scene he had been afraid he would stumble in on. Zara, his Zara, the mother of his children, was sitting on the floor, on the felt, turned into a stone idol. She did not even react to his entrance.

Abo saw that during the night, Zara had become pinched and drawn beyond recognition. She was no more than a skeleton of the Zara whom he, by prior mutual agreement, had stolen away one night, her parents being convinced that their daughter was a beauty worthy of becoming the precious jewel of a wealthy family in a neighbouring *auyl*.

Abo and Zara had followed their hearts and decided the question for themselves. Put an end to any argument on the matter.

But now… but now this beauty, who had made Abo so happy – Abo, the guy with the strange name, the top dog in the neighbouring *auyl* of Kegesi – and had given her Mr Right two golden children, Ajna and Bolo – this beauty was sitting on the floor, turned into a stone *balbal*.

Abo looked at her and did not recognise her. While he stood there, tears suddenly gushed from the two small slits that just yesterday had been two beautiful, intelligent eyes; an implausible abundance of tears of desperate, inconsolable grief. At the same time, the woman remained a stone *balbal*. Extraordinary! The fine blue satin fabric covering the small breast with its two modest bumps instantly grew dark from the mother's tears.

42

Some sixth sense told Abo that now was not the time to ask Zara what had happened. He should not even look at her face, especially not her eyes. Those deep eyes, always sparkling with love. He must not.

Some sixth sense told Abo that he should now turn to his Creator, and to him alone. He raised himself onto his haunches and, placing his palms together, pleaded with his Creator. 'Oh Lord, Creator of Eternity and Infinity, tell me, how have I sinned before you? You, my Creator, made me as I am. The descendants of my great-grandfather Ḳara-Aspan, they say, exceeded one hundred and fifty people. Maybe there were many more than that. Who has counted them? Our people believe that it is wrong to carry out a census. Or rather, they used to believe that. Oh, my Lord, my Creator! When I was called up into the Red Army, a snot-nosed kid...'

Some sixth sense told Abo that he should stop now. He should halt the surging tide of his thoughts.

He had been taught how to halt the surging tide of his thoughts by – Afghanistan. Or rather, by Master Ivanov, known in common parlance as Ivasi. Back when they were stationed at a place on the high bank of the Volga, Ivasi had apparently noticed that the cadet Ḳara-Aspanov had fallen into deep thought about something. Stepping right up to him (Abo was then just one of the snotty-nosed new recruits), Ivasi had bellowed in a voice like summer thunder, 'Private Ḳara-Aspanov! Empty that pot of yours! All the trash that's piled up in your head – chuck it out. There's no place for trash in our business. Remember that! Remember it for the rest of your life! Thoughts are trash! Rubbish! In a word, shit. Got it?'

The red nose of the Great Master threateningly touched the bridge of the cadet's nose. As a method of instruction, it was very, very effective.

Abo, of course, got it. Even without little lectures like this, they were kept out on the parade ground until last thing, and when the cadets finally returned to their dormitory, they were barely able to drag their feet. Reaching their iron cots, they fell straight onto them and slept the sleep of the dead. After three months of this, there was not a single light left on in the head of any of the cadets. Just emptiness. Just a few springy movements.

Over the course of the first six months of their new posting, though, the Great Teacher's good-for-nothings showed the world such miracles that all the specialists in the combined overseas units (there were every kind there) began to gasp and groan with astonishment. Abo understood this, because out of all the 'volunteers', he was the only very clever one.

Now there he was, Abo, sitting there, hardly breathing, so as not to wake up Zara, his Zara, the mother of two innocent victims, two angels, Ajna and Bolo, who were sleeping deeply after returning from a hell made by human hands.

***

43

Ajna and Bolo were deeply asleep. Abo realised that Zara was also asleep – sitting up, in the pose of a graven idol. Sleeping. 'The poor thing', he thought. 'She's exhausted. If even I, hardened and battle-scarred, am suffering as I am, what is it like for her, with her tender-hearted, compassionate nature?'

How beautiful she was... Abo wrenched himself away from his wife's face. He knew that the look in his eyes was piercing, and Zara was very sensitive – perhaps too sensitive. His look was heavy – like lead, as Ivasi himself used to say. Ivasi. In the seventh month of their tour in Herat, the Teacher decided to mark the fact that they had now killed one thousand of their 'prey', as they called the Afghans, Americans, British and French killed by his unit. Not the rank and file – the riff-raff – but the officers, engineers, highly qualified men with sought-after skills. They had even killed a general, by all accounts, a Hindu by origin.

Ivasi decided to hold this important event in the reading room of the city's only library. The men were amazed to see that among the invitees were as many as eight generals, who dazzled proceedings with their presence. There was even – and this they found particularly difficult to believe – one lieutenant general from the engineer corps.

The very last to be presented to the elite guests – for dessert, as Ivasi himself put it – was Abo, the Falcon from Tien Shan, a name the Teacher gave him in a moment of improvisation. In front of everyone, Ivasi hugged Abo tightly, pressing him to his chest. 'He should not have done that', thought Abo, even at that very moment. Because from the Teacher, whom he sincerely adored, came a whiff of sharp, cheap eau de cologne and the revolting stench of moonshine. In that second, Abo, a man from the steppes, conceived a hatred of his idol. That was all it took. Abo was even sorry that Ivasi had disappointed him. But it was too late.

Sitting here now in his hut, he remembered clearly how back then, in distant Herat, he had wanted to challenge Ivasi to a duel. Abo, this now insignificant, demoted major, wanted to duel with the cast iron master, the virtuoso of his craft, Ivasi. Right there, in the library, in front of those brilliant generals and colonels. It was laughable, of course. At that moment, though, Abo felt his superiority over Ivasi and thought, 'the evil Teacher must be punished'.

Abo scolded himself sharply, and hauled himself out of his reminiscences and back to the rented house on the nameless street near the penultimate bus stop of route 526 in the city of Almaty. Finally back in the real world and his rented apartment, and seeing his children sleeping peacefully on the felt and his wife Zara sleeping sitting upright, he thought, 'How can I set my children free from this nightmare, this all-consuming nightmare from hell? My darling children. How? How?'

There was only one answer. The one at which he had arrived three long, painful days ago. Retribution. Retribution! There was no other way.

Abo knew that his only support on this frail planet Earth was Zara, a very sensitive soul, very delicate. He looked cautiously at his wife, sitting there asleep, and wondered if she was only pretending to be sleeping.

'She's the only one', he said to himself. 'My Zara is the only one who was able to pick up quickly from me the ability to take rest on the go. Sleeping on the move, or sitting on a camel, or sitting on a horse, used to be the lot of many Kazakh women. Was. So… now…'

***

Zara knew everything. Three days ago, some sixth sense had told her that Abo, her Abo, who gave her existence its meaning, had taken a decision. From the changed timbre of his voice, from the strange looks that sometimes flashed in his eye, from the way he spoke to her, sometimes going far away into a completely different world, she began to expect him to do something bad, something strange, something terrible, even. Her beloved.

Zara had known since childhood that puppies are blind for three days after birth. Now she seemed to herself to have been as blind as a new-born pup. 'You stupid woman, Zara!' she told herself. 'Run quickly! Run!' And then, 'What for? Where? Why? From whom?'

There was no answer. But the question became more and more insistent, more and more strange, and, it seemed, meaningless. 'Why? From whom?'

A voice that seemed to belong to someone else altogether suddenly prompted her. 'Go to the *auyl*. Your native *auyl*. Go to Kegesi. Kegesi!'

An unnerving memory came back to her. One day, in an ordinary conversation, she had accidentally confused the Kazakh Kegen with the Japanese Kegesi, and her husband had frowned at her, his look grave and suspicious. They had quickly laughed, though, and to their hearts' content. Those were the happy couple's young years, before Ajna and Bolo were born. Why had they laughed? Because it was funny, that was all. They did not need another answer; they were confident in their future.

'What is Kegesi?' Zara had asked again.

'It's a city in Japan', guffawed the demoted major from TSTS-17.

Zara knew, Zara was sure, Zara never doubted that a happy future was waiting for them. Zara smiled. 'Tell me about Japan, too. Where is Japan? Where is Kegen?'

A playful feeling took hold of her and she threw her husband a flirtatious look. He smiled too, and exactly repeated his wife's words. 'Tell me about Japan, too. Where is Japan? Where is Kegen?'

'Show me Kegen' became a password to sensual pleasures for the young couple. At those words, both would smile, and both would instantly be joined into a single "orgiasm", as Abo liked to joke, though he knew the right word well enough.

***

45

'The high mountains have their own character, like my Abo.' Zara screwed up her eyes and stared at Mount Talġar, towering over the city. 'Talġar is like my Abo. Five kilometres high. You can't tell...' Zara was not aware that she was smiling. 'Talġar is like my Abo – good.' At that moment, though, she noticed a trail of white cloud, hanging like a little flag on the tip of Talġar's conical peak. She frowned. 'Ah', she said. 'This means that Talġar is preparing a surprise for us women of Almaty. We can expect a little present from its very top – nasty storms, hail the size of a man's fist. Wait, Zara, wait! Wait, Zara, wait! Wait, Zara, wait. Your know your lot in life... your destiny... your destiny... your destiny... your destiny is to be patient and wait, to be patient and wait, to be patient and wait, to be patient and wait. To be patient!'

Zara recalled the nightmare that had begun exactly three months previously. Nine blows in three months. And what blows, what blows – typhoons. Hell, real hell. Every blow a typhoon. In every blow – the devil incarnate. In every blow – an orgy of a hundred devils and a thousand, thousand demons.

Zara's head slowly began to whirl. She hugged the trunk of the apple tree under which she was standing. 'Oh, my Lord, my Creator', she said, and slowly, so slowly, slid to the ground.

Abo found her. She woke up to find that Abo was carrying her into the house in his arms. Zara was ashamed, and immediately decided that Abo must not – must NOT – think that she had fainted. She did something a lot of women might do: she pretended that she had deliberately been having Abo on, that she had not been asleep, and she began to laugh, letting out peals of silvery laughter in her very pretty, very sexy voice.

This – her pretty, silvery, sexy laugh – turned into something wholly unexpected – the coming together of two loving hearts. Or perhaps not so surprising. She knew that Abo, her Abo, would never miss even the slightest opportunity.

When Zara was finally convinced that Abo had once more fallen into his heroic sleep, and the children were still dead to the world, Zara, moving gently and quietly so as not to wake her husband, got up and went out into their skimpy, regulation one-tenth of an acre garden.

Here, in the skimpy little garden, the truth of the position her family was now in dawned on her. 'No! No! No!' she exclaimed, not noticing that she was crying out as loudly as if the executioner himself were standing in front of her. 'I won't let it happen. I won't. I won't!' Up to that point, her resolute anger had been unfocused, lacking in real venom. Now, though, she suddenly recalled that a hard look had crossed Abo's face while he was playing with the children, and there had been something strange in his laugh. Something indecipherable, and sinister. 'Nothing good will come of this', she thought. 'Nothing good.'

And then, *apropos* of nothing at all, she thought, 'No! No! I will not hand my children over! I won't allow it. I won't let anyone... not even Abo... I won't!'

That was the strangest thing. The way Zara all of a sudden, resolutely, at the top of her voice, cried out into the emptiness, 'I will not give my children to anyone! Not even to you, my beloved, my Abo. I will not let it happen! I will not! I will never give them up!'

She then surprised herself even more by deciding – again, *apropos* of nothing, as far as she was aware – that she would indeed take the children away. 'Yes, I will. I'll take them away. I'll take the children to my *auyl*. I'll take them to my parents. My parents will make them better. In the *auyls* there are healers. They'll cure…' She stopped, and finished sadly, 'Abo, alas, won't acknowledge any kind of healer there. He's said so himself. He won't let me. So I'll…'

***

'Poor, poor moon, my moon', thought Abo. 'You're so full today. You're so bright today. You're so lonely today. Moon, bright moon, up above the Whole Wide World, you alone are pure, you alone are just. Help me. Help me!'

'So lonely today. Moon, my bright moon, up above the Whole Wide World, you alone are pure, you alone are just. Help me!'

He recorded with surprise that he was once again standing on his own, at night, on Camel's Hump. 'When did I come here? Why did I come here?' As usual, he talked to himself. 'I seem to have slept all day at home. I never do that. Well, well. True, Zara and I did go out into the master's skimpy garden a couple of times. Zara… she seems to sense my intention. She's very, very sensitive to me. That means that I really must do it tonight. This very night.'

Abo turned back towards the south. A feeling of wonder took him. There was the moon, in her place, full and round, but now she seemed to be pinned to the very tip of Mount Talġar, lighting it with her brilliant light. The white summits of the Tien Shan ridge were so close that between himself and the white ridges, just at that moment, there was no million-strong city of Almaty. Just the big, white moon hanging on the peak of Talġar, and Abo himself, standing there with his burden from hell. 'It's as if my soul is looking for an ally', thought Abo. 'My soul is an orphan. And the moon… the moon is also an orphan. You see, Abo? The moon has been left all alone. All the stars have abandoned her, betrayed her.' Aloud, he said: 'I'm the only one who understands you.'

Now, like a pickpocket, there crept into his soul an unusual feeling of pride, and Abo allowed himself a certain arrogance. 'I'm talking to the moon, but the moon, when all is said and done, is only a satellite of Earth, and Earth, when all is said and done, is just one of the Sun's satellites. And the Sun, when all is said and done, is only one of seven billion suns, among which there are supergiants, thousands of times more powerful and thousands of times more massive than our Sun. So, you, Abo, don't be like a snot-nosed street kid! Know your true place! And know, Abo, that your Creator is the Supreme Mind, ruler of Eternity and Infinity. And between us, between the Higher Mind and me, no one and nothing should come!'

Then Abo remembered that he had wanted to consult with the hoopoe-like man – though perhaps he had been a little unjust in calling him Hoopoe.

When Abo approached Hoopoe's hut, he saw a feeble light in the ground-level window, and his spirits rose. 'That means he's home', he thought.

Abo stooped down low to knock on the window, and then straightened up in surprise as the dim light went out altogether. He stood there for a while, and had just set off on his way back when a woman came out of the hut, almost at a run. Abo recognised the wife of Hoopoe. She was sobbing, and threw herself onto Abo's neck and began to wail rhythmically, lamenting as Kazakh women do when their husbands have died.

Abo stooped once more to try to calm the unhappy woman. The woman, though, continued wailing, wailing rhythmically, lamenting as Kazakh women do when their husbands have died. After a while, Abo realised that her husband had not in fact died; he was still alive, but had abandoned his family, his six little sprats, in order to save his homeland, his Kazakhstan, from catastrophe. Her husband, whom Abo had named Hoopoe, had decided to dismantle the infernal machine buried between the Aral and Caspian seas. That was what all this was about.

Abo asked her, 'What is your name, *žeņeše*?'[9]

The woman abruptly stopped crying and answered calmly, 'Sajra.'

'What a fine-sounding name, thought Abo. 'Almost like my Zara.'

Abo stood up straight, and for some reason his voice became loud and decisive, as if he had been arguing with someone and won. 'Only people such as your husband…' He faltered, wondering what the man's name was.

Sajra readily prompted him. 'Asan. His name is Asan. My falcon', she added unexpectedly. 'My falcon.'

'Only such people as your husband,' resumed Abo, 'your falcon, will be able to save mankind. The lot of all the rest is to exist and live out their days, and then to disappear without a trace. So be proud, be proud of your falcon, Sajra! You're a lucky woman, Sajra.'

With that, he straightened up, and, without even saying goodbye, set off towards the white summits of the Tien Shan ridge.

***

The beauty from the Turkmen *kishlak*[10] of Kôk Ajla was also called Sajra. That summer, their famous unit TSTS-17 had been stationed in a mountain gorge near the city of Herat.

One day, his Teacher Ivasi whispered to him, 'Our mission in this gorge is to test an infernal machine. I'm only telling you because you're special to me. You're a special man in our special unit.'

---

[9] *Žeņeše* – form of address to an older sister-in-law or, generally, an older married woman.

[10] *Kishlak* – Turkmen village.

The Teacher Ivasi evidently thought that he had said something incredibly witty, because he spent a long, long time emitting reverberating guffaws and endlessly repeating, 'You're a special man in our special unit.'

He then puffed himself up in a manner befitting an important official, and although there was not a soul to be seen except the two of them, whispered gravely, 'Only the two of us will know about this infernal machine, understood? I've got clearance from the top brass for just the two of us to know. So button your lip.'

This was how Ivasi tended to express himself. He was not the most literary of men.

Three days later, the Teacher Ivasi and his favourite pupil Abo paid a courtesy visit to the mullah Mùrat, whose stone house was enclosed by a stone wall. They took expensive presents with them.

Abo was always a welcome guest of the mullah Mùrat and his numerous servants. They called him 'Muslim Bala', which meant a young Muslim.

The Teacher Ivasi and his favourite pupil tried to follow all the rules of propriety befitting (as they understood it) honoured guests. All the grandsons, granddaughters, great-grandsons, and great-great-granddaughters of the mullah Mùrat were given expensive, precious gifts, while the mullah himself received an *akalteke* stallion – the dream of every Turkmen. The beauty Sajra, meanwhile, presented (on behalf of her grandfather) a precious gift for Ivasi's wife – a set of very, very expensive earrings. After all, you could not expect Turkmens from the small *kishlak* of Kôk Ajla to know that their honoured guest, Ivasi-Aġa, as Sajra called him, was a committed, notorious bachelor.

The Teacher Ivasi and his pupil Abo then spent a long time exchanging Eastern courtesies with the mullah Mùrat and his descendants. After this the meal was served. At a generous, abundant *dastarhan*, an ever-growing supply of delicious, diverse national dishes and sweets appeared in turn. Next it was time to praise the merits of the guests and, of course, the hosts. Then, when the blazing Asian nozzle known as the Sun began its slow cooling process, the guests reminded their generous hosts that they were still soldiers, after all, and this area was full of all sorts of *kaffirs*,[11] and they were, alas, forced to interrupt their happy stay with the great, wise old man. And they went out beyond the high stone fence.

The entire family, of course, had to see their special guests off, from the six-month-old still in nappies to the white-bearded great-grandfather. At this point, the chief guest Ivasi had a bright idea. He would like to take a picture. 'As a nice keepsake', Chief Guest Ivasi repeated several times. A small (as Turkmens viewed these things) family contingent, consisting of a mere seventy-two souls, came out into the narrow, crooked street in the *kishlak* of Kôk Ajla.

---

[11] *Kaffir* – non-believer or infidel in Islam; in Kazakh colloquial speech also a synonym for dishonest, ignominious or cruel.

Abo was amazed when his Teacher Ivasi-Aġa turned out to be not just a notorious bachelor, but also a notorious amateur photographer.

Abo was amazed again when his Teacher, thoroughly enjoying his back-up profession as a photographer, suggested that he, Abo, should stand next to the elder, the mullah Mùrat, and then with an edge of something like sarcasm, declared with a smile, 'My photos will open a direct way to paradise for all of you!' He said this in Russian, of course; in a near-whisper, he added, 'You're not to translate what I just said into... whatever language they speak round here. It stays between us.'

The surprises went on coming. Ivasi now beckoned Abo over with his right index finger, and evidently finding it hard to suppress his excitement, whispered, 'There! You see that tank over there, the one covered in black armour-plating? No gun barrel. That one. You see it?'

Abo nodded.

'Now you've seen it, remember it. That's a miracle-tank, a twenty-first-century weapon. Do you hear me?' The great Teacher had a habit of not pronouncing a few letters in some words. 'You hear me? It's a tech-miracle. The twenty-first century! You hear me? Tech-miracle! Black beetle! Just between you and me, you can call this the three hundred and sixty-sixth miracle. You haven't forgotten those three hundred and sixty-five methods of enemy destruction that I taught you greenhorns? That black beetle is the three hundred and sixty-sixth miracle.'

Abo nodded again, and committed it to memory forever. Tech-miracle. Black Beetle.

At this moment, while the Teacher and his diligent pupil were whispering, the mullah Mùrat apparently conceived a desire to say something to his main guest. He beckoned them both over – Abo as well.

Abo was only nineteen years old at that time, and as a young eastern man would, he looked at Ivasi for guidance. Ivasi, preening himself a little, nodded to signify that Abo should go to the mullah. He even gave him the gentlest of pushes. 'Go. When a *saxaul*[12] calls you over, just go.'

Abo recalled now how, on Afghan soil near Herat, his Teacher Ivasi had got in a muddle over the words 'aksakal' and 'saxaul'.

The white-bearded leader rose from his seat, warmly hugged the slender young man, and, putting his hands together, blessed him and wished him happiness.

At that moment, Abo felt a strange blast of warm air, coming from he knew not what. He turned round, and there, looming big and black was the blackened black beast, the Black Beetle – the tech-miracle.

Just one week later, the mullah was dead. The head of a family of seventy-two living souls, born to live, yes, who also should have lived long lives. It was

---

[12] *Saxaul* – dry, prickly tree growing in the desert and semi-desert, a symbol of endurance; *aksakal* is Russian for *aḳsaḳal* means a respected elder.

said that this venerable steppe elder suffered greatly, cried out a loud, inhuman cry, and in the end shot himself with a hunting rifle right in his grey-haired, wise old head.

Ivasi's team of forty-nine 'eagles' had gone on a mission to the mountainous region of Faizabad, home to the highest peaks of the Pamir-Himalayan ridge, the so-called 'ten-thousand metre peaks'. They met with great success, and returned having lost only three of their number but wiped out more than three thousand locals. They came down into the *kishlak* of Kôk Ajla, and there that good soul Abo learned that of the vast family of the mullah Mùrat, only Sajra remained alive. Sajra, of whose glowing beauty Abo had forbidden himself even to think. Sajra, even to think of whose beauty was a sin.

When acquaintances from the *kishlak* of Kôk Ajla told this terrible story, Abo, iron Abo, almost lost his mind, and when he learned how the orthodox Muslims, who condemn suicide, themselves were forced to 'help' the weak-willed to escape this fragile, cursed world, his indignation knew no bounds. He was ready for anything.

Abo, unbending Abo, about whom they said, 'That stone monument there, and our Abo – they are one and the same; you won't move either one or the other' – this same Abo started to cry like a child. No; he did not merely cry – he broke into floods of tears. He broke into floods of tears, and set off at a run towards the Turkmen *kishlak*.

With tears still on his cheeks, Abo sprang like a panther over the high stone wall, which was there to keep out unwanted intruders, and found himself in the courtyard of the family's fortress. He immediately felt as if he had accidentally fallen into hell, a place everyone on Earth talks about, but no one, fortunately, has yet seen.

In this hell he sought out Sajra and found her still alive, only… it would have been better not to have found her. Better not to have seen her.

This Sajra was a terrible copy of the fairy-tale princess, the fairy-tale fairy, with whom back in his early childhood he had frolicked in his imagination, poor, desperate dreamer Abo.

There in front of Abo, the same Abo who only yesterday had celebrated a happy event – his promotion to the rank of major – in front of this Abo, appearing in all the splendour of his new military uniform, lay a beautifully dressed skeleton.

The skeleton, with hopeless, lightless eyes, looked at Abo and tried to say something, tried to move its almost lifeless lips, but… but the almost dead lips could open only slightly, to reveal the pearl-white teeth that just yesterday had been in the dreams of all the young Turkmen lads in the surrounding *kishlaks*, and of one other – the young Kazakh, who had managed over and over to suppress his surging, inappropriate, personal feelings: Abo.

***

Completely out of the blue, Lieutenant General Ivasi, with two stars on his chest and rather the worse for wear, appeared at the high stone gates of his venerable *kunak*,[13] the mullah Mùrat. Extraordinarily bad timing. Abo had just closed the eyes of the unfortunate beauty and was on his way out.

Both, naturally, were taken aback.

'You... You? What are you doing here?' This was the lieutenant general.

The lieutenant general waited for Abo to become flustered and, if not exactly frightened, then at least embarrassed. The rest of Ivasi's subordinates would have done just that. Abo, though, his pet, his little brat, unexpectedly growled, 'What are *you* doing here?'

These words – not words, bombs – exploded right in the lieutenant general's face. He was a lieutenant general! And a famous warrior with two gold stars on his chest. What rankled most, though, was that this pup, as Ivasi himself still thought of this home-grown hero – this pup had allowed himself to walk straight by his commanding officer – and not just any commanding officer, but the officer in charge of special unit TSTS-17, the man known throughout the armed forces as Ivasi.

Ivasi was at first confused, but quickly managed to become enraged. In his rage he allowed himself to start screaming – quite literally. 'Hey you, puppy, come back here!'

That was all it took.

This was the Teacher's first mistake. The Teacher had allowed himself to give way to anger. 'Anger is your greatest enemy!' he used to tell his chicks. 'Don't let that old Baba Yaga in!'

His next blunder was to pitch right in with a stream of foul language. He had a reputation for this – indeed, he was a leader in his field. It seemed that he had decided to get in the first blow to the groin. His pupil, though, dodged aside with lightning speed.

Things continued to develop. Over the course of the next minute, the Teacher worked out that he was making mistakes: not one of his famously deadly blows had reached its target. On the contrary, on the handsome young face of the already hated pupil, a smile had come out and started to shine. A smile full of insolence and mockery.

The Teacher decided to deploy one of his secret blows (legal ownership of which was properly his) in order to smash his rat of a pupil for good – which being translated meant to kill him. He walked around a little, made an apparently unsuccessful jump at Abo, appeared to stumble, and just as it seemed that he on his way down, he struck out suddenly. He was confident that his lightning-fast subterfuge would have the desired result, so one can imagine his momentary shock when he saw Abo still alive, and still smiling. What a disgrace! He had been disgraced, and worse, his shame had been witnessed by

---

[13] *Kunak* – a good friend; a blood brother in the Caucasus.

a bunch of *chuchmeks*[14] who had appeared from somewhere and were gawping at the fight between the man who yesterday had been the teacher and the man who yesterday had been his pupil. Where did they come from?

Ivasi's momentary shock led him to make an even more rash decision. He shouted, 'Hey, you, *chuchmeks*! I order you to kill this traitor!'

In so doing, Ivasi foolishly sentenced himself to death. One of the *chuchmeks* blasted a shotgun at point-blank range into Ivasi's belly.

***

'Time is definitely a relative concept', thought Abo, looking at his watch and seeing that it was four in the morning. 'Where on earth have I been, for it to be that time?' He remembered talking to Hoopoe's wife. He remembered thinking (or maybe he had said it out loud, to Hoopoe's wife?), 'People like Hoopoe will save mankind.' Abo felt himself smiling as he recalled the strong objection in the voice of Hoopoe's wife: 'His name is not Hoopoe! He is Asan. And I am Sajra.' 'OK, OK, OK!' Abo had backed off hastily. 'As you wish.' As sneaky as a sucker punch, the thought erupted in his mind, 'Sajra – there; Sajra – here; and I have my Zara. Why do beautiful women…' Abo did not dare bring this idea to its logical conclusion. He had managed thus far to keep his wife's name – Zara – off the list of doomed women. 'Zara, my Zara.'

Abo realised, or felt, that he was standing not far from his hut number 526, and frightful sounds were striking his consciousness, like treacherous bolts of lightning. The sounds of crying. No, not crying – cursing. Ajna and Bolo were cursing not with words, but with the intonation of their voices, plaintively cursing this irrational world. Ajna and Bolo, his angels.

Ajna and Bolo were crying. No! It wasn't crying, it was… a plea to deliver them from this curse – the curse of life. Deliver them! Quickly. Now! This minute! Right now!

Abo's heart trembled, and for the first time in his life, the courage of the great warrior Abo failed, and he ran. To his shame, he ran away.

It had been four o'clock in the morning, and now two hours later he got out of the overcrowded, decrepit bus and found himself in the square at Almaty-1 train station. 'Why did I come here?' he asked. 'When?'

An hour later he caught himself at Barakholka Market. An hour after that, he found himself at the bus station, sitting and waiting for someone, or something. Most surprising of all, though, at exactly nine o'clock, he showed up at work. Marina Petrovna saw him and almost choked. Quickly pulling herself together, she tried to make a joke. 'Comrade Ķara-Aspanov, you are late. One minute late. Advising you of this is Reserve Staff Sergeant Marina Petrovna Belyaeva!'

---

[14] *Chuchmek* – ethnic slur in Russian for Asians, Siberian Mongoloids or Caucasians.

It was a harmless little sin for Corporal Marina Petrovna Belyaeva to pass herself off as a staff sergeant. Abo tried to smile condescendingly, but realised that he had not succeeded. Marina Petrovna, imagining herself to be the big boss, simply because she was at that moment sitting in the office of the acting deputy director of Nursery Number Two, struck an official pose, and said, 'By the way, Ķara-Aspanov, let me share with you the glad news that we have a new director!' Seeing that her announcement had not had the slightest effect on Abo, she contrived to take offence, and with a kind of sadistic exaltation declared, 'He has many fine qualities. He is, for example, very businesslike. He is the younger brother of the late Nùrdin Saidov – Kamardin Saidov! You already know him.' Marina Petrovna looked at Abo with a vindictive exaltation, but once more acknowledging that she had not, apparently, got through to wild-man Abo, she summed up her bombshell in a few blunt words. 'As you know, he is a very, very vindictive being.'

When Marina said the names of Nùrdin and Kamardin, Abo suddenly recalled with great clarity the tableau of the three lying dead on the yellow rug: Anna Andreyevna Petrenko, Nùrdin Saidov and Bajbaķ Malšybaev. In his memory arose a photo-sharp picture of each of the slain. He remembered the scars, such very fine scars. And how the heads of all three, as if someone had given the order: Attention! were turned to the right. And one more memory – the sound of his own inadvertent cry: 'The work of a master!'

This Abo, currently lying on his iron work-issue cot, said to that other one, the one who four days previously had stood on the edge of the yellow rug, 'What a fool you are, Abo! You are an idiot.'

This Abo, currently lying on his iron work-issue cot, as usual commanded himself: sleep for four hours! But for the first time in all his adult years, his body, alas, did not obey its master. On the contrary, against his will, unwanted visions descended on him, visions of things which he feared above all else and from which, that very morning, he had fled in panic. He saw Ajna and Bolo, stretching out their chubby little hands towards him, crying, sobbing, screaming in desperation. They were begging him, pleading with him, shedding floods of tears and pleading with him to save them, save them from this nightmare.

Abo, their father, himself knew what the nightmare was like, and to his eternal shame, he did not know how to save his Ajna and Bolo. How was he to save them? How? How?

Abo could see very clearly, as if it were really happening, his beloved, tormented Zara, turning into a stone *balbal* at the head of his children's bed. In the petrified eyes of his wife, Abo intuitively read a prayer: 'Have pity on me. Give me just one teardrop.' *Give me just one teardrop.* Abo could not catch to whom this cry of Zara's soul was addressed – whether to him or to the Creator himself.

He saw that Zara had run out of tears. The whole supply had been used up. Such a thing can happen, then.

Abo tried again, and this time on the command of 'Sleep for four hours!' he fell asleep and slept soundly, as only Abo knew how.

***

Zara, that stone *balbal*, crafted millennia ago by unknown artists, saw how her husband, Abo, came into their hut towards morning. She saw how he sat down and crossed his legs, frowned slightly and stared at their suffering, screaming children. Zara saw how he also then turned into a stone *balbal*. The stone *balbal* sat for a long time, then slowly, quietly got up and walked out of their temporary family home.

Abo had exuded a tranquillity which frightened Zara. Her fear served to confirm in her own mind that she had understood everything. Abo had made some kind of decision. That meant, of course, that Zara, too, had a decision to make. What? What must she do? Zara did not yet know.

Two hours later, this particular fit was over. The children, almost simultaneously, calmed down. Almost simultaneously fell asleep. Fell asleep exhausted and, Oh my Lord, my Creator! visibly aged. Zara stared long and intently at her children, her Ajna and Bolo, then jumped up as if she had been scalded. Her six-year-old Ajna and four-year-old Bolo suddenly seemed to her to be wooden dolls, carved in the shape of an old fisherman and his aged wife.

Strange things started to happen. Zara, perfectly calm, went out into the master's garden. Juicy red apples, the famous Almaty Oporto, were lying around under the apple trees. The mistress of their rented house appeared only once a month, as she put it, 'to collect her thirty roubles.'

Zara picked up a bright red ripe apple and gobbled it down at once, as if she were a starving first-year schoolgirl.

Next she went into the dark, narrow pantry. She waited for her eyes to adjust to the darkness, and when she was able to distinguish the various bits of household stuff, she pulled something out of a hiding-place, something wrapped in a white linen cloth. Slowly she unwrapped the linen cloth, and there was a black axe with a white handle.

Now Zara, one of the most tranquil creatures on earth, abruptly tested the dull steel axe blade with her right index finger. Apparently still satisfied with its condition, she smiled, reassured.

Then she came out of the shed with the unwrapped axe, the axe with the white handle and the blue-black blade, and made her way to the dry ditch at the end of the plot, where there was a standard Soviet lavatory, constructed of a variety of planks. She stood still for a minute, then entered the toilet. There she noticed for the first time in her life that toilets have a hole in them the shape of a human heart. She gave an unreadable smile, then returned to the narrow, dark cubbyhole, carefully wrapped up the weapon (which is what it had been, in this instance), and equally carefully put it back in its former hiding-place.

55

Now she felt very clearly that it was up to her to take some kind of action. She must not put the fate of her Ajna and Bolo into anyone else's hands, not even Abo's. That was clear. Zara waited patiently. She waited for Ajna and Bolo to wake up. She settled to waiting.

Zara knew that the lazy southern Sun, having reached its zenith, would sort itself out a nice long rest, luxuriating in the peace up there, and then, only when it had rested sufficiently, would it lazily begin to descend to the horizon. 'The Sun has a watering hole down there', concluded Zara.

Zara had a gold wristwatch, given to her by Abo to mark the twenty-fifth birthday of his, as Abo put it, 'support'. He never spoke his love aloud; he declared himself in a soft, sincere smile, a light touch of his palm on her smooth back. Zara knew that their relations were simple, but sincere.

At four thirty Ajna woke up. At four forty – Bolo. Both children were serious, reserved, polite. Ajna was a naturally happy girl. At least she had been, until recently, until about three months ago, when this hell started.

This hell had begun suddenly, as all misfortunes do, three months previously, while they were visiting relatives of Abo's in Kegen (or, as Abo jokingly called his native *auyl*, Kegesi). For its first victim, this hell had chosen Abo – not by chance, it seemed. Abo seemed to guess at once where his hallucinations were coming from. Towards evening, probably trying not to give away what was happening, moaning and sighing quietly, he had suddenly saddled up his favourite horse Bajšübar, and taken himself off to the mountains. He returned from the mountains the next morning, noticeably thinner, with clouded, colourless eyes.

Zara looked hard at the children. While the fit had been in progress, the children seemed to age horribly. Now, though, to her surprise, they looked as if nothing untoward had happened. Or was she mistaken? 'Bolo seems fine', she thought. Ajna, though, was still showing signs of her suffering. She still looked like a girl who had aged suddenly, or perhaps an old woman who had been rejuvenated. 'Zara', she said to herself, 'Have you lost your mind? Everything's OK! It's you, Zara – you're losing your mind.'

Zara once more looked hard at her children, still afraid of what she might see. This time, everything seemed to be fine. Except that Bolo's face seemed swollen. 'Is there something wrong with me?' Zara asked herself. 'Is this all too much for me? No wonder people say, fear has big eyes. That's enough, Zara. Dress the children and go straight to Kegesi.'

The last bus to Kegesi, according to the schedule, was supposed to leave at six thirty in the evening. It was now four twenty. 'We'll have time', Zara fretted. 'We have to.'

When Zara and the children reached the bus station, they still had half an hour left, but the bus was already revving its engine. Zara took the children's hands and went in hot pursuit, but the wretched, clapped out old bus, staggering and stumbling the way a drunk runs away from a policeman, roared off so zealously that the only man there (he had been seeing someone off, perhaps) let out a loud, sneering laugh, and said, 'You shouldn't have slept in!'

***

Abo fell soundly asleep at the second attempt, and slept, as the saying goes, like a dead man. He woke up in an extremely cheerful mood, which was perhaps surprising. He had the notion that just before he had woken up, he had been singing, singing his favourite tune 'Găkku'[15] over and over, without words. 'Găk-ku, Găk-ku, gă-gă-gă-gă-gă …'

He remembered how, in the eighth year at school, his classmates had enticed him into amateur dramatics. He had even taken part in one concert, singing the song 'Găk-ku, Găk-ku, gă-gă-gă-gă-gă' and thereby winning considerable success with the girls. After that, though, he had given it up. 'It's not something a real žigit[16] should be doing', his great-grandfather, Ķara-Aspan, had said.

And now… now Abo woke up in a good mood, even singing… to himself.

In this unfamiliar, playful mood, he conceived a desire to become better acquainted with the new director, Kamardin. He washed thoroughly, and made his way straight to the office of the newly minted lord. Abo had more than once heard from the omniscient Marina that this other Saidov, younger brother of Nûrdin, also worked as a bursar, of State Nursery Number One, in another district. Abo knew Kamardin as a slovenly, poorly educated, frivolous, vulgar oddball. And now here he was, that oddball, the new director. Director of State Nursery Number Two. Well, well.

Kamardin had not, apparently, been expecting a visitor, and was slumping in his chair. He pulled himself up lazily and sat up properly. Abo had an inkling that Kamardin was inwardly offended. He imagined Kamardin thinking, 'Who does this night watchman think he is, insolently dropping into my office without an invitation?'

The playful mood that had possessed Abo now took on an aggressive tone, and Abo began to mock the 'big man', as this semi-literate upstart undoubtedly considered himself. Abo wasted no time in taking the bull by the horns. He asked rudely, 'Hey, pen pusher, where's your Girl Friday? Or don't they let you have one? You're just a worthless, unworthy basķarma?'[17]

Abo saw that his words, and more importantly, his tone, had knocked Kamardin out of his stride. He forthwith gave up expecting to find any logic in what Kamardin did.

He saw how it would all go from here.

---

[15] 'Găkku' – popular Kazakh folk song.

[16] Žigit – generally denoting a 25- to 40-year-old male, the term can also be used as an honorific indicating bravery, endurance, fortitude and being true to one's word.

[17] Basķarma – early Soviet title for *auyl* chiefs, here used mockingly, something like 'boss-man', 'big boss'.

Kamardin would rise from his massive, fake leather chair, and his two hands would automatically feel for the gun or dagger which he, of course, always had about him. Having made sure that he was armed, Kamardin would confidently, slowly approach Abo, and, with an undercurrent of pent-up anger, ask, 'What's this, my friend? Are you tired of living?'

'And you?' Abo would ask. Abo knew that throwing the question back at the newly made boss would enrage him. Even if the newly minted boss did not strike Abo, he would come very close to his enemy and, standing nose to nose, start squeaking. 'My friend! I see that you are very, very tired of living!' And he would make a feint, as if to land a blow.

Abo, though, would get in first, and give him a gentle thump. Not a solid punch; he would hold back. Kamardin would find this insulting, and strike out in earnest. Abo's reply would be stronger than before, but still take the form of a feeble half-punch.

This reply in the form of a feeble half-punch would inspire Kamardin, who would then draw his pistol from his pocket and attempt to smash Abo on the head with all his might.

This was when the artist in Abo would wake up. The artist, having skilfully made himself go pale in apparent abject fear, would begin to apologise. He would say, 'My dear Kamardin! Don't kill me, don't kill me! Forgive me! I'm so stupid. Forgive me. I am an unworthy good-for-nothing! So distinguished a person as you should not dirty your noble hands on me.'

That would do it. Kamardin, like all nonentities, was a lover of flattery, loved it when other nonentities grovelled in front of him. This nonentity, who had come to believe that he was the centre of the Earth, would relax, but just in case, just so that this unworthy scum understood his rightful place, he would give Abo one last boot with his right foot.

Abo would allow Kamardin the chance to kick out at him, but at the last second, with an easy, lightning-fast movement of his right hand, would knock Kamardin to the floor. He would then assume the appearance of a lunatic and put on a show, running from corner to corner of the spacious office. Forced by the crazy behaviour of his subordinate to resort to using a gun, Kamardin would fire his pistol twice – without, of course, actually hitting him; all Kamardin wanted to do was make Abo snap out of it.

Abo, meanwhile, having taken on the role of a coward driven beside himself with fear, would be dashing all over the happily spacious office and, in that terrible state, run out into the corridor. From there he would run to the ground floor, and from there, out into the grounds of State Nursery Number Two. Naturally enough, the semi-moronic boss would come full tilt in pursuit of the shameless and fully moronic night watchman. In the yard, after letting Saidov catch up a little, Abo, still pretending to be mad, would run into the room where all the support staff were – the cleaners, nannies, cooks – and, suddenly developing an appalling case of the hiccups, would say to the newly minted director, 'You chancer. Who did you sell those thirty children to – the ones you chose from the poorest families with the most children, spinning them your lies? Where are they now? And how many miserable children have you sold through your Nursery Number One? Eh?'

Saidov, still with a gun in his hands and standing dumbfounded in the doorway, would gape stupidly at the staff and Abo in turn.

Abo, taking advantage of this moment, would fly off like a speeding bullet, on his way cannoning into his boss as if by mistake and dealing him a mighty blow in the stomach. In doing this, Abo would make sure that the raging Saidov did not turn up his toes for good.

Saidov, disgraced in front of all these good people – and worst of all was that they were his subordinates – would slide his gun into his trousers and start brandishing his precious dagger. Spotting this, Abo would slip out the back way in the direction of the summer dining room, made of logs from Tien Shan. He would have a clear goal in mind – for the thick log currently masquerading as the director to throw his sharp dagger at Abo. Abo, having precisely estimated the dagger's death path, would dodge aside in a hundredth of a second, further disgracing their log of a new director.

And that is pretty much what happened.

A burst of female laughter rang out. The enraged male, maddened and shamed by the female derision, pointed himself like a bull at the toreador, and rushed off (his turn to be the speeding bullet) in the direction of Abo.

Abo, at the very last moment and having done his sums carefully, calmly moved one step, just one little step to the left. That was all it took. The enraged bull, with all the momentum afforded by his weight, smashed his narrow forehead against the stone wall. As is well-known, a lump of stone does not care who hits it with his head. When head hits lump of stone, there is only ever one winner. The lump of stone.

So sad. For Kamardin Saidov, it was not to be. His career was cut short. His funeral, though, was lavish, and in some ways, triumphant. An orchestra played, even though he was a Muslim.

Abo went out of the massive iron gates of State Nursery Number Two, and for some reason found himself thinking, 'Three plus one.'

***

People were swarming around the bus station, and the constant buzz of all their voices was unsettling. Zara felt that her nerves would not hold up, that she might fall apart, that some kind of death struggle might seize her. In normal life she was tranquillity itself. 'What is happening to me?' she asked herself. Without meaning to, she stopped moving. This seemed to contravene the law of the bus station anthill – that everything must be done at a constantly frantic pace – and a huge man with curly hair, muttering angrily under his breath, rudely shoved Zara aside. Aside was crowded too, though, and a lady promptly jabbed Zara hard in the ribs with her elbow. Only now did Zara realise that she had let go of the children's hands. She let out a frightened gasp, and, pushing with great force, cleared everyone out of her way, including the same huge, curly haired man, and rushed frantically back towards the entrance of the bus station.

In the square by the bus station there was more room. Coming out into the square, Zara started to scream, frantically calling the children by name. 'Ajna! Bolo! Ajna! Bolo!'

Ajna and Bolo turned out to be close by. 'Mum! Mum!' they answered her. Ajna's voice sounded completely calm, Bolo's somewhat muffled. Ajna, in her little girl's way, even gave her mother a very polite, very gentle, telling-off. 'Mum, what were you doing? The whole of Almaty must have heard you yelling.'

This gentle remark of her daughter's sobered Zara up. She pulled herself together and began to hug and kiss her children, as would any mother in the Whole Wide World who had lost her own children and then found them again.

Zara sat the children on a bench and asked an old Kazakh woman to look after them, for the love of God; then herself began to run once more from place to place, through all the halls and buildings, visiting every ticket office – all in vain. The queues were enormous, and hanging around every ticket office were gangs of suspicious-looking young lads that made Zara think of hunting dogs. (Zara was not to know that these lads, who put her in mind of hunting dogs, would come along each morning and buy up all the tickets, then resell them all over the course of the day at exorbitant prices.)

Zara began to feel very tired, and decided to have a short rest on the bench where she had left the children. She was most surprised to find the huge man with curly hair sitting on the bench and talking peacefully with them. For some reason, this made her very angry, and she muttered quietly but fiercely, 'Children, what are you doing, talking to a complete stranger?'

In unison, the children chorused, 'Mum, mum, don't be cross! He's a nice man. Granny was nice to us too – she bought us ice cream.'

The huge man, on closer inspection, turned out to be not so much a man as a young lad of eighteen, maybe twenty at the outside. Zara was even more surprised when the huge curly man, seeing her coming, half-rose from the bench and smiled awkwardly. 'Forgive me, please, I'm just... waiting for my older brother from Kegen.'

The word 'Kegen' startled Zara. Her heart missed a beat, and she almost stopped breathing. 'Are you... are you... also from Kegesi?' she asked, looking at the huge curly lad, this *local* lad, with bulging eyes full of surprise. This bewildering question had the effect of confusing the huge curly one, and he in his turn stared at Zara. The young man from Kegen seemed to be the first to realise that he was looking straight into the eyes of a strange woman, because he suddenly blushed, and turned away.

'It's my fault', thought Zara. 'I am a Kazakh woman, and a Kazakh woman should not look straight into a man's eyes.'

60

From this awkwardness, arisen in a twinkling, Bolo rescued both Zara and the huge and curly, but at the same time bashful, young man from Kegen, by starting to whine, 'Mum, I'm hungry!'

***

Abo knew that when the Sun had scrambled its way to its highest point, the decrepit buses of route 526 would become noticeably emptier. In this knowledge, he walked calmly and quietly to his stop. Calmly and quietly waited for his bus. Took his seat. Or would have done, except that he had to stand – there were too many pensioners on board. 'These are Komsomol members', he thought to himself, 'summoned by Khrushchev and thrown in their millions out onto the Kazakh steppe. Cheated and thrown out – pensioners from the Almaty cotton mill. Cheated and forgotten. Nobody needs them now. What a shame. What a shame.'

Abo calmly and quietly got out at his stop, and equally calmly and quietly made his way to his own home, or rather, the home he rented. Entering the house, he was somewhat surprised to see that Zara and the children were not there. Abo calmly decided, though, that Zara had taken them off to work with her. He had something to eat, and then calmly and quietly got ready for bed. Just then, though, he remembered that today was the day – the day when the monthly allowance of cottonseed oil was given out, the coveted three hundred grams of cottonseed oil, obtained by means of a coupon which Anna Andreyevna Petrenko, director (deceased) of State Nursery Number Two, handed out personally at the end of each month.

Abo grinned wryly. 'Off you go, Abo, off you go. The mistress can't make a meal without cottonseed oil. Come on, up you get.'

He quickly found the coveted voucher for the whole month's allowance of three hundred grams. 'What generosity our Soviet authorities show us', the veteran of Afghanistan thought sarcastically. 'Three hundred whole grams of cottonseed oil for thirty days.'

The Afghan veteran calmly walked about three kilometres and came to State Grocery Store 526. 'How about that. Grocery store 526 on street 526.' The veteran gave yet another wry grin.

The battle-scarred Afghan was not at all surprised to see a long queue, the tail of which stretched along the street for a hundred metres or so, maybe a whole one fifty. Abo told himself to relax. 'This is normal', he said. 'For a man hardened in the hell of Afghanistan… actually, this is ridiculous.'

He noticed that the long queue consisted mainly of pensioners from the Almaty cotton mill. Young Komsomols from Khrushchev's call-up. 'Called them up, brought them here, then left them here with no family.' And then: 'Ridiculous. This great long queue for three hundred measly grams of cottonseed oil? Ten grams a day. This great long queue? Ridiculous.'

The long queue was ridiculous, but it was not the most ridiculous aspect of this episode. Nor was the fact that he was going to have to stand in the merciless Sun for several hours. It was the way the saleswoman, a fat woman with a head like a small button, treated her customers, who by now were practically dying on their feet.

Then again, for a man who had passed along the 'illogical road of genuine, bleeding hell' (as someone had once described Afghanistan) to stand there for three at least, maybe four hours, was genuinely ridiculous.

It paled, though, in comparison with what came next. The battle-scarred warrior had been standing there for exactly three hours (and a bit), and was the last in the queue (he checked; there was no one behind him) by the time he approached the chubby saleswoman with the small child's button-like head. She gave him a theatrically scornful look and declared, without explanation or warning, 'All gone! That's it. Good sir, there's no more oil. All finished!'

Abo could see clearly that the aluminium tank was still full.

This circus clown of a woman with a small button-like head was, in Abo's opinion, no more than an unfunny joke. He did not even contrive to get angry. He was still in a perfectly normal state of mind; his mood was even playful. He made a joke. 'Last man gets the lot!'

The chubby saleswoman with the little button head did not relent. Very spitefully and insolently, she yelled, 'Be off! Get out of it. There's no oil for you!'

Abo still contrived not to lose his cool. He was still able to smile, and parried her blow by saying, 'I have the same kind of token as everyone else.'

Button-Head screamed furiously at him, 'Get lost, you devil's brat!'

At this, my Abo, my patient Abo, before he even knew that he'd done it, leapt like a panther over the low rail, and, again not realising that he was doing it, hefted the aluminium tank and poured all the cottonseed oil slowly and carefully over the saleswoman with the button head.

And that was that.

***

The huge and curly young man, who had appeared entirely by chance and who had, as Zara noticed at once, a very sincere smile – this young man sent by the Creator himself, apologised that he had not himself worked it out, and took the children and Zara to the nearest cheap snack bar. It was cramped and stuffy in there, and the flies had plainly adapted to every kind of toxic substance and become, to all intents and purposes, immortal. Zara was terribly embarrassed to discover that she had left home with no money for the journey. True, they had as much money at home as a hen has teeth, but even so. And now a complete stranger was dipping into his pocket for them. Her self-flagellation did not last long, though. Zara remembered what Abo had made his mind up to do – Abo, that dear, loving, doting father. Zara would not allow it. 'No! No! No, and again no!' This to herself. 'My children... our children... can be cured.

Their great-great-grandfather, Ḵara-Aspan, will cure them. There's a reason why people call their great-great-grandfather the Holy Hermit! A good reason!'

As women do, though, Zara then began to accuse herself. 'I'm being irrational. Irrational!' And then: 'But I'm their mother. I'll do anything for Ajna and Bolo. Anything at all!'

The huge curly man turned out to have a name. Zara was very surprised when he told them it. 'Tắte',[18] he said very politely, 'my name is Ḵajsar. Your name is Zara. You are the great-granddaughter of the Holy Hermit.'

Zara's head started to spin. 'How…? Do you know me?'

'Not only you. Abo aġa,[19] too.'

'Abo aġa?' repeated Zara. And again: 'How?'

Zara thought that her fear must be showing in her face, because the young lad who had identified himself as Ḵajsar became visibly embarrassed, and said in a timid voice, 'I, too, like you, am from the tribe of Alban, the clan of Ḵyzyl Bôrik. Your legendary husband is also from the tribe of Alban, only from the clan of Ḵoṇyr Bôrik. By blood, I'm closer to you. We are relatives, tắte! Relatives!'

Zara was particularly struck by the fact that this new-found relative had called Abo, her husband, 'legendary'. She even asked again, 'You said "legendary"?'

The new-found relative sincerely and proudly, even solemnly, said, 'What else? He's twice a hero of Afghanistan! Everybody knows that! But… unfortunately, he was unfairly demoted. Very unfortunately.'

Zara's mood suddenly blackened, as she remembered why she had had to spirit the children away from their own father. What was she doing, sitting here? 'You're stupid, Zara', she told herself.

With a sharp movement, she seized the children's hands and, without even saying goodbye to Ḵajsar, rushed off. 'Where am I going now?' she asked herself, but did not answer her own question. 'Just run!' she told herself. 'Just run!'

Zara began to accost strange men with silly questions. 'Are you going to Kegen?'

Or:

'Will you take us to Kegen, please? My father will give you a sheep! A large fat-tailed sheep. You know how much a fat-tailed sheep will fetch at the market, don't you?'

Many people shied away from her, frightened; some angrily muttered curses under their breath. But Zara was persistent; so persistent that one moustachioed man of about forty at first scolded her, calling her a gypsy, and then, the third

---

[18] Tắte – depending on the region, a form of address to an older woman, or man, meaning 'aunt', 'sister', 'uncle'; may also signify 'mother' or 'father'.

[19] Aġa – respectful form of address to an older man, which can be translated as 'brother', 'uncle'.

time she approached him, softened and stopped, and asked, with a tolerant smile, 'Where did you say? Kegen?'

'Yes, yes, Kegesi. Kegesi', replied Zara, automatically copying her husband, who always said the Kazakh name 'Kegen' Japanese-style. Her husband's words flashed through Zara's mind: 'Kegesi – the name of a small Japanese village, incinerated along with Nagasaki by the atomic bomb'. Granted, Zara did not know the meaning of the word 'incinerated' or 'Nagasaki'. She liked the sound of the words, though, and her brain had retained them forever.

The moustachioed man of about forty, having allowed a pause of decent length, repeated his question. 'Kegen, you say?'

'Yes, Yes, Yes!' Zara was prattling in her excitement, and shining with joy.

'Kegen is a long, long, lo-o-o-ong way. Two hundred kilometres. You realise that?' Taking a long, hard look at the young woman with the fine figure, the moustachioed man getting on for forty continued, 'Very, very far indeed. How do you intend to pay me?'

Zara was a very pure young woman, and thus very naive. Delighted that this moustachioed man of about forty had agreed to take them, she blurted out, 'I'll pay you whatever you want!'

And that was that.

The moustachioed man of about forty smiled to himself, and said, 'Get in.'

When they had gone seven or eight kilometres from the bus station, the man abruptly stopped his boneshaker and declared in a solemn voice, 'Well. We seem to have run out of gas.'

The shock was just about enough to stop poor Zara's heart. Like a fish thrown up onto dry land by an angry typhoon, she opened and closed her delicate little mouth. Her unglossed lips started to tremble, like those of someone dying of malaria. Somewhere far away, she could faintly hear Bolo's pleading voice:

'Mum! I want to pee.'

As if in a dream, there came into her mind snatches of things seen: some kind of very tall bush... A ploughed field, and beyond the field, the glinting white walls of typical Kazakh houses with red tiled roofs... Her children, Ajna and Bolo, running away somewhere through the ploughed field, Ajna pulling Bolo along by the hand... and this was when Zara felt the moustachioed man of about forty grip her with iron hands and begin to drag her into the bushes.

Anger, a great anger, peculiar only to women who love, swept through Zara's whole being. And...

...screaming from her unfathomable anger, she miraculously tore herself free of the beast's foul embrace. And...

...stumbling and falling, stumbling and falling, she ran, following the direction her fleeing children had taken.

But her strength gave out, and she lost her breath completely. The moustachioed man in his forties with no heart and no shame caught up with her.

***

The strange incident with the cottonseed oil somehow brought Abo a peace beyond understanding. When he returned home, that is, to his decrepit shack, Abo was not even surprised at the absence of his wife and children. He peacefully lay down on the patterned felt rug, and instantly fell into a peaceful sleep. He knew for sure, though, that he would wake up at exactly five.

Indeed, he did. He woke up at exactly five. He at once realised that his former peace of mind had deserted him. He found himself seized by anxiety – a terrible anxiety, the cause of which was eluding him. 'What is it?' he asked himself. 'Why am I so anxious? Why? This has never happened to me before. What is it? Why?'

Abo was somehow sure that Ajna and Bolo would come home in the dead of night. 'Why only Ajna and Bolo?' he wondered. What about Zara? Why did Zara have to come back separately from children? Why?

Abo decided that these were stupid questions, and did not start looking for answers to them. He sat down, folding his long legs under him, adopting the position known in Kazakh as *maldas*. Once he had assumed the *maldas* position, Abo could pass several hours turned into a stone idol, or (as he saw himself) a smooth, sleek python.

On these occasions, Abo would close his eyes and disengage himself from the world around him. Today, though, before he disengaged, he had time to mutter, 'Ajna and Bolo will be here by morning'. His next thought was, 'Then it will be easier to bear this inhuman pain, this diabolical trial. Be patient, Abo, be patient. Patience. You will deliver Ajna and Bolo from it first, and then… Oh, my Great Deliverer… Your will be done.'

By the time Abo finally mastered himself, it was already getting late. 'It lasted five whole hours', he thought. 'Good for you, Abo. Good for you! You held out. You held out through the tortures of a whole host of brutal butchers enjoying every minute of their work.'

Abo could feel something vile piled up in his mouth, like grains of sand and stones of different sizes. Most unpleasantly, blood was seeping from them. Human blood. Abo felt the urge to vomit, and threw up small, white pebbles. Only then did he realise that they were fragments of his own teeth. Teeth which, Abo knew, had been the envy of all the eagles of TSTS-17, the elite unit famous all over Afghanistan. 'I'm in such agony, I've ground my own teeth to bits', he thought. 'Well, Abo, the end is coming.'

A thought suddenly struck him with appalling force. If he had survived this hellish pain only with great difficulty, how would Ajna and Bolo possibly bear it?

Abo felt exactly as if someone had just thrust a red-hot needle into his brain. 'Who's there?' he asked. 'Who are you, who needs to force your way into the deepest layers of my brain? What are you looking for in that grey mess? What are you bringing me – something wonderful, or more grief?'

'Grief, obviously.' Abo answered himself. He made an attempt to be playful. 'It means, dear Abo, that a Big Bad Monster has plunged into the most precious sanctuary of your human existence, into your brain. Kindly note that you are in a perilous situation.'

Abo was sure that these deliberations had occupied no more than a few minutes. He was amazed, then, to discover that he was standing all alone on the Camel's Hump, in north-west Almaty. 'When did I get here? How? My dear Abo, answer me.'

Dear Abo, Abo in his playful mood, was unable to answer his own questions, for the simple reason that at that very moment he remembered the children. 'Ajna and Bolo won't be back until about daybreak', he reminded himself. 'So I can afford to stay here on my *minber*[20] until midnight.'

Abo went on making fun of himself. 'Dearest Abo will also get home just before daybreak.' He was using sarcasm and humour as a protective shield against the decision he had made... He had made up his mind and would not change it. Tragedy was coming.

Somewhere in the hidden depths of his soul, he could vaguely guess at what it was, this terrible, inhuman act of 'heroism' towards which he was being pushed by the false reality presented as a sacred necessity by the corrupt media. Even as his patriotic duty.

Poor Abo.

Poor Abo, of course, could not even guess why he had hauled his butt (as his peers would say) into such a wilderness, such troubled times, and why he was standing on his favourite Camel's Hump. He could not guess.

He could not guess. But in the most secret corner of his consciousness, as in the infinite space of the cosmos you might see a single star, now disappearing, now reappearing, there beckoned to him, teasing him perhaps, one such star, one hope, one tiny ray of hope... This weakly twinkling star seemed to hint, 'Your children, Ajna and Bolo, will recover. Do not lose faith in the Creator. Do not lose your faith.'

Habits learned in Afghanistan forced him to face the truth. To look straight into the dirty, muddy, drunken eyes of reality. The eyes of a bribe taker. Of a chancer. A huckster. The eyes of a politician. The eyes of politicians had always provoked disgust in Abo, the legendary warrior.

Abo easily caught sight of the little star which was winking on and off, up there in the Great Bear. Kazakhs sometimes called this constellation the Seven Robbers. A popular legend said that these seven robbers stole the only daughter of a poor man and still keep her hidden from human eyes, so that an outsider's greedy look will not damage her bright appearance.

Abo had known since childhood where to look for this heavenly beauty. First you needed to get a fix on the Seven Robbers. That was easy enough – there they were, bending their long neck over Greenland; the handsome steed

---

[20] *Minber* – rostrum; a reference to the shape of the Camel's Hump hill.

had made his way to his watering hole. Now the horse's four hooves – there; there they are, shining brightly, opalescent. Now if you screw up your eyes and look long and hard above the middle star of the bent neck... there! The mysterious beauty!

Winking, mysterious, this playful little star likes to fool those who are bold enough to try to climb up to her. Abo, of course, was no exception. 'She is waiting for her beloved, her betrothed', he said to himself. 'She's waiting for him. She will show her face only to him.' Abo knew deep inside himself that he was, against his will, now, at this moment, smiling.

Abo was in a deep trance, trying to forget himself.

To forget this accursed world. To forget this accursed reality.

The closer the hour of judgement came, the crazier became his wild thrashing about. Thus, I know for sure, the male camel rampages in early spring, the rutting season.

In his deep trance, Abo was looking for an excuse not to think, God forbid, about how the upcoming disaster would end. Don't think! No! No! No! Maybe that was why he, for the thousandth time in his life, gave himself over entirely to thinking about the Great Creator of Eternity and Infinity.

Eternity and Infinity now appeared before his eyes, first in the form of the Milky Way, a cluster of millions of suns and billions of stars, spinning, tumbling, each around its sun.

Abo, my dreamer Abo, for a long, long time and to his heart's content, wandered, moving from one constellation to another.

Then his heart, the size of a fist, shuddered, and for a moment froze, for Abo had noticed with horror that staring fixedly and greedily at his beloved Milky Way was the two-eyed Hunting Dog.

The Hunting Dog, like the Milky Way, was an old friend of our dreamer, Afghan Abo.

The dreamer Abo knows that the Hunting Dog has two eyes. One of them, the left, is bulging, and the other, the right, is squinting. The left is black and appears very, very deep, and the right is narrowed with cunning, as if winking. Eternity's own eternal game.

The dreamer Abo knows that while he was in Afghanistan, digging around in the army reading room, he came across, maybe randomly or more likely through the natural order of things, a newspaper article by the Japanese author Makoto Miyoshi. Miyoshi boldly claimed that the black eye of the Hunting Dog is nothing other than the throat of an insatiable black hole. The black hole is waiting patiently for the Milky Way to come closer so that it can swallow the whole Flock of Swans, as the Kazakhs call the Milky Way. The Flock of Swans is the way the white swans fly, returning from the south-east to the north-west in the early spring. To be swallowed by an insatiable black hole. So it is with people. And with whole peoples.

***

Something strange was preventing her from breathing. She felt herself wheezing desperately. 'What is wrong with me?' she asked herself. 'Who was it who wanted to strangle me? I remember someone choking me with a rope. Who was it? A rope. A rope. Yes, that's right, a rope.' Zara automatically felt her neck with her right hand and, for the moment intuitively, concluded, 'That villain tried to strangle me.' A thin, very strong rope was still around her neck. 'Wicked, wicked man. Find him and kill him.' The more she uttered the word 'kill', the more tightly the rope squeezed Zara's tender neck.

Piecing together fragmented details of the crime committed by that scumbag, the moustachioed man of about forty, helped Zara begin to gather her wits. Her every move was horribly painful, and she felt weak all over. She pulled herself up to a sitting position on the dirt of the ploughed field. Her female essence, her human essence, was broken, crushed, killed. She, proud Zara, had been unable to defend her honour. 'Better that I had died', she cried to herself. 'Spat upon, reviled... how will I look into Abo's eyes now? I should throw myself under a tram or a bus. I have no other choice. No other choice.'

Then she remembered her children. She whispered their names again and again, automatically, unconsciously, and forgot the state she was in. She tried to stand up too quickly, and was knocked over by a sharp pain like a lightning bolt, and fell back onto the ploughed earth.

Zara broke out in tears. For the first time in her life. The first time in her whole life. Her character was so resolute and unyielding that behind her back her girlfriends called her *kara tas*. The girl of flint. Now Zara, the girl of flint, wept inconsolably for a long time, and then, with a giant effort of will, managed to get to her feet.

She stood, fell, stood up again. Swaying from side to side, Zara, the girl of flint, managed to take a few unsteady steps; she lurched forward, then back, then stumbled sideways. A thought slipped like a thief through her mind: 'What will people think, seeing me in this state? People will take me for a drunkard. Oh, the shame of it.'

That was still the state she was in two hours later, when the exhausted July sun finally slipped into the arms of the snow-capped Alatau mountains. Zara, still staggering, limped her way to a hut on the edge of a settlement of immigrants from Ukraine. Here there lived an eccentric named Vasil, with Maria, his steppe-born, plump, kind-hearted wife.

Her strength ebbing with each step, Zara dragged herself up to the gates, an entrance constructed from Tien Shan spruce logs. She caught her breath, and, standing with great difficulty on her weak legs, began to beat her feeble right hand on the impervious gates, which were soaked from the frequent rains.

The husband and his wife could not hear her faint knock. After a while, though, sensing an attempt by an alien being to intrude onto the space which he was guarding, Bars, the household's fanged wolfhound, let out a few relatively friendly growls, and then unleashed a volley of barks, as if to say, 'Heavens, how slow are these two-legged animals to get the message!' At the same time, he felt the need to observe doggy etiquette, and so gave exactly three loud woofs and then fell quiet. That should do it. The alien had no doubt now realised that no one poked their nose onto territory guarded by Bars.

Zara did indeed work out that access to this area was denied, and made an effort to get herself to the neighbouring huts. She could not. She had been reduced to such a state of emaciation and weakness that she started to moan weakly, and fell down on the road trampled by Vasil and Maria Shmytko's cows and pigs.

***

Vasil and Maria Shmytko were known in the suburban settlement of Podgornoye as decent folks, honest and principled, although, unhappily, childless. Despite their childlessness, they were respected by everyone as hardworking citizens. And now, unexpectedly, as if from heaven and surely at the behest of the Holy Virgin, two angels had descended to their childless, barren hearth. Such pretty little things, so neatly dressed.

Vasil and Maria first of all gave them a hearty and generous meal, and only then asked them who they were, why they had turned up alone without parental supervision on the outskirts of this village, who were their father and mother, what were their names, where did they live, why had they, Ajna and Bolo, run away from someone or from something and appeared, tired and out of breath, at the gates of their home. And why had they chosen to knock on this door, in particular?

Ajna, the elder, answered all the questions exhaustively in her beautiful Russian. The husband and wife started to smile contentedly, and continued with increased enthusiasm to ply the 'angels' with every kind of dish from a rich and exclusively Ukrainian menu.

After their hearty feast, Ajna and Bolo fell quiet. It was to their credit that they chose not to chatter to each other in a language incomprehensible to the hospitable couple. They expressed their thanks in the international language, then went over to the wide sofa, and, as if by prior agreement, both fell instantly asleep.

Vasil and Maria also found themselves thinking and doing the same things, as if by prior agreements of their own. They were both filled with indescribable joy; they were smiling broadly with pleasure. They moved the boy sleeping like a dead man onto a proper, wide bed, leaving the girl where she was. Still quietly smiling, they covered them with fresh-smelling sheets so clean that they crackled.

Then they grew serious, and together stepped up to look into the face of their Saviour. Both turned instantly pale, and slowly, faithfully crossed themselves.

After this, Vasil and Maria were unable to fall sleep. Joy surged inside them, and they gave themselves up to sharing long-forgotten memories, talking by turn and not interrupting each other, as was their custom, reminiscing about life on their native farmstead, Vesyoloye, near Uzhgorod.

In the morning, Vasil and Maria got up without having to fall asleep, as Vasil liked to put it. They dressed and had a drink of tea, and then Vasil fiddled about for a long time in their Stalin-era Moskvich, finally managing to start the old banger, as the couple fondly called their 'personal means of transportation'. At exactly nine-thirty in the morning, with Vasil, as always, at the wheel, and Maria, as always, by his side, and the little children 'sent down by God himself' in the seats of honour in the back, they moved off in the direction of their beloved Almaty.

The *auyl* of Podgornoye formally continued to be called a suburb, but in fact it was only some three hundred metres from the capital.

Vasil and Maria, still smiling with joy and talking to each other about something they had long since already known, did not notice how their 'personal means of transportation' was already rushing along the city streets and avenues.

In a splendid mood, even humming some Ukrainian song under his breath, the good citizen of Uzhgorod, who in less than a day had been made young again, rolled his 'means of transportation' into the paying car park in front of the Central Department Store. Here, with a smile that hid a nice secret, he whispered something in his better half's ear, and in the same good mood headed for the store's main entrance.

He returned fifteen minutes later, happy – radiant even – and hugging a large stuffed teddy bear and a goggle-eyed Barbie doll.

Bolo was given the big teddy, and Ajna the Barbie.

Both immediately started to shine.

More than either of the children, the big boy Vasil was in heaven. Watching her other half this last day had made Maria feel like a young girl again, who accidentally put a spoonful of sugar and a spoonful of pepper into her mouth at the same time.

Then Vasil, still radiant, nosed his old banger all over the narrow, pointlessly meandering streets of Almaty-1. With great difficulty he found the right crooked street, and on this crooked street he found house number 526.

We could relate how the radiant Vasil and Maria entered the hut, and how the tall, slender Kazakh greeted his children; how Vasil and Maria, the unknown benefactors who had brought them home, were honoured with brief but heartfelt words; how Abo, Abo the Immutable, became flustered as, scrabbling around to find paper and pencil, he wrote down the address of the noble Ukrainians and promised to come to visit them; how Abo, terribly embarrassed at the squalor of his home, apologised, though apologising was alien to his nature, and saw the benefactors safely on their way.

Or we could miss it out, and move on.

***

Abo had been sure that the children would come back on their own. He was right, with one minor amendment: they had been brought back by a Ukrainian couple.

As a Kazakh, Abo was seriously upset. Unexpected visitors had arrived, and he had not been able to treat them properly. It did not matter that he had not invited them. As a Kazakh, he was supposed to usher them to the holy *tôr*, the seat of honour – and he did not even own a holy *tôr*. Worse than that, he actually had nowhere at all to seat these noble strangers who had brought his children home, alive and well, and moreover had done so in their own transport, winding their way for ages round the dirty, crooked streets. He could not even find two decrepit chairs, so as to invite his guests at least to sit for a while. It was a mortal disgrace to the householder, even if the house was just a wretched hut. (I, the author, have a relative who found himself in a similarly humiliating situation, and hanged himself. These things do happen. My people have a saying: 'Honour is above death'.)

Abo, as a Kazakh and as a human being felt humiliated and insulted. But this was not important. What was important was the thing that Abo had decided to do. He had, after all, decided... except that now, all of a sudden, he could not remember what it was. 'What was it I decided to do?' he asked himself. 'Specifically, what was it? You don't know? You'll forget your own name next!'

Abo flinched, realising that he had turned momentarily into a stone *balbal*. 'Wake up!'

And wake up he did. The children, it turned out, were not in the shack. He quietly went outside. There they were, in the skimpy back garden, between the six apple trees. They had started up a game. 'Well, look at that', he thought.

The sight of his children playing aroused a fatherly feeling in Abo, and he smiled to himself – and after all, he knew what he was about to suggest. He called the children over to him. Ajna and Bolo ran up to their father, whereupon he unexpectedly (and to the children, he may have sounded rather solemn) said, 'Let's go for a walk.'

They walked to their hearts' content. First, Abo took the children to the zoo. Ajna and Bolo spent ages hanging around the elephants. There were three of them – mother, father and, best of all, baby. He was so funny, this clumsy little elephant, and so cheerful. Maybe his mood was helped by the special attention his kind-hearted visitors were giving him. That was what Abo thought, anyway.

One of the visitors said that the baby had turned out to have a sweet tooth. He loved ice cream.

In a fit of generosity, Abo gave the children lots of money to buy sweets. Ajna dashed off five times for ice cream, and Bolo, inevitably, overdid it somewhat, setting a family record for treating the baby elephant and his dad and mum.

Then the little family, marching slowly and impressively as if they were on the parade ground, made their way over to 'Monkey Kingdom'.

When the family trio reached the middle of the Kingdom, Ajna exclaimed enthusiastically, 'Fantastic!'

In the kingdom there were, as was written in chalk on what looked like a school black board, thirty-eight species of the closest relatives of the builders of communism. A large mural of the builders of communism – 'Workers and Kolkhoz Women' with cheerful, intelligent faces and eyes radiating happiness – stood right next to the thirty-eight.

A representative of one of these species, a huge male gorilla, impressively underlining his superiority over the rest of the two-legged beings, came up to Abo. And here was a strange thing: the male stared searchingly straight into the eyes of his fellow being and winked at him with his left eye – specifically his left eye. With his dark brown right eye, Abo noticed, he was asking in a very severe, demanding way, 'What present have you brought for me, my relative? Where is it?'

Abo, my Abo, for the first time in his life trembled with shame. There, looking at him with such boldness was his Great Teacher, the lieutenant general in charge of a special kind of special purpose troops, tester of the ferocious TSTS-17 itself – Ivasi.

For a split second, his leader's behaviour confused Abo, and he even started to boil with anger, but noticing the enraptured gazes of his children, quickly cooled down. Smiling, he pulled from the right pocket of his jeans a whole ten roubles, and gave Ajna and Bolo their orders. 'Buy a whole rouble's worth of bananas –' and then, realising that the fat saleswoman would undoubtedly try to hoodwink the children (after all, she had tried to twist even him round her finger when he had treated the children to a very expensive and creamy ice cream) he said, 'Remember: count the change on the spot!'

Thus Abo, for the first time in his life, felt like a generous father, and bursting with pride at his sudden openness of spirit, issued further orders:

'Have a good walk, my children. Walk! Life is beautiful. You could live... how you could live. If only –'

He seemed to choke suddenly, and, still staring first at Ajna, then at Bolo, with wide, deep eyes, he stopped abruptly.

Abo, my Abo, felt a light dizziness. This also was a first – dizzy for the first time in his whole, distinguished life.

One can say that without doubt Abo, my Abo, enjoyed several happy hours that day, hours that were the equivalent of several months lived by an ordinary man. He needed those hours, so that as judgement hour approached, he would not allow his heart to soften. 'Do not take away my hardness, O my Lord, my Creator.'

When they left the zoo, though, without knowing why, he started to play the fool. He spotted a couple of young Kazakhs, about thirty years old, thirty-five at most, dressed in identical black woollen suits notwithstanding the hot, stuffy weather, with all the buttons done up, exactly like junior officers at a general's reception.

Abo turned himself into a jester. Grinning and playing the part of a hopeless moron, he went up to the two young men. 'Hey, lads, I see that you're here for a reason. I see that you're from... up there', and he glanced heavenwards, a sign that might be interpreted as indicating the offices of high authority and discipline. 'I ask you very, very earnestly, to please take these two away – the girl and the boy. Take them away.'

The two lads gawped silently.

Abo continued to clown around, egging on the soldiers in their black suits. 'Take them away, take them away! It would be very, very bad not to get them away from trouble. Disaster, even.'

One of the two appeared to decide to say something. Holding himself in a superior manner, he hissed, 'What do you mean, take them away? What does that mean?'

Abo was still clowning around. 'He's going to kill them.'

'Who's going to kill whom?' The second guy wearing a black woollen suit in the forty-degree heat now joined in.

'Their own father wants to kill them.'

The two men in black asked, in perfect unison, 'Who?'

'Their father.' There, at any rate, was an honest answer.

The two men in black, puzzled, asked, 'Who is this animal?'

Abo had apparently, without realising it, been waiting for this question. In a firm, confident voice, he said gravely, 'Me. I'm their father.'

The two men in black, throwing their cigarette butts onto the asphalt in unison, in unison and with animal ferocity methodically ground the hapless butts into the asphalt. Then, without looking back, they went off with a familiar marching step into the depths of the zoo.

Still in the same playful mood, Abo tenderly called Ajna and Bolo, who were playing a little way off, to join him, and they all walked along a narrow path in the Park of Culture and Rest named after ... who else? Like all the parks in the vast Soviet Union, the park carried the name of Maxim Gorky.

In Gorky Park, Abo gave Ajna a whole three roubles and, hugging his children in turn, in a deliberately cheerful voice commanded them:

'Riiiight! Quiiiiick, march! Play! Buy whatever you want – sweets, ice cream! And play, play, play, play! I'll be right here. On this bench. I'll sit and wait for you. For a hundred years, if need be. Understood?'

'Hoorah!' cried the children – his children – in unison, and scampered off happily to the stall where they sold ice cream and candy-icicles.

The lazy, sleepy-headed Asian sun seemed to have no plans to move from where it was. In his mind, Abo compared the Sun to the worn-out neddy of the legendary jester, and beardless conman, Aldar Kôse.

This lazy Asian sun, playing hide and seek with a thin, barely noticeable haze, started to jump – prance, even – around Abo.

Abo felt a kind of phantasmagorical chaos in his mind. An excerpt from one of his favourite melodies started up in his head, and then suddenly stopped, as if a nervous lady had flipped off a gramophone.

On, off; on, off. 'Fate is playing with me just like that', thought Abo. 'So much blood on my hands... a sea of blood... civilians... and *shuravi*...' As if on a screen, he saw in his mind a picture of the *shuravi* Ivasi. Ivasi, with a crooked and insolent smile, silently asked, 'You okay, Afghan? Grin and bear it, eh. What do they call you these days – *arġymaķ*?[21] Turkmen old-timers' name for you, I hear.' Ivasi disappeared, or rather, was rubbed out.

Only then did Abo notice that the Sun had managed to hide behind the eastward-leaning and crested neck of the indefatigable *arġymaķ* Talġar. Figures swam slowly, oh so slowly, on the screen of his memory: Ivasi (366 ways to kill your fellow creatures)... the mullah Mùrat... the whole Turkmen Kôk Ajla clan (the first experimental victims of TSTS-17)... Beautiful Sajra... how that poor girl suffered, several times begging Abo to kill her. 'Do a good deed – kill me', she had sobbed. 'She... so proud, so beautiful', remembered Abo. 'She... but by then Zara and I were writing to each other. A young soldier should not play away and at home. She called me brother, I called her sister. Poor Sajra... How she suffered... begged me to kill her. When you think that for a Muslim, especially a Muslim woman, suicide is an unthinkable sin... how great was her suffering.'

At this point Abo came out of his reverie. He noticed that an old lady was sitting on the bench with him, timidly, slightly sideways on. She was well-dressed, very clean and neat. 'Noble. From an aristocratic family', thought Abo. 'Probably a doctor. Or a retired doctor – doctors don't usually go out on breaks during work time. Maybe you should ask her about types of radiation sickness? What do you think, Abo?' A different, stronger Abo answered the weak Abo at once. 'No way! Only the Creator can answer that question. The Creator's answer is the whole long history of Mankind.'

***

The weak Abo was subconsciously afraid of the inexorably approaching zero hour on which the other, strong Abo had so resolutely made up his mind. The weak Abo, like a coward, avoided even the thought of retribution; the taking of retribution, though, was the decision made by that desperate lone wolf of this great country, a country that had somehow acquired the strange notion

---

[21] *Arġymaķ* – purebred horse highly estimated for speed, beauty, strength and endurance.

that she was allowed to decide the fate of all mankind. The time for carrying out the sentence pronounced by that brutal but special martyr of the great Ivasi tugged at the weak Abo, pulling him.

The weak disciple of the great Ivasi walked more and more slowly, procrastinating. But when he had returned home with his happy children, even the weak Abo fell to thinking. The strong Abo gave the weak Abo a good telling-off, and then also fell deep into thought, turning in his traditional way into a stone *balbal*. He was thinking so deeply he did not notice that Ajna and Bolo had fallen asleep right there on the floor. The weak father picked his daughter Ajna up off the floor, hugged her, pressed her to his chest, and then, with fingers like iron tentacles, expertly pressed two of her arteries. Once more he pressed his daughter to his chest, then gently laid her back down on the thick rug. Next he picked up Bolo, his little boy, whom he had so lovingly spoiled, and repeated the ceremony. Then the great warrior of the land of the Soviets immediately turned back into a stone idol, a *balbal*. A stone *balbal* is seen by the Kazakhs as a symbol of Wisdom and Decisiveness.

The strong Abo did not come round for two hours, by which time it was already deep into the night. The strong Abo knew that the weak Abo had been banished completely. The strong Abo came out of his hut and thoroughly performed the ritual of ablution. The apple trees in the garden seemed like dark, silent giants. That meant that tonight there would be no Moon until after midnight.

On this moonless night, all the stars were shining brightly, freely. They looked so big. So clear. The cool of the night helped the strong Abo in its own way. 'You had no right', he told himself, 'to give Ajna and Bolo over to be eaten by the Jackal. The age of the Jackal must be overthrown. Don't let the Jackal triumph, Abo! Don't leave your tiny children to the humiliating mockery of the age of the Jackal! You have saved them. You have saved your angels. This is your purest act of heroism!'

The strong Abo inclined his head to all four sides of the world in turn, bowing to the fairy-tale bright and clear stars. All the stars, it seemed, started to wink approvingly, even to smile with joy. Then, still feeling a fierce determination, the strong Abo went back into the house. First he took Ajna into his arms and pressed her to his chest, kissing her three times on the forehead. Then he laid his daughter gently back down on the rug. The strong Abo repeated the whole ceremony with Bolo. Then he crossed his legs and bowed to the children, three times to each. His own children! In his heart, though, his own children were already far away, and, quietly saying *bi-smi llahi r-rahmani r-rahim*,[22] he resolved to proceed to the fulfilment of his Great Obligation. At this very moment, though, Ajna, who was still no more than deeply asleep, started hiccupping

---

[22] A rendition of the first verse of the Qur'an: 'In the Name of Allah, the All-beneficent, the All-merciful'. [Ed.]

and moaning, and then, for the third time in a month, screamed loudly, 'Papa! Papa! Save me! Papa! Papa! I can't... I can't bear it!'

Save me! Please, Papa, I beg you! I beseech you...

The father, a weak and confused and grieving father, hugged his daughter, and, standing up to his full height, began to rock his five-year-old daughter, lamenting, *ăldi-ăldi, aḳ bôpem.*[23]

With a desperate cry like that of a calf who realises that he is being led to the slaughterhouse (a horror that Abo had witnessed for himself when his beloved and not usually foolish father had foolishly taken him to see calves being brought into the famous Semej meat-processing plant), Bolo woke up.

The already weak and wretched father of two incurable victims of TSTS-17, himself loudly sobbing, decided to shout down his two exhausted, beloved children, Ajna and Bolo. Stammering, he cried, 'I will save you, I will! I swear it. I will find the strength... I will find the strength! I will save you!'

After that, time began to be counted off in seconds, and then fractions of seconds. Abo, driven to despair, had time to think, 'It's a good thing that Zara's not home.'

Time accelerated to fractions of fractions of seconds. The figure 365 suddenly flashed in Abo's brain. The number 365 meant 365 (+1) ways in which one human being can kill another.

Feverish now, with two fingers – two steel pincers, as the virtuoso Ivasi himself had said, admiring the iron fingers of his most talented pupil – lightly, leaving no trace, causing no pain, and most importantly, without his victims realising, the strong Abo took the angelic souls of his beloved children, Ajna and Bolo.

Now time slowed down. Every second, every fraction of a second, turned into minutes and hours.

The wretched Abo slowly, like in a slow-motion film, stood up to his full height. Bowing his head so as not to dent the low ceiling of the hut, he went out of his house. Outside, he straightened up and stood for a minute in the pitch darkness. Then he took a few steps at random and – a miracle! – realised that he was standing on Camel's Hump.

From here, the whole of space always opens up. You can see everything from here.

From here, the strong Abo clearly saw how his darling Milky Way, like a mesmerised rabbit, was reluctantly but inexorably approaching the dark eyes and insatiable jaws of the Hunting Dog. Abo could clearly make out the rabbit and the dog. In this moment, a moment that stretched out forever, Abo grasped the majesty of the Universe.

It now seemed to Abo that spread out before him was the carpet with the yellowish tint, the well-known carpet which had served to adorn the spacious,

---

[23] A chorus often found in Kazakh lullabies (*besik žyry*), meaning 'hush, my beloved baby, hush'.

very spacious office of the director of State Nursery Number Two in District Number One in the small (a mere one million inhabitants) city of Almaty.

On this great big rug lay three corpses. The three corpses of three prominent figures – the immortal Anna Andreyevna, the immortal Bajbaķ Malšybaev, and the immortal Nŭrdin Saidov, who were more than confident – they knew, beyond any doubt, that they were eternal, immutable, and that they had the right to play with the lives of dozens or even thousands of defenceless children from the poorest families and *auyls*.

The heads of all three were turned slightly to the right, as if at the command, 'Attention!' On the necks of all three, just visible, were tiny traces of blood.

'The work of a master!' Abo had said then.

'The work of a master!' Abo now hissed, through closed teeth.

On this same wide carpet appeared, or perhaps one should say was revealed, the outline of the hunched over, very tired beggar Kamardin Saidov.

Now the old campaigner, the warrior Ivasi materialised on the carpet, looking around him like a coward. Gone was his old confidence. He glanced shiftily at Abo, and smiled a guilty, repentant smile. The smile was pathetic and somehow artificial.

Abo continued to wait. He was waiting for someone else. The mullah Mŭrat and the sad and beautiful Sajra appeared. Sajra, in spite of all sorts of prohibitions, stared boldly and proudly at Abo, as if she wanted to say something to the young soldier, the handsome young soldier, the still unbroken, desperate young soldier Abo.

Abo, though, was waiting for his wife, sweet, darling Zara, unhappy Zara, who had wanted (as her husband well knew), to save the terminally ill, tormented Ajna and Bolo from the attempt her husband was compelled to make – at any cost – to save them. To save them.

Abo would have liked to go to Zara, to embrace her, and, most important of all, to kneel and ask her forgiveness. Forgive me, please forgive me.

But Abo, this Abo, who intended to bow down before his wife and beg her to forgive him – forgive me, please, for everything, for everything, for everything – this Abo took a step, and that step turned out to be no ordinary step. His left leg stretched out and found itself on the surface of a huge star – a planet in his own darling Milky Way; his second foot landed on another planet, and then the third step... the fourth... fifth... and thus Abo leapt from constellation to constellation, and spiralling, spiralling, he came to the heart of the cluster, where he tried to shout at the top of his voice to warn his darling Milky Way of the danger... of the danger... of the danger of the approaching Hunting Dog... the voracious Hunting Dog... voracious Hunting Dog... Amen.

Translated by Richard Coombes

KALIKHAN YSKAK
(14.03.1935 – 3.08.2014)

Kalikhan Yskak was a Kazakh writer, literary critic, translator and playwright. He studied journalism at the Kirov Kazakh State University (now Ál-Farabi Kazakh National University: 1952–57) before going on to study screenwriting at the State Committee for Cinematography in Moscow (1967–72). He subsequently worked for newspapers and journals, which led to positions managing both the drama section of the Writers' Union of Kazakh SSR and the Literature Department at the Áuezov State Academic Drama Theatre. He oversaw the prose section of the *Žŭldyz* journal. His prose works include 'Ķoŋyr kùz edi' (A Quiet Autumn) published in 1963, several short story collections: *Dos hikaâsy* (About My Friend, 1963), *Meniŋ aġalarym* (My Brothers, 1965) as well as novels: *Tùjyķ* (A Taciturn Person, 1975), *Ķara orman* (Black Forest, 1980) and *Aķsu – žer žannaty* (Aķsu – Heaven on Earth, 1989). He has written screenplays, such as *Sarša tamyz* (Snow in the Middle of the Summer, 1968), *Ùšy-ķiyrsyz žol* (Road of a Thousand Versts, 1969) and *Ķaraša ķazdar ķajtķanda* (When the Geese Return, 1985), and more than twenty plays, including an epic *Ķazaķtar* (Kazakhs, 2000), about the origins of the Kazakh Khanate. He has translated Ivan Bunin, Anton Chekhov, Aleksandr Kuprin, Leo Tolstoy and others into the Kazakh language, and had his own works published in the Russian, Uzbek, Tajik, Chechen, Ukrainian, Slovak and Bulgarian languages.

In 1992, Yskak won the State Prize of the Republic of Kazakhstan for his novel *Aķsu – žer žannaty*. His other awards include the title of an Honoured Worker of the Republic of Kazakhstan (2000), Ġabit Mùsirepov and Žambyl Žabaev international literary prizes, as well as the Parasat Order (2007).

A Quiet Autumn

It was autumn. There was a sprinkling of that unending drizzle we call 'white rain'. The road was impassable. This is the most unattractive and miserable time in the Altaj. A thick mist had screened the high mountain summits and had now hung its wings over the gentle slopes. It was as if the mountains had sunk and resigned themselves to the beauty of the area now being judged by sullen ridges and clumsy knolls. Down below, there was no longer anything left of the former dense forest, there were only maybe clumps of trees showing green here or there; these outliers were stubbornly making their way up across the slopes, gradually, by degrees, merging with each other and forming dense forest thickets on the terraces and saddles of the mountains.

I was entering a grove consisting entirely of larches, when I became aware of a loud, rattling sound. Soon, out from behind some trees came a large cart, heavily laden with silage. When it joined the main road and came closer, I saw that the horse was being driven by a young woman. White-faced, with a tightly knotted, white down shawl on her head, she didn't immediately see me, but then she quickly pulled in the reins, as though trying to find out who I was, striding along the deserted road at such an inclement time, and looked at me keenly.

'Ķasym, dear, can it really be you?' she asked in surprise. By her black eyes, fringed with long lashes, and by her pure, resonant voice, I immediately recognised Altyn.

'Not lost, are you? Where are you coming from? Where are you heading?' she bombarded me with questions. She spread out the truss of dry hay she was sitting on and indicated the place beside her.

'Do get on, get on!' she added impatiently.

Meeting her on the road had never even crossed my mind. And yet this beautiful, shapely woman with a slender waist, eyes as black as blackcurrants and rosy cheeks 'like peaches and cream', as they say, had often appeared in my memory. Now I found with chagrin that she'd sunk markedly in height and noticeably put on weight; her face had become rounded and lost its matchlessly fine features. I greeted her guardedly, although she was friendly and, to all appearances, very pleased about our unexpected meeting. I don't know what made me behave with such unusual coldness towards her: perhaps the changes that had taken place in her caught me unawares, and perhaps it was a manifestation of the habitual discomfiture which had never left me during our past meetings. I could think of nothing better than to bark out in reply:

'And where have you sprung from yourself?'

'What do you mean – where have you sprung from? This is our way of life...' She had evidently sensed, after all, a change in my attitude to her. 'You saw me in the days of your golden childhood, and a whole lifetime's gone by since then. It's a human trait to change: something new appears in people, and something else goes forever...'

And, as if not wishing to pursue her idea, behind which there evidently lay something not very pleasant, she tried to turn the conversation onto a different course:

'But you haven't changed at all, you wretch! Still the same boyish face – no moustache, no beard!' She burst out laughing, but fell silent straight away, seeing that I was quite unable to feel at ease. She did up the collar of her light quilted coat, which had kept on coming open over her full breasts, and stared in silence at the light chestnut horse slowly pulling the heavily laden dray.

'What do you mean – where have you sprung from?' she repeated, pensively now. 'It's here in our Topķajyṇ I've been living, ever since those days. I work on a livestock farm. And what brings you here yourself?'

'I've got things to do here... I've been walking from Sarymsaķ, and hadn't come across a single vehicle going my way, I'd barely made it this far.'

'Aha', she nodded, without taking her eyes off the road.

***

She was two years older than me. We'd gone to the same school, been in the same class. Altyn was reputed to be the prettiest of all the schoolgirls. She sang beautifully. Her songs ring in my ears to this day, having found a place in my heart forever. All of my loftiest dreams took shape to the melodious ringing of her voice. All it took was for some familiar motif that she used to perform to start ringing in my soul, and rising up at once before my eyes would be Altyn herself, the days of my distant childhood and my home.

I'd completed the course at our *auyl*'s[1] seven-year school and, at the insistence of my parents, who didn't want me to tie myself to back-breaking labour too early, I went away to the Topķajyṇ boarding school. Before me lay study in parts thirty kilometres away from our *auyl*.

The head of the boarding school proved to be an inordinately fat, middle-aged man with a cataract the size of a grain of wheat in one eye. He looked through my application and school report and, humming some plaintive tune under his breath, leant back, almost sprawled, on his chair. He looked for a

---

[1] *Auyl* – socio-economic formation considered to constitute the heartland of the nation and a basis for an ethnic and cultural union of the nomadic community. Consisting of 50–70 yurts in the eighteenth century, it developed into its current permanent state of 'rural settlement' (of a minimum of 100 dwellers) when Kazakhs adopted a settled mode of life in the nineteenth and twentieth centuries. *Auyl* can also be used as a synonym for 'native land' and 'homeland', concepts revered by the Kazakhs.

long time at my worn-out boots and my trousers made of mangy foal's skin, dyed with *estek*.[2] It was obvious that I wasn't to his taste. There seemed to be a puzzling question in his eyes: 'Does this ragamuffin really mean to carry on at school?' He finally stopped wheezing through his fat nose and, scraping his chair noisily, straightened up.

'Hm-m, you say you want to go to school? Well, all right, we'll take you into the school, but a place in the hostel's going to be a bit difficult... Hm-m!... It's something that, as you know... In short, everything will depend on your begabiour.'

That's what he said, 'begabiour'. It looked as if the conversation had taken quite a lot out of him, because he tossed my documents onto his desk and leant back once again. Long, wearisome minutes trickled by: the headmaster reclined in his chair with his eyes closed, and I sat on a bench and awaited a final decision. I understood perfectly well that without a place in the hostel, it wasn't worth my even thinking about continuing my studies.

'Have you somewhere to put up?' he suddenly asked me. 'If not, then today, so be it, one way or another you can stay overnight in the hostel. You can come in tomorrow.' All of a sudden, he started snoring, sitting right there at the desk.

I realised that the ice had begun to break. It wasn't worth testing my fate any further, and I quietly tiptoed out of the office.

...For the first time I found myself alone and far from home. Unfortunately, I had no relatives in Topķajyṇ. I didn't have the courage to go to strangers and ask if I could stay the night. I spent a long time mooching around the *auyl*, and only well towards evening did I head for the school. The hostel was located in a long, sun-dried brick building. Towering in the middle of an enormous room reminiscent of a hall was a black stove that looked like an enormous monster. Squashed up in a row, like lambs on a common leash, stood some iron beds. The bedclothes hadn't been tidied up. Five or six boys with close-cut hair were sitting around a scuffed table, poring over their textbooks and exercise books. As soon as I came in, they lifted their heads from their books and scowled at me, like cats that had seen a dog. Another boy, thin and lanky, with a forelock falling down onto his forehead, was lying on his bedclothes in his boots. He twisted his head on his thin neck, examining me from head to toe, then licked his lips with his thick, rough tongue.

'What, joined the school, have you?' he asked me.

From the tone of his voice I realised that before me was one of the school's ringleaders. Afraid he might turn me out, I nodded hurriedly:

'Yes.'

'What class are you in?'

'Class eight.'

'Re-eally? So, we'll be studying together! Well, come in, come in! Handily, I'm by myself here... There aren't enough beds, we sleep in pairs. Come in, why

---

[2] *Estek* – woodland herb; its roots are a source of orange dye.

are you standing in the doorway? And we'll find a place for your sack: I've got a roomy trunk!' Without allowing me to collect my thoughts, he came over, gave me a friendly slap on the back and sat me down on his bed. You might have thought he'd recognised a kindred spirit in me. 'And I expect your sack's stuffed full of *bauyrsak*?'[3]

'No, no, it's got clothes in it.'

His brows at once sank discontentedly, the amiability went from his face, and little wrinkles appeared on his forehead. But he tried all the same to conceal his disappointment.

'Never mind, never mind! You won't die of hunger here. Everyone here brings a sack soaked in fat and full of *bauyrsaks* from home. The fatty food already makes me feel ill!' He pulled a wry face.

Yes, if there *had* been *bauyrsaks* in the sack and I'd put them down in front of you, I'd have watched you set about stuffing your face with them, I thought. Look how coy you've become!

Lanky didn't think of spending any further time on me. He turned to a rotund, swarthy boy sitting over a textbook, and barked:

'Hey, Žarykžùldyz,[4] you're not so tall, you can sleep with the new boy. I can see it'll be a bit cramped for him and me on my bed.' He took my sack and unceremoniously flung it onto the next bed.

The other boy started blinking his eyes, which were round like cups, and only mumbled timidly:

'Why are you throwing things?'

I was furious, thinking, You miserable lump! If I came across you in the *auyl*, I'd show you how to chuck someone else's sack around! Well, never mind, you're an old hand here, you can keep your chin up for the moment! (They say this round-backed fellow now works in the *auyl* as the agent for the collection of wool. I've long been meaning to get him back for my old grievance, given the opportunity.)

I'd barely had the time to recover, when into the room, clicking her heels, came a small, fair-faced woman, who set about giving everyone a loud telling off.

'What's going on here? Why are you lying down?... Why aren't the beds made?... And why are you sitting on the bedding in your outdoor clothes?' she pounced on me. 'Having a nice sit down!...'

'Oh dear, Kùlǎš *apaj*,[5] I'm tired of telling them the same things over and over again!' Lanky cut in, licking his lips. 'They don't do as I say.'

'Who doesn't? Point him out to me!'

Lanky hesitated, not daring to name anyone specific.

---

[3] *Bauyrsak* – fried wheat dough found in the cuisines of Central Asia, a must-have treat for guests during occasions.

[4] *Žarykžùldyz* – lit. 'bright star'.

[5] *Apaj* – respectful form of address used when talking to an older woman.

'Send two boys to my place, get them to bring some water!' the woman ordered and, treading firmly across the floor in her heels, left the room.

The doors only had to close behind her for Lanky to stretch out on his bed again and pick up his book. The others, too, buried themselves in their books.

'Well, who's going to go for the water?' Lanky asked after a time.

The room grew even quieter, and nobody raised his head from his book, as though exams awaited them all the next day. Lanky's eyes once again rested on the rotund, swarthy boy.

'Hey, Žaryķžüldyz, it's your turn to fetch water today! Ķasym here's got nothing to do either, so take him with you. Let him get to know our way of life.'

Žaryķžüldyz rose from his seat reluctantly.

'Oh well, I'll go, if I must.' I replied, too. After all, anything's better than sitting among lads you don't know, looking as if you've got a splinter in your foot and don't know how to get it out.

The other lads heaved a sigh of relief, noisily slammed their books shut and pushed them as far away as they could.

Žaryķžüldyz and I led a grey horse with thin, protruding ribs from the stable and started harnessing him to an impossibly rickety cart on which there stood a barrel. As soon as the stave touched his jaded back, the grey nag showed his vice. He started desperately thrashing his docked tail around and remained standing where he was: not a horse, but a bit of hide that still needs knocking into shape. Every time the hefty stave rose into the air, Kôkšolaķ – that was the nag's name – instantly braced his whole body and arched his croup, making ready to kick out at any moment. I didn't think Žaryķžüldyz should have taken his anger out on the horse. In situations such as this, as the people say, a beaten dog rounds on a peaceful crane. The saying's spot on, but not everyone can understand the meaning of the words.

'Oh, I hope your spleen gets twisted! Well, what's the point of tormenting yourself and us? By the time we get to the river and back, it'll be midnight, won't it? The question is, who needs it?' Žaryķžüldyz was beside himself with anger. But Kôkšolaķ wasn't in the least concerned about his moaning. He flicked his sides a couple of times with his tail, and as though of his own free will, moved off.

Žaryķžüldyz proved to be a garrulous fellow (I later learned that his real name was Ķomšabaj). It transpired that ever since he was a baby, he'd been constantly wet beneath the nose, and that was why the *auyl* kids, inexhaustible in coming up with various inventions and names, gave him the nickname Žaryķžüldyz. The white trickle beneath his nose was done the honour of being called a bright falling star. But the funniest thing was that one of the lads only had to say: 'There's a star falling!' for the flow from Žaryķžüldyz's nose to become even more copious; he sniffed loudly and kept on wiping the abundant moisture with the backs of his long fingers. But the 'trail of the star' above his lip never dried up. Žaryķžüldyz was entirely untouched by the barbed puns of his classmates, there was no vanity to him at all.

While we were making our way to the lake, he imparted a good many useful things to me. First of all his account was of the thin, lanky boy who had sent us for the water.

'Don't particularly do as he says, or else he'll be on your back. He'll start giving you orders: do this, do that. He'll give you no peace. His real name's Ķydyrhan, but we call him Humpy. I tell you, he's an artful dodger like the world's never seen. He grovels in front of the teachers and the matron, even in front of the cook, but acts bossily with his classmates and stirs them up against one another – just to gain some benefit from it all for himself, if only a scrap. He's as slippery as a spoon dipped in oil, you can't keep track of what he's going to come up with next.'

'And who's the woman who gave us all a telling off?'

'Oh my, that's Kùlǎš – the main woman in charge of things!' Žaryķžùldyz ran his fingers under his nose. 'She only has to say "boo", and the whole school freezes! She's a matron – one, a teacher – two, the headmaster's wife – three! What else? Yes, she has control of the food and clothes that are issued to the school. If she takes a dislike to you, assume you won't get any decent clothing. But if truth be told, she's a dunce, a real dimwit! She once barely completed seven classes, but now – what do you know? – she teaches us in class eight. Exploits the fact that her husband's the headmaster. Oh my, you don't know our life yet', Žaryķžùldyz sighed with such a serene air that he might have been taken for the most tranquil person on earth. 'There isn't a man in the *auyl* to give Majmùryn[6] a rap on the knuckles, and there isn't a woman to make him see reason, and that's why he's got too high an opinion of himself – Majmùryn may not be a God here, but he's not far short.'

'And who is this Majmùryn?' I asked.

'I'm telling you – the headmaster! Surely you've seen him?'

'Yes.'

'That's him – Majmùryn. His real name's Ķalmataj. On paper, the school has four horses, four cows and one yearling bull. And all the rest that you'll see in our set-up belongs to Majmùryn. His sheep number thirty or forty head, there's a horse and a mare with a foal, and I think he has five or six cows. In the summer, all of us in the school store up hay for his livestock and firewood for their house. Any surplus he sells wherever he can: in the district capital, in the *auyls*... He's helped himself to everything, the devil! As you can see, we're the ones that even bring water for his house.'

'But you weren't taken on as his workmen, you could refuse to break your backs for him!'

'Oho! Just you try disobeying! No, hear me out first... A few days ago there was an inspector here from the district council. Someone must have written to the council about our desperate state. The devil got into me and I poked my nose in with a complaint to the inspector that there was no order in the

---

[6] Majmùryn – lit. 'fat nose'.

hostel, the food was bad and the bread they baked was undercooked. And what came of it? The inspector left, and I was knocked into the middle of next week. "You've evidently got so fat that now you're being picky about the state's bread! Maybe there's someone else among your friends who's dissatisfied with the way you're fed here? It's no problem for us to expel that sort from the school!" The way they had me up against the wall, I was ready to squeeze both feet into the same boot. You try sticking your neck out here: they'll turn you out of the school, and if they don't succeed in doing it straight away, Majmùryn will start failing you in history.' Žaryķžùldyz wiggled his shoulders as though he were feeling cold. 'If you want to be in the boarding school, then keep quiet...'

We were a long time getting to the river. We used up all our strength in filling the barrel. Finally, we got onto the cart and touched the reins, but Kôkšolaķ didn't bat an eyelid. He stood as if rooted to the ground, not reacting at all to our chucking and twitching on the reins. But Žaryķžùldyz only had to whack him on the side with all his might a couple of times for the horse at once to sink down and spring backwards. The cart struck a tree, a dry, cracked wheel split apart, the spokes flew everywhere like chips of wood, and the next instant the cart lay on its side, while the water poured out of the barrel in a roaring torrent.

'I hope you croak, damn you! I hope you turn to stone once and for all! I hope you swell up and burst like a shrivelled bubble!' Žaryķžùldyz poured out a no less roaring torrent of oaths on Kôkšolaķ, but to all appearances the poor horse had, in his time, been obliged to hear worse curses than these: he didn't swell up, nor did he burst – on the contrary, he angrily flattened his ears against his head and made ready for the next engagement with his tormentor. Žaryķžùldyz tried every means to force Kôkšolaķ to get under way, and, seeing that all his efforts had been to no avail, he banged his stick on the ground and sat down by the edge of the road.

'No luck at all!' he muttered furiously. 'I'm going to get it from the bursar now for the cart. Sit down!' he said to me, 'there's no point in standing... We'll get out of this somehow...'

***

It was quiet. Above the *auyl*, now hidden in a narrow, wooded ravine, the twilight was descending; showing through it, indistinctly black, were the houses, scattered disorderly. Sparks were flying from the clay tandoors that were set up in the courtyards. At times the curt barking of dogs would reach us, and rare summoning voices of women rang out, calling the cows returning from pasture. Somewhere on the edge of the *auyl*, a girl's sad song could be heard.

'Altyn's singing!' Žaryķžùldyz roused himself.
'Who's she?'
'One of us, from school.'
'She's a good singer', I responded, 'a good singer, wherever she's from.'

Indeed, the song which had disturbed the quiet of the evening suddenly seized all my attention. The pure and tender voice pierced my heart. A breeze blew gently; the recently opened panicles of feather grass trailed in the wind like the fluffy threads of a silk bridal veil, then, after gently swaying, froze motionless once more. Rising up like an overturned cauldron in the very middle of the ravine was a mountain crag. Its snow-covered summit hung sleepily over the silent gullies that cut across the mountain slopes. The full moon, which had appeared simultaneously with the glow of sunset, seemed to be hearkening reverently to both the evening's quiet and the girl's tender song; in any event, it had settled itself comfortably and, it appeared, for some time, like a welcome guest, on the shoulder of the crag.

The song was approaching us, gradually gathering inspired strength.

A dress with a fringe along the hem and a slender waist –
the light wind, dallying, won't leave you be…

This refrain reached our ears, breaking off in a strange sort of way and betraying the spiritual unrest of the girl singer. In between times she was singing the folk song 'Bir bala' ('An Unknown Girl') – which I'd heard every single day in my own *auyl*. But now this old melody, which had already been on the point of boring me, awakened in my soul completely new and hitherto unfamiliar feelings. Maybe the reason was that we didn't have such a skilled singer as Altyn in our *auyl*, or maybe I'd already started missing my family and was feeling the pull of home, but suddenly my heart began aching badly. And the song, just like that wind that wouldn't leave someone be, was suddenly flying up nearby, now sounding powerful and resonant, now dying away in the distance, like the barely audible rustling of the grass. And there was nothing in the world more beautiful than this melody, floating over the evening *auyl*.

Some time passed, and in the deepening twilight there appeared the girl herself. Her white dress fluttered weightlessly in the air. She was driving before her a mottled yearling heifer.

'Altyn!' Žaryķžůldyz hailed her loudly, leaping to his feet. 'Altyn!'

The dappled heifer gave a start in surprise and, holding its tail up clear of its body, it hurtled back towards the cowshed. The song came to an abrupt end. The girl stood for a moment or two peering into the darkness, and then cautiously enquired:

'Is that you, Žaryķžůldyz?'

Žaryķžůldyz gave a loud sniff and mumbled:

'Yes, it's me.'

'What are you doing here?'

'We came for water.'

Altyn walked up closer to us, tossing back a strand of black hair from her forehead. The moon was dazzling her eyes, and in the moon's light, there was the flash of a slender white face. Her cheeks were pink, and clearly visible were the little dimples on her cheeks. Her delicate lips seemed coated in snow-white sour cream. Beneath her brows as slender as the new moon sparkled eyes as black as blackcurrants. It wouldn't be at all surprising, it suddenly occurred to me, if from those clear eyes rolled the transparent morning dew.

Altyn saw the cart lying on its side and burst out laughing.

'Oh, wetnose, you've got yourself into hot water again!' she teased Žaryķžůldyz lightly, turned around and set off calmly in the direction of the *auyl*.

I thought she was one of those supercilious *auyl* girls who have a high opinion of themselves. But her soulful song was still ringing in my ears... Altyn walked away as though dancing; it seemed to me as if her bare white calves were touching the panicles of the feather grass in play. And I imagined, too, that as she went, she was laughing at our haplessness, I could read it now even in her gait. Indeed, she had song with her, she was led by freedom, while we were offering up prayers to a grey nag, and our peace depended on the whim of a capricious animal... A kind of hurt took hold of my heart. More and more, Altyn seemed in my imagination to be a wilful girl who knew no sympathy for the misfortunes of others. I don't know what Žaryķžůldyz was thinking about at that time, but it occurred to me that the girl from the song that had just rang out was Altyn herself.

A dress with a fringe along the hem and a slender waist –
the light wind, dallying, won't leave you be...

***

In the end, I wouldn't leave Majmůryn be and he was forced to accept me into the boarding school.

The first day of lessons arrived. Of all my classmates, it was Altyn who aroused the warmest feelings in me. She sat at her desk alone, at the back. She didn't make a fuss, she was laconic, and she didn't even join in with everyone else's merriment at the mischief of one or other of the pupils. She was even-tempered and conducted herself with a particular kind of dignity, standing out sharply in this respect from the other girls her age. The classroom was congested, and there weren't enough places for all the pupils. I'd been counting on sharing a desk with Žaryķžůldyz, but a boy every bit as rotund and swarthy as he had already settled next to him and, naturally, didn't want to give up his place. I didn't venture to approach Altyn, particularly as a few minutes earlier she'd sent Humpy packing when he'd tried to sit down next to her.

'What, has your place flooded? Sit at your own desk!' Altyn gave him a shove in his scrawny chest. 'Go on, go on!'

The bell rang, and Majmůryn rolled into the classroom.

'What are you hanging about by the door for, like a stuffed dummy?' he asked me in a hoarse voice.

'There's no room.'

'Sit next to Ķabdyġalieva!' He jabbed a finger in Altyn's direction. 'Don't worry, she doesn't bite.'

This was all Majmùryn had to say for chuckling to sweep through the classroom. To my misfortune, I hadn't managed to take a single step before my trousers, made from dried foal skin, began their awful scrunching. The class rolled around laughing. With his huge belly quivering, Majmùryn was choking, too, emitting sounds like the quacking of a duck: 'Wakh-wakh, wakh-wakh!...' I didn't know what to do – laugh or cry. Altyn was the only one not laughing at me. But in her gaze, which was fixed upon my orange trousers, I read alarm.

'Oh, what a handsome couple!' exclaimed Humpy from the front desk, as soon as I'd sat down next to Altyn.

By now the class was roaring with unrestrained laughter. I was ready for the earth to swallow me up. Altyn had evidently resolved to give me some support – or perhaps she didn't want people laughing at her – and she intervened decisively in the subsequent course of events.

'What's so funny? A pair like any other!' She swept her eyes scathingly over Humpy. 'Just look at that, he's completely lost it!'

After the laughter had quietened down somewhat, Majmùryn cleared his throat and proceeded with the lesson. He laid the history textbook out before him and, casting glances at the open pages, read an entire chapter out loud to us almost without pausing for breath. This exercise took quite a lot out of him, his voice fell, and his forehead was covered in perspiration. On concluding the chapter, Majmùryn slammed the book shut and rose from his chair.

'I have some urgent business, I'll be away for a short while. Don't make a noise, read the textbook!' Without waiting for the lesson to end, Majmùryn left the classroom.

And of course, no one even thought of reading the textbook. Barely had the door closed behind Majmùryn before a hubbub began and laughter rang out.

Although I suffered no little ignominy because of my trousers, they did me an important service nonetheless. Majmùryn evidently told his wife about what had happened in his first lesson, because on the very next day Žaryķžùldyz came running to get me.

'The bursar said you were to go and get some clothes!' he shouted in joyful excitement while still some distance away.

The school's bursar was an elderly man by the name of Zejnolla, clumsy and unsociable, like a bull given to butting. He went about all year round in a shabby winter coat with a collar made of cat fur. The children addressed him respectfully as *aġaj*,[7] but behind his back for some reason they called him The Man in a Case. Only after some time did I learn the origin of this nickname, but for the time being I thought he'd been given the name for his meanness.

---

[7] *Aġaj* – respectful form of address when talking to an older man.

Anyway, this Zejnolla regarded anyone as a waste of space, if, for some reason, they weren't to his liking; he'd look at them first with one eye, then with the other, but never with both. It was clear that I fell into the category of precisely those people he considered a burden. At the sight of me, his face became contorted and began an agonised twitching, his whole body bent, and he started sorting through the footwear collected in a large box; then, as if tearing off a piece of his own flesh, he tossed me a pair of working boots, size forty.

'*Aġaj*, they're a bit too big for me, I think', I began, but fell silent straight away, seeing the gaze of his bloodshot eyes fixed upon me.

'Do you think shoes of a smaller size grow on trees? There's enough like you here to fill two boarding schools. If you don't want them, don't have them!' he droned, turning away from me in a sulk.

Žaryķžüldyz, who was standing outside the door, shook his head at me in despair, giving me to understand that I shouldn't contradict. The bursar, meanwhile, was sorting through trousers and jackets, picking them up one after another, then looking me over from head to toe and, folding the clothes up again, stuffing them deep into the box. It was clear that he begrudged giving out what would have been my size. But he was nonetheless forced to hand over the very last trousers and jacket.

'Don't argue with him, got it?' Žaryķžüldyz whispered in my ear, having after all come inside the storeroom. 'He's Majmûryn's father-in-law, isn't he! Take what you're given and don't get into arguments. As you know, "an impoverished soul takes good care of another man's wealth." There's plenty of clothes of every kind in this storeroom, but look, what do we go around in? Come, let's go back to the hostel!'

The boots of thick rawhide were too big; the tips of my toes were almost a whole span short of the toecaps, which were round, like flasks for mare's milk. When I took a step, the boots made a hollow banging noise on the ground, and it seemed to me as if my feet were going to break off at the ankles. Žaryķžüldyz made me walk backwards and forwards, cast an eye over my gait and commanded me to take the boots off. Then he turned our mattress over, unstitched the seam, pulled out a lump of cotton wool, scrunched it into two balls and pushed them into the toes of the boots. We'd adjusted the boots to my feet after a fashion, but with the trousers and jacket the situation was worse. What size clothes I'd been given God alone knows, but the waist of the trousers could be pulled right up to my chin, while the bottom of the jacket hid my calves. I seemed to myself like a horse that's been led out to a *băjge*,[8] wrapped from head to toe in a horsecloth.

'There's nothing to be ashamed of', Žaryķžüldyz reassured me. 'As long as things hang on your shoulders and don't fall off your hips. The good new outfit's the one that's warm, not the one that looks nice, got it?'

---

[8] *Băjge* – an ancient type of horse race popular with Kazakhs, six to hundred kilometers riding depending on the type of *băjge*.

But I wouldn't have parted with them even if the jacket hadn't hung on my shoulders, and the trousers hadn't stayed on my hips. The new clothes were an absolute fortune for me in comparison with the rough trousers made from foal skin and the boots with holes in them, about to fall apart at every step. I felt as if I were on horseback.

***

From that day on I felt myself to be an equal among my peers, involved, as it were, in a new and interesting life. And everything that happened in that little *auyl* bearing the name of Topķajyŋ – which meant 'birch grove' – all the concerns that made up the life of the boarding school, which had now become my home, seemed to me to carry in them the breath and rhythm of the enormous world. I found myself among a multitude of people. We, the lads, lived and slept in one room, two to a bed. It was similar to the way we mounted up two to a horse in our *auyls*. We ate in a cramped canteen, where one would get more food, another less, and sometimes there were grievances, too, fights would break out, but we would probably not have agreed to exchange our boarding school life for any other, even one utterly wonderful. I felt I was maturing dramatically, learning more and more about life and gaining confidence. I started trying to find myself friends – that's human nature for you: each of us forms their own social circle, seeks people among whom they can breathe more easily, live more fully. Of course, at that time you don't yet know people well, don't have a grasp of what there's more of in them, good or bad, you don't weigh up their actions, as if on scales, to pronounce a definitive opinion on this or that person. Most often, it's like this in childhood: you've taken a dislike to someone and you start steering clear of them, without having even fully discovered their qualities. Or else, on the contrary, inspired with fellow-feeling, you start gravitating towards someone, you're involved with them heart and soul, and wish them success in everything. It can be the case that this person isn't always right in their actions, doesn't always treat people fairly, but you stick up for them all the same. I had two friends – Žaryķžüldyz and Altyn.

Žaryķžüldyz was the first person to take an interest in me when I'd only just arrived at the school, and that really meant something to me. We slept on the same bed, and you might say we had no secrets from each other. Žaryķžüldyz liked literature, but was good at Russian and maths as well. For me, a boy who had grown up in an isolated Kazakh *auyl* and who couldn't string two words together in Russian, it seemed impossible to know Russian better than Žaryķžüldyz. Now, when a lot of time has passed, I can confess that I not infrequently used to copy Russian and maths homework from Žaryķžüldyz.

The three of us, Altyn, Žaryķžüldyz and I, would do our lessons together. I didn't notice any particular enthusiasm for any one subject in Altyn. Now I could say that her gentle, receptive soul was made for song; she was someone with an inclination most of all for art.

91

In those days I was trying to write poetry. One day I dashed off some lines which I considered to be an undeniable poetic success:

The boarding-school's dress is uniformal,
Two hundred grams of bread's the normal.
Neither hungry, nor well-fed today,
But the road keeps running far away.

Once, while doing a lesson, I recited the poem to my friends.
'No, that's not a poem!' Altyn concluded after listening to me.
'Why?'
'I've never come across a poem like that! And I think you're wasting your time. You're unlikely to make a poet.'
I was upset by her judgement – direct, sharp, devoid of any kind of respect for my enthusiasm. Even Žaryķžůldyz, who'd perhaps only nodded his head while listening to my creations before, came down hard on me this time with murderous criticism:
'Write either in Russian or in Kazakh', he said. 'And the words you chose aren't poetic, I don't think. What's more, there's no adjective like "uniformal". And so, more correctly it would read: "The boarding-school's dress is uniform, two hundred grams of bread's the norm..." And if we're talking about the content... In short, it's a poor poem... You shouldn't write about the school like that. Maybe you haven't accepted it yet, but for me it's both my home and parents.'
'Now you've taken a completely different side. There's truth in the poem. You criticised Majmůryn to me yourself, by the way.' I decided to direct his attention to his own recent words, but Žaryķžůldyz stood up to me:
'It's true I criticised Majmůryn, but not the school! And if there's something here that's not right, that's his fault. But the school... You leave it alone, Ķasym.'
And it's true, writing poetry had proven beyond me. My 'creative travails' ended with the lines quoted above, and I didn't write any more for the time being. I feel ashamed now to remember my first poetic exercises. Nonetheless, those four lines dedicated to the boarding school spread quickly among the children and were sung like popular satirical songs. Of course, they came to the ears of the headmaster.
'No good is evidently going to come of you!' Majmůryn's wife, Kůlǎš, rounded on me after a day or two. 'A boy who's not fated to live goes running to the grave himself! That must have been said of you, you wretch!...'
She sat me down to peel potatoes for a whole day. The punishment proved to my benefit, because in the evening I got an extra helping of soup. And in another couple of days Altyn altered my jacket and trousers – adjusted them to my size, so that I started looking a real dandy. It was just my boots that were a bit big, and in games I couldn't keep up with the other children.

There were about fifty boys and girls at the boarding school. They were clothed and fed by the state. Altyn was an orphan, too. Maybe the idea that she'd be able to count only on herself in life forced her to be collected and serious-minded. She took care of herself, dressed neatly, was a skilled seamstress and an excellent embroiderer. Altyn complained to no one and confided in no one. To me, it seemed that she had some sort of secret...

A year had passed since the end of the war. And as ill luck would have it, that year had turned out to be uncommonly arid, food had become a problem again, and people had continued to experience need. Relations, close and distant, would come from the *auyls* to visit the children and they wouldn't come empty handed: some would bring *ķurt*[9] and *irimšik*,[10] others dry *talķan*[11] or a cup of butter. We were fed tolerably, but the delicacies brought from home were dear to us. We all missed our native parts. Sacks and saddlebags were emptied at once by the whole gang, because food was considered common property in the school. Rarely did anyone hide anything of what they'd been brought from their *auyl*. And if they did, then people like Humpy 'unmasked' them in an original way: they'd find it and eat it all themselves to the very last crumb.

One day the Sun shone on my street, too. Šalym arrived in his old, rather too large hat with big, drooping flaps. I was in seventh heaven, I was so happy.

'Oh, my beloved little imp, you're alive and well?' As he came towards me, his sparse little beard was twitching in time with his words and his sharp little eyes were shining with tears.

Šalym was quite a character. His name was Ybyraj, and he was my father's elder brother. There had at some time been someone by the name of Ybyraj in our family, and so Hanšajym *apa*[12], according to custom, didn't dare call her husband by that name. She called him Šalym, which meant 'my old man'. Gradually, our entire *auyl*, consisting of ten houses, began to call him Šalym. The old man was already nearly seventy, God had given him no children, and so he considered me his son. What's more, the Kazakhs have a highly developed sense of kinship and are quite sensitive to orphans. For Ybyraj I was the embodiment of the house of his dead brother Raķyš, so he simply worshipped me. He was no eminent man. He'd been a cowherd all his life. From an early age he'd tended the herds of the local landowner, had been a placid, obedient workhorse, as they say, and had remained one: nobody had

---

[9] *Ķurt* – hard, salty dairy product made from drained yoghurt-like beverage, *katyķ; ķurt* comes in different shapes.

[10] *İrimšik* – a type of cottage cheese that is served as dessert.

[11] *Talķan* – a nourishing product prepared from ground and dry-fried wheat, barley or corn mixed with sugar and butter or sour cream.

[12] *Apa* – depending on the region, aunt, sister, mother, or grandmother; it is also a common respectful form of address for older women in general.

heard so much as a sharp word from him, let alone of any great deed he might have performed in his life.

'You probably heard that after you left, I had lumbago and I gave up work', he groaned. 'But the foreman wouldn't let me go, persuaded me to keep watch over the crops. "It's an easy job," he says, "there'll be a horse underneath you." Now I could kick myself for agreeing, my dear little imp. The job's turned out to be hectic. The harvesting's on, and you can't take even one step away. Your *apa*'s been making my ears ring. "Our boy's missing home," she says, "go and see how he's getting on, whether they're bullying him at the boarding school." And so I got away from work. You're not going hungry here? They're not bullying you?'

He spoke quickly, not letting me even open my mouth. He had a critical look at how I was dressed, as though he'd seen me off to the school in expensive clothes and was now concerned I might have lost some part of my finery. He asked me about absolutely everything! And he didn't forget to report the *auyl* news either.

'Your *apa*, Allah be praised, is well, and sent this *talķan* for you', he pointed with his chin at a small sack lying at his feet. 'This year, unlike former times, your *apa* doesn't have enough *ķurt-maj*.[13] The damned grey cow has completely had it, even the bull doesn't look at her nowadays. She might at least have some shame in front of people... It looks as if she'll stay dry this year, too. Before winter comes, I'm going to slaughter her for meat, and I'll bring you the best pieces from the rump. I've had enough, how long can I keep looking under that shameless creature's tail? Life's improving, and if we're alive, we'll get another cow. Allah be praised, we've not yet lived to see the day when the cauldron in the house is empty. Is that right, what I'm saying?'

He ran through all of our kinsfolk living in the ten households and then moved on to the affairs of his nephew, Ķabyken.

'As you know', he leant towards me confidentially, 'as you know, he didn't mind having a drink before. Well, but now the rotten egg's lost his head completely. He fills his belly with booze and loafs around the *auyl* aimlessly. He doesn't know what he's prattling about – as the saying goes, a white pooch jumps into his mouth, and out of it comes a grey bitch. He's a stain on our family... I'm ashamed to look people in the eye. Before coming here to see you, I dropped in on him, but you know his wife... Not a woman, but a raw ox-hide that even a knife has no effect on, let alone words... She's got milk from four cows, but begrudged you a cup of butter. It's a wonder the earth doesn't swallow up these people who don't know compassion. Let them be that way... They're not people, but black stone, even if there is a human soul in their bodies... I drop in on them, look around, and Ķabyken in the corner of the room. I wonder whether I should tear the skin off his stupid head and give him a smack in the mouth, but then I remember: I've got a journey ahead

---

[13] *Ķurt-maj* – collective term for dairy products such as milk, *ajran*, *ķurt*, *irimšik*, etc.

of me, and it mustn't be defiled by an ill deed. You mustn't do a thing like that when you're going to see your son... Otherwise he'd have caught it from me, blast him!...' He took a little breather, having given vent to all his annoyance, and wiped away the sweat which had appeared on his forehead. Then he started bustling once again: 'Well, all right, that's enough about that. And I've stayed too long. As you know, you've got to keep an eye out for the crops. If the livestock trample down the corn, there'll be no end of trouble. And the foreman will be upset with me. Well, so long!' He got onto his horse and struck it with his whip. But, after riding a few steps away, he turned back.

'As you know, we're little people, even if we do understand everything in this life. Don't fool around here, do as your elders say, work properly. I see you've been dressed and shod like a bridegroom. Even I couldn't have got you new things like that. Our people's power's feeding and clothing you, teaching you sense... The power of our people... You've got no father or mother, my colt, so don't go doing anything that might prevent you from being at the boarding school. Be a good lad, my colt! Well, so long!' He started beating his heels against the belly of the bay horse and set off at a trot, but I hadn't had time to go into the school building before Šalym was back again.

'As you know', he leant down from the horse, 'the dust doesn't rise under a lone traveller's feet. And so, share the *talķan* with your friends. They're children just like you, and they miss their homes as well. A man becomes a man among other people. And what can you do without people? And so, you mustn't be greedy, my colt! Well, so long!...'

He began to ride away, but immediately exclaimed loudly:

'Oh, I've got a head like a sieve! How about that, I've come back to you so many times, but almost forgot... As you know, your *apa* will always have something laid in for you...' He wedged the handle of his whip in by the pommel of his saddle and started fumbling in his bootleg. 'Where ever has it got to? Not slipped under the lining, has it? How many times have I asked the old woman to fit some kind of inside pocket to my jacket? She doesn't pay any attention, the old girl! So now you have to faff around, looking for a needle in a haystack. Aah, there it is!...'

Still, quite some time went by before he extracted from the leg of his felt-lined boot a fifty-rouble banknote. For me fifty roubles was nothing less than a fortune! Never had I been such a rich man! Šalym was almost ready to go again, but changed his mind and took a snuffbox from his pocket. He held his thumb out upright, poured some *nasybaj*[14] onto it and began drawing it noisily, by turns, first into his right, then into his left nostril.

'Do you know where they sell tobacco here?' he asked, moving on to his own needs. 'This snuff was given me by Matrei, and either it's mixed half and

---

[14] *Nasybaj* – tobacco snuff mixed with dried plants (juniper, saxaul, meadowsweet, birch tree) believed to be a mental and physical stimulant.

half with dust, or else it was picked when it was green, but there's no strength in it... Well, never mind though, snuff's not marble, it'll turn up somewhere or other. Well, so long! I'll be going, I've stayed too long. As you kn... kn... know... Achoo! As you know, we've never had any money. Buy books and exercise books with what I'm leaving you, my colt! Well, so long! Achoo!...'

It was a real struggle for Šalym to part with me. As it was for me with him.

**

It turned out to be a rainy autumn. But not for nothing do they say that even a blizzard means freedom for children and dogs, and still less could rainy autumnal days (not really rain, just a continual, tedious, light drizzle) lessen our vim. Saturday and Sunday are special days for boarding school children, as on those days everyone rides or walks back to their homes and *auyls*. It becomes quiet in the hostel, just the three of us remain: Žaryķžŭldyz, Humpy and me.

On those two days Žaryķžŭldyz never got up from his bed. Wrapping his back up in his fustian blanket, as though the wind were blowing through the hostel, and keeping on running his fingers under his nose, he'd spend entire days trying to solve mathematical puzzles of some sort. And he loves nothing better than to be left to practise solving problems. And Humpy never emerged from the kitchen. He'd collect the sugar and butter meant for the pupils who'd gone home and hid them in his red trunk. Then, until deep into the night, he'd be ceaselessly chewing something, chomping loudly and breathing heavily through his nose.

My favourite thing was doing nothing. I'd lie in bed with my head covered by a thin blanket and my nose buried in my pillow, giving myself up to sweet dreams. What can be better than lying in a warm bed, listening to the rain beating monotonously on the window pane and your heart echoing it? Not life, but paradise! Your dreams carry you far away, you fly all around the world and visit unknown lands, forgetting that you're lying half-starved beneath a thin blanket. Sometimes you fall asleep, exhausted by the endless train of picturesque scenes passing in succession before you, and then you have a fabulous dream. Ah, how lovely, how nice!...

I always dreamed about Altyn. And she and I would always be soaring together, high in the heavens. The stars would be twinkling beside us. Holding hands, we'd fly through the clouds. Sometimes, from behind thick clouds, fat Majmŭryn would suddenly appear, tear Altyn from my arms and disappear with her. Worn out by an uneven struggle, I'd fly headlong towards the earth and wake up, falling from the bed onto the floor. Satisfying myself that my misfortunes had taken place in a dream, I was inexpressibly glad of this fact. I'd clamber up onto the bed and shut my eyes, trying to have my recent dreams again. But no matter how tightly I closed my eyelids, the sweet visions returned no more. Instead of them came others, in which I'd be saved from the pursuit of now a frightening monster, now an enormous snake, now one-eyed Majmŭryn.

And again, I would wake tired, with a bad headache, and lie in bed for a long time with my eyes open, unable to understand where I was.

Some people dislike it when it's overcast. But for me, bad weather was a blessing. To each his own. I would sit down by the window, look at the endless, spitting rain and give myself up to long dreams…

Žaryķžüldyz did sums. Humpy shovelled down bread. I sat by the window. Clouds floated quickly and non-stop across the sky. The last days of November. A quick, cold wind chased rubbish down the street: yellow leaves, the dry stems of grasses, bits of paper. The old birch tree swayed in front of the window, and a noisy flock of crows flew above its crown in a vain attempt to settle for the night. A sheet of paper is held up by the butt of the tree. Perhaps it's one of the sheets on which my unsuccessful poetry is written?

Yes, I'd begun writing poems again and wrote a lot. And they were all dedicated to Altyn. Beneath that old birch tree, the three of us – Žaryķžüldyz, Altyn and I – did our homework. Beneath that old birch tree, we confided our dreams to each other. Beneath that birch tree, I wrote for the first time a short story, dedicated to Altyn as well. But nobody other than me knew about that. I simply didn't dare show Altyn my latest creation.

That unforgettable autumn, Almataj, Majmüryn's younger brother, returned to the *auyl* from Almaty, having graduated from his institute. He started teaching literature to the senior classes. He was a thin, swarthy *žigit*[15] of medium height, about thirty years old. His eyes were large and clear, and shone sadly under high eyebrows. Visible next to his Adam's apple was a ribbed scar the size of a fish scale, the result of some old illness. Naturally, this mark gave rise to a nickname, something the boarding school children were really good at. He hadn't had time to look around after his arrival, before he was already being called Tyrtyķ – Knotty. He was notable for his terseness: either he was a reserved man by nature, or else he'd decided to be cautious with us. He didn't permit himself to shout at the pupils. Apart from the class register, he held nothing in his hand, neither book nor exercise book. He knew the lessons by heart and spoke without a single hesitation, something which prompted our respect.

I don't know why, but I took a liking to Almataj from the very first day. I waited impatiently for his lesson and listened attentively to everything he talked about. I wanted to show what I could do as well, and I never missed an opportunity to ask questions, often interrupted him and was forever volunteering to answer during lessons. But the strange thing is that, however diligently I answered him, he never gave me a mark higher than a four. This was all the more surprising, since some of my classmates got 'excellent' without having understood the material, and having done nothing more than learn it

---

[15] *Žigit* – generally denoting a 25- to 40-year-old male, the term can also be used as an honorific indicating bravery, endurance, fortitude and being true to one's word.

by heart. But the teacher turned a blind eye to this. His attitude to the pupils'
knowledge aroused in me both disappointment and condemnation.

One day, Almataj – I couldn't call him Tyrtyķ – kept me behind after the
lesson. I was in the second shift and it was already dark outside, it was late. He
shut the door tight and sat down next to me. He put his hand on my shoulder
and began looking silently into my face. His gaze was intent. Several agonising
minutes passed before he started to speak.

'It seems to me, boy, that you're in a hurry to become an adult', he suddenly
said.

I didn't understand what he meant. Nothing could be read on his face, not
approval, not a shadow of annoyance, not a hint of irony. He turned his sad
eyes away and fixed his gaze on the toes of his boots. His long fingers passed
over my shoulder and touched my hair. A shiver ran through my body, as if
it had been touched by cold mercury. I involuntarily struck him on the hand.
He evidently hadn't noticed what he was doing himself, suddenly realised and,
embarrassed, moved away from me.

'Is Altyn a relative of yours?' he asked quietly.

'No.'

'Maybe you're from the same *auyl*?'

'No.'

Almataj rose, went across to his desk and, standing with his back to me,
started leafing through the register. Then he turned to me again.

'You aren't annoyed with me?'

'What about?'

'About the marks I give you.'

'No.'

'And if you're frank?'

'No.'

'That's good. Don't compare yourself with the others. I know back to front
who digests how much material. Some want nothing more than to graduate
from the school. They need a mark, and that's all. And some... I mean, you
dream of becoming a writer, don't you? That suits me, Ķasym. Your dream
can't be given a "three" or a "four". The main thing is your love for literature.
Have you thought about that?'

'I don't know.'

'I've heard you write short stories.'

'Who told you that?'

'Ķomšabaj.'

'No, I don't.'

'And if you're honest?' He gave me an intent look.

'I haven't.'

'Well, all right... Which writers do you like? Who have you read the most?'

'I read everything I can get hold of.'

'I'll give you an interesting book. If, of course, you'd like to read it.'

'I'll read it.'
'Let's go to my room, then…'

***

It was the first time I found myself in Majmùryn's house. It was completely full of furniture and decorated with rugs. There was no room to swing a cat for things. I strode mechanically into the room, hesitated, glancing at my enormous, dirty boots, and then stepped back towards the threshold.

They'd just finished having dinner in the house. Majmùryn rose up like a hill as he reclined in the *tôr*[16] with two or three cushions under his elbow. His shirt was unbuttoned, the top of his vest was black with sweat and looked like a cloth through which dirty water had been strained. Damp, black streaks stretched from his nipples to his navel. Majmùryn turned over, picked up the terry towel lying by his head, crumpled it up, shoved it under his armpits and, with energetic movements, began wiping the sweat away. His wife, who was carrying a tray full of *bauyrsaḵs* into the kitchen, saw me by the threshold and stopped in surprise.

'What are you here for?' Kùlắš asked, then gave a nod of understanding, took a handful of *bauyrsaḵs* from the tray and thrust them upon me. You might have thought that I'd come to ask for a handout. I was prepared with one kick to send both her tray and her herself to the devil, but at the very last moment something restrained me. Or rather, I was stopped by the words of Šalym who had asked me not to do anything that might deprive me of the opportunity to be at the boarding school.

I turned to the door, prepared to leave, but at that moment, from a side-room, came out Almataj. He threw a stern glance at his sister-in-law and asked me:

'Where are you going? Come through to my room!' Almataj took me by the sleeve and dragged me almost by force into his room. He moved a chair towards me and cried through the door: 'Bring us something to eat!'

Not a minute had passed before the tray appeared in front of us. On top of the *bauyrsaḵs* lay some cold lamb. Almataj followed Kùlắš with frowning eyes and then turned to me again:

'Well, have some dinner!'

But I didn't even reach a hand out towards the food. I couldn't forget how a few minutes before I'd been humiliated in this house. My entire body was tensed. Almataj seemed to understand the state I was in, took a small piece of a *bauyrsaḵ*, chewed it reluctantly and moved the tray aside. He rose, pushing his chair away noisily towards the wall, and dragged out from under the bed a large suitcase, made to look like crocodile skin. He opened it, rummaged

---

[16] *Tôr* – honourable place located opposite the entrance at the back of a yurt or a room, reserved for guests or for the oldest man in the family.

99

among his things, took out a tattered book and placed it upon the table. On the cover, which had seen better days, was an inscription in Roman characters: *The Kazakh Language*. The book didn't excite any particular enthusiasm in me, because I'd held a similar one in my hands before, even a rather newer one. Strange, I thought, was it worth inviting me home for the sake of this book? Almataj evidently realised what I was thinking.

'This is the very interesting book that I promised you', he said. 'Mind you don't lose it. This book was a present from my very best friend. And one more request: don't show it to anyone, even your own father. Read it and return it into my hands, got it?'

'Got it.' I replied.

'That's good.'

I put the book away in my bosom and set off back to school.

I leafed through the book and didn't find there was anything unusual about it. I read the first few pages, got my head around the method of word formation expounded in it, and realised that it was written in an original way, but no more. Why ever had he offered me this textbook? At the end of page ten a sentence broke off, the next page was missing, and page twelve began like this: 'As we were leaving our native parts, the time was approaching midday.' This page was as thumbed as could be, had turned yellow, and was held together in places with glue. I began reading on:

> Quick dark clouds were moving away south in a continuous train, like a caravan, the Sun was gradually drifting out from behind them and casting its warm rays onto the earth. But all the same, the cold wind blowing from the left penetrated clothing and pierced right through the bodies, as though reminding travellers that September had come. There were two of us.

That is exactly how the story began; I remember those lines by heart to this day. It's not even only the beginning I remember well, but the whole short story.

I don't know until what time I was reading the book, but in my memory has remained the deep empathy I experienced with the author. 'That *Šuġa* was indeed a fine girl!' I repeated in my mind, saying goodbye to the work's heroine. I would probably have sat over the book right through till morning, had I not been turned out of the school by the night watchman. I put it away in my bosom again and set off for the hostel. From then on, I spent my nights with that book, as though with a bride, carried it under my shirt, hid with it under my blanket, and in the end read it from cover to cover in a week.

Neither the name of the author nor the titles of the stories were given in the book. It was even hard to establish where one work ended and where another began. Sometimes a story would break off in the most interesting place, then there'd come some grammatical rules – they'd stretch to several pages, as though leading the reader away, forcing him to think about there being a textbook in front of him – and then there'd come the text of the story once more. I read the book, unable to tear myself away, like a lamb grown thin after a hungry winter falling greedily upon the first grass of spring.

It was as if scenes from the life of my native *auyl* had come to life before my eyes. I plunged into the maelstrom of a life in which there was much that was both good and bad, in which there lived and fought for a bright future both old men and young, people of stern temper and of gentle spirit, the unjust and the honest, the raging and the meek. I cried over Šuġa dying of anguish, I grieved with that poor devil Äbdirahman; I was beside the old man Ajranbaj, who was like my own Šalym, and the old woman Raušan, who, like two peas in a pod, reminded me of my grandmother, Hanšajym; I listened to Ajdarbek and Zejnep's conversation as though sitting next to them by the hearth; I was grateful to Ämiržan for his wise words and precise thinking; I laughed wholeheartedly at the pranks of the *žigit* Ķùrymbaj. This was a huge and lively world! It could be said that I forgot about myself. It was as if my thoughts had found wings. And at the same time, I regretted that I hadn't had the chance to take part in the life the author had depicted so subtly and brilliantly. I regretted that I hadn't been born some fifteen or twenty years earlier. Who was this man who had reflected so masterfully the life of the steppe-dwellers, a period encompassing almost a quarter of a century? He had presented the reader with a great and interesting story, as though pouring mare's milk to the brim of a *tegen*[17] and setting the full bowl before him. There, quench your thirst, have your fill of this life-giving drink. There's the taste here, and colour, and breath of life, nothing's been lost or forgotten, and not a single drop's been spilled. I reread the stories several times, and I even copied 'Šuġa's Memorial' into my exercise book.

Then I asked myself why Almataj was hiding this book. Why didn't its cover correspond to its contents? Why were the stories set out in such a way that you wouldn't immediately suspect their presence? I pondered on this puzzle for several days and nights in a row. As we'd agreed, I took the book back to Almataj and handed it to him in person. Then I asked him about what had been tormenting me. Almataj wasn't in the least surprised by my questions. He took the book from me and in turn, asked:

'Have you read Chekhov?'

'A little.'

'Then consider that you've read the works of the Kazakh Chekhov', Almataj answered.

'And is he alive now?'

'You'll find out when the time's right, Ķasym.'

Nothing more did he say to me. I returned to the hostel, and my concern now was the exercise book into which I'd copied the story. I didn't trust myself with it, or my friends. I cut my padded jacket open, put the exercise book inside

---

[17] *Tegen* – large bowl for mixing dough, pouring milk etc.

the quilted lining and sewed it back up with thick canvas thread. Like this, it seemed to me, my treasure would be perfectly secure. In the daytime I'd be wearing the jacket, in the night it lay under my head. It got to the point where at night, on hearing the slightest rustling, I'd grab at my quilted jacket, afraid that someone would try to steal my favourite story from me. Finding some free time, I'd go away from the people, unstitch the jacket, take out the exercise book and reread 'Šuġa' once again. Then I dreamt of meeting the author. I wanted to tell him about my impressions and show him my exercise book. I presumed he lived in Almaty, and if I were to find myself in the capital, I'd be sure to seek him out. But ten whole years went by before I learnt the whole truth about the author of these stories that had caught my fancy.[18]

***

There are times when a man can find no peace and he's gripped by obscure, troubled feelings. He lives in expectation of something unusual, something to soothe his soul and bring a feeling of complete satisfaction. What is that inexplicable force which so disturbs a man and draws him far away? Maybe the name of that force is love? I believe that neither a sage who knows the secrets of life, nor a poet familiar with man's spiritual upheavals could answer this question. It's better to proceed from the very stuff of human nature, from the very wonder of earthly life, which is heading far away, onward and in the direction of hope.

I was captivated by this inescapable thirst for life, which is hard, incidentally, to convey on paper. A weakness of man is that he's at times incapable of fully expressing his innermost thoughts. Moreover, the thoughts and feelings that worry you may prove to be the most commonplace for the people around you. In the days of my childhood I never met a single person who would have believed that I was aiming to become the living soul whose concerns would encompass looking for the solution of the most complex questions of human existence. Nobody believed it was exactly those problems that worried me.

That's not hard to explain, though. I was an orphan who dreamt of getting an education and becoming a fully fledged man. Who doesn't want that? The responsibility for my studies was taken on by the country; what more can be wished for by a boy who's grown up in a small, poverty-stricken *auyl*? Live, study, learn some sense... You're still a boy... Altyn, too, probably saw me as a silly little boy who was not yet capable of forming his own judgements about life. She did, indeed, treat me like her small, younger brother. She pitied me more than she was drawn to me as a kindred spirit, she wished me well, but never shared her innermost thoughts with me as an equal. It's unlikely she sensed how ardently and anxiously my heart would beat when I saw her.

---

[18] The author of 'Šuġanyṇ belgisi' ('Shuga's Memorial') is the well-known Kazakh writer Bejimbet Majlin (Beimbet Mailyn), who fell victim to Stalinist repressions.

And if she did sense it, she undoubtedly took it for a naive, boyish affection, for a manifestation of the childhood friendship which attends us in our life at school.

The only one of the adults who could read my thoughts like a book was Almataj. Yet he demonstrated it not through words, but through his gaze. Even after I'd read his book and returned it to him, Almataj didn't condescend to have a candid conversation with me. He was, after all, quite a reticent, terse man, and seemed to me a most enigmatic sort.

Yes, he was a mysterious figure for me. I saw in him a man given to profound reflection, to which, as it seemed to me, the gaze of his shrewd and always sad eyes bore witness. All in all, in the whole of his unremarkable and listless person it was his eyes that were the sole attraction, involuntarily drawing to him anyone who met him. The whole of his life appeared to lie in those eyes – deep-set, tenacious, seeming to pierce right through you. During lessons, those eyes followed every movement Altyn and I made. I'd wait while Altyn was confirming the homework with her girlfriends, and his sad black eyes would look at us greedily, demandingly; I'd listen to Altyn clarifying to the girls some new material set as homework, and his sad black eyes would be sternly and fixedly registering our smallest movement. Almataj could be recounting something or answering someone's question at the time, but his focused gaze would never let us out of his field of vision for an instant. Those deep-set, unblinking, black eyes could read a person's thoughts, leaving you defenceless, as though turned inside out. I involuntarily tensed and grew tired under that importunate and at the same time perspicacious gaze. Altyn, too, started to feel awkward about the unsought and excessive attention paid us by Almataj. I only had to relax just a little, to take just the slightest liberty in a lesson, for her to tread on my boot underneath the desk, letting me know we were being watched.

Altyn stood out from the other girls of her age – she wasn't so easy-going and carefree. She attended school regularly, studied diligently, and after classes, socialising with no one and without getting held up on the way, she would walk back to the hostel. She would raise her shoulder blades, draw her head down into her shoulders and walk, never lifting her eyes from the ground. It was as though something were crushing her, lying on her like a back-breaking load. Sometimes, with the onset of twilight, she would go to the school, open the doors and spend a long time wandering alone around the empty classrooms. Worrying about her, Žarykžüldyz and I would head for the school as well, but right behind us would come Almataj, too. He would observe us silently and just as silently go off home. We thought he was watching us on purpose, something which was done in the boarding school in those days. There was a strange attitude there to any of the boys appearing beside a girl. A terrible commotion would start up, the teachers and pastoral staff would immediately set about discussing such events as something quite out of the ordinary. The most commonplace meeting of a boy and a girl was perceived at the very least as a wolf approaching a sheep – inevitable trouble was expected every time. Because of this we were obliged to socialise with the girls only during classroom activities. Otherwise we risked becoming a topic of discussion at a class meeting or, even worse, at a meeting of the teachers' council, from which, of course, nothing good could be expected.

Our mentors, who in lessons 'sowed' us with the seeds of true friendship and humanity, did everything, time and again, to divide us into two opposing camps, just as soon as there was mention of relationships between boys and girls, methodically killing in us the manifestation of our first pure feelings for one another. When I remember that far-off time of childhood, my heart becomes tight with hurt, because that attitude to us on the part of the teachers and pastoral staff led to our constantly bullying the girls, teasing and upsetting them, and sometimes even humiliating them with an incautious word. The girls behaved affectedly, too. Gasping and groaning upon hearing any word from us that might give grounds for imagining some intimacy, they'd demonstratively block up their ears and run out of the classroom, like a jittery herd of saiga scenting danger. And all this was done merely to look 'proper' in the eyes of the pedagogues. Now I think of how many first feelings were killed, stifled in those days, feelings which failed to blaze up with pure fire, failed to captivate our hearts with a childlike aspiration to exalted, inimitable adoration of a chosen girl! Again, I see the curious and loving eyes, I hear the beat of our hearts, I mentally pronounce the words which then tightened our chests. Perhaps, I think, we lost those sparks inside us which, with time, would have led to conscious friendship, would in the future have formed strong and loving families.

The human soul has its winters and summers, too, it's chilled by blizzards and warmed by fine, sunny days. Warm words once spoken are preserved in it for a whole lifetime, a single glance, one tremulous movement, a memorable gesture, are all committed to memory. They come to mind later on, during your adult life, as an undying echo of the start of your journey, as salvation, as the life-giving currents of your relentless movement along the line of fate – all the things that are never repeated later in human life, however fully it measures out to you, both good and bad. In the long ascent through life there exists but one bow, one single knot that will hold you when inhuman tiredness comes and if you find yourself falling, plunging down from on high. The light of that moment will lend you new strength, proving the permanence of the human spirit and the inexhaustibility of the human soul.

I must still have been a silly little child, and I don't remember that first long winter I lived through in the boarding school well. It's barely remained in my memory at all.

And now, as I'm riding on the cart which is being driven by an already grown-up Altyn, I feel myself to be a man vainly trying to draw together the ends of a broken noose. I want to give up this useless and bitter endeavour... May the reader forgive me for jumping to a different topic, or rather, moving on to a different time point in the lives of Altyn, Almataj, Žaryķžŭldyz and Humpy...

Spring comes late to the Altaj, as if testing the patience of all living things to the full. But on the other hand, it chops the remains of winter right down to the ground; brings down to the earth at a stroke so much warmth that everything all around loses its head, experiences hitherto unknown bliss, forgets itself in fabulous contentment. The earth is covered in such tender, lush greenery that the snowy summits of the Altaj freeze in astonishment before this tumult of spring, as though they hadn't been neighbours all their lives with the taiga forest, so dense that even a dog cannot at times poke its muzzle into its solid green thickets. The magic of spring! The miracle which excites endless rapture in man and gives birth to tremulous astonishment. At this time my native parts become particularly dear to me, precious to the point of tears.

My *auyl* is in the Altaj. In the long winter it withdraws into itself, as if sunk into a deep sleep, but in spring, with the first rays of sunshine, it instantly comes to life. We take off the heavy clothes we've grown tired of over the winter and bid farewell to the stove which has warmed us in the long nights of snowstorms.

In spring it's hard to resign yourself to the approaching exams. You're drawn to the outdoors, and you have to summon all your strength of will to keep yourself within the four walls of the classroom. A day seems like an entire week, while a week drags on as if it were a long month. But everything has its season, studies come to an end, the last exams are sat and pupils make their separate ways home. The schoolyard falls quiet, and life in the hostel comes to a standstill. Only we remain, the few complete orphans, like lame sheep who stay in the fold when the whole flock is hastening to open pastures. Whatever the care the country has surrounded you with, it's still hard and bitter to acknowledge that you have no parents waiting for you with open arms. Your soul grows cold from loneliness. Bitterness fills your breast and burns like fire. You feel as if somebody has wronged you, sadness comes upon you and entices you into its toils. Now the most insignificant word from people around you wounds your heart, reminding you of your orphan's lot over and over again. I've noticed that orphans are sensitive and reserved folk, and it takes no little effort to draw such a child out, to win his emotional favour.

To this day I remember distinctly that hot summer when we were making hay. We lived cooped up in a hut made of branches. Žaryķžŭldyz and I on the grey nag Kôkšolaķ would rake the hay up into haycocks, and during a short break we'd have our simple lunch – milk and *ajran*,[19] delivered from the collective farm.

Kôkšolaķ used up all my strength – you might have thought he'd been created by nature specifically to wear people out. There is a saying: 'You lead

---

[19] *Ajran* – sour drink made of cow, sheep, or goat milk fermented with lactic bacteria, often thick and used both as food and as a beverage.

a nag to a dwelling, but it strives to make off to the wilderness.' Well, Kôkšolaķ was the classic embodiment of this adage. However you entangled his legs, however watchful an eye you kept on him, the dock-tailed creature would all the same contrive to get first into the collective farm crops, then the boarding school's melon field, or would even escape completely into the *auyl* and hide there in a shed, where the stinking liquid manure was knee deep. If Kôkšolaķ ran away, it was hard to catch up with him and if he disappeared, then, as they say, you could go and chase the wind in the field. The nag's back was completely covered in scabies, and you couldn't mount Kôkšolaķ without a horsecloth, while leading the stubborn beast on a rein was almost unthinkable.

...I was sleeping that sweet, pre-dawn sleep, when somebody dragged me out of bed by my legs. It was our bursar, Zejnolla. He had a furious look about him. He told me off, using foul abuse, throwing in, as he did so, a few strong words in memory of my father, whose bones had already rotted in the ground long before. It transpired that our Kôkšolaķ had ravaged the melon field again. I made to begin proving my innocence, but Zejnolla lashed my bare legs with his whip, now already accusing me of disobedience, which was, in his eyes, all but a mortal sin. The other lads were woken by the noise. Spilling out of the neighbouring hut came the girls. The matron Kǎmila rushed to my aid.

'What are you shouting about?' she fell upon Zejnolla. 'An animal's an animal! What do you want, the boy to keep watch on that nag in the night and not get any sleep? Don't be a bully, got it?!... You should be ashamed of yourself, raising a hand to a poor orphan!'

'I wasn't appointed to keep track of *žetim-žesir*![20] And what all kinds of limping old women say has no authority over me!' Zejnolla didn't let the opportunity slip to underline the fact that Kǎmila *apaj* was a lame widow. 'I know my job! We need to have good order!'

Tears came into the matron's eyes. She was silent for a minute, not knowing how to reply to Zejnolla, who had no conception whatever of such qualities as leniency or respect for people.

'May God punish you for that!' she said quietly, and, turning away, began raking the ashes over with tongs, searching for coals. 'That sort of thing doesn't go unpunished...!'

'If I see the animal in the melon field again, don't expect any mercy!' The bursar's eyes, red with anger and surrounded by a grey line of pus, had almost popped out of their sockets. Running into the hut came Kǎmila *apaj*'s red-coated puppy, which poked its nose towards the crockery standing by the fireplace, but was immediately sent flying by a kick. The blow from the bursar's kersey boot, swollen with dew, was a heavy one, and, with a wild yelp, the poor puppy flew out through the door opening and hurtled headlong into the neighbouring hut. At the same moment Altyn came running into ours. She must have only just got out of bed, because her hair was half-plaited, and

---

[20] *Žetim-žesir* – lit. orphans and widows, also an ancient derogatory term for 'slave'.

visible through the unbuttoned collar of her dress was the top of her brassiere, constricting her taut breasts and setting off her white body. Having run into the hut, she instantly tore the whip out of Zejnolla's hands.

'You're like a wolf that's got into the sheepfold, taking liberties!' she threw into his face. 'Who do you think you are?! Get on your horse and go, while you're still in one piece!'

'You... You... You've cut your teeth, I see!' Zejnolla was taken aback by the unexpected onslaught, but he pulled himself together at once and, frowning, advanced on Altyn. She, however, had no thought of waiting to see what else he might come out with, but ran outside and used the whip to deal several blows to the head of the bursar's horse, which was tied to a tree. The horse recoiled, broke the long bridle rein and, snorting, galloped off.

Zejnolla almost exploded with anger. But he didn't venture to say anything sharp to the girl and, all dark with anger, cleared off, stamping his boots heavily. The words he was muttering as he went carried to us:

'I'll get even with you, you good-for-nothing girl!... I'll show you!...' He didn't even think of returning for his whip, as a man should, so as not to allow it to remain in another man's hands, let alone a woman's.

I was ready for the earth to swallow me up in my shame. How weak and indecisive I was! And just think – it wasn't the other lads who'd defended me, but Altyn! A weak little girl had not only stood up for me, but had put the man who'd wronged me to flight as well. I felt humiliated, pathetic and worthless. I was ashamed.

The Sun was rising from behind a hill. The morning chill had started to ease. The lads were already haymaking, and the buzzing of a saw could be heard from the nearby wood. I lay in the hut, rolled up in a ball. Kǎmila *apaj* came into the hut twice, suggesting I have some breakfast, but I didn't get up from my bed.

'You don't throw a fur coat into the fire because you're upset about a louse! Get up, Ķasym, have something to eat! It's time to go to the farm for milk, otherwise we'll be left with no lunch', she rebuked me, bustling around outside. 'Ķomšabaj's come, he's been sent to make hay. You and Altyn will probably be going to help him.'

***

A winding black road. The cart rolled along, rocking a little. The river had dried up, and mosquitoes, which had appeared with the first warmth, were buzzing about in a swarm. Kôkšolaķ strode on, brushing them off incessantly with his docked tail. In piles of earth, swept up onto the ruins of the houses which had once stood on both sides of the road, mottled wood mice were busy collecting dry cedar buds. One, taking fright at something, left a little green ball behind and hid in a crevice, but the bud was picked up at once by another mouse, which hurried towards its burrow. A woodpecker was tapping on a tree trunk; at times, stopping its pecking, it would wipe its long beak on the bark. The impression was that it wasn't cleaning its beak, but sharpening it. A little bird of some sort, grey with a yellow throat, was accompanying us, hopping from branch to branch – it looked as if its nest was nearby. Altyn sat with her legs hanging down over the side of the cart, quietly humming some tune or other.

She'd been in a bad mood of late. Almataj's family had taken away her tranquillity. It had all started at the end of the academic year, when Majmùryn had tried to stop her taking the history exams. Then his wife, Kùláš, had become involved, getting her husband to give Altyn a 'satisfactory' mark. But from that day on she'd begun, under various pretexts, to take Altyn away into her house and make her do housework. And now Almataj had been hovering around for a whole week at the haymaking. He'd helped to rake up and stack the hay, but while doing so had tried to stick close to Altyn to exchange at least a couple of words with her. Now it was my turn to keep a close eye on his every move. I was tormented by jealousy, and I couldn't look at Almataj with indifference. 'And what is it he's trying to hunt out here?' I thought discontentedly. 'What does he want from our Altyn?'

Almataj and Altyn would lay the hay onto a sled, and I, on Kôkšolaķ, would drag it to the spot where a stack was being erected. I lashed the horse mercilessly every time to get back again more quickly. 'The sweat's pouring off us, you might let us have a little rest', was Almataj's request, but hearing his words, I drove Kôkšolaķ on even quicker. Obstinacy was winding me up. I'd get carried away working right through until evening and only relax when Almataj went off to the *auyl* for the night.

One day, returning yet again from the stack, I saw Altyn was crying. Almataj was walking rapidly away down a path. I didn't venture to ask about the reason for the tears, but sat down beside her by the haycock. Altyn didn't wipe the tears away, as though she hadn't noticed my presence. I waited for a while, poking around in the earth, then tossed some hay onto the sled myself and dragged it to the stack. But when I came back again, Altyn greeted me with a smile. Not so much as a trace remained on her animated face of the recent bitter tears and inexpressible anguish. Altyn's character was generally changeable – she would flare up in a trice, and cool off just as quickly; if a minute before her face had been cold, in the shortest possible time it would be radiating joy, pensiveness would give way to friendliness. But all the same it seemed to me that, concealed behind her clear, bright smile there was alarm. In the evening she gathered the girls around her and spent a long time singing songs, and all of them were sorrowful, sad ones. Almataj, though, appeared in the fields no more…

Altyn kept on humming some simple sort of tune. It was reminiscent of the never-ending song of the prankster Aldar Kôse,[21] which he would drag out to test the patience of people he didn't like. I sat restraining myself for all I was worth from glancing round at her, from looking at the expression on her face. Then there was the rustling of hay – clearly, she'd changed her position or climbed down from the cart. Next, I felt hot breath above my neck. I'd never thought anyone's breath could be so hot. It seemed as if I'd been hit by a wave of fire, and a tremor ran through my body. Now she was bound to say something to me. But what?

'Ķasym?'

'Yes.'

'Tell me why you're so silent.'

'No reason...'

'Let me have the reins.'

'Why?'

'You have a rest. You must be tired of whipping Kôkšolaķ.' Altyn sat down beside me and took the reins and switch out of my hands. 'Have a little rest.'

The cart pitched on a rut, and Altyn caught me with her elbow. I was dumbfounded. For a whole year we'd been sitting at the same desk, doing our homework together, walking beside one another, but not once had I experienced such a heady feeling. I was ready to set out on a never-ending journey on this shaking cart with the hateful Kôkšolaķ in the harness, just as long as Altyn was always sitting beside me. How could I reveal this dream to her?

'Yes, yes, have a little rest', she repeated once more. She turned to me and burst out laughing. Dimples appeared in her cheeks, and her cheeks became more pink than usual. 'Spread the hay out, lie down and put your head on my lap...'

I saw nothing but her pure, clear eyes above me. The whole world for me now was those eyes. My head started spinning. A light little cloud seemed to be jumping in time with the motion of the cart, at times there rose above me the crowns of tall larches, rocked by the wind, while stretched out even higher was the light-blue sky, ever so pure, like Altyn's eyes, and soaring in it was the black dot of an eagle – exactly like the pupil which was sparkling with a dark mysterious light in Altyn's eyes. I lay on my back and never took my eyes off the eagle. I lay motionless, fearing that this scene might disappear, vanish into thin air at one clumsy movement from me. I even started thinking cautiously. But my heart was booming, it was simply dancing, ready to burst out of my chest.

The cart rocked gently and the larches accompanied us, their crowns waving smoothly. The clear sky had overturned above us. The eagle was going ever higher. I shut my eyes. Still the same scene: the clear sky, the eagle soaring

---

[21] Aldar Kôse refers to a Kazakh folk fairy tale character, who is a swindler cheating the rich, greedy, evil khans and helping the poor people.

in the heavens, Altyn's smiling, unfathomable eyes... I felt a hot palm on my forehead. Altyn passed her hand over my hair. My face began blazing.

'Ķasym?'

'Yes...'

'Tell me why you're so silent.'

'No reason...'

'Are you daydreaming about something?'

'Yes...'

'What?'

'I don't know... And why are you so silent yourself?'

'I'm daydreaming too.'

'About what?'

'About you... I'm dreaming of seeing you in ten years' time, when you've become a real person. Is my dream to your liking?'

'Yes.'

'What do you want to be?'

'I don't know...'

'You're still a little kid, Ķasym. Otherwise you wouldn't have said you don't know. You'll finish school, and maybe you'll go to Almaty. What are you going to be? A teacher, an engineer or a writer? Do you have a dream, Ķasym?'

'And what do you want to be yourself?'

'Who are we?... We'll make do with what we get. There's no need to choose', Altyn sighed. I opened my eyes. She was looking at me intently with her elbow leaning on my chest. Both of her plaits were hanging down from her breast and I felt a tickling in my nostrils from the scent of her hair, which had lightened in the Sun. Above me I could see her clear eyes, the fine arcs of her eyebrows, her restlessly moving full lips. Again, I was hit by a wave of heat. And suddenly I wanted to share my innermost thoughts with her.

'Altyn...'

'Yes?'

'Do you want me to tell you?...'

'What?'

'About my dream?'

'No, don't! No!' Altyn bent down and kissed me on the lips. 'This is enough for you.' Then she hugged me tight and pressed me against her. And suddenly I burst into tears, drowning my face at her breast, gasping for breath and trying not to breathe. I cried for a long time, sobbing bitterly... This must have been the manifestation of my first boyish feelings, my answer to Altyn's questions. Or maybe those tears were my recognition, and at the same time appreciation, of the first caress I'd had occasion to experience in my life. Evidently the one and the other. I subconsciously sensed I was now losing Altyn, she was unattainable for me, like a strong bird describing circles and already disappearing in the heavenly blue. And there is no return for it from its element...

***

I went back to the haymaking by myself. Altyn stayed in the *auyl*. She didn't want to stay, but Majmúryn's wife insisted upon it, having found work in her house as always. I went back in a bad frame of mind. I was uneasy at heart and didn't even feel like eating. Towards evening there was a change in the weather, the sky became shrouded in cloud and with the onset of twilight it started raining, with hailstones. We'd covered the hut in advance with a thick layer of green grass, so the roof didn't leak, and we went to bed that evening unusually early. It rained hard all night without a break, and right through until morning I tossed and turned in my bed, unable to get to sleep. Uneasy thoughts wouldn't let my heart be.

'Oh my, Almataj's kidnapped our Altyn!' came someone's cry just before morning. 'He's carried our darling off!'

I rushed headlong out of the hut. Žaryķžúldyz ran out after me. Together we tore to the hut where the girls were living. The shouting, it turned out, had come from Kǎmila *apaj*, who'd left for the *auyl* to do her laundry after dinner and come back again towards morning.

'The unfortunate child, even without this her life's not been a happy one!' she wailed, entirely in the power of rage. 'She was left without parents at an early age and came to know the life of an orphan, and then some! There it is, an orphan's lot! Almataj, how could he?... It was Majmúryn who thought of all this!...'

I froze as though struck by lightning. What became of me next, I don't remember. Later I was told that I grabbed Kǎmila *apaj*'s long kitchen knife, which she used to cut bread, and ran off in the direction of the *auyl*. I was apparently shouting that I'd spill Majmúryn's guts out. Halfway there I was caught, it turns out, by Žaryķžúldyz and Humpy on the horse, and they carried me back to the haymaking by throwing me over the saddle. Without them, I would probably not have managed to escape misfortune.

The hut was in semidarkness when I came round and opened my eyes. The wind was blowing and light rain was falling. There was a rumbling in the mountains at times, as though a mudslide were approaching. The forest was humming. The roof was dripping. Someone noisily threw a truss of hay onto the hut, a little stream of water poured onto the floor, and then the dripping stopped. Face down beside me lay Žaryķžúldyz with the palm of one hand beneath his cheek. He had evidently dozed off without realising it. By his head was a white sheet of paper. I picked it up and saw that there was a poem jotted down on it. The handwriting was that of Žaryķžúldyz.

Our dearest Altyn, the noblest of girls,
Her loss was quite unforeseen, I fear!
A cold, cold bed in an alien world
Is already awash with your tears.

With all my heart have I loved you for ay,
Sworn an oath for all time to be true,
In sorrow must I curse myself today –
No more shall I ever be with you!
O sorry fate, how pitiful my lot,
Why thirsted I once for great change?
You left my dream in unfreedom to rot,
Did not grant even hope in exchange.
Have you truly conspired to betray me,
O my youth, my bright joy from above?
With the bitterest pill love does slay me,
How am I to live without my love?…

Not much of a poem, of course, but in those difficult moments it seemed to express my bitter thoughts exactly. At that minute there was no better poet for me than Žaryḵžŭldyz, and there was no better poem than his work. On reading those lines I learnt for the first time of the feelings that Žaryḵžŭldyz, like me, had for Altyn.

I folded the sheet in four and put it into my pocket. In the morning, Žaryḵžŭldyz spent a long time searching for the missing item. I didn't admit to him that I'd taken the poem.

That year I left the school. At first, Žaryḵžŭldyz begged me not to abandon my studies, but then, seeing my determination, he gave it up as a bad job. There were tears at our parting. Then he came with me half the way. We said goodbye, wished one another success and happiness and set off in different directions, but, after going a respectable distance, we went back to each other and began saying goodbye again. It was then that I first called Žaryḵžŭldyz by his proper name – Ḵomšabaj. I took the sheet with the poem out of my pocket and offered it to him, but he didn't take it.

'I guessed you had it', he said. 'Keep it. In memory of our boarding school life.'

I didn't linger at home either. I insisted Šalym sell the grey cow and I used the money to travel to Almaty.

I later learnt that Almataj never did make an appearance in the *auyl* of Topḵajyn, but found work as a teacher in the *auyl* of Ŭlken Naryn. It was said that he and Altyn got on well and lived in perfect harmony.

And now, exactly ten years after those dramatic events in our lives, and quite unexpectedly, I had met Altyn. And again we were riding on a cart, sitting next to each other, and our shoulders were touching when the cart lurched on ruts. Altyn would sometimes urge the horse on and twitch at the reins, then would freeze and sit in silence, as though listening to the tapping of the raindrops. Sometimes a lump of clay would slip off the wheel rims and plop onto the ground.

The heady, sour smell of the silage took my breath away. The cart rocked on the rain-worn road, and it seemed to me that it was aiming to get Altyn and me closer to each other. Every time our shoulders touched, Altyn's long eyelashes would quiver, she would quickly lift her clear black eyes to me and immediately move away towards the edge of the cart. But however hard she tried to stay sitting a respectable distance away from me, the shaking cart would bring her closer to me again and again.

Life is interesting. At that moment I pictured it in the form of a winding dirt road on which there are a good many ruts. Some people pass along the road in a hurry, negotiate it all in one go; others make their way along it slowly, every step causing them difficulty. Some stray on the journey and lose themselves, others contrive an unthinkable struggle, filled with drama, still others meet their fortune with ease. And whoever they are, people don't realise that they're going along the same highway of life, bound together by meetings and partings.

The *auyl* was already visible up ahead, and my heart was beating harder. I recognised the familiar outlines of the houses; the *auyl* didn't seem to me to have changed, it was still the same quiet little Topḳajyṇ. I knew very well, however, what lay hidden behind this seemingly peaceful scene. The houses looked out through the trees, reminiscent of sleepy eyes hidden behind their lashes. I knew about this ruse of the *auyl* of Topḳajyṇ too.

'Does Almataj teach in the school here?' I asked.

'No.' Altyn barely moved her lips. 'He works in the same place, in Ülken Naryn. It's a year now that we've been living apart. We're divorced. One son between two, first he pulls him his way, then I pull him mine. Sometimes I want to be more decisive, but I feel sorry for Almataj. He hasn't got anyone else. True, it's hard for me as well when my son's not with me. I'm alone too...'

'Why didn't you get on?'

'I don't know, Ḳasym. How can I put it to you... It's evidently all down to the fact that it wasn't through mutual desire that we got together. There was nothing that he's done to make me feel bitter. I'm probably to blame for everything myself... Hey, Sara, come over here!' We were already by the outermost little houses. A young woman wearing a raincoat and a tightly knotted scarf on her head looked around at the voice and started coming towards us. 'That's Kămila *apaj*'s middle daughter. Married with two children. She works with me as a calf-tender. You see how swift the flow of life is! Sara, could you take the silage to the farm, please? Unharness the horse and put the harness in a dry place, or else tomorrow it'll chafe the animal's neck. I'm going to go home, I have to entertain a guest.'

We set off along a street that was familiar to the last little pothole. Around a corner appeared the hostel in which we used to live. It was full of life now, too: children were constantly running in and out of it. There was some elderly woman bustling about by the canteen.

'Take the firewood into the lobby, it'll get damp here!' I recognised Kămila *apaj*'s voice.

The hostel hadn't changed a bit – the only thing missing was the old birch tree by the window, the mute witness of my first boyish love. There was only a short, dry, black trunk, but bursting up out of it were some young shoots, and they were straight and unshakeable. It seemed as if the youthful branches had set themselves the aim of making up for what had disappeared.

'You should have put rubber boots on, I'm afraid your feet must be wet.' Altyn's voice interrupted my thoughts.

'It's all right, we'll get dry at home', I replied. But Altyn paid no attention to what I'd said, ran a dissatisfied eye over me and remarked:

'You're thin. Not ill, are you?'

'My health's fine. As you know, I always was thin.' I remembered the touching way Altyn had looked after me and felt warm at heart.

'Let's cross to that street', Altyn pulled me by the sleeve. I saw that rolling towards us, like a lopped tree trunk, was Majmúryn. I flinched in revulsion. We turned aside.

'Is that one still working here?' I murmured.

'He used to teach in the reception classes, then left to work at the livestock import warehouse. Something along the lines of a steward. The pay's better there.'

Majmúryn went past, sunk in mud right up to his ankles in his kersey boots. The slurping sounds of his heavy footsteps stayed in my ears for a long time. It seemed to me, as before, that his every step defiled the earth.

***

Altyn led me to a little house under a wooden roof standing on the very edge of the *auyl*. We opened the doors, and at the table I saw Ḳomšabaj. He was, as before, swarthy to the point of blackness, had put on weight and become so round that he looked like a black cauldron, but there was a flash of sparks in my eyes, as though I'd seen something radiant, like the face of the Sun. Maybe these words sound high-flown, but there are times when people find themselves in the power of unrealistic comparisons.

'Who's this I see? Is it really you?' He came up to me with clumsy, waddling steps, and gave me a firm hug. 'Look how you've shot up, you son of a bitch!'

'Žaryḳžúldyz, when are you going to stop turning up at twilight in the house of a single woman?' Altyn started nagging him. 'How many times do I have to tell you?'

'Stop it, don't turn me out, not this time at least!' Žaryḳžúldyz answered her. 'You can see Ḳasym's here, let's have a heart-to-heart! What do you think, do I come here to you from a good life? Our group's done for. There aren't the people even to sing at a concert, let alone put on a show. And as you know, we've got a public holiday just around the corner.'

'Have you come to talk me into it?'

'Well what else am I to do? Help me out! Well, all right, let's put our problems aside and listen to Ķasym instead. What brings you here, old friend? Tell us!'

'I've come home for a short stay. Decided to look in on you.'

'Excellent! All's well with you, then. No, we've not seen one another in ages, but we've read your essays and short stories in the papers and journals. We're happy for you. Sometimes we even boast and tell everyone we were at school with you and were even childhood friends.'

'Why don't you tell me about yourself', I interrupted him, 'you haven't given up poetry? Any success?'

'What are you talking about?' Žaryķžůldyz burst out laughing with an awkward wave of his hand. 'What poetry? I'm a mathematician! I went down a different path.'

'He's headmaster of the boarding school', Altyn chimed in. 'He hasn't the time for poetry now.'

'That's right, the prose of life!' Žaryķžůldyz brightened up.

After the initial animated enquiries, little by little, we became more subdued. Quietness descended on the room. I learnt that Ķomšabaj had still not got himself a family and lived alone. And he was living in Kămila *apaj*'s house. He apologised for having no opportunity to write to me – work at school took up all of his time. I remembered his poetic exercises and threw an involuntary glance at Altyn. I was now convinced that being plump suited her – it lent her even greater femininity. Altyn's cheeks were glowing again in the warmth and her face had become even prettier, with the dimples coming and going on her cheeks.

We sat for a long time and had a good heart-to-heart. Altyn, finally free from constraint, was lively and joyous, like in the old days. She'd always been like that, open and encouraging candour. Looking at her now, I wouldn't have guessed she'd led a difficult life in which there'd been more woe than joy.

'Dear Ķasym, a guest, as they say, is a man from God, and you could have stayed here for the night as well', Altyn said to me after dinner. 'There's enough room in the house. But I can't offer you that. You know for yourself our *auyl*'s ways.'

I was happy with her words, direct, as always, and full of dignity. We went out into the entrance hall.

'Ķomšabaj, hold on!' Altyn led him into the next room. The door was open and I involuntarily overheard their conversation. 'You're not looking after yourself again. Here, take this shirt, I've washed and ironed it. And leave the one you're wearing.'

She came back into the hall and said goodbye to me, and I went outside. A few minutes later Ķomšabaj caught up with me. The long-extinguished fire of jealousy suddenly stirred inside me. Conversation started up again, and we'd talked about many more things before we reached Kămila *apaj*'s house. I couldn't restrain myself and asked Ķomšabaj about the reason for his bachelor life. He didn't start speaking at once.

'It's strange, but for some reason, when I was a student, not one of the girls took my fancy', he told me. 'And now it seems as if it's too late. Women of my own age have long since had families, and younger girls seem to me incomprehensible somehow, I can't find any common ground with them. With age you get embarrassed about it all somehow... And you're apprehensive too, afraid of putting your foot in it. All in all, there's no way I can get married. You couldn't understand me in this respect. You know what they say: if your head doesn't ache, you can't be bothered with God. That's the way it is with you...'

'And what about Altyn?'

'Altyn is still the same Altyn. You know I've loved her for a long time. Maybe, if truth be told, this is where the reason for my bachelor life lies too. Don't ask me any more, don't trouble my heart.'

'Don't be offended. After all, it's – how can I explain it? – a friendly interest, no more. And no less. But tell me, have you spoken to one another about it?'

'In hints', Ķomšabaj gave an embarrassed laugh. 'I can see she's agitated, but she doesn't show her feelings. You know her character for yourself. But I haven't had a frank talk with her, I'm not brave enough. Yet I can sense all the same that she's not indifferent to me either.' He sighed and fell silent.

***

The quiet autumn. I sat by the window and looked outside. There was a long, unending drizzle of rain. Drifting before my inner eye were far-off autumnal days. The wind was blowing in gusts outside, caravans of storm clouds were rushing across the sky, trembling leaves were flying in the air, crows were crying restlessly – it was all, incredibly, like a half-forgotten picture from the life of the little *auyl* of Topķajyŋ. The sky was sinking ever lower, the shadows of twilight were creeping across the ground. Just such a sky had once also hung over my dear Topķajyŋ. Falling from on high were the cries of migratory birds. It seemed to me as if the birds were flying from a distant *auyl*, lost in a hollow in the taiga. It was as if they were bringing tidings from my distant childhood.

On the table lay a manuscript. The work on the book was complete. But my native *auyl* was still before my eyes. Two *auyls* had merged into a single whole; the *auyl* where I was born and the *auyl* where I attended the boarding school. As alike as two drops of water, two teardrops. I missed Ķomšabaj and Altyn. A whole year had gone by since the time of our meeting in Topķajyŋ. A quiet joy possessed me, finding concord with spiritual sorrow. Two teardrops as well. It's strange, but when meeting friends you muffle that warmth up inside you, you converse in a detached sort of way, with feigned indifference. But finding yourself at a distance from them, after a certain time you miss them beyond measure. I missed Ķomšabaj and Altyn. Each of us had in their heart a good deal they'd have liked to tell a friend. We'd led a life that was far from simple, and behind us there remained the tracks of inexperienced travellers, the ruts of our road through life, while ahead stretched the continuation of the journey, marked by new milestones, where there are plenty of potholes, ups and downs, as yet invisible to the eye. The unknown lures you on, the past evokes warmth. Will we succeed in negotiating the road that lies before us? What will tomorrow, our new step, bring us? I had but a hazy idea of my future. And not because it was shrouded by a veil of mystery or uncertainty of some kind, but because I perceived life as a miracle which would set before me a multitude of new problems and impose different demands upon me. What discoveries await Ķomšabaj and Altyn? I didn't know what their lives were like now, what was worrying them, what new things they'd discovered in themselves and the people around them. I was sad not knowing if Ķomšabaj had been able to open his heart to Altyn. Before me lay the newly completed closing chapter of a new book. The autumn was drifting, and there was a long, unending drizzle of the rain we call white.

Translated by Hugh Aplin

SAYIN MURATBEKOV
(15.10.1936 – 13.03.2007)

Sayin Muratbekov was a Kazakh writer. He studied journalism at Kirov Kazakh State University (now Ăl-Farabi Kazakh National University; 1957–63) and literature at Maxim Gorky Literary Institute in Moscow (grad. 1971). He was editor-in-chief of the *Žŭldyz* journal, head of department for the *Ķazaķ ădebieti* newspaper and director of the Bureau for Propaganda of Fiction of the Writers' Union of the Kazakh SSR (1962–72). From 1972 to 1977, he worked for the Central Committee of the Communist Party of the Kazakh SSR before taking up the positions of editor-in-chief of *Ķazaķ ădebieti* (1977–80), secretary and then second secretary of the Writers' Union of the Kazakh SSR (1980–84; 1988–91), director of *Žazušy* publishing house (1984–86) and a deputy of the Supreme Soviet of the Kazakh SSR (1984–89). Muratbekov was among the leaders of the 'Nevada–Semipalatinsk' movement (Kaz. Nevada–Semej; 1992–96). His works include short stories and novels, such as *Meniŋ ķaryndasym* (My Sister, 1961), *Auyl oty* (Lights of *Auyl*, 1964), *Kôkoraj* (The Youth, 1967), *Otau ùj* (Home, 1968), *Žabajy alma* (Wild Apple, 1972), *Dos izdep žùrmin* (I'm Looking for a Friend, 1973) – and *Eskek žel* (The Unceasing Wind, 2004). He was regarded as a master short story writer, and some of his works have been translated into more than a dozen languages.

In 1990, he won the Mùhtar Ăuezov Literary Prize for 'Ķalyŋ ķar' (Heavy Snow), and in 1998 received the title of an Honoured Worker of the Republic of Kazakhstan. He was a laureate of the State Prize of the Republic of Kazakhstan (2006) and a recipient of the Independent Tarlan Award for *Žabajy alma* (2003).

The Smell of Wormwood

1

My far-away, forgotten childhood…

And yet I remember so very clearly that thin boy with a limp, in his tawny, parched fur jacket. Sometimes I close my eyes and I can see, as clearly as if it were real, that boisterous gang of young boys, tearing through the mountain *auyl*,[1] and there he is, running along at the tail end, dragging his bad foot and trying not to fall behind. But he does fall behind anyway, and again I hear his voice calling: 'Hey guys, hang on, will you! Come along with me, I've got a story. You'll see, it's more interesting than yesterday's!'

In the spring of 1942, Aân's mother died and he was left alone with just his grandmother – his father had been drafted into the army at the very beginning of the war. And Aân's grandmother had brought him to our *auyl*, hoping for help from her distant relatives.

We were playing at war on the only driveable street, tossing 'grenades' of dust, wrapped in scraps of paper, when he came out of the house for the first time. Old men and women passing by grouched: 'Will you look at those stupid children: one war isn't enough for them, so they've started their own. As if there weren't any other games. The wild little imps!' It was a windless day, the dust hung in the air for a long time, veiling the Sun, and we attacked our 'enemy' with shouts of 'hoorah!', so engrossed in our game that we didn't notice anyone or anything else. It was our commander, Sadyk̦, who halted all of a sudden on the boundary line where the curtain of dust ended and asked:

'Hey, who are you? Where did you come from?'

Well, at that, all the guys abandoned the game – this was such an unusual question for our *auyl*, where everyone had known everyone else since they were little children. Looking round, we saw an unfamiliar boy in a white waistcoat and short trousers. He didn't look like someone from those parts, and we were especially struck by the forelock of coarse black hair drooping down onto his forehead.

---

[1] *Auyl* – socio-economic formation considered to constitute the heartland of the nation and a basis for an ethnic and cultural union of the nomadic community. Consisting of 50–70 yurts in the eighteenth century, it developed into its current permanent state of 'rural settlement' (of a minimum of 100 dwellers) when Kazakhs adopted a settled mode of life in the nineteenth and twentieth centuries. *Auyl* can also be used as a synonym for 'native land' and 'homeland', concepts revered by the Kazakhs.

A new kid in our *auyl* was too exceptional an event altogether, so we forgot about the game in an instant and crowded round Aân, each of us trying to shove his way through a bit closer and get a good look at this *auyl* newcomer. At that moment Aân was like a combined theatre and circus for us *auyl* children.

'Listen, who is he, eh?'

'But where's he from, do you know?' we asked each other, jostling with our elbows and excitedly examining Aân from head to toe as presumptuously as if he were a thing.

He, in turn, gazed at our dishevelled appearance, and there was a hint of bewilderment in that gaze. We were fine specimens then, as filthy as piglets. Our trousers and shirts, beneath their layer of dust, had lost their original colours and were hanging in tatters, as if they had spent some time in the teeth of a pack of dogs.

Aân's clothes were not conspicuously new or high quality, but his neat, clean appearance was as astounding to us as regal luxury.

'Look at him, the little snot-nose, he's already sprouted a forelock!' Esikbaj, the first to express an opinion, concealed his envy poorly.

We didn't think it was funny, but we laughed anyway, trying to back up our pal against the stranger. The laughter sounded phony, as if we had been coerced; Aân blushed deep-red and didn't say anything.

'But I know who he is!' Sadyķ declared loudly. 'You came yesterday evening, didn't you?' he said, addressing the new arrival. 'And you had a dark-grey cow. Am I right?'

'Yes', said the boy, nodding seriously. 'Only she's not all that dark. You saw her in the evening, but in the daytime she's a lot lighter, and we have a calf too.' I fancied I saw an ironic smile glide across his lips.

But Sadyķ carried on with his questions:

'What's your name?'

'Aân.'

Some of the guys moved their lips, trying to memorise this name.

'You come with us, we'll be friends', Sadyķ declared, and without waiting for Aân to agree, he grabbed him by the hand and pulled him along.

The new arrival glanced at the dirty, scratched fingers and cautiously disengaged his hand. Right, I thought, now it'll start. Sadyķ's not likely to swallow an insult like that.

'Guys, where can I get a swim around here? It's roasting hot', said Aân, not giving Sadyķ a chance to take offence.

'Well, we've got this little spot where water's just great', simple-hearted Sadyķ replied for all of us. 'Want to go there now?'

'Yes!' said Aân, nodding.

Sadyķ led the newcomer off to the creek, extolling all its virtues in glowing terms along the way. The guys swarmed around Aân, all trying to get a word in to elevate themselves in the eyes of this outlandish boy. But Sadyķ was still the one in charge.

'Do you know how long I can sit under water? Until you count to sixty', he lied through his teeth, but at that moment our supremely honest Sadyķ genuinely believed himself.

'And I've got a white shirt too, by the way. Only it's lying in a big trunk. Mum says I can't put it on. Just wait until you grow a bit, she says, then wear it as much as you like', put in Scratcher Ķasym.

He got that nickname because in a fight he always went for the face with his nails. He wept buckets, but kept straining all the while to sink his nails into your eyes. So, most of the guys tried to avoid tangling with Scratcher Ķasym. And Esikbaj was the only one who wasn't afraid of his nails.

Just then Esikbaj was slouching along enviously on one side. He was the strongest scrapper, sinewy, with long arms, which was why some of the little kids sucked up to him all the time. But now it was like he wasn't even there – the guys had focused all their attention on this spick-and-span newcomer. And so Esikbaj plodded along in proud isolation, muttering contemptuously to himself.

'Right then, come here! Scratcher!' he barked, just as soon as Ķasym closed his mouth.

Ķasym approached Esikbaj apprehensively, holding his fingers curved like a golden eagle's claws, just to be on the safe side.

'So, maybe you've got heaps and heaps of gold in that trunk of yours, too. Ah-ah, put those claws away, you cat. And hold your head like that.' And Esikbaj gave Scratcher a loud flick on the head with his finger.

Scratcher's head chimed like a ripe watermelon. And Esikbaj kept flicking it again and again, putting all his skill and strength into it. Ķasym burst into tears of rage and flung himself at his tormentor. But Esikbaj moved faster than him and punched him on the nose.

Ķasym squeezed his nose in his hand and plodded back to the *auyl*, hunched over and shuddering. And Esikbaj glanced pointedly into Aân's eyes, as if to say: bear that in mind for the future, no one messes with me.

Aân responded by looking around at all of us with an enquiring expression, seeming to ask: what's going on here with you? But no one wanted to tangle with Esikbaj, so we looked away. And in any case, devious Ķasym wasn't all that popular.

'You're strong, of course, but why do that to him?' Aân asked Esikbaj, shaking his head.

Esikbaj snorted sarcastically and moved aside again. He didn't dare do more than that just yet. Today Aân was still an unknown quantity, even for him.

That day we swam, sunbathed and swam again, playing by the creek until evening, and we grew as accustomed to Aân as if he had lived in our *auyl* from the day he was born.

In short, in the first few days Aân won everybody over. And we took a special liking to his gentle, easy-going character. Of course, everyone started slyly cosying up to him, wanting to be his friend, but Aân treated everyone in the same affable manner, making it clear that he wanted to get along with all of us. A few squabblers tried to get under his skin and provoke him, but Aân merely knitted his brows and moved well clear; the answer he gave to the most persistent troublemaker was this:

'I don't want to fight. Because it's stupid, and because my granny has no one but me. If I fight, she'll be upset.'

And the troublemaker departed in peace. He had already been convinced that Aân was no weakling on the day we met him. We wrestled on the sand then, and the newcomer pinned everyone down. Only Esikbaj managed to best him.

This unruly brawler spent four days nursing the idea that Aân was the same as everyone else, so he could be beaten according to the usual routine. Once he was convinced of this, Esikbaj started hassling Aân. But inciting the intelligent and good-natured Aân into a conflict wasn't that easy.

'That's enough! Drop it, will you', Aân would say good-naturedly, shrugging it off.

But one day Esikbaj's patience ran out and he slavered spit on his finger and ran it across Aân's face.

Aân wiped his face with the back of his hand and asked in a serious voice:

'So you just can't get by without a fight, then?'

'What, with you, you mean? I've seen plenty like you!' Esikbaj blustered and tried to flick Aân on the forehead, but Aân dodged away in time.

'Let's go to the gully. I won't fight in the middle of the street. My granny's bound to find out if it's here', Aân said calmly.

'Think that'll save you? I'll decorate your face so your granny can read it like a book!' Esikbaj assured him.

We set off after them. Delighted with himself, Esikbaj went down into the gully first, declaring:

'Right, come here, smart guy. Now I'll show you.'

Aân took off his shirt as he walked along, carefully hung it on a saltwort plant and readied himself for combat. The fighters were well matched in height. Esikbaj reached out with his arms first, putting them around Aân, hugging him close and trying to tumble him over. But his opponent remained firmly on his feet, and it was already clear to us spectators that Esikbaj couldn't prevail in a fair contest. Realising this, Esikbaj contrived to grab hold of Aân's forelock and started forcing his head back. Aân gritted his teeth against the pain and slowly collapsed onto his back. Then Esikbaj planted himself on top of Aân and started pounding him with his fists. His back hid Aân's face and we could only see Aân's legs desperately churning up the dust. Then suddenly Esikbaj gave a terrible howl and slipped over to one side.

Aân had a grip on Esikbaj's wrist and he twisted it slightly as soon as Esikbaj gave any sign of lashing out. In front of our very eyes the invincible

Esikbaj was grabbed by the scruff of his neck like a mischievous kitten and his face was gently shoved into the dust, twice.

'Is that enough now?' Aân asked.

'Ai, oi! Of course it is!' Esikbaj yelled, afraid the winner might change his mind.

Aân didn't beat his enemy when he was down. He calmly put on his shirt, smoothed down his forelock with his hand, and climbed back up, without even once looking back.

Then autumn arrived and we went to the first class of school with our teacher, old Imanžanov, who had trembling hands and inflamed eyes that watered. The old man brought with him some sheets of paper, which was precious at the time, and taught us the alphabet.

I shared a desk with Aân and was the first witness of his scholastic achievements. His abilities were evident from the very beginning: I recall how, after all the tiresome ones and zeroes, our teacher wrote the first letter on the board and we stuck our tongues out as we copied it onto our sheets of paper. Our fingers, so strong and firm in our street games, could barely control a pencil. But while we were still struggling with our stubborn fingers, Aân was already squirming impatiently on the bench and asking old Imanžanov what to do next.

'Don't be in such a hurry, all in good time, Aân', our teacher reassured him, delighted to have a live pupil, who was eager to learn.

After the lesson Aân declared indignantly:

'Why didn't he write out all the letters? I'd have learnt them all at once and written to my dad.'

We understood his feelings: every one of us was just waiting for the moment when we could sit down at a table and write a letter to our father or brother at the front. Our old teacher seemed to sense this and was unstinting with his efforts and his patience, and soon the great day arrived. During one of the breaks we thronged behind Aân who, all on his own, traced out the words: 'My dear dad...'

From then on, when Aân got back home from school, he made himself comfortable on the floor and wrote a letter, slavering on his indelible pencil. After the second line his lips would turn as purple as if he had been swimming in the creek.

Almost every day a letter left the *auyl*, addressed to Aân's father. Sometimes there were two, if his grandmother had sat down on the bed and dictated her own letter.

We envied Aân, because we still hadn't learnt how to put words together on paper to form meaningful sentences. But our new friend didn't act even the slightest bit superior with us. We used to come to him and say:

'Aân, help me. I really, really want to write a letter to my brother.'

And he would reply magnanimously.

'Take mine and copy it. Only put your brother's name instead of my father's. Okay?'

We would nod affirmatively and dash home in eager impatience.

In this way all our classmates gradually started sending letters to the front. And the letters were like twins, because they were essentially composed by one and the same person.

It seemed as if our teacher had just been waiting for his pupils to learn to write letters and soon he took to his bed, half-paralysed. There wasn't another teacher (and how could you find one for a little mountain *auyl* during a war!), so we began compulsory school holidays that dragged on for a long time.

During that period, which in my memory is fused into a unified whole, something else happened as well. One day Aân was driving a bullock home from pasture and on the way he decided to break it in for riding. The normally meek bullock flew into a wild rage and flung Aân off its back. The unfortunate rider sprained his foot badly and spent about a month lying at home. This sprain proved calamitous for Aân and he was never able to escape its consequences.

He spent less and less time messing about with us, until he became a mere observer of our games; he used to sit somewhere out of the way, peering enviously as we rushed around the *auyl*, impersonating the Red Army.

And then winter came, the first snow fell, and the time of snowy mountains and sledges arrived.

2

Our *auyl* nestles at the foot of Mount Eškiôlmes. In their effort to steal closer to the summit, the leading huts have crept up onto the slope and froze there, at the very beginning of the journey: that's the impression you get when you look at the only street in our *auyl*. In summer its upper end abuts on the thick mane of wormwood that covers Mount Eškiôlmes, and in winter children come hurtling down over the trampled snow on sledges, their jolly voices ringing out above the street until late in the evening. Winter in our *auyl* is wonderful; deep snow falls, and at the same time it's sunny and warm at the foot of the mountain. What a delight it is to go hurtling through the supple air, with snow clogging your eyes and squeaking under the runners, and you can see your friends hurrying back up, dragging their sledges, their cheeks aglow with heat...

The sledging that day was the same as on any other. It was getting close to the evening already. The Sun had grown swollen and heavy with its red juice, ready to drop down behind Mount Eškiôlmes at any moment, and it tinged the snow with a gentle, pink glow. The cattle that grazed on thawed patches of ground were following their usual path, down from the sunny summit of Mount Eškiôlmes into the *auyl*. An aura of peace hung over everything, as if all troubles and tears had disappeared, at least for these few hours. And so, the alarming wail of despair startled everyone. It was answered by weeping so mournful that it sent chilly shivers running down our young spines. And a minute later we realised that grief had chosen as its prey the house where Aân lived.

Well, it can't be helped – even misfortune provokes a surge of curiosity in children. We tumbled off our sledges and ran to take a look at someone else's misery. Those who managed to learn the whole story first whispered knowingly:

'I heard that Aân's granny has died.'

They passed the word on to the others as zealously as if there was a *sùjinši* – a reward for conveying good news – in store for us, and of course they kept their eyes fixed on Aân, afraid of missing the most important part.

Aân was standing in the doorway, as white as the snow that our sledges had just been hurtling over, and blinking rapidly. The women from neighbouring houses had raised the lamenting clamour; they were keening on all sides, some from the heart and some simply for appearances' sake. But Aân stood there motionless, deaf and dumb, simply batting his eyelids and occasionally giving in to a chilly shudder. Plucking up our courage and urging each other on, we crept up to him. He greeted us in silence, merely casting a bewildered glance at the sledges we had dragged along behind us.

The Sun hid behind the summit of Eškiôlmes. Colours faded and the air turned twilight-grey. And we devoured Aân with our eyes, waiting for when he would start crying. Someone even asked the question out loud, as if trying to prompt Aân:

'Hey, why isn't he crying? His granny has died.' But, without saying a word, Aân stepped out of the doorway and then walked past the windows and around the corner. As you can easily guess, we dashed after him, intrigued by his behaviour. He looked back and said:

'Well, what is it, guys? Want to listen to a story?'

He said it as if not only his grandmother, but all of our grandmothers, had departed from this world together and we were in need of consolation from him.

'Well, shall I tell you a story?' he asked, smiling sadly.

'Yes, do!' Sadyķ blurted out.

'Probably a funny one would be best', he said to himself and started pondering, rubbing his cheek against the sparse fur on the collar of his jacket.

And we all clutched our sledges tightly and gaped at him with our mouths hanging open.

Aân heaved a faltering sigh and began as if he had forgotten that we were there and was speaking only to himself.

'It was a long time ago... Once upon a time there was a boy... an orphan...'

The story he told us was a long, pensive one, because he was making it up right there in front of us. It was a sad story. But the orphan showed he was no kind of pitiful whinger, he didn't give up, and we actually laughed a couple of times, forgetting that Aân's grandmother had died that day.

She was buried the next day. Following local custom, the small number of men who had been excused from military service interred Aân's grandmother and then went tearing down into the *auyl* on their horses, leaving Aân beside the grave. He stood there all on his own with his head bowed. And this time, too, his eyes were dry, as if he hadn't learnt how to cry yet. Then he picked up a lump of clay mingled with snow off the grave mound and flung it aside, as custom required.

'Granny, may the earth be as soft as down to you!'

He blew on his frozen fingers and trudged off down the road into the *auyl*. That same day Aân moved in with old Bapaj, who was a distant relative of his grandmother. Bapaj rode out of the gates first, his sleigh heaped high with brightly coloured blankets and pillows. He was followed by Aân, leading the light-grey cow. The cow took one step, then another and balked obdurately, sensing that she was being led away forever from her old, familiar stall. Well, any excuse for action was good enough for us. We abandoned our sledges and the whole gang started shoving the cow from behind.

'One, two – heave!' shouted Esikbaj.

The cow goggled her huge eyes, filled with bovine melancholy, shook her head and flicked her tail, as if she were being bitten by horseflies, and pretended she was going to butt Aân, but then accepted the inevitable, mooed pitifully and plodded after him, sniffing at the flap of his fur jacket.

'She's a clever creature, she understands everything', said Aân, as if he were trying to justify the cow's behaviour to us.

We escorted him to his new home and then went back to our sledges.

Aân didn't come back out to see us until the next day. He stood out of the way and watched with his eyes glowing as the guys came flying down the slope on their sledges.

'I used to have a sledge too. Back in the city', he told me after I made a dashing turn and braked to a halt at his feet.

He said it as if we had accused him of something.

'I tell you what, Aân, take my sledge and ride down', I suggested, unable to bear his gaze.

'Well, maybe I really could have a go?' he said uncertainly, but then his face lit up. 'Right, who wants to race me?'

Limping along, he dragged the sledge up the slope, flopped onto it belly down and slid down in an instant.

'Thanks', he said as he got up. 'Ooh, it's so fast! I didn't even have time to think.'

'But my sledge is even faster', Sadyķ boasted. 'Try a ride on mine, Aân.'

'Give me your sledge then', said Aân, delighted.

After that he perched himself on Esikbaj's sledge, and before he had even pushed off the other guys all started shouting eagerly:

'Aân, Aân! What about my sledge? Take my sledge!'

'Ooh, that's enough sledging!' Aân exclaimed, breathing deeply and fitfully, obviously tired because he was out of practice.

'Right, and for that you'll tell us another story', Sadyķ joked.

'All right then, I will', Aân said with a smile. 'And it will probably be better than yesterday's. Well, more cheerful, I suppose.'

When twilight fell, we gathered at Bapaj's house and kicked up such a racket taking our seats on the porch that the door immediately swung open and an old woman's voice cried out:

'Oi, what a disgrace! I wondered what all that tramping was. I thought they must have driven the collective farm herd in under my windows. But it's you, ruffians! Right, quick, march out of here, you miserable wretches. Ooh, I'll teach you!'

She brandished her dry, little fist, and that was enough to make us vanish from that yard in an instant. We stood in the street, glancing at each other in bewilderment. So much for our stories! was the message written on the guys' faces. Then Sadyķ came up with an answer.

'Guys, let's go to the stable! We can climb up on the roof and listen to as many stories as we like!'

Well, how come we hadn't thought of that before? There was hay piled up on the roof of the stable, it had been lying there, soft and fragrant, since early autumn. Just sit there and listen. We'd never find a more comfortable place, no matter how hard we racked our brains. Attaboy, Sadyķ!

We yelled out 'hoorah!' and dashed off to the stable like lunatics, spurring each other on. Aân ran along at the back, limping on his bad foot. Clambering up the brickwork onto the roof wasn't very difficult, especially for guys with hands that were just itching to climb up onto something. It was really great on the roof, and for a few minutes we tumbled about on the fragrant hay, laughing and squealing, burying ourselves in it completely, intoxicated by the smell of summer. Then the guys somehow all went quiet at once and started arranging themselves comfortably in a circle. The storyteller himself sat down in the centre, after first gathering together a huge armful of hay for a seat, and directed a keen, intent gaze towards the black ravine, which we could barely make out in the dark night – and what could be made out in that pitch darkness? But Aân's eyes pierced through the night, he could see something exceptional, something incomprehensible to the other boys. And we got an eerie feeling.

'It was a long, long time ago... in distant times. There was a boy... an orphan...', Aân began.

His muted, murmuring voice was spellbinding. Sitting there, we didn't stir a muscle, believing every single word, although we knew perfectly well that it was nothing more than a story, made up by one of us. Down below us the horses snorted and whinnied quietly, shifting their hooves about. But we no longer responded to the everyday sounds of the real world, we had been transported to an exotic country that extended through the darkness at the foot of Eškiôlmes.

After that it became a custom: as soon as the evening started drawing in, we would take our usual places and Aân would start telling his next story.

On one of these evenings Sadyķ appeared on the roof with a newspaper and a handful of tobacco, filched from home. Taking his seat staidly, in the way that he thought real men sat, he manufactured a huge, clumsy roll-up, as crooked as a goat's leg, took a little box with a single match in it out of his pocket and lit up amateurishly. We watched him wide-eyed; he took his first drag, broke into a long paroxysm of coughing, then brushed away his involuntary tears and casually declared:

'Now we can begin. Let's hear your story, Aân!'

'Hey, I'll have a go, too, first. Let me have a drag!' exclaimed Scratcher Ķasym, who was sitting beside Sadyķ. He reached out impatiently for the roll-up.

Our Sadyķ was magnanimous. He held out the cigarette and Ķasym pounced on it as greedily as if his very salvation lay in this dose of smoke. But he started coughing and sneezing so hard that we started making fun of him, and someone declared, in a moralising tone:

'Serves you right! You shouldn't be so greedy.'

And then Esikbaj intervened.

'Let me have it, Sadyķ, I'll show you how to smoke', he demanded grandly.

'Help yourself', said Sadyķ, making another grand gesture. Esikbaj breathed in excitedly, filling his mouth with tobacco smoke, and released it gently through his nostrils. And then he looked round at us with a superior air, as if to say, *there, that's how it's done, you boobies*. At this point my patience ran out, and the other guys followed me, and soon all that remained of the 'goat's leg' was a tiny little butt that no one dared to put in his mouth.

The next day each of us brought along his own tobacco to the roof. Panting eagerly, scattering tobacco and rustling newspaper, we each crafted a misshapen roll-up and puffed black smoke up into the night sky as we listened to Aân, and after that his stories acquired even greater fascination. Smoking elevated us in our own eyes, we thought of ourselves as sophisticated individuals hearkening to the wisdom of one of our brethren. Then one of us got caught by his mother while he was stealing tobacco, and our parents sounded the alarm. Tobacco and newspapers were stashed away in the family hiding places. But we had already become men of the world.

'Guys, hey guys, have you noticed what dumb Tùrdaġùl smokes?' Esikbaj asked when we convened a council to discuss this tragic matter.

Oh yes, we knew that very well, and from then on a handful of dry horse dung (may the reader forgive me!) became one of the indispensable items that that we always carried around in our pockets. And once more we blew up smoke to the stars as we paid heed to Aân's voice.

His stories seemed miraculous to us. They had everything in them: valour, chivalrous might, intellect and beauty. But their greatest attraction was that Aân made us the characters in them. According to his words we flung ourselves intrepidly into the attack against the fascists, one of us against a hundred – no, against a thousand – no, damn it, one against a million, with fantastic steeds snorting under us, and magical swords of pure silver glinting in our hands. Frightened to death, the enemy fled in panic before me, before Sadyķ and naturally, above all, before Esikbaj. Scratcher Ķasym, who sniffed constantly, forgot all about his snot and the fact that he still hadn't scoffed the bread cake filched from the dinner table, because just at that moment he was demolishing the fascist hordes in one fell swoop all on his own.

Listening to Aân, we forgot about our meagre dinners and scanty clothing. All that seemed a mere trifle compared with our heroic deeds. And when a story ended and Aân's final word faded away, we would start passionately discussing the tumultuous events that had just ended. The constant refrain was:

'I gave it to them, eh? Fantastic!'

'What about me?'

And the conversation inevitably turned to the genuine war. Esikbaj or someone else would say:

'If I had a magic sword like that, I'd go to the front and give the fascists a thrashing, I'd mow them all down.'

Or something of the kind. And Sadyķ or someone else would add something like this in a pensive voice:

'Just imagine it: my dad, surrounded by fascists. And then I appear with my magic sword. "Dad," I say, "it's me, Sadyķ!" And crash, wallop! I smash the fascists, every last one of them! Ah, wouldn't that be great!'

The rest of us agreed with him, each also dreaming of helping out his father or his brothers at the most critical moment...

Sometimes Aân made up a frightening story. Then the night around us was filled with the clanging of bronze wings on which wild, beast-like birds soared aloft, and the alleyways, the ravine and gullies all positively swarmed with one-eyed monsters, demons and other creatures of darkness. The night was electrified with horrors: we fancied we heard howling voices carried on the wind blowing from the direction of a gully, and the very bravest of us only had to cry out 'ha!' for the rest to howl '*oj-baj*!'[2] and bury ourselves in the hay.

To this day I still can't imagine what Aân was feeling as these stories took shape in his mind. Perhaps he was oppressed by loneliness and sometimes, when despair triumphed, it seemed to him that he was besieged by misfortunes, and they assumed fantastic forms in his young imagination... I can only guess about that. But in such cases his stories always ended happily, because he believed in the triumph of good.

At the same time, no one else could cheer our spirits the way Aân did. Unfortunately, it only happened very rarely. But when he did set about telling a funny story, with a faint smile revealing his sparsely set, bad teeth, we squirmed in laughter, thrashing our legs about, choking and clutching our stomachs. It felt as if there was no war going on in this world, and at that very moment our fathers and brothers were alive and well, sitting at home, safe and warm...

'Aân, just one more... It's no problem for you', we would implore him when he fell silent.

---

[2] *Oj-baj* – an exclamation approximating 'oh, my!'

But despite all our pleading, he never told more than one story. He would get up, brush off the hay that was clinging to his fur jacket and reply guiltily:

'It's late already, guys. Time for bed. They're probably damning us at home.'

It seemed to us that Aân was simply putting on airs and playing hard to get, that making up stories wasn't all that difficult, you just had to know a special method, and Aân knew that method, and we simply lacked the courage or were simply too lazy to interrogate him about it properly, and then make up stories ourselves. But it clearly wasn't really such an easy business after all. Aân thought, sitting in the sunshine somewhere, while we blithely careered down the slope on our sledges, and in the evening, weary and contented, wet through from the snow, we went to the stable to listen to what else our friend had prepared for us.

As a reward for a new story one of the guys would give his sledge to Aân in the morning – it became a custom. Well, that's the way it was at the beginning, and at first we were very conscientious, but then the impulse cooled and one day, when someone's turn came, he said:

'You know what, Aân? Why don't I give you my sledge tomorrow? You don't mind, do you?'

'Of course not', replied Aân, dismayed.

The new departure was infectious. After all, who wants to part with his sledge even for one day, when the snow is glittering so brightly and the sledge glides over it so fleetly, and the wind howls in your ears? So now, if Aân managed to get even one ride on a sledge, because someone's conscience was roused and he said with a heavy heart: 'Aân, maybe you'd like to take a ride?' – that could be regarded as a stroke of luck.

Aân would drag the sledge up the slope, but it no longer brought him the same joy, and after sliding down, he returned the sledge to its owner. It seemed as if he only took it because he understood everything and didn't want to make the shamefaced boy feel even more awkward. And afterwards he would stand at the bottom of the slope for a long time, burying his nose, blue from the cold, in the collar of his fur jacket, knocking one heel against the other and silently following our fun and games.

Sometimes Bapaj's old wife would stick her head out of the gate and shout:

'Hey, Aân, where are you out there? Where has he got to, that gadabout? Ah, that's where you are! Get along and tether the cow, and pen the ducks and geese. Oh yes, I completely forgot: then water the mare. And don't forget to put down some hay for her!'

'I'll do it all, granny', Aân would reply and walk into the yard, looking back constantly, as if afraid of missing the most interesting part, and almost always coming back.

But in the evening Aân came into his own. He obviously waited impatiently all day for the Sun to set, and when it sank down behind the summit of Eškiôlmes and it started getting dark, his face brightened up and he would say:

'Right, now for the stable. I've made up such a fine story today! Far better than yesterday's!'

Sometimes he couldn't bear to wait and would summon us to listen to his story in the daytime.

'You must be fed up with sledging by now! The same old thing every day. What's so interesting about lying on your belly and spoiling your clothes?' he began, thrusting out his lower lip scornfully.

But he was no good at pretending, and we realised what was going on and didn't fall into his trap. Except perhaps for one little simpleton who happened to pipe up:

'Maybe we should go after all? My felt boots are soaked right through.'

And that strengthened Aân's resolve...

'What kind of sledges are these anyway?' he snorted, wrinkling up his nose. 'They're not even a good excuse for sledges. I'd like to get my hands on a sledge with a steering wheel and a motor, and headlights, too. One you can ride uphill in, not just slide down. That's what I call a sledge!'

'Eh, you're making it all up! Sledges like that, that can go downhill and uphill, don't exist, do they?' we asked in amazement.

'Sure thing they do! Well, like a flying horse. Well, like the horse Tajburyl!'

'The horse Tajburyl? The one the great hero Ḳobylandy rode on?'

'Well, yes. These sledges are like that. Downhill or uphill, it's all the same to them!'

No one dared to argue with Aân: if he claimed it was so, then sledges like that really did exist.

If only I could have the kind of sledge Aân's talking about, each one of us thought.

3

Aân had a strange character. Once I came out into the street late, before going to bed – I'll just get a breath of fresh air, I thought – and I saw someone rushing down the slope on a sledge in the darkness. The sound was as if Mount Eškiôlmes had started creeping along. What kind of weirdo is that, I thought. Who's got it into his head to go sledging at this time? The sound came closer and closer, and then a little black figure appeared, coming straight at me. The moonlight lit it up, and I recognised Aân. His mouth was extended in a happy smile from ear to ear and the flaps of his fur jacket were fluttering urgently, as if Aân was hurrying to make up for lost time and get in some sledging for the future as well.

I called to him.

'It's you!' he exclaimed excitedly. 'Look, Sadyḳ gave me his sledge until tomorrow. Let's ride!'

'You what, have you gone crazy, sledging at this time? It'll be midnight soon, and you go sledging!'

'You mean you don't know?' Aân asked in amazement. 'You really don't know that the best time for sledging is by the light of the moon? That's when a sledge acquires special abilities. Well, like wings.'

That was something I didn't know, so I was flabbergasted and didn't say anything.

Meanwhile Aân ran up the slope and came rushing back down a little while later. And when he appeared in a broad strip of moonlight, I fancied that he really was flying. Well, not really high, of course, about a centimetre off the ground, but he *was* flying, damn it!

'Hoorah!' Aân shouted triumphantly, raising one arm in the air.

Probably a sledge really does grow wings in the moonlight, I thought, and ran home to get my own sledge. I started rummaging in the darkness of the hallway and, as always happens, buckets and basins crept under my feet and the cursed things clattered.

'Hey, there's someone moving about in the hallway', my mother said on the other side of the door. 'Probably the dog's got in again.'

She opened the door when I'd finally found the sledge and was all set to run. But my mother nailed me with the strip of light that poured out of the room.

'Ah, so it's you, making that racket! And what do you want in here, if you don't mind telling me?' my mother asked.

'Mam, I just want to go sledging for a while.'

'Isn't the day enough for you?' my mother asked angrily. 'What an idea to get into your head, when good people are sleeping. You're not a thief, are you, to sneak about sledging in secret?'

'Aân's sledging out there, he says...'

'Aân, Aân, he can go to blazes, that Aân of yours. All I ever hear is: "Aân said... Aân this... Aân that!" Put that sledge down now and march to bed, quick.'

She grabbed the sledge and flung it into the corner with a crash, and I got a hefty clip round the ear.

Terribly distressed, I plodded into my room, got undressed and lay down beside granddad, but I couldn't get to sleep for ages. The sound of sledge runners slithering over snow was still ringing in my ears. And when sleep finally did overcome me, I dreamt of Aân, flying uphill on a winged sledge, to the summit of Eškiôlmes ...

Winter pampered us for a long time with good weather. Then a day came when the sky was obscured by dark clouds and a cold, stinging wind started blowing out of the steppes. That evening the lamps were lit earlier than usual in the *auyl*. But we didn't abandon our tradition; as if nothing had changed, we gathered on the roof of the stable and started making roll-ups, preparing to hear another story. I remember that Aân's face was glowing with quiet joy.

'Guys, something amazing happened to me. If I tell you, you won't believe it. Early this morning I saw my dad', he said in the voice of a man who has received a wondrous gift. 'Really, really. Yesterday they put dad's coat on my bed, and it smelled of my dad. Like the smell of wormwood. When granny was alive, she used to say: "Do you know where I gave birth your father? I had him on Wormwood Hill, right up on the very top. I followed the cattle up and I had him there". And obviously the smell of wormwood must have stayed with my dad ever since then – so bitter, so bitter and good. I buried my nose in the coat and lay like that for a long time, until I fell asleep. And I dreamt of dad, strong and cheerful. Looking at me and laughing all the time.'

'I sleep under my dad's coat. And it smells of wormwood too', one of the guys remarked.

And then the conversations started about our fathers and brothers – in short, about what the clothes they'd left behind smelled of. And the interesting thing was, everyone agreed that their fathers and brothers smelled of wormwood, too. As if they had also been born on Wormwood Hill, which was not far away from our *auyl*. And then everyone gazed at Aân, leaving the final word to him.

'Guys, also I smell of wormwood. Probably because I'm a lot like my father. That's what everyone says. You can sniff for yourselves', Aân said self-consciously.

We sniffed at the air: and it was true – we detected a distant smell of wormwood coming from Aân. It was rather bitter, quite impossible to confuse with anything else. Or maybe we just imagined it, since we were used to believing every word Aân said.

'Yes, he does smell of wormwood', Sadyk̦ declared authoritatively, laying all our doubts to rest.

As you can guess, Esikbaj couldn't bear the thought that someone else smelled of wormwood, but he didn't. He sniffed his sleeve and chest thoroughly and announced:

'If it comes to that, I smell of wormwood too!'

After that everyone started sniffing their sleeves, and voices from all sides claimed:

'I smell of wormwood too!'

'So do I!'

'And so do I!'

Let it be said that we were all quite delighted with this new discovery, and no words can express the joy of it.

Eventually the guys settled down and Aân prepared for his story, clearing his throat.

'Wait', said Esikbaj, 'I want to ask Scratcher why he didn't give you his sledge. It was his turn yesterday'.

'My sledge broke… ' Scratcher K̦asym whined.

'Aha, it just happened to break yesterday. Not any earlier, but yesterday. Amazing how it managed to break right on time. A fortunate coincidence, isn't it?' asked Esikbaj, doggedly pressing his point.

'Well, give him yours if you want to so much', Scratcher K̦asym snarled, realising that he had been found out.

'I'm not mean', said Esikbaj.

'Guys, that's enough! It's such a trivial thing', Aân put in.

'Don't interfere, Aân. He has to be taught a lesson', Esikbaj persisted, grabbing the shaggy cap off Ķasym's head and flinging it down the roof onto the ground.

'Now what's that for? He'll catch a cold. I can get by without a sledge', Aân interceded for Scratcher.

'He won't catch a cold. Just let him clear out of here, quick' – and Esikbaj half-rose menacingly. 'Well, who am I telling?'

Scratcher Ķasym reluctantly climbed down off the roof, picked up his cap, pulled it right down onto his eyes and said before he left:

'I'll tell Tùržan on you. And he'll give you what for!' And he walked off, reviling Esikbaj and the entirely innocent Aân for all he was worth.

His brother Tùržan had been well known for his violent character even before the war. A month ago, he had come back from the front with one arm missing, and now he believed he could do anything he liked.

'I'm shell-shocked', Tùržan used to say. 'I spilled my blood for all you so-and-sos!'

And boys really caught it in the neck from him – that was why Scratcher Ķasym threatened us with his brother's vengeance. But just then we weren't afraid of anyone – we were waiting for a new story.

That evening Aân went back to his stories about the orphan boy.

… He had ridden for probably a thousand kilometres on the ugly colt, when suddenly it spoke in a human voice: 'You see the high mountain? It's the highest in the world. But that's nothing to me. I've got folding wings. I just have to wait for the night to fall. But in the daytime even a bird can't fly over it, because it's afraid of scorching its wings in the rays of the Sun. That mountain there, reaching right up to the Sun, do you see it? But when the Sun sets and it turns cold, we'll fly. Only be careful not to fall, hold on tight and better squeeze your eyes tight shut. Then I'll tell you when you can open them. I'll say, And now you can open your eyes – you understand?' Anyway, that night they flitted over to the other side of the highest mountain and saw a cave. Someone was sleeping in it beside a campfire. 'This is where that one-eyed monster lives', the colt told the orphan boy.

Aân stared at us wide-eyed, as if he'd just seen us for the first time, and lowered his voice to a whisper, as if that one-eyed monster could hear him. He did this so artfully that cold shivers ran down our spines and the sharp, black silhouette of Eškiôlmes seemed to be the very same mountain behind which the one-eyed monster was wheezing and snoring in his cave. And the cold wind blowing right then seemed to be caused by his snoring. The mountain was swaying gently in that wind, rising and sinking with each breath in and out, like the fabric covering a nomad's yurt. We were afraid to breathe, we breathed as cautiously as we possibly could, and I could see that no one dared to turn his head towards Mount Eškiôlmes ...

And the wind blew hoarsely, sometimes flinging into our faces handfuls of wet snow, seemingly from out of nowhere. Heavy black clouds gathered over the *auyl*, flying there from all over the heavens, and hung low over the houses. A dog started barking and howling like the one-eyed bogeyman's faithful guardian. It will wake the monster now, and then watch out, I thought, shuddering involuntarily.

And then, at the most interesting part, one of the guys howled:

'Help! Fire!'

A slim serpent of fire was creeping along the edge of the roof. As the wind drove it on, it picked out precisely the most convenient route. Evidently one of the guys had tossed his cigarette butt away and it had landed on the hay that had been spread across the roof at the beginning of autumn.

We spilled off the roof, plopping down like overripe fruit from a tree swayed by the wind, and scattered at a run. Aân was the last one to jump, I only remember his cry of pain from far behind us:

'Oi, my foot! My foot!'

It's shameful to admit it, but at that moment we had no time for him – each of us was thinking about his own safety. Especially since doors were slamming all over the *auyl*, with howls of 'Fire! Fire!' Grown-ups came running to the stable and Tùržan's figure loomed over at the front. His hoarse, angry voice stood out above the general hubbub.

'I'll give them what for! I spilled my blood for them, the snot-nosed kids!'

I darted behind the bushes beside the road and when I glanced out from my safe hiding place, I saw Tùržan dash to the spot where Aân was lying, writhing in pain.

The dark silhouette started jerking in a frenetic dance. I heard a whip whistle through the air and almost simultaneously Aân's imploring voice:

'What for, mister?'

'I'll show you what for!' Tùržan growled.

Then he gave Aân a parting kick with his coarse tarpaulin boot and dashed into the stable, where the horses where neighing in alarm at the scent of burning.

The fire found it hard to master the wet hay, and the grown-ups who had arrived dealt with it in a jiffy. After that, one of the men noticed Aân, lifted him up in his arms and declared reproachfully:

'Just look how badly he beat the boy! The vicious beast, taking revenge for his arm on a boy.'

The men surrounding them clicked their tongues in sympathy and condemned Tùržan. Realising that the grown-ups' anger had been diverted into a different channel, we cautiously crept out of our refuges and, for the sake of safety, gathered well out of the way, not looking each other in the eye. We felt guilty for running off in such a cowardly manner and abandoning our friend in distress.

'Guys', someone began, clearly wanting to make excuses.

'Guys, guys... Shut up, all right?' Esikbaj interrupted him rudely.

Aân was carried to Bapaj's house and, after hanging about for a while, feeling dejected because our conversation was flagging so badly, we all went home.

When I showed up, the grown-ups were still awake. My grandfather was sitting huddled up on the made-up bed, and my mum and granny looked visibly upset. They seemed to have been waiting especially for me to get back.

'There he is now, the great hero, feast your eyes on him', my granddad said angrily. 'Only why didn't this coward feel the lash of Tùržan's whip? He's the one who deserved it!'

What excuses could I offer for myself? I just stood in the doorway, silently running my finger across the wall, as if that was a highly important occupation. My stomach was aching with hunger, but I didn't have the courage even to hint at supper. And most importantly, I felt that I was a despicable individual, unworthy of even being fed.

'Poor Aân, completely on his own, with no one to stick up for him. His father's at the front. And Bapaj and his old wife need watching all the time themselves, they're so doddery', my mother muttered. Then she turned to me and said: 'Sit down and eat something, you good-for-nothing.'

'I don't feel hungry somehow', I mumbled, sidled to my bed with an air of self-renunciation, got undressed quickly and dived in under the blanket.

I fell asleep surprisingly quickly, but still managed to hear my grandfather mumble:

'If I could just drop fifty years, I'd teach Tùržan a lesson. That son of a bitch has become a really vicious brute.'

On waking up in the morning, I saw my mother pouring milk out of a jug into a half-litre jar. As if sensing my glance, she turned around and said:

'Get up now and have breakfast. And I'll take the milk to Aân. He's probably famished. They say he's still flat on his back, the unfortunate boy.'

I ate hastily and ran off to see Aân. My mother was still sitting in Bapaj's house, whispering about something with the old woman, who was spinning wool. Every now and then they both glanced at the sick boy. Aân was lying on a crude felt pad: his bed had been made up beside the stove, but he was still squirming in chilly shudders under a threadbare blanket sewn out of scraps of cloth. Aân's face was swollen from the drubbing and there was a massive, crimson bruise on his cheekbone.

'Well, how do you feel?' I asked, sitting down close beside him.

'Not too bad', Aân replied, barely able to move his tongue.

We fell silent – and what could we possibly talk about just then? We simply kept casting glances at each other. And I involuntarily started listening to the grown-ups' whispering.

'Well, how's his foot? Have they set his foot?' my mother asked.

'No chance of that! Our old man has been chasing about like a scalded cat since yesterday evening. And he went running off again this morning. But what's the point, who's going to take on that job in our *auyl*?' the old woman grumbled.

'But what about the bone-setter Asylbek? They say he's a good healer.'

'Ah, Asylbek's gone into the city, as if he did it deliberately. Bad luck never comes by halves. And that young imp's a fine one too', – the old woman nodded in Aân's direction. 'Out wandering about until midnight. Always wanting to shove himself ahead of the others. Damn all his games to hell. And we have to answer for the tearaway. He's like a millstone round our necks. If only the war would end soon, so his father could come back. Then we could die in peace. He's ruined all the blankets in the house. He wets himself in his sleep, like a little baby, even if he does know how to write letters', the old woman said, leaning down closer to my mother.

She was rather deaf and thought she couldn't be heard at all, but in fact her droning voice carried right across the room. Aân blushed and tears welled up in his eyes, and although I looked up at the ceiling, pretending not to pay any attention, he turned to face the wall and pulled the blanket up over his head.

'*Ojboj*,[3] it all comes from his illnesses', my mother said in the meantime, getting up, 'never mind, he'll get well in time… I think I'll be going, the small of my back's aching. Anyway, if there's anything you need, don't be shy. If we have it, we'll help.'

Bapaj's old wife put down her yarn and followed my mother out to see her off, or maybe for something else. The important thing was that we were left alone. I felt a desperate desire to help Aân somehow and I'd come up with what I thought was a subtle plan.

'We can't beat Tùržan, he's a grown-up, but you know what we'll do: we'll thrash Ķasym. That'll make Tùržan really angry. There are lots of us and he can't catch everyone', I suggested, trying to console Aân.

'What's Scratcher got to do with anything? It's not his fault', Aân said to the wall.

'Maybe not. But he's Tùržan's brother', I replied excitedly, amazed that a smart guy like Aân couldn't appreciate such good revenge.

'And Tùržan's not to blame either', Aân muttered, still not looking round.

'Then who is to blame?' I asked, flabbergasted.

'The war, that's who! It's all because of the war.'

'Oh, sure! He was crazy before the war. All the grown-ups say so. If you don't believe it, ask anyone you like.'

'Now I'll never smoke again to my dying day', Aân suddenly declared.

'But all the same, Tùržan is vicious, he's a total psycho', I said, refusing to back down.

Aân turned around gingerly and said:

---

[3] *Ojboj* – exclamation of indignation or sympathy.

'Hand me that coat over there... No, not that one, the one beside it... the black one' – and he pointed to an old coat hanging in the place of honour.

I moved over the only chair, stood on it and took down the coat off its nail.

Aân took hold of it tenderly and nestled his cheek against the rough fabric, rubbing it to and fro. His nostrils flared sensitively.

'It smells of wormwood. It's my dad's. I hope he'll come back soon', he said in a quiet voice. Then he sighed and handed me the coat.

'Hang it back up, or else granny will see and scold me. She'll say it's a thing, not a toy, and then go on and on! She won't shut up until the evening.'

He stretched out on his back and said nothing for a moment, touching the bruise on his cheekbone. Then he added:

'But dad will come back soon. I know it.'

About ten days later he got out of bed and started walking a bit. When he came out into the street, we could see immediately that his foot was in a really bad way.

Just like before, Aân would come to his favourite spot at the foot of the snowy slope and watch the guys sledging from a distance. He followed every movement we made with rapt attention and if something funny happened, he laughed wholeheartedly. As if he was just as healthy as all the other guys. But when Sadyḳ offered Aân his sledge, Aân shook his head and refused outright.

'My foot hurts', he sighed.

4

Sometimes in the evening, after supper, I set off to Bapaj's house, walking languidly after running about all day. More often than not at that time, Aân would be sitting beside the little iron stove, tossing bundles of straw into the flames. During the war firewood was hard to come by – our region was in the steppes – and we had to heat our houses with straw. Sometimes, grain was threshed with a stone roller and then large straws, as long as reeds, were left, and sometimes you could come across an ear with some grains still on it. Straw burns easily, it melts silently in the flames, but the ear crackles and shoots out sparks, so when you hear that familiar crackling, you can reach into the fire with a stick and rake out the ear with its toasted grains. And at that moment it seems like nothing in the world is more delicious. And this was what I often found Aân occupied with.

If I showed up at Bapaj's house during supper, Aân didn't dare to invite me to join him at the modest table; he nodded silently at the felt pad lying abandoned beside the stove, at the same time glancing sideways anxiously at Bapaj and his old wife. I would huddle up in the corner and from there I watched the progress of supper in this house that seemed so strange to me. The old folks usually ate talḳan[4] and the boy had those roasted grains of wheat to add to his supper.

---

[4] *Talḳan* – a nourishing product prepared from ground and dry-fried wheat, barley or corn mixed with sugar and butter or sour cream.

'You're still young, not like us old folks. And you've got strong teeth too', Bapaj's old wife used to say sensibly.

Aân would nod, as if agreeing, and wash down the wheat grains with tea, then turn his tea bowl upside down, come over to me in the corner and ask in a quiet voice:

'Want to hear a story? It's brand new. I only made it up today. Well, will you listen to it?'

'Do you have to ask?' I replied indignantly.

'Okay, listen... Once upon a time there was a boy... He was absolutely alone...' Aân began, and the minutes that followed were miraculous for me.

Thank God, neither Bapaj nor his old wife ever interfered. They ate their *talḵan* soaked in butter and drank unbelievable amounts of tea with great gusto. Then the old man, exhausted by all the tea, would go over to the bed and knead the pillows for a long time, burping in satisfaction and sometimes joking:

'What are you whispering about, eh? You great conspirators! Probably planning to steal someone's daughter, are you? Do you confess?'

And his old wife grumbled to him in the same tone:

'They say a bad dog never stops barking, it goes on and on. Our lad's like that; always droning on and on without a break.'

Before going to bed, she would turn down the already feeble flame in the kerosene lamp, murmuring:

'I'll never save any kerosene with you idlers chattering all the time.'

Eventually they would go to sleep and we would amuse ourselves with stories for a while to the sound of their snoring. Aân would take his precious store of scorched grains out of his trouser pocket, blow the chaff off his palm and share them with me.

'They're delicious, aren't they?' he would ask.

I agreed with him, although the only desire that the taste of burnt grain aroused in me was to spit out this excessively 'refined' dish in secret.

Sometimes I managed to bring him a small piece of stale, dry bread. His pupils dilated like the pupils of a cat that has spotted a mouse, but he tried to eat calmly, maintaining his dignity.

One day, after a heavy snow shower, one of the guys suggested a game of snowballs. We elected two atamans and divided up into two equal teams. And at that point Aân, who had resisted staunchly so far, gave in and asked to be included in the game.

'Why would we want someone lame like you? You aren't even allowed to run. What point is there in playing with you, judge for yourself', one of the atamans declared.

Tears welled up in Aân's eyes, he turned away and plodded off dejectedly, limping more badly than ever. I felt so sorry for him that I couldn't stop myself and went running after him.

'Aân, where are you going?'

'Well, it's...' was all that Aân said, afraid of bursting into tears.

I set off beside him and neither of us spoke for a while. We walked along like that until we came up to Asylbek the bonesetter's house, where Aân heaved a sigh and turned into Asylbek's yard. I decided to stay with him to the end and followed him in.

Old Asylbek was clearing dung out of his shed. When he spotted us, he leaned on his spade and asked from a distance.

'What do you want, lads?'

'*Ata*[5], please, do something about my foot. I want to run', Aân implored him.

'Bapaj told me about it... But you refused yourself. It's probably too late now and the foot will stay crooked', Asylbek muttered reproachfully.

'*Ata*, do something. I really want to run', Aân repeated.

'Eh, do you think it's that simple to set a joint back in place? And it will hurt, hurt really badly! If I was a real doctor, it would be a different matter... But old Asylbek is just a *auyl* bonesetter, that's all', said Asylbek, keeping his probing eyes fixed on Aân.

'*Ata*...' my poor friend wailed again.

'So be it, son, so be it, I'll do my best', said Asylbek, suddenly all business. 'Go on into the house, my little nephews, go on in. Hey, old mother, give our little nephews something to eat!' the bonesetter shouted, turning towards the window.

His wife appeared behind the dark windowpane and nodded as if to say: I hear you.

We went into the house and timidly took off our coats. The lady of the house sat us down, rigid with embarrassment, at the head of the table and regaled us with *bauyrsak*[6] and *ajran*[7] to drink. I had to eat for two, because Aân couldn't swallow anything. A little later Asylbek himself appeared.

'Well, have you had a bite, little nephews?' he asked cheerfully in the doorway.

Aân nodded.

'That's good' Asylbek continued, removing his galoshes. 'Wife, put out a clean blanket for us... That's right. And you, my fine eagle, lie down. Boldly now, boldly! You wanted this, no one coerced you. So you have to be a man right to the end!'

He smeared his little patient's sick foot with sheep tallow and massaged it for a long time. I could sense every cell in Aân's body tensing up. He watched from under half-lowered eyelids as Asylbek's deft hands worked away, lifting

---

[5] *Ata* – lit. 'grandfather'; respectful form of address to an older man.

[6] *Bauyrsak* – fried wheat dough found in the cuisines of Central Asia; must-have treat for guests during special occasions.

[7] *Ajran* – sour drink made of cow, sheep, or goat milk fermented with lactic bacteria, often thick and used both as food and as a beverage.

his head to get a better view of what Asylbek was doing with his foot and holding it up until his neck got tired. And the bonesetter massaged the leg and talked, trying to distract Aân's attention, then suddenly made a movement that I didn't notice. I only guessed about it because Aân screamed blue murder.

'Oi! That hu-urts!'

'Well now, that's all', said Asylbek, stroking the painful spot. Then his wife brought a clean piece of cloth and the bonesetter bound up Aân's foot tightly, even leaning back to admire the work of his own hands.

'Beautiful, eh? Now all the other kids will envy you.' Then he added seriously: 'We'll hope for the best. And in any case, take it easy with the foot.'

Spring came.

The collective farm was short of manpower, and we went out into the fields together with the grown-ups. At first our responsibilities seemed simple: sit on a bullock harnessed to a plough and urge it on every now and then with a little switch. And behind you women leaned all their weight into the plough, because their husbands had gone away to the front and there was no one else to do this work.

We started ploughing at the crack of dawn. The bullocks plodded slowly across the wet, thawed-out earth, dragging the ploughs after them, the women trudged along after the ploughs and a thick black trail stretched out behind them – a layer of overturned earth.

But then the ploughshare would sink in deeper than it ought to, and the bullock would stop, unable to overcome the additional resistance. It had wasted away and exhausted its strength over the winter, because it carted both hay and grain in winter too. And now it stood there, trembling with the strain, drooling hungrily, and that was when the work of the boy sitting on its back began.

'Right, move on!' the boy yells, lashing the bullock on the back and the rump, where the blood has only just clotted from the previous lacerations.

The bullock strains with its final ounces of strength and drags the plough on farther, until the next hitch. And so, from morning to evening you shout yourself hoarse, sitting on the sharp, bony back of a bullock. Your throat dries out from all the shouting, your arms dangle down, flooded with lead, your stomach's empty, and all this sets your head spinning. And you hear a weary reproach from behind:

'What are doing there, sonny?'

And you raise your lash again. The bullock shudders under the blow, but its stride remains as sluggish and feeble as ever. You want to tumble off and collapse onto the ground, weeping and hammering on it with your fists.

The woman plodding after the plough can sense your condition. She takes the switch out of your hands and lashes with it herself, driving the beast on, and tells you sympathetically:

'Hold on tight, sonny. Make sure you don't fall.'

She herself has dark circles under her eyes from exhaustion, her stride is uncertain and her fingers are trembling. But as soon as one of the women starts up a song, she joins in too:

Oh, Kôkše Mountain is so high,
It's so hard to get a message from a dear one
Who is far away[8]

Someone joins in from another plough, and then another, and the song drifts quietly across the field, like a sad sigh, rising up from the secret depths of the soul. And at this saddest of songs our throats tighten, we feel sorry for the women, and ourselves, and the completely blameless cattle. But our manly pride forbids us to cry!

This is what Aân said after the first working day, when we were lying flat on our backs in our dugout:

'Anyone can cry. If you're a real man, you have to keep a grip on yourself.'

Our dugout is dark, as black as a cave. The kerosene lamp doesn't make any difference, its light is so feeble that we can't even see our own supper. We simply recognise it from the taste – *talķan*. After our perfunctory meal, we collapse, still dressed, onto the meagre layer of straw that serves as our bed and fall asleep immediately. Our sleep seems to last no longer than a minute. No sooner have we closed our eyelids than foreman Tûržan sticks his head into the dugout and shouts:

'Hey, you tearaways! Rise and shine!'

His voice has turned hoarse, because nowadays he bellows twice as much as usual. And now he shakes almost all of us by the shoulders, yells in our ears and lugs our bodies over to the exit like rag dolls.

And it all happens all over again. Once again, you're up on a bullock's spiky backbone, and once again you're shouting:

'Move on! Move on!' – and once again you raise the lash and strike the bullock until your arm goes numb. By lunchtime you start dozing off from exhaustion and hunger, and when you do doze off, you plunge down onto the ground, onto the crumbly fallow soil. Then the bullock halts, pleased to have a break, and the woman stops and walks up to you with a compassionate expression on her face. Cursing the war, she helps you get to your feet and clamber up onto the beast's steep back.

Aân also suffered the same lot, only for him it ended really badly. He shrieked and fell silent, realising that he was obviously fated to suffer agony with his bad foot for the rest of his life. He lay there, huddled up, only asking not to be touched when one of the grown-ups tried to remove his *šoķaj* – a simple shoe made of tawed leather.

---

[8] The song is a combination of the folk song 'Kôkšetaudyņ biigi-aj' ('Oh, Kôkše Mountain is so high') and verses added during the war.

143

They lifted Aân up and carried him to the brigade field camp. And they left him in the care of the cook until the first cart arrived.

Before even an hour had passed, the cook came running, frightened out of her wits, called me aside and whispered.

'What a character that boy has. So young, but you know what he did? He almost strangled himself! Yes, yes, I saw it with my own eyes. I glanced into the dugout, and he was holding his own throat and squeezing it. As Allah is my witness, I got such a fright. "What are you doing? What's wrong with you?" And then, just imagine, he closed his eyes and pretended to be asleep... The poor boy! I'm afraid for him. I wish you'd have a word with him.'

I dashed to the field camp at top speed and the panting cook trotted behind, admonishing me:

'Tell him: who has a calm heart now? We all have our own grief. One person has this, another person has that. You tell him: say he mustn't do that!'

Aân was lying on his back with his eyes closed.

'Aân! Aân!' I called in a whisper and sat at the head of his bed. He opened his eyes and spoke, looking up at the ceiling:

'You know, I wanted to die. Why am I like this, I thought. And then I remembered about my dad...'

Without finishing what he was saying, Aân stuck his nose into the unbuttoned collar of his shirt and, smiling feebly, said:

'It smells of wormwood too. Bitter, so bitter... When dad comes back, he'll think of something... He'll take me away to the city. They have doctors in white coats there. He'll tell them: "Cure my son". And they'll cure me so that however much I run and jump, it'll be okay. And then he'll take me to school...'

Aân got carried away with his dream and started telling me how he would live with his father when he came back, and I listened and forgot about everything else, because this was just as interesting as the stories he made up.

'You'll see: soon the war will end and dad will come back. Just as soon as they crush the fascists, he'll come back', Aân said firmly.

I believed him unreservedly; well, about his father coming back soon. I really wanted this man I didn't know to come to our *auyl* and put an end to my friend's loneliness.

Early in the evening a cart trundled up with seeds for sowing and after it was unloaded, it took Aân away to the *auyl*.

Childhood was definitely a hard time for me and my peers. The battles were blazing somewhere in lands far away (it was hard for us to imagine those places, overgrown with thick forest and covered by steppe land that wasn't like ours), but the war was going on everywhere, and we had our own wounds, both large and small. Afterwards scars covered them over, but even now those scars can start aching once in a while. There's probably not a single person in our *auyl* who was spared by misfortune at that time.

Tùržan was followed back home from the front by a few other men. And each of them brought back the terrible mark of war. Some came with a leg missing, some with no eyes, some, like Türžan, with an arm missing – but even so their return was a celebration for the entire *auyl*. Because in place of some who went to the front, only death notices came back. But life treated the boy Aân with exceptional cruelty…

I remember that sultry day in the middle of the summer when his father's death notice had arrived. The war was coming to an end and all the talk just then was about how the ones who were still alive would come back in a little while, and that made the event seem especially tragic to me.

Aân was running after us along the dusty street, limping heavily on his bad foot. He was holding up the trousers dangling on his emaciated body and shouting:

'Hey, you guys, hang on, will you! I've got a new story. You can't even imagine how interesting it is! Where are you going, guys?'

But in the heat of the game we had no time for him. Awkward and weak, he was a burden to us at moments like this. He fell behind our horde as it rampaged along the street, and then plodded on in complete isolation. That was when the man from the *auyl* soviet found him. They say the courier hesitated for a long time, not knowing how to hand him the notification, while Aân gazed at him in alarm, completely unable to grasp what this man wanted. Eventually, the courier thrust the terrible slip of paper into Aân's hands and dashed away, almost running.

From a distance we saw Aân read a piece of paper, then read it again, and again, as if he couldn't believe his eyes. Then he folded it into four, put it in his pocket and started watching our horseplay as if nothing was wrong. I sensed that it was something bad.

'Well, see you. I'll be off', Aân said and started limping towards the edge of the *auyl*.

'I don't really feel like going home', I said and set off after him, but he didn't seem to hear, as if he had disconnected himself from everything going on around him.

He went to the stable. It was stuffy there, with a smell of decayed dung. Fat black flies were buzzing. Behind a beam running across the ceiling, fledglings were cheeping. After the bright light of the street, the stable seemed absolutely dark. I stood for a little while, letting my eyes adjust, then set off along the passage between the stalls, holding my hands out just in case.

Aân was sitting on a pile of hay in the farthest corner, with his face buried in his hands. Then he wiped his eyes and walked out of the stable. I plodded after him again. His eyes and nose had turned swollen and red, but he smiled and said:

'It's really hot, eh?'

A week went by after that, and one morning, after I'd driven our young goats to pasture and come back to the *auyl*, I saw the guys crowding around Bapaj's yard and a cart with a plump bundle of household bits and pieces lying on it. The guys were talking quietly and glancing at the gates.

'Aân's going away to an orphanage', announced Esikbaj, standing at the edge.

'What did you say? Where's he going?' I asked, not understanding anything at first.

'They say they're going to take him to the station. And he'll get a train there.'

Aân came out of the gates, dressed for a journey. He was accompanied by Bapaj and his old wife and a driver, the owner of the cart. As he walked along, Bapaj was telling the young man he must make sure to get the boy to the station.

And the old woman hugged Aân and burst into tears.

'Be happy, my little dear', she said, wiping away her tears. 'You grew from good seed. Your parents were wonderful people, be just like them. If we're still alive, come and see us.'

'Write when you get there. You know how to write' said Bapaj. 'It's a pity there's no buyer right now, or I'd have sold the cow. I'll take her to the market and send you the money.'

'Why sell the cow?' the old woman asked in surprise. 'When Aân grows up, she'll be useful for the household. Don't listen to granddad, my child. He's gone completely gaga. When you come back, you'll have a cow with calves.'

'What would I want with a cow?' Aân asked, then he turned to us and started saying goodbye.

'I'm going to write letters to you, to everyone! To you, and you...' he said, shaking our hands.

Then he climbed onto the cart and the driver started the horse.

'Right, walk on!'

Esikbaj clung on to the cart and saw Aân to the end of the street. We stood there for a long time, watching the cart stir up the grey dust behind it as it carried Aân away. Aân took off his cap and waved his last goodbye to us, and then he was completely hidden by a bend.

'Guys, let's play a game!' Scratcher Ķasym said, as if nothing had happened.

'I've got a headache' said Sadyķ setting off towards his own gates.

'And my mum's calling me to do something', said another one of the guys.

So that day the gang split up long before the evening...

We remembered Aân and his stories for a long time. Sometimes, we got together on inclement winter evenings and reconstructed all the stories he had told us word for word.

Not long ago, I walked out into our *auyl* street the way I did as a child, and I suddenly fancied that the one-eyed monster whom the brave orphan boy fought was sleeping just below the shaggy cap of Mount Eškiôlmes, setting it shuddering with his snores. Where is that boy now, is he alive?

A gentle gust of wind brought the familiar pungent scent from Wormwood Hill. And I thought, If Aân's alive, he'll definitely come back here. Because sooner or later the bitter smell of wormwood will lure him here.

Translated by Andrew Bromfield

KABDESH ZHUMADILOV
(b. 24.04.1936)

Kabdesh Zhumadilov is a Kazakh writer. He began his studies at the Faculty of Philology of Kirov Kazakh State University (now Ăl-Farabi Kazakh National University) in 1956. However, he was recalled to his home region of Xinjiang after two years in Almaty. Zhumadilov returned to Kazakh SSR in 1962 to complete his education, graduating in 1965.

Zhumadilov worked for *Ķazaķ ădebieti*, the newspaper (1965–67), Žazušy publishing house (1967–76) and the State Publishing Committee (1976–81). His first poems were published in a Xinjiang newspaper in 1954, and two years later his debut short story 'Žamal' appeared in the journal *Šuǵyla*. A collection of poems, titled *Žas dăuren* (Young Years), was published in 1967, shortly followed by his first short story collection, *Ķazdar ķajtyp barady* (The Geese are Returning, 1968). The year 1969 saw the publication of a novel, *Kôkejkesti* (The Essential). Since then, Zhumadilov has been regarded a master of realistic prose writing, with deep knowledge of Kazakh history and ethnography. He has focused primarily on historical themes and the lives of Xinjiang Kazakhs, such as in the novels *Soņǵy kôš* (The Last Departure, 1974–81), *Atameken* (Fatherland, 1985) and *Taǵdyr* (Destiny, 1988).

Soņǵy kôš was awarded the Múhtar Ăuezov Literary Prize (1983) and *Taǵdyr* won the Abaj State Prize (1990). Zhumadilov is the recipient of the highest award for writers in the Republic of Kazakhstan, the title of People's Writer of Kazakhstan (1998), and of the Parasat Order (2005).

A Beggar Man

As was his habit, Ajdarbek got off the bus as soon as he arrived at one of the streets in Almaty's city centre. He carried his accordion in a box on his back, and a travel bag was suspended from his right shoulder. Both hands were busy holding onto the handgrips of the crutches that supported him. The Sun had just risen, and was visible through the high-rise buildings. Ajdarbek stood there for a moment, resting on the crutches and breathing in the fresh May morning air thirstily: it had not yet been toasted by petrol fumes and smog. His knee was bent, so that his right foot did not touch the ground. Then he began walking, starting as abruptly on his way as a chained horse jumping suddenly. His place of work was not far from the bus stop. Limping along the familiar road, he descended into the pedestrian underpass at the junction of four streets.

There were several shops and stalls inside the underpass. People came and went all day long. There was a shoemaker's; a photo stall, where old photographs were restored and framed; and other stalls selling newspapers, magazines, books and sundries.

As Ajdarbek passed, his shopkeeper 'neighbours' nodded their heads and waved their hands in greeting. He didn't stop at any of the stalls, but headed to one of the damp, empty corners of the underground passage. He leaned against the wall and set his backpack and the accordion down slowly. Inside the backpack was a folding chair; he rested his crutches against the wall and took a seat on the chair.

Waiting a bit, gathering his breath, he exercised his fingers, opening and closing them to encourage flexibility after clenching the handgrips for so long. In the mornings, pedestrians were rare in the underground passage. Only the sound of cars on the road above them could be heard through the concrete. Ajdarbek sat motionless for a few minutes, then said to himself: 'So… let's start work.' His 'work' was not difficult: he took a newspaper out of his bag, folded it in front of him and put his time-worn hat on top of it. Then he reached into the old box, the colour of which had completely faded, and lifted up his brown accordion, still in good shape. He treated the accordion as though it were some kind of sacred object, setting it carefully on his knees. He hung the accordion strap around his shoulders and ran his fingers over the keys, sounding different melodies.

What music should I begin the day with?, he wondered. Ajdarbek's repertoire included more than a hundred songs in Kazakh, Russian and Tatar, but he was not in the habit of playing them all together. He preferred to choose the music

148

as though he were performing at an official concert. The type of music he played on any given day depended on his mood; the music might be solemn, or melodic, or melancholy. Lately, before playing, he assessed the passers-by in different groups according to features such as ethnicity and age. For example, when he played 'Katyusha', the patriotic Russian folk song that had gained so much fame during the Second World War, no veteran passed him without turning his head in approval. Recently, on 9 May – Victory Day – he started the day with 'Katyusha' and ended it with other war songs. (During holidays, people were more generous.) Mentally, the titles flashed in sequence: 'Waltz of Love', 'Birdsong', 'Waves of the Danube', 'Moscow Evenings', 'Ġaliâbanu'... in his mind's eye, they were illuminated brightly. When he noticed a group of young people descending the steps, he immediately began playing 'A White Bow', a well-known song about a high-school sweetheart.

The beginning of the day went well. Passers-by threw five tenge or ten tenge into his hat, and, occasionally, twenty tenge. It was different every time: some people gave trifling amounts, as if they wanted somehow to discharge their duty: as soon as they tossed their change, they hurried away. Others stayed a little longer, listening to the tunes. There were also those who acted covertly: pretending to browse books in the stalls, they walked around slowly, listening attentively to the music... There were those who could not seem to find any change in their pockets; they made a big fuss rummaging through them, turning them inside out and looking for small coins rather than go through the 'shame' of asking the beggar for change of a big bill. Ajdarbek never blamed such people. He understood that nowadays many were not able to make ends meet, that the standard of living was unequal: one was rich, another was poor. The rich never walked through the underground passage, however. They stayed above it, riding the asphalt roads, zooming back and forth in their cars.

Initially, Ajdarbek had been ashamed of his chosen occupation; sometimes, in fact, he was ashamed to such a degree that he wanted the ground to open up and swallow him. Yet he had become accustomed to it: 'I'm not a person who begs for change and does nothing', he would say, 'I am a beggar who sells his art... When you pay for art, it does not matter whether it's acting on a stage or performing music in the underpass. The difference is that ticket prices are considerably more expensive at the concert hall – but here it costs nothing. You may listen almost free of charge. At the philharmonic, tickets are sold at the box office, and the shows are specially advertised; but my box office is... my hat! And my audience exceeds that of any concert hall, tenfold.'

This was exactly what people said about life, that it's unstable: one day it greets you, smiling; the next, it turns its back. Alas! There was a time when people referred to him as a 'gentleman from Seŋgirtau'; now here he was, sitting in the underground passage. Once he had held a post as a manager of a cultural centre. He was responsible for staff, including automobile club coordinators, a film technician, a librarian, a security guard and several others. His regional chapter had organised a club for art aficionados; every weekend, they would put on concerts for the public. Not a day went by in which Ajdarbek did not participate in a concert in Seŋgirtau. Whenever or wherever you saw him, there he was, cradling his accordion at the centre of any *toj* – any feast.

That was all gone now, like a dream.

How strange; after four or five years, his festive life in Seŋgirtau had come to an end. First, the regional authorities did away with the collective farm and all its cattle, claiming various reasons – all still incomprehensible to Ajdarbek. When the cattle had gone, people's wealth went with it. The once well-organised system of collective farming was disbanded, and the farmers were left with nothing. After a few years, Seŋgirtau became a deserted, unpromising region. It merged with the neighbouring district, and people without work scattered to different places. As the saying goes, 'hungry bellies have no ears': nobody needed live music performances any more. The cultural centre remained empty, and eventually the doors were locked for good.

Ajdarbek was left without work. He played his accordion at weddings and other occasions, but these kinds of parties were not regular. Even when they did occur, people didn't pay enough for his services: payment was provided in the form of showing respect by inviting him to the table. He would sit at one edge of the *toj dastarhan* – the festive table – and enjoy a good dinner. Thank God, his wife Ķajša had not lived long enough to bear witness to his impoverished state – this dreadful period that saw him become useless and homeless. She had died several years earlier, from a terrible disease in the district, which had spread near the atomic bomb testing sites in Semej. People would die without symptoms, seemingly healthy, without feeling anything awry or becoming ill. Ķajša had only collapsed once, while chatting at the dinner table.

Since then, Ajdarbek had been living with his thirteen-year-old daughter, Ajgùl. His eldest son, Ajķyn, went to study in Almaty. Dear God, who had expected him to gain admission to university? The previous year, he had visited the university by himself, taken the entrance exams and become a student of industrial transport. Ah, how difficult it had been to see his only son off! Travel was too expensive, and neither father nor son could afford to make the journey either way. Ajdarbek had pondered the situation: 'What's the matter with me?' he asked himself. People say, clever dogs never show how they die. If I die, then let me die far from Seŋgirtau. I should move to Almaty and live with my children...'

Driven by these thoughts, Ajdarbek had sold his cow and left for Almaty the previous summer along with Ajgùl. He'd packed his clothes in a case and put his brown accordion on his back. My music won't die, he thought. I'm sure to find a job in the big city. However, this wish did not come true. He travelled back and forth, knocking on many doors. He visited every art institution and organisation, seeking positions, but there were no vacancies. The organisations were making their own staff redundant, and barely surviving. Wherever he went, he encountered anxious, angry people: 'My dear young man, you've got such high demands', scolded the director of one of the philharmonic orchestras.

'We are not taking on even popular performers, despite their achievements. And here you are, having worked only in the position of a district centre manager!'

Such remarks actually had a calming effect on Ajdarbek. His efforts to find a job with cultural organisations and concert halls were fruitless: it was impossible, after all. Even finding menial work was hopeless. In addition to all the newcomers to the city searching for jobs, the citizens of Almaty themselves – robust, experienced professionals – were mired in joblessness.

Ajdarbek was able to arrange for Ajgùl to study at a boarding school in the city, however; and Ajķyn lived in a university dormitory and received a stipend on account of his achievements, though that sum did not cover his everyday expenses. Ajdarbek himself had fixed up an old hovel that belonged to a close friend of his, on the outskirts of the city, and was now living there.

Autumn changed into winter. As it is said: 'Misfortune never comes alone.' The first day it snowed in Almaty, Ajdarbek was hurrying to an interview for a security guard position. While crossing the street, he slipped and fell. Luckily, a kind Muslim man helped him up and took him to the hospital. Alas, his right femur was fractured. Ajdarbek thought he would have to stay in the hospital until he recovered, but discovered this was not common practice. The doctors put a plaster cast on his leg and let him stay for a few days, and then told him: 'Now you may go home. We'll need to remove the cast after two months, so please get in touch with us by that time.' They said this as though a wonderful house with a comfortable bed awaited him.

All was in God's hands. Moreover, misfortune tells us what fortune is. This broken leg led unexpectedly to Ajdarbek's new career. After leaving the hospital, he had limped to the bus stop on his way back to his 'house' on the outskirts. It was difficult labour for a person unaccustomed to the use of crutches, and of course the ground was still slippery. As he approached the bus stop, his crutches slid, and he collapsed against a nearby tree. The fall, and his broken leg, caused him so much pain that he almost lost consciousness. He sat there for a few moments, just to catch his breath. His old marmot-leather hat, which Ķajša had sewn for him, had fallen off his head and lay upturned on the pavement; he was unable even to pick it up. Just then, an elderly Russian woman passing by threw ten tenge into the hat. Not long afterward, another elderly man threw five tenge…

'Ah, troubles!' Ajdarbek said to himself, feeling humiliated. 'They think I'm a street beggar! Do I really look like one?'

However, he didn't hasten to retrieve his hat. This novel situation seemed to invite some interested hesitation: 'Let's see what happens.'

Over the next half-hour, he collected sixty tenge. Perhaps he had been lucky enough to encounter only very kind people, or those who might have sympathised with the 'disabled on crutches'. This sum was not meagre: it meant two loaves of bread, two litres of milk. If you economised, this amounted to two days' provisions. An idea struck him. 'I'm hungry, yet here's one way to survive in this big city! Who knows me here, after all? Who am I ashamed to be seen by?'

Thus, Ajdarbek became a beggar by circumstance, perhaps by destiny. As soon as he became accustomed to the crutches, he went to set up at the railway station, carrying his accordion on his back. There were more people there, and the income was not bad – enough for his daily sustenance, plus enough to spare for his children to have a meal or two. Sometimes, he was able to give Ajkyn and Ajgùl some extra pocket money. However, the railway station had drawbacks: there were many guards about, for one thing; they chased away anyone who might, they probably reckoned, injure the city's image. Another risk was that there were many arrivals from Semej, and he might meet someone who knew him.

This had actually happened once. Ajdarbek nearly came face to face with an acquaintance from his *auyl*,[1] who was in the crowd heading towards the platform. In former times, the man had been a regional Party leader; now he might have been working as a trader. He was so preoccupied with his baggage that he didn't notice Ajdarbek, who quickly turned his back to him. God had saved him, for the man was a talkative sort, and hardly a sympathetic character. One glimpse of Ajdarbek, and all of Seŋgirtau would soon be abuzz with the rumour that he was begging in Almaty... Since then, he avoided the train stations, and usually begged for change at bus stations and markets, and in the underground passages.

Ajdarbek also feared being noticed by his children. He could endure humiliation as though on a dung heap, but these apples of his eyes, he felt, shouldn't have to witness his poor condition. He lied to them that he was working as a security guard, and they believed him. Whereas he had long since ceased to feel shame. He was desperate; what was the use of feeling ashamed? Was he begging because everything was going so well for him? Ajdarbek also knew that he was not the only one suffering so, that many people were facing similar personal disaster. If you don't have anything, why shouldn't you ask for help? He was not stealing, or using power to extort what he needed, but receiving alms given voluntarily. Stealing is a sin; giving alms, a blessing. How many people, then, would be blessed when they gave to him? He was thus also blessed. He was pursuing God's path: he was God's employee, collecting taxes on His behalf...

After reaching this conclusion, however, Ajdarbek began to feel uneasy about one thing. He felt guilty before Heaven. 'This is not God's way', he

---

[1] *Auyl* – socio-economic formation considered to constitute the heartland of the nation and a basis for an ethnic and cultural union of the nomadic community. Consisting of 50–70 yurts in the eighteenth century, it developed into its current permanent state of 'rural settlement' (of a minimum of 100 dwellers) when Kazakhs adopted a settled mode of life in the nineteenth and twentieth centuries. *Auyl* can also be used as a synonym for 'native land' and 'homeland', concepts revered by the Kazakhs.

thought. 'It's not honest.' After the doctors had removed the cast from his leg and explained that the bone fractures had converged well – which Ajdarbek could feel was true – he had continued, for three months now, to support himself with the crutches when he left the house. It was true that his leg ached after walking for a very long time, but in general he had no complaints and didn't use his crutches at all when he was at home. But he had become too accustomed to them when he was outside, earning money: the crutches fit his current work description. They were weapons in the defence of his image. These days, people were, in the main, not interested in music, but the crutches evoked pity and mercy.

Ajdarbek was becoming ashamed of his *haram*[2] deception. Nevertheless, not long afterward, he calmed himself: 'My leg was genuinely broken, after all. Nothing is wrong with using the crutches until it heals perfectly...'

He had already heard so many beggars and panhandlers telling lies and speaking nonsense. They had an endless number of ways to justify themselves, every day:

'My house burned down...'

'I just got out of the hospital...'

'I was robbed, so I can't go home... I can't return to my *auyl*...'

They would make such declarations without hesitation or any trace of the lie on their faces. By comparison, Ajdarbek and his crutches were small-time! A person did not tell lies purposefully, though. He had read that in India, among some people, begging was a specialist trade that had been passed on since the time of their ancestors. To earn people's pity, they might even disable their own children on purpose. Oh God, save us from being beggars who pass down beggary from generation to generation!

With these casual thoughts in mind, Ajdarbek was looking down and playing 'Ġaliâbanu' melodically. Suddenly he felt someone staring at him, and raised his head. It was the local police sergeant, a Kazakh man with protruding lips who had something of the appearance of a Dungan.

'So, you've returned', the sergeant said, using the informal, junior 'you' in his address and smiling importantly.

'We should only return to familiar places', Ajdarbek replied.

'Are you making money today?'

'As usual, my income is in the hat!' Ajdarbek pointed at the scattered small change in his upturned hat.

'You people really have fantastic lives!' said the policeman, staring at the money with fireless fisheyes. 'You don't exert yourselves, you don't pay any taxes...'

Ajdarbek kept silent, although he was eager to retort, If you think it's so fantastic, let's swap roles. But what was the use of arguing with anyone in a position of power?

---

[2] *Haram* – 'forbidden' in Islam.

'All right then, continue about your business', said the sergeant. 'I'll be back in the afternoon.'

Ajdarbek sighed. 'I'll be back' – after midday, for there were fewer people around then – actually meant: 'Prepare something to drink'. If he didn't obey, he would get into trouble. The policeman could certainly force him to leave his spot in the pedestrian underpass. This sergeant thus became his 'third child': yet another expense.

The man selling the books opposite Ajdarbek, Šamġon *aġa*,[3] waved at him. 'Ajdarbek', he shouted, sticking his head out of a little window in his stall, 'you must be thirsty – come, have some tea and warm your stomach!'

Ajdarbek counted up his coins and put them in his pocket before heading over to the stall. The Tatar woman serving lunch in the neighbourhood had given him some *samsa*, a savoury pastry, as payment for 'Ġaliâbanu', and he took them to have with his tea.

Šamġon *aġa* was from Oral, in west Kazakhstan. He was seventy years old, and dapper – he shaved daily, looked after himself well and was neat and tidy. He had once worked at one of the publishing houses nearby. Now, he sold books. It seemed that he had done a brisk business that day, as he looked very cheerful. He laid a table on a box in the corner of the stall, which was barely big enough for two people. On one plate, he set out some sliced bread and fresh spring onions; on another, he placed some baked potatoes and two chicken legs.

'Come and sit!' he said, gesturing towards a chair in the corner of the stall as Ajdarbek entered through the tiny doorway. The lights were always on in the underground passage, where one never saw the Sun. Šamġon *aġa* unplugged a tin kettle and poured two cups of tea. Then he reached into the other corner and took out a half-full bottle of vodka.

'A few ounces?' Šamġon *aġa* looked at him enquiringly, but without waiting for a reply, poured the vodka into two glasses anyway. 'Brother, let's toast to our prosperity!'

Ajdarbek had ceased drinking long ago – not on account of his health, but for reasons of economy. He had crossed off 'drink' from the family budget, and could not even remember the last time he had been offered a drink so convivially, as a guest. The thought made him sad, and he drank the firewater in a single gulp.

'How are the kids? Studying hard?' asked Šamġon, biting a spring onion crisply.

'Thank God, they're fine. They are my support now', replied Ajdarbek, reaching for the onions. 'God is merciful. Both of them study well. My son is in his second year, my daughter in the seventh grade.'

---

[3] *Aġa* – respectful form of address to an older man, which can be translated as 'brother', 'uncle'.

'The young will grow; once poor, they will become wealthy', said Šamġon *aġa*, quoting an old saying. 'Think of your children, may they live long; you shall have many good times!' He pushed the plate toward his guest.

After downing the 'few ounces', the pair of them talked cheerfully about a number of different things.

'Many Tatars live in Oral', Šamġon said. 'Maybe that's why, when you play "Ġaliâbanu" and "On the Banks of the Sarman", which I listened to in my childhood, I am delighted to hear them again.'

'I'm sure you made great friends with the Tatar girls!' said Ajdarbek.

'Ah, what *doesn't* happen, when you are young?' replied Šamġon. 'Tatar girls are so attractive... As the poet Ķasym Amanžolov wrote: "The Šaġan River is green / I'm lying proudly on my back."[4] We used to walk a lot with the girls in the moonlight.' Šamġon *aġa* sighed nostalgically. Then he asked: 'Ajdarbek, how old are you?'

'Forty-six.'

'Oh, you are still young! My eldest daughter is a year younger than you! Did you study at the conservatory, or did you learn music yourself?'

'What conservatory!' laughed Ajdarbek. 'I attended a musical college in Semej. My late father was a teacher. I was bad at many subjects, so he bought me a *dombyra*[5] as well as an accordion, to challenge me. It was my father who awakened my interest in music...'

'Well, music is in your genes, then. If you are not gifted in an art, merely studying it will not bring good results... If fate were kind, you would be playing in an orchestra, even giving solo concerts!'

For a few years now, no one had spoken to Ajdarbek in this manner, and Šamġon's kind words touched his soul. He kept silent for a moment, and then said: 'What can one do... no one knows what fate has prepared for you...' He swallowed hard in response to the lump in his throat. 'People say my grandfather was a rich man who was sent to Siberia in the nineteen-twenties, and died there. My own father was a schoolteacher. Then everyone gained freedom and started a business, while here I am, sitting with nothing...' The beggar man's eyes were full of tears; he was on the verge of weeping.

'Now, stop it!' urged Šamġon, looking straight at Ajdarbek. 'The main thing is that we are independent! We are no one's slaves. Think of your children!'

At this moment, Ajdarbek stiffened. 'My fear is that our children mustn't be beggars *or* slaves!' he replied energetically. 'Ah, well, let's get back to our work. Today I must pay the "tax" to the sergeant...'

---

[4] The verses were translated by the National Bureau of Translations from Ķasym Amanžolov's (Kasym Amanzholov) poem 'Oral'. [Ed.]

[5] *Dombyra* – the most popular musical instrument among the Kazakhs, made of wood and stringed with animal's intestines. It can be of different shapes, with 2–4 strings and 8–24 frets, the most typical one being of oval shape, two-stringed and with 12 frets.

The days passed slowly, one by one. After thinking hard, Ajdarbek decided not to use his crutches any more. For one thing, it was uncomfortable to use them for walking, as well as in the bus, where it was also inconvenient; for another, the dishonesty of using them when he was really healthy disturbed him too much. If beggars require uniforms, they must be thought through in different ways – but he could not continue doing what he was doing. He found another way: his clothing. He began carrying a walking stick and wearing dark glasses. He reasoned that the stick could double as a weapon for defence, and the dark glasses protected his eyes from light. If strangers believed he had a visual impairment, so much the better. It worked to his advantage to play the part of the 'blind musician'.

As soon as Ajdarbek got rid of his crutches, his range extended: he began travelling to more populous parts of the city instead of always staying in one place. He had realised that a certain number of people came through the underground passage over time, and those who had already given change to a beggar would not turn their heads towards him again for a long while. Like a shepherd seeking better land for his sheep, he had to change 'pastures' regularly. Now, he went to the market sometimes; played near the bus stations; and even visited mosques and churches. Eventually, he learned that Christians visiting churches were more generous than Muslims coming to or from mosques – perhaps because music and the mosque belonged to very separate spheres. On Orthodox Easter Sunday, Ajdarbek played old Russian songs so skilfully that he earned exceptionally well.

He also learned that the number of beggars had increased over the past few years. There were familiar faces, but also many new panhandlers, palmists and various ķimalaķšy.[6] There were refugees from neighbouring countries, such as Uzbekistan and Tajikistan. Ajdarbek despaired when saw these new groups of beggars and poor people; his strength ebbed. He did not begrudge them the potential decrease in his own earnings because of their presence; he worried about the future of his people.

Ajdarbek returned to the underground passage after ten days, and his 'neighbours' greeted him with dropped jaws: he had no crutches! He carried a handsome walking stick! He had shaved, and his appearance was very neat. He had become a complete stranger; the only constant was his accordion.

'You are very handsome, Ajdarbek!' called Šamġon aġa cheerfully. 'We've been missing your music. Please, play "Ġaliâbanu" again!'

Everyone was very supportive, and requested their favourite tunes. Ajdarbek was thrilled. He hadn't felt himself so alive and cheerful in a long while. As if it were old times, he played his accordion vigorously, and filled the underground passage with different melodies. Deeply engrossed, he would square his shoulders as he played, seemingly as ready to fly as a hawk. His

---

[6] Ķimalaķšy – fortune teller who uses forty-one beans or stones or sheep dung (ķimalaķ means sheep dung in Kazakh) sorted in piles, to predict the future.

long fingers travelled the keys, up and down, such that observers were unable to follow them. His old, brown accordion was in tune that day, and eloquent! Sometimes it would whistle like a swan; at other times, it bawled like a camel calf… He didn't notice anyone in the crowd watching him, didn't even glance at the passers-by. He just played from his soul – and for rather longer than usual.

Everyone seemed to have gotten up with their right foot first on this day: it felt charmed. He was feeling divinely inspired. While playing his music, he suddenly looked in his hat. It was full of change; coins were even scattered on the newspaper spread under it.

Now in his stride, like a racehorse in the final stretch, Ajdarbek turned to waltzes and began playing one of Oginski's *polonaises*. As he was ending the piece, he noticed someone approaching him: a man in a uniform, epaulets and all. He trembled at the thought that it might be the sergeant, but no, the man was a major in the armed forces, a Kazakh of around thirty years old.

'Excuse me, *aġa*, may I speak with you, please?' His voice was soft, but his manner was lively.

'Yes, you may', Ajdarbek replied, arising. 'I'm listening!'

'I've been listening to you for some time. Your performance is perfect!'

'You sound surprised', said Ajdarbek, who meant it modestly. 'But I am not a beginner on this instrument.'

'Yes, your technique is excellent. Where did you study music?'

'I do not have such an extensive education, but I did finish music school; nowadays they call them "colleges".'

The expression on the major's face altered somewhat when he heard this. He drew nearer.

'How wonderful! We are going to form a national ensemble in our military district. Would you like to join us as an accordionist?'

Oh, God! thought Ajdarbek. What is he talking about? Am I dreaming? He couldn't believe what he was hearing, and stood there, startled.

'There are many musicians who have degrees; however, there are few musicians as highly skilled as you are.'

Ajdarbek grew quiet, too emotional now to speak. The major appeared to understand his silence in a different way; looking at the coins in the hat, he said: 'Certainly, we can't offer you a big salary. But we can provide you with accommodation, and your travel within the city would be free…'

Ajdarbek relaxed at last, and realised the major's intention. 'Oh, my brother', he said, 'I'm not counting your money – I'm actually surprised by this unexpected news! It's just that I've been missing the stage, and longing for it!'

The major was that rare military man who conducted himself gently, eschewing a commanding air that might be considered commensurate with his rank. This is no ordinary fellow, thought Ajdarbek, but an angel from the skies! The major did not conceal his delight, and added: 'Then, *aġa*, we are agreed! Tomorrow at eleven in the morning, we are having a meeting. Please do come.' He took out a notebook, jotted down the address on a sheet of paper and handed it to Ajdarbek.

That evening, Ajdarbek left early. On the way, he visited the barber and had his hair cut, his moustache trimmed and his beard rounded. Then he visited a Russian bath. Back home, he took out the suit he had once worn onstage, which he had attempted to sell on several occasions, unsuccessfully. He cleaned and ironed the black trousers and matching black jacket, the white shirt and black bow tie, then polished his black shoes. Like the war veterans putting on their military uniforms on Victory Day, Ajdarbek wore his suit and looked himself over in a neighbour's mirror. He hardly recognised his reflection. As the saying goes: 'Leaves beautify the trees; clothes, the man'. He hadn't looked in a mirror for ages, in fact. He observed that he had grown thin, and that his suit was looser than it had once been. His temples were now greying, too. But he had been a handsome man; he still was.

He was sure that luck would be with him now, that the angel-major had not appeared in vain, that merciful God was helping him.

He had predicted correctly. The committee tested his knowledge of music and asked him to play his accordion. They assessed him unanimously as a highly skilled musician, registered him in the orchestra and handed him a certificate that designated him as a 'musician of a military ensemble'.

That afternoon, many passers-by might have puzzled at the sight of a middle-aged man carrying an accordion along the street, his eyes full of tears. For Ajdarbek, six months of frozen winter ground melted all at once; the tears were washing away the insults, the poverty, the depression, the suppressed indignation. It turns out that happiness and unhappiness are just a breath apart.

Ajdarbek hurried to his children. He longed to tell them the news, to make them happy with it.

He longed to make them proud.

Translated by Mitchell Albert

ASKAR SULEIMENOV
(29.12.1938 – 15.05.1992)

Askar Suleimenov was a modernist writer, literary critic and playwright. He graduated from the Kazakh Pedagogical Institute (now Abaj [Abai] Kazakh National Pedagogical University), where he later also pursued a doctoral degree (grad. 1962). He worked in the editorial office of the *Žuldyz* journal, at Ķazaķfil'm (Kazakhfilm) studios, at the Writers' Union of the Kazakh SSR and at the Äuezov Kazakh State Drama Theatre.

Suleimenov's first literary essay came out in 1961, soon to be followed by 'Tùr turaly birer sôz' (A Few Words about the Form), published in *Žuldyz* in 1963, where he manifested his literary aesthetic principles. His much-debated literary views were first laid down in a collection of essays on literature and art, *Bolmyspen betpe-bet* (Face to Face with the Being, 2001). In prose, Suleimenov challenged the literary stereotypes of social realism and sought to create a literature in modernist form, with content deeply rooted in the national culture. His novels *Besin* (Noon, 1980), *Adasķaķ* (The Wanderer, 1988) and *Besatar* (The Gun, 1996), which revisited historical events from a new perspective, earned him recognition in the literary community. His plays, including dialogue-dramas *Kek* (Revenge, 1980) and *Situaciâlar* (Cases, 1989–94), reflect the modernist tendencies in playwriting. He also wrote film scripts, including *Ķùlager* (Kulager with Bolat Mansurov), *Baânel – Ķozy Kôrpeš Baân Sùlu*, and *Arġymaķtar men adamdar* (Stallions and People). Furthermore, Suleimenov translated plays by Berthold Brecht, Molière, Ernest Hemingway, Tennessee Williams, Mikhail Bulgakov, Said Ahmad and others into Kazakh. He was posthumously awarded the State Prize of the Republic of Kazakhstan for *Situaciâlar* (1996).

The Old Man

'Úkeṇ, Úkeṇ, yes, Úkeṇ, well now, it's that same Úkeṇ, yes, Úkibaj, Úkibaj Omarov, Comrade Omarov...'[1]

Nyǵmet Safin, pleased that he had actually remembered the name of the old man sitting by the door, stretched his numb shoulders with relief. The old man, however, didn't even look at him, but continued to sit motionlessly, staring straight at the floor.

This short old man, as thick-set as a tree stump, had been employed in all manner of positions at the collective farm: he had worked the fields, spent time on the nature reserve and tended the horses. If Comrade Safin's memory wasn't playing tricks, the old man was now seventy-one or seventy-two; he had been retired some two or three years previously and had not been seen by the younger man since then. 'Oh, this wretched job', Nyǵmet said, dressing himself down. 'We are forever scurrying about, either with the farm or other affairs and yet the distance between us and the people only seems to increase.'

The scrawny man, who looked rather like a seasoned *tazy* Kazakh hound, was energetically wiping his brow in a gesture of self-chastisement, while his long fingers emitted a loud crunching sound. Nyǵmet then stretched once more, leaning back as he did so, and looked at the old man again. Omarov was wearing kersey boots; the cotton wadding from his *šapan* coat, tied together with a thick rope, peeked out here and there from tears in the fabric, while the man himself was slumped in the embrace of an old red couch that had seen better days.

On the one hand, Comrade Safin was surprised: this same Úkibaj, whom he had known three, five, ten years before, would have shut anyone up if ever anything had been amiss; he had witnessed on numerous occasions how Úkibaj arrogantly believed he could say whatever he thought without reproach. This was also the case when he had worked as gang foreman and at the stud; many times, Nyǵmet had had to shield him from various important individuals, whom Úkibaj would have otherwise placed in a most awkward situation. However, he had never seen him like this: a god-fearing, meek and mild old-timer.

Nyǵmet recalled times when the old man had not only got into altercations, but had even caused a right hullaballoo. Now, though, it was as if he had taken a vow never to stand up to anyone again. Safin, in part tired from sitting on his hard chair and in part on edge, bothered that he might have missed his lunchtime *šubat* drink of camel's milk, called out to the old man:

---

[1] Úkeṇ and Úke – respectful forms of address originating from the name Úkibaj.

'Well, Ùke.'

The old man didn't stir.

'Well, Ùke, just listen, at least', he said, raising his voice a little more.

The old man didn't stir.

'Oh, Ùke, you're so stubborn', Nyġmet said at last, trying his best to soften his voice, although it was already showing signs of displeasure. Luckily for Safin, the words that burst from his wrinkled throat emitted only distant echoes of his suppressed irritation. The reason for this, and it is worth sugar-coating, was that Comrade Safin had been seriously offended by his visitor's behaviour; some worthless old man had come to his office and sat himself down not so much as one should in the presence of a manager or official, but rather solemnly and importantly in the place of honour, as if visiting a younger son and waiting for the latter to afford him all due distinction and solemnity.

Comrade Safin was about to shout at him, a habit he had developed back in a time that could never be returned, but then he recalled an establishment employee who had come visiting only recently; he had shown him a newspaper article about a local governing authority, entitled 'Strike Them Down'. Nyġmet himself hadn't gone deeply into all the finer details of the story, but what he had understood had held him back. The second reason lay in the whip this stump of a man was holding and which Nyġmet had been eyeing cautiously. They say that even for the holiest of men, discretion is the better part of valour. The old man couldn't be hauled up in front of a collective farm meeting – he had distanced himself from his work there. There was nowhere for him to be excluded from; he was not a part of any organisation and even if he didn't use it on Safin himself, what if the old man were to use this whip to hit the desk behind which he was sitting? To be honest, the possibility of such a thing happening was, of course, nothing more than a minor concern, Nyġmet knew this, but could he really afford to disregard the fact that the party's control committee had been spending the past three days trying to find breaches where there were none and looking in depth into the collective farm's affairs? Could he really, even for an instant, forget, in recent years especially, that any blurted word was likely to be blown out of proportion and spread to all quarters?...

'No, no, Comrade Omarov, you can't do that. I have the greatest respect for you, you know how highly I regard you.' If he were now to cut him off or, heaven forbid, shout at him, then anyone who had their ear to the ground and knew the art of filing complaints might suddenly blow this up into some battle royal and take the matter straight to the district party committee. Although Nyġmet was in his middle-aged prime, he had not achieved official status easily and his career had had occasion to flounder; it was as if he was looking at the desk in Älžanov's office as an outsider, all covered in beautiful green baize, and, hovering there by himself, he scratched his Adam's apple. Pretending to continue scratching, he undid the top button on his brown twill service jacket, then tore off a page from the calendar hanging on the wall. The date was 22 March 1961.

The reverse side of these pages contained heartfelt poems, excerpts from novels or various useful tips. Comrade Safin, however, didn't dwell long on this small scrap of paper that promised to shed light on every worldly mystery; perhaps deciding to enjoy reading it back at home, he placed the page in his chest pocket, among the pages of his savings book, bound in shiny paper. Then, he began painstakingly sorting the reports, statements and letters that had been strewn over the desk, and placed them in the filing cabinet. He took a key from his coat hanging on the rack behind the old man and, accompanying each motion with a rhythmic click, he locked all the drawers in the filing cabinet. He looked over at the old man, who was sitting as before, staring down at the floor.

From time to time, he would scratch his bald pumpkin of a head with the handle of his whip. Nyġmet cleared his throat and then began to cough even more proactively. Then, perhaps in an attempt to suppress what was left of the tickle in his throat or possibly because he had a bout of hiccups, he sang 'Up in the Hills'[2] in a low voice. To be more precise, he didn't sing it, only wanted to. This was because he didn't hear his own voice. Lighting up a thin, reed-like Dzhambul cigarette, Nyġmet stood a little confused and then sat back down on his stool.

However, the fact that Comrade Safin had chosen his words carefully for Ùkibaj and that all these carefully chosen words were wrapped in the softest of intonations, which, if one were to consider it, were uncharacteristic for his own voice and completely lost on Ùkibaj, he did not comprehend either what Nyġmet had already said, or what he had yet to say but was secretly holding back. But in this situation, Nyġmet, likewise, had no reason to be angry at Ùke. This was because this silent, meek behaviour was not a persona the old man had chosen consciously, rather it had befallen him unexpectedly; this condition, the origin of which was a mystery, had enveloped him from the head down and ground down this short, little man by about noon, when he had stumbled here with his bear-like gait and had seen Espaj sitting opposite Comrade Safin.

Espaj was a neighbour of his and also a pensioner and he was able to receive his 15 roubles. However, the cunning Espaj, not satisfied with this sum, had taken to herding the collective farm's hundred head of sheep. Which was why Ùkeṇ was surprised to see him here with his round, cartwheel back: So, where's this chancer's flock and why is he traipsing around these offices? No other thoughts flashed through Ùkibaj's mind. He stopped, not knowing how to gauge the movement in Nyġmet's chin, which resembled that of a horse before a race. At that moment, Comrade Safin had addressed Espaj:

'Well then, are we agreed, aḳsaḳal?'[3]

---

[2] A line from the song 'Tau išinde' by Kazakh poet and composer Săken Sejfullin (Saken Seifullin; 1894-1939).

[3] Aḳsaḳal – traditionally, a well-respected and powerful elder in charge of the community. Nowadays, a reverential form of address to elderly men in general.

Espaj nodded his long neck enthusiastically in agreement. Just the once, but that was enough for Ùke to lose his composure. He failed to notice how Espaj greeted him as he was leaving and even how he himself had sunk down into the red couch. The only thing he said to himself, and then it was under his breath, was 'You're done'. Saying 'You're done', he was carried back to the Terisakkan spring and found himself alongside the red stallion, which was drinking from the water. However, as they say, only the Devil carries no hope; even when he was left alone with Comrade Safin in his office, where the walls were adorned with pictures of heads of sheep (or perhaps they were cows), he never lost hope that he wouldn't hear the words that had been uttered earlier to Espaj.

Deep in these thoughts, the old man began counting the taxes he might not have paid. While he was doing this, sombre thoughts began to seep inside him and then completely overcame him, settling deep within his chest, with its covering as thick as the hair on a young camel. But it turned out that this old workhorse had already paid all his taxes. Hoping that, perhaps, he had some other debts and that this was the reason he had been called to the district office, his stubby fingers fidgeted. Comrade Safin coughed and Ùke looked straight over at him; in so doing, he turned his head so sharply that it looked as if he had wanted to rip it off together with all the thoughts and doubts that had entered it. Until recently, he had evidently been hard of hearing, but now he could hear quite clearly. He began hearing Safin's words even before they had reached him; he captured them at the very moment they emerged from his mouth.

'Yes, Ùke, you have probably heard this already. You need to hand over your red stallion to the collective farm.'

And that was it. He saw Safin's pale lips moving, parting then coming together as if he was eating morsels of meat, and he heard these lips forming words that were then fired in his direction. Only a moment before, when he was gasping for breath and tormented by pain as if he had been slashed with a knife, these words might have burned his insides to the ground. Now, however, when he finally heard them, he instantly forgot all about them. Again, he was transported back to Terisakkan, to the place he had travelled back to just before, at the mercy of his grey pacer. There, he saw Safin plunge his hands into the bulging pockets of his breeches and walk proudly up and down. Then, as if unable to find anywhere else, he stood in front of the only window in the room. Safin's voice then struck Ùke once more:

'Is now the time to be keeping your own horse? A cow and calf, five sheep and no more', he said in Russian.

'So, you're saying we can't keep horses?' Ùke said after a pause, his head drooping so sharply that his beard touched his chest. It couldn't be said that he hadn't heard the question. He had heard and understood it. He also knew that this lad was not one to play a joke. Even if he had, he would not have made a point of calling him into the office to taunt him. He was forced to respond with a question of his own for the simple reason that he had nothing else to say.

Hearing the question, he was going to sit there casually as if it was nothing, but alarm bells rang in his heart.

'Of course', Safin said and, with that, it suddenly became light in the gloomy office. Safin had moved away from the window and was now sitting on his haunches before him.

'Who can't?'

'You, Espaj, me.'

'What about the executive committee?'[4]

'What does the executive committee want your horses for? It has a car.'

'Yes, but I don't have a car.'

'All the same.'

'Why is it all the same?'

'Let's not argue about it, *aksaḳal*, alright?'

'How about you take my cow?'

'Not allowed.'

'Take the calf.'

'*Ôjdôjt.*'[5]

'What, you get the squits from beef, you mean?'

'No, I told you, Ùke. It's not allowed.'

'Why am I not allowed?'

'What aren't you allowed?'

'Why aren't I allowed to keep a horse?'

'What makes you better than anyone else?'

'Not me; it's my horse that's better.'

'*Nuishto?*' – 'So what?' said Safin in his clumsy Russian.

The old man understood the meaning of the individual words *so* and *what* because he had heard them before. However, when Safin, his boxcalf boots squeaking as he walked, had combined the two together, the old man became confused; for him, it would have been the same as a fox and a hound eating from the same bowl and playing together.

'So', the old man said.

'What do you mean by *so*?' Safin said.

'S-soo', the old man said.

'What do you mean by *s-soo*?' Safin said.

'Ah', the old man then said to himself, folding his whip in two and shoving it into the leg of his boot. What this deviant's *so what* actually meant was 'who cares that your horse is better?' Ùke had then been about to explain to this young man that he had been with horses ever since he could remember and that, if he were not allowed to be near horses, he wouldn't touch his food; even the most difficult of days wouldn't seem so pointless if he wasn't able to stroke a horse's mane... He wanted to put all this across in every last detail and with

---

[4] A Soviet authority.

[5] *Ôjdôjt* – an expression of suspicion, doubt, irony.

the same meticulousness that one needs when cutting thin ribbons of leather, but when he saw the look in Safin's eyes he abruptly decided against his sudden idea. He had heard that Safin was suffering from tuberculosis. And perhaps he was. The deviant's eyes were tired and reminded Üke of the desolate eyes of a bitch who has just produced a litter.

Üke had heard that people with this disease could be stubborn and dedicated. They might not have much energy, but they have the tenacity of a gopher; if they bite, they will never let go.

All the old man's hopes he had been summoned because of unpaid taxes, dissipated. Now he had learnt the real reason from Comrade Safin and he understood precisely what this all meant. All the same, to make absolutely sure he'd understood what he'd heard, he had sought possible ways out, but Safin had offered no rescue. The only thing he said was that *s-soo what*?

What he meant by this was 'who cares that your horse is better?'

The old man shoved his *tymak*[6] under his arm and left the office.

The old man left and was surprised at himself. His old body, wizened like an old *ķüryķ*,[7] had become weightless; before, his feet had burned treacherously after only a few steps, but now they were cold; his heart, too, had once been up in his throat, but now it wasn't beating so strongly. What could this all mean? the old man thought, sensing his body growing cold as if he had swallowed a big spoonful of mercury. Only his eyes felt hot. Üke couldn't understand this either.

There wasn't a single day in the year when an *auyl*[8] like Torlan would display any signs of exuberance. On the grey *auyl* road that ran from the mountains, Üke caught sight of a single car and children with school bags, running directly in front of it. When the car drew nearer, the children turned and scattered like rabbits to both sides of the road and the car sped past them. Üke, however, didn't hear a sound. He slapped his hands over his ears and even tried poking his stumpy fingers in them. Apart from the fact that his lungs were full of petrol fumes, he could not have heard either the pattering of the children's feet or the sound of the car. 'Heaven forbid', Üke said and pulled his hat down tightly, raising the earflaps. 'Of course', he said, 'it is easier to die when you know what the illness is.'

---

[6] *Tymak* – fur cap with large ear flaps for a cold season made of lamb, hare, marten, sable, steppe fox and fox leather, the latter being the most esteemed.

[7] *Ķüryķ* – light pole with a rope and a lasso or a loop at the end used for catching horses.

[8] *Auyl* – socio-economic formation considered to constitute the heartland of the nation and a basis for an ethnic and cultural union of the nomadic community. Consisting of 50–70 yurts in the eighteenth century, it developed into its current permanent state of 'rural settlement' (of a minimum of 100 dwellers) when Kazakhs adopted a settled mode of life in the nineteenth and twentieth centuries. *Auyl* can also be used as a synonym for 'native land' and 'homeland', concepts revered by the Kazakhs.

If Üke had opted for the direct route, he would have turned right after the bridge. However, reaching the old post office building, he turned to the left onto a path that ran along the foot of a green hill. He had only just remembered that Žaḳaṇ's[9] wake was being held at six.

Žaḳaṇ, rest his soul, had been his peer, a *tôre*[10] from the neighbouring Ḳùmkent collective farm. The poor soul had been bedridden for three months, not eating or drinking, fading away and finally giving up his soul just the day before. It had all been down to cancer of the oesophagus, which had grown especially vile in Žaḳaṇ's later years.

Üke's head suddenly began to itch furiously and he removed his *tymaḳ*. At that moment, a barely audible hum came to him from up above. The old man took no joy from this and found no astonishment in it either; he had simply forgotten that, only recently, everything that had been classed as noise had been inaccessible to him. Then, despite the fact that the Sun was not particularly bright, Üke shielded his eyes with his *tymaḳ* and looked up at the warm, pale-blue sky until his neck went numb. Although the old man failed to see the silver wings that appeared four or five times a day from the direction of the Betpaḳdala plain, studying the two trails, stretching wilfully across the sky, he concluded that these were indeed evidence of a plane, and he replaced his *tymaḳ*.

He saw wild hawthorn bushes at the top of the hill, their branches dotted with items of clothing; nearby, three or four lads were throwing up lumps of earth. Gravediggers, most likely.

'A sad time', Üke said. 'Those who once rode stirrup to stirrup with me are no longer here. There are some fine men, but Žăke is no longer with us. Who is there now to urge on his stocky roan stallion? Go on now, attack me, you poor beggars, go on! He used to say. Others were alive and kicking but this good man, someone everyone had been able to depend on, had now gone.

'Having dug out clumps of fresh, red earth from the ground, sufficient to load a camel, these young men were now making him a new home. Soon they'd cover him with it. His roan stallion was left without a master and he would leave behind a disconsolate old woman and children.

'The roan stallion no longer had a master, but there was always Nyġmet, who wouldn't leave him uncared for. That Nyġmet had become a real philanthropist with his care home for horses.'

The rain had fallen only the previous evening. The blessed earth had dissolved like ground millet in tea, but it had now begun to dry and return to its normal appearance. It breathed steam, much like a smoker. For a moment, Üke recalled Safin and his thin cigarettes and then, how the day before, he had washed Žaḳsylyḳ's body with two or three other old men. He was surprised that his old calves were still as strong as a bull camel's. He thought about this

---

[9] Žaḳaṇ, Žăke, Žaḳa – reverential terms of address for someone called Žaḳsylyḳ.

[10] *Tôre* – descendant of Genghis Khan, considered to be Kazakh aristocracy.

166

body and how it would now be making its final journey. Oh, the old man said to himself, but today I won't be able to attend the wake. He didn't begin to explain to himself why. He knew his path that day would lead to Terisaķķan. He knew that all the *auyl*'s old men would speak ill of him. They would be surprised he hadn't come and they would have words. But what was there to be done? He only had to think of his red stallion and his crooked legs led him ambling away towards it.

'May Allah have mercy on your soul, Žaķa', Ùke said, walking away from the graveyard. The three or four lads shook the dust from their clothes and stretched their overworked bodies.

Only now did the old man notice that the wild hawthorn bushes, which had never even been marked by the mangiest *auyl* dog, had now blossomed.

The old woman was sitting on the veranda at the front of the house, three small girls around her, and picking at some old wool; the poor thing obviously wanted to make a rope for the red.

'Have you got any *kôže*?'[11] the old man asked and lay down on his old blanket.

'That's right, you just lie there as if you've kept yourself busy all day... Oh, and Žaķsylyķ's son came round again; where have you been idling your time away?'

Despite saying this, the old woman still rose from her seat and brought him his *kôže*. It was corn *kôže*, into which she had added some *ajran*.[12] It was very cold and the old man started coughing.

'When are you going?' the old woman asked.

'Where?'

'To the wake.'

'It's time you called people here for your own wake.'

The girls, who were making mud cakes from the earth, the daughters of Ùke's younger brother, the driver, didn't understand what a wake was. They likewise didn't know why the old couple were giving each other the evil eye.

The three-year-old Raâ, whom he usually praised by calling her his sunshine girl, unlike any other child in the entire district, approached the old man.

'Beard', his sunshine girl said, hanging from Ùke and grabbing his chin. This evidently meant that he had to bite his beard while she would pull it in all directions. Ùke pushed the child away and she fell to the ground, although she did not cry. Ùke's red jenny was munching what was left of last year's alfalfa. It would usually be harnessed, but the old man removed the saddle.

---

[11] *Kôže* – soupy meal made of meat, cereals or pasta; some varieties made with fermented milk may be served cold.

[12] *Ajran* – sour drink made of cow, sheep, or goat milk fermented with lactic bacteria, often thick and used both as food and as a beverage.

'Don't let the foal out', he said to the old woman and, his legs dangling to the sides, he urged the jenny out into the pale-steaming steppe in the direction of Terisaķķan.

It was about fifteen kilometres from the *auyl* to Terisaķķan. Terisaķķan was a natural spring. It was here that his red would be put out to graze after the autumn races and the winter hunting. The Sun was now setting and the horizon near Mount Myņžylķy was glowing crimson like spilt blood. As far as the eye could see, the steppe was covered in a light-purple haze that rose up to the jenny's knees. It seemed as if the old man and his donkey were floating in milk. The lowing of cattle returning from pasture could be heard all around, like the belching of a rabble of lowlifes who have eaten their fill; the old man tied the flaps of his hat tightly under his chin. Once they had left a decent distance between them and the *auyl*, the donkey's initial zeal subsided; having left his whip at home, the old man's only instruments were the bind reins tied at his waist and the end of the buckles on the leg of his boot.

The obstacle hobbling the donkey's progress was not so much its stubbornness as its adorable offspring, a black foal with a white streak on its forelock. The old man, however, had failed to understand this and he lashed the donkey like a bird of prey would with its beak, flaying the skin. By the time the old man had reached the Bazarbaj burial ground, it had become totally dark. At this point, the donkey refused to take another step and suddenly brayed so piercingly and so loudly that it seemed its insides would burst. This enraged voice, which emanated from the very depths of the creature's maternal substance, was akin to a curse.

'Oh, this mortal coil!' the old man muttered, sliding down and sensing goosebumps spread across his body. His remark was directed at the jenny, but he remembered Žaķsylyķ and his now masterless roan stallion. Then, for a long time, Ùke contemplated the pale shadow that had rapidly distanced itself from him. He looked so intently that his eyes hurt; a fear overcame him and it seemed that the darkness was devouring not the donkey, but his red stallion. The old man then turned sharply and ran like a madman, his *šapan* gown flapping as he went.

***

Reaching Terisaķķan, Ùke removed his *tymaķ* and *šapan*, kicked off his kersey boots and waded into the spring, which was as large as a house. His bones creaked as he entered the water; wading out further, his coarse feet rubbed on the sharp stones on the bottom. He stopped shivering, not thinking for a moment that what he was doing was rather odd. He regained his breath.

Where the water was deeper, the silver moon lay face up on the surface, glimmering like a black mirror. Ùke bent over the moon and drank some water. He drank in large gulps and so greedily that he began to choke.

Then, he washed his face, ears and under his arms through his undershirt. He looked over at Mount Ķanžuġan,[13] where the red's father had died. Several trees grew at the peak of the mountain. However, either because the light of the new moon was dim, or because his eyes had lost their previous keenness when the twilight was battling with the pending darkness, he couldn't make out these trees. A peak as round as an egg rose before him, or perhaps it was in his imagination. On that day, covered with a thin, blue-black mist, it was not as impressive as it had been; it seemed as if it had grown melancholy, weighed down by the quiet pensiveness of that silent March night, and, bent double under its burden, it had become shorter.

'The Earth is also like a man', the old man then said. 'The blessed Earth has a body; it rages, it feels anger and, at times, it feels vexed. The peak had heard the bay's neighing when it was a foal and now, perhaps, it had felt the threat hanging over its red offspring.'

Saddened and grasping at anything that might give him solace, and eventually managing to reassure himself, here, alone in these vast expanses of the steppe, illuminated by the moon, he was still unaware that all these bitter attempts at consoling himself at his loss would be only one of his transient spiritual states, which might crumble like bricks made of sand. The old man, who until only recently had come over in a cold sweat before Nyġmet and whose heart was now breaking from inconsolable weeping, recalled how, nine years before, in April, his leopard-like[14] bay stallion had swept unhurriedly over the sandy lower reaches of Kendirli. Whenever this image appeared before him, he would perk up quite considerably. He became even happier when he saw what he thought was his bay stallion in the heated throng of a game of kôkpar,[15] readying itself, neighing, to rush forward at any moment.

'My foal', the old man said. 'My leopard, my foal...'

Once again, tears welled up in his eyes, like that time he had seen the flowers blossoming on the hawthorn bush.

People familiar with the obdurate temper of both the old man and his bay horse, would put on a show of bluster but only to keep up appearances; they would never genuinely try to compete with them. Therefore, the old man would burst forth, dissecting the crowd, only at the start and the middle of the game of kôkpar, so that the audience would remain riveted on the contest; he would save his victory gallop with the carcass for the end of the game, when the žigit[16]

---

[13] Ķanžuġan translates as 'washed in blood'.

[14] The old man compares his stallion to a leopard, a common comparison in Kazakh culture, denoting strength.

[15] Kôkpar – is a sport in which a headless goat carcass is advanced by players on horseback toward the opposing team's goal.

[16] Žigit – generally denoting a 25- to 40-year-old male, the term can also be used as an honorific indicating bravery, endurance, fortitude and being true to one's word.

of the neighbouring collective farm's political department had resorted to all manner of deceptive tricks.

That spring, his house had stood in the foothills of Mount Ķanžuġan. He had been the only person living there. Emerging from the crowd and endeavouring to get home as soon as he could, the old man had taken the direct route and had not loosened the reins until he saw his light roan *tazy* hound, running out to meet him. On that occasion, he had either listened to the breathing of his bay steed, which had not been on top form, or he had looked back at the cavalcade of riders, stretched out behind him. When his house had been very close, the bay horse had kept slowing and had then come to a stop. The old man had not given this much thought, thinking that the dog Aķķoân had probably run across the road ahead. However, when the bay horse had become seriously anxious, it was only then that the old man had looked ahead to see they had reached a broad trench that three tractors had dug the autumn before. There was no chance of turning back. The horse, hesitating a little, had then jumped and nearly reached the opposite side when, at the last moment, rider and mount fell back into the trench in different directions. He remembered hearing his horse's piercing shriek – the cry of his premortal agony.

He also remembered slashing his steed with his big knife when the horse had croaked pitifully in its attempt to get up.

He couldn't remember anything else.

The old woman had handed out the meat from the bay horse to the neighbours, retaining a small piece of *ķarta*.[17] A few days later, she had boiled it, but the old man had not even touched it. It had made him sick as if he had been forced to drink broth made from a relative whom he had driven to certain death. He had been about to kick the low, round stool, giving way to his old habit of not holding back his anger, but then he had seen his old wife, her back turned slightly away from him, wiping her nose on the corner of her scarf.

Üke had been beside himself all summer and autumn that year, right up to early October. Spring had arrived and the dense reeds of the Žamanaj region had captivated the stallions, young and old. The old man had tried to protect his mare from them by keeping her tethered; in his eyes, it had become a bay colour. He had feared that something would not go right and, therefore, had viewed the mare's belly with some doubt. Finally, her finger-thick teats had extended.

'S-soo what', the old man said, looking out at Ķanžuġan. He remembered the district office, the bulging pockets of Safin's breeches and the man himself blocking out the March daylight. This was the first time he had recalled the office, Safin and his pockets since leaving the *auyl*, only now they generated no fear and no anger for him. This was because, at precisely that moment, this vision appeared to him like a melody that he had heard many years before; it

---

[17] *Ķarta* – horse intestines, cleaned, turned inside out and stuffed with horse fat, onion, garlic and black pepper.

was a melody as painful as a judgement, only one that, of course, had been consigned to the past. And why? Had he not heard it that day? Had he not almost suffocated that day from what he had heard? He didn't know. The only thing he did know was this: the main thing in this melody was a judgement. Seeing as he had heard this judgement, he accepted it and believed there was no reason to torment himself over and over. If he had not submitted, it would have been another matter, but although the poor devil didn't agree with Safin's words, he did acknowledge he had to obey them. After all, he had no other way out.

There had been plenty of things in his long life, as long as a sheep's intestines, which he had not agreed to and about the same number of things to which he had had to submit. Every time he had been forced to agree to things, it was as if he'd been forced to swallow sharpened knives and he had grown accustomed to it. Therefore, the old man had not been in the least concerned when the silhouette of Safin's bulging pocket had blocked out his view of the Ķanžuġan mountain peak where his bay stallion had perished. An extreme sorrow stirred once more in the old man's heart and, at that moment, Ķanžuġan, which he had been looking at all that time, suddenly appeared to dissipate like a sweeping mirage, to which the old man, without changing the intonation in his voice, simply said 'S-soo what?' Recently, having considered these two regurgitated words separately and finding it hard to understand them, he had not focused on their threatening meaning. The old man didn't realise that it had not been a mirage that had blotted out Ķanžuġan, rather his own tears that he was shedding here at Terisaķķan; tears that fell one after the other over the bristles of his beard. Therefore, in the impenetrable darkness that was a feature of the July nights, the old man stood cautiously, warily and in total silence, as if his ears had been chopped off, and thought about where this mirage might have come from in the middle of the night.

Then the old man pronounced his 's-soo what' once more, not really thinking about to whom and why he was saying it.

However, Mount Ķanžuġan, which had been the pasture, the cradle and the grave for his leopard-like bay stallion, never did rise up before him.

This old Sozaķ night, thick as a mother mare's first milk, with a fresh half-moon reclining easily, seemed to have swallowed up both Ķanžuġan and the old man's 's-soo what' in the process.

Ùke's throat was dry. He swallowed and tasted his bitter tears. He told himself this was not a mirage, but his own tears. He wiped his tears on the sleeves of his undershirt, yet Ķanžuġan still did not appear. He looked around. The same picture remained: opposite him, a mere stone's throw away, lay a dark, winding path; a little further on, a swaying brush of reeds and, to the left, the distant lights of the *auyl* flashing. The moon lay at his feet. It was then that the old man remembered he was standing in water, only he was unable to move. Grief had stuck him like glue to the bottom of the spring. Oh, but not only had

Ķanžuġan disappeared, but the place where it had stood was no longer there, as if a giant razor had shaved it clean off down to the root.

Now, the old man became genuinely anxious.

The earth that bore both death and life, suddenly fell into a sleepy reverie and fear overcame the old man's body. This fear, without the slightest reverence, had shackled the old man's body with the hands of night in an iron grip. What was this sudden panic? He didn't know. Perhaps it was the spirit of his bay stallion or, perhaps, it was the dense underbrush of reeds that had not fed the bay horse but had grown thicker over the autumn, and which was seeking his sole heir, the red stallion. 'Oh, why should you be looking for the red?' the old man said. 'The bay's time has come and gone, but the red still roams these parts. It is nibbling on goat's beard and dandelion somewhere nearby.'

The old man suddenly began making excuses to the night and the earth, which emitted no noises other than the hungry calling of a curlew and the croaking of the frogs. However, the hand of fear did not release its tight hold. The old man broke out in a sweat. When the cold sweat ran down his spine and began creeping like a centipede across his brow, he heard the neighing of the bay horse. It was exactly like the neighing of his dead steed, abrupt and sporadic; reflecting its playfulness and its character. At first, this sound carried from a long distance away, from the dark sands of Kendirli; then, occasionally breaking up, it could sometimes be barely heard at all. All at once, it burst from right under his feet, from the mirror-like waters of the spring and then carried across the sky, echoing over the land overrun with reeds, and resonating the song of the bay horse that no longer existed, its lost soul, its majesty and courage. The sweat that had come over him before proved to be just light perspiration; now, though, he was completely wet through.

Then, he looked over once again at Ķanžuġan. Again, it could not be seen.

'What on earth is up with it?' the old man said.

His bay horse had previously visited him in his sleep; he had seen it and had woken up, as if from a nightmare. However, he had never heard the horse's voice so clearly in waking life. The fact that its voice had suddenly emerged in this world and on this day, rocketing sonorously up into the air under the cover of darkness that night, as clean as a prayer mat, and spilling all around, when he had been choking from his grief, unable to find a place for it in his heart, sent a feverish shudder through the old man. This shudder struck his body in a single blow like a lash above the knees. At that instant, the bay stallion snorted. The old man's favourite, now gone, snorted just as it had snorted before, impatiently asking for food and flaring its nostrils. This time he heard the sound behind him and much closer. What was more, there was no echo.

A flock of ducks flew directly over his head. When the report of their many wings, akin to the quick fingers of a young *dombyra*[18] player, drawing unfathomable melodies from his instrument, began to fade away, the clinking of fetters could be heard.

'Oh, my precious red, it's you', the old man exclaimed.

Although the red stallion was eight years old and the old man had ridden the creature eight spring months and eight summer months, he had never heard it neighing.

'Just like his father, with the same voice. Oh, my precious, heaven forbid, the same fate should befall you', the old man said, beginning to recite a *surah* from the Qur'an, but then swallowing the continuation. He had forgotten that he had only just been frightened to death. Now, though, his knees were no longer shaking; only his heart chimed and rang as if it had been touched by a red-hot branding iron.

***

Uke came out of the water. He wrapped his legs, numb from the cold, in dirty calico wraps; he could not feel his lower limbs and stamped his feet a little before pulling on his boots. With his *šapan* gown thrown over his shoulders, the old man set out to the Žuǵy Valley, from where the clink of the fetters was coming, continually foundering as he trudged in the untrodden slush.

That night, the world in which the old man found himself was both indifferent and unmoved. It had turned peacefully quiet, like a dreaming child that has yet to know grief. This world knew only itself, its origin, the March damp that roamed the slush and the verdant song. This world was like a woman immediately after giving birth, who has been relieved of her burden, has had her fill of the traditional *ḳalža* broth,[19] and now quietly dozes in a glow of perspiration. This woman-like world was also tired, but this tiredness consisted of the waters of life; the world drank gently, finding serenity. It didn't much care for the red horse that had neighed, seeing the pale shadow at Terisaḳḳan; it didn't much care either that its legs were fettered; it didn't care for the old man and that he was as old as Ḳanžuǵan, apart, of course, from the fact that the latter was a mountain peak; and it didn't care for the profound sadness in the man's soul, as desolate as Ḳanžuǵan itself. The world that night would not pray to another because it was the world at night and it knew that others would pray to it.

---

[18] *Dombyra* – the most popular musical instrument among the Kazakhs, made of wood and stringed with animal's intestines. It can be of different shapes, with 2–4 strings and 8–24 frets, the most typical one being of oval shape, two-stringed and with 12 frets.

[19] *Ḳalža* – traditionally, meat of a fat sheep slaughtered for a woman who has only just given birth; *ḳalža* broth is believed to help regain strength post delivery.

A short while later, the old man caught sight of an islet of reeds. Perhaps because they rose from the oil-black water of the spring, their heads had not yet opened and their stalks appeared light. They were all striving, stretching upwards to the warm sky and the new moon.

The old man walked among the reeds and bowed before the Almighty; the reeds also bowed to the Almighty, but they were growing; the old man, however, was humbled. On his head he wore a discoloured *takiâ* skull-cap, soaked with sweat; on his shoulders was his threadbare *šapan* gown, from which the cotton wadding protruded from the holes; the legs of his trousers hung over the top of his kersey boots. He was walking towards his red stallion which was a mere commodity to Safin, a tick in a box; for the old man, it was the only inspiration and pride that remained in his life. He was walking towards his red horse, that had come to know its strength, its freedom and all the flavours of the sprawling steppe around it through the medium of the shackles that bound it.

As he went, the old man grasped several reeds and pulled; they offered no resistance and snapped crisply. 'You are still young, like babies whose teeth have yet to show', the old man said. He told the reeds that they should never bow down to orders or violence and did so like a mentor, who considers it his duty to warn the shoots that were still growing in strength. In so doing, he overlooked the fact that he, too, much like these young reeds, was yielding and breakable; his own joints had not only stiffened like the gnarled bones from an *asyķ* game of knucklebones but had already begun to wither. Ùke, however, had no opportunity to even think about this. The thing was, he was in a tremendous hurry. With each short step, it was as if he was kicking away every unwanted, superfluous thought that might assail his mind. Emerging from the waters of the spring, the old man noticed that as soon as his head became laden, his legs would become heavier. He feared that his thoughts would continually plague him and he wouldn't be able to make it to the valley of alfalfa, where the red horse was passing the night. However, when he was among the reeds and after he had emerged from them, these cursed thoughts that migrated from no one knew where stuck to Ùke like leeches. In these moments, he was unable to repel this mighty onslaught of leeches and had no choice but to put up with them. Without enthusiasm, but without anger either. His only escape was to flee. He ran, scurrying like a fox cub, and it seemed that the thoughts that had stuck to his head had failed to take a hold on his legs.

The old man was overjoyed to have overcome his thoughts. What is more, he was happy when he sensed a hope that he could rid himself of the lead lump in his chest. He didn't know how exactly to get rid of it, but he sensed he would resolve upon something important and would come to the right decision. With that, he launched into a run once again.

Passing by the stream that had dried up some three or four years earlier, the old man emerged at Žuġy Hill. Stopping, he began reciting an excerpt from a *surah* he had remembered and, in a surprisingly constrained voice, he said, 'Oh, my precious'. Then, from down below in the hollow, he heard the snorting of a horse and the silvery jingling of a chain. These were, without doubt, the fetters of the red, although it was another horse that was snorting – a mare. The old man, whose white shirt had become untucked and now hung down to his knees, first walked, then ran and ended up tumbling head over heels into the hollow. He tumbled because his heart had turned cold. His heart had turned cold because, in May, he had had to get through the shepherds' festival and he had wanted to field his red stallion at the races. Now, though, this slatternly creature had rolled up...

'What the...!'

The red stallion felt no alarm on seeing the black-and-white shadow come tumbling down the slope. He knew who it was. That day, he had been seriously delayed. The red had been waiting a long time. He had been waiting for him because this man would always remove the rattling chains that fettered and so irritated him and would then mount him and ride away without a saddle. The red stallion, presenting its sides to the light tickling of the evening breeze, would launch into a slow trot.

As the black-and-white shadow rolled ever closer, the red stallion neighed and, knowing that this man might remove the shackles from their heavy embrace, whinnied and pawed at the ground. However, the old man didn't look at him. He rushed to drive away the mare with the large croup which the red had encountered just beyond this hollow and which, after that, had fawned over him, never leaving his side. The roan mare, whose undercoat had only now begun to moult, had aroused heated shivers within the red stallion, an unfledged boldness and playfulness that captivated him. On that day, running late and tumbling down the slope to boot, as if he were fleeing a pack of wolves, the old man, muttering and moving in a strange and uncustomary manner, spattered the churlish joy of the red that he had encountered in the twilight. However, the young mare, which had only now found a mate, had no intention of heeding the cries of the old man, who could only threaten her by gesticulating with the flaps of his *šapan* gown. The mare stepped back and hovered a short distance away.

Then, with the words, 'Oh, my God, you won't get one over on this lusty lass', the old man shackled the roan mare in the red's fetters. Then, thinking that this was not enough, he secured its legs with the rope that had been tied around his waist and sat down on his haunches on a nearby hillock. The red stallion, sniffing at the old man and the mare in turns, and finally realising it would not get assistance from one or favour from the other, just stood there in confusion. Were it to leave at that moment, it would be parted from the mare and, if it remained... Well, it had not drunk any water all day and its legs were no longer fettered. The red stallion, as if becoming angry, roused itself, perked up its tail and headed out in the direction of Terisakkan.

The old man paid him no attention. He sat there quite lost, looking as if he had received an almighty clip around the ear. The thing was that having tethered the roan mare with the fetters, he had remembered why he was here.

His red horse had become the subject of dirty dealings. However much he guarded him against the roan mare, his time would come to an end either that day or the next, and this thought pierced his heart like an arrow. The old man failed to see the red stallion gallop away over the hill and he also failed to hear the round Earth shudder as if it was unable to withstand the swinging of a heavy club. He lay on the alfalfa that felt cold from the pre-dawn dew and didn't move a muscle or utter a sound. There was the roan mare, the moon and the sky, obscured in places by light clouds. Of course, there was the night, bewitched by the lonely cry of a curlew. All this, however, lost all significance the moment the old man remembered why he had come.

'Where will I go tomorrow and where will I end up?' the old man said in a voice that squeaked like the sound from a *ķobyz*.[20] I must be out of my mind: here is a lover of the races; he loses all that he values and what is he thinking?! Like hell you'll put him into the races. Oh, what the...!' the old man said and perked up, realising he might be ridiculing himself. 'Yes, you put yourself into the race, or that skinny cow over there. Nyġmet never did take it. Nyġmet never did take it, so put in your grey donkey. Go on, I tell you. What's the matter, you with your head all drooping like an old owl. You can gallop later, your old beard flapping as you go. In any case, that cow won't gallop fast, so don't worry about holding back the reins; you just step to it. You might not last for six laps, but you're sure to come first after one.'

It really did seem to him that he was taking part in a horse race up on a cow and that he could really hear the noise and cries of people beyond the *auyl*, gathered on the plain, all overgrown with sagebrush.

The old man sincerely regretted thinking of this. He was angry at himself for so cruelly belittling himself, but what else had there been left for him to do? It had not been he who had cast the nets; his only fault had been to get caught in them. However, the old man did not have the strength to start delving into the cause of his current state of mind. The only thing he did was to turn over onto one side, as his warm feet had grown numb.

The alfalfa was as cold as ice. The old man lay curled up, his long-unshaven face pressed up against the cold alfalfa. The old man, his chest lashed by spite the size of a mountain, thought that his life, as long as a July day, had already decreased to the handle length of a small mattock; there was now not long for him to wait until the hour that his night-time prayer would arrive, he had been paying for it with the grey hairs in his beard and the depth of his wrinkles; this night-time prayer would take him away from Kendirli, from his grandson Abylaj and from this cool night, serene for humble souls. However, this thought didn't scare the old man. Since his only son Serik had died in the war, fought such a long time ago, he knew that everyone in this celebration known as life

---

[20] *Ķobyz* – ancient Kazakh musical instrument, with a wooden body, two to four strings, and bow made of horse mane. It is the main attribute of the *baķsy* rituals in healing people and is considered sacred.

has their morning, their afternoon and their evening. 'If the world swallowed up a strong, young *žigit* without a second thought, then it is hardly likely to pity anyone else, now is it?' the old man had said back then.

'Yes, my evening prayer is today', the old man now said. 'Tomorrow the night-time prayer will come; tomorrow.'

The old man was not pained that death was on his heels and watching him from behind the branches of the trees and the hollows; he was not pained either that Safin was depriving him of his last true joy. What pained the old man was the way in which he was doing it.

He knew that this year, the farm had failed to meet the meat production plan and this meant the authorities were following their usual practice of doctoring records and making up for the missing hundredweights with a knife to the throat. That said, he was not against what they were doing. He was ready to swear on the vast expanse of sky overhead, on the young mare, who had yet to pass a single drop of milk from her teats.

'The winter was harsh, sheep were lost and that meant we didn't meet the plan. So what that we didn't, I say! Who will reproach you for this or accuse you, you scoundrel?! It's meat you need, right? Well, that's fine. So, take that dappled cow there. Go on, *take it*, I said. It's meat you need, isn't that right, Nyġmet, my dear fellow? Not my horse, not the races, not the whinnying of my red stallion; it's meat you need!!! You'll weigh the meat on the scales, but what about my sorrow, eh, the sorrow that burns this old throat of mine? What scales will you throw that on and what god might show you favour? But your family line won't peter out, will it, Nyġmet? That's why I am angry and not because I am grown old and thinking about death; I tear about and my soul is rent in two, like a hunted fox that has been smoked into a corner. If death doesn't fear me, then why should I be afraid of it? We have served our time and have outlived the prophet by an entire *mùšel*.[21] A man who has reached this age should not fear death but life, for how is this old man here, who is no longer able to keep a steady hold of his whip, supposed to stand up and fight a big fellow like you?' The old man spoke, barely able to hold back tears.

The old man who, prior to that moment, had been unable to restrain himself, felt considerably better for having got this burden off his chest. However, the heartfelt pain that Safin had been aggravating for such a long time did not subside. Moreover, when waiting for his red stallion, who had left to drink from the waters of Terisaķķan, he had involuntarily raked up the fire once more. He blew his nose and untied the roan mare, which had been looking about over at the hill all this time. It transpired that the old man, too, had been shackled, only by his passion for the red stallion; these shackles had now fallen

---

[21] *Mùšel* – life cycle. The Kazakhs believe that life consists of 12-year cycles and the beginning and ending of each *mùšel* is seen as an important landmark in a person's life. Prophet Muhammad lived up to 63 years of age, and for Kazakh men it was considered a considerable age.

away. The old man knew this well which is why, at this time when he felt empty and despondent, he saw himself in the same pitiful state as that ginger cow. And that was why he had released it.

But who would release him; who would loosen his shackles?

He didn't know. He really wanted to know but he didn't. Not only did he not know, but he had no idea who else could possibly have a clue. The old man had never shown anger when he had not had something or had received less than he was due. He had never worried if he was given more, either. He always said that no family ever gets by without having to pay its dues. Today, though, at that moment, seeing the red circling the roan, he realised that he mustn't give away everything. A person might hand over a lot or a little, but he cannot hand over himself because, all others aside, does a person not feel a need for himself?

At that moment, perhaps it was spite or perhaps tears, but something like a hot lash burned the old man's chest as he got up, trying to avoid this beating, and he realised the true value and significance of the red stallion.

Who's the red? Who am I?

Then, driving away the red, he removed the fetters from the roan mare.

He returned to his place and sat down, placing the shackles by his side.

Then, he repeated: 'Who's the red? Who am I?'

After that, the old man was unable to say a word. He had wanted to say plenty more, so as to lift the burden from his heart and rid himself of the lump in his chest, but he could not find the words. It has to be said, though, that the old man didn't really have a need for these unuttered words. This was because these six words, each one of them like a *saķa* bone,[22] encompassed the entire life of this old man who so loved horses.

'Who's the red? Who am I? I could hand myself over for meat. I would, too, but you wouldn't accept that, would you, you son of a bitch. You wouldn't take it, for I would hand myself over otherwise. A horse is the wind; a horse is a spirit that takes control of you, the moment you touch its withers. A spirit, yes. The spirit of the steppe, the steppe itself. If I ran from the steppe and handed over the steppe for meat, wherever would I go?! Oh...' the old man was about to say, but he was unable to finish, for he had become overcome with tears and fell back down to the ground.

He was overcome with overwhelming grief. The sky, dotted with motley clouds, came down like a ton of bricks. It came down and crushed his heart that was out of its mind from spite and tears.

As he lay there, the old man sensed an aggressive strain in this chest. Had this come from the sky? Or had it come from the bay and the red, father and son? He could not see it, only sense it. It threw him to the ground but the indifferent, wrathful earth refused to open its embrace to the old man. It was as if it spoke to him: 'You just lie there and cry as much as you like. Only don't go

---

[22] *Saķa* – a major, weighty *asyķ* (knee bone of a sheep or mountain argali), selected to hit other *asyķs* arranged in a row in the target game *asyķ atu*.

asking me for patronage. I may bring forth patrons, but I am not one of them. All I know is that each person has their own destiny and their own fate. You see, I am not one for subtlety. You want to loaf about there, be my guest, only don't you dare encroach upon the flowering tune and the flowering melody that frolic in my heart. What was it on about? It seemed to be saying, 'Drop dead, clear off.'

***

The old man got up. The shackles lay on the ground, shimmering in the cold. The red stallion neighed. Then it touched its lips on the roan mare's side, nibbling and kissing it while looking indifferently over at the old man.

There was no moon and the curlew could no longer be heard. All that could be heard was the roan mare crunching and chewing on the young clover.

The night was as black now as the burnt base of a cooking pot; it was as indifferent and aloof as a dead body.

The old man tried to make out Ķanžuġan. This time, the peak made no attempt to conceal itself. However, it continued to lose its majestic appearance. It seemed diminished, as if cut back, much like a giant grave that has been bent over and fallen into a deep sleep.

Then, placing a bridle on the red horse, the old man decided not to find a higher spot to help him mount, as was his usual custom, but instead jumped straight up onto its back. Then, hanging the shackles over the saddle in front of him, he set off towards the *auyl*.

The red stallion was well aware of the vagaries that might be concealed on the long-untrodden paths in these parts. It pulled its neck a couple of times and, feeling no resistance from the reins, it turned sharply round and emerged from the undergrowth.

They set off along the path.

The light in the *auyl* had diminished. The night lights would generally flash and glisten, but these appeared to look out coldly and menacingly. Although they could be seen, here and there, from afar, each one of them looked askance, never once blinking.

The red knew that the old man would not let it loose on the way to the *auyl*. If it had tarried only a little, its entire body would have burned from the waves of fiery lashes. Stepping carefully, it then found the path under its hooves and, hearing the old man's customary command it set out, first at a gentle trot and then, with a snort, it galloped ahead... The old man was about to stroke his own head, but his hand touched a bare skull. A bare, wet skull. It appeared that his *taķiâ* skull-cap had blown off.

The rain had been falling for some time, but the old man had failed to notice. He failed to notice it now, too. He had bent down close to the red horse's mane, not because he had wanted to shelter his face from the jets of water that were falling on that moonlit night like slaps of the back of a hand, but because that was his habit.

The old man could hear a refrain. It was either a fragment from a *kùj*[23] melody, a keening lament, or the call of the bay stallion. This refrain could be heard much like the weeping one time of his thin, swarthy grandson, who had left for Almaty to study. What refrain was it?

The old man could smell fresh blood, gushing from a lifeless body. Now, he could only hear the sound of hooves, working the earth and the moment he heard these sounds, he instantly grasped the essence of the decision that had been flashing and then receding in his mind all evening. *Slaughter it!*

'I'll slaughter it!' the old man cried out, for a moment burying the sound of the rain and washing away the sound of the hooves on the dirt.

The old man could hear a refrain. It was either a fragment from a *kùj* melody, a keening lament, or the call of the bay stallion with scorch marks the colour of dropwort. Generally speaking, it was a bloody refrain. But what refrain was it?

But he had nurtured him!

He had wanted to instil boldness in his puny little grandson, put fire in his eyes and teach him to have courage in his soul.

How could anyone be deemed a man if he hasn't galloped at full pelt on a horse?

Could the earth really live without the sound of hooves?

Where now would he gallop, when and on what?

The old man could smell fresh blood, gushing from a lifeless body.

A light struck his eyes. He shuddered, for it turned out he had reached home. The light had come from the headlights of a motorcycle, the bundle of noise that belonged to his younger brother Mùķan. He was fixing something on it, but then came over and took the reins of the horse.

'Where have you been?' the younger brother asked. The old man, however, didn't hear him. He was about to take a swing and launch the shackles at the blinding light that the motorcycle had set on him but, at that moment, the thin, pale-faced old woman came out to meet him. She had covered her head with the top of her gown; the small girls sheltered from the rain by clinging to the hem of her dress and getting under her feet.

'What were you thinking, you miserable wretch, bursting into the *auyl* on horseback like that?'[24] she said, taking the shackles from his hands.

'Bring me a knife', the old man said. He said it not to his younger brother, but to the old woman.

'What did that miserable wretch say?' the old woman asked, turning pale.

'Bring me a knife', the old man said. Getting down from the red, he strode quickly through puddles over to the noisy motorcycle and gave the headlight a

---

[23] *Kùj* – traditional musical piece for folk instruments, usually based on plot.

[24] Bursting into a *auyl* on horseback is associated with bringing bad news.

good kick. The lamp smashed into many pieces, but the bulb remained intact. The old man kicked it again.

Everyone was familiar with the old man's temper. He might have repeated himself one or two times, but if he had ever had to repeat himself a third time, then everyone knew they would surely get an earful. The younger brother brought the knife. The old man cut a lock of hair from the forelock of the red stallion, which was nuzzling up for food; he first licked the lock of hair himself, then moistened it first with his own saliva, then with the red horse's saliva; then he gave it to the old woman. Only now, it seemed, did the thin, pale-faced old woman understand the thoughts going through the old man's head. Shoving the girls away with a shriek, discarding both the shackles and her stick, she tried to wrestle the knife from the old man's hands, saying,

'You wretch, what has the poor stallion done? You'd do better if you slaughtered me. Go on, cut me down, rather than disgrace yourself before Abylaj.'

It had been the same knife that had spilt the blood of the bay horse on that previous occasion.

The old man didn't push her away, but he didn't let go of the knife either. Looking at his little thimble of a wife, peering out from the dark, her pale complexion and her pale shawl which had both turned grey, he spoke through his sobs: 'What am I to do, Răba? Tell me, what am I to do now?'

The rain fell without end. In fact, its bubbling and seething, if anything, intensified. When lightning flashed, the youngest of the three daughters, Raâ, the old man's sunshine girl, unlike any other in the entire district, cried out in fright and finally caught sight of her grandmother, whom she had been about to lose from view. The old woman was standing, holding the old man's hand, as if in greeting. The red stallion stood indifferently to their side. She didn't make out her father, even though he was standing alongside. She didn't see the shackles either, which were hanging over his shoulder.

Translated by Simon Hollingsworth, edited by Simon Geoghegan

ABISH KEKILBAIULY

(6.12.1939 – 11.12.2015)

Abish Kekilbaiuly was a writer, politician and public figure. He graduated from the philological faculty of Kirov Kazakh State University (now Ál-Farabi Kazakh National University) in 1962. He began his career as a journalist (1962–65), before taking up the positions of head of the Records Office for Culture and Inter-Ethnic Relations of the Kazakh SSR (1965–68), managing editor of Ķazaķfil′m (Kazakhfilm) studios (1970–75), head of department of the Central Committee of the Communist Party of the Kazakh SSR (1975–84), Deputy Minister of Culture of the Republic of Kazakhstan (1984–86) and Second Secretary of the Writers' Union of the Kazakh SSR (1986–88). He was also elected deputy and chairman of the Supreme Soviet (1991). On the eve of Kazakh independence, he was State Advisor to the President of the Republic of Kazakhstan (1993–95) and an elected deputy of the Mǎžilis (Mazhilis), the lower house of the Kazakh parliament. He served as the first Secretary of State (1996–2002) and a senator (2002–15).

Kekilbaiuly was widely credited with being one of the leading writers in Kazakhstan. He published over fifty books, including epic historical novels *Ùrker* (Pleiades, 1981) and *Eleņ-alaņ* (At Dawn, 1984), and was awarded the State Prize of the Kazakh SSR (1986). *Aņyzdyņ aķyry* (The End of the Legend, 1971), *Šyņyrau* (The Abyss, 1971), *Hanša-dariâ hikaâsy* (The Story of Hansha-Darya, 1968) and *Kùj* (1967) are regarded as his most prominent works, in which Kekilbaiuly delves into the Kazakh national psychology. He translated a number of works into the Kazakh language, including Guy de Maupassant's *Pierre and Jean* and *A Life*, Shakespeare's *King Lear*, *Romeo and Juliet* and *Coriolanus*, and Michael Frisch's *Don Juan*.

He was a member of the Academy of Social Sciences (2009), a Hero of Labour (2009), and a People's Writer of Kazakhstan (1987), and was awarded a number of Orders, including Otan (1999) as well as Tarlan Award (2003).

Lucky Tortoise Grass

If you are destined to enjoy good fortune, things are sure to go smoothly from the start. In the time it would take his sluggish wife Saķyp to make the tea, the entire *auyl*[1] would have managed to migrate and set up their yurts in a new place. Today, though, the black kettle came to the boil faster than usual. The nimble-footed roan, which by dawn would have always been far from the *auyl*, was today standing by the yurt as if it had been tethered for the night. It gazed pensively at the distant caragana bush by the ravine. Looks like I'm going to meet good fortune today, thought Ķarabala, threading his foot into the stirrup. Then, fiddling with the thin, horse-hair reins, he rued his words: Oh my, what am I thinking? Lest I commit an offence before God for thoughts like this. He recited a prayer to himself, three times over. Then, striking his heels into the roan's sides, he quietly uttered, 'Oh, Allah, save and have mercy on us.'

He had not slept for the past two or three nights. There was nothing worse for him in all the world than having to ask anyone for anything. It would be good if they gave him what he wanted, even if that meant having to make countless requests and belittle himself. But emerging empty-handed from a door, through which you had entered full of hope, is a fate worse than death. Thanks to his black hammer and anvil, he seldom approached others for anything; it was generally they who came to him. He would remain in his blacksmith's shop on the edge of the *auyl* from early morning to late at night. He wouldn't go to feasts and gatherings like the other old men of the *auyl*. He did go to funerals, however. On those occasions, seeing the chatterboxes blathering away about any old thing even here, when the deceased lay on the right side of the house, he would grow angry inside. Today, however, the stay-at-home, taciturn Ķarabala was taking to his horse. He had decided to go, not just anywhere, but straight to the district centre. He had decided to visit the central council offices…

He had been made to go by that bully from the meetings, that windbag from the high podiums, that whinger who had been the first to sign all the collective declarations, the man known to all by the name of Oņbaj. However

---

[1] *Auyl* – socio-economic formation considered to constitute the heartland of the nation and a basis for an ethnic and cultural union of the nomadic community. Consisting of 50–70 yurts in the eighteenth century, it developed into its current permanent state of 'rural settlement' (of a minimum of 100 dwellers) when Kazakhs adopted a settled mode of life in the nineteenth and twentieth centuries. *Auyl* can also be used as a synonym for 'native land' and 'homeland', concepts revered by the Kazakhs.

many chairmen were elected in the *auyl*, Oŋbaj would be the first to defiantly oppose them and grapple with them before anyone else. If ever a loud abusive dispute broke out next to the council offices, you could be sure that Oŋbaj would be at its centre. He was always arguing or showering people and their most distant ancestors with curses and expletives and no one would match him in this regard. He was a dab-hand when it came to swearing and cursing, both in Kazakh and in Russian. Not a year had gone by since an old Korean tailor had moved into the *auyl*, but already by the autumn Oŋbaj was outside his shop, trading curses with him in Korean like a trooper.

Recently, Oŋbaj had sent his son to fetch Ķarabala the blacksmith. Ķarabala had barely crossed Oŋbaj's threshold before he started taking him to task:

'What kind of relatives are you? You don't even take an interest in whether we're still alive or not. You only need me to argue with others and spray them with expletives on your behalf. I've been chained to this bed for six months and I haven't even had so much as a stray dog come round to see me. I no longer have the strength to lean against this bloody, wizened old walking stick. The authorities have to allocate me a car because I'm an invalid, do you know that? So, off you go to the district centre and get it sorted. In this day and age, if you don't go forty times to every official, kissing their feet and singing their praises, you'll never get anything done. I can't go myself because my body has become an accursed burden for me. After all, our grandfathers were suckled by the same mother, and you're not trying to tell me you have no use for me now, eh? What difference will it make if you go a day without bashing your hammer against that sorry anvil? You have to go for me, my *ķirdas*.[2] If you don't do what I ask, then the moment I die and you come round here to mourn with that big nose of yours snivelling and dribbling and whining, "Oh, brother of mine", I'll give you what for with this crutch right over your head!'

Ķarabala's thin whiskers shuddered at the idea of what could possibly be going through his *ķirdas*'s head if he was even dreaming of beating seven bells out of someone even after he had died. On the other hand, he pitied him. There was nothing but skin and bone left on him. He was a close relative, there was no arguing with that. Very close in fact; he couldn't entertain thoughts of requesting his daughter's hand for his son because of their blood relation. Plus, they were of the same age. Oŋbaj had been a hothead from a very early age. He was barely more than fifteen before he got into the habit of mooning about like a baby camel outside the yurts whose owners had adolescent daughters. There was one agile and fair-faced old man who had often chased and thrashed him. Oŋbaj returned from the war, leaving a whole leg behind him, but even with one leg, he still managed to cut a dash from one end of the *auyl* to the next. On top of his own six children, he had fathered a number with the *auyl*'s three or

---

[2] *Ķirdas* – term for people of the same age or contemporaries. In Kazakh culture, relations between *ķirdases* are affectionate, allowing the taking of liberties and undue familiarity, and often accompanied with poking fun at each other.

four widows and they all were remarkably like Oŋbaj with his chest puffed out like a camel. In his childhood, when he got into fights and, on occasion, came off worse, he would get to his feet, brush the dust from his trousers and say, 'All the same, I still haven't lost.'

And indeed, as he claimed, Oŋbaj never lost anything in life either. Until recently, his smallholding had been well-established. This year, however, since the onset of winter, he had not ventured over the threshold, chained as he was to his bed. With age, his old wounds had evidently come back to haunt him. Since Oŋbaj had become bedridden, life at the council offices had become a lot calmer. That said, unaccustomed to keeping his mouth shut, he wasn't going to keep his mouth shut at home. In a word, people came to hear that Oŋbaj had said this, or Oŋbaj had said that. There were those who got irritated by it and grumbled, saying 'What does that one-legged troublemaker want?' or 'When is he finally going to give up the ghost?' while others pitied him: 'Why doesn't the poor old man give it a rest? He'll only end up unloved and shunned by all.' There were plenty who were irritated but very few who felt pity. Accustomed to arguing and quarrelling with everyone, he was now battling with his illnesses; his torments there for all to see, he had grown weak and his strength was slowly ebbing away.

His children had inherited more of their mother's apathetic listlessness than his energy and quick-wittedness. Every last one of them was a reticent, indecisive, timid little creature. His eldest son had worked as a driver, but his car had suddenly been taken away from him. Oŋbaj blew his top: 'It's all because I took to my bed; if I'd been able to get up, I'd have given that miserable official a clip round the ear and told him what for!' He then laid into his son in the most colourful terms, asking him why he had said this and why he hadn't said that. He just mumbled back, barely audibly, 'Alright kôke,[3] stop it already!' The driver-son was then sent off to work as a lamber with some remote flock.

Clearly realising that his timid son would never achieve anything on his own, Ķarabala had been called for. Oŋbaj had always felt sorry for his childhood companion. 'However much you work and sweat, you'll never be a match for Ķali, who just hangs around the *auyl*, playing cards all day. His wife and children tend to the sheep, but he takes all the glory and accolades for himself. I don't know what it is he shows at those exhibitions with that unsightly mug and sagging nose of his, but he goes to them all, be they in Almaty or even Moscow, and always on his own. Every time he comes back, he's laden with rugs and Indian tea. He's the only one who's prepared to listen to all the flattering blathering of all the great and the good there. You, though, hear nothing but the ringing of your anvil and the thudding of your hammer for days on end.'

---

[3] *Kôke* – a respectful form of address to a patron, supporter and protector; it can be applied to both males and females.

This was only the second time in his life that Ķarabala was going to the district centre. Once, in the year the war started, he had been called up along with all the other young men to the enlistment office. There, he was told either that his knees were disjointed or that his ankles were crooked, but the bottom line was that he was deemed unfit for military service. Apart from these two visits, he had also travelled out to remote *auyls* to visit relatives on his wife's side.

Although he had decided to head out on that day, he was plagued with doubt and worry and was not himself. If Oņbaj were to speak about someone, he would never have anything positive to say. So perhaps that was why Ķarabala imagined that the bosses in the council offices he was heading to were each as bad as the other. The first of them, according to Oņbaj, was a complete rogue with a quivering Adam's apple and the eyes of a black borzoi dog. They said he was a sly one who would never show kindness without something in return. The second official was a learned man who classed himself as a noble, blue-blooded descendant of Genghis Khan; even when his own father came to see him, he would make him wait in the reception for a couple of hours. The third, it was said, was a really cunning sort who allegedly abided by all the laws but actually pedantically studied the details of every document he was presented and had thus hidden away plots of government land and property for himself and his family. As they say, he'd wipe anyone's mouth with dry straw instead of giving what one was asking from him. According to Oņbaj, there wasn't a single decent person living in the district centre, apart from the crafty old charwoman, who would never hesitate to serve you a mountain of food and a bottle of vodka for a wink and a rouble. And now, Ķarabala had somehow to persuade these shrewd, miserly operators to allocate Oņbaj the invalid a car. How on earth would he find the strength to overcome these mountainous hurdles and get these people to hand over something they wouldn't be particularly keen to part with? Ķarabala was only persuaded to take to his horse and travel to the district centre because he was afraid his childhood chum would be mortally offended if he were to turn him down. He was afraid he would be accused of caring more for his steed than his *ķirdas* and not wanting it to shed more of its salty sweat than was necessary.

The roan would normally run like the wind when sent out to pasture, but ambled along slowly if ever a rider took to its back, as if wanting to give its master plenty of time to count every last sagebrush along the way. Wherever one looked, there were tortoises, plodding about in the grass, their rear ends raised high. Hearing the sound of approaching hooves, they would freeze and pull their heads under their shells; once the sound had just passed, they would start crawling on their way again, their heads bowed low. A tortoise the size of a frying pan appeared in front of Ķarabala. It had somehow managed to keel over onto its back when emerging from a hollow, its feet now twitching uselessly in the air. Extending its short, wrinkly neck in a strange manner, it was trying with all its might to turn itself back over. A blade of grass was sticking out of its mouth. Its tiny grey eyes, no bigger than a grain of wheat, were staring straight at Ķarabala. This tortoise enchantress, which was God knows how many centuries old, seemed to have been lying in wait to see what this Kazakh astride his horse in his shabby *tymaķ*[4] fur hat was going to do.

Ķarabala was about to lean down from his horse and turn the poor creature over with the handle of his whip, when suddenly he remembered the old superstition that anyone who takes a blade or a clump of grass from a tortoise's mouth in springtime will see his wishes come true. He climbed down from the roan and drew closer. With the word *Bismillah*,[5] he took the grass. It was a single blade, no thicker than a needle. It looked like a stem of wild carrot that grows in sandy soil. He placed it on his palm and then turned the wide-eyed tortoise over onto its front. He got back on his horse, rode off a little and then turned to look back. The tortoise, which people believe has miraculous powers, was edging forward among the trampled and still prostrate sagebrush bushes. Can you believe it? Am I to believe what I'm seeing? This means I am the Creator's favourite slave! What did I do to deserve Allah's kindness?! Ķarabala's heart leapt at the sudden thought. He even forgot the fear deep down that had tormented him only a short time before, when he had thought, Oņbaj will give me a right old drubbing if I return from the district centre empty-handed. He wrapped the blade of grass in a prescription note for some medicine his wife had given him, seeing as he was going to the centre anyway, and placed it in his inside pocket. He didn't even notice how he lashed the croup of his lazy roan with the whip that hung from the long sleeve of his shirt. The lazy horse broke into an idle trot.

'Red gelding! Oh, red ge-e-elding! The *žigit*[6] and his girl went gathering coal...' This song always brightened Ķarabala's spirits and it seemed that even his stiff, black moustache had become softer and fluffier. He would always sing it when he was in a good mood. He had learnt the words to this absurd song from Oņbaj and they would burst out of his mouth of their own accord. At feasts and gatherings, Oņbaj would start by getting into an argument with the person nearest to him for no reason whatsoever. Then, with his sleeves rolled up above his elbows, he would start drinking. No sooner had the full glass touched Oņbaj's thin moustache than it would be placed straight back on the table, empty. After a while, if Oņbaj lost an argument, his eyes would flash maliciously and his jaw muscles would grow tense. If, however, he came out on top, beads of sweat would appear on his brow and he would leap from his seat, leaning on his crutch and, with a wave of his hand holding a full glass of vodka, he would loudly sing his song in a penetrating voice: 'Red gelding!

---

[4] *Tymaķ* – fur cap with large ear flaps for a cold season made of lamb, hare, marten, sable, steppe fox, and fox leather, the latter being the most esteemed.

[5] *Bismillah* – the first word in Qur'an; it means 'In the name of Allah'.

[6] *Žigit* – generally denoting a 25- to 40-year-old male, the term can also be used as an honorific indicating bravery, endurance, fortitude and being true to one's word.

Oh, red ge-e-elding!' The women at the table would laugh. Ķarabala never did understand what this red gelding was and what it had to do with the *žigit* and his girl and who had forced these poor devils to gather coal during peacetime. He certainly had no idea what was so funny about it. Whatever it was, these absurd lines had stuck in his memory and, if Ķarabala was in good spirits, he would immediately start singing this song. But this ditty, which amused everyone who heard it when Oŋbaj sang it in his jovial manner, came across as a dull drawl in Ķarabala's rendition, like the gait of his lazy roan, sending him off to sleep as he rode along. The song had a way of releasing a man from his troubles, like a single bowl of cold *šalap*,[7] downed on a sultry day in July.

Ķarabala's father had been a camel herder who had lived in a lone yurt out in the steppe. Ķarabala had grown up a timid child and always cowered behind his parents' legs at the sight of strangers. Now, he continually looked about him, worried that someone might hear him as he rode the deserted steppe on his own, singing his song, and might spread mocking rumours: 'It turns out we didn't know that Ķarabala could sing so sweetly when there's no one around!' That spring, the feather-grass steppe was deserted. The pale sky overhead had yet to clear itself of the winter clouds. As if realising it was the only four-legged creature on this endless steppe, the lazy roan snorted loudly and frequently. Ķarabala smiled to himself for no apparent reason.

The things he recalled! One time, a smart, business-like secretary from the *auyl* council had torn him from his father's arms, almost by force, and taken him to school. The school was located in an old mosque, where a former mullah taught the children. This small, square, white, limestone building with protrusions at the corners used to be called the *Aķ mešit*, or 'white mosque', but this had been changed to *Aķ mektep*, which means 'white school'. The people, however, never called it white mosque or white school, rather they named it *Aķ škol*.[8] About twenty children from all around congregated in the Aķ škol. The twelve-year-olds Oŋbaj and Ķarabala were the oldest. Oŋbaj was a particularly capable student, while Ķarabala was not up to much. He had no problem in the arithmetic class when he had to count camels, horses, sheep and goats, but when it came to crows on wires, boxes of apples picked in an orchard or the speed of two cyclists riding towards one another from different towns, he became dreadfully confused. But as far as Oŋbaj was concerned, it was as if he had ridden a bike, zealously gathered apples and counted crows from the day he was born. He added when told to add, subtracted when told to subtract, multiplied when told to multiply and divided when told to divide. After the Aķ škol, he studied for seven years in the neighbouring collective farm. Ķarabala, however, didn't even manage to finish the Aķ škol and went no further, remaining as illiterate as the day he began.

---

[7] *Šalap* – a drink, *ajran* (sour drink made of cow, sheep, or goat milk fermented with lactic bacteria) diluted with water.

[8] *Škol* – Kazakh pronunciation of the Russian word *shkola* (school).

189

Oņbaj turned into a handsome *žigit* and would wet his hair into a side parting and don a black suit and white shirt before leaving the house. His hair, combed and moistened with water, his snow-white teeth, his smiling eyes and his leather boots that he polished every day all gleamed like the coat of a lamb, licked clean by its mother. But Ķarabala, with his top button raggedly undone, remained as slow and sluggish as ever. Almost every more or less decent-looking girl in the *auyl* received letters from Oņbaj, written in verse. His pockets were full of handkerchiefs the girls had embroidered for him.

He was incapable of sitting still at meetings and gatherings. His eyes burned like hot coals and his cheeks blazed. Not a meeting went by where he would not make a speech. It was all the same to him if it was a ceremony, a report meeting or a gathering to discuss sheep shearing, haymaking, lambing or the removal of the *kùjek*.[9] The chairman would call his name as soon as the report had been presented. The people would whistle and applaud, and everyone seated in the hall and on the praesidium would cluck their tongues and bob their heads in admiration. Visiting representatives from high-standing institutions, most pleased with the way this spirited young *žigit* instilled hope in his listeners, would shake his hand and slap him on the shoulder.

If it hadn't been for the war, Oņbaj would probably have gone far. Every time Ķarabala thought of this, his heart would ache with pity for the man. He was never envious when he heard compliments made about his *ķirdas*. He thought, who else was there as praiseworthy as Oņbaj, for there was no greater *žigit* among them. Ķarabala, who had hidden behind his father's legs as a small boy, would now never be far from Oņbaj's side. When people admired and praised his *ķirdas*, Ķarabala would grin from ear to ear. Even when the doctors deemed him unfit for military service and he had had to make his farewells with Oņbaj, who stood ashen-faced at the head of a column of soldiers, he had been unable to stop the tears streaming from his eyes. All Oņbaj had been able to do was curl his lips in a crooked smile, shake Ķarabala's hand and remain standing there, looking somewhat confused. All his strength gone, Ķarabala had made it back to the *auyl*. It took a long while for the image of Oņbaj's ashen face and broad forehead[10] to leave him. He felt pity for this *žigit*, as stately as an ivory statue and energetic and capable to boot, setting out to face a shower of bullets. Accustomed since childhood to see Oņbaj as an exceptional lad above everyone else, of all the young men lined up on the square Ķarabala pitied him alone. He felt awkward staying behind in the *auyl* after Oņbaj had gone to meet certain death. He hid away from other people, afraid they might wonder why he was any better than the other lads who were now up to their knees in blood.

---

[9] *Kùjek* – sheep or goat breeding season running from September to November. A felt apron called '*kùjek kiiz*' is placed on breeding rams to prevent them mating too early, which is removed at the *kùjek* season.

[10] Kazakhs believed broad forehead to be a sign of an intelligent man.

For the next four years, he never ventured away from the hot coals of his furnace or his black anvil. Oŋbaj returned a year before the war ended. Only on that day did Ķarabala emerge from his soot-caked smithy into the daylight. He could not hold himself together when he saw his *ķirdas*, lying on a down-filled cushion, a pair of crutches leaning against the wall and a solitary boot, worn down on one side, standing by the door. He sat down, embarrassed, and shook his *ķirdas*'s hand, whose military uniform made him look even bleaker. With one finger, Oŋbaj stroked the end of his handsome moustache and greeted Ķarabala, 'Well, all well with you, is it?' Everyone in the house stirred uneasily, as if his words had actually meant, What could have happened to you, seeing as you stayed behind here in the *auyl*? But Ķarabala paid no attention. He interpreted his *ķirdas*'s knotted brow in his own way. Could it really have been easy for Oŋbaj, once the centre of attention, to return with only one leg? Instead of their previous bold sparkle, his large, cup-like eyes now contained something harsh and severe. No matter who spoke, Oŋbaj would abruptly interrupt them all.

In the autumn of that year, Oŋbaj, who now rode with a solitary leg in the stirrup and his crutches tied to the saddle behind him, was elected *basķarma*, chairman of the collective farm. The one-legged chairman's election was both sudden and unexpected. It seemed that he knew and could see things that others could not. The people who once admired him, now felt resentment. The women who cut the hay, afraid the farm chairman might make a sudden appearance, stopped gathering by the haystacks to look for lice in each other's hair. The old men who worked on the threshing floor stopped filling the hems of each woman's skirt with mounds of grain after the end of prayers as a sign of a good omen. Those who worked in the council offices walked about on tenterhooks. Oŋbaj's collective farm was the first to fulfil its loan plan, too. With Oŋbaj's arrival, even the bachelor's tax plan was fulfilled earlier than anywhere else. Under Oŋbaj, livestock grazed on higher ground that had once stood unused. Under Oŋbaj, they cut the grass where previously only the argali mountain sheep and saiga antelope grazed. Under Oŋbaj, a major irrigation ditch was made to drain water from new fields and barley, millet and wheat were planted. Under Oŋbaj, a red racehorse was bred in the *auyl*, which no horse could beat in the *bájge* races.[11] Under Oŋbaj, money was paid for working days. Under Oŋbaj, the local wall newspaper was published on time. Under Oŋbaj, even Ķarabala came to meetings regularly. This was perhaps because he became a member of the collective farm's management board and, every other day, some minion came to invite him to the council offices. However, despite all this, the rule of the one-legged farm chairman, which had caused a great stir not only in the *auyl* but in the whole district as well, proved to be short-lived.

---

[11] *Bájge* – traditional type of horse race popular in Kazakhstan; the distance can be from six to one hundred kilometres, depending on the type of *bájge*.

Oŋbaj was one of the people who had called for the consolidation of small holdings. However, after the three neighbouring collective farms were amalgamated, it was not Oŋbaj who was elected but the chairman of one of the other farms. Oŋbaj became a mere deputy and these two managers would look askance at each another in the future meetings. They almost began writing letters of complaint about one another higher up the line. In the end, they stopped concealing their mutual animosity and started openly trading hostilities. The chairman was sent to a nearby collective farm and Oŋbaj the deputy was sent to an outlying farmstead. Oŋbaj gave it all up and refused to leave his house. A month later he was invited to the district centre where they offered him a job as a meat packer. He refused, telling them that watching over scales was the last thing he needed. Then they offered him the post of tax collector, but he turned this one down, telling them counting kopecks was the last thing he needed. After that, no one came looking for him any more.

For a considerable time, Oŋbaj waited in hope. He was annoyed, vexed and upset, and he even thought about forwarding a request to the *aksakals*, the respected elders. In the end, he went out looking for work himself. At that time, as luck would have it, a survey expedition arrived in the *auyl*, looking for oil or water or something similar. God knows what they saw in Oŋbaj, but they took him on as a storekeeper. Back then, you name it – the collective farm needed it; there was never enough petrol, tyres or spare parts for trucks and Oŋbaj now had access to all three resources. If Oŋbaj took a liking to an applicant, he would shower them with a savoury word or two in Russian and give them what they needed. If, however, the applicant failed to leave a favourable impression, he would spit and blurt out a choice discourteous remark, telling them to hand over whatever it was they needed to their brainless *bastyk*.[12] Be that as it may, when the drivers and tractor operators were desperate for fuel, it was not to God they would turn, but to Oŋbaj. There was no way the applicants were going to let Oŋbaj's words drop, so they would relate every word he had said to them back to their farm bosses. His words soon spread about the *auyl*: Oŋbaj said this, Oŋbaj said that. People used to say, 'If our man says anything, he always hits the nail on the head' or 'Our one-legged chairman knows what to say'. Now they would say, 'If Oŋbaj speaks, it is only to rub the truth in your face'. Only the supplicants themselves knew how much petrol could be had via the back door for the empty tanks of the farm tractors and trucks, but these same supplicants would always start the rumours and gossip.

What Oŋbaj said about the officials followed them everywhere like a fireball. What could the officials and farm chairmen do? Hearing their drivers diligently relay Oŋbaj's offensive words back to them, they would flare up as if they had swallowed hot embers. They would go red in the face, then turn pale; they would feel annoyed and then threaten, That scoundrel! Well, we'll see! Threaten they did, but there was nothing they could do... The first chairman

---

[12] *Bastyk* – senior official or boss.

was a resentful type and he decided: 'What we need is that bum's healthy leg to get caught in a mantrap.' He bought a whole crate of cognac from the district centre as well as a crate of vodka from the *auyl* shop, slaughtered a plump sheep and invited Oŋbaj's Russian manager to his home, along with a core group from the collective farm. But the manager himself was a cunning one, too. He praised the official's pretty other half and his litter of children, he praised the *ķuyrdaķ*[13] and the *bešbarmaķ*,[14] without even knowing how to eat it, and he praised the seared ram's head with its bulging ears, which had been placed before him.[15] He praised the *ķymyran*,[16] which he declared was not too tart but just right and he praised the *ķymyz*[17] for being just the right sourness. He ensured the strong liquor didn't go ignored or without compliments either. In the middle of the night, having slapped the master of the house on the shoulder, he embraced all the men and women in the assembled company and, with tears of feeling welling up in his eyes, he was barely able to make his farewells and leave his hosts. However, when talk at the feast turned to the storekeeper, the Kazakh Oŋbaj Bisenov, all he did was laugh curtly and cluck his tongue. The chairman then began bad-mouthing the storekeeper with subtle hints, but this only sparked laughter; he recounted some stories about the man's antics, but the manager simply chuckled once more. He then openly spoke out against Oŋbaj, but the manager simply nodded and smiled. Realising that his words hadn't had the slightest impact on his guest, the chairman cussed at him openly in Kazakh, to which the manager just rolled about laughing, embraced him heartily and kissed him, calling him a 'splendid chap'.[18] During the beanfeast, he repeatedly said only one thing about Oŋbaj, articulating the Kazakh in his inimitable Russian pronunciation: 'Oŋbaj Bisenov is a smart man.' This apparently meant that 'rumours from your *auyl* haven't reached ours'. Thus, it proved impossible to deprive Oŋbaj of his cushy little number.

A senior official is a senior official and he has plenty on his plate. The hay needed to be mown, the grain needed to be cut, and the feed needed to be

---

[13] *Ķuyrdaķ* – national dish of fresh meat and offal (lungs, liver, heart and kidneys) fried in fat. It is usually prepared to mark the slaughter of livestock.

[14] *Bešbarmaķ* – national dish, a main meal for guests; traditionally made from a sheep slaughtered for the occasion.

[15] According to the Kazakh tradition, it is customary to present honoured guests with a boiled sheep's head. Prior to boiling, it is thoroughly cleaned; the wool is burned off, the horns and teeth are removed, and the lower jaw and tongue are separated from the rest.

[16] *Ķymyran* – a common name for different variations of sour milk drinks, including fermented cow's or camel's milk, or a mixture of *ajran* and water, or *ķymyz* mixed with cow's milk and water, etc.

[17] *Ķymyz* – beverage of fermented mare's milk highly esteemed for its refreshing qualities; it is the main drink for special occasions.

[18] The term used is *malades*, a derivation of the Russian *molodets*, purposefully using a Kazakh pronunciation of the Russian term.

moved to the silos... In a word, they had to meet the plan and this meant that the trucks and tractors had to operate. This required petrol, tyres and all manner of nuts, bolts and spares. The old scythes, sickles, ploughs or even the hay mowers, harrows and droppers were not what they used to be and they prayed to God that Ķarabala would not fall ill. However much he kicked out and however much he hated Oŋbaj, the chairman had no choice but to approach him with outstretched hands, because Oŋbaj held everything needed for the farm equipment in his hands. It was far from uncertain if even God himself had these requisite capabilities. Oŋbaj knew full well that he could cock a snook without having to suffer the slightest consequence. At the end of the month, quarter or year, he would refuse to speak to the drivers, the foremen, the mechanics or even the engineers. Until the chairman himself came with a pleading expression on his face, Oŋbaj would sit around at home, doing nothing. The dispatch manager would allude to the fact that 'Bisenov knows this only too well'. So, there was no option for the official but to gather all the elder statesmen of the *auyl* and go *en masse* to see him. On these occasions, Oŋbaj would not say a word and simply present, hand over or pour out even more than was needed. If they smiled at him and called him Oŋeke[19] or if they said, You know how it is, he would not only give them fuel and spare parts, but also advice and detailed explanations about where to build enclosures, where to dig wells, where they should mow the hay or where best to put out the horses, camels or sheep to graze. Generous with their words of gratitude, the officials would return satisfied. Their joy, however, would be short-lived. Only when everyone had calmed down at last, with the plan fulfilled, somehow or other, rumours would appear in the *auyl*, such as, If it wasn't for Oŋbaj, we'd be in a right pickle. Now again, they had to grit their teeth and put up with the well-doer, consoling themselves only with the words, Just you wait!

In the end, three or four years after dropping like manna from heaven, the survey expedition went back to where it had come from and many gloated over the fact. They were pleased in the belief that the spiteful Oŋbaj had had his tongue and arms cut from him. Although his arms had indeed been cut from him, Oŋbaj still had his tongue, but the poor man really did have a hard time of it all. Initially, it had been smart officials that were needed, now it was young, energetic ones. Oŋbaj found himself forced to count kopecks, a job he had refused before; then he had to watch over the scales, another job he had earlier turned down. But that was nothing; the one-legged *žigit* who had once turned his nose up at the stench of singed wool was now forced to collect stinking pelts and sheared fleeces. He would stand by the cast iron scales in the cold warehouse building, leaning on his crutches and keeping count by hitting the table with his knuckles. The one thing people had plenty of these days was pelts and skins of various descriptions. And Oŋbaj had the strongest *nasybaj* snuff in his pocket, too. In one corner of the enormous warehouse, half shrouded in

---

[19] Oŋeke – reverential form of address to someone called Oŋbaj.

darkness, white, red and maroon bottles could be found, their bottoms forced into the damp earth.

There was plenty of rumour and hearsay going around behind Oŋbaj's back. There were many visitors who popped into Oŋbaj's warehouse and word got out that the one-legged man could barely make it home of an evening; he would frequent places where people congregate and emerge, swaying to and fro. He couldn't restrain his behaviour either. The man once revered as a talented speaker was now referred to as an acid-tongue, a hothead and a bickerer. At one time, people had been drawn to him but now they avoided him. Poor Oŋbaj would walk alone along the broad street, waving his crutch around in front of him, screaming and wailing all manner of absurdity.

On these walks, he would be sure to turn towards Ķarabala's house. Throwing both crutches in different directions at the door and jumping along on one leg, he would make his way to the *tôr*,[20] where he would topple to his side and prop himself up with a cushion. Saķyp would do her best to curry favour with Oŋbaj, laying out the best *kôrpe* blanket[21] and offering the best cushion in the house. Stretched out on the *tôr* seat, Oŋbaj would eat fatty *ķuyrdaķ*, drink tea and take a hair of the dog from a half-litre bottle that the lady of the house had brought out from the *kebeže* chest.[22] He would pour some out for Ķarabala too. Ķarabala was never one for strong liquor. He would only have to down a small shot from a table glass and he would instantly start giggling for no apparent reason. If he were talked into having any more, his head would drop to his chest and he would start snoring. Oŋbaj had no wish to lose the one pair of ears that actually listened to him, so he would pour his *ķirdas* just the one glass, Ķarabala would begin to laugh in fits and starts, while Oŋbaj would continue drinking alone, talking to himself.

He looked into his *ķirdas*'s face, as if seeing him for the first time and announced, 'Oh, *ojbaj-aj*,[23] you really are so unfortunate! Oh, so unfortunate! Why can't your broad forehead shine with success, for it would make a fine guiding light for the farm's flock. You have the strength and you look no worse than anyone else. Your portrait would grace any newspaper, with its whopping great nose, handsome whiskers and round mug. Instead of showing off the likes of you as *our star*, they choose people like Ķali – unsightly, little beggars who have seen better days, like pieces of meat gnawed down to the bone. It turns out that fortune has no sense of fairness; one person gets lucky while another doesn't. Happiness is nothing but a one-eyed giant. He doesn't know

---

[20] *Tôr* – honourable place located opposite the entrance at the back of a yurt or a room, reserved for guests or for the oldest man in the family.

[21] *Kôrpe* – traditional quilted blanket, with one side decorated with a patchwork of multicoloured pieces of fabric.

[22] *Kebeže* – traditional wooden chest for storing produce and crockery or a box for carrying bales on a camel.

[23] *Ojbaj-aj* – exclamation of indignation.

whom he is carrying on his shoulders until he sees him with his solitary eye. But the moment he does, he throws him off, lifts him up by the scruff of his neck and tosses him aside! It probably won't be long until we see these Ḳalis and their like flying head over heels!' Saying this, he tipped the contents of his glass into his mouth.

It seemed that neither vodka nor bitter onion, neither fatty ḳuyrdaḳ nor thick, milky pekoe tea could douse the fire that raged inside him. He would only finally quieten down once he had got it all out of his system. Oṇbaj brought a piece of bitter onion to his nose. He sat there for a while and then suddenly cried out, 'Oh, my! If it was back in the old days, I would have helped you go far. Oi, my old ḳirdas, who'd have ever doubted it?'

Saḳyp was pouring the tea but even she shuddered with a start and listened in. 'Hey, what can I say? I only have myself to blame', said Oṇbaj after a while, using all his strength to lift the cushion from under his elbow, as if taking something out on it. 'When they amalgamated the collective farms, it turns out they wanted me to be the chairman. Instead of keeping quiet, I chose that time to give the secretary a hard time. I was complaining about the excessive paperwork at a district meeting and I failed to notice that I was poking the first secretary's eye with my stick, so to speak. From that time on, the management looked askance at me. I could never seem to find common ground with them, just as soured milk cannot ferment into ajran[24] the second time round. Why on earth was I so ambitious back then?! Now you can't be too modest or too ambitious, too crafty or too smart. Perhaps too much wealth will do you no harm, but being too smart certainly will and you can put paid to your own happiness. What God gives us will do, it's fine. What He gives us and then takes back, that's fine too. The worst thing, though, is when God promises to give you something and then changes His mind. That is something you'll never forget until your dying day. That's how it is, my ḳirdas.'

Looking enquiringly across at Ḳarabala, Oṇbaj sloshed himself another glass from the bottle. Then, having downed the contents, he tossed it to one side and, leaning on his old ḳirdas's shoulder, jumped up onto his one leg from where he was sitting. Saḳyp instantly picked up the crutches that were lying by the doorway and shoved them under his arms. Oṇbaj began to sing at the top of his voice. First, he sang an obligatory, sad and heart-wrenching Russian song. Although his small audience did not understand the words, they were still touched profoundly by the song. The more Oṇbaj sang, the more animated he became. His placid, shaggy moustache, flat around his mouth, suddenly jumped to attention. A flame flickered and sprang to life in his once bleary, melancholy eyes. His thin lips, only recently burned by the vodka, began to turn brown, like wind-dried jerky. Oṇbaj straightened his shoulders and puffed out his chest, as if he were standing on his own two legs and not resting on crutches. When the

---

[24] Ajran – sour drink made of cow, sheep, or goat milk fermented with lactic bacteria, often thick and used both as food and as a beverage.

Russian song was followed by a bewitching Kazakh number, the kind-hearted Saķyp felt tears welling up. Ķarabala's eyes were also moist. Oŋbaj became even more passionate when he saw the effect his singing was having on these simple souls. The pure tears in the eyes of these simple-hearted folk had the effect of a refreshing breeze on Oŋbaj, cleansing his soul of his smouldering regrets and the bitter vodka that burned his throat. Placing his hands on their shoulders, he said, 'Oh, my poor things! I'm the only man in our entire clan of ten families or so, who has even a modicum of intelligence. God forbid anything should ever happen to me; who would step in to protect you all?'

Ķarabala became even more upset and began to weep bitterly. He felt a lump in his throat and blubbed like a child, 'You are a pillar of support for me!' He spoke sincerely, sorrowfully and with feeling, reflecting the true grief he now felt. Having opened this old wound, and taking large strides with his crutches thudding against the floor, Oŋbaj left the house. The thud of the crutches could be heard for some time beyond the window of the squat little house attached to the smithy, as if someone were driving nails into the hard, black earth out there.

That night, Ķarabala was unable to close his eyes. This great hulk of a man, who in life doggedly ignored his numerous hardships, was certainly not one to be troubled by trifles. Thank God, he never had time to get bored. Thank God, Saķyp who may have been lethargic and sluggish, had never openly opposed him. She had given him a son and a daughter. Their son had married and now lived in his own home, working as a horse breeder. Their daughter had been married and lived in the neighbouring *auyl*. They lived decent lives. If people said, Ķarabala, do this, he'd do it. If people said, Ķarabala, go there, he'd go. Thank God no one had yet ever rebuked him for doing anything wrong. Perhaps this was the reason, but he was seldom ever troubled about his work. Only on the odd occasion when Oŋbaj came round did the *auyl* blacksmith think that the world beneath his feet might suddenly vanish. The many things he didn't understand began to pump fear into his submissive heart. He could not understand why things were going so badly for his *ķirdas*, whom he revered like a god. Judging from what Oŋbaj said all the time, there was clearly a place in life for squabbling and scheming, he thought. There didn't appear to be anyone in the *auyl* who could call him a *kaffir*.[25] Everyone was the same as everyone else; they were simple folk. And yet, he saw how Oŋbaj was living his life.

Perhaps life was indeed not what Ķarabala knew, which meant that there was more to life than a crooked anvil and a black hammer. Probably not everything you encounter in life may be of use to others, just as not everything they themselves encounter may be of use to them. If this were not the case, would Oŋbaj really have been in such a state? Perhaps it all came down to that

---

[25] *Kaffir* – non-believer or infidel in Islam; in Kazakh colloquial speech also a synonym for dishonest, ignominious or cruel.

stray lead bullet from that Hitler bastard. The father of that Hitler really had a lot to answer for. It was as if that bullet had not only blown off his *ķirdas*'s leg, but cut the wings from his soul and all the hope that they carried. Otherwise, Oŋbaj, who was a cut above the rest in terms of gumption and ability, would never have cut short his education on his return. Who knows where he'd have ended up or who he'd have become? That stray bullet had wounded him and this sultan among *žigit*, the best of the best, had ended up living alongside docile, timid and submissive people like Ķarabala. Now his old *ķirdas* didn't know what to do with himself. Ķarabala would come over all hot under the collar whenever he started thinking about this.

As for himself, he had reached a ripe old age by wearing whatever he could lay his hands on and consuming whatever he had been destined to eat, and it had never really bothered him. His father, too, had never really racked his brains over what to do when this son of his had been born. He had never opened any sacred book on the matter and never cried out an *azan*[26] when giving him his name. He had been born a swarthy looking *bala* and so that is what they called him: Ķarabala.[27] And yet, even though Ķarabala had now become an old man, no one in the *auyl* addressed him reverentially as Ķareke. The people said simply that 'Ķarabala did that', 'Ķarabala made that' or 'You should get Ķarabala to do that'. If at times someone came to see him from another *auyl* and addressed him as Ķareke, he would instantly come over in an uncomfortable cold sweat. He would never take the *tôr* seat at feasts or gatherings, but sit somewhere near the entrance, resting on his elbow without ever receiving any reverential treatment. Surely, everything has its significance and purpose? Who, for example, would think of making a ploughshare from old tin or a spittoon out of stainless steel? He now constantly saw Oŋbaj's present condition as precisely such an incongruity.

Sometimes he would think how unfair God could be, but he would instantly come to his senses and say *tăuba, tăuba!*[28] to himself, asking forgiveness for his sin. He could hardly believe that it had been he, this lowly little craftsman, who had plucked the thin blade of grass from the tortoise's mouth, as if there weren't another more worthy human being on this earth. It had been he, the one who had barely managed to get through three years in school and who had barely enough brains to write the first four letters of his father's name, tailing off with a dash of sorts, instead of a signature when receiving his salary. Such good fortune never falls into the hands of just anyone. But it would have been better if someone canny and quick-witted like Oŋbaj had chanced upon the lucky grass. If Oŋbaj had been the one to find the magical grass, perhaps he

---

[26] *Azan* – the muezzin's call to prayer.

[27] *Bala* – boy or child, *Ķara* – 'black' or 'swarthy', making Ķarabala – 'a swarthy boy'.

[28] *Tăuba* – penance for forgiveness of one's sins, in this case referring to the sin of blasphemy.

would have spread his wings and flown, like back in those fiery years of his youth.

He had been a young, eminent and handsome *žigit*, whose face would have been etched in the minds of those who had seen him even just once and whose stature would have remained in the memory of all who had heard of him. Perhaps, instead of just the neighbouring collective farm, he might have gone on to study in the next district or another region, or even Almaty or perhaps even Moscow? Surely, he would now be sitting importantly, a scholar with a broad, gleaming forehead, in one of those big scientific institutions! Perhaps he would have arranged for all the lads with at least some ties to this *auyl* to be accepted to study there. Everyone in the *auyl* who fell ill or had some business in town would have stayed at his house. Oŋbaj could even have become a big cheese, like the characters you only ever hear on the radio or see in the pictures. It was he who would have been able to change the course of a great river to be turned in the direction of this place, to the land of his ancestors and, having done so, this barren land would not have been quite so useless and there would be so much more than just camels wallowing in the dust. If that had been the case, Ķarabala would have told his childhood chum: 'Hey, don't forget your *ķirdases*, you haughty old dog. We, too, deserve to get something out of this, seeing as you have the power of the law in your hand. My son Ķuatbek is a horse breeder, and a pretty good one at that. He has red and blue pieces of paper[29] burning a hole in his pocket. He takes right after me, for he is just as indecisive, but he wants to buy a car. However, it turns out you have to wait in line twelve months to get one. Not only that, but they say in addition to having money, you also need friends in high places. In short, there's plenty to keep us busy. No matter what we do, you yourself know that this affair is beyond me and my son alone. Be a sport and give us a hand, would you? Our little Žaŋyl, who I think you once saw sitting on her potty, is now married with children. However, she doesn't have a decent house like other folks. Can you help her out? The other *auyl*s are all alike. In our *auyl*, though, a huge number of shacks have sprung up with windows that look like black burrow holes. Just bear that in mind, alright? Bounty is as accessible to us as the peaks of the snow-covered Ķaratau. Come on, all you need to do is pick up the phone.'

These were nothing but dreams. As it was, Ķarabala the blacksmith wasn't doing that badly and worse off than others. In any case, if Oŋbaj were to become a big cheese, Ķarabala would do very nicely as a result. Ķarabala would have been more than happy even if Oŋbaj were to ask the people he met, 'Ķarabala the blacksmith was my *ķirdas*. Is he still with us?' And he didn't want his old friend to be all annoyed and unpleasant either.

When he thought about this, he pictured Oŋbaj as he had seen him three days previously, all skin and bone. His face, which had once been a bright, wheaten colour, was now pale and wrinkled. His arched brows had now thinned, the

---

[29] Soviet roubles.

199

hairs sticking out in all directions. His eye sockets were now so sunken they could have housed glass bottles. In short, he had a baleful appearance. Only his spiteful, toxic tongue reminded everyone that this skeleton-thin man, sitting wrapped in an old blanket, was the Oŋbaj of old.

Ķarabala struck the roan with his heels. Luck had to be on his side on this day. There had to be a reason why he had stumbled upon the tortoise grass. Who knows, but if poor, crippled Oŋbaj could see his wish come true, perhaps he might be able to pick himself up again.

He reached the district centre by about noon. By asking around, he found the office where Oŋbaj had told him to start. A fidgety woman sitting in the reception room poked her head through the door of the official's office and spoke to him at length. The official indicated that Ķarabala should go in. Sitting impassively at the head of a pine table, with a coat around his shoulders, was a broad, hefty, swarthy man with a dry, sinewy face. He asked how things were, flashing a white metal tooth. While listening to Ķarabala, the official rummaged around in a wire urn, retrieved a paper bag and spat into it. Ķarabala was just about to finish relating his business when the metal-toothed official jerked his head sharply to one side, as if intending to unscrew and tear his long neck from its body, and pensively ran his fingers twice from his chin to his forehead and back again. Then he smirked, baring his metal tooth. Ķarabala sat there and thought, Just as people said, he really does look like a frisky hound, standing guard over a trap.

'I know, my good man', began the sinewy face. 'We are talking about that troublemaker Bisenov, right? I have his letter here, in which he's bad-mouthed every last one of us, from our distant grandfathers and great-grandfathers seven generations back as well as every one of our seventy-seven foremothers. He deserves to suffer a little more just for that alone. However, seeing as you've come... We have received the paperwork granting him a car, but the decision to release it in the middle of the year is down to the head of another department. If they give the all-clear, we are ready to go. You have a kind face, nothing like that quarrelsome old goat; you should pop into that department I told you about.' He looked askance at Ķarabala, as if gauging how his decision had been received.

Ķarabala rose awkwardly from his seat.

'Did Üšķyn make it through the winter alright? How did the lambing go?' asked the sinewy face.

'Not bad, praise be to Allah.' Ķarabala had seen this man with the sinewy face and long neck somewhere before. Closing the door behind him, he looked back once more but couldn't place him.

The second office he visited had many more people than the first. Chairs were lined up on both sides of a long room and they were all occupied. Most of the people held bulky files on their laps, unlike Ķarabala, who had come empty-handed. It looked like this official was running late, because a bright-faced young woman was continually answering the ringing telephone, saying, 'No, he's not here yet. There are a lot of people here to see him.'

Every time she turned to answer the phone, she cast a sideways glance at the reception area. The young men sat ceremoniously with their bulky files and looked at the young secretary in anticipation. A short while later, the official appeared in the doorway. He was a slim, sleek, swarthy *žigit* with a stern look in his eyes and sharp cheekbones that gleamed like knife blades. He strode in importantly, as if he were corpulent and barely able to carry his own weight. Not deigning to glance at anyone, he glided through to the *tôr*, behind a door padded with black imitation leather. Opening the door, he would address his secretary. While he was talking to her, his gaze fell on Ķarabala, who was sitting on a chair by the entrance. He raised his thick brows and for a moment looked surprised. Then his gaze warmed a little and he nodded in the old man's direction. 'I hope you are well, my good man', Ķarabala spoke affectionately, scraping the chair beneath him.

He may have said the appropriate words, but he blushed deep crimson; everyone else turned to look at him. The official went back into his office. Shortly thereafter, he rang his bell and the secretary opened the door to his office. Turning around, she turned to Ķarabala and said, '*Aķsaķal*, please step inside.' Ķarabala got up, cast bashful glances at the other people in the room, as if asking their forgiveness, and headed into the office.

It was a large room, full of gleaming furniture; there was more than enough room for a horse to gallop through, as they say. The agile, swarthy, hawk-faced *žigit* jumped up from behind his large desk and rushed over to greet Ķarabala, taking his hand. He led him over to a small, narrow table in front of his large desk and sat him down in one of the armchairs to the side. Ķarabala had never sat on anything other than a hard stool before and he sank fearfully into the deep seat. He removed his fur hat from his sweaty head and cast it onto the small table before him.

The swarthy *žigit* with the hawkish appearance sat in silence, listening to his visitor. He made a note on the paper that lay in front of him. After the old man had finished talking, the official pressed his buzzer and the secretary appeared from behind the door.

'Connect me first with Esenķùlov and then with Žùzbaev.'

'Right away.'

No sooner had the secretary closed the door behind her than the telephone rang. The swarthy boss reached for the receiver. 'Hello. Ah, I see... Then make a start on the paperwork. We'll think of something. Very good.'

The thin, swarthy *žigit*, his skin drawn tightly over his cheekbones, spoke clearly. He had hardly managed to replace the receiver when the telephone rang once again.

'Ah, yes. Hello... Those three cars are still there? That's good. We'll give one of them to a disabled man. A directive, you say... We'll see. We'll see the best workers won't go empty-handed, don't you worry.'

It turned out that the man at the other end of the line was the talkative sort and wrinkles appeared and flashed on the swarthy man's forehead.

'The boss isn't there yet. I'll tell them myself when it arrives. Tell them I've given the order.'

The official's face looked grim. He was obviously accustomed to getting his own way. He rapped his fist quietly on the desk from time to time. Ķarabala enjoyed watching the ashtray with its white-tipped cigarette butt jump with each thump. The swarthy *žigit*'s open, no-nonsense and authoritative tone was probably what Oŋbaj would have described as 'rectitude'. Even the ashtray was frightened of him. Having finished his discussions, the official turned to Ķarabala.

'*Aķsaķal*, go back to the office you visited earlier and collect your papers. Then go and see comrade Žùzbaev. He'll sort you out. Do you have anything you want to ask?'

'No, my good man. Thank you very, very much. All the very best to you.'

'And thank you, too. Last year, you successfully dealt with an important assignment. I was entrusted with heading the erection of a monument to our war veterans. If it wasn't for your help, we would have brought shame on ourselves.'

Only now did it dawn on Ķarabala. Last year the Party organiser had been constantly on his case and hadn't given him any rest until Ķarabala had constructed some glittering piece of metalwork. He had probably been talking about this. The swarthy official rose to shake his hand goodbye.

Žùzbaev was the trade boss. Ķarabala reckoned that only shrewd operators, capable of jumping through the eye of a needle, worked in trade. This one was a self-important camel of a man, with flared nostrils and curly hair. When he spoke, he would forever move his stump of a hand, which had been shot off by a bullet, back and forth across the table.

'Right then, *aķsaķal*, this car is for you personally, is it?'

'No, no. I have a disabled relative. It is he who sent me.'

'Well I never! So, you've just been at the chairman's office?'

'Yes, that's right.'

'We haven't yet received the quota of cars for the disabled this year. Although admittedly, there are three cars standing at the depot. The office of the regional Party committee passed a decision that they would be given to those who got the greatest yield from their ewes and we were ordered not to touch them until then. Now, you see, they say one has to be given to a disabled person. The first secretary will be coming tomorrow and will give me an earful. Of course, that's not your fault. But what's to be done?'

'I don't know, but those chaps said it was possible.'

'Of course, we have to do some good. But then we have to observe the word of the law as well. You have to respect the law, don't you? So, what's to be done?'

'If it's against the law…'

'No... no. This is no fault of yours.'

'So... What's to be done?'

Žùzbaev found himself in a difficult situation. Having rummaged through everything on his desk, he moved to the drawers, where he found a printed sheet of paper. Donning spectacles as large as a yurt's *šaṇyraḳ*,[30] he started reading it. Then he struck the desk with an unsightly, fat finger.

'It turns out it isn't against the law. But the office has come to a decision... So, you're from Üšḳyn?'

'Yes.'

'You herd livestock?'

'I'm a blacksmith.'

'Ah, right. What is your name?'

'Ḳarabala.'

'How long have you been working as a blacksmith?'

'I was born there. I have worked at the smithy since childhood.'

'Do you remember the famine of fifty-three?'

'Of course.'

'Do you remember one March when a large number of vehicles got stuck in the frost on the hill on the approaches to your *auyl*?'

'Too right, I do. I remember it like it was yesterday! They were stuck there until the frozen earth thawed, if I remember correctly. Most of them had broken drive shafts and I was kept busy with work for a whole month.'

'Well I never! I heard there was a blacksmith in Üšḳyn with hands of gold. So, it was you.' Ḳarabala blushed. Žùzbaev, noticing his embarrassment, also felt somewhat awkward.

'I was there in all that turmoil. We unloaded everything off the truck, gathered camels from your *auyl*, packed them up and ferried feed to the next collective farm where the sheep were dropping like flies.'

'Hey, so you must be the man from the district executive committee! Comrade Žùzbaev.'

'Yes, I did work at the district executive committee.'

Both fell silent. Only then did Ḳarabala recall that restless, swarthy man. The winter had been harsh that year. The spring was just about to arrive but there had been a sudden snowstorm. The livestock, weak from the winter, had begun to drop. Everyone in the *auyl* had been saying that comrade Žùzbaev himself would come, bringing feed for the livestock and provisions for the residents. One day, a roaring and a rumbling could be heard from the black ridge in the west. Up on the bare hill, where there was no shelter or cover of any kind, a large column of vehicles had got stuck in the snow. Žùzbaev, who headed the convoy, instructed comrade Oṇbaj to gather together all the horse-drawn transport he could muster. They went round every house, looking for pack-

---

[30] *Šaṇyraḳ* – upper dome of the yurt; in this context used to indicate the ridiculously big size of the spectacles.

saddles. For two days, Žùzbaev scampered back and forth on his skewbald horse between the ridge and the *auyl*. He knew no rest and gave the villagers no peace either. Putting on some homespun, patchwork gown, tied around the waist with a hair rope, he tirelessly helped saddle up the cargo. Then, seated atop an enormous camel, he led the caravan himself. For many a year after the old and young remembered this indefatigable man who, despite being a big boss, had still rolled up his sleeves and worked as an equal alongside everyone else. The people said that back then he had lost his temper with Oŋbaj, saying, 'You might have a firm hold over your farmstead, but you are callous and you have no pity for your neighbours.'

Much was said about this man, who had proved himself decisive and swift both in word and in deed. It was said that he had later been demoted. So, this was the office where he'd ended up. The silver-haired, broad-chested, swarthy man with flared nostrils looked out of the window and fell into a reverie.

'Well, what on earth are we to do? Alright. Seeing as you've come... Is there someone who could drive the car?'

'The disabled man's son is a driver.'

'Then get him to come here and he can collect it.' The two men got up and shook hands in farewell.

'So, how are things this year in Úšķyn?'

'There was plenty of snow over the winter.'

'Then this year things will go pretty well, I'd say.'

Once he had finished his business at the office, Ķarabala set off to the edge of the district centre, where he had left his horse. Passing by a house where people were bashing pots and pans, he remembered he had not had any lunch and this was most likely the teahouse that Oŋbaj had waxed lyrical about. Ķarabala was just about to jerk open the door, when a woman screamed out from inside:

'We're closed for a break! Come back at five.'

'I'll have probably made it back to my *auyl* by five.'

'Let him in. Turns out, he's a traveller,' came another voice from within.

Ķarabala entered the teahouse and sat down at a table by the door. An undernourished woman with a chest like a chicken's approached him.

'What will you have to drink, sir? And to eat?'

'Oh, anything to take the edge off my appetite, my dear.'

'Perhaps you'll have something more to get your appetite going?'

'I'm not after a bottle, if that's what you mean.'

The right corner of the chicken-chested woman's mouth jerked crookedly. Soon, she brought over an aluminium bowl of borscht and a main dish with rice, topped with a mound of lungs, liver and some other black substance. Then, with a sway of the hips, she went back to join the other women in their white coats who were whispering in the depths of the room. This whispering intensified discernibly. All it took was for one pockmarked woman in the centre of the huddle to say something amusing and the women seated with their backs to Ḳarabala laughed till their fat sides shook.

Ḳarabala started eating faster in order to make his exit sooner. He broke out in a sweat, although he was eating food that had gone cold long ago. One or two plump flies, full to the brim from simply licking the mountain of dirty dishes, took it in turns to land on his ears; they did not bite him but just buzzed, as if to say, What are you in such a rush for?

If there was one thing Ḳarabala couldn't stand more than anything else in the world, it was flies. He also couldn't stand frivolous women, who laughed in the presence of men. Once, sometime before, when he was still at the military enlistment office, he had been troubled by a green fly with shaggy legs as well as a young female doctor. Of course, the enlistment office was a serious institution, but it was wrong to make all the young men strip naked and stand around in their birthday suits. They were shy and didn't know what to do with themselves from the shame, covering their confusion with their hands, while women in white coats entered the stuffy, sweat-filled room, tapping their stilettos as they went. A young, attractive woman with an elegant figure entered the room where they stood and sat silently on the edge of a wobbly table.

He stood there and thought to himself, 'Oh, Lord, it would be better to be sent out into trenches with bullets whistling overhead than be forced to stand naked like a statue before this angel in white.' The men approached one by one. As his turn drew nearer, he began to shake. When his name was called out, he thought he heard thunder clap in the middle of a clear sky and he scurried closer to the table.

'*Aġa*,[31] remove your hand', said the woman, baring her teeth in a smile.

His throat was dry and he was about to say, 'My dear, but this is so embarrassing…' but the woman frowned. At this point, a green-winged fly flew through the window and settled on the back of his head; his head began to buzz. No matter how he shook it this way or that, the fly entertained no thoughts of flying away. Annoyed, he lifted his hand from his nether regions and, not just anyhow, but with all his might, slapped the nape of his neck with the palm of his hand.

All the while, the crafty woman was watching him with all her attention. Then she turned around and he could see the back of her head. She was shaking with repressed giggles. Then she sat down at her table and simply laughed out loud for everyone to see. Seeing the woman laugh, the naked young men in line behind Ḳarabala delighted in the opportunity to snigger and guffaw at the tops of their voices as well.

The attractive young woman who had only just seemed an angel in Ḳarabala's eyes now appeared before him as a downright demon. He was convinced this very same woman from the enlistment office was among the huddle of women

---

[31] *Aġa* – respectful form of address to an older man, which can be translated as 'brother', 'uncle'.

laughing softly at the back of the canteen. Rapidly finishing the food in front of him, he got up and hurried over to the coat rack. He rushed for the door, shoving his fur hat under one arm and his black overcoat under the other. Hardly had the panel door slammed back shut, when the women seated deep in the room burst out into gales of laughter. The more distance Ķarabala put between himself and that accursed building with its buzzing flies and cackling women, the more he calmed down. He jumped onto his roan, which was waiting for him in the yard of the livestock office, and headed homeward. Only when the district centre was left behind the black ridge did Ķarabala's spirits pick up again and he started singing: 'He-e-ey! Red gelding! Oh, red ge-e-elding!' When he sang the words, 'The girl and the *žigit* went gathering coal…' he clapped his hand over his mouth and yawned so broadly that his jaw almost cracked. Then he said to himself, 'Oh, Allah …'

The roan broke into a canter, probably because it could sense its home *auyl* lying up ahead. Leaning back, Ķarabala sat low in the saddle. From time to time he would repeat to himself, 'There, you see how well things worked out in the end!' The three bosses in the offices no longer seemed to him to be quite so high and mighty. They had heard him out attentively and had fulfilled his request. It turned out that two of them knew him personally. Ķarabala was also sure he knew the one with the metal tooth and the sinewy face. But where *had* he seen him? He hadn't seen him at his mother-in-law's funeral. He didn't think he'd seen him at his father-in-law's wedding feast when he'd taken his second wife, either. Perhaps he had been one of the authorised representatives who had arrived on those frothing horses. How could he remember them all? And they only came to see him when they needed bits of metalwork for their vehicles doing anyway. Yes, that was it! The year before last, some men had come to see him just before nightfall wearing canvas capes. Without even approaching the seat where their host was sat, they had begged and pleaded with him to help them there and then. 'Our shock absorbers have gone. *Aġa*, please help us out.' They had arrived in the twilight hour and it was nearly morning before they departed, when the air had only just begun to turn grey. They had evidently just returned from a hunting trip in a canvas-covered car. The canvas had been soiled with blood; they had wiped it clean with clumps of green grass. He remembered seeing this gap-toothed bloke, running around next to the car. It had probably been him. He must have had some fresh teeth fitted in the intervening years. Whatever the case, Oņbaj's long-cherished dream that had been tormenting and giving him no rest, had finally come to pass. The insurmountable task that the sharp-tongued, quick-witted Oņbaj had been unable to achieve, having travelled repeatedly to the district centre, cussing every last person and yet returning each time empty-handed, had proved to be a mere trifle for Ķarabala! And yet he found it so hard to string two words together that he would find his shirt wringing with sweat from the effort. This, of course, had all been down to the miraculous blade of green grass, thin as a needle, which had been poking out of the tortoise's mouth that morning. His ancestors had been right all along! Absolutely right. Something good was finally coming Oŋbaj's way. His heart would probably leap for joy when Ķarabala handed him the document granting him permission to pick up the car. He would probably burst into fits of laughter and say, It turns out that you are good for something after all, you poor wretch. Let him laugh. Let the poor soul have his fun...

When Ķarabala entered the house, not a sound could be heard coming from his darkened room. Oŋbaj was seated in the *tôr*, half prostrate, propped up with two cushions on either side. Everyone else in the house was tiptoeing around him in silence, as if they weren't among the living but barely discernible ghosts. A cunning grin flickered on the face of the weak, shaking Oŋbaj, who had barely been able to sip his tea. He pointed to an empty space by his side, as if to say, Come and sit next to the *tôr*. Ķarabala had barely managed to bend his knees to sit and was about to open his mouth to speak, when Oŋbaj interrupted him with a smile, 'You don't have to tell me; I know it all already. First, have some tea.' He then drank his tea himself, his whiskers wiggling as he did so. Ķarabala was incapable of swallowing anything, such was his impatience to impart his news.

Oŋbaj turned his tea bowl over, pulled up the satin blanket that had slid from his shoulders, wrapped himself up again and only then did he ask, in a most placid voice, 'Well, how did it go? How are those buggers; the bureaucrats, I trust they are all in good health?'

'Yes, it would seem so.'

'They probably met you with open arms, right?'

'Thank Allah!'

'Well, yes... I know them well.'

Oŋbaj brought his snuff on his thumbnail almost up to his nose, but then lowered it again.

'What did that thieving hound with the metal tooth have to say?'

'It turns out he has prepared the paperwork for you.'

The derisory smirk in Oŋbaj's eyes immediately disappeared but surprise and doubt still quivered at the ends of his arched brows.

'And did you see that dandy senior official, too?'

'I did.'

'I bet he was bleating like a ewe that can't give birth, right?'

'Quite the opposite. He sorted everything out straight away.'

This time, Oŋbaj straightened up and fixed Ķarabala with a penetrating gaze, as if he were about to angrily scream at him, 'Who do you think you're trying to kid?'

'And what did that beefcake with the stump have to say, then? I bet he led you on with his empty promises, right?'

'It turns out that there were three cars at the depot. He told me that we could take one of them. Here's the paperwork.'

Oŋbaj cautiously unfolded the piece of paper. He took his spectacles from under his pillow and read it over, slowly and carefully. He turned it this way and that, shook his head and snorted. In the end, a smile broke out on his lips.

'Well, wouldn't you know it – all it needed was for you to go see him and that Šyġajbaj,[32] who's so tight he wouldn't even give you the morning dew, has turned all generous!'

Ķarabala felt as if a heavy burden had been lifted from his shoulders. He felt quite light-headed with relief and was about to relate the tale of the lucky tortoise grass but, seeing how Oŋbaj's pale, grey face was swelling and flushing, as if he were coming out in nettle rash, he stopped himself. No one in the house seemed interested in the good news he had brought, for they were all staring open-eyed at the host on the *tôr* seat. Oŋbaj suddenly clutched at his side, as if he had been stabbed with a knife. He slowly sank back onto the patchwork cushion, his face glazing over in a cold, blue colour. After a brief pause, he spoke in a weak voice, 'Alright. Thank you. You can go home now.'

Ķarabala got up, put on his fur hat and took up his whip. Reaching the doorway, he turned and looked back. Oŋbaj still had that pale, bluish look about him. A nasty, crooked smirk seemed to have taken hold of the right side of his mouth. Leaving the house, Ķarabala felt around in his coat pocket to make sure the lucky tortoise grass was still there. Only then did he remember his wife's prescription. He took the reins of his roan and slowly headed off to his end of the *auyl*. It's probably true what they say about the road always seeming longer in the dark. He thought his house was still a long way off, although it was a mere stone's throw away. As he rode, Ķarabala lamented forgetting to buy his wife's medicine in his haste to get back home.

Translated by Simon Hollingsworth, edited by Simon Geoghegan

---

[32] Šyġajbaj – traditionally greedy character from Kazakh folklore.

SABIT DOSANOV
(b. 12.01.1940)

Sabit Dosanov is a writer, literary critic and playwright. After graduating from the Faculty of Journalism at Kirov Kazakh State University (now Ăl-Farabi Kazakh National University), he worked as an editor for the State Committee for Television and Radio Broadcasting, and as prose editor for Žazušy publishing house. Subsequently, he was appointed director of the Kazakh branch of the USSR Literary Fund (1985–89), general director of the Centre of Folk Art and Cultural Services (1991–95) and managing editor of Ķajnar publishing house (1996–97).

His first essay and short story collection, *Ķajyrly taŋ* (Good Morning), was published in 1966, followed by two more short story collections, *Bǔlbǔl ǔni* (The Trill of the Nightingale, 1968) and *Ķyran ķalġymajdy* (Eagles Don't Doze, 1971). In 1970, he published a monograph devoted to the problems of modern Kazakh literature, *Sony izder* (Fresh Traces), and 1978 saw the publication of *Tau žoly* (Mountain Road), a novel. This was followed by a non-fiction short story 'Žer taġdyry' (The Fate of the Earth) in 1979 and another novel, *Ekinši ômir* (The Second Life), in 1982. He then published further monographs: *Ķazyna* (Treasure, 1984) and *Žǔrektiŋ otyn sôndirme* (Don't Let the Fire in Your Heart Be Extinguished, 1988). His other novels include *Žiyrmasynšy ġasyr* (The Twentieth Century, 1998), *Aķ aruana* (The White Aruana, 2001), *Aptanyŋ ekinši kǔni* (The Second Day of the Week, 2003), *Ķylbǔrau* (Cattle Collar, 2003), *Ǔjyķ* (Quagmire, 2005) and *Tǔjyķ* (Deadlock, 2007). A number of his works have been published in Russian and *Aķ aruana* has also appeared in French.

Dosanov is an Honoured Worker of the Republic of Kazakhstan (1999) and a recipient of the State Prize of the Republic of Kazakhstan (2012) as well as the Parasat Order (2009).

By the Wayside

I

The suffocating heat swam hazily through the city, swallowing everything in its path. It invaded the nose, burned the lungs and refused to grant a single, much sought-after, invigorating breath of fresh air. Instead of quenching the thirst for something cool, each new breath brought with it only heat. For a whole month there had been no wind or rain. The leaves on the trees had prematurely yellowed under the scorching Sun. The earth had cracked and dried, lifeless and pallid even in the shadows of trees. Feet would sink in the pavements, sticking in a boggy mire of asphalt. Layers of heavy, grey dust covered the beautiful city in the foothills of the Alatau. Only at daybreak did a fresh breeze draw in from the mountains, even then barely perceptible.

At the start of each day, before the invasive humidity had set in, Ajdyn ran to the newspaper kiosk, as was his age-old routine; he would always start the day with a newspaper. The white-haired Russian woman in the kiosk knew him well. She had an excellent memory, despite her age, even knowing which papers he would buy. He had begun flicking through the newspapers right by the kiosk when he suddenly heard a familiar and distinct, low and husky voice behind him:

'Ajdyn!'

Turning sharply, he could scarcely believe his eyes.

'Ajdyn, is that you?! Don't you recognise me?' said a swarthy *žigit*[1] of medium build with a pot belly, who had approached tentatively. Thin, wily eyes looked studiously at Ajdyn.

'What do you mean, *don't you recognise me*? Gafur!' Genuinely pleased at their meeting, Ajdyn was about to extend a hand in greeting but then, submitting to the impulse, embraced his friend warmly.

'Well, this is unexpected! You disappear for years and then you suddenly turn up out of the blue!' Ajdyn's exuberant voice was already making the passers-by turn their heads. He pointed to the five-storey building nearby. 'What are we doing standing about here? Why don't we head up to mine?'

Entering the apartment, Gafur instantly realised that Ajdyn lived alone. It was clean, even excessively so, but there was no sense of a woman's touch about the place, which would have given the impression of a family home with all its comforts. The apartment gave the distinct impression of being a bachelor's

---

[1] *Žigit* – generally denoting a 25- to 40-year-old male, the term can also be used as an honorific indicating bravery, endurance, fortitude and being true to one's word.

pad, from the shabby walls, which had once been painted blue, to the empty sideboard and the bed, which had been made in almost military fashion.

'Sorry, but where are Rymžan and Ajbar? Why are you here on your own?'

'I... I lost them... both my wife and son...' said Ajdyn after a brief pause, barely able to hold back his tears. 'Four years ago', he inhaled deeply and then added, barely audibly, 'A car accident. Rymžan and Ajbar had gone to visit friends in Šymkent. Their bus turned over at the Ķordaj Pass and they both died...' The lump in his throat interrupted his sentence.

Gafur touched his friend's hand. 'And you've been on your own ever since? You never remarried?'

'No, I never wanted to. You know how much I loved Rymžan and how we got married... You remember, right?' A reproach could be heard in Ajdyn's voice. 'You were the best man at our wedding after all.'

'Of course, I remember! And I remember the grand feasts you put on when Ajbar was born and when he first went to school...'

'Ajbar died instantly, but Rymžan passed away in the district hospital in Georgievka, where she had been taken after the accident. Before she closed her eyes for the last time, the last thing she said was: "It will be so hard for Ajdyn now. He relied on me for everything".'

Both fell silent. The tea had long since gone cold but Gafur, who knew his tea and who liked to take it strong and hot, and always demanded that a mere sip be poured into the bottom of his drinking bowl at a time, drank the cold, weak tea, pretending it was much to his liking.

'So, how are things with work? You still in the same place?'

'No, they let me go because of the job cuts.'

'How come? The cuts shouldn't have affected you!' Gafur even rose to his feet in indignation.

Ajdyn simply nodded impassively. 'You think?'

'You graduated with distinction and you always worked at the same place. You have plenty of experience, which is more than can be said of us. No, no, say what you like, but you are one of the bright ones. I recall back in the Soviet years, how you took part in the All-Union Meeting of Inventors in Moscow. That was you, right? Do you think that there are many engineers in Kazakhstan as talented as you?'

'Those that remained were the ones who came later, but we were laid off.' It seemed that Ajdyn was quite calm about it all.

'But that's so unfair. You've still got a good while to go until your pension kicks in, right?'

'I'm afraid I won't make it to my pension', said Ajdyn quietly. 'The people in the know say that the last five years of your salary are reviewed before calculating your pension. I've been without work for two years now and I have another twelve years before I can claim a pension.'

'Then you need to take on any work you can get, whatever it is.'

'Now is hardly the time to pick and choose. I worked for a while as a caretaker, but I lost that job not long ago.' A bitter, ironic smile appeared on his face: 'It turns out someone else also needed that job.'

'Come on! Don't despair. We won't leave you out in the cold. If I found you work, would you move to Astana? You can exchange this three-room apartment, right?'

'I can't leave my Rymžan and Ajbar', Ajdyn interrupted. 'I fear you won't understand, but…' Ajdyn could hardly breathe.

There was silence again. Gafur began getting ready to go.

'Think about it', he said, this time not quite so forcefully. 'I'll look for work for you in Astana. At a pinch, I'll speak to my boss.'

'I'll think about it', Ajdyn replied, smiling amicably.

'Come to see me in Astana. Here are my details.'

'Look at you', exclaimed Ajdyn, inspecting Gafur's business card. 'You've even got a mobile phone.'

'You know I don't need this business card, nor the mobile phone. My boss does all this… Oh, incidentally, is there any news on your dissertation? Did you manage to complete your defence of it?'

'No, I didn't.'

'Why not? You finished it ages ago.'

'You know, I'm not one for all those titles and the song and dance', Ajdyn smirked.

'Yes, I know. But I've heard from many people that you could eat some of those in your field for breakfast, even the specialists. If only I had your knowledge, I would move mountains.'

'It's not knowledge but money which rules the world now.'

'Yes, unfortunately you're right. Okay, I'll be off. The boss will be wondering where I've got to.'

'How much longer will you be in Almaty?'

'The boss and I are flying to Moscow this evening. He's then flying abroad for his holiday and I'm going to have to bring back his new Jeep to Astana.'

Ajdyn walked Gafur to the bus stop. It was a hot morning and the sky was clear. However, the weather in Almaty is like the mood of a capricious woman; it can change dramatically, sometimes forty times in a short day. Leaden clouds suddenly obscured the Sun as if from nowhere, it became stuffier and even the wind that had blown unexpectedly from the south-west simply lifted the dust from the asphalt and burned people's faces. Heavy, warm raindrops slowly hammered the ground.

Ajdyn stood there for some time, deep in thought, not knowing how to interpret this change in the weather.

II

Perhaps he was tormented by his hunger or his thoughts, as tormented as the clouds above, which pestered him continually, one after the other. Perhaps the humidity was weighing on his chest. Or maybe it was his meeting with Gafur which had raked up the fire in his soul. He couldn't make head nor tail of it all and lay awake well into the night.

God, when will this losing streak come to an end? Can you not see, Lord, how these never-ending misfortunes shackle and stifle me? Help me, Lord! Offer me support! Don't turn your back on me for good! I have done my best to follow the path you have laid before me!

Turning from side to side, he only managed to nod off to the creak of his old wooden bed by morning. He woke exhausted, shattered. The bright rays of the midday Sun that had forced its way through the holes in the old blinds made the little room in the concrete house unbearably hot.

He barely managed to move his strangely shaking legs as he staggered, swaying from side to side, to open the window. It was even hotter outside and the hot air flooded into the room, delighted, as if it, too, were seeking refuge from the scorching rays. Ajdyn's heart began to ache once more and his eyes misted over. Only then did he remember that he had scarcely eaten in two whole days. He remembered the broth that he had set aside for these moments of extreme hunger. 'I think there must be something I can eat in the fridge', he thought, and with this in mind he made his way to the kitchen, keeping himself upright by leaning with his shaking arms against the wall.

He opened the fridge door and stood, dumbfounded. The fridge was completely empty. All that had been left were a few pieces of bread and a yellow saucepan with brown, burnt spots. He heated and ate the remains of the soup he had boiled a week before from some scrawny bones and turned off the fridge.

'I should wash and clean it. I don't have any butter or even a cup of milk for my tea to store in it. Will a day come when I can boil another bowl of broth from bones?' There was nothing left in the house to sell. 'Perhaps someone will buy this fridge from me on the cheap?'

Having eaten half a bowl of soup and two pieces of bread, Ajdyn bucked up a little and broke out in a sweat. He needed a drink. He didn't want to use the last of the stewed tea, so he boiled the water, brewed some grass he had dried the day before, and drank some herbal tea. He didn't want the tea to be bitter, so he added a pinch of salt, as he had long since run out of sugar, and the tea took on a fermented, leathery flavour.

The ninth residential district, built forty years ago, was on the outskirts of the city, on the windward side. Ajdyn lived on the top floor of a dilapidated five-storey building. Entering his sitting room, he noted a black mark the size of a button on the pipe that ran from the ceiling to the radiators. This reminded him that in spring the pipe had worn thin in this place and leaked. He touched the spot and realised that the hole had, of its own accord, plugged itself from the build-up of scale. 'God sides with the poor', he thought.

Lying on the settee, Ajdyn began to think about the next day and what he would do for food. 'Today is here, but what awaits me tomorrow?' he mused.

'The day before, I sat on the black market all day long, with the last of my riches laid out, in the form of antique books; I made only a measly three hundred tenge. I had spent ten on the journey. I bought my newspapers. How many days would the remaining two hundred and seventy last? People are so strange, they won't buy these books for a tenth of the usual asking price, even though they were scarce in Soviet times, sold only under the counter. The final resort – my thirty-volume medical encyclopaedia. With luck, I might be able to live some time with that money.'

The television set had long since stopped working and as if to spite him, the radio fell silent, too. How would he buy his newspapers now? Ajdyn felt like he had been stranded on an uninhabitable island and he now went to his neighbours for the latest world news. Stagnant water in a pond turns sour over time. The same can be said of a person if they never speak with anyone; over time they lose themselves. The weeks in which he had not spoken with anyone became months, and Ajdyn felt he was turning into an unsociable, withdrawn and sullen hermit. His personality and habits began to change and he started to find certain unpleasant traits in himself. Frightened by this, Ajdyn had taken to conversing more with his neighbours when the opportunity presented itself; loneliness to him was worse than poverty. However, there had been times when there had been no one to exchange a word with. This was now a time of 'you scratch my back and I'll scratch yours' and the people had now become more particular about whom they would pass the time of day with. There were only two people who would happily chat with Ajdyn. One of them was a retired colonel who lived across the hallway, while the other was a journalist who owned the first apartment, and who had been made prematurely redundant.

When the heat had subsided and the shadows grown longer, Ajdyn ventured out into the courtyard, but there was no one there. Not knowing what to do with himself and already considering returning home, he suddenly caught sight of another neighbour, a young Tatar. Today, the lad, who previously had only greeted him with a cursory nod of the head, was especially polite and extended his hand.

'How are you, old friend? I haven't seen you for a long time. Have you been away?'

'Where have I to go? I just sit at home.'

'I looked for you.'

'Why?' asked Ajdyn in surprise.

'I heard you say that you had no work and I wanted to help you, so I spoke with some people I know and asked about a job for you.'

'Really?' Ajdyn was cautious.

'There is a job going; a real job! It's hard work but the pay's good', he smiled slyly.

Ajdyn interrupted his neighbour impatiently: 'Rafik, come on, tell me what it is!'

'You're a good driver, aren't you? Wait down here tomorrow morning, bring your passport and driver's licence and...'

'And then?' Ajdyn wanted to learn what this job was as soon as possible.

'Then I'll introduce you to my *žigits*. They're six brothers. You'll be the seventh. You'll fly to the United Arab Emirates.'

'What for?' asked Ajdyn, his face dropping. He knew that you needed money to travel abroad.

'They're businessmen and they trade in cars. They'll buy a number of foreign models and you'll simply drive one of them back with them.'

'How long will we be gone?'

'Each trip lasts seven to ten days. They pay a hundred dollars a day. They also pay for the flight, accommodation and even meals.'

'Well now! That sounds like an excellent job', said Ajdyn, his heart leaping with joy. God has not deserted me after all! So, my hopes were not in vain!

'For the sake of your neighbour, you can even miss prayers, they say. I did my best and found this job for you', said Rafik with a self-satisfied grin.

'Oh, Rafik, I will never forget your kindness. Thank you so much.'

'A *thank you* doesn't cut it. We'll drink to it when you return.' Ajdyn got the hint and laughed. 'Of course. You bet we will!'

'Alright then. See you tomorrow.'

Rafik's blue eyes sparkled merrily, his cheeks flushed on his red burly face and he quickly departed. 'God arranged this meeting. Is this a dream or can it really be true?' Ajdyn rubbed his eyes. Making sure it was not a dream, he stood for a while outside his front door, gradually regaining his senses.

III

Having loaded the cars purchased in Dubai onto the ferry, they delivered them to Iran. They set off the following day, when the morning air was cool. Six drivers sat at the wheels of six cars and they sped away over the smooth road surface. Ajdyn was one of the six. The seventh man, the boss, made himself comfortable on the back seat of the first car.

Having left the Iranian port town of Bandar Abbas, they made a short stop for a snack. Over lunch, the boss explained their onward route.

'After one thousand and seven hundred kilometres, we'll arrive in Sirak, a village on the Iran –Turkmenistan border', he explained. 'Then, we'll drive through the towns of Mary and Chardzhou and reach the Uzbek border. Our next stop will be the village of Farat in Uzbekistan. Then comes Bukhara, Navoi and finally we'll be back in Kazakhstan. It's hot out there and the road is hard, but we won't stop until we reach Sirak. If anyone gets tired, don't be shy – speak up. I can take the wheel and let you get some rest. Right then, *žigits*, to your horses!'

The men started their cars and headed off. Ajdyn was entrusted with an Audi that was only two years old. To all intents and purposes, it was a new car. The interior was clean and looked as if it had only just left the factory.

The engine was immaculate. Indeed, a new car is like a decent horse. Despite the heat, Ajdyn didn't feel at all tired. Quite the contrary, he sped along in high spirits, his thoughts racing faster than the car itself. He pictured the stack of green notes he would receive upon arrival in Almaty. 'I'll be rid of that tormenting hunger and poverty.' His dreams soared and his heart leapt for joy.

'How wonderful the scenery is and how varied! From tropical greens to desert yellows. But it is all equally beautiful and a joy to behold. Thank you, Lord, for everything!' He wanted to sing for the first time in years. Admiring the view on all sides, he began to sing Estaj's song 'Ķůsni-Ķorlan'.[2] Rymžan had loved this song. Ajdyn was no singer, of course, but he had a pleasant voice. When Rymžan had been alive, he had sung this song at parties. Those times had been carefree, when they had not worried about tomorrow, about there being nothing to eat or to wear. When Rymžan and Ajbar had been alive, Ajdyn had been the happiest man in the world. Now, his life had been split into the *before* and *after*. How deceptive this world could be! His life had flashed by in the blink of an eye and was now replaced with mere existence. His heart now ached for his irretrievable happiness. However, he had to continue this existence...

They reached Farat late in the evening and stopped at the house of an Uzbek man. The boss gathered them together before they went to bed.

'*Žigits*, you are all tired from the journey, but there is not long to go. Be sure that you get plenty of rest. I will wake you myself in the morning.'

Hearing these words, Ajdyn fell into a deep sleep. When he awoke the next morning, he discovered that his fellow travellers and the cars had all gone, all without a trace. He asked the Uzbek, who wailed as if he was mourning the dead:

'Oh my, they are nothing but fraudsters. It's one thing that they didn't pay for last night's pilau and accommodation, but they took two bundles of fabric with them, too. We made clothes from that fabric and sold them to make ends meet. What are we going to do now?'

'A car – do you have a car?' Ajdyn could not understand what had happened. But they were decent lads! They wouldn't do this, surely?!

'Yes, I have a car. But what's the use? We'd never catch them!'

'But if we did?' He believed that it would be better to act than to do nothing.

'It's impossible. Even if we did catch them, it would achieve nothing. Your own Kazakhs would shoot you down and leave you to rot in the steppe.'

'What should we do now?'

'What should we do? We'll find something to eat. And what will you do? Return home while you still can.'

'But how can I when my pockets are empty?'

---

[2] Estaj Berkimbajůly (1874–1946) – Kazakh poet and composer; his song 'Ķůsni-Ķorlan' is dedicated to his beloved Ķorlan, whom he could not marry due to their different social status.

'In that case, find yourself some temporary work to earn enough for the journey.'

'I have no documents', Ajdyn suddenly recalled in horror. 'The boss took all our documents, saying it would be better to keep them all in one place.'

'Well, you're done for, lad.'

'Yes, I'm well and truly done for!' He pronounced the words without even considering their meaning.

The extent of human cruelty and betrayal had shaken him. He felt pain, stinging, endless and all-encompassing. It ripped his heart and burned his insides. He sat motionless for some time, almost out of his mind. His vision darkened and he couldn't see anything. When fate wants to strike, it does so with merciless ferocity. Regaining his senses, he looked around him; the old Uzbek had disappeared without a trace. In faint hope, he tried the handle on the entrance to the house where he had spent the night. It was firmly shut. He rang the bell. No one answered. Not knowing what to do, he took himself in an unknown direction.

IV

Three months had passed by the time that Ajdyn finally made it back to Almaty, all skin and bone and quite lost. And yet another misfortune awaited him at his apartment, where he had lived so many years. His wooden door had been replaced with a metal one. Where there was once one lock, two had been pierced in its place. Unable to understand what had happened, Ajdyn rang the bell. The door opened a few inches.

'What do you want?' asked a chubby-cheeked lad with unkempt hair.

'Please open the door', said Ajdyn. 'This is my apartment.'

'Are you out of your mind? Get the hell out of here, or I'll call the police!' and he slammed the door in his face.

Sensing something was amiss, Ajdyn's heart pounded, his blood boiled and he went to see his neighbour the Tatar. Rafik himself opened the door. Ajdyn complained to him that strangers had taken over his apartment.

'Yes', said Rafik in a detached manner, 'after you left, some people came and began full-scale repairs on the place. They only moved in recently. I asked them what was what, and they told me they had purchased the apartment.'

'What should I do?'

'Go to the police.'

Ajdyn followed Rafik's advice and went to the police station. The young policeman who Ajdyn had brought along questioned the fat man with the unkempt hair, but it transpired that the documentation was all completely above board. They then went on to the cooperative of apartment owners, but there, too, the documents had all been drawn up in the proper manner.

These documents confirmed that Ajdyn had sold his apartment through a broker for three thousand dollars.

'*Aḳsaḳal*,[3] I am sorry, but there is nothing I can do to help you', said the young policeman and he went on his way.

Bad luck never comes alone. When it rains it pours, thought Ajdyn. He refused to comprehend what had happened.

This cannot be! Am I really to end up on the street? Who am I? There is really no end to people's inhumanity. Have they no fear of God?! Why? Why has all this happened to me? What have I done? God Almighty, why do you choose to punish me like this? What bad thing have I done? Can you really leave a man in this situation? Am I so guilty that no forgiveness is possible? What have I done to deserve this? What?

His head span from everything going through his mind and his eyes welled up. His knees shook and he made it to a bench, barely able to move his legs, and sank down without an ounce of strength remaining.

The Sun was setting…

V

Early in the morning, a motley crew of all manner of nationalities would disperse in different directions and gather once more only with the fall of evening. Ivan, constantly drunk, with an enormous, grey-red nose and clearly the leader of the gang, was a Russian. His right-hand man, the stocky Šavhat, who was blind in his left eye, was a Tatar. Tohtahun, a lad of medium build who was covered in cyanotic pimples, was an Uygur. The short, stocky Pak was a Korean. The lanky, spindle-legged chatterbox Yuldaš was an Uzbek. The tallest of them all, Timofei, so thin and long-legged that the others had nicknamed him Antenna, was a Ukrainian. These were the people who the fair-faced Ajdyn came to acquaint himself with.

Their current abode was a small basement in the residential district that had earlier been used for storage. Šavhat had brought his friends here from the rooftops or drain covers which had previously been their homes.

'You've got the nose of a bloodhound', Ivan had once said to Šavhat. 'The things you find! If it weren't for you, this rabble would never have found such a place.' Ivan spat with relish and the globule flew past Ajdyn who was sitting opposite, only just missing him.

'The boss is right', echoed Yuldaš, accustomed to agreeing with Ivan at every turn. 'Could there be a place better than this?'

'What the hell do we want anything better for?'

'Why?'

'No one will allow us to live anywhere better.'

'Yes, that's right.'

'The businessmen will just take it away.'

'That's enough! Shut it, all of you!' barked Ivan, his face like thunder.

---

[3] *Aḳsaḳal* – traditionally, a well-respected and powerful elder in charge of the community. Nowadays, a reverential form of address to elderly men in general.

The gang, which had been buzzing like a hive, instantly fell silent.

This group of people, popularly known as 'the homeless', have their own, unwritten laws. Knowing they wouldn't make it alone, they had recently decided to live together. During the day, they would trawl all corners of the city of half a million people and congregate in this cellar each evening. This residence was a khan's palace for homeless vagrants.

The daily routine was always the same and today was no exception. As twilight would fall, they would return 'home' one after the other.

'Hey, Alik, light a candle, would you?' ordered Tohtahun, who was sitting below, clearing his nose loudly through short, fat fingers.

'My name's Ajdyn, not Alik', he muttered in retort.

'Shut it, for fuck's sake! The boss is on his way and if there's no light, he'll give you what for! Then you'll forget your name, for sure!' said Tohtahun in a threatening voice.

No sooner had Ajdyn lit a candle when Ivan walked in, wiping his hooked nose with his index finger.

'How are you doing, my falcons? Everyone here?'

Yes, thought Ajdyn, the boss is in a good mood today. He has a habit of calling us falcons if he's had the good fortune to get a drink. Otherwise, he'd be screaming and shouting, calling us dogs or pigs.

'We're all here', said Šavhat, licking his cracked lips with the large tongue that his mouth never quite succeeded in containing.

'Well, what have you got? Throw your pickings into the kitty. Let's sit! Antenna, that tap isn't going to, you know, blow up on us, is it? You're a plumber, after all, right?' said Ivan and burst out laughing malignantly. 'It won't blow up, right?'

'Yes, I worked as a plumber at the apartment cooperative', Antenna replied proudly. 'Don't you worry, it won't blow up!'

'So why did you leave?'

'Well, they paid peanuts and, even then, never on time! So, I nicked a couple of meters and sold them on. And, well, that cost me four years. My bitch of a wife sold the house, found herself another bloke and buggered off to another city. That's how I ended up here.'

'I couldn't find work in Tatarstan, so I came to Kazakhstan. I was told you could make money here', said Šavhat, keeping the conversation going. 'You can't trust anyone. I did get behind the wheel of a Kamaz[4] in the first year, truth be told. They were shipping metal to China. Those damned customs officials, though, milked us for everything they could and it all went down the tubes from there; I lost my job and all my documents.'

'So, you wanted to get into business?' snorted Pak. 'I was in business too and even mortgaged my house. The business went bust and my home went out

---

[4] Kamaz – Soviet make of truck.

the window! Well, not out the window, but to some wise guy. He took my wife with him, too. Yeah, all women are bitches! They're only in it for the money!'

Yuldaš echoed, pointing his finger at Ajdyn: 'Those damned kalbits[5] are right when they say, Don't trust your wife or your horse. I returned from Siberia to find mine in bed with a lover. Both of them stark naked.'

'What happened then?' asked Timofei with a spray of spit.

'Stop interrupting, you moron', snapped Šavhat.

'What man would stand for such humiliation?' Yuldaš went on. 'I went for my knife and wanted to run them both through. That bitch, she was a sly one, ran off and hid in the next-door apartment. That bastard lover of hers, though, got what was coming to him. They clapped me in prison, good and proper.'

'But why did you go to Siberia?' asked Pak.

'You dumbass, it's obvious. I went to sell fruit and veg.'

'What's there to hide: I was suffering from the vodka', said Tohtahun. 'I just can't do without the blessed stuff!'

'Boss, and what about you...' Timofei bit his tongue.

'What, you want to interrogate me, do you?! You wanna know it all, is that it?' growled Ivan.

'Boss, the Kazakhs have a saying: If the people demand it, the khan will slaughter a camel', said Šavhat, Ivan's second-in-command of sorts and who sometimes allowed himself to take liberties.

Ivan, warmed by the strong vodka, took a liking to the word *khan*.

'Well, bugger it! If you really want to know, what is there to say?' he said, stroking his hooked nose with two fingers. 'I'll be damned! Honest to God, my life is similar to the fate of this Charlie here, to be robbed of a century of freedom. Vodka is my friend and my foe.'

Understanding that Charlie was Tohtahun's nickname, the others now realised why Ivan had taken him under his wing.

'Alright, that'll do for today. Time to turn in', said Ivan irritably.

All at once, everyone took to their corners on the straw without undressing.

Soon, the poor, sleeping vagrants began their nightly contest of who could snore the loudest as they left yet another day behind them.

Ajdyn spent another two months in this den as the poor relation. He had had to be as quiet as a mouse in the company of these men who were stronger than him. All the same, the group never did accept him and he could never get himself established among them. In the end, they threw him out.

If before he had simply been discontent, now his life became hell.

Once, he had found a wallet on the ground. He opened it impatiently and couldn't believe his eyes, seeing a wad of crisp, new five-hundred tenge notes. His head span from the good fortune that had befallen him. Gathering himself, he counted the money to find five thousand tenge. Having long since gone without a hot meal, he almost ran to the canteen opposite, already sensing the

---

[5] *Kalbit* – ethnic slur in Russian referring to those of Central Asian nations.

taste of something good in his stomach. At that moment, two vagrants caught up with him. They had colourful Chinese bags over their shoulders.

'Hey, you!' said a blue-eyed insolent lad, coming up to him, 'give us the money, you bastard!'

'What money?' replied Ajdyn, anxious.

'We saw you find that money on the street', said the second lad, blocking Ajdyn's way.

Ajdyn ran but the two bullies caught him in an instant and set about him. However hard he tried to resist, he was no match for the two of them. He fell and they began beating and kicking him. Nevertheless, Ajdyn refused to let go of the wallet, which he held in an iron grip. The hooligans could not unclench his fist but then a sudden, sharp pain forced him to open his hands. They had cut his fingers with a razor. Having got their hands on the money-stuffed wallet, the two ruffians disappeared in the crowd. Not a soul had come to help! Not a soul had even attempted to intervene.

Washing his bloodied hand in the irrigation canal, Ajdyn fell under a large poplar in the courtyard. Darkness had already fallen and the people had all gone to bed. Ajdyn, however, could not sleep for a long time. All his ordeals and the abuse he had had to endure over the past few months passed before his eyes. He recalled standing with some unemployed people on Sejfullin Street[6] before joining the gang of homeless men and being chased away with uproar and a dog.

A month before he had discovered a tin can in a rubbish bin and had rejoiced over his find like a little child. This joy, too, had been short-lived. Quickly opening the tin labelled 'Pate', he had assuaged his hunger a little, but later almost died from food poisoning.

He had encountered his fair share after that, too. Once, in the midst of a foul, awful night, when they say a decent master wouldn't let his dog out of the house, Ajdyn had been woken by drunks returning from visiting friends. They kicked him, saying,

'Hey, you bastard, get up and get lost.' One was a fat, slant-eyed Kazakh who stood threateningly close. Throwing back his hair from his eyes, the other was also closing in, intimidatingly.

'Come on, please let me sleep here until morning.'

'Get lost right now! Get lost, I tell you! You're dirtying our entrance!'

As he emerged from the entrance, he heard the voice of the woman who had been with the thin-eyed Kazakh:

'God, that tramp really stinks!'

With that, the metal door had slammed shut. Overcome with drowsiness, Ajdyn laid out a dirty newspaper on the ground not far from a garage in the yard and fell asleep.

---

6   Sejfullin Street is a road in Almaty where people can pick up unemployed men for short-term jobs.

That lunchtime, Ajdyn had been rummaging about in a rubbish bin, collecting bottles, when he heard a familiar female voice. He didn't dare look straight over, but just glanced over out of the corner of his eye. He recognised her at once: it was Naġima, Rymžan's college friend. Ajdyn couldn't bring himself to raise his head until she had gone some distance away. He stood there some time, like an ostrich with its head in the sand. He had been familiar with the stench from the rubbish before but now he sensed it acutely and it turned his stomach. Looking at his old jacket and filthy trousers with holes on the knees and running his cracked hands over the stubble on his face, he felt like a cornered animal. There were red flags wherever he looked and there was nowhere left for him to run. Guns were being fired and evil, pursed eyes gazed out over the sights of rifles that released a flurry of deadly bullets.

He despised himself and cursed his misfortune. He wanted to cry but no tears would come.

VI

A year had passed since Ajdyn had acquired his homeless status and become a vagrant, but it was only now that he realised this, once the cold autumn had set in. They say, A man can grow accustomed to a grave in three days, and this is so very true. It turned out that he had gradually become accustomed to his dog's life, which at first had seemed incredibly hard. He had suffered from hunger and all manner of humiliation. Despite this, he had not wanted to part with life and he had continued his existence as best he could. Now, though, he had begun to tire of it.

Realising that this harsh life had no intention of showing him mercy, he began to feel more and more distressed. His heart ached and his soul shed tears of blood.

Who needs me in this world? If I were to leave it, not a soul would notice. Perhaps the Earth would even be cleaner without me! I have become a worthless being; no one needs me and I have bestowed no warmth on anyone. Every bug has a hole, a place to live and offspring to care for. But what would I leave in this life? What is the point of my existence? There is none! There's nothing more to say! I am simply done with existing. Enough! I have to leave this life while I am still a person! How long must I bear this filth and humiliation? It would be better to die than put up with all this, he thought. From that day on, Ajdyn would think about one thing only: when and how he might die, and this thought would come to overpower him.

Previously, especially in the first years of living with Rymžan, Ajdyn had been terrified of death. However, since he had lost his Rymžan and Ajbar, he had come to look death squarely in the face and it no longer held any fear for him. Latterly, he had come to think that death was better than this accursed dog's life and he submitted himself completely to the idea.

Perhaps he dreamt of Rymžan under the influence of this thought. In one dream, just like in their happier years, they were strolling around the Medeu district. Ajdyn wanted to embrace and kiss Rymžan, but she ran from him. Ajdyn ran after her. They waded through dirty water. After a while, they reached the Keŋsaj Cemetery, going around the hill at Kôk Tôbe. Reaching the last grave, Rymžan fell. Ajdyn wanted to lift her up but at that moment he awoke. His right leg was in agony. He ran out onto the street. On closer inspection, he saw that a deep wound, the size of a hen's egg, had appeared on his right knee. This, he realised, must have been the work of a rat, which had devoured the flesh from his leg.

Barely able to walk on his bad leg, Ajdyn sat on a bench in a courtyard. Not knowing what to do and where to turn for help, he looked around. He saw a newspaper at his feet and reluctantly picked it up. It was a copy of the local *Almaty Akšamy* paper from 5 May 2000. He listlessly skimmed over the first two pages and his eyes fell on a brief article, titled 'Homeless vagrants'. He began reading:

Recently a great many people have been made homeless. They have nowhere to live, no means of existence and no opportunity to find work. Not all of these hardy men are alcoholics or drug addicts. They have become estranged from society due to the harsh realities of everyday life. Without a place to live, they are forced to live in cellars and on rooftops, eking out whatever existence they can. Our society does not seem to provide social care nor empathise with these people. With this problem in mind, Professor Fyodr Zavyalov and Doctor of Economics Elena Spiridonova from the Demidov University in Yaroslavl have studied the problem of homelessness. Their painstaking work has helped find relatives of 83 per cent of homeless people, the parents of 27 per cent, brothers and sisters of 64 per cent and children of 54 per cent. The conclusion reached is that people simply lack generosity. The research has found that many homeless people are well educated and they are capable of working as drivers, fitters, lathe operators, electricians and so on. They want to live normal lives but, with no fixed abode, they don't possess the correct papers. The main reason for losing their homes is a criminal record. They live by whatever means they can: 43 per cent get by on earnings made by chance, while the rest collect bottles, scrap metal, raw materials and the like, while in the summer they sell fruit and vegetables they have stolen. Only one fifth of homeless people receive an old-age or disability pension. All their earnings, obtained with great difficulty, go on food, alcohol and cigarettes. How much more do they need for medicines, clothing and soap, for example? One positive thing has been revealed: homeless people spend 17 per cent of their earnings on newspapers and magazines! That is some comfort.

Ajdyn put the newspaper down on the bench and looked around. It was already late in the morning and yet there were still no people in the yard. He had not felt the pain in his leg while he had been reading, but now the agony had become intense.

Ajdyn sat for a while in contemplation, his face turned to stone. He pulled a comb from his pocket and tidied his hair and messy beard. He looked around and, with determination, took a knife from his other pocket. The sharp blade in his good hand, glistening in the newly risen Sun, pierced his soft body. Closing his eyes, Ajdyn cut open his own stomach.

He held his spilling guts with his hands and slowly began to slump. His eyes were half closed and his lips foamed. At that moment, the Sun, which had been hidden behind the clouds, re-emerged, illuminating everything. The pain had gone. A blinding, brilliant mirage appeared before Ajdyn; a white swan slowly emerged from a translucent haze. It was flying towards him, mourning her partner. A sad melody could be heard, a lament or a quiet elegy. The swan soon transformed into Rymžan, dressed in a long white dress. Ajdyn wanted to embrace his love and moved forward, but fell. Flapping her wings, creating a cool breeze, Rymžan smiled down at him. Her captivating smile filled Ajdyn with incredible joy, happiness and long-anticipated peace. All those dark days and nights which had brought him so much grief were now far behind him.

Ajdyn suddenly got to his feet and finally touched his Rymžan. His body was light and he melted away in the shimmering mirage.

Life on Earth continued as before, as if nothing had happened. It had found no place for him and so had sent him to the heavens. Its deceptive beauty glimmered, the Sun shone, the moon rose in the sky and day became night.

A short life had flashed by, besieged by perpetual cares and troubles…

Translated by Simon Hollingsworth, edited by Simon Geoghegan

MUKHTAR MAGAUIN
(b. 2.02.1940)

Mukhtar Magauin is a Kazakh writer, literary scholar and historian. He graduated from Kirov Kazakh State University (now Ăl-Farabi Kazakh National University; 1962), where he also received his doctorate degree (1965). He was head of the literary criticism department of *Ķazaķ ădebieti* newspaper, *Žŭldyz* literary journal and Žazušy publishing house. His first short story, 'Kešķŭrym' (In the Evening), was published in 1964 in *Žŭldyz*. He published several monographs, beginning with *Ķobyz saryny* (The Ancient Melody of Ķobyz, 1968) that treats about the forgotten literature of the Kazakh Khanate period (fifteenth–eighteenth centuries). His next two publications, *Aldaspan* (1970) and *Ķazaķ tarihynyŋ ălippesi* (The Primer of Kazakh History, 1995), sought to foster national unity through the rekindling of the historical consciousness. Magauin was blacklisted by the Communist authorities for a period of time, and the majority of his now renowned literary works were published after the collapse of the Soviet Union. His major works include *Kôkmuñar* (1972), *Alasapyran* (Havoc, 1980–82), *Šaķan šeri* (1985), *Sary ķazaķ* (The Blond Kazakh, 1991), *Ķypšaķ aruy* (The Beauty of Kipchaks, 2004), *Žarmaķ* (The Split, 2007) and *Šyŋġys han* (Gengis Khan, 2011–17). His selected works were collected into thirteen volumes that appeared in 2002. Magauin translated several short stories and novels into Kazakh, including those by William Somerset Maugham and Henry Rider Haggard.

Magauin is a laureate of the State Prize of the Kazakh SSR (1984) and a People's Writer of Kazakhstan (1996). In 1997, he won the International Prize for Writers and Cultural Workers of the Turkic World awarded by Sulejman Demirel, former president of Turkey.

Death of a Borzoi

1

Towards the end he became absolutely feeble. But even so he crept up to the mound twice – first from one side and then from the other, dragging his exhausted body, racked with pain, across the ground. The slopes of the mound were shallow, its sides had been smoothed by the steppe wind and powdered with fresh, virginally white snow. A white, silent mound... It exuded an aura of bitter loneliness and grief. In summer, when the crumbly earth was the colour of a hare's back, it had smelled differently here. Something familiar and kindly could be sensed in that smell – or so, at least, it had seemed to the borzoi. At that time, he had come running here often. And he had kept wandering around the mound, poking his nose into the yellowish earth mingled with small stones. The smell that he could distinguish was weak and vague. It was not a pleasant smell. It was the way foxes smelled two or three days after their skins had been torn off and they had been dumped in the steppe, as far away as possible from any dwellings. Crawling about in the stinking foxes' carcasses were little maggots, ants and fat, lazy bluebottles... The borzoi was fastidious and that smell made him feel sick. But here beside the mound he also sensed something different. Mingled with the smell of rotting flesh, detected so clearly by his sensitive nostrils, was the smell of his master. He was lying in this earth! Hard though it was to imagine, it was true. He knew, he had seen everything with his own eyes.

The borzoi felt a sense of relief. His master was here, close by... And he would wake up in a little while. Perhaps tomorrow. How much longer could he go on lying here? But this hope, almost a certainty, gave way to alarm. What if he had already got up and walked away? And was sitting at home, as he used to do? But no. Snow had fallen the night before, and there weren't any tracks in it. Which meant that he was here.

Straining his entire body, the borzoi started scraping away at the base of the mound with his sound paw. Under the layer of fluffy snow earth appeared. Not yielding and damp, exuding a dense, warm, living odour, but crusted hard, the way the earth was at the entrances of animals' abandoned burrows. It had caked together, frozen and turned as solid as stone. His claws made no impression, they did no more than scratch it. The borzoi stopped scraping and froze, gazing at the elongated mound. Cold. Immovable. Like a black boulder that has grown roots deep into the ground... No, not like that. There, deep inside it, his master was lying. His master was lying under this mound!

226

He turned his head and glanced down into the depression, at the ravine overgrown with bushes. In summer a stream of icy water flowed from a spring in a narrow crevice at its beginning. The bottom of the wide-sprawling ravine was covered with green grass then, grass so tall that the backs of the yearling foals could barely be seen in it. But now both the ravine and the spot above it where the *auyl*[1] camped for the summer had been completely blanketed over with snow. The only dark spot, in a little hollow protected from the wind, was a crooked wall – all that remained of the old encampment. When the *auyl* was preparing to move on the last time, a sick lamb, covered in short, sparse wool, had been left lying at the foot of that wall. It had stayed lying there, it didn't get up again. And it would never get up again. It would never munch on the luscious young grass or drink its fill of the spring's transparent water. All that was left now at the spot where it had been lying were thin, little, white bones that had never been given a chance to grow strong...

It was like a flash of lightning, like a blow from a whip. A previously unfathomable secret was suddenly revealed to the borzoi. And it was so monstrous that his ears stood up erect and he froze motionless, staring at the mound. Enough time to gnaw through a large shinbone passed before the borzoi emerged from his stupor and recovered his senses. But then all his joints turned feeble and limp and his body started trembling rapidly. His throat went dry, the fur on his back stood up on end and chilly shivers ran down the nape of his neck. He squatted down on his hind legs, lifting his face up to the sky. His mouth opened of its own accord, and a long, dismal, lingering sound burst out of his throat. The silence of the steppe was shattered as that groan soared high above the Earth.

And that groan, that pitiful lament for what had been lost irretrievably, was terrible and never-ending...

2

How bright the world was! How large and wide! And the sky – how blue and high it was! And the Sun! Be careful, of course, not to look at it directly, but even so – how warm it was, how gentle! The white puppy sitting in the hot Sun beside the wall of the shed surrendered to his impulse and started whimpering in pleasure. It was so dry and soft here, lying on a bundle of straw mixed with scraps of dried horse dung... What bliss!

Close by was a puddle filled with melted water. A yellow puddle, yellow water. The puppy got up, walked over and slurped cautiously – once, twice. The

---

[1] *Auyl* – socio-economic formation considered to constitute the heartland of the nation and a basis for an ethnic and cultural union of the nomadic community. Consisting of 50–70 yurts in the eighteenth century, it developed into its current permanent state of 'rural settlement' (of a minimum of 100 dwellers) when Kazakhs adopted a settled mode of life in the nineteenth and twentieth centuries. *Auyl* can also be used as a synonym for 'native land' and 'homeland', concepts revered by the Kazakhs.

water had an unpleasant, salty taste, and a disgusting smell of cattle dung. The puppy snorted. No, this water could not be drunk. He had already learnt that all things could be divided into those that could be eaten or drunk and those that were unsuitable for that purpose. There were far more of the unsuitable things, unfortunately...

However, the puppy's disappointment was short-lived. He started skipping over the crumbly snow. The snow had turned dark and was covered with a layer of refuse and soot, his paws sank down deep into it and water immediately ran into the little hollows of his tracks. But granules of ice glittered intensely around their edges: although they couldn't be eaten, they could be licked. But they had no taste at all and they made his tongue feel cold. The puppy turned away. He wasn't feeling hungry – before they let him out into the yard, they had given him plenty of milk and he still felt full.

Meanwhile, his old place at the bottom of the wall of the shed, where he had been warming himself in the sunshine, had been taken by a speckled hen and her bustling family. And she was clucking, rustling straw and raking through the refuse with all her might. Her little chicks, yellow and tousled, squeaked as they rushed about this way and that and dived under their mother's legs. She only had to give the signal, and they went flocking to answer the call, jostling as they tried to overtake each other: 'Gimme! Gimme! I want some, I want some!' An instant later the covey of little round bundles of fluff would scatter again. But then the call would come once more: 'I found something! I found something' – and the chicks went dashing to their mother, stumbling and falling on their way. It was interesting to watch these amusing creatures. But it must be even more interesting to play with them...

The puppy wagged his short little tail and gave a friendly yap: he dashed down a snowdrift, burying himself up to the chest in crumbly snow. But the hen immediately raised the alarm: 'Run for it! Run for it!' The chicks, who had been darting about jauntily, went racing to the speckled hen, dashing into the safety of her protection. The chicken spread her wings bellicosely: 'Get away! Get away, you mangy puppy!' she clucked.

This was an awkward turn of events! The puppy pulled up short. One little chick stuck its little black beak out, but immediately disappeared back under the distended feathers. Well, well... The puppy took two or three uncertain steps anyway, sank down onto the ground, lay there for a while and yapped, then got up and yapped again. And at that the hen became really furious. Apparently she no longer intended to limit herself to simply clucking 'Get away! Get away!' and had readied herself to attack. The puppy was totally disconcerted, but entirely unexpectedly, perhaps simply in order to be contrary, he took a step forward. The hen rose to meet him, her wings spread out menacingly. It seemed as if she was about to dart straight at the puppy... But instead of that the speckled hen suddenly turned her tail towards him and retreated unhurriedly behind the shed, preserving her dignity and clucking her 'Get away!' And the chicks went with her...

The puppy, saddened at losing his chance to gambol about for a while and let off steam with some racing and chasing, also turned round and started plodding towards the outskirts of the *auyl* on his own.

The earth had not dried out yet. In the hollows and depressions sky-blue puddles glittered, steaming lightly. White patches of snow still lay in the dense thickets of meadowsweet, but everything all around had changed and taken on a strange, new, surprising appearance. Only just recently everything here had looked so dreary and sullen, but now it had lit up with a bright smile and was scurrying in jubilant haste to drink its fill of the golden juice of the Sun's rays. There was a fresh, invigorating fragrance in the air. Where was that sweet smell coming from?

The puppy realised that it was oozing out of the scrubby little plant with the slim stalk and fluffy cap that he was trampling. He lowered his face and thrust his nose into the fragrant herb. It probably couldn't be eaten, but it was delightful to smell... On all sides of him there were clumps of tender, springy stems forcing their way up out of the damp depths, and each one of them had its own kind of scent. The puppy especially enjoyed sniffing at the taut arrows of feather grass, which were growing there in abundance. What a smell! His entire puppyish being was seized by incomprehensible joy and he rolled about, wallowing ecstatically in the soft, caressing verdure. Then he stretched out on the ground with his legs splayed wide, presenting his little belly to the Sun.

He stretched out, warmed up a bit, fell into a doze and had a dream. He saw a yellow chick standing in front of him and cheeping, inviting him to play. Such a tiny, little baby bird... Naturally, he replied with a jolly bark, and then they both started chasing each other around. But how fleet-footed that little chick was! It simply couldn't be caught... The puppy didn't fall behind though, he kept chasing after that little scampering bundle of yellow so hard that the wind whistled in his ears. And eventually he caught up with it. Now he could grab that tiny, fluffy creature. It would easily fit into his mouth. A chick was just the very thing for eating, wasn't it... What an unexpected discovery! Yes, yes, a chick was good for eating! But suddenly the little yellow bundle stopped right in front of the puppy's nose and posed there fearlessly, refusing to give way. 'Gr-r-r!' the chick suddenly exclaimed. 'Now it's your-r-r tur-r-rn to r-r-run away!'

The puppy shuddered and opened his eyes. Standing over him was a huge dog, a black mongrel, snarling and baring its teeth. The puppy licked his lips as if everything was perfectly fine, gave a long yawn and stretched. Then he yapped in a thin little voice and started getting up. But the black dog leaned down to the puppy, tumbled him back over onto the ground, and after that... Before the puppy could even understand what was happening, his body was seared with scorching flames, a reddish-green mist started swirling in front of his eyes and everything around him started swaying about.

'Hey, *ket*! Get away! Go away!'

The desperate howl mingled with the clatter of horse's hooves growing louder as they approached. The weight pressing down on the puppy's chest disappeared. He scented his master, who had arrived just in time, and started whining and groaning pitifully. His master dismounted hastily. And then his hands took hold of the puppy and lifted him up off the ground... But although the touch of those hands was gentle and cautious, it stabbed into the trembling little body painfully, piercing through it like a spear. The puppy started whimpering and groaning again, as if he was still caught in the jaws of that huge, black dog.

Leading his horse by the reins, the puppy's master held him tenderly against his chest and carried him like that all the way to the house, then tormented him for a long time, smearing something on his unbearably painful wounds. Eventually the puppy's master bandaged him up and laid him on an iron bedstead standing in the centre of the room with nets stretched around its sides. And now those same hands fed the puppy and carried him out into the fresh air three or four times a day. The puppy spent the rest of the time lying motionless on the bed. There wasn't much space there for getting up and walking around, and he wasn't strong enough yet to jump over the nets. And he didn't feel like doing that anyway...

Two or three weeks later the wounds on the puppy's body had healed up. But his heart had suffered a wound that could not be healed. Naturally, it was quite beyond him to comprehend that injustice, cruelty and violence exist in this world, and even though you may be entirely in the right, that will not be enough to protect you when you are assailed by misfortune... Of course, it goes without saying that he was not able to understand all this. But from that time onwards, everything unfamiliar aroused his mistrust, or even outright hostility.

3

When the puppy had already recovered and returned to his carefree life, a boy arrived at his master's house, and he proved to be a real scamp. As soon as he had jumped down off the bullock cart, he went dashing straight to the puppy. But the puppy had already learnt to divide all people into two kinds: his masters – who included, by the way, the woman in long clothes who filled his bowl right up to the edges every day and busied herself about the house – and outsiders, strangers. The puppy shied away from the boy and hid behind his master. But the puppy's master didn't even glance at him, although he hugged the boy close and kept kissing him over and over again... Freeing himself from that strong embrace, the boy reached out for the puppy again. What was the puppy to do? Since the puppy's master had shown such great affection for the boy, the puppy had no right to run away from him. And the puppy's master actually squatted down on his haunches and encouraged him: 'Lašyn, Lašyn,[2] come here to us!'

---

[2] Lašyn means 'falcon'.

The boy's hands turned out to be soft and gentle. He fondled the puppy and lifted him up. Crooning 'my little doggy', he started stroking the puppy's head and back, and then brought his own face close to the puppy's little face covered in white fur and sniffed, drawing the air in through his nose. He took no notice of his mother, who had led the mare back home, because the time had come for her to be milked, although as soon as his mother spotted him she had begun calling: 'Ädil! Ädiltaj!'[3] He clutched the puppy close to his chest and ran into the house.

Early that evening a lot of people gathered here. It was crowded round the low, round table with a heap of fresh, ruddy *bauyrsaks*[4] towering up on it, and all those dazzling white lumps of sugar. Ädil set Lašyn on his knees and fed him *bauyrsak* and sugar lumps and they were surrounded by the sounds of a feast, with contented guests making jolly conversation and sipping on their extra-strong, dark-brown tea, primed with camel's milk.

'He's grown into a genuine *žigit*',[5] said the *aksakal*[6] Omar, smiling as he looked at Ädil. 'Many long years of health and happiness to him!'

'Right, Kazy, you must celebrate your joy for forty days',[7] put in the pockmarked shop manager Esenžol, who had brought Ädil. 'The teachers said that your Ädil was the very best of all the pupils who completed the class, and there were twenty-five of them who completed classes. They said he can solve the problems for the second and third class and he has learnt all the textbooks off by heart. Now he won't keep pestering you any more – "tell me a story..." He'll read all the books in the Kyzylotau[8] himself before autumn...'

'He takes after his father... As the saying goes, a man following in the footsteps of his ancestors will hone his arrows sharp...'

'But I think the *pwaise* for that is due to my *wittuw sistew Kamiwa*', Esenžol's wife, Ajsùlu, chipped into the general conversation. She blurred her l's and r's, and now that she had stuffed her mouth with *bauyrsaks*, she had to struggle hard to get out every word as she chewed on them. 'She's so *capabuw*... Just *wook* at how many dung cakes she has laid up in her *yawd*... Oh, and she's so *diwigent awound* the *househowd*, so *vewy diwigent* ...'

'Be quiet wife, you'll have your say later, don't interrupt the *aksakal*...'

---

[3] Ädiltaj – term of endearment for the name Ädil.

[4] *Bauyrsak* – fried wheat dough found in the cuisines of Central Asia; a must-have treat for guests during special occasions.

[5] *Žigit* – generally denoting a 25- to 40-year-old male, the term can also be used as an honorific indicating bravery, endurance, fortitude and being true to one's word.

[6] *Aksakal* – traditionally, a well-respected and powerful elder in charge of the community. Nowadays, a reverential form of address to elderly men in general.

[7] This refers to a Kazakh saying that one celebrates a great occasion for forty days.

[8] Kyzylotau ('Red tent') was a mobile library in the remote parts of the USSR.

'What do you mean by *owdewing* me about *wike* that? You *awways tweat* me wike a *thown* in your side... If you think I'm bad, find *youwself* someone *bettew*...'

'Be quiet, I say! Let the people listen to the worthy man.'

'A man following in the footsteps of his ancestors will hone his arrows sharp', the *aḳsaḳal* Omar repeated and paused. 'The late Ämir, Ḳazy's father, was a *žigit* among *žigits*. And he kept superb borzoi dogs. So fleet that they ran down a fox like a whirlwind – not borzois, but panthers. E-eh, you wouldn't believe it from anyone else until you could see it for yourself. Now you want to make all the livestock thoroughbreds. I can't undertake to speak about livestock, but even in ancient times the Kazakhs had the very purest thoroughbred hunting dogs. Mamaj, for instance, had a hunting dog called Besḳara. The son of a certain *baj*[9] offered him five mares with their foals for the dog, but the stubborn man still wouldn't swap. And after that, that was what the borzoi was called – Besḳara, in the sense of 'five head of livestock', although the dog had its own name before then. As I recall, he was grey, with dark stripes – a real tiger. He had such a deep, broad and mighty chest that he didn't lie down on his belly, but only on his side. He had a huge head with powerful cheekbones. No other dog could compare with Besḳara in size. Believe it or not – it's up to you – but wise men whose fame runs from region to region or daring *batyrs*[10] who know not the same fear as other mortals, are born among people. Allah is great! And just so among animals there are some who stand out from their brethren from the day of their birth. Besḳara was such a dog. My winter meadow and Mamaj's were next to each other, so I saw him with my own eyes: in one winter Besḳara took thirteen wolves. And as for hares and foxes – there was no counting them. He even often went after the wild mountain sheep. Later Mamaj kept a grey borzoi bitch at home, he said she was from Besḳara. The borzoi bitch lived to a great old age and died in the year the war ended, in spring. She sensed that death was close and went away, no one knows where to. People are right when they say, A good dog doesn't want to be seen dead. Mamaj was in mourning for days. When some men die, their families don't grieve as much for them. And to tell the truth, although she wasn't Besḳara, that borzoi bitch was the genuine article. You can't find thoroughbreds like that now. How could people ever find the time to look after a dog properly, or keep a hunting bird...'

'Yes, that's the way of it', said Ḳazy. 'Who would pasture the state's livestock then, and mow the hay...' A cough erupting from deep inside Ḳazy's chest choked off his breathing and he left the phrase unfinished.

'Who would drink the vodka then?' Esenžol put in, and his pockmarked face wrinkled into a crumpled smile.

---

[9] *Baj* – rich person, landowner.

[10] *Batyr* – originally term for 'hero' or 'valiant warrior', roughly equivalent to the European knight; nowadays the term signifies military or masculine prowess.

'Why don't you just keep quiet! You'll *obviouswy* never make a good shop managew', said Ajsůlu. 'And what kind of shop is that, without any vodka, Oh *Lowd?*'

'Well it's a good thing that there's none of that hellish stuff on the table', Omar said, nodding in approval to Esenžol. 'Well done to you for not bringing any.'

'I would have brought some', Esenžol chuckled, 'only it all ran out, there isn't a single bottle at the depot. This is a backward region, so they tell us. They say: you still live according to the old ways, but you're beginning to get a bit more savvy about culture, too. One crate used to be enough for our *auyl* for the entire winter. Apart from the two of us, me and the farm manager, no one ever even tasted the stuff. Well, but last autumn I got in three crates of white vodka with red wine – and it disappeared in a flash. Even Ḳazy, the last time he went to the district centre, got as thick as thieves with the cursed stuff. In the summer, when everybody goes off to the high mountain pastures, the only hope I have left is the *aḳsaḳal*... But he's never even tried a sip in his life, he says it takes away the power of the namaz.'

'May Allah forgive you, you idle prattler', Omar sighed. 'Even for those who don't observe His precepts, vodka is still a depraved thing.'

'Eh, *aḳsaḳal*, you've never tasted it, that's why you reason like that. Ḳazy over there tried it once and saw that his entire life until then had flown by in vain. And that's good for me: I have someone to chink glasses with. As Allah is my witness, soon he'll give his wife away for half a litre...'

'Stop harping on about it. You're always prattling about something! Yes, it happened, I did take a drink – so now what of it?'

'Drink, and make it often, good luck to you...'

'It's just like it used to be in the old days with *ḳirdas*,[11] they're always making fun of each other', said Nůrila *bǎjbiše*,[12] Omar's wife, a dark-faced, gaunt old woman in a white *kimešek*.[13] She wanted to change the subject.

'When *ḳuwdases* get *togethew*, things get *jowwy*', Ajsůlu put in.

The puppy, completely gorged on *bauyrsaḳs* and sugar, suddenly yapped as if in approval of her words.

'That's old age for you', said Omar, shaking his head. 'I started talking about one thing and switched over onto something else... What was it I was talking about?'

---

[11] *Ḳirdas* – term for people of the same age or contemporaries. In Kazakh culture, relations between *ḳirdases* are affectionate, allowing the taking of liberties and undue familiarity, and often accompanied with poking fun at each other.

[12] *Bǎjbiše* – first wife in the traditional polygamous family; also elderly wife, respected woman, as well as form of address to a hostess.

[13] *Kimešek* – traditional headdress for married women. It comes in different forms depending on the region and the social and marital status of the person wearing it.

233

'About how there are some dogs that even a man couldn't be compared with', Esenžol joked.

'Yes, I remember now... an animal and a man both resemble their forebears. Ädil here, for instance – with his liking for dogs he takes directly after his grandfather, the late Ämir...'

'And what's more, old Mamaj, whom you were talking about, is a maternal relative of mine', said Ķazy. 'I got this puppy from him when I went to Baķanas this winter. He was the only puppy to be born, and to be honest, Mamaj didn't want to let him go. He said: "My grandson's grown up, he'll go out hunting soon, he'll need a dog..." So I pressured him, I almost took the puppy from him by force. "It will be instead of the *ķyryķ serkeš*,[14] according to the tradition", I said... But the puppy... In your opinion, what is he worth?'

'I've seen quite a number of good dogs, but I've never tried hunting. What kind of connoisseur am I?'

'All the same, compared to us, you're a man of experience. Ädil, let the puppy go... Say your word, *aķsaķal.*'

'What can I say... A big chest – that means he has good stamina for running. A short neck and prominent cheekbones – that means he is sharp-toothed and strong. Back legs with low, stocky calves – that's a sure sign of speed. I don't know if he'll take a wolf, but he'll present us all with fox-fur caps, you mark my words...'

'May all you have said come true! The first cap is yours!' Ķazy exclaimed.

'Mamaj was right not to want to part with him', Esenžol remarked.

A little while later a dish of meat arrived at the table, crowned by a fatty sheep's head with dangling ears, boiled so thoroughly that in places the bones of the skull showed through. But Ädil and his white puppy had already given up the struggle and dozed off by the wall, cheek to cheek.

4

Carefree, halcyon days arrived in Lašyn's life...

Ädil's father warned him:

'He likes wandering about, he's very fond of his freedom and just can't sit still at home. Not long ago that bastard Bardasoķ,[15] Esenžol's mongrel, almost tore him to pieces. If I hadn't turned up, he would have worried the poor little devil to death. I had to put Lašyn on the bed, the one you used to sleep in when you were little. It took him twenty days to get back on his feet. So you be careful not to let him out of your sight.'

But in any case, Ädil was already quite inseparable from Lašyn. Three houses in the midst of the uninhabited steppe – that was the entire *auyl*; there

---

[14] *Ķyryķ serkeš* ('forty goats') – tradition which holds that a *žien* (nephew or niece) can ask a *naġašy* (maternal relative) for any three things at the latter's disposal and the *naġašy* has to oblige.

[15] *Bardasoķ* – lit. 'go and catch'.

weren't any other children here, apart from Ădil, and the puppy was his only amusement, apart from his books. On the very first day he attached a fox's tail to the end of a long *ķuryķ*.[16] Although Lašyn didn't have a clue what it was, nonetheless he resolved to give it a bite – just to be on the safe side. Ădil lowered the end of the tail almost right down onto Lašyn's nose, let him sniff at it, teasing him, then suddenly started spinning round on the spot, holding the *ķuryķ* out at arm's length. Lašyn went dashing after the tail, but it kept flying round in a circle, always staying out of his reach. When it sank down a bit lower, billowing gently through the air, so that its tip almost touched Lašyn's little face, the little puppy would put on speed, but the tail always went soaring back upwards again. The puppy dashed round the circle as fast as he could go. Right, now that thing was going to be caught in his teeth at last! But the elusive tail soared upwards yet again and went flying in the opposite direction. The puppy reversed direction, too. His paws were beginning to feel as heavy as lead, and he was running more and more slowly. But the tail, billowing gently through the air, still didn't move too far away from him. The unfamiliar but pleasant smell it left hanging in the air behind it excited the puppy, igniting a flame of incomprehensible passion in his soul. The thrill of the hunt, assimilated together with the blood of his ancestors, spurred the puppy on again, and he launched himself into pursuit of the fox's tail with even greater fervour.

Then suddenly the fluffy tip of the tail was there in his jaws! The puppy chewed on it and tore at it with relish, dragging the tail across the ground, worrying it and growling. But suddenly the cunning tail slipped out of his teeth again. The puppy launched into pursuit again – and so on many times more, over and over again...

Ķazy's house stood in a spot sheltered from the wind, at the foot of a hill that was overgrown right up to the very summit with feather grass and meadowsweet. The hill merged smoothly into the plain, and when the wind blew, the dense grasses on the hill rippled as if green waves were running through them. Water from a lively little spring babbled along the bottom of a ravine that dissected the plain, and young rushes rustled and murmured along the stream's meandering bed.

Ădil's main responsibility was to drive the mare home at the appointed time for milking – she grazed among the tall grasses that were swelling up with fresh juices, building up their strength. And the puppy, whose head was all that could be seen of him – a white spot flickering among the green stems – rushed after Ădil, hopping and skipping. On the way back he broke into peals of jolly barking as he pursued the little mare. And when she broke into a gallop, Lašyn fell behind, becoming extremely agitated and getting under Ădil's feet.

'Why do you take that stupid puppy along with you?' Kǎmila asked angrily. 'How many times do I have to tell you, the mare mustn't be upset before milking, it makes her lose her milk.'

---

[16] *Ķuryķ* – light pole with a rope and a lasso or a loop at the end used for catching horses.

But Ädil remained as inseparable from the puppy as ever, and the puppy never missed a chance to have some fun with the mare. It was only after Ädil's mother ran out of patience and gave him a heavy clip to the back of his head in a fit of temper, saying: 'Just look at him – so little and so stubborn!' and gave the puppy a hard whack with a stick that happened to be within reach that the little rascal started paying any attention to her admonitions. His father made a beautiful patterned collar and then Ädil led the puppy along with him, restraining his fervid eagerness in good time. But out of force of habit the puppy still started barking as soon as he saw the mare, and the mare, either cowed by his belligerence or taking pity on him and fearing that he might explode from all this frantic barking, went dashing headlong into the *auyl* in the same way as ever. And so it could happen that while Ķazy, after stuffing his saddle bag with books, spent half a day getting to the *auyl* and going out to cut the hay, and at least a day riding round the flock of sheep scattered across the *žajlau*[17] – it could happen that during that time Ädil and Lašyn would feel the rough edge of Kämila's tongue more than once, and also suffer her swift reprisals.

Running along beyond a depression some distance away was a chain of rounded hills, divided by low passes. Dense groves of curly osiers grew everywhere there, and glinting among the thickets of reeds there were springs – transparent and pure, with ice-cold water. The docks growing on the broad meadows were so tall that they could conceal a camel that had sunk down onto the ground...

When summer had moved past its mid-point and the sky had turned incandescent, flooded with an intense, sustained, sultry heat, and the tips of the grass had begun drying out and turning yellow, Ädil started wandering farther and farther away from home and on into the hills during his rambles. Thus far the ravine had been the boundary line for Lašyn, but now a new and unfamiliar world was being revealed to him. A multitude of unfamiliar smells assaulted his nostrils. They included the acrid smell of rotted dung tumbled about in the dust, and the heady smell of a luscious meadow, and the subtle, delicate smell of crimson, yellow and sky-blue flowers, and the damp smell of turf, threaded through by fine roots, and the bitter smell of decomposed wood... This multi-layered aroma set the puppy's head spinning and he yapped joyously in unaccountable exultation as he rolled about on the ground, gambolling round Ädil, whining as he ran to and fro and frolicking in his absolute delight. And the farther they went from the *auyl*, the more often they encountered the scents of all sorts of different kinds of living creatures. There was the smell of a horse here and the smell of a cow there, and a man had walked by this place, and then here there was the smell of the fluffy tail that had flown round and round after the *ķùryķ*... Yes, yes, that tail had been here, where the earth was dug up, then

---

[17] *Žajlau* – highland summer pastures; winter pastures are called *ķystau*: both are integral to the nomadic lifestyle of Kazakhs.

it had circled round a prickly bush and headed off somewhere in the direction of the hills. Lašyn wanted to go chasing after its tracks, but Ádil's voice rang out behind him, ordering him to come back and, like it or not, he had to turn and retrace his steps.

In the small groves of trees on the slopes of the ravines it was cool and even quite humid. The earth here was damp, the grass was soft and silky and there was a smell of briers, hawthorn and hops, but all these smells were swamped by the smell of black currants. It cost Ádil no effort at all to fill his little pail right up to the top with the large berries covered with a misty-blue glaze. Then he found a little spot where the grass was a bit taller and stretched out, setting his head on a thick, exposed root. He lay there on his back under the branches of black currants that hung right down to his face, and from there the sky shone though between the separate leaves with their triple serrations, which tore it into little patches of light-blue, giving it a dappled appearance. But it still looked glorious, and not very distant, he only had to reach up his hand, rake apart the foliage – and there it was, right at his very fingertips... There was an immense abundance of berries in any case, but when he looked up at them from below, he could see even more. They were no longer concealed by the leaves, and they crowded really closely against each other, glistening like little black beads. Crossing one leg over the other, Ádil unhurriedly grabbed entire handfuls of berries and dispatched them into his mouth. And when no berries were left where he could reach them with his hand, he moved to a new spot, shifting himself with his elbows. But soon he was no longer eating the berries by the handful, but lazily plucking one at a time, bursting them almost reluctantly with his lips and straining the slightly bitter juice through his teeth. And then, setting his hands under the back of his head, he lay there for a long time without moving, looking up at the blue sky that paled when clouds drifted across it. The white puppy, imitating his master, would also stretch out flat on the ground, snuggling his chest close against the damp grass; he felt cool here and froze with his head laid on his outstretched paws, not making even a single rustling sound. He wasn't bothered by anything, except the flies and gnats. If not for them, how sweetly he could have slept his fill, how many pleasant dreams he could have had! But after Ádil and the puppy had lain there like that for a while, relaxing in total bliss, the boy would exclaim 'Up we get!', as if he had suddenly remembered something, and jump up off the ground. Wagging his tail, the puppy would jump up after him and shake himself bodily. Jumping over the trickles of spring water that glittered among the darkened, rotten, exposed roots and fallen tree trunks and snapping the clinging threads of hops with a crack, they scrambled out of the blanket of endless underbrush. It was sultry and stifling in the ravine. The Sun blazed down from its highest point, scorching Ádil's forehead, and he bound up his shaved head with a handkerchief, then he and the puppy ran towards the pass. Here there was a cool breeze blowing, and beyond the pass lay the *auyl*...

Lašyn was six months old now; he had stretched out and grown heavier, so that he looked more like an adult dog. By this time he had realised that there were quite a lot of things in the life and customs of his masters – and not only of his masters, but of all the two-legged creatures – that were beyond his ability to explain. Previously everything, or almost everything, that he encountered had seemed entirely understandable and reasonable to him. But now, when he started pondering, first one thing and then another simply defied comprehension.

Take that mare, for instance. She had four fast, strong legs. She never stumbled or fell, as Ädil did. And if she started galloping, then no man could ever catch up with her. One day the grey mare flew into a temper at something and started kicking out with both of her hind legs so hard that the fence gave way and collapsed onto the ground. What if the man had got in the way of her hooves? What would have been left of him? But despite that, the horse continued to obey the man and did what he told her to do, carrying out all his orders. Even little Ädil was her master. What could Lašyn make of that?

Or take the cow, for instance. She had two horns sticking up on her head – they were thick and sharp. One day Lašyn was circling round her calf and she suddenly bellowed and came rushing at the puppy. If he hadn't jumped aside and run for it, she would have crushed all his bones to dust. But what of it? The cow also served the man submissively. And the poor old camel, who was such a terrible monster, with two big humps – he could easily lift a load that was too heavy for even ten of the two-legged creatures, but he also performed the man's work for him submissively day after day. And he roared, he roared with all his might, the poor creature, but he wouldn't cross the man, not for anything in the world.

And what about the big, black hound that had almost bitten the puppy to death in spring? He had huge back teeth, if he flung himself on anyone, no one could fight off his attack. But even he did as the man told him. He was obedient and even pathetic – he wasn't allowed to enter the house, for instance, as Lašyn was, they didn't let him past the doorstep. And the most important thing in life – food – was also completely in the power of the two-legged creatures. They ate all the sweetest and most delicious things, and they ate as much as they wanted. Of course, Lašyn never suffered from any shortage of food, but looking at the black hound's hollow sides and seeing the way that he prowled round the yards of the houses, trying to sniff something out, Lašyn realised that he didn't get a chance to stuff his belly full very often.

Day by day more and more riddles appeared on all sides. Just take the iron bullock cart in which certain people had come to the *auyl* one day! There wasn't a single horse or camel harnessed to it, it ran along all on its own, and as well as that it made a growling sound like the rumbling of distant thunder. And on another occasion an immense bird had landed in the steppe. Lašyn had gone dashing to the bird, along with the men from the *auyl*, who had saddled up their horses. Some other men had climbed out of the iron bird and stood there for a while, talking to the men on horseback and asking them about something, and then got back into the bird, which had turned out to have an appalling voice and, what was more, when the bird flew up into the air, it blew up an entire dust storm. If Lašyn was left alive, it was only because he had moved faster than the horses who were retreating in the face of the fierce blast of wind and had managed to run out of the way...

The more mysterious men seemed to Lašyn, the more he believed in men's power. And there was also a certain event that occurred, following which he completely stopped being surprised by the way everything in the world was subservient to men, and acknowledged men's absolute and indisputable superiority...

This was what happened. After yet another excursion for black currants, he and Ädil were on their way back to the *auyl*, and no sooner had they rounded the tall bushes of honeysuckle with which the shallow slope was overgrown than they saw the black dog Bardasoķ right there in front of them. Only two steps away, the length of a horse's rein. The gaunt hound was plundering the reserves of seeds and straw collected together by field mice, impatiently raking away the soft earth with his paws. He scraped away for a little while, then stuck his nose into the burrow and sniffed, growling with greed. Then he went back to work, growing more and more excited every time, probably scenting that his booty was near... Ädil froze in astonishment at finding the dog engaged in such a strange occupation. Well, Lašyn's heart skipped a beat too at the sight of his sworn enemy. Every little bone and every little joint in his body started trembling and he cowered under Ädil's feet, taking shelter there. And then Ädil recalled what his father had told him about this black bandit who had almost torn Ädil's puppy, his dear little Lašyn to pieces when the puppy was still very little...

He bent down, fumbling at the ground with his hand. Hearing a rustle, the dog jerked his head out of the burrow, but it was too late. No sooner had he turned his head towards the danger than a sharp, hefty stone hit him in the side. The dog's desperate yelp echoed back from the knolls and he broke into a run, hunching up his back from the pain. A second stone, slightly smaller than the first one, went flying after Bardasoķ and missed, plopping down somewhere in the clumps of meadowsweet. 'Damn!' exclaimed Ädil, slapping his thighs in annoyance. Only then did Lašyn, who had not been expecting such turn of events, awake from his stupor and gather his wits. And then he was overcome by fury. He started barking in a thin little voice and rushed after Bardasoķ, who was skedaddling for all he was worth. Lašyn pursued his old enemy for quite a distance before reluctantly halting in obedience to loud calls from Ädil, who was running after Lašyn, pleading with him to come back. And it was a long time before he was able to gather his wits and recover from the shock that had overturned all his previous ideas about life, about his own existence, about who was strong and who was weak... If Ädil, the smallest of all the two-legged creatures that he knew, was capable of this, then what were the others capable of?

'Where did I come from, who am I, where am I going?' No, of course, complex philosophical questions such as these did not arise in the puppy's mind. But after the events just described, Lašyn was convinced that there was someone in this world who possessed mighty, invincible powers. By controlling those powers, he could do anything he wanted. And the owner of these powers was called man.

5

Ķazy gave a dry, hacking cough as he unfastened the hook on the swollen door. Skipping past his master, Lašyn darted outside. And after darting outside, he screwed up his eyes, which were blinded by the incredibly bright light. Everything all around, which had been dirty-grey or brown only yesterday, had changed today: the distant hills, and the yard, and the roofs of the sheds – they were all covered in a blanket of festive white. Shivering slightly in the fresh air, Lašyn took two or three steps forward. Something crunched lightly under his paws. He looked back. There were tracks printed out clearly behind him. And there was his master, walking over to the barn, and there was a clear line of marks stretching out behind him too. Lašyn stood still on the spot for a while, bewildered by this new discovery, before following his master's example and setting off towards the barn. And then he saw more tracks, and they looked like his own, only a bit smaller. He poked his nose into them, and it turned out that they had been left by Bardasoķ. From the look of things, Bardasoķ must have been circling around here, searching for something that he could eat.

The air was pure, without any strange scents, and the crisp frost made it denser – Lašyn felt strength flooding into his chest with every breath. He ran the length of the yard several times, flinging up the dry, glittering snow. He wanted to go dashing to the spring, and then through the pass that was like the crooked curve of a camel's shoulder, and gambol about in the open space. It was only the fear that Bardasoķ might be wandering about somewhere nearby that stopped him. And apart from that, seeing that his master had led out his horse and was tying him to the outside of the fence, he decided that his master must be preparing to go somewhere and he might take Lašyn with him.

The puppy, only so recently lanky-legged, dock-tailed and paunchy-bellied, had already developed into an almost adult borzoi. He had grown sturdier and put more flesh on his bones, his chest had broadened out, his belly had tightened up. His head, disproportionately large in comparison with his body, could withstand any attempts at fault-finding by the experts: the crown was high and intelligent-looking, the ears were large and adequately broad, dangling down like shaggy burdock. And his straight, white teeth were long and sharp where they ought to be and short and strong where they ought to be, the kind of teeth that you couldn't help admiring when he opened his mouth – those teeth looked capable of gnawing through a bone from even the very strongest camel. After Ädil went back to his school, Ķazy looked after the growing puppy. Avoiding giving the borzoi food that might make him put on fat, Ķazy had waited for the first sprinkling of snow. But as ill luck would have it, autumn had dragged out. Long bouts of drizzly rain set in and dreary, dank winds started blowing. However, if the dog wasn't taken out hunting before he was a year old, the muscles on his neck would lose their flexibility and set hard, and then he would never become a nimble dog with a tenacious grip. That was what especially concerned Ķazy. And when at last the first snow did fall, he tossed and turned all night in bed, got up when it was still dark, hurriedly saddled up his horse and fed Lašyn with broth, and having managed to do all this in the short time needed to boil milk,[18] he rode out of the yard.

He chose the slopes of Žauyrtaġy to hunt on. And what a multitude of different markings Lašyn saw on the fresh snow there! Large and small tracks, for the most part with forms and smells that were entirely unfamiliar: sometimes they intertwined and sometimes they stretched out in long lines, and sometimes they ran off in different directions. He was ready to go dashing off along every track, only his master's command held him back and restrained his impatience. But then a track appeared that looked like the track left beside the barn by Bardasoķ, only not so big. The borzoi caught the scent of the long, fluffy tail that he had chased after in the summer... Lowering his head to the ground, the dog began trotting over the stony ground. But his master didn't follow him, on the contrary, he called the borzoi back in a low voice. Then he pointed in the opposite direction and swung his horse round. Lašyn realised he had made a mistake, but soon he was dashing confidently along the track, running ahead of his master.

Not far from a plateau among low hills sparsely covered with pea shrub, the bushy tail had suddenly slowed its pace and started weaving about in search of prey among the snow-sprinkled bushes. Here and there they came across mouse burrows that it had dug up; earth that hadn't frozen yet was mingled with crumbly snow. The bushy tail had sometimes climbed up onto a hill and sometimes dived down into a hollow, spending a long time there weaving from side to side. The inexperienced dog, who stuck diligently to the track, probably circling back to the same spot about ten times, eventually grew tired of chasing after an animal that was either far too cunning or simply stupid – and all without any result... But when Lašyn's master approached him, the fervour of the hunt blazed up inside him once again and he trotted on along the track, which now turned uphill. No sooner had he passed the crest of the hill than down below, at its foot, he spotted an animal that darted into the thickets of pea shrub bushes – the same animal that he had been searching for unsuccessfully for so long. And the animal's tail really was long and bushy, and the animal's appearance was like a dog's in some ways. But the animal was fiery-red and it resembled a flame fanned by the wind... It was impossible not

---

[18] An age-old Kazakh unit of time.

to be lost in admiration at the sight of it, spread out on the white snow like a hot, red flame... Just for an instant Lašyn froze, but a second later, he was flying downwards like an arrow, flinging up the snow with his strong paws.

The distance between them was shrinking rapidly and the characteristic scent of a fox reached the borzoi's nostrils. Lašyn could clearly see the animal's back ahead of him. 'I'm fast!' the young borzoi exulted. 'Oh, how fast I am!' Although the vixen's legs were short and it ran with a scurrying motion, it still ran so fast that it was quite impossible to overtake. Lašyn had already been only a lasso's length away, but then he noticed that the gap between them had started to grow. The vixen was heading across the depression now, slipping away little by little in the direction of the hills. If she could just reach the stony slope, she would be saved... But unfortunately for her, the dark figure of the dog's master appeared up ahead. He had clearly decided to steal a march on her and was galloping to cut her off. The vixen also summoned up all her strength, but the man, lashing on his horse and shouting at the top of his voice, managed to cut off her path. The animal swerved to one side and started running at an angle, managing to gain a small distance. Now she could hope that, having got a start on the horseman, she would be able to slip away across the slope to a safe place. And after a while the horseman, galloping along the foot of the hill, really did start falling back. The borzoi was no longer a danger to the vixen either, and it seemed that in just a moment she would be beyond their reach...

But at that very moment a broad depression opened up ahead of the vixen. And she realised that she had made a fatal mistake. The land along the depression was overgrown with tall, dried-out, coarse grass, sprinkled with a fine layer of snow. In summer this place had been a green meadow that had never known a sickle and the luscious grass, growing free and untrammelled, could conceal a horse up to its very head. But now this meadow, faded and withered, represented an almost insuperable barrier for the vixen with her short legs. What could she do? Not seeing any other way out, she dashed straight into the depression; on its sleep slope the grass was not so thick. But the dry stalks pricked and scratched her belly, and the vixen skipped up into the air as she ran, flinging her whole body upwards. Yet those brittle stems were no obstacle to a young, long-legged dog full of energy, and his speed was not reduced. The distance that the vixen had managed to gain by squeezing everything possible out of her four legs was rapidly shortening. 'I'll catch her!' the borzoi exulted again. 'Just a little bit further... and I'll catch her!'

The vixen was in a lather, with her tail hopelessly bedraggled. It was no longer bushy and fluffed out in the wind, but trailed along behind her, slowing her down in addition to everything else. 'Now!' the borzoi thought triumphantly. 'Now I'll grab her!' His teeth clacked in anticipation of the moment when the tip of that fiery-red tail would be caught in his jaws. But at that very moment the steep, grassy slope broke off and the vixen's paws touched smooth ground, made bright by its mantle of snow, with spears of feather grass sticking up here

242

and there. Summoning up her final strength and almost fainting from the fear that had thrust its sharp claws into the back of her head, the vixen sprinted forward. Death, clacking its jaws, dropped back a little, but for how long? The distance between the fox and the dog was no longer than a horse's rein. And in addition, so much strength had been spent on conquering the steep slope... Her paws had grown heavy and they parted from the ground without their former lightness. But the horror of imminent death drove the vixen on.

Behind her the snow crunched regularly, the sounds getting louder and louder, proclaiming the steady approach of her enemy, and the heavy, snuffling breathing that the vixen could hear so clearly testified that sharp, remorseless teeth were ready to sink themselves into her delicate body at any moment. Sweat clouded her eyes and reddish mist swirled all around. Not even hoping that it would deliver her from danger, but instinctively, simply out of habit, the vixen hoisted up her tail – and it rose up in the dog's path, the final obstacle and her only defence. The young borzoi was guileless! Thus far he had chased the vixen not at all in order to grab her and tear her to pieces. This pursuit was a kind of amusement for him. He wanted to overtake the vixen, pinch her gently in his teeth, roll her about on the snow and tumble about, playing a game. When the red tail blossomed right in front of his eyes, he took this for a new game too and strove with all his might to grab that tail. But the tail swayed from side to side and didn't allow him to take possession of it. No sooner did it flutter right in front of his muzzle than it immediately darted off to one side. The borzoi turned his muzzle and took aim – now he would grab it! – but the tail had already shot upwards and flitted out of reach. Out of sheer inertia the dog went hurtling past, and the cunning little beast had already turned aside, to the distance of a *ķiryķ*. In his eagerness the dog galloped in pursuit, close on her heels. But that red flame flared up somewhere on the left, then on the right, and then on the left again – the borzoi's jaws grabbed at empty air, he swung his head and saw that the vixen had gained a distance that he couldn't cover even in three good bounds.

This pursuit had drained Lašyn's strength. And while he was scrambling up the steep slope, puffing and panting, the vixen suddenly swerved off towards some thickets of meadowsweet, ran round them, finally exhausting the borzoi, and launched herself forward along a straight line, still fanning out her bushy, wily tail. A moment later she had skipped through the narrow little saddle between two hills and disappeared from view.

Lašyn stopped. His chest was bursting, his tongue had swollen and didn't fit into his mouth. His legs ached and wouldn't obey him, as if they didn't belong to him at all, and his head was spinning. The line of tracks running off up the slope, the intertwined branches of the bushes, the hills white from snow – everything was drifting and swaying about... But suddenly the borzoi gave a start, although for an instant he couldn't believe his eyes. The very same vixen that he thought he had finally lost track of came darting out from behind a rocky ledge and hurtled towards him at full speed.

No doubt the cunning little beast had not suspected that the dog chasing her was still *kôk asyk*, that is, 'green' and immature, and was capable of breaking off the pursuit at the decisive moment. Yes, the vixen had not expected that... After skipping through the saddle, she had dashed to one side along the rocky slope, on which she left no tracks, and doubled back round the hill. In this way she was counting on wrong-footing the dog who had been gaining on her. But her own cunning was her final undoing: out of the blue the enemy she had managed to deceive so adroitly popped up right in front of her face.

It was all over, the vixen sensed that she had fallen into the claws of death. In desperation she went dashing back, but Lašyn had already managed to recover a bit and catch his breath, and he overtook her in two bounds. Now that tail trailing along the ground was in his jaws. The vixen turned back and bit the borzoi on the muzzle. And the dog, who didn't have the slightest intention of causing the fluffy little beast any harm, flew into a fury when those sharp teeth sank into him. Breaking free, the vixen went hurtling off again, but there was nowhere she could find salvation from the monster hovering over her! With a single bound, the dog seized her again, catching her by the hip and striking her against the ground. And then he crushed her in his fangs, once and twice, so that her little ribs crunched...

And then his master arrived. Jumping down off his horse, he ran up to the dog, who was worrying the lifeless vixen: 'Enough, my boy, that's enough!' He grabbed the borzoi's prey out of his jaws, lifted up the vixen by the tail and smashed her head against the ground.

'May your hunting spoils be multiplied threefold!' he exclaimed, smiling at the dog.

Naturally, Lašyn didn't understand the meaning behind those words, but he grasped the most important thing: his master was grateful to him and very pleased.

And so the borzoi learned to kill and realised that he would be praised for it. For him this was the beginning of a life full of constant battle and canine prowess, bloody skirmishes and invariable victories.

6

Soon the borzoi's fame had spread throughout the entire district. And among the men living in the nearby *auyls* it was a rare individual who failed to adorn his head with a brand new fox-fur *tymak*[19] that winter. Everyone was pleased and they all sang Lašyn's praises, especially old Omar. 'Now I don't feel the cold as badly as I used to, in my trashy sheepskin cap', he kept repeating. 'Now I feel warm, and it's all thanks to Ädil for raising such a fine dog, may he prosper, and may he always get top marks at school and be the first among his fellow pupils!' He repeated these words most often when he called in to Ķazy's

---

[19] *Tymak* – fur cap with large ear flaps for a cold season made of lamb, hare, marten, sable, steppe fox and fox leather, the latter being the most esteemed.

house to hear the latest news about his young favourite. The sheepherders and watchmen from the winter pastures in the district either dropped in to see Ḳazy themselves, or sent him greetings through a messenger, but one way or another each one of them managed to obtain a fox from him. And Bekḳali, the farm manager, even acquired two fox-fur *tymaḳs*: he wore one in the *auyl* and the other when he travelled to the collective farm's board of management or to the district centre. And only the shop manager Esenžol was left without a fox. 'First let him stop short-changing people on his abacus', Ḳazy had supposedly said. 'And let him stop his cheating and tittle-tattling!'

Once, not long after that first hunt, Ḳazy left the *auyl* together with Bekḳali, who was in a hurry to reach the district centre with the annual report. They came back home about two or three weeks later and on the evening of that day the inhabitants of the four houses, which together were referred to as the 'central estate' of the farm, gathered at Ḳazy's house. In an exception to the usual rule, on this occasion three bottles of transparent liquid were lined up at the centre of the large table. But at this well-laden table there was none of the lively animation that had filled the house with light and joy after Ädil's return. Most of the talking was done by Omar and all the others, including fat Bekḳali, who was not even thirty yet but already had a bulging stomach and fat, greasy, glistening cheeks, and pockmarked Esenžol, as sly and tricky as a red vixen, and Ajsùlu, who couldn't pronounce the r's and l's in her words – all of them assiduously poured that transparent liquid into themselves. Even Kämila and Bekḳali's wife sampled it once. Lašyn noticed that both of them winced and wrinkled up their noses when they did it. The transparent drink probably didn't taste very good, it must be bitter... But the borzoi's master certainly didn't say no to it. He poured it for his guests, encouraging them to drink up, and he didn't forget about himself either. Whenever he started coughing with a harsh, wheezing, whistling sound, he immediately tipped another little glassful into his mouth. And then Lašyn's master behaved in very strange manner: although his guests had not gone home yet, he slumped over onto the cushion, fell asleep and started snoring. That wasn't like him... Not at all like him. Something had happened to him, some change in his life...

Ḳazy often went out hunting, especially if there had been a light sprinkling of snow, on which an animal left fresh, clear tracks. At the crack of dawn he and Lašyn set out in search of game if there had been what the Kazakhs call an *uzaḳsonar* or a *ḳansonar*, or a *kelte sonar*:[20] by reading the snow like a page of an open book, an experienced eye could tell how long ago an animal had passed by and how far away it had already gone. And sometimes, without waiting for the weather, Ḳazy simply relied entirely on his dog and the dog's

---

[20] *Sonar* – refers to a day convenient for hunting, usually the day after snowfall (when animal tracks are clearly visible): *uzaḳsonar* is the day following a night when it stopped snowing at midnight, *ḳansonar* is the day following a night when snow kept on falling until the morning, and *kelte sonar* is a period when fine snow sprinkles down night and day.

nose, gumption and speed. And for good reason: even on the least successful days they returned home with at least a pair of hares. Lašyn had grown sturdier, his body had become springy and resilient, his muscles had filled out and his very size and appearance inspired involuntary fear in strangers. But at home in the *auyl* he actually behaved rather timidly, perhaps recalling the terrible fear he had once experienced there in the jaws of a certain black dog...

But one evening, when Ķazy, who coughed incessantly now, had taken some of his bitter drink, lain down and covered himself snugly in order to break into a sweat, Lašyn went darting out of the door and stopped dead on the threshold: Bardasoķ was in the yard. He was rummaging greedily in a heap of refuse. Bardasoķ noticed Lašyn too. Standing sideways on to the borzoi, he merely turned his head, bared his teeth and growled. Lašyn, however, heard more fear than menace in his growl. Rather surprised and reassured by this, he looked more intently at this dog that he hadn't seen for such a long time. Bardasoķ seemed to have shrunk in size and had a scruffy, pitiful kind of look. He had evidently also compared his own strength with the borzoi's and realised that if there was going to be a brawl his prospects were poor. He put his tail between his legs with a low, dull growl and took off at a run towards his own home. The borzoi was suddenly overwhelmed by fury. In a few rapid bounds he overtook the black dog and grabbed him in the same way as he flung himself on vixens, sinking his teeth into Bardasoķ's groin, slamming him down on the ground and falling bodily on top of him. But the dog proved to be stronger than a vixen. Howling desperately, he bit the borzoi anywhere he could, and only stopped resisting when Lašyn's sharp fangs closed on his neck. Hoarse gurgling sounds bubbled up in his throat and his paws jerked convulsively, scraping at the ground.

Blood flooded the borzoi's eyes and he carried on throttling Bardasoķ, blind to everything in front of him. He was only brought back to his sense by a sudden blow. For a brief instant Lašyn thought that his spine had cracked and broken in two – Esenžol had given him the fiercest kick he could manage with his steel-tipped boot. And the shop manager immediately took a swing for a second kick, but Lašyn dodged that one, releasing his victim and jumping aside, only he didn't run – he halted and stood there facing Esenžol with his teeth bared.

Ķazy, who had heard the noise of the dogs' brawl, darted out into the street and dashed at Esenžol, limping on one leg.

'Hey, what are you beating my dog for?' he shouted.

'Beating it? Why, I'll skin the hide off it!'

'The hide? Why you... Who are you?'

'Ah, so you don't know yet?' Esenžol laughed. 'You'll find out. I'll make sure you do. You'll go the way of your *naġašy*.'

'My *naġašy*'s got nothing to do with you', said Ķazy, suddenly quietening down. 'And don't go threatening me. People say you can bend the truth, but you can't break it. I spilt my blood. Everyone knows that. There!' Ķazy bent down slightly and slapped one palm against his wooden leg.

'Eh, sweetheart, we know all about goody-goodies like you! Angels with little wings, that's all you are.' As Esenžol's voice rose higher it started trembling, growing more and more agitated until it broke into a shout. 'Do you think everyone's gone blind and let their guard down? Not everyone! We have eyes and ears too! What kind of books are you collecting in that Ķyzylotau of yours? Eh? What kind of books are they, I say?'

'What do you mean, what kind of books? The kind that Soviet publishing houses publish.'

'They're published by traitors like that *naġašy* of yours! You're all cut from the same cloth... Do you think I don't know what kind of books Esenžan's son, the student, got from you this summer? All German and American. And what do you force on the people who can read here? Old books, old ones! Books that mourn for the past, they wrote about them in the newspapers! They should have been burned ages ago, but you keep them hidden away. Maybe you can tell me what for? Eh? Nothing to say? Say nothing, then. But honest people won't keep quiet!'

'Shut your foul mouth, you despicable scum!' Ķazy exclaimed, grabbing Esenžol by the collar.

Their neighbours had already crowded around them on all sides.

'There, you worthy people! Just look!' said Esenžol, raising his hands. 'Just look! His borzoi tore my dog to pieces, and now he wants to kill me. You can bear witness!'

'You piece of shit!' Ķazy hissed through his teeth. 'Maybe I really should smash your face!'

'You just try it, go on...' Without any effort, Esenžol freed his collar from Ķazy's unclenched fingers and pushed Ķazy away. He looked down at his enemy where he had collapsed awkwardly into the snow. 'You miserable drunk!' he exclaimed abruptly, then snorted in disgust and walked away.

The words spoken during this altercation were beyond Lašyn's comprehension. But it was quite clear to him that the reason for the quarrel was his brawl with Bardasoķ. When Ķazy seized Esenžol by the collar, the fur on the borzoi's back stood up on end and he would have gone rushing in to help his master if the people who had come up hadn't stopped him. But even so Lašyn had been sure that his master would come off best against the scrawny, diminutive shop manager. Only things hadn't worked out that way...

Lašyn usually attached no importance to the way people behaved towards each other. The two-legged creatures weren't all alike, of course. Kǎmila, for instance, took advantage of the fact that she was bigger than Ǎdil and hit him now and then when they were alone together, after which the boy went out to drive home the mare or to fetch water. And one day, when Kǎmila was being especially hard on Ädil, Ķazy flung the boot that he happened to be taking off just then at her... Lašyn attached no importance to all of that, though. But the skirmish for which he had been the cause convinced the borzoi that, like all living creatures, people were divided into the strong and the weak... In spite of that, Lašyn's respect for his master was not diminished in the least. Realizing that Ķazy was ready to intervene for him in a critical situation, even when his enemy was stronger, Lašyn loved him even more than before...

7

Now, after his narrow escape from death, Bardasoķ didn't dare even to come close to Ķazy's house. Whenever he spotted Lašyn in the distance, he promptly hid. And as for Ķazy, although he had suffered defeat in his clash with Esenžol, he wasn't at all intimidated in his presence. Every two or three days he walked into the shop, took a crisp, crackling piece of paper out of his pocket, handed it to Esenžol and then stuffed a bottle filled with that bitter drink inside his outdoor clothes...

The borzoi liked it when he and his master set out in the direction of the shop manager's house, which adjoined the shop. As soon as Bardasoķ sensed their approach, he became extremely agitated. He ran into the porch, darted back out and then hid again, and when his final doubts had disappeared, he preferred to scram and leave the yard altogether. However, Ķazy didn't call into Esenžol's house. Instead, he opened the door of the cramped, little shop in which there was not enough room for two people to turn around, already lowering his hand into his pocket right there in the doorway...

While the walk in that direction was to the borzoi's liking, the walk back was not. As soon as Lašyn had moved away a bit from the shop manager's house, Bardasoķ clambered up onto a heap of dung and burst into hoarse, furious barking, directed at him: 'Frightened, are you? That'll teach you! Get out of here while you're still in one piece!' If Lašyn stopped and looked back, the black dog immediately fell silent. He might even cower down under the gate with his tail between his legs. But as soon as the borzoi set off after his master, the black dog started up again. At first that had made Lašyn angry and he wanted to dart over that way and teach the insolent coward a good lesson, but he soon stopped taking any notice of him. There was something else that did bother Lašyn though. When his master got home, he would knock the cork out the neck of the bottle by striking the glass bottom hard with the palm of his hand, fill a table glass right up to the rim and drink it down in a single gulp. After that, Lašyn could sense that something in him changed... No, he didn't do anything to offend the dog or lay a hand on Kämila – she already tiptoed round the house, quieter than a shadow, in any case... Ķazy simply grasped his head in his hands and sat there without moving for a long time. But no matter how docile he seemed, at those moments Lašyn felt a bit afraid of him.

The houses were few and far between in the *auyl* located next to the farm. The shop that supplied the inhabitants with tea, sugar, various foodstuffs and clothes never had more than three or four customers the whole day long. But Esenžol invariably spent the prescribed period of time sitting behind the counter – from ten in the morning until six in the evening. He clicked the beads on his abacus, calculating and recalculating something, unpacked things or bundled things up. The only break he allowed himself was an hour for lunch, apart from his time off on Sunday. But then, if sheepherders happened to arrive from the distant *kystaus* on his day off, he wouldn't take the lock off the door, no matter how much they pleaded... 'The shop is sealed, I have no right to violate the procedures of the state', he would tell them coolly. 'I only have one head on my shoulders, dear people.' And they had either to go back home or wait until the next day. These men, who tended livestock all year round without any days off, were used to that kind of treatment. It never even entered their heads to be outraged or to complain. And although it was said that Esenžol sold his goods for inflated prices and short-changed his customers into the bargain, people turned a blind eye to it all, thinking themselves lucky to even have a shop like that out there in the remote steppe, and if Esenžol skimmed off ten or fifteen kopecks, they were none the poorer... The steppe-dwellers had big hearts, it wasn't their way to be petty about things and nurse hard feelings!

One day Ķazy came back home without his usual bottle. The bitter drink had run out. He wouldn't have believed it, but Esenžol himself had shown him the empty crate. There was nothing to be done: thoroughly annoyed, Ķazy hobbled back home, limping more badly than usual. Although his master was gloomy, Lašyn was in a cheerful mood. He scampered about beside his master, crunching the snow that had turned hard after a blizzard and even wallowing in a snowdrift once or twice. There was a sparse scattering of granules drifting down from the sky. That meant snow would start falling before the evening and they wouldn't spend tomorrow sitting at home.

Ķazy seemed to guess what the borzoi was hoping for. He took his horse to the spring to drink, then tethered him beside the wicker fence and brought out an armful of fragrant hay. Then he went into the barn and put his saddle and its trappings in good order. And it was only after the crimson-red Sun, glowing dimly through the low clouds, had sunk below the horizon, that he and Lašyn went into the house.

The room was dark and dreary. Ķazy pulled off his boot and set it by the door, then took off his artificial leg and shoved it under the bed in his usual manner. He lay down in front of the stove, on top of a felt rug spread out over a double-folded quilt, setting his elbow on a pillow. The dog settled down at his master's feet. The window was veiled more and more thickly by the darkness of night, which crept into the house through the hoar-frosted panes of glass. Only glimmers of light from the flames that crackled and hissed as they consumed the pressed dung under the top of the cast-iron stove flickered on the walls and the low ceiling. From time to time the gusting wind blew into the chimney, driving the flames back inwards, and they spurted out from behind the shutter of the stove in sharp little tongues. And then the room was lit up with startling harshness for a moment. The borzoi saw his master, still as morose and taciturn as ever, lying there and gazing into the corner with mournful eyes.

The dried dung in the stove gradually burned out, shrinking into dark lumps covered with grey ash, and the darkness on all sides grew thicker and thicker. Only the scorching-hot, cast-iron stove still glowed with crimson heat under the kettle and the *ķazan*[21] that gave an occasional glug. There was meat boiling in the *ķazan* and the smell of cooking horse flesh tickled Lašyn's nostrils, addling his head sweetly... But his master suddenly got up and disappeared into the next room on one leg. He came back holding a *dombyra*.[22] Lowering himself back down in front of the stove, he sat there in silence for a while, and then started playing a melody that Lašyn had never heard before.

Ķazy's fingers did not strike the strings, but merely ran over them, barely even seeming to touch them. For some unfathomable reason the dog felt chilly shivers running over his body. A strange, incomprehensible sorrow filled his heart – a sorrow that seemed mingled with anticipation. An expanse of land covered in green, swaying grass appeared before Lašyn's eyes, and hilltops, and the yellow steppe, scorched by the Sun. He and his master seemed to be tramping across an unmown meadow, then crossing an endless ridge of hills that ran off into the distance, and then rushing down into the vast, boundless steppe. The tender, blue sky radiated a cool freshness and the horse trotted along steÄdily and cheerfully. Dust span out from under its hooves in a fine yarn and immediately dissipated, as if dissolving into the air. There were countless numbers of tracks left by wild animals scurrying about everywhere. But he and his master kept moving forward in a straight line, taking no notice of them. Ah, how many smells there were! Lašyn waved his nose about, catching the smells of wild flowers, the smells of wormwood and feather grass, the smells of familiar and unfamiliar beasts. Over there a hare darted out from under a bush in fright, and over there a vixen had taken refuge under the brownish trunk of a shrub of meadowsweet... But the thrill and passion of the hunt had been extinguished in the borzoi: he didn't fling himself at the vixen, he didn't tear at her with his fangs and choke her, pressing her down against the ground. No. A single, solitary feeling had completely enthralled him, a single, solitary dream... What this feeling was and what this dream was, Lašyn himself did not know. Over and over again the passes and hills were followed by new passes and new hills, and there was no end to the yellow steppe... And he and his master kept rushing onward, on and on...

Then suddenly everything ended. Unable to catch his breath, Lašyn's master suddenly stopped short and started sputtering and coughing. The song of the *dombyra* broke off... The door crashed open like thunder and Kӑmila

---

[21] *Ķazan* – traditional cast metal cooking pot with a rounded bottom.

[22] *Dombyra* – the most popular traditional musical instrument among the Kazakhs. It is made from wood and stringed with animal intestines. It comes in various shapes, with 2–4 strings and 8–24 frets, the most typical one being of oval shape, with 2 strings and 12 frets.

appeared, enveloped in clouds of frosty air. She had obviously got chilled to the bone setting the livestock down for the night, and before the door had even closed her nagging rang through the air. Ķazy held the cough inside his chest and said nothing, breathing with a whistling sound. Still nagging, Kǎmila flung off her outdoor clothes as she walked, squatted down, holding her hands out to the fading stove, and warmed herself up a bit, then lit the kerosene lamp, moved the round table over to Ķazy and spread out the tablecloth. She set the lamp on the table closer to the door, then took a colander and a large dish with a half-effaced inscription, and started taking the meat out of the *ķazan*.

As he carved up the horsemeat, Lašyn's master tossed the dog a fat marrow bone. There was a little piece of meat left on it – about the size of a small child's fist – and Kǎmila muttered something disapprovingly. Ķazy still said nothing even now, setting down a vertebra covered with a good finger's thickness of meat in front of his wife. Kǎmila, however, failed to appreciate this and immediately started jabbering angrily about something. Her little, pink mouth, the size of a thimble, never closed, her black pupils seemed to glitter with malice and her pretty face turned dark. Looking at her from out of his corner, the borzoi could not even enjoy his bone to the full. He fancied that he could sense something suspicious, and he felt a chilly breath of dread on the back of his neck... He only calmed down a little when his master's wife had finally got everything off her mind and gone quiet. His master and Kǎmila started eating, but they were both sullen and preoccupied. Lašyn caught a bone that was thrown to him in mid-air...

Ah, how wonderful even those joyless times would seem when the borzoi recalled them later!

8

Early-early in the morning, when the temptation was so strong to doze on until the dawn, Lašyn and his master got up, and with the first pale light glimmering in the east, they set out on their way. The snow that had fallen briefly the evening before had been blown into low spots by gusts of wind, and now it stood out in white patches against the background of the darkened crust that covered the entire steppe from end to end. The plain had a mottled, cheerless appearance, as if it had been sewn together out of dirty rags and the intense, pre-dawn cold rendered the air as ferocious and keen as a steel blade. Undulating gently in places and rising up higher in others, like the surface of a river on a windy day, the steppe was frozen in oppressive silence, and on all sides there was nothing living to delight the eye, apart from sparse black shrubs of meadowsweet that appeared first in one spot and then in another. But owing either to the cold or the anticipation of bloody skirmishes, a light tremor had run through the borzoi's entire body the moment they stepped out of the house.

The *auyl* was left behind them. Lašyn gradually revived a bit and started running with a livelier, more rapid stride. He moved on in front of his master, a lasso's length ahead, deviating now to the right and now to the left, and looking around vigilantly. Ķazy realised that it was not easy on such a day to pick up a trail or to catch a fox, but even so he seemed to be hoping for a stroke of luck. Maybe fate would smile on them and good fortune, as the saying had it, would grease the strap of their saddlebow.

The Sun appeared behind them, in the gap between the horizon and a long, ribbon-like cloud. It was as big and round as the lid of a *ķazan* and as red as iron heated in the fire. Its bright rays, beaming out in all directions, seemed not to warm the sky and the Earth, but instead to bring more cold to them. Even so, however, the world was transformed. The dead, frozen steppe drew in a breath and came to life. While the shadowy side of the crests of hills still looked as dark and ominous as ever, the sunny side began glittering and sparkling in gold and pink. And as for the hollows in which the snow that had fallen the evening before had accumulated – they started scintillating like the purest silver.

A little while later, when the long, gloomy shadows of early morning had shortened and brightened slightly, as if thawing out a little on the pale snow, a hare darted into sight up ahead of them. It was a long way away, but Lašyn's paws had been tingling for a long time and although the hare, sensing danger, immediately went dashing up a hillside, the dog launched straight into pursuit from a standing start. At the pace he set it only took him a very short time to get close to the hare. As Ķazy spurred on his horse, he felt no doubt that soon now he would slit the hare's throat, splashing scarlet blood across the snow, and attach the little white carcass to his saddle by its hind legs. Lašyn was seeing the same visions... But what happened was something quite incredible. Hearing the crunching of snow growing louder behind him, the hare flew as swift as an arrow. Lašyn strained every sinew to the limit, but the distance between them did not grow any shorter. They both darted out onto a plateau that had been smoothed out into a level platform. But for all the wind's efforts to tamp it down, the snow here was still quite loose. It supported the hare, but the dog kept sinking into it over and over again. Lašyn saw that the hare was slowly but surely pulling away from him...

In his time, he had caught so many foxes and hares that he had learnt one thing very well: animals differed from each other – some were slow movers, quite incapable of running fast, while some were as fleet as the wind, and therefore not everything was decided simply by whether the pursuit was begun from a short or long distance away. This long-legged white hare, who had already started moulting from its tail, which was significantly darker than its body, was clearly a quite conspicuous exception among his brethren. It repeatedly bunched itself up into a tight little bundle and then stretched itself out above the ground, rushing along so fast that no living creature could possibly have kept up with it. But the pride of a dog who had never known defeat would not allow Lašyn to admit that he had been beaten. No way! It might be sooner, it might be later, but he was going to catch this hare, grab it and eviscerate it... He strove hard to run evenly, the blood of his countless ancestors lent him ardour and he endeavoured merely not to let the hare out of his sight.

Ascent after ascent, hollow after hollow... Lašyn's legs grew heavy, but he didn't give in. Eventually, after they had cut across a depression that was overgrown with wheatgrass and sprinkled with loose snow, and then started running uphill again, Lašyn noticed that the hare was only a lasso's length ahead of him. And it wasn't running as agilely as it had been. And its long ears were drooping down wearily... The dog strained hard, summoning up his final ounces of strength and putting on a spurt of speed, and the distance shortened. But the hare, crazed with terror, darted out into the pass first. And immediately after darting out like that it went hurtling down towards a black expanse of pea shrub bushes. The exhausted dog merely gnashed his teeth when he saw the hare dive into the thicket of pea bush. The frozen branches lashed the borzoi across the face and he had to struggle hard to force his way through them. Meanwhile the agile hare had finally slipped away from him and disappeared without trace. Entirely without trace, because inside the thickets of pea shrub bushes that stretched across the slope for as far as the eye could see, there was a multitude of hares' trails – tangled together, meandering and intersecting – and it was impossible to make out which was the single correct one. Panting hard, with his tongue lolling out, Lašyn swung his muzzle this way and that way, realised that he had lost his long-eared prey and turned back.

With the flaps of his fur coat flying in the wind, Ķazy drove his overheated horse on along Lašyn's tracks. When he saw the borzoi, he jumped down off his saddle, twisting his wooden leg through the air awkwardly. The first thing he did was take a close look at the dog, examining his face and jaws and his frantically heaving chest. He couldn't spot any spattered blood. How could that be? He was more amazed than annoyed. Until now Ķazy had believed no animal could possibly be found that his dog would allow to get away. Probably the problem was the crust covering the snow, which broke under the borzoi's weight...

The hare-hunting season was already over. But according to signs in which some believe, and some don't, if you come across a hare when you ride out from home, you must run it down without fail. Otherwise that day's hunting will turn out to be a failure and probably nothing decent will turn up on the following day either... Well then, what point was there in dilly-dallying any longer? Ķazy checked the dog's paws: they were sound, but the dog himself seemed dejected and there was a guilty, shamefaced look in his eyes. His neck and sides were soaked with sweat and his armpits were damp with perspiration. In places his fur was dusted with hoar frost. Taking off his coat of unshorn lambskin, Ķazy spread it out on the snow and muffled the dog in it. Then he took out a large piece of fat-tail sheep's suet and put it in the dog's mouth.

When enough time to milk a mare had passed, Ķazy saddled up his horse and turned him towards the *auyl*. There was nothing to be done, he had to accept the fact that today they had been unlucky... But Lašyn apparently had other ideas. His strength had been restored and he had got his breath back. The borzoi dashed on ahead in his customary manner, prowling about, turning left and right, zealously searching for a trail. Without any success, however. They moved on in his manner for quite a long distance, until they reached a broad upland plateau where sheep were grazing. In places the snowy crust hardened by the frost had been pierced through by their sharp little hooves, and the grainy snow was mingled together with earth and fine crumbs of ice. Dark pellets of sheep's dung, warmed by the Sun, were sinking into the snow. Here and there scraggly blades of feather grass that had survived the attacks of numerous flocks of small livestock were trembling, bent over in the wind.

At this pasture the borzoi, who seemed to have abandoned all hope of coming across a trail, detected the presence of an unfamiliar smell. The smell was fresh, the animal had clearly only just passed by this place. Lašyn circled around on the spot, sniffing, and immediately spotted the trail. An ordinary dog's trail, left on the snow loosened up by the sheep's little hooves. But the smell... No, of course that wasn't a hare. And it wasn't a fox. The imprint was too large... It was an enemy. Yes, an enemy... The dog became excited; the fury only recently provoked by the loss of the hare started seething through his veins again. A fine tremor ran through Lašyn's body from the tips of his ears to his tail and the fur on his back stood up on end; after standing there for a moment, the borzoi set off.

The enemy had chased after the flock, which had scattered across the pasture. Lašyn trotted unhurriedly, in order not to lose the trail he had picked up. When he climbed up to a pass, several kilometres farther on, a motley flock of sheep, made up of black and white spots, came into sight, scattered across the hillside. The sheep were grazing out there in the open among the scattered, dark shrubs of meadowsweet and the thawed-out patches that had appeared in the snow. And Lašyn could see the sheepherder sitting on the opposite slope, counteracting his boredom and amusing himself by building a mound out of stones. His horse, with its legs hobbled, was nibbling at last year's grass down below...

Suddenly Lašyn spotted a large, sturdy grey dog directly ahead of him. The dog kept trotting rapidly for a while and then halting behind some outcrop or little hillock. As if he was trying to hide... The borzoi's fighting spirit was roused and his long, lingering, frenzied bark cut through the freezing silence. Lašyn gave voice two or three times – that had never happened before – and went dashing headlong down the slope. From somewhere behind him he heard his master's encouraging shout.

The grey wolf halted the moment he sensed danger and immediately turned towards the high, bald hills. It was probably not only the man doggedly galloping after him that disconcerted him, but also the large, broad-chested dog – glancing back frequently at it, he unintentionally slowed his own stride and he didn't manage to get very far, the dog caught up with him at the very first pass. Ķazy's voice, the voice of Lašyn's master, lashed him on and when the borzoi, sensing that the enemy was afraid of him, ran down the wolf, out of force of habit he sank his teeth into the wolf's groin, just as he did with a fox.

And then he tried to fling the wolf up into the air and slam him hard against the ground. The wolf proved to be far heavier than Lašyn had expected. And his body was brawny and sturdy, he immediately made it quite clear to Lašyn that he wouldn't be subdued that easily. The wolf's backside jerked when Lašyn grabbed his body in his teeth. And in that same instant his sharp fangs snapped shut right beside Lašyn's ear. The wolf had miscalculated when he reached back and he fell just a little short of sinking his teeth into the borzoi's face. When he struck out at the dog for a second time, with his eyes flooded with blood and his long white teeth exposed in a glittering grin, Lašyn managed to dodge. The wolf gulped down empty air, but he had managed to free himself from the borzoi's iron jaws. A loud shout rang out as Ḳazy galloped up on his horse, and the wolf broke into a run, leaving a bloody trail behind him. Lašyn dashed after him, infuriated. But he had already realised that the opponent he had encountered this time was anything but weak. And he had also realised that only his own speed and agility had allowed him to remain unhurt. But he felt no fear, on the contrary, ferocity lent him strength and daring.

After Lašyn almost bit Bardasoḳ to death, the borzoi had become an eager fighter. The dogs who accompanied their masters when they came into the *auyl* from the surrounding winter pastures found themselves constantly harassed by him. Fast, adroit and agile, as befitted a dog of his breed, Lašyn prevailed over guard dogs the size of a yearling calf, who were every bit as strong as he was. On occasion the borzoi did feel the sting of their fangs. But from any skirmish he always emerged victorious in the end. And usually any dog that had once been defeated by him never risked paying another visit to the *auyl*.

Recalling his previous victories over shaggy guard dogs, Lašyn decided to employ a well tried and tested tactic. What he needed to do was bide his time and grab the wolf just below his ear or on his throat. The wolf, sensing that he couldn't escape by fleeing, had stopped placing any reliance in his legs. He saw that his only chance of surviving lay in overpowering his opponent in a bloody duel and his eyes blazed with a sullen, pitiless flame. The wolf and the dog ran along almost beside each other, each following the other's slightest movement, with their faces almost touching, trying to seize the right moment to attack. They ran well ahead of Ḳazy, who was following on behind them. That was what the wolf had been waiting for: he suddenly stopped running and bounded straight at Lašyn with quite incredible speed, while his own inertia continued to carry him forward. And once again the borzoi was saved by his agility – the wolf managed to sink his teeth into the dog's side and tear out a lump of flesh from between the ribs, but that was all. Blood gushed out of the wound... However, Lašyn did not even notice that in the heat of the skirmish. He fancied that his side had been scorched by a flame, but even that sensation disappeared immediately, dissolving in the fury that was now raging in every fibre of his being.

And even so, he did not fling himself at the wolf yet. It was the wolf, with that same sullen, pitiless flame blazing in his eyes, who kept leaping at the dog, who had frozen in near-immobility. And neither of them made a single sound. There was only the burst of rapid breathing erupting out of the wolf's jaws and his teeth snapping, grabbing the empty air.

Lašyn was waiting for his chance. He was well aware that his enemy was strong and experienced. He only needed to catch the wolf out in a single false move to finish the duel with a crushing pounce. Everything depended on his restraint. And his opportunity came. The wolf, now believing that he was a lot stronger than the dog, abandoned patience and caution. A sudden lunge... But Lašyn dodged nimbly and flung himself at the wolf in turn. He was aiming for the throat. But he miscalculated and plunged his teeth into the wolf's thick neck. Nonetheless he had taken an unbreakable, vice-like grip. His teeth had sunk deep into the wolf's body. The wolf also attempted to grab the dog by the shoulder, but his teeth only tore away a scrap of skin, covered with smooth fur. Lašyn carried on forcing his fangs deeper and deeper, intending to wrench the wolf's neck round and fling the beast to the ground. But the wolf wouldn't yield. And his muscular neck was strong, Lašyn's fangs seemed to have grown into it and become firmly stuck there. But Lašyn could sense that the wolf could not hold out in that position for long and he snarled furiously, trying to close his jaws together. He must not let the wolf break free... Suddenly he heard the clatter of horse's hooves and his master's resounding voice behind him. The wolf braced all four paws against the ground, slackening his resistance and yielding slightly, and Lašyn, feeling a new upsurge of energy, instantly twisted the wolf's neck. The wolf fell, jerking his legs awkwardly in the air. But even so he still didn't surrender, he still tried to get up and throw the borzoi off himself, and lumps of snow, mingled with earth, flew out from under his paws.

But just then, muttering under his breath 'God help me', Ķazy tumbled off his horse rather than jumping off it. The knowledge that his master had come hurrying to him gave the borzoi strength. Stumbling and falling as he ran, Ķazy pulled a broad hunting knife out of his boot-top and slashed the wolf across the belly.

He had to set the end of the handle of his whip in the borzoi's mouth to get the tightly clenched jaws to open. Lašyn had a wound, rather large but not dangerous, on his side: the skin had been ripped off his ribs and a lump of flesh had been torn out... It would heal. And the wounds on his chest and shoulder blades – they were just scratches that would close up in five or six days. Ķazy was simply glad that he managed to stop the blood draining out of the dog's body.

And indeed, Lašyn really did recover soon. Of course, the wound on his side, the size of an open hand, carried on suppurating for quite a long time, but eventually a hard scar formed over it... However, Ķazy, who had been chilled by the cold wind during the hunt, took to his bed.

9

The snow melted, the steppe turned green and the sky, turning blue, seemed to expand, becoming both deeper and wider. Ķazy's family loaded the old felt yurt that had been stored in the barn for a long time onto the creaking, dried-out cart, took their place in a line of camels burdened with the same load and set out for the *žajlau* for the haymaking. Ķyzylotau had been transferred into the management of Esenžol's wife, Ajsùlu, who couldn't pronounce her r's and l's, but Ķazy was not upset about that. Sensing that his illness was getting the better of him, he preferred to lead a quiet life, avoiding vain fussing and fretting, and drinking fresh *ķymyz*[23] from his mare.

The haymaking *auyl* – that was what they called the five or six yurts, home of the herdsmen whose job it was to lay in hay and fodder for the collective farm's flocks. The sheep that they pastured were divided up among the neighbouring flocks for the summer, so that each family was left with two or three dogs who were temporarily deprived of their usual occupation. Many of them were simple watchdogs, but there were a few half-bloods among them. Some of them turned out to be old acquaintances of Lašyn's, those he had thrashed more than once, and he made the acquaintance of the others in the same way now. The owners often stood up for their bitten dogs and things might get as far as a quarrel, but not the kind of crude altercation that had blown up between Ķazy and Esenžol in the winter. Dogs were dogs, after all, was it really worth insulting each other because of them? One day, after everyone had settled down at the *žajlau* and got used to the place, in the evening twilight three strangers arrived at the *auyl* in a fast, rattling cart that moved all on its own. They took Ķazy away with them without hanging around for long. However, Lašyn didn't attach any importance to that. He was in the prime of his life, at his most mature and vigorous, when a new, enticing, uncharted world of feelings about which he had previously no idea was revealed to him for the first time. And the reason for all this was a bitch – a half-blood by the name of Ùšar. Once she came on heat, all the male dogs in the *auyl* started chasing hard after her.

Then what bloody battles boiled up! Lašyn was often left alone, and it was not so very easy for him to hold his ground against an entire pack of enraged dogs! The fur flew in clumps, some shaggy dogs the size of a yearling calf lost an ear, others fled from the battlefield bleeding profusely and even Lašyn spent a long time afterwards licking his deep wounds. But nonetheless, after besting all his rivals, he was left in sole possession of Ùšar. The other dogs merely circled about in the distance as they watched them frolicking and disporting themselves, without daring to interfere. But before the borzoi could relish the fruits of his triumph to the full, Ãdil arrived for the summer holidays, together with the other children from the *auyl*. And the first thing he did was to drive away the other dogs with a stick, take Lašyn by the collar, lead him to the yurt and tether him to the doorstep with a leash made of hair. Even though the

---

[23] *Ķymyz* – beverage of fermented mare's milk highly esteemed for its refreshing qualities; it is the main drink for special occasions.

borzoi was delighted at the appearance of his little master, he couldn't approve of this kind of behaviour. But neither his pitiful whining nor his restless barking touched Ädil's heart. He only released the dog after all the canine passions in the *auyl* had died down.

Ädil had changed in many ways. Naturally, he had grown in a year and now he had a fringe hanging down onto his forehead, but the most important thing was that he had become unusually serious for his age. He didn't talk much and tried to act like a grown-up in everything he did. He wasn't attracted by games with the other children. There were about a dozen books, some thick and some thin, in Ķazy's house and Ädil turned his attention to them, taking each one in turn. There was one that he was never parted from at all, reading it to himself and out loud, with expression. And when Ädil's resonant voice rang out in the yurt, the door would swing wide open at a light blow from a staff, and old Omar would walk in: he had moved to the *žajlau* with Ķazy and now performed the duties of scythe sharpener.

After settling down on the *tôr*,[24] squatting cross-legged, he would listen to the boy and ask:

'What bold *batyr* are you reading about – what is his name?'

'Alpamys.'

'Clever boy, my little pigeon… They say God is a support to the lonely man. He was also the only child of his father and mother, like you. He did not burn in the fire, he did not drown in the water, arrows did not touch him and the sword did not slash him, he went into battle alone against an army of many thousand, because he was a *batyr*, a bold hero who knew no fear. There are no more bold *batyrs* like that any longer, they have died out, and there is no such strength as that in man any longer. But on the other hand, there is knowledge and wise books – they give a man might and strength and bestow wings upon him, they grant him a lion's heart and kindle stars in his breast. Study, *ķaraǵym*.[25] If God supports you, you will become a genuine *žigit*, a worthy man. Prepare for that day and be wary of reaching it with nothing. Study. If you study well, you will achieve what you wish.'

And they would both say nothing for a while, pondering. Eventually Omar would say:

'And now, Ädilžan,[26] show respect for an old man and carry on reading…'

And that was repeated almost every day.

Sometimes, as he used to do the previous summer, Ädil would take Lašyn with him and walk far away from the *auyl*. But he no longer leapt over the holes and bushes that they came across. He no longer waved a willow wand about as he ran, shouting at the top of his voice and listening intently to the

---

[24] *Tôr* – place of honour, located opposite the entrance at the back of a yurt or a room, reserved for guests or for the oldest man in the family.

[25] *Ķaraǵym* – affectionate form of address to a younger person.

[26] *Ädilžan* – term of endearment for Ädil.

echo as it returned his voice, reflected by the hills and rocks, or tumbled about and frolicked in the luscious grass. If he saw a knoll that was a little higher than the others, he would clamber up, seat himself on a rock and sit there, gazing in silence at the winding road that had been made across the steppe by the wheels of jolting carts, and which disappeared on the horizon; a tranquil breeze would blow, stirring the short fringe on his forehead. At moments like that Lašyn wallowed in bliss, settled comfortably beside Ädil on some mossy rock, exposing his chest, as the boy also did, to the breath of the steppe wind and warming his back in the Sun.

At the time when the tips of the grass started wilting, one day after lunch Ķazy came back to the *auyl* with Bekķali, who had driven out to the district centre. Ädil was reading his book to old Omar and he had just reached the place in the poem about Er Tarġyn[27] when the bold *batyr*, badly injured and abandoned by his fellow clansmen, is lying in the mountains of Bůlġyr...[28] Hearing voices, the boy went running out of the yurt. His father, who had just got off his horse, embraced him and Ädil burst into tears, burying his face in his father's chest.

That evening the entire *auyl* gathered in Ķazy's four-winged yurt.[29] And they were all bright and cheerful, especially old Omar. He struggled hard to maintain the air of gravity appropriate for an *aķsaķal* who has been rendered wise by life. As soon as a new guest entered the yurt, he would turn to Ķazy and say in a voice loud enough for everyone to hear:

'The truth bends, but it does not break... No, those words weren't spoken in vain. If you are unharmed and have returned home, if you have escaped from the grip of adversity, it means that there is justice in the world. Clearly, Allah heard Ädil and his mother. Let us then give thanks to the Creator, the All-Merciful, the Almighty!' And Omar kept putting a little wad of green *nasybaj* snuff behind his lip and then taking it out again, recalling as he did this the ancient hardships that had fallen to the lot of the people, and also the recent terrible war, and again he thanked God that all of these disasters were behind them now.

As for Ķazy himself, he did not speak much, remaining silent for most of the time. He only hugged Ädil close to his chest, stroked his hair and ruffled the fringe on his forehead, which had grown longer over the summer. Sometimes he tried to smother a cough, and then it was painful to look at him... His appearance had changed a lot, he had become hollow-cheeked and pale. And

---

[27] Er Tarġyn – the protagonist of a heroic epos of the same title.

[28] Bůlġyr – a mountain from the *Er Tarġyn* epos.

[29] Four-winged (*tôrt ķanatty*) refers to a yurt with latticework walls (*kerege*), consisting of four sections. This, alongside the more spacious six-winged, was the most widespread type of yurt among ordinary people, while eight or more winged yurts were common among the rich and aristocracy. The thirty-winged yurt is the largest one, commonly used by the leaders to hold meetings.

he had grown a tar-black moustache. It suited him, but seemed to emphasise the thinness of his face even more.

Ķazy did not succeed in recovering from his illness after his return. When the *auyl* moved its encampment to Suyķbùlaķ,[30] he laid his cheek on the pillow from which he would never lift it again. He died in the middle of the night. At that time heavy rain was falling at Suyķbùlaķ, the work in the fields had halted and all the adult men were at home. Close to the encampment where the *auyl* had stationed itself, on the top of a shallow-sided hill, they dug a grave as deep as the height of a man. They held a *žanaza*[31] for the deceased and in the morning they committed his body to the earth. There was not a single person who did not shed a tear. Old Omar trembled and his voice kept breaking as he read the funeral prayer. Only Ãdil stood there silent and pale. When the body, wrapped in a white shroud, was lowered into the grave, his eyes turned moist. As his elders had told him to do, he scooped up a handful of damp earth, threw it into the grave and then walked away without waiting for the end of the funeral.

When Lašyn's master, who had fallen asleep in his bed the evening before, failed to wake up in the morning, the dog was not very alarmed. And when they carried him away and buried in the ground, Lašyn did not feel any particular anxiety. There were so many incomprehensible things in the lives of people! His master would sleep long and well, and then awaken from his sleep and come back home. After all, there had been times when he went away before, but he had always come back. And this time he had not gone far away at all. He was lying right behind the *auyl*. And he would get up tomorrow, if not today...

However, the more often the borzoi visited the grave mound, the more his heart was oppressed with bleak melancholy. Something vague was beginning to weigh down on him. Something that was like dread – what if his master carried on lying there for a long time, what if the house started feeling empty without him, like that time in the summer, when he had disappeared for an entire three months... Recalling that time, Lašyn felt lonely and abandoned. And when Omar *aķsaķal* seated the five or six young children who were going off to school on a cart harnessed to a bull and drove out of the *auyl*, the borzoi tagged along after them. No matter how hard Ãdil tried to drive him away, the dog kept following him. And he only turned back when Ãdil jumped off the cart and threw a stone at him.

Lašyn felt hurt, he had been abused when he was not guilty of anything... But as for understanding what Ãdil was feeling as he rode away on the jolting cart – of course, that was beyond him.

---

[30] Suyķbùlaķ – settlement, nowadays the district centre of the Žarma district in eastern Kazakhstan.

[31] *Žanaza* – Muslim funeral prayer.

10

Ķazy was still sleeping in the same way at the top of the hill. Sleeping without waking up. Without even trying to call in at home even once. And meanwhile the leaves had withered, the haymaking *auyl* had dispersed and the people had gone off to their *ķystau*. Kămila and Lašyn had also gone back to their home at the farm. But Ķazy was still where he had been, lying in the ground close to the old encampment.

The house was filled with emptiness, every one of its three little rooms. Lašyn wanted to run as fast as his legs would take him away from this place, away from this eerie emptiness. But it was dismal out in the steppe. Continuous rain had set in. Although you couldn't really even call it rain. It just drizzled and drizzled from morning until evening, never stopping for a single minute. If only there could have been a genuine downpour, or the sky could have cleared – anything but this constant scattering of fine little drops, with the distance veiled in unbroken mist. And if the rain did break off briefly, the wind started blowing – a dank wind that chilled you to the very bone…

Lašyn felt cold. And miserable.

And hungry, if truth be told. Lašyn no longer ate his fill as he had done previously. Sometimes Kămila even completely forgot that he existed. Once, when the borzoi tried to remind her that he was there by getting under her feet, she actually kicked him, something that had never happened before. She kicked him and drove him away, like some kind of beggar… Well then, Lašyn didn't pester her any more after that. He settled down in the corner behind the stove, curled up into a ball and waited patiently for his master. The moment the door opened, his head leapt up off his paws, but it was always a stranger who walked into the house. If Lašyn heard men's voices he would leap up, push the door open with a jolt and go flying out into the yard… But he didn't see his master among the group of men talking.

Lašyn tried to be patient and bear it, but he just couldn't adjust and get used to living like this. His only hope was that his master would come back eventually.

One day Esenžol came into the house in the evening twilight. Kămila, who had been sullen and unsmiling for a long time, cheered up a little. There was meat glugging in the *ķazan* as it boiled. Esenžol said something and laughed as he stepped inside and made himself comfortable on the *tôr* as if that was perfectly natural. Kămila hastily laid the table and started taking the mutton out of the *ķazan* and putting it in a dish. Esenžol took out a bottle of the transparent drink from under his clothes and stood it on the tablecloth. When he laughed, his pockmarked face crumpled up, bunching into a tight knot. And when the fragrantly steaming dish appeared in front of Esenžol, the first thing he did was to fling a whole heap of bones down in front of Lašyn. And what bones they were – juicy marrowbones, with little pieces of meat that had not been sliced off by the knife! For the first time since they had returned from the *žajlau* the dog was able to satisfy his appetite and eat to his heart's content.

And the feeling of anger and resentment towards the shop manager lingering in Lašyn's heart disappeared, it simply evaporated, and he felt grateful to their visitor for his kindness. With his empty stomach filled by this delicious food, Lašyn felt pacified and content, and he started falling into a gentle doze. Then his eyelids seemed to glue themselves together and he fell asleep.

He couldn't tell how long he had slept before he was woken by a strange moaning sound. The lamp had not been extinguished. The table had not been cleared. The dish holding the remains of the meat was still standing there in the middle of the table, with the empty bottle standing beside it. Lašyn started sinking back down into slumber, but then he heard the same sounds again. He realised that it was Kǎmila's voice and the moaning was coming from the next room. It sounded as if someone was strangling the woman and she was choking... The dog's sleep vanished in an instant and he jumped over the table and went dashing to the rescue. By the lamplight falling through the open door, he saw that Esenžol was lying on Kǎmila, forcing her down on the bed. The borzoi dashed straight at him, jerking off the blanket. And then his sharp fangs sank into that fat, naked backside right up to the gums.

An agonised howl rang around the house. Kǎmila and Esenžol jumped off the bed in terrible turmoil and agitation. But when the dog went rushing at Esenžol again, instead of helping him, Kǎmila, as naked as the day she was born, attacked Lašyn. But she wasn't holding anything in her hands at that moment and the growling dog with bloodshot eyes refused to back down. Eventually Kǎmila grabbed Ķazy's stick, which usually stood at the foot of the bed, and drove the borzoi out into the street. For the first time in his life Lašyn was forced to spend the night in the yard and not under the roof of his own home, in the warmth...

From that day on Lašyn's life was wretched. His bowl was permanently empty. The only way left for him to survive was by eating refuse on the rubbish heap: sometimes he actually went hungry for two or three days. But even on the hungriest days he didn't go prowling round the yards like Bardasoķ or sniffing out something that could be eaten in stinking kitchen swill. It was better to avoid starving to death by living on mice. One day he was even fortunate enough to catch a hare not far from the *auyl*.

It proved far harder to survive the inclement autumn weather. The borzoi sought refuge by digging himself into the straw heaped up behind the barn. But straw provided poor warmth for a dog who had grown up indoors. Especially early in the morning, when the grass was white with hoar frost and the piercing wind started blowing even more viciously; Lašyn trembled and shuddered, wishing the earth would open and swallow him up. And on rainy days the borzoi had a really hard time of it. He installed himself beside the wall of the barn on the side facing away from the wind and greeted the dawn like that. He did not even try to whine or beg Kǎmila to open the door, knowing that she wouldn't relent in any case.

There was only one person in the entire *auyl* who treated the borzoi compassionately. Old Omar, who noticed that Lašyn was spending the night out on the street, under the open sky, took the dog into his own house and gave orders for him to be well fed. Omar was hoping that the borzoi would sleep at his house, but there was no chance of that. The dog seemed to be just waiting for the door to open so that he could dash headlong out into the street and go back to his previous spot by the barn.

Omar *aksakal* tried again more than once, but the dog never took to living at his house. He just ate and then went back home. How could he stay – what if his master came back? Lašyn was ready to stay by his side and never leave him now. To run after him everywhere, wherever he might go. Just as long as he didn't lose him again... But his master still didn't reappear. Occasionally, sometimes every other day, sometimes every three or four days, sometime after midnight or in the pre-dawn twilight, someone would tap cautiously on the windowpane of Lašyn's old home and Kǎmila would open the door. The first time it happened the borzoi, certain that the person who had turned up at such an hour was his master, immediately jumped up, ready to go running to him, but he only saw Esenžol slipping into the house. Soon Lašyn became accustomed to the gentle tapping at the window and the creaking of the door in response. He stayed in his spot on the hay and didn't move. The dog had never been fond of Esenžol, but he sensed that it was inappropriate for him to interfere. Lašyn was naturally easy-going and he kept his discontentment hidden deep inside.

Once, in the middle of the night, snow started falling in thick flakes. It was a windless night, warmer than usual. The emaciated dog spent it in a half-doze, buried in the straw, and only opened his eyes when the snow stopped falling. Everything on all sides was absolutely white. In the purified, transparent air the outlines of the hills were etched with remarkable clarity and they looked as if they had retreated from the *auyl* into the far distance during the night. The borzoi stretched his numbed body right out and shook himself noisily. And then he filled his chest completely with the fresh, invigorating air and jumped on the spot, and then he jumped again... Something long-lost awoke inside him and he felt a vague desire to snuggle up close against someone. He ran around the yard. Someone went into the house and didn't come back out for a while. The snow had already obliterated the footprints leading to the door, but the ones leading away from the yard stood out clearly, even the patterns on the boot soles were clear. It was Esenžol. So there was obviously no news yet from Lašyn's master...

Lašyn stood there for a moment, gazing at the outlines of the distant ridge of rounded mountains, and then he set off reluctantly, seemingly almost against his own will, walking slowly out of the *auyl*. On the outskirts he stopped and lingered for a moment, then started trotting resolutely towards Suykbùlak.

11

The surface of the snow that had fallen overnight had already been speckled all over by the tracks of numerous animals. Everything here was in plain sight: who had passed by, when and where he was going to – Lašyn could tell all that at first glance. Here a yellow weasel had gone trotting by on three legs. His tracks disappeared not far away, under a shrub of meadowsweet, but they would reappear on the snow again about ten or fifteen paces farther on. Ah yes, here they were. Now the weasel had turned off to the right. But that was of no interest to Lašyn. A little animal like that, what was he worth? But that trail there, cutting across the first one, was a polecat's. They weren't very big, but they were strong and agile – and terribly audacious! His master loved them. If they were following a fox's tracks and they came across a polecat's, they never failed to turn off and follow him. But Lašyn was in a hurry now. Sometime later there would be a chance to go hunting for polecats with his master... A fox's trail. He was probably running along friskily and waving his bushy tail playfully. He had gone off to one side too, and there was no point in following him. And that was a fox cub. Forget him, let him carry on gambolling about. And then another fox. A fresh trail, he had run by here only quite recently. From the tracks it was easy to tell that it was a dog fox. Ah, and now he was stretched out somewhere on the snow, glittering in the Sun like a fiery-red flame... Somewhere close by, there was only one or two hills between them. That was a shame!

This was impossible, Lašyn's heart succumbed and he went dashing along the trail. And the moment he clambered up the first ridge of hills and started peering into the distance, while concealing himself behind an outcrop of rock, he actually saw the fox wandering about among the pea-shrub bushes in a depression.

The dog set off immediately, dashing straight at it, cutting across the shallow slope at an angle. The fox was caught unawares and before it heard the rustling and took to its heels, Lašyn was only the distance of a cast lasso away from him. He didn't let the fox get far and pinned it down with the full weight of his body.

But the strange thing was that the dog didn't have his former fervour. Why had he chased after the fox? Why had he caught it – for whom? What need was there to kill the fiery-tailed creature? He didn't know. The fox lay there motionless, stretched out at full length in front of Lašyn. A drop of blood dripped out of its nose onto the snow. The borzoi glanced around – was there anyone nearby? No. No one. But what did 'no one' mean? What about his master? He was really close, wasn't he? Recalling why he had left the house, Lašyn abandoned his prey without even giving it another glance and set off, running with long, elated bounds in the direction of Suyķbùlaķ. He knew the shortest way there. He only had to follow a narrow depression and skirt around a steep spur of the hill, overgrown with prickly briars and honeysuckle.

While he was still in the depression, Lašyn fancied that someone was watching him from somewhere nearby. The borzoi glanced back, but he didn't see anyone. And he didn't notice anything disquieting or suspicious. Without delaying for any longer, he ran on. But the unpleasant, alarming sensation arose again. Lašyn shuddered all over and looked around apprehensively. No, there was nothing that ought to put him on his guard... But he still felt as if the mysterious owner of some unknown, supernatural power was squeezing him ever more tightly in a cold, monstrously huge vice. It was a fiendish, invisible device, grasping Lašyn tightly from all sides... The borzoi started trembling as if he had been seared by the cold breath of some unknown being. He sped up. The rocky spur overgrown with scrub was already behind him, now he only had to climb up into the saddle between two hills and he would be close to the spot where his master was lying... And suddenly Lašyn stopped dead in his tracks and froze in surprise. Someone was standing directly opposite him, leaning against a rock. A shadowy figure, with a blur instead of a face, and the outlines of his body were blurred and indistinct, too. But it was Ķazy – with a fox-fur *tymaķ* on his head and a polecat fur coat thrown over his shoulders. He seemed to be looking at Lašyn and smiling. And calling Lašyn to come to him – without a single word or sound, but Lašyn could understand everything... A joyful bark burst out of the dog's jaws and he sprang towards his master, conquering Space in a single bound. But there was a sudden clang and Ķazy disappeared. And the mysterious something that had been squeezing Lašyn from all sides in its monstrous vice suddenly sank its teeth into his front right leg at the point where ulnar bone protrudes.

One of the sheepherders who had lingered on in the *kùzeu*[32] until the cold weather set in must have set a trap for a wolf and forgotten about it...

12

Lašyn was overwhelmed by confusion. He flung himself upwards in desperation. The iron vice didn't release him, its jaws didn't part. He jumped again – but only succeeded in dragging out from under the snow a cast-iron, toothed wheel that was attached to the trap by a long, iron chain. The heavy load dragged his leg back down towards the ground and the borzoi somersaulted over, crashing down onto the rocks hidden under the snow. His ulnar bone crunched and snapped. Lašyn's eyes flooded with blood, he half-rose and flung himself on the trap. The greyish steel, reddened slightly by rust, grated under his teeth. But the dog's teeth proved powerless, quite incapable of forcing those iron jaws apart... The borzoi bit at the unfeeling metal in his wild frenzy. Soon the trap and the snow around it were covered in blood. The jaws of the vice didn't open – on the contrary, they seemed to close even more tightly. Exhausted, the borzoi collapsed onto the snow. And he lay there like that for a long time, hearing nothing and seeing nothing.

Eventually he opened his eyes. The former fear and confusion had left him. Now he regarded the trap that had taken a remorseless grip on his leg as one of the dangerous creations of human hands. He recalled that there been another

---

[32] *Kùzeu* – autumn pastures.

trap exactly like this one, only old and broken, lying in their yard. That cheered the borzoi up a bit and gave him hope.

When he recovered consciousness, in addition to the pain, Lašyn felt extreme hunger: in the last few days not a single scrap of food had come his way. He thought about the fox that he had caught, and although he had never tried fox's flesh, he felt sorry now that he hadn't eviscerated his prey and satisfied his hunger with it. His eyes happened to slide across the spots of blood that had dried into a crust on the snow. Not only beside the trap, but for a distance of two or three metres, everything was covered in blood. And then Lašyn lifted himself up slightly and started gulping down the congealed blood lying on the snow. A few minutes later not a single drop of it was left.

The hunger abated a little, becoming duller, and the borzoi started feeling more cheerful. He realised that he couldn't break free from the iron jaws unassisted, only his master could free him. And his master would free him. If only Lašyn could get to him...

The toothed wheel that was attached to the trap as a drag proved to be incredibly heavy. Every step cost Lašyn an appalling effort. The ends of broken bone rubbed against each other and crunched. Perhaps everything would have been simpler if the foot clutched in the trap had stayed there, clamped in the iron teeth. But it did not wish to part from his body and was held firmly in place by the strong tendons and muscles. Every limping step that threw the borzoi's weight onto his right front leg set coloured circles spinning in front of his eyes and dissolving into a grey mist. Still, Lašyn edged forward inch by inch, with the heavy drag sometimes catching on rocks and sometimes getting caught in bushes. At moments like that Lašyn thought that he would stay stuck at that spot and never move on. But he continued on his way, suffering immense agony. On one occasion the drag got jammed between tree trunks and he simply couldn't free it. Enough time was wasted on his vain efforts for meat to become well-cooked in the *ķazan*... But eventually the borzoi realised that he had to pull the wheel back in the other direction in order to drag it free somehow and force his way onwards, out of the thickets. Having learnt his lesson, he tried to scramble his way through where there were no bushes or rocks to hinder him.

But the trap grew heavier with each step. No matter how even the terrain that the dog was struggling across might look, time and time again unexpected obstacles appeared beneath that treacherously smooth mantle of snow. And it was even harder to clamber up to the top of the hill where his master was lying. Previously the borzoi would have conquered this low knoll in a few bounds, but now it seemed to have grown into a steep mountain. The only good thing was that by this time his wounded leg had frozen and been transformed into an icicle. It merely dangled there, alien and lifeless, without causing him any pain. Summoning up the final remnants of his strength, the borzoi dragged himself upwards. The Sun was declining towards the day's end when he finally reached the sacred mound...

13

The borzoi howled for a long time. He howled with brief pauses, sobbing dolefully, just like a female camel howls when she loses her little colt. The surrounding knolls echoed his howling back to him. How could Lašyn not howl when the most terrible secret of all secrets had been revealed to him... Man, the lord of everything living on the face of the Earth, who breathed life into inanimate iron, transforming it into the likeness of a fleet-footed horse, or a bird that soared higher that a falcon, man, who was almighty and all-merciful – he also died! Like a little lamb or a field mouse. That was why Lašyn's master had been lying at the top of the hill for so many days and nights. And there was no one in the whole wide world who could help Lašyn as he lay there bleeding to death, weakened by hunger, with only hours left to live... The borzoi howled in mourning for his master. He howled, taking his leave of this world, of the vast expanses of Earth and heaven...

Death came sooner than he expected and not in the way that he expected. A hungry she-wolf with three fully grown cubs, who had been circling around the *kystau* for a long time, breathing in the smells of smoke, human dwellings and hearty food, heard the dog's doleful howl and immediately went dashing towards his voice. The howling guided her unerringly to her goal. After choosing her hiding place, she realised even from a distance that there were no people nearby and she was facing a solitary dog who had lost his way in the steppe. Concerned that a victim who was simply walking into their jaws might cause them unnecessary trouble by taking to his heels, by mute agreement the four of them first surrounded the hill from all sides, creeping stealthily, and only then did they fling themselves on the borzoi, with hungry flames blazing in their eyes and their long, white teeth bared in rapacious grins.

On that day Lašyn had suffered so many disasters, a secret so appalling that it destroyed all hope had been revealed to him and he was already so exhausted by his suffering and pain, that he could no longer be surprised by anything and felt afraid of nothing. His life had lost all meaning for him. But he was still alive, and life has its own laws. The borzoi didn't surrender, he didn't offer up his head in submission to his fate and in anticipation of the death-dealing blow...

The first attack by the wolves, who had decided that the solitary dog was easy prey, came to nothing. Only the she-wolf proved adroit enough to tear at Lašyn's loins. The borzoi's fangs clashed together menacingly, flashing through the air with lightning speed and preventing the young predators from even touching his body. The wolves withdrew, but they immediately flung themselves on their victim with redoubled fury.

The dog was alone and there were four of them. His movements were restricted by the trap, there was nothing to hinder them from attacking him, pressing their rabid onslaught harder. The pans of the scales were weighted unevenly. The she-wolf, well-experienced in savage skirmishes, was already convinced beyond any doubt that she would drink her fill of warm blood and eat her fill of fresh meat. Her caution abandoned her. Everything merged together, fusing into a confused jumble that wheezed and clattered furiously, floundering about in a cloud of powdery snow. The borzoi was at the very bottom, pinned down by the wolves. But he managed to postpone the moment when the wolves would tear him to pieces by making an imperceptible movement that ripped open the she-wolf's belly.

The young wolves only noticed their mother spinning around on the snow, trying to grab hold of her own side, straining to reach her belly with the entrails tumbling out of it, when the borzoi had already been finished off and his bones hastily gnawed clean. The dog had turned out to be extremely scrawny and their empty stomachs had not been filled. On the contrary, their appetite had only been tantalised and the hunger tormenting them had only increased. When the young wolves saw the blood gushing out of that terrible wound, they immediately pounced on the she-wolf.

In only a very short time there was nothing left of the she-wolf who had given birth to them, suckled them on her own milk and raised them to be strong and pitiless, except for the short tip of her tail and the four, hard-frozen pads of her paws.

14

On the top of a crookedly slanting hill resembling a *taķiâ*[33] that stands above one of the deep ravines dissecting the foothill belt of Žauyrtaġy, a low mound of earth has been piled up. Every time the *auyl*, in its nomadic wanderings round the green *žajlau*, sets out its encampment nearby, the *aķsaķal*, leaning on a stout, knotty staff, leads a teenage boy to this mound, goes down on his knees, facing the *qibla*[34] and in a guttural voice recites a prayer. And he strokes the mound with his hand in memory of the departed. And on those days when the boy feels the sharp edge of his mother's tongue, he comes here and sits for a long time in silent solitude, sometimes shuddering convulsively. That mound is the grave of Ķazy, who once trod this Earth, although he had only one leg. And the youth is his son, Ädil.

And here, right beside the grave, is the spot where the blood of the borzoi dog Lašyn was spilt. But no one knows about that, of course. Nothing remained after Lašyn except for the fox-fur *tymaķs* on the heads of the men of the *auyl*. But even they became worn out a long time ago and have been replaced by simple lambskin caps and cheap fur caps... For after all, Lašyn was the last of the thoroughbred borzois in these parts.

Translated by Andrew Bromfield

---

[33] *Taķiâ* – short, rounded skullcap for men, typically worn in summer or under the *tymaķ* (winter cap) in winter.

[34] *Qibla* – the direction in which Muslims should face when they pray, towards the Ka'aba in Mecca.

BEXULTAN NURZHEKEYEV
(b. 22.02.1941)

Bexultan Nurzhekeyev is a Kazakh writer. In 1965, he graduated from the philological faculty of Kirov Kazakh State University (now Äl-Farabi Kazakh National University). He was a teacher and then a First Secretary of the regional committee of the Komsomol in the Panfilov district; he was also an instructor of the Central Committee of the Lenin Young Communist League of the Kazakh SSR, editor-in-chief of Žalyn almanac and *Žŭldyz* literary journal, and from 1976 to 1980 worked as deputy head editor of Žalyn publishing house, where he is now senior editor.

His first short story, 'Kinäli mahabbat' (The Guilty Love), was published in *Žŭldyz* in 1965, followed by several short story collections: *Kŭtumen ôtken ġŭmyr* (Expectation, 1974), *Bir ôkiniš, bir ŭmit* (Regret and Hope, 1980), *Erli-zajyptylar* (Husbands and Wives, 1987), *Äjeldiṇ žoly žiṇiške* (A Woman's Path is Delicate, 1998) and *Bejtanys äjeldiṇ ķupiâsy* (The Secret of an Unknown Lady, 2002). What distinguishes these works is a realistic portrayal of family life and Nurzhekeyev's observations of the intimate feelings of women. His second-most visited theme is Kazakh history. Nurzhekeyev wrote his first essay on national history and ethnography, 'Ôzender ôrnektegen ôlke' (The Land of Rivers), in 1982. The subsequent years saw the novels *Žau žaġadan alġanda* (Hard Times, 1993) and *Aj, dùnie-aj* (Oh, World, 2015), which reflect upon the historical hardships experienced by the Kazakh people. A thirteen-volume selection of his works came out in 2014. He has also published two collections of essays on the prominent Kazakh historical figures and artists: *Oj-ŭškyn* (2002) and *Ôner ķŭdireti* (2013). His prose has been translated into Russian, English and Turkish.

Nurzhekeyev was awarded the State Prize of the Republic of Kazakhstan for Literature in 2018 for his historical novel, *Aj, dùnie-aj* as well as the Orders of Ķŭrmet (2000) and Parasat (2008).

Death of a Soul

They used to say that to lose a woman is like having the handle of your whip break. Whoever said that clearly came from a time when whips were still highly prized.[1] For a man who makes a living in the saddle, rearing livestock, a whip without a handle could hardly serve as a whip at all. That is why a single man, living without a wife, is compared to a whip without a handle. Ķajran, who had just committed his wife to the earth and was deep in contemplation, now came to understand the profundity of these words. For Ķajran, however, it seemed he had buried his wife not today, but long ago, some seventeen years before.

***

Back then, Ķajran was involved in archaeological expeditions and would spend more than two months in the Ķaraġandy region. He missed his eldest son Maķsat, his younger son Mùrat, his sweet little, nine-year-old daughter Ôrim and his wife Ùldir terribly. And quite rightly. How could a forty-one-year-old man in his prime not pine for the thirty-eight-year-old love of his life?! Things were not made any easier by the bitter, snowless Arķa[2] frost that would arrive in October to batter and beleaguer him. God knows, but had he been younger, perhaps he would have shot off to Almaty at will, without a backward glance.

The manager was a worldly-wise man but long in the tooth. Perhaps it was because of his long marriage, but he had grown a little cold, accustomed to the twists and turns of family life, and he seldom thought of his wife and children. And it seemed that he didn't pine after them quite like Ķajran did after his family. Nevertheless, he was a companionable, cheerful man who preferred to be surrounded by amiability and attention and a jolly, hearty table with plenty of guests. He always felt very much in his element in homely surroundings, he cracked jokes freely and sang pretty well, too. And seeing as he hailed from Žaņaarķa itself,[3] he had friends, acquaintances and relatives in

---

[1] The whip is considered a key attribute of a man, a symbol of his dignity and plays a significant role in socio-cultural life.

[2] Arķa relates to Sary-Arķa, an area in central and northern Kazakhstan.

[3] Žaņaarķa – district in the Ķaraġandy region.

every *auyl*.[4] Customarily proclaiming, 'Right, lads, today we are to be guests in yet another wonderful home…', he would take his three affiliates with him pretty much every evening. Ķajran was the most senior of the three. Among the diggers were students from the university at Ķaraġandy, and one or two of them turned out to be locals.

On one occasion they had been busting a gut for ten days or so to ensure the current year's assignment was completed, and the manager once again dragged them along to see the latest of his acquaintances. The head of this particular family was the same age as their boss and similar to him in disposition and temperament. The house with its adjacent outbuildings was located on one of the tributaries of the Sarysu River, overgrown with rushes and willows, and close to the main road that ran through those parts. The master of the house's four sons, four daughters-in-law and a single grown-up daughter greeted them most hospitably. During the comprehensive privatisation of the country, they had managed to carve off a pretty healthy slice for themselves. Having entrusted a flock of sheep to one son, a herd of horses to another, a herd of cows to the third and having placed the eldest son at the head of them all, the father, with all his four sons, held the entire district in his hand; in the palm of his hand when open but in his fist when clenched. The *ķymyz*[5] and *ajran*[6] flowed freely there, summer and winter alike. A happy family, Ķajran noted, that had created a heaven on Earth with their own bare hands. Despite being intrigued by their expertise and their forbears' skills in rearing livestock, he was struck most by the fact that the four sons, the four daughters-in-law and the master's only daughter, too, were blessed with pure voices and all sang beautifully. The eldest son broke into song first, announcing that he had written it himself. Good lord, the melodiousness, the length and the *leitmotif*; it was all so harmonious and brought joy to even the most trained ear. Other composers would have burst with *braggadocio*, having written such a song, and, God knows, they would have either given you one in the eye or knocked the living daylights out of you should you have ever put them down. Often, if someone were to get carried away and say, 'How talented are our people', a certain mistrust would be awakened in Ķajran. Oh, talk about laying it on thick! he would think. Now though, having listened to the fine young horse

---

[4] *Auyl* – socio-economic formation considered to constitute the heartland of the nation and a basis for an ethnic and cultural union of the nomadic community. Consisting of 50–70 yurts in the eighteenth century, it developed into its current permanent state of 'rural settlement' (of a minimum of 100 dwellers) when Kazakhs adopted a settled mode of life in the nineteenth and twentieth centuries. *Auyl* can also be used as a synonym for 'native land' and 'homeland', concepts revered by the Kazakhs.

[5] *Ķymyz* – beverage of fermented mare's milk highly esteemed for its refreshing qualities; it is the main drink for special occasions.

[6] *Ajran* – sour drink made of cow, sheep, or goat milk fermented with lactic bacteria, often thick and used both as food and as a beverage.

herder, like it or not, he had to acknowledge his minor indiscretion and rebuke himself, not without a certain bitterness, Oh, what a fine people we are, unable to appreciate the gifts and talents in our midst!

Ķajran had probably never felt quite so uninhibited and at ease in someone else's house as he did here. At the height of all the excitement and perhaps because the host had performed a song, Ķajran sang too for the grateful audience. After her elder brothers and their wives, the younger Ķarlyġaš also sang two songs. Everyone knew one of the songs but Ķajran had never heard the other, which was full of yearning and grief. Who knew what sadness the girl wanted to impart; she was still unmarried, although she was already twenty-five. It seemed she was trying to hint at something with her song for, as she finished her performance, she surreptitiously studied each and every person present, as if wishing to ascertain if they had understood anything. Or perhaps she was trying to glean their impressions of her singing. Whatever it was, it did not escape Ķajran that some grief was troubling the girl. So, what was it, then? Perhaps in her youth, she had been deceived by someone, perhaps she hadn't found a fine young man to swoon over her. Or was it that she had loved someone and that love had not been reciprocated, or... He found his imagination running away with him.

'There is plenty of space in the house and there is enough bedding to go round', boomed the host, as the evening ended, persuading them to stay the night. And once they had made up their minds, more *ķuyrdaķ*,[7] rich tea and sweets were offered. Taking the opportunity to stroll out into the courtyard, Ķajran walked straight into Ķarlyġaš, who was preparing the samovar.

'Oh, forgive me, my dear! I didn't see you in the dark', he exclaimed, resting his hand on her shoulder.

'It's no big deal, *aġa*![8] I wouldn't have been offended if you'd bumped into me on purpose', Ķarlyġaš replied with a laugh.

'Heaven forbid! After the bright light, it takes a while for your eyes to get used to the dark. And do you think I'm so tired of living that I'd deliberately go around knocking over such a lovely young girl, especially one who sings so delightfully?'

'It turns out, *aġa*, that you're not such a bad singer yourself!'

'No, no, my dear. That was just to keep the evening going... Well, not to keep it going, rather out of respect, you could say. I am not really one for singing, especially to an audience, as I feel rather uncomfortable standing up in front of people. Therefore, I beg you not to be too quick to laugh at what should be seen as respect for the audience.'

---

[7] *Ķuyrdaķ* – national dish of fresh meat and offal (lungs, liver, heart and kidneys) fried in fat. It is usually prepared to mark the slaughter of livestock.

[8] *Aġa* – respectful form of address to an older man, which can be translated as 'brother', 'uncle'.

'No-o, *aǵa*, I am not laughing at you one bit! Many people perform songs using only their vocal cords, but you sing from the heart. And I have a singular and special regard for a man who sings and speaks from the heart.'

'However many compliments you care to bestow on me, I know full well that I am no singer by any stretch of the imagination.'

'If you say you know full well, then you are very much mistaken. Songs are not written to be performed by singers alone. In truth, a song is created for the listener. Therefore, only the listener properly understands and deeply appreciates a song. Judging by your words, I think you are a most sophisticated listener.'

'There, Ḳarlyǵaš, you are mocking me again. You could say just *listener*, without all the superlatives to go with it.'

'Alright, be just a listener. Although you are a listener with an understanding of songs and of art. Isn't that right?'

'My dear Ḳarlyǵaš, please don't say such things! I am much the same as the next man and there is nothing special to set me apart from others. Whatever you do, please don't make me feel awkward.'

'What a curious man you are! You are the first Kazakh I have met who won't accept praise. Incidentally, it's a trait that suits you very well. Most importantly, it's not feigned, rather something you were born with. Indeed, I was thinking what it was that had made me single this man out, and there it is…'

'Ḳarlyǵaš, are you making fun of me again?'

'Not a bit of it, *aǵa*! I really have a lot of respect for you. How come I've never set eyes on you before, or have you been shutting yourself away amidst the chaos and stench of city life?'

They walked around the yard together retreating a little further from the bustle of the outhouses and the heat of the fire-breathing samovar. Ḳarlyǵaš proved to be not so much a plain-speaking girl, rather one who was open and bold, not concealing her thoughts, asking directly what she wanted to know. She was decisive and self-assured, without the false modesty one sometimes encounters. He must have been looking at this fair, tall girl throughout the day without really noticing; perhaps it was the languid light of the celestial bodies above, or the gleam of one light against another. However, when his gaze fell onto her slender body, Ḳajran fancied her snow-white bosom was especially well illuminated. In that minute, as if returning to his senses, he recalled Üldir. Her, bosom, too, was a special kind of white. Even when the lights were out, it would still shine a dazzling white.

'*Aǵa*, what are you thinking about? You miss your family, I suppose? Being such a long way away from home must be hard for your wife and children.'

'Yes, it is difficult. I miss my daughter especially. She will be nine in November. I often start thinking about her, the scent of her hair and her cries of *Papa! Papa!* and it's as if she were standing right beside me. My two sons are a couple of monkeys, too. I've never reproached them for anything; I don't want to break their spirit and see them grow up as spineless milksops. There's a very apt folk saying, A good person may well end up a nasty piece of work and a good-for-nothing – a spineless milksop!'

'I've never heard that before. It is not easy to grasp straight off.'

'When I heard it the first time, I didn't fully understand how a *nasty piece of work*, meaning a malicious type of person, could be classed as good. However, when I got to thinking about it, it turns out that many consider meticulous and demanding people malicious. In a word, a person who knows and demands what others don't even want to think about. As for a spineless milksop, it is well known that a good-for-nothing sort is incapable of taking a stand between right and wrong. You see what kind of philosophy our people have?'

'You, *aġa*, are unlike any Kazakh who grew up in the city. No city-bred Kazakh could reason like that in their native language.'

'Oh, come on, there's no need to belittle indiscriminately this poor urbanised Kazakh! You see, I may live in the city, but in my heart, I linger each day on the *auyl* roads. My father is past seventy and lives in an *auyl*, as does my mother and she is past sixty. I am always with them in spirit, although, to my misfortune, I seldom visit. Every time I get a pang of yearning for them, I embrace my children and blank it out, even if only for a while. I deceive myself like that. There are times I feel incredible delight when I watch my two sons larking about. They could turn the whole house upside down and I wouldn't say a word. Say what you like, but children are the true source of a man's happiness. Everything else is just transitory. Love for one's children is one of the most profound feelings that never wanes.'

'In that case, my esteemed *aġasy*,[9] where do you keep your love for your wife, who gave you these children – in some remote backwoods miles away?'

'What do you mean by *backwoods*? She remains in her place. Shouldn't love for one's children and for their mother be complementary rather than contradictory feelings?'

'You won't be offended if I ask you something, would you?'

'Not at all.'

'You've been talking a lot about your children but not a word about your wife. Does that mean you don't miss her?'

'What makes you say that? With our Kazakh steppe mentality, it is not considered seemly to be constantly talking about our wives in the company of strangers. Besides, a feeling of yearning for one's children naturally implies a man has a wife, and everyone understands that.'

'*Aġa*, it seems you are explaining very simple things in a very scientific kind of way, so it's difficult to talk with you without choosing one's words carefully. A person will always be wary of saying something out of turn and putting their foot in it.'

'Ķarlyġaš, I can't say I noticed you being particularly wary.'

---

[9] *Aġasy* – affectionate for *aġa*, used here in a mockingly reverential form.

'Well, I am the kind of person who prefers not to keep their thoughts to themselves and I wear my heart on my sleeve. Perhaps it is out of respect, or maybe the way you set out your thoughts so precisely and exactly that I feel the need to take your feelings into account and to follow your lead in the conversation.'

'Well, I've done it now, eh?! I didn't have the faintest idea I was so charismatic.'

'Perhaps you have an unknown power that acts on me alone?'

'Can that really be the case?'

'If not, then how else can you explain it?'

'Ķarlyġaš, you really must have decided to pour scorn on me.'

'Not you; I am scorning myself, you see.'

'Please explain how I'm supposed to understand that.'

'There's nothing to understand!'

'So, that's how you take my feelings into account and follow my lead, is it?'

'Yes, that's right. Just like that, aġa. Is that not enough? Only now am I beginning to understand what a wicked person I am. Really quite nasty, in fact.'

'Oh, stop it, Ķarlyġaš, don't say such things! What's got into you? What makes you say that? Anyway, we'd better head back. People may start looking.'

'Well, if they do, then they'll most likely be looking for you. No one will be looking for me.'

At that moment, Ķajran was overcome with a sense of doubt. That's enough, he said to himself, setting himself at ease. She knows I have a family and children; she's hardly likely to go in for something like that. Or… or has she been with a man before? Ashamed by his own thoughts, Ķajran stole a glance at Ķarlyġaš, under the cover of darkness. As if sensing this, the girl also looked straight back at him.

'Ķarlyġaš, has something changed? Only just now, we were having such a nice conversation.'

'I'm tired, aġa. I may live among a good couple of dozen people, together with my parents and brothers, but loneliness has finally worn me down. I am twenty-five but not one lad has ever courted me. I have never experienced young love and certainly not adult love. Hand on heart, aġa, tell me what sort of life is that?'

'If you've always been a picky one, perhaps you are the one to blame?'

'No, I am not so haughty. It's just that I've yet to meet a man who has fallen in love with me so that I might fall for him myself. Now, if someone like you were to come along, for example, that would be another thing. Alas, though, I have never met such a man thus far. Who knows, perhaps I never will.'

'Don't talk like that, Ķarlyġaš. You have your whole life ahead of you.'

'Aġa, white lies really don't become you. The life ahead really cannot be the one we want it to be. I fear that in the end I'll have no choice but to marry a widower or a divorcee.'

'But that's a life, too. It's better than nothing.'

'If I were looking for something better than nothing, I would probably have already found him. It's just that I don't have the strength to overcome my passions! Why don't you understand that? Or don't you want to understand it?'

'Such passions will truthfully tell you to go to the one you love. What's not to understand here?'

'My passions play these mean tricks on me; what am I to do if I like someone who has a wife and children? Tell me honestly, assuming I were to fall in love with you, could you then leave your family and marry me?'

'Of course, I wouldn't marry you.'

'But why not?'

'Because I married my wife for love. And she married me for the same reason. Added to which, we both love our children. Consequently, we have added to our earlier loving feelings our love for our children and all these feelings have simply grown incredibly stronger.'

'But what about the opinion that married life makes a married couple's feelings for one another grow cold?'

'But feelings can also grow stronger with each passing year. Just now, I told you they have grown stronger thanks to our children.'

'So, people lie when they say things grow cold?'

'Who knows, life doesn't set hard and fast rules; you can expect one and the other...'

'If you look at it scientifically, you want to say?'

While Ķajran hesitated, not knowing how to respond to the girl's venom, Ķarlyġaš, without saying another word, turned and walked off towards the house. Only she knew why she acted as she did. For her to have been so upset with Ķajran, one would have had to assume that their relations had been intimate and long-standing. But this was not the case. So, what was going on? Nevertheless, Ķajran was pained by the awkwardness that had arisen; he somehow felt guilty despite not knowing what he was guilty of. Involuntarily, he raised his eyes to the starry night sky, whose dancing lights flashed their lashes and impassively winked at him, as if silently telling him, How are we to know?

Ķajran returned to Almaty in mid-October. Emerging from the train in the morning and rushing home, he suddenly remembered with dismay that he had left without his keys. He hadn't stopped to think that, upon his return, the children would have already left for school and his wife, for work. He popped into the nearest shop and called Ùldir's work, where they told him she had taken the day off. Even though I didn't warn her, she clearly worked out when I was returning and is getting things ready, he thought, a pleasant sense of yearning running warm through his body. Leaving his luggage with the neighbours, he thought it would be best to wait at his friend Degdar's place, whose house was just around the corner. Perhaps I should call ahead to find out if he's at home or not, he lingered for a moment. Hey, it's not far so, if he's not in, I'll come back and, by that time, Üldir herself will probably be back, he concluded.

Since the country had gained its independence, Degdar had been busy trading in the crazy market, opening a chain of kiosks and small shops in different parts of the city, and he was seen as the most forward-thinking and business-like *žigit*[10] in their circle. Ķajran had consulted his old friend about getting his savings together and opening an outlet of his own, so he thought this would be as good a time as any to discuss the matter further.

He approached Degdar's front door and had barely managed to press the bell when he heard something creak and fall to the floor on the other side. There was clearly someone in the apartment, but no one was coming to open the door. He pressed the bell again, this time holding it down for longer. A barely audible commotion could now be heard coming from the other side of the door.

'Degdar, it's me', he said, raising his voice. He could hear the suppressed whispering of a woman, saying, *Don't open it!*

'Ķajran!' came Degdar's voice, from the other side. 'Sorry, but I have someone round. When did you get back? Oh, this is really awkward, but I am sure you understand.'

'It's nothing, don't worry. I arrived on the morning train and left my keys behind, that's all. Üldir's not at home or at work. She'll probably turn up any minute now. Sorry for the intrusion, alright?'

At the same instant as he turned to leave, he again imagined he heard a woman's frantic whispering. He felt he'd heard that voice somewhere before; it was not so much the voice as the whispering that was familiar. Descending from the second floor and passing the first, he felt his ears ringing and his spine shivering in a cold sweat: that whisper was just like Üldir's! It was her, he had no doubt. His hands shook, his knees began to buckle and he almost fell to the floor right there and then. He had no recollection of how he had made it out onto the street. Turning to look up at the second-floor window, he stopped abruptly, realising that they might be looking at him from up there. 'Please, let it not be Üldir! Please, let it not be her!' he said to himself, not really understanding why. Then he turned back into the entrance of the building again. The thought flashed through his head, 'I'll smash that evil bastard's door in and disgrace him in front of all his neighbours', but he reined himself back once more. 'What if it's not him? The shame would be too much... It's probably not her; they couldn't do a thing like that, surely?! Üldir is probably sitting at home, waiting. I'll just go home', he decided. With this thought, and without a backward glance, he headed for home. He disappeared behind the corner of the building opposite and looked back. 'They probably saw me leaving from the window. If it is Üldir, she'll come running straight out. Why carry the

---

[10] *Žigit* – generally denoting a 25- to 40-year-old male, the term can also be used as an honorific indicating bravery, endurance, fortitude and being true to one's word.

burden of doubt around with me forever, when I can hang around here and make sure once and for all', he decided and walked around the building to hide behind the corner, from where he had a good view of Degdar's entrance.

Precisely twelve minutes later, Degdar poked his head out of the entrance. Emerging, he turned to face the second-floor window. Someone gave him a sign from up there and Degdar, turning sharply, walked as directed to the house opposite. Ķajran had a gut feeling that he was checking to see if the coast was clear, already a bad sign. His throat was dry, his body shivered, and it was all he could do to hold himself together. Then, guided by rage, discretion, calculation or cunning – he didn't know what, Ķajran slipped across to the last entrance door of the neighbouring building so that Degdar wouldn't notice him.

Degdar returned a few minutes later, searching all around. Concealed in the entrance to his own house, he spent a while looking around. Ķajran's fears grew stronger. He was already quite certain Degdar had been following him and no one else. Failing to notice anything suspicious, Degdar confidently returned to his apartment, his figure becoming darker and then disappearing altogether. When Ùldir shot out of the entrance like a bullet, Ķajran stood motionless, like a statue, glued to the spot. He was unable to close his open mouth, nor move from where he stood. His mouth ached, his body was not his own and he dared not take a single step for fear of falling. As for Ùldir, she did not turn in the direction that Degdar and Ķajran had taken, but hurried across to where Ķajran was hiding. Absolutely livid at his wife's goings-on, Ķajran emerged from the entrance and blocked her way.

'Aah!' she cried out and fell to the ground.

He wanted to hurl the worst insult he could think of at her but, as ill luck would have it, the words would not roll off his tongue. Instead, he just looked at her with as contemptuous a stare as he could muster and, without turning, walked off in disgust. He punched and kicked at the door to Degdar's apartment on the second floor and, venting all his bitterness and rage, screamed: 'Come out, you bastard! I'll kill you! You dog! You reptile!' Only when the neighbours threatened to call the police, did he reluctantly drag himself away. He imagined that Ùldir had made it home by that time. How would he now be able to cross the threshold where she would be waiting? And how would he even be able to look at her? What would he say to the children and what would he say to his unfaithful wife? Would it not be better to kill himself than enter that home? A good dog doesn't want to be seen dead, they say, and why was he worse than a dog?

As if a gaping, black hole was waiting to swallow him up whole, he found he could not take a single step in the direction of home. Turning to the west he loped off out of town. How am I to go on? What am I to do now? he asked himself, furiously and grievously offended. Naturally, he tried to calm himself and weigh things up sensibly, not allowing his emotions to get the better of him, but sordid thoughts continued to gnaw away at him: So, they both made it a rule to meet at Degdar's?! That means she's been playing me along for a good while...

There was a small bar on his way, on the western end of Abaj Prospect, and Ķajran went in; he ordered an entire bottle of vodka and downed it. He pushed the food he had ordered as a chaser around his plate with his fork, but it seemed to stick in his throat. Neither the vodka nor the food had any effect and he felt precisely nothing: it had gone neither to his head nor to his feet; he was neither drunk nor full. It was as if it wasn't him doing the drinking and eating but his aggrieved honour, his pent-up rage and his righteous anger.

He decided to walk, rather than take public transport. Where should I go? In which direction? These thoughts circled in his head. Perhaps end the bloody thing once and for all and go and hang myself?!

Should I get divorced? What would then become of my little foals?[11] At the end of it all, without them, my life really wouldn't be worth living! What kind of life would I have if they weren't around?

Oh, my little foals! My colts! Did I really ask God for you to come into the world so this would happen? Without you, my life is worthless! How can I tell you the truth, the awful truth, by blackening your mother's name? But if I don't tell you, how could I explain it? 'A mortal offence is death to the soul'; how on earth could I share a bed with her? And if I don't, what do I need a wife like this for? It's not just being with her, but her whole appearance, even her breathing turns my stomach... So what is your wretched father supposed to do? What's to become of you, what's to become of her, what's to become of me? What am I to do – how do I go on living?

Not knowing down which dark alleys his legs were taking him, Ķajran just kept walking, weeping disconsolately like a small child. His tears were mixed with bitterness and bile, which seemed to burst from his chest but appeared to be weakening and diminishing with each step. Looking around, he realised he was walking along Abaj Prospect again. But where could he go, who could he see, why was he wandering around? These were questions to which he had no answer. But life still remained, warm within him. Damn it! He could have dashed it all to hell, but what about the children? They may have had different bodies, but their souls were as one with his. How could he betray his children and never see them again because of this harlot of a wife? If he left home, it wouldn't be her who was punished but him! That would hardly be fair, would it?

He had truly loved her and had evidently made a mistake in believing that she loved him, too. Now his children were his only happiness. But she was their mother. A child who loses their mother is a true orphan. How could he turn his own children into orphans? God curse such a father! So, what was he to do? Throw himself back into the arms of this unfaithful woman? If he had not seen and confirmed it with his own eyes, he might have had some doubts and things would have been different, but how could he go back now knowing

---

[11] 'Foal' and 'colt' are diminutive terms that Kazakhs use for their children.

exactly what had happened? What kind of a man and what kind of a person would he have to be to do that? Blinded by passion, he used to sometimes call her his 'Ray of Sunshine'. Now, though, he would never be able to call her that until his dying day; he was quite sure that she was no ray of sunshine. *Oh, sweetheart!* she would babble to him when half-asleep. This word would no longer engulf him in some illusion of happiness, because a passion that is for sale serves only he who owns it; there was no guarantee that she hadn't used this same word with someone else. Therefore, there could be only one punishment for her infidelity and that was divorce, meaning the destruction of the illusion of happiness that he himself had erected. However, would the children of a divorced couple be happy? Unlikely. They would only begin to recover once they had survived the ordeal and become adults themselves. But at the same time, forgiving his wife's infidelity for the sake of his children would be tantamount to acknowledging infidelity as an inalienable part of life. He couldn't regard it as a mistake; mistakes are made when you have to choose one path out of many that are tangled together in a time of great hardship. There was no way that Üldir had found herself in such a situation. If she wished to divorce him because she now found him repulsive, that was up to her and she would have to decide for herself. And she would have to explain everything to the children, too.

He wandered the streets back and forth, until, deep into the night, he became exhausted. His legs could walk no further and his head had started to throb. Even his thoughts, lying scattered in confusion, were fatigued. What will be will be! he said to himself, grinding his teeth. I swear by the spirit of my ancestors: I'll do this for the sake of the children!

With his mind finally made up, he approached his house. He hesitated a little by the door, in an attempt to suppress his agitation. Twice he raised his hand to the bell, but he lowered it both times. Finally mustering up the courage, he pressed the button. He listened out and then pressed it again. 'Papa!' he heard his eldest son's voice, swiftly followed by the chirruping of his younger son and daughter. Fighting back tears, Ķajran lost his bearings and couldn't work out which way the door opened and on which side of the door he was actually standing. The blinding light, the clattering of the door opening, the arm of his eldest son instantly clasped around his neck, the sonorous squealing of his little daughter, who wasn't yet tall enough to embrace him, almost sent him out of his mind once and for all. He stepped forward and tripped over something. It was his own luggage. He had no idea if the neighbour had brought it over or if the children had popped over for it. The most important thing was that the children knew he had returned. The little ones had not gone to bed, patiently waiting for him to return. The little dears!

Carefully peeling off his two pining sons who had wrapped themselves around him from both sides, he picked up and kissed his nine-year-old daughter. Breathing in her scent, he couldn't keep his tears from falling down his cheeks and dropping on his daughter's hair.

'Oh, my Ôrimtaj!'[12] he whispered, pressing her up close, 'My little poppet!'

'Papa, why are you crying?' his daughter asked him, wiping his face with her hand. 'Has someone upset you?'

'No, my darling! I've just been missing you, that's all.'

'I'm going to sleep with Papa!' Maķsat, the elder son declared.

'Me too', cried Múrat, butting in.

'Papa, no. Me!' sobbed Ôrim loudly.

The four of them wouldn't fit together on one bed, so they laid out a thick blanket on the floor and settled down on it one after the other.

'Bagsy I get to lie on Papa's right', cried Ôrim.

'Then I'll go on the left', said Múrat.

'Alright, then. I'll curl up at the end', interjected Maķsat, with a display of conscience.

They were curled up very snugly, for sure, but Ķajran couldn't close his eyes till morning. It was the first time he had slept away from his wife in his own home. The next day, not without premeditation, he came home a little later. He ignored both his hot tea and his dinner, sniffed his sleeping children's heads and went into the bedroom. Ùldir followed him in. However, he did not look at her.

'I'll sleep separately. Make me up a bed down here', he said, pointing to the floor by the wall. 'I don't want the children to ever know or have to deal with the fact that we are sleeping separately. That's the last request I want to make of you.'

And that is how they behaved for a week. Ùldir put up no resistance and did as she was told, probably assuming that he wouldn't keep it up for long. As had been his custom, Ķajran would come home from work, have dinner with his children, look over and ask them about their homework, all without ever letting on. After this situation had extended to a month and more, Ùldir's female side got the better of her out and she blurted out:

'So, are you going to be like this for the rest of your life?'

'From now on, I will live not for myself but for my children. As for you, if you want a different life and a better husband, you can go off and look for one. The way is clear and you are free to do as you please! From now on, I don't need you or any other woman', he pronounced in a low, indifferent voice.

Without a murmur, Ùldir froze to the spot. It was not Ķajran's words that frightened her, but the tone he had used, which she thought sounded as cold as the grave or as icy and impassive as a dead body. She sensed a dread that is hard to explain.

***

---

[12] Ôrimtaj – the diminutive form of Ôrim, a girl's name.

After graduating from the history faculty, getting married in his final year at university and then being employed at the Institute of Archaeology, Ethnology and History in Almaty, Ķajran had been delighted to have found a means of making a living that would ensure his family's table would never be bare. His bride Ůldir had still been a student at that time. Together, they rented a tiny corner in the Compote district of the city, as the locals liked to call it.[13] The makeshift dwelling where they settled and the dark, narrow streets were more reminiscent of a remote *auyl* than a city neighbourhood. Fearful of walking out at night, Ůldir did her best never to venture out after the Sun had set, neither to the cinema nor to the theatre. She would never go herself and she would not let Ķajran out either. You are all the theatre I need and I am all the theatre you'll ever need! she used to joke. Ķajran put her way of speaking bluntly about what was on her mind down to her Russian-language upbringing,[14] and he didn't attach any particular importance to it. In any case, the facts of life for them lent themselves to this. The mischievous and tender Ůldir never let the wiry, coltish Ķajran out of her embraces. Ķajran himself didn't really want to be set free anyway. He thought this bliss would never end.

Maķsat and Můrat came into the world when they were still living in their temporary accommodation. It was only when Ůldir gave birth to their daughter Ôrim that the Institute allocated them a three-room apartment. That was a time when the guests were many and the table was full. Shortly afterwards, Ķajran defended his thesis. Immersing himself completely in his research, after his tutor had been appointed director of archaeological expeditions, Ķajran accepted his invitation and chose a relevant subject for his doctorate. At first, things went quite well, but, after the collapse of the Soviet Union, the country's close-knit fabric of scientific research also began to fray and split, and holes began to appear here and there, until eventually the whole thing disintegrated altogether. Sometimes wages were paid, sometimes they weren't. Ķajran completed his doctorate with considerable effort and prepared to defend it the following spring. But then Ůldir's betrayal, unfortunately, noticeably crippled his enthusiasm. However, he pulled himself together and did his best to hide his troubles. To a certain extent, he succeeded, too.

He managed to defend his doctorate that spring, a month later the doctorate was confirmed and, with the onset of summer Ķajran had already set out for Žaņaarķa as the head of an expedition. While he was on this trip, Ķarlyġaš personally invited him to visit. The attention and esteem bestowed were no less than they had been the year before. There was likewise no change whatsoever in the young beauty's words or designs. Ķajran, however, made a firm vow to

---

[13] The Compote district was so called because it contained street names that translate as Cherry Lane, Pear Street, Garden Street and so on.

[14] Kazakhs generally, and Kazakh women in particular, would tend to keep their opinions to themselves, while Russians in the Kazakh understanding were seen as being more direct and outspoken.

himself: If I can hide Ùldir's sordid behaviour from others for the sake of my children, then I'm damned if I can't conceal my true feelings from Ķarlyġaš for their sake, too. I am going to give my children a good upbringing, as if nothing has happened, not tear them away from their mother, so no one can say I am not fulfilling my paternal responsibilities. And having thus made his decision, he reined in his free will and went to work.

'Anyone who didn't know wouldn't have noticed it, but I can sense you're harbouring a secret. Tell me what it is, you're not unwell are you, by any chance?' Ķarlyġaš asked directly as they were strolling after tea.

'Whatever gave you that idea?'

'Well, there are odd times when you appear to drift away, as if something is gnawing away at you. You laugh happily enough but then suddenly check yourself and your gaze slides off into the distance.'

'And what: are you secretly monitoring all this or something?'

'Of course!'

'What for?'

'Why else do people do such things? It's probably because I have fallen in love with you! I like you, you see. Naturally, you love your children, not me. You say you love your wife too, in an attempt to deceive me. I can see from your actions and your behaviour that you're not telling me the truth. Let's say you do love your wife, but perhaps your wife doesn't love you back. You know that. Knowing this, you go around forever deep in thought and looking anxious. That's because you have no wish to abandon your children. That's what I think... Forgive me if I'm wrong and I'm prying into what's none of my business.'

The thought suddenly flashed before him that he would tell her the entire truth, but he instantly rejected the idea; to slander my wife would be to slander myself, he thought.

'My wife has some problems with her health, that's why I am worried', he said, finding a more believable way around the issue.

'So that's it! Oh, life shows no mercy and happiness is so short-lived!' Ķarlyġaš murmured, as if to herself.

...Having returned to Almaty once again in the cold autumn, Ķajran made it a rule to come home late every day. Over time, his wife came to see him either as some kind of shadow around the house, or as an apparition. At first, he was fearful and worried that one of these days he would show a sign of weakness to Ùldir. Gradually, an irrepressible feeling of disgust awoke in him, along with a concern that he might accidentally expose the children to his unhealthy dislike for their mother. Ùldir evidently sensed all of this and, one day, making neither her own bed, nor Ķajran's, she sat with her back to him, as if in some silent protest. Ķajran was about to lay his bed for himself, when she shot up and snatched the blanket from his hands.

'That's enough!' she screamed, flinching. 'I don't want to put up with your abuse any longer!'

'Well, if you don't want to, then no one is forcing you to. You are welcome to go wherever you please!'

'Why should I be the one to go? Why don't you go?!'

'Then ask the children to go with you. Tell them honestly what happened and let them decide who should leave.'

'What a black heart you have!'

With these words, Üldir set about making her and Ḳajran's beds without saying another word. And from that day, it was as if she had lost any hope she might have once harboured for Ḳajran. She now did all the housework without question. Sometimes, Ḳajran might have exchanged words with Üldir, without looking her in the eye. He spoke amicably only with the children, spoiling them as he had always done. Ten years later, the eldest son Maḳsat was married on his twenty-fourth birthday. Clearly hoping that this event would inject some variety into their lives, Üldir zealously and indefatigably immersed herself in the wedding preparations. It was as if there was not the slightest thing going on between her and Ḳajran; she was jovial, radiated happiness and spoke at length with people, asking them about this and that. However, the moment the wedding ceremony was over, the cold relations returned once more. About two years later their first grandson arrived. 'Let's call him Mănken! It was one of Abylaj's[15] names that Tôle Bi[16] gave him' declared Ḳajran, delighted. Neither the ḳaidas[17] nor anyone else from the wider family had any objections. Ḳajran celebrated the event like a truly happy man. That said, neither Üldir, nor the children, and not even Ḳajran himself could determine if he was indeed truly happy or if he simply seemed to be happy. Ḳajran himself had no wish to dwell on the matter. The only formula that remained in his head was My children's happiness is my happiness! Life went on and the second son Mùrat was married at twenty-five. They enjoyed the wedding parties of their children and seemed very happy, and no one, not even the ḳaidas who went from wedding to wedding and from party to party, could discern the couple's family secret. What was outwardly an entirely comfortable existence evoked no particular suspicion among others. However, instead of growing mellower, Ḳajran became colder and colder as the years went by, his heart now like a castle made of stone.

One day, his daughter, now a student, looked at her father and asked:

'Papa, there isn't anything causing you any pain is there, by any chance? Or perhaps you're having problems at work?'

---

[15] Abylaj Khan was a Kazakh khan who headed the national liberation struggle against the Dzhungar conquerors during the seventeenth and eighteenth centuries; the liberator of Kazakh lands and unifier of the three žùz (tribal unions headed by their own khan).

[16] Tôle Bi – the name of one of three celebrated bies (judges or adjudicators).

[17] Ḳuida – co-in-laws. Usually parents and relatives of a married couple refer to each other as ḳuida, and have particularly warm and respectful relationships; in Kazakh society one would be honoured to be called ḳuida, and pleased to treat their ḳuida with all the due respect in response.

'No, daughter, Everything's fine.'

'I'm not so sure, Papa. Sometimes you don't listen to me, as if you were thinking about something else entirely. You may be sitting next to me, but your thoughts are miles away, as if they are floating somewhere in the distance.'

'Perhaps, Ôrimtaj, I simply wanted to hear you worrying about your old dad. My two sons are married and you have turned into a fine catch yourself, so I just have more to worry myself over, you see. However, these are nice worries. You'll understand when your time comes. I am a happy man, after all: I have a wonderful daughter and my sons Maķsat and Mùrat, isn't that so?'

'And you have a wonderful wife in Mama!'

'Yes, my dear…'

'Mama, sit down for a moment, would you? Listen. Surely you want to hear how lucky our Papa here is, right?'

'Just a minute.'

Ķajran and Ôrim both sensed a hint of tears in Ùldir's voice.

'Mama's crying', said Ôrim, sighing sadly. 'I feel like crying too, Papa. We really are so happy: me, Maķsat and Mùrat, all of us, because we have such a Papa as you and such a Mama! Come here, Papa, and let me kiss you on the forehead. Oh, come on! Look, now Papa is crying. Now you've made my eyes all watery. But crying from happiness is also happiness, isn't it? Isn't it, Papa?'

'That's right, darling, that's right! And your poor old father will do whatever it takes to ensure your happiness continues forever and ever, my ray of sunshine!'

If anyone understood the true meaning of these words, it was probably Ùldir, as she came back out from the kitchen. But Ôrim, her eyes wet with tears, was, of course unable to fathom the underlying reason.

And so, life went on. Ķajran and Ùldir married off Ôrim the following year, just after her twenty-third birthday. Ķajran was now fifty-five and Ùldir fifty-two. They had set up their sons in nests of their own and sent their daughter off to pastures new. The day after her daughter left home, Ùldir's blood pressure shot up and she was taken to hospital. Ķajran, however, did not visit her once. Given the true nature of their relations, he thought it would have been an abomination to do so.

From that time on, Ùldir's illness returned more and more frequently. At first her ailment laid her low just once every two or three months, but she always got back to her feet. Then she started falling ill on an almost weekly basis. In the end, her condition became so bad that Mùrat and his wife moved back in with their parents for good. Not that Ùldir got any better. With the new year, her speech became increasingly slurred and by the end of November, she was back in the hospital. It seemed she wanted to finally have it out with her husband, for she tearfully asked her daughter to ask him to come. 'Let's go!' his daughter said, taking him by the arm. As his daughter insisted, he could not refuse.

Üldir was lying on her side in a separate ward. She signalled to her daughter that she wanted to be left alone. Then she beckoned to Ķajran to sit closer to her.

'Y-you... h-have... p-pu-nished me cru-uelly', she said with great difficulty through her tears. 'B-but th-thank y-you for n-not t-telling the ch-children... P-please d-don't t-tell them after I h-have g-gone and my soul will r-rest easier...'

'I won't. But there is something you should know: you also punished me and, thanks to you, I have lived seventeen years as nothing more than a fixture in the family, with children but with no wife of my own.'

'Y-yes... B-but...'

'Remember, it was you who committed the sin, but we bore the burden of punishment together. I did this for the sake of my children. So, don't you judge me!'

'N-no...' Üldir dejectedly shook her head. Her chin jerked fitfully and her eyes fell tightly shut. Ķajran was unsure how long he had sat there waiting for her eyes to open again, but they did not. He waited a fair while, and then got up and hurriedly left the ward.

Two days later, on 27 February 2011, Üldir's soul left this Earth.

***

They say that back in the prehistoric past, long before the modern era, our ancient ancestor Arys had two sons, one called Aķ and the other Pan, who by the cruel hand of fate froze to death in the lower reaches of Mount Han Tăṅiri. Since that time, February has been known as 'the two brothers' or *Aķ-Pan*. Perhaps in light of this, February has always been associated with another meaning: the end or the conclusion. It is in this month that winter ends. And it was in this month that Üldir's life ended. Only time will tell if death can ever unravel the tangled knot of life.

Translated by Simon Hollingsworth, edited by Simon Geoghegan

SOFY SMATAYEV
(b. 24.06.1941)

Sofy Smatayev is a writer and playwright. He graduated from the Moscow Institute of Steel and Alloys in 1965 and worked as a metallurgical engineer at a number of USSR plants, before being appointed as an engineer and subsequently senior engineer at the Institute of Metallurgy and Enrichment of the Academy of Sciences of the Kazakh SSR. He worked for the *Žŭldyz* journal and for the Central Committee of the Communist Party of the Kazakh SSR. For a number of years, he headed the National Book Chamber. He wrote poetry before taking up prose, and his first published book is a collection of poems and ballads, *Astana ottary* (The Lights of the Capital, 1962).

Smatayev is a prolific writer, author of nine novels, including *Elim-aj* (My People, 1978; three volumes), *Bŭlaḵ* (Spring, 1979), *Mǎṅgilik bastauy* (The Origins of the Eternal, 1987), *Biz ḵŭlmyz ba, kimbiz?* (Are We the Slaves?, 2003), *Žarylḵap batyr* (about eighteenth century military commander, 2003) and *Alau* (Flame, 1974), as well as several short story collections. He has authored eighteen plays, including *Taġdyrlar* (Destinies, 1976), *Sen kimsiṅ?* (Who Are You?, 1977), *Žŭldyzym meniṅ žoġary* (My Lucky Star, 1985), *Zar zaman* (Hard Times, 1977), *Abylaj Han* (about eighteenth-nineteenth century khan, 1985) and *Kôgildir taksi* (A Blue Taxi, 1993). He wrote libretti for several operas: *Žŭmbaḵ ḵyz* (A Mysterious Girl), *Žambyl* (about Žambyl Žabaev, a poet and epic poem narrator), *Žaâu Mŭsa* (about a poet and composer), *Ajbibi men Nŭrbota* (Ajbibi and Nŭrbota) and *Bojdaḵtar* (Singles). Twenty-three volumes of his selected works have been released; the first seventeen volumes in 2008 and a further six in 2009. His works have been translated into fourteen languages. He is a professor, recipient of the Alaš International Literary Award (1992) and of the Ḵŭrmet (2000) and Parasat (2007) Orders.

The Song

What a sad song it was!

In those minutes, a bluish, misty haze would cloud her eyes. Staring unblinkingly with blurred, frosted sight, fixed on what she could not see, her eyes seemed to be brimming with tears. And yet no one would ever see her cry. The outcast, ragged girl, whose tremulous voice sent a chill through our small boys' hearts, captivated and held complete control over us.

Oh, if we could only understand but one word of her song! We would try to sing along, timidly and out of turn, grasping for anything familiar from our own Kazakh songs but, one by one, we would fall silent, ashamed of our faltering voices. This embellished melody which our ears were not accustomed to and which lifted the unfamiliar, burring sound of this alien language into the overcast sky, enchanted and ached within us, speaking of something intimate, dear and lucid to our now-exposed hearts.

That miracle enchants me even today, though I still cannot understand it…

The girl would always come from the other side of the irrigation channel. She would wade through the icy water, timidly dipping her bare feet, purple from the chill, into the dark, icy current, her hand holding onto her frayed hem as she went. Only once she had emerged onto the snow-covered bank would she warily cast a sideways glance at us. She would come closer, hunching over tremulously and suspiciously. And she comes now, so many years later, wading through that dark water, onto the white snow and towards me, but only in my memory…

***

It was late autumn in 1948. Back then we would never tire of racing, screaming, running and shouting through the *auyl*[1] houses. From the faintest sign of dawn till after the dusky twilight, we found no time to rest in our irrepressible scampering, at times even forgetting to wipe our noses on the sleeves of our sorry jackets. It was during this period of my childhood when we met, when life flashed by at pace and our interest in everything was insatiable.

---

[1] *Auyl* – socio-economic formation considered to constitute the heartland of the nation and a basis for an ethnic and cultural union of the nomadic community. Consisting of 50–70 yurts in the eighteenth century, it developed into its current permanent state of 'rural settlement' (of a minimum of 100 dwellers) when Kazakhs adopted a settled mode of life in the nineteenth and twentieth centuries. *Auyl* can also be used as a synonym for 'native land' and 'homeland', concepts revered by the Kazakhs.

I remember that distant morning clearly. It began with a deluge of jubilant cries that could be heard past the windows in our street.

'Alaķaj! It's snowing! Hurray!'

'Now that's what I call a snowfall! Look at all that snow!'

The young always find great joy in the first snowflakes, the first rain and the first grass and this joy is equally unbounded wherever a person lives under the laws of the vivid world of childhood. This joy transcends time, space and everything else that people have dreamt up at different times and for different reasons.

You jump over the threshold, your blackened feet flashing, and there you see the first, fluffy snow! The white, weightless butterflies blind you as they fall from the depths of the grey, hazy sky. Hurriedly, you raise up your hands and the flakes trustingly drop into them, melting the moment they touch. You bend down, gather the snow from the ground and press it into firm handfuls, laughing happily as you go. You raise your hot face to the sky and open your mouth wide; your cheeks and forehead are seized by the cold, while the tip of your tongue senses only the pure, fresh moisture. The first snowfall is a special time in childhood.

Launching snowballs at one another, we would forget everything else, for only one, indescribable, heaven-sent joy meant anything for us in this world and that was snow, snow, snow!

Suddenly, a song could be heard. It was so unexpected. The delicate voice of a child, full of yearning, floated from afar but was discernible and real; the unfamiliar tune, rather than fade away, became stronger. It mourned and pined.

Although the blinding flakes of snow continued to fall generously, in that minute, we failed to notice them. We stopped playing and hesitated for a moment, exchanging uneasy glances. Then we rushed as fast as our legs would carry us to the place from where the song was emanating. We ran, afraid of missing out on something important, afraid of being left behind. We feared that the melody would fall silent and suddenly disappear. That it would be lost forever. We dreaded the thought that we might not make it.

And that was how we came to surround this strange girl. She stood there with her bag on her shoulder, completely motionless. The hem of her shabby dress hung in tatters. She was barefoot, which came as no surprise to us; at that time, the only thing the hardy soles of our feet ever wore was the earth, baked by the Sun, iced over with the first frost or dusted with snow. Not even her clothes surprised us; in those post-war years, we weren't dressed much better ourselves. But the song! A familiar rhythm suddenly pierced through the quivering, delicate and mournful voice and the words that were alien to our ears spoke melodiously and rang out like silver, illuminating our own pain, as yet unknown but already laid out for us. It was then that I saw the trembling moisture that clouded her gaze and I was awestruck. This seemingly sick, suffering infant soul was trying to pour out from those intense, wide eyes, but it could not and so it suffered and instead broke out in this wonderful song.

When the melody slowed a little, a shadow appeared to run over the girl's grey features, but then the song took flight once more and the singer's unwashed face lifted up and shone.

The melody ascended to the purest sound and then it broke off, as if cut down by a knife.

It was Tileuķor who had interrupted the song. The bully Tileuķor. He was the ringleader among us. We hadn't noticed him bending down to gather up snow in his hands; all we saw was Tileuķor rush forward and shove snow down the back of the girl's dress.

The unfinished song broke off as if of its own accord, yet the girl didn't move.

As one, we all turned to Tileuķor, scowling at our leader. Tileuķor lowered his head and hid his hands behind his back, but we were waiting for an explanation. And yet the girl, pale and with slightly quivering, copper lashes, remained motionless among us slant-eyed and swarthy lads.

At that moment, Tileuķor raised his head and smirked.

'I know her!' he said and fell silent.

Tileuķor was older than all of us and he always knew everything. He enjoyed keeping what he knew from us.

'That girl is a German!' he cried at last. 'I saw her yesterday. At Andrei's house. That's her!'

We all knew what a *German* was. A one-eyed evil spirit with crooked fangs. *German* meant war. *German* meant death. It was the cause of the daily keening, wailing and weeping in which we had grown up.

Instantly, the pale face of the girl with sullen cheeks, strewn with her colourless hair, became that of a demon child.

'Look at you, showing off like that!' we hissed through our teeth. 'So, who are you, then? Ah, so you're not talking, eh?!'

We looked at one another and instantly understood what the other was thinking; nearby was the clay pit used for making bricks, full of snow! Enough snow for an entire war. A war with this German. We rushed to the pit, with the one word, throbbing in our heads: *German! German! German!*

So much snow! It came up above the ankles and almost up to the knees!

But why was she not running away? Her bag had slipped from her shoulder. The girl stood there, the two spots of her bare feet turning the blinding white snow a crimson, blood-like colour.

Suddenly, our leader, the bold Tileuķor, waved his hand and rather vapidly gave the order:

'Let's go! To hell with her!'

He was the first to clamber from the pit.

At that moment, the girl smiled. Shaking her head, she flicked back her curly fringe from her forehead and began to sing the same song. Her voice became louder and more resonant. Her unknown yearning became more tender; her sadness – more lucid and lighter. We stood on the edge of the pit, our mouths open, and the girl was with us once more; we had forgotten what had happened before.

Involuntarily, I looked to my right and my gaze fell on Tileuķor, who was standing silently by my side. His face was wet from the falling snow. Then I realised: it was not snow. My chin began to quiver. I sensed that I would burst into tears at any moment. I didn't remember Tileuķor's father who had died in the first year of the war and I didn't know why I would weep – pity for Tileuķor, pity for myself, or the song of this outcast girl, but, barely able to keep myself in check, I pulled Tileuķor back by the sleeve and, at that same moment, his fist cracked into my skull.

The light faded, everything went dark and my head span. I fell.

When I pulled my hands away from my burning face, I saw that there was no one there but the girl.

She stood very close and was now smiling at me. I lowered my heavy head and understood; her face, pale and blue from the cold, remained before me and smiled over me in a way I could not understand.

Everyone had abandoned me. They had left me with this German girl. I didn't cry but she was smiling. I had caught it bad for no apparent reason and not because of her at all. For some reason, this German girl found it all very amusing...

Trying to settle my shaking, I got up and immediately lashed out at her little face with all my strength. My hand appeared to meet rock. What I saw at that moment would remain in my memory forever. Blood gushed from the girl's nose and yet there was neither fear nor affront in her blank, wide eyes, only surprise. Dumbfounded surprise. Her nose that was dripping with blood and her pitiful mouth, warped into something akin to a triangle, were nothing compared with her eyes, which expressed no pain whatsoever. I realised that no person with eyes like that would ever be able to sing. Ever!

My shoulders shook from loud, uncontrollable sobbing.

***

That day, I came down with a fever. The illness took a firm hold of me and I was confined to my bed for most of the winter. The younger grown-ups decided that I had caught a chill; the older ones determined that some wicked person had put a curse on me. It was completely quiet in my gloomy, shabby little room. My peers never came to see me. From time to time, I could hear the barely discernible, muffled voices of the lads out in the street and the excited cries of my friends on the ice slope, but that was all.

That winter I discovered something that still brings me joy; my mother was a wonderful storyteller. Of an evening, having driven in the animals and fed them, she would throw coal into the fire, put the kettle on the stove and, with a smile, she would hurry to sit beside me on my bed. Before beginning a new tale, she would invariably tighten her white headscarf. I still recall that heart-warming motion and her familiar, low, monotonous voice.

Of course, it was then that I first climbed up onto Želmaâ, the pacer camel, along with the legendary wanderer and sage Asan Ķajġy,[2] to travel all the countries of the world in search of the Promised Land. There were times when I would go hunting with Ķûlamergen himself, whose arrows never missed their mark. One strange tale that my mother used to tell was the story of the lament of Măriâ the orphan. In this story, I knew what my kind mother could not have known: I knew what the lament of this unknown Măriâ sounded like. It was sung in an unfamiliar language by a girl in rags. And this lament was the song that no one would ever hear again.

And yet I waited for the song, greedily listening to the children's voices, barely audible beyond my window. I heard the song in my dreams and sometimes I dreamed of the outcast girl's eyes. I would awaken frightened and stare out at length into the darkness, afraid to close my eyes and see her gaze once more, indifferent, surprised and quite devoid of pain.

The melody never did sound again on our street, however hard I strained to hear it. The orphan girl never crossed our threshold either and did not appear beside me.

It was always others who came instead. Relatives would come, neighbours would come, the young *auyl* nurse would come. At first, she would examine me and say something to my mother in an authoritative whisper; my mother would listen patiently and nod, humbly sighing. The nurse then came more and more seldom, until she no longer visited at all. However, I continued to lay on my creaking bed and stare out the window for days on end. The lopsided window had been struck through with a cross; it had long been left in disrepair and was misted over with the moisture that had settled on it.

Suddenly, very close by, out on the street, the song could be heard. I sat up. At first, the delicate voice tried to calm its shaking and, when it finally settled, it rang out loud and clear.

'*Apa-a-a!*' I called out in anguish. '*Apa-a-a!*'[3]

But my mother was not at home.

I don't know how I managed to grasp the metal bedknobs, but somehow, I crawled on my faltering legs, tripping and gasping for breath, and looked for some clothes. With my bare feet in my father's rubber-hemmed deerskin boots, I stumbled over to the door.

The daylight blinded me. I screwed up my eyes to settle my dizziness. Overcome with weakness, I stepped out. I didn't fall.

---

[2] Asan Ķajġy (Asan the Sad) – a semi-mythological character, *žyrau* (poet), but also a *batyr* – 'warrior' – and a counsellor to the khans and rulers. He was an adviser to several khans and the first ideologist of the Kazakh Khanate. According to legend, he rode his camel, Želmaâ, across the steppes in search of the 'Promised Land' for his people and found it in south-east Kazakhstan, where the Kazakh Khanate was established in 1465.

[3] *Apa* – depending on the region, aunt, sister, mother, or grandmother; it is also a common respectful form of address for older women in general.

The song now drew me forward with an irrepressible strength. I rounded the corner of the house and saw the same scene as before: I saw the scrawny little singer, surrounded by my friends.

When I finally came right up to her, gasping for breath and dragging the heavy boots with great effort, the girl cowered and fell silent. I took her hand with shaking fingers. She looked at me with a frown and pushed me forcefully in the chest. I fell flat on my back.

With a single bound, Tileuķor shot towards the girl, but I cried out in terror: 'Do-on't to-ouch her! Do-on't to-ouch her!' I barely heard my own scream.

I looked at the faces of my friends, who had crowded around me and lifted me from the ground, and laughed. I felt so at ease now! She had pushed me over! We were now even; she had relieved me of the guilt that had been eating away at me. I was growing weak from my uncontrollable laughter, from the early spring Sun and the free wind; I was unable to stand any longer, but my chums held me tightly under the arms. I was barely able to speak, but I uttered,

'Sing! Let her sing…'

The girl lowered her head. And then her lips quivered and the song, rising slowly, began its ascent to the heavens. Suddenly, I could see a powerful man's hands lift up the girl and raise her to the skies. An unfamiliar woman's face appeared with incredible clarity in my diseased imagination, looking at the young singer with motherly love and pity. I imagined strange lands where I had never been, while the song continued to draw me into the unknown, leading me to places seen never before, far, far away.

***

She would always come from the other side of the irrigation channel. We saw her delicate figure from a distance and rushed to meet her.

From that same day, my health took a turn for the better. I quickly re-joined the lads' games, always fun, noisy and boisterous.

The grown-ups decided that I had managed to pull myself together, while the elderly persisted in thanking the Almighty for His mercy, seeing some divine predestination, but no one except me knew of the mighty power of forgiveness that had relieved me of my illness.

The blessed summer came and the gold and blue sky shone unrestrained. In the midst of our perpetual merriment, I recall seeing Emma, the young, singing girl, standing in the centre of it.

We already knew that her father, a German communist, had died a hero's death in the Battle of Stalingrad, while her mother had frozen to death in a terrible blizzard out in the steppe in the early spring of '46, saving a flock of sheep. And, quite obviously, people more often than not offer tender embraces in times of tragedy. The *auyl* had become accustomed to Emma. I can still see the dark hands of the villagers stroking little Emma's blond locks; I can see the hands of other mothers washing her hair; I can see hands offering her a piece of bread or a small handful of grain. With every beat of my heart, I recognise that I am increasingly indebted to the villagers till my last breath; the plain-hearted simplicity of their day-to-day lives will forever be an example of kindness and sympathy.

We never recalled the fact that Emma was an orphan; for us she was no different from the other children who had grown up after the war without a father's affection. Many of my friends had been dealt the same hand.

Emma was no longer the lonely, outcast little girl that the post-war wind of orphanhood had blown across the steppe like a tumbleweed. Her face had come alive, the harsh shadows had disappeared and her eyes now sparkled. We now heard her laughter, sonorous and resonant. She couldn't get her tongue around the words to sing Kazakh songs and Tileuķor and I were her best friends.

One day, our entire gang lay on the sweltering bank of the Ķarasu Creek, our copper-brown bodies, pimply from spending so long in the water, facing the Sun. Tileuķor poked his bare foot into my side:

'Hey! Look – your father's coming...'

I jumped up and rushed forward, pulling on my trousers as I ran. My father was a train driver and there were times he would leave for two- or three-day shifts, which was more than enough for me to miss him terribly.

I rushed to embrace him and thrust my nose into his driver's overcoat, greedily breathing in the incredible, pungent odour of coal and fuel oil that had been absorbed into the fabric.

'That'll do, son. Just look how you've made your nose all dirty.'

My father would always say the same thing but would bury his face in my curls all the same. He would look at me, his brown eyes laughing, but he would speak very strictly:

'You only ever have time to run about all day long. You've probably forgotten that you're off to school in the autumn, haven't you?'

'I remember! I remember, I'm going to school!'

'Well then, take these. And make sure you don't lose them.'

With that, my father pulled two wondrous pencils from his pocket, blue at one end and red at the other. It was as if he had presented all the riches in the world to me alone! Back then, it was no easy matter buying even a regular pencil. Dizzy with happiness, I jumped up and down on the spot.

'Go on, off you run', he said, with a gentle nudge in the back.

Touching heads with my father, I raced off to join my friends, sensing how he was watching after me with a smile. However, I was too preoccupied with my excitement to look back; I ran, shouting:

'Look! Look! Pe-encils! Red and blue! Coloured pencils!'

The kids had been watching us the whole time. When I ran up, no one paid me the slightest attention. Some turned onto their other side, without even a cursory glance at my incredible pencils, while the rest got up lazily and ambled over, only hesitantly and, even then, as if they weren't really interested. Only

Tileuķor extended a hand, carefully handled the red end of the pencil and, in an unnatural voice, clearing his throat, said:

'There, now, make sure you study well.'

I turned to Emma. She wasn't looking in my direction. Her blonde hair was scattered over her shoulders and, without moving the locks from her brow, she lay silently as she intently watched my father walk away. I think it was only then that I understood everyone's aloofness. It is possible to forget about another person being an orphan or fail to notice them, but there are a great many reasons in this world why orphans themselves cannot forget their own deprivation.

I was stupefied by this insight. Not knowing quite what I should do, I timidly tugged at Emma's shoulder.

'So, you're going to study then?' she asked, looking at me indifferently.

'Yes, I am! And so will you! We're all going to study! We'll be off to school soon. We'll sit next to each other, okay?'

'I don't have any paper or pencils', she said coldly and turned away.

'Here! One's for you! And one's for me! Here, take it, Emma!'

In disbelief, she held the pencil tightly in her hand, shook her head and quietly began to laugh. She broke into the same song, only quickly and playfully and then, suddenly short of breath, she fell silent, looking up to the sky and smiling. A white bird circled high above us in the endless, ethereal, blue sky. It flew at such a high altitude that it looked like a mere speck.

That evening, when we had all returned to our homes, Emma timidly approached me and, looking to one side, placed the same pencil back in my hand.

'But why?' I asked, unable to understand.

She just stood there, without turning away. Eventually, she said:

'Keep it with you for now. I'll pick it up later. I don't want to go losing it or anything.'

'Alright. I'll hide them together. Yours and mine. I'll take good care of them!' I promised.

'Hide them', she said, without turning away.

***

Ten days passed.

Early that morning, when the large round table had been moved to the middle of the main room and our entire family had sat down for tea, the door suddenly swung open. Tileuķor, panting, nodded to me and instantly disappeared into the hall. I put down my tea bowl, from which I had been about to drink, and shot out after him. I had never seen Tileuķor looking quite so flustered.

'Emma is leaving...'

'Where to?!'

'They say that some m-m-m...' Tileuķor hesitated as he tried to pronounce the Russian word. '...co-mission. There you go.'

I couldn't understand a thing.

'They're taking Emma away to an orphanage.'

'Just a minute... I'll be right back...' I muttered, not budging an inch.

I eventually ran back into the house and scattered blankets, clothes and pillows in all directions, but the pencils were nowhere to be found. I rummaged under the bed, on the table and rushed from one corner to the next, but in vain.

'What are you looking for, son? Has something happened?' said my father.

'Can you please explain what is going on?' said my mother.

I was unable to say a word to my parents in reply!

Finally, with the pencil in my hand, I rushed headlong out into the street, leaving the door wide open behind me.

We ran to the station. It was less than a mile away from our *auyl*, but it seemed so much further in those protracted minutes.

My friend had long legs and had dashed off ahead, only to turn to wait for me, evidently out of pity.

'Hurry up!' he cried. 'Stop dawdling and get a move on!' But we were too late.

My legs no longer wished to do my bidding and I was clean out of breath from the running. Hot, salty sweat filled my eyes.

Suddenly, out in the distance, against the humped slope of the mountain, we caught sight of a train. Its green carriages, gleaming merrily in the morning Sun, were drawing ever nearer. Passenger trains would wait no more than two minutes at our station. In those two minutes, I realised that human life is sometimes measured in moments.

The train barely slowed as it arrived into the station and departed almost immediately again, leaving nothing more than puffs of black smoke in its wake. I fell to my knees exhausted, only having made it half way, and I scratched in the light-coloured steppe earth with my nails. I could hear Tileuķor's confused, consoling voice; it echoed in my ears. I heard the piercing screech of the train followed by my own intermittent breathing. For a moment, it seemed that a miracle had occurred and I could hear Emma's song. It played out within me like the yearning for a dream which is destined never to come true, like a last *sorry* to a childhood never to return; its ghostlike echo would ring out in my life for a long time thereafter. However, I would never hear Emma's song again.

***

Each time I sit down at my writing desk and each and every time I open the drawer, I will stare at length at the pencil, red at one end and blue at the other, with which I have never written a single word in all these years. This is Emma's pencil. Each and every time I will think one and the same thing: will I ever be able to put together a song that I could dedicate to Emma, the little singer from my childhood?

Translated by Simon Hollingsworth, edited by Simon Geoghegan

TOLEN ABDIK
(b. 4.09.1942)

Tolen Abdik is a Kazakh writer and playwright. He graduated from the philological faculty of Kirov Kazakh State University (now Äl-Farabi Kazakh National University) in 1965 and began his career at the *Ķazaķstan pioneri* newspaper (now *Ùlan*), before being appointed as head of the department of prose and deputy editor for the *Žalyn* almanac, and, later, managing editor at Ķazaķfil'm (Kazakhfilm) studios. He was a manager of the literary department of the Central Committee of the Communist Party of Kazakhstan (1979–89), editor-in-chief of *Ķazaķ ädebieti* (1989–94), assistant to the President of the Republic of Kazakhstan and deputy director of the Internal Policy Department in the Presidential Administration of the Republic of Kazakhstan (1996–2009). Since 2009, he has been editor-in-chief of *Ôrkeniet*, an academic journal.

His first short story, 'Rajhan', was published in 1964 in a collection of short prose forms by young Kazakh writers, titled *Taŋgy šyķ* (The Morning Dew). His first solo collection, *Kôkžiek* (Horizon), came out in 1969, followed by *Kùzgi žapyraķtar* (Autumn Leaves, 1971), *Aķiķat* (The Truth, 1974), *Ajtylmaġan aķiķat* (The Undisclosed Truth, 1979), *Oŋ ķol* (Right Hand, 2002), *Äke (*Father, 2006) and *Parasat majdany* (The Battlefield of Sanity, 2002), as well as the novel *Ôliara* (Timelessness, 1985). Abdik is widely credited with being one of the leading realist writers in Kazakhstan, who masterfully employs modernist and postmodernist literary devices. His works have been translated into English, German, Latvian, Estonian, Ukrainian and Russian, as well as into a number of Turkic languages. His plays *Biz ùšeu edik* (There Were Three of Us, 1985) and *Ardager* (The Veteran, 2011) have been staged at the major theatres in Kazakhstan.

Abdik was awarded the State Prize of the Republic of Kazakhstan (2004), the Kazakhstani PEN Club Prize (2003) and the Franz Kafka European Gold Medal (2003) for 'Parasat majdany'. He is an Honoured Worker of the Republic of Kazakhstan (2002) and recipient of the Parasat Order (2013).

The Battlefield of Sanity

To be, or not to be – that is the question;
Whether 'tis nobler in the mind to suffer
The slings and arrows of outrageous fortune
Or to take arms against a sea of troubles
And by opposing end them; to die: to sleep –
No more, and by a sleep to say we end
The heartache and the thousand natural shocks
That flesh is heir to: 'tis a consummation
Devoutly to be wished – to die: to sleep –
To sleep, perchance to dream – ay, there's the rub
Hamlet[1]

You have to make the good out of the bad because that is all you have got
to make it out of.   *All the King's Men*[2]

I obtained some diaries from an acquaintance of mine, a doctor. The most
wonderful thing was that the author of the diaries was also an old acquaintance.
No matter how spacious the world is, all the paths in it intersect. What a mighty
God we serve!

In the pride of youth, we see life as a noisy bazaar. It develops in cycles.
We have a lot of friends around us: your friend's friend becomes your friend.
In the bustling whirlwind of youth, we remember certain things but forget
others; we cultivate close links with some people, but break up with others. I
still remember one man: tall, thick, fair-faced. Probably he was weak-nerved,
because he turned as red as a beet at the slightest joke, every time. Everyone
treated him with undue solicitude, as if he was a foreigner in our company.

He did not interest me at all; a few random conversations at the table left
nothing in my memory except for the sensation that this was a very delicate,
mild man, fairly well-read, probably from an educated family. You could feel
that he was a gentle spirit. This trait seemed special to others, but in reality,
it was his weakness. He did not enter into a conversation; he could sit silently
for hours.

---

[1] William Shakespeare, *The Tragical History of Hamlet, Prince of Denmark*. The Second
    Quarto (1604–5); Act III, Scene 1. In: *Hamlet*, Ed. Ann Thompson and Neil Taylor. The
    Arden Shakespeare, 2006: pp. 284–5.

[2] Robert Penn Warren, *All the King's Men*. Harcourt, 1996: p. 391.

We did not communicate very well, and, after many years, my impression of meeting this man was that we had travelled together on the same ship for a time, compelled to communicate politely, but did not make any mutual attempts to become closer. Then the journey was over, and afterward we never had to meet again.

Now I am reading these diaries, which consist of several notebooks, and I cannot fathom that he is their author.

Going by the records, it is impossible to acquire at least some idea of his private life. Diaries express their author's reflections and complex emotions in a pure way.

Only in the very last notebook are the vague contours of his destiny drawn. There, some of the events of his life are described colourfully. All his correspondence had been transferred carefully to the pages of this notebook. It seems that the author of the notes assumed that, one day, they would fall into someone's hands and attract attention. I believe that I am meeting this secret desire of the author, offering the reader precisely the last part of the diary – in my opinion, the main part, where the brightest features of his soul are expressed extraordinarily, capturing the tragic fate of those who seek truth in this life, yet face dark, insurmountable contradictions. Perhaps it might be useful to those who are lost in the struggle between hope and doubt, truth and falsehood.

It would probably be inappropriate to name the author of these notes. We shall consider that he is one of many unknowns among our contemporaries, who might live next door to us, yet remain a secret to all.

1

13 March

It seems that something in my life has changed. But what, exactly, I do not know yet, and it worries me. Maybe it started a long time ago, but I did not notice it – I have just started to realise it. Everything is possible. I do not know. Or, my nerves have shattered, so there is no order in my thoughts, I forget what I just thought about. And in the diary, there are entries from 3 March, but the following days, 4, 5 and 6 March, are not recorded. Only on 7 March do they continue. And what I did during those missed days, I do not remember. I have heard about memory failure before, but with what it is connected, I do not know.

It happens like this: the longer life lasts, the more people, meetings and events disappear into oblivion. Even what you once attached great importance to falls into this darkness; even the names of close people in childhood, in adolescence, are forgotten. You cannot remember old friendships. Everything evaporates like air. Truly, our lives are like water, flowing into nowhere. Human memory is a mistery.

Ask the doctor about the reasons for this, and the response will be 'overwork'. Maybe the doctor is right. In this world, you've got a lot to deal with. And if you think about it all, you will find yourself lost, like a traveller at a crossroads. The mysteries of being are incomprehensible. You cannot blame either God or Man. On one hand, God created the world and all the people in it, and instructed them on charity, faith and kindness. What else do you need? But, on the other hand, how can we *not* feel compassion for a man who acts according to God's commands, but suffers the consequences alone?

Both good and evil are skilful debaters! It is unlikely that you will be able to convince anyone of anything. Each will come out armed with the strongest arguments, and each builds a little hut in the magnificent House of the Lord and proclaims his own Paradise in it. But the person squeezed into a small hut can barely stand up at full height. Bent and pushed, I feel my constant humiliation, the reasons for which I do not know. Everything closes off the splendour of God's world from me: I can't enjoy the play of sunlight, Nature's charms, the fragrant infusion of herbs in the spring air, as I once did. Immersion in my inner world, perhaps, is the reason for this. A tent-like world deprives me of the remnants of joy. 'Our perishable world', to cite Maġžan Žùmabaev's poem, 'is a prison for those who think.'[3]

2

15 March

They say that a person can adapt to Hell in three days. It is possible that this is so. And in fact, to become accustomed to the agonies of life is simply necessary. Otherwise, how can we exist in this world? But the habits of sin, lie, injustice and cruelty are dangerous. For example, we no longer pay attention to the daily newspapers, which publish details of all the monstrous abominations perpetrated by people who have lost their humanity. But I am even more frightened by the fact that other people, the ones living next door, say, do not feel any disgust. Perhaps it is the same foolish bravado of youngsters who, out of a deep longing to know the darkest secrets of life and death, run up and touch a corpse?

I have long ceased to read the newspapers. They write horrible stories that are simply unimaginable:

'He raped or killed his mother'
'He raped or killed his young daughter'
'She killed and threw her newborn child into the trash'
'A millionaire married her son'
'The maniac killed people and ate their flesh'
'A necrophiliac had sexual relations with the dead'

---

[3] A quote from a well-known epic poem, *Batyr Baân*. The poem does not exist in English and the quote has been translated for the purpose of this anthology by the National Bureau of Translations. [Ed.]

Such terrifying things are happening throughout the world, and I cannot handle it anymore – I am vomiting from all this, as if I swallowed multiple stews. From disgust, the blood in my veins becomes cold, as if I fell into a sewage ditch without any possibility of washing off the shit!

And yet the peaceful citizens next to me live quietly. They try, with nasty tranquillity, to treat all this with understanding. Possessing some secret wisdom, they are ready to legitimise all this world's shit.

There are ancient fairy tales about dragons, which demanded human sacrifice from time to time. People desperately chose the most beautiful girls, so that these monsters would be satisfied. Thus, for a while, they could buy peace and security for themselves.

It seems that such universal and unopposable monsters still dominate mankind, making it tremble with bloody wars, formidable typhoons and earthquakes, sending out epidemics of terrible diseases and mass starvation, and collecting their ruthless tribute from the human race. Not content with all this, the universal dragon demands that human spirituality itself be sacrificed to it.

Balzac was right when he remarked, 'Pain [is] the most abiding of our sensations…'[4]

Well, yes, the newspapers inform us eagerly about impending nuclear, ecological and cosmic catastrophes, even presage the possibility of a new Great Flood – and this is all presented not as cheap sensationalism, but as quite reliable scientific forecasting! The exact time of any global disaster, as a rule, is never indicated. But we tremble even at a single thought about it.

Of course, it is quite possible to assume that someday the Sun will go out and that human life on Earth will disappear: the wonderful child of the universe will vanish, taking with him into the chaos of nonexistence all his joy and suffering, hope and despair, all that makes the universe beautiful. How can we reconcile ourselves to the fact that human kindness, mercy, compassion, love and self-sacrifice, all amassed for hundreds of thousands of years, drop by drop, will disappear into this post-historic darkness? All of it will pass into the void of cold space?

However, no matter how much you puzzle over this, nothing in the world will change. God only knows what the end of mankind will look like. Maybe the story of Noah will be repeated, and there will be a worldwide flood? And maybe *nothing* will happen again. Something else will come up, and life will begin again from insignificant bacteria. And it will take another few billion years for man, with his high intelligence, to appear. No one knows.

And yet, if this world is destined to perish, and if it lives out its last days, oh, how I would like to leave it in the fire of cosmic devastation, retaining to myself, in my soul, even the remnants of that high human dignity and respect,

---

[4] Honore de Balzac, A *Women of Thirty*, Chapter II. Translated by Ellen Marriage.

and not be erased from the face of the Earth as an unnecessary, biologically vile slug, ravaged, mired in sins.

3

25 March

They say that disease of the body comes from bad food, and disease of the soul from gloomy thoughts. Whichever it was, I'm already on my seventh day in a hospital surrounded by a high, concrete wall. A small single room, a shelter for many who have been here before, serves as my refuge. It looks as ugly and wretched as the hospital-issued clothing. The whole view of the world of God is fenced off by the wall of a high-rise building, and only a small piece of sky shines in, through a narrow strip on the right. There you can distinguish the top of a mountain peak; this alone connects me to the other world.

Lest the irrevocably passing days disturb the soul, I decided to forget about this diary, and did not take pen into hand. But today I could not resist, and there is a special reason for that: a rather strange, inexplicable situation made me turn again to my notes.

In the morning, preparing to take my medicine, I reached for a glass of water on the nightstand and suddenly saw a folded sheet of paper there. I'll never forget this moment. A sheet of yellowish, cheap paper, with some indistinct yet familiar handwriting on it, as if it belonged to someone I knew – but I do not remember who. With an unintelligible fear, as if dealing with an explosive, I unfolded the paper and began to read:

My unfamiliar friend!
You have forced me, prompted me, to deepest thought. I apologise for daring to read your papers without your permission.

It's easy to understand that you have set out, courageously, on a very risky mission, known in the language of sceptics as 'searching for the meaning of life'. Yes, the matter is in fact very risky, and thankless, and hopeless. However, I do not want to upset you. On the contrary, I wish you a safe journey to the extravagant world of the spirit, where very difficult trials await you. Good luck, my brave friend!

To my mind, the existing opinion that human life represents an age-old struggle between good and evil is by no means indisputable. It is impossible to place them on different sides. It's just as impossible as grabbing anyone out of a street crowd and determining with certainty how much 'good' and how much 'bad' he contains. Such a notion would be naive. To his enemies, he is a scoundrel; to his loving wife, dear and priceless, a kind and sympathetic fellow. But even love and hate are selective in relation to a person. That is, in man we accept not only good things; we do not deny the bad. How many examples there are: a 'good' friend with a 'bad' side, a good man who allies with a villain and vice versa, two decent, virtuous people who are mortally hostile to each other.

Hence life is not only a confrontation between good and evil, but also a clash of good with good, and evil with evil. So we are forced to admit that good and evil are conditional, subjective, completely different for different people.

Yet this is just an insignificant part of the problem I have posed. The most important, the most curious thing, is that the components of this notorious pairing, 'good and evil' – like Siamese twins – are inextricably intertwined. They cannot exist alone. There is, you know, in Chinese philosophy, the concept of *yin* and *yang*: light and dark, Heaven and Earth, top and bottom. They are cyclical, one eventually passing into the other. The world exists in the revolution of these transitions. If we apply this philosophy to everyday human affairs, then the following is obtained:

It is believed that water is the basis of life. To water gardens and irrigate fields and pastures, people erect dams, build reservoirs, accumulate water for their own use. This is a manifestation of yang, of creative beginning.

But that same water, at the time of the spring flood when rivers overflow, demolishes the dam, washes away houses and destroys in its path any living thing: those same gardens and fields, wild and domestic animals, people. Having reached a critical point, the 'good' element turns into a destructive force and acts as its opposite quality: yin. Gradually, however, the high waters calm down, the rivers return to their former shores, and the life-giving water again becomes a boon to people. But the wait also begins for the next spring, when the strength of yang can again turn into destructive yin. So it goes, from year to year, in an endless cycle of time, the element in question being water, all the same water!

What conclusion can we draw? Good and evil are the same phenomenon, only with different characteristics in different situations. Is it possible to separate them, put them into different vessels? And how much is it necessary to do so? Think about it.

My unfamiliar friend! This is just the beginning of a conversation. Don't you think we can speak a lot? It would be very good and useful to become closer, to share our secrets. We shall open our souls to each other! Should you decide to write me a reply, put your letter in the bottom drawer of the table in the corridor.

Your unknown peer

I was surprised and slightly troubled; I do not know why, but I read the letter again from beginning to end. Like a cold stream, fear penetrated into my heart. How did the letter get to me, on the ward? After all, I am alone here. Did someone come here in my absence? Did someone read my diary? He could come into the open, and become acquainted!

Anxious, I walked around the room, not feeling my legs. But – calm! Calm down. Think it over. Okay, the situation is clear. There are enough cranks around nowadays. And do not forget that you are in a psychiatric hospital.

Calming myself in this way, I decided not to attach much importance to the incident. At eleven o'clock I went for an autogenic training session. It was conducted by a young, fair-skinned girl whom I had not seen before, very pleasant. When she spoke, her upper lip curved into a sweet flicker. She smiled at the same time, showing pearly teeth. Her look was radiant, bright; you seemed to be washed in those rays when she looked into your eyes. Those smile-serious lips intoned:

You are relaxing… you are seized with a pleasant feeling, of bliss… you seem to be plunged into a light sleep… plunged into a dream… plunged into a dream…

From afar you can hear music – quiet at first, then more and more sonorous, growing. This is unworldly delight. Under this melody, the child falls asleep; you fly to your dreams. Your feelings obtain freedom and soar into the air, hovering above the clouds like a bird. It is a feeling of lightness and infinity. Infinity…

And now you are sitting on the soft, shaky shore of the azure lake. The Sun is shining brightly. You smell the fragrance of fresh herbs, of the blooming *žajlau*…[5] and the spirit of warm greens tickles your nostrils.

Someone in the distance is waving their hands.

Suddenly:

'Wake up!' a voice rang. 'You are already awake… you are vivacious… your body has become light as air, your muscles filled with elastic force, your eyes full of brilliance; you are ready to fly… Wake up!'

I reluctantly opened my eyes, yawning and stretching, and I saw the girl psychotherapist with the smiling eyes, looking at me as though at a little child.

'Very good! Well done', she said cheerfully, and it's unclear to me whether or not she was praising us or herself – for she had completed the autogenic training session successfully.

At first I was uneasy, embarrassed by the fact that some intimate secrets of my soul had become available to an outsider. I began to look around quietly, suspiciously, but then immediately calmed down. Everyone else, just like me, came out of the trance, yawning and stretching. So, I was not alone in this situation.

---

[5] *Žajlau* – highland summer pastures; winter pastures are called *kystau*: both are integral to the nomadic lifestyle of Kazakhs.

4

26 March
Something is wrong with me. At night, I had a bad dream. I walked along the dark corridor. There was some rubbish, boxes, in my way. I brushed the wall with my hand so that I wouldn't stumble. It seemed I was in a hurry to get somewhere, and was trying to walk quickly. Suddenly, something sharp slashed my neck. I hardly had time to notice it – it could have been a dagger stuck into the wall. I did not seem to feel any pain, but was aware of my head rolling from side to side, and automatically grabbed it with my hands. It turned out that my neck had been cut almost completely, my head now attached to my body with just one strip of skin. The feeling was disgusting. Then I had to move forward, with one hand clutching my head and the other stretching out as I probed the wall like a blind man. I advanced very carefully, lest the head fall off my shoulders and roll into the darkness.

The corridor lasted forever. Was I really doomed to wander forever? But at last, I entered a spacious room. It looked like the hotel lobby, with a high ceiling. I sat down cautiously in the armchair and made a decision: I wrenched my head off completely and put it down on the next chair. People passing by looked at me in surprise. Embarrassed, I picked up some newspaper and quickly covered my head. What a shame! I thought. How do I hide this head?

I had to hurry somewhere. But where would I go, without a head? I raised the corner of the newspaper carefully and saw that my head was still lying there. I ought to get rid of it soon... Then I woke up.

I lay awake for a while. My heart was beating wildly. I was puzzled by one detail of the dream: how could I see my head if it was torn off and lay to the side? This was completely absurd. But everything was so clear! I remembered every sensation.

For a long time, I could not sleep. The half-darkness of the room and the thin light of the window generated a delirious anxiety. I felt a light breeze.

The nightmare clung to me, lingering like an annoying fly. I only had to close my eyes, however: immediately, I saw my own head thrown back on the chair, with shreds of red meat in place of the severed neck.

5

27 March
What can be more terrible than when a person begins to fear himself? Your inner world becomes wild and incomprehensible, like an eerie forest in which you are lost. You feel panicked that you will never get out of it. Suddenly you feel that you are alive no more, that someone else is wandering in a dense wilderness. You have become an outsider to yourself. One day, like a mouse, your own soul flees in fright and looks with timid amazement at the outer world. No matter how terrifying our lives might seem at first glance, there is something consoling in it for us. Look – this is the Sun! And here are crowds of people! More natural feelings gradually return to you, and it seems again

that you have goals, a reasonable starting point and a cause for everything happening in your life.

Now my first priority is to find the person who wrote me that strange letter. It is necessary to stop this game, this imaginary mystery. Like a scout in an enemy camp, I sneaked through the courtyard of the hospital and gazed intently at everyone who came to meet me. I was sure that if they just looked into my eyes, I would recognise my 'pen friend'.

During the search for my mysterious peer, I made the following discovery: we live life very superficially, knowing little about other people. While I was looking for my peer among the madmen in our hospital, I came across so many different types! But before, they had all seemed the same to me.

A reddish-haired man, who had seemed to me to be a gloomy, silent individual, actually turned out to be a great chatterbox. Before introducing himself, he grabbed my sleeve and began to pour out the names of his ancestors and boasted of their great exploits, telling me extensively about which of them had gone before the Tsar of Russia, and which had become an outstanding scientist. He made me exhausted.

One fat man, carefully tending the pathetic remnants of hair from his temples to the crown of his bald head, threatened me at each meeting: 'Hey, little brother, do you know who I am? In this country there is no Kazakh who does not know me. Where did you come from?'

There was one more freak, a hard case. He said he was Jesus Christ, descended from Heaven to bring order to Earth, but that people were frightened of him and hid him in the hospital, the United Nations being the mastermind behind this crime. In general, the poor fellow spoke pitiable nonsense.

Meanwhile, the weather becomes warmer and warmer. Although sometimes a damp wind blows, piercing one to the bone – like a patient's breathing.

One day, just before dinner time, there was a fight in the courtyard. A large, bearded man suddenly attacked a long-haired guy. The attendants could barely manage to pull them apart. Witnesses gave different versions of the reasons for the fight. The nurse's version was that the bearded man had been infuriated by the fact that the head physician, passing through the courtyard, stopped by and greeted the long-haired man. Waiting for the doctor to leave, the bearded man attacked the young patient, growling menacingly: 'Why did he say hello to you, but not to me?' When you consider all that, you will surely think, what is the difference between life behind the concrete fence and life in the courtyard of this psychiatric hospital?

After dinner, I went to see the doctor for an examination. A small, bespectacled man, he sat up straight in a chair. He scrutinises a person as though they are in pain, but he is thorough and accurate – a good specialist. He took my blood pressure, listened to my heart and lungs. Then he began speaking about life. He asked me what I did before being admitted to the hospital. It seemed as though he was bored, and looking for a suitable companion. We talked about the little things, aspects of hospital life – the fact that the night before, the hot water had been turned off, for example, that the weather was unpredictable.

Then the conversation turned to medical topics. I was given a lecture on psychopathology, focused particularly on split personality. The doctor gave, as an example, the case of a good family man and a good worker during the daylight hours who, at night, turns into a dangerous maniac, raping women and murdering people. Another example: a respected pilot who, for several years, had been luring young girls into seclusion and raping them. He was caught at the crime scene after murdering one. Who would have suspected that a member of such an elite profession, a man who commanded airliners, could lead another life – a secret existence full of vile crimes? There was no shortage of such examples. It turns out that the emergence of a 'second person' within a person, so sharply different from the first, is nothing but a manifestation of the profound pathology of his psyche.

Personally, I am predisposed to think that in our times, when 'normal' and 'abnormal' are mixed indiscriminately, it is absolutely impossible to determine the border line between illness and health. An odd tooth is considered pathology; but when people betray a loved one or blood relationship or friendship – this is called not a manifestation of pathology, but an everyday life occurrence. It turns out that we are used to this absurdity. Otherwise, what pathology can be worse than betraying our moral values?

Today's moral situation: frenetic selfishness, biological egoism, bestial cruelty, demonic envy, callousness, boasting and bragging by the powerful... is this not pathology?

Can you meet a man today who would like to get rid of his flaws, which number more than the hairs on his head? Stop a hundred people on the street and talk to each of them; they will all present themselves as near angels. Who are the rapists, then, and where are they?

6

31 March

Today I got a letter again. I feel as though I shall destroy myself. Although I swore not to look in the bottom drawer of the nightstand, I could not resist. I initially resisted. But by noon, I had rushed along the corridor to the nightstand. And here I am, limp, like a half-stricken animal, caught in a noose.

In my hand I have a letter.

Frankly, letters, for me, are like a challenge to a deadly duel. I do not want any fight. If not for this last letter, there would have been at least a little breathing space in my battle with that dark force. I would have accumulated enough mental strength for confrontation. But the invisible enemy launched an insidious attack.

Here it is. The second letter.

Unfamiliar fellow!
I did not wait for your answer. I had to write the following letter. Once
again, I ask you to excuse me for reading your diary without your
knowledge.

From the diary, it became clear to me that you only believe one-sidedly,
so to speak, in the good of man, and do not believe in evil. In my opinion,
truth consists of believing in both. Can you not see that our world is
caught between these two forces? A cart pulled by a horse wearing a
double bridle, one of them necessarily evil. But it does not have what
you think is an exclusively malicious essence, which only brings trouble
to people. Take, for example, death. It is, without doubt, considered an
absolute evil thing. But think, my friend, what would our lives be like, if
there were no death? If the old and sick did not die, the lives of villains,
criminals, tyrants threatening all mankind would not cease. What Hell
would be on Earth! Thanks to the efficacy of death, the flywheel of the
eternal engine of life can spin. And if people did not have the brutality
that enables them to kill, then how could they protect themselves from
bloodthirsty, two-legged predators? Here we are afraid of the deadly
venom of the snake, but how many beneficial medicines are made from
that same snake venom? So now, please tell me: is the venom of the snake
'good' or 'bad'? It is impossible to hang on to only one of these labels.
It would be wrong, and unintelligent. To understand whether we are
confronted by good or evil, we must enquire of any given phenomenon
whether or not it is useful or harmful.

Now, about lies and deceit. We hate the lie; we know that. But if lie
could speak, we would hear this: 'Hey, my dear! Thanks to me, you are
alive and well and feeling so self-assured. If you always told the truth and
only the truth, you would all have gnawed at each other's throats by now!
How many times have you been saved, thanks to me, and how many of
you are safe now, thanks to me? You cannot live without me for a day!'

You can have no objection to her words. Because what you have heard
from Lie is the real truth.

In your diary, you often mention 'decency' and 'purity'. I'll tell you a
story I heard from a friend:

An intelligent and good-looking woman put the horns on her
husband. We shall not be distracted by the details; I shall only say that
the facts of adultery in our time have become quite ordinary. But bad
luck: the poor woman contracted a venereal disease. And maybe, if
this unfaithful person had secretly pursued an appropriate course of
treatment, she would have been cured and the story could have ended

happily on that note. However, she became seriously depressed, and came to believe herself unworthy of her husband, whom she had disgraced. So she committed suicide. As a result, her husband and child were left without a wife and mother.

The deceived spouse grieved deeply. He had been destroyed by a monstrous mistake committed by his deceased spouse, who considered her husband to be the purest person in the world, to whom it was impossible to atone for her guilt, and therefore only one thing was left for her to do: hang herself. But do you know what? Her husband had loved her greatly; he would have been able to forgive everything. He had, in fact, plenty of sins in his own past – he could not consider himself a model of purity.

You can live happily despite such disloyalty and shortcomings, but former happiness cannot be returned. What an error! What prejudice! They destroy the world, cripple life on Earth. What are we trying to achieve, poisoning our consciousness with some concept of sublime purity that does not exist in nature! What stupidity! The husband grieved. The end.

To achieve happiness, a person must first clearly understand for himself who he is and what he is. He will have to admit that he is not a saint at all, but an ordinary, mortal sinner. Without acknowledging all this with humility, no one can be spared vain, foolish and hopeless spiritual self-torture.

When I think about it now, it seems that I have only to stretch forth my hand, and the bird of happiness will fly to it and sit on my palm. Well, with all my heart, I want the bird of happiness to fly to your hands too.

I remain your well-wisher, and hope that you shall reply with a letter.

Your unknown peer

I remember that when I read the last lines of the letter, the sheet trembled in my hands. 'Quiet! Be calm', I commanded myself. But a storm of indignant feelings did not let me calm down. Disorderly thoughts, like panic-stricken animals during an earthquake, scattered in all directions, and I could not concentrate on anything. What is it? Is someone trying to drive me crazy? Or does he have other intentions?

Soon I did manage to calm down, and began to delve more closely into the contents of this second message from the stranger. Then a new turmoil swept over my soul. The fact is that much of the letter was *true*. However, the threat lurked therein. The most terrible thing is not a complete lie, but a lie covered up in the shell of truth. The most dishonourable bastard is one who wants to appear in the form of a humble truth-seeker. This is the hardest thing to cope with.

And yet, the stranger chose his direction incorrectly. If the desired object is in the east, then a person heading west will never find it, no matter how resourceful and persistent he is. To find it would require a change of direction.

Of course, I also know that everyone can be good and bad, but this does not at all serve as proof of the inseparability of good and evil. We must distinguish between these two principles.

If a horse is white and black, we call it 'piebald'. Does the concept of 'piebald' exclude the independent meanings of the terms 'white' and 'black'? No, of course, not; in the colour of one animal, two different colours are combined. So it is with good and evil: no matter how you mix them, in any combination, they cannot merge into one indivisible, single concept.

There are also other crafty, crooked thoughts in the letter, which are curious because they contain not some deep truth, but a hidden, corrosive paradox.

In the burning war of reason for the apprehension of truth, there is no room for art and ornamentation. Here you need bare, unadulterated truth, without embellishment. Beauty distracts from truth, and, in essence, is hostile to this war. A beautiful but stupid man; a beautiful but unfaithful wife. Beautiful, but false words... How many times has a lie defeated us, dressed in the garments of beauty? How many gracefully tailored false thoughts, like a frivolous guide, mislead people?

P.S. Gottfried Benn: 'Hegel, Darwin, Nietzsche – they became the real cause of the death of many millions. Words are more criminal than any murder. Heroes and crowds are paying for their uttered thoughts.'[6]

7

1 April

I am overwhelmed with endless suspicion, and suspicion breeds a sense of desperation.

What a bad person my 'unknown peer' is. He goes everywhere, spies on me. It seems to me that when I read his letters, he looks at me through a crack somewhere. He is too well informed about me, as if reading my thoughts, which I do not even have time to put into my notes.

I have already cooled down somewhat in my desire to catch him, to expose him. Trying to outwit someone who is more intelligent and more resourceful than you is completely pointless. Likely, now, he is somewhere nearby. It is very possible that he is in close contact or even in collusion with a nurse or the attending physician. He knows everything.

Day and night, I can think only of him. Last night I had a dream. He came forward, at last. Wearing exactly the same hospital clothes as mine. Even the slippers were the same. He was standing with his back to me, and said:

'Well, we meet at last.'

'Yes. So we meet at last', I repeated, as if imitating him.

---

[6] Unless stated otherwise, all quotations given in the text have been translated into English from the Kazakh by the National Bureau of Translations. [Ed.].

I wanted to see his face, but I could not. I pretended I was not surprised, and waited secretly for him to turn around. I believed that if I kept silent, he would turn to face me. However, he stood there, like a statue, and did not move.

'Well, enough! Enough of this game of hide-and-seek!' I said. I was out of patience. I put my hand out to turn him by the shoulders.

But what was this? My hand refused. As if it was tied to my body. I made an incredible effort. It did not work! It was like it wasn't mine. And then a weight piled on my chest, began to suffocate me... I groaned – and immediately woke up, in a cold sweat. The nightmare of suffocation overtook me in the small hours.

I wanted the dream to return, to look again at him, remember at least some distinctive features of my 'unknown peer'. But all in vain. I lay in bed, my eyes shut tightly, and did not see anything else. And what if I saw his face? I would not be able to cling to someone just because I dreamt of him.

8

2 April
I am like a hunter who, pursuing an animal, loses his way on the unfamiliar steppe. What to do? At night, I cannot sleep. The deadlock brings me to depression. In the morning I get up, all broken. I am finally ready to surrender.

This protracted war of nerves is not for me. I cannot stand it, and decide to write a reply:

> My unfamiliar peer! [I began the same way as in his letters.]
> I dare to hope that you will forgive me for not answering your letters immediately. But the whole point is that the questions that you raise are known to me, and I answered them myself, too, long ago. It seemed to me that there is no need to enter into a discussion with you. However, I later discovered that this is not the case. Many of your starting positions are very different from mine. Of course, this does not matter much – it is naive to believe that, in our populous world, everyone should think and act in the same way. But at the same time, it is impossible to sit idly by when someone tries to distort your convictions. And so, I decided to answer you.
>
> Life is a fight. In this struggle, humanity first took part – like all living things on Earth – only physically, using its muscular strength. But then we invented all sorts of weapons, and began to exterminate each other much more successfully, in large numbers. Now, in our day, a war of wits has entered into force, and has flared up in all parts of the world. This is the most dangerous war. In an era of universal collapse of spirituality, no one will be saved.
>
> You seem to have announced this war to me... and I must accept the challenge. Now let's get to the point.

311

You call on me to believe in evil, just as I believe in good. But the fact is, my dear, that I actually admit the existence of evil in humans. Faith is a preference; it is a choice; it is a spiritual merging with what you see as the highest value. Dostoevsky said: 'Where there is no faith…, there is no love to humankind.'[7] So what is your faith, to which you are calling me? What do you want? Do you want me to become a believer in evil? He who does not believe in good shall never be able to do it himself.

Here you persistently repeat the idea that we should not hang the labels 'good' or 'bad' on anything in the world. But if a person does not learn to separate one from another, how does he differ from an animal? And the very concept of humanism is a result of this human trait: to be able to distinguish between good and evil. After all, humaneness is the basic code of inter-human relations at all times, and among all peoples. Mankind cannot exist without it. (True, there are many among us who brazenly and openly violate this code, but we cannot say that only evil rules the world.)

I cannot admit that your philosophy of death is successful. If it is a matter of natural death, which comes to man at the end of life, given to him by God, as a concession of place in life to the next generation, then to such 'evil' mankind has learnt to react with understanding.

But there is unjust death. Ruthlessly, it takes a person's only loved one, cutting off his life halfway. And to some villain and maniac, it gives an innocent sacrifice to mockery, torment and death. The bloody tyrant: in the name of his triumph and insane rapture in his own power, death throws to the mass grave of history thousands and thousands of murdered people… And all these varieties of unspeakable death do not fit into your death apologetics. Which are aimed only at one thing: to cast doubt on the concept of good. And even this goal is far-reaching; we must fight for good.

Your ideas about Lies also sound paradoxical. Yes, in human history there were times when people lived in lies, and survived thanks to them. Perhaps there are still many such people. But this is not because a lie has such dignity, but because society itself is based on lies. If this were a truth-based, just society, then Miss Lies would be immediately exposed, and she would not dare behave so arrogantly and haughty as you describe it.

At the end of the last letter, you told the heartbreaking story of a woman who hanged herself for deceiving a decent, faithful, loving husband. And he was far from being an angel. The poor woman was the victim of her error: she believed in the existence of moral purity. But I perceive this example as a clever, sophistic trick, an impure mind game. After all, you can give examples where, after the betrayal of his beloved wife, a husband commits suicide. Therefore, your conclusion that the

---

[7] Fyodr Dostoevsky, *A Writer's Diary: 1873–1876.*

alleged cause of all ills is moral purity – which does not exist in Nature – has no basis.

It is a mistake to assume an equal ratio of the forces of good and evil. And that we must try to just keep this balance, and then everything will be in order. Nothing like this! There can never be a balance of evil and good. Good is more precious. A wise man said: 'There are many ways to commit evil, and the only way to do no evil is to do no evil.' And that's all. Try to do good, because bad will happen without any effort.

And I am far from thinking I can prove something to you, or, even worse, to instruct you on the true path. All of the above has only been an answer to the controversy almost forcibly imposed on me. In your views on the world there is something deeply offensive to my soul, affecting my best feelings. And it is very difficult for me to simply exchange opinions with you, and I do not want any rapprochement and friendly communication. Therefore, I advise you to find yourself another, more suitable intellectual partner.

The stranger

9

3 April

I could not even imagine that my 'unknown peer' would cling so fast to my soul. Day and night I think of him, like of a beloved. I feel his round-the-clock presence with all my skin, with all my nerves, and at times it seems to me that I hear the close knock of his heart.

I continue to follow some of the people walking around the courtyard, but in this shadowing I just waste my time. Every night I spend in insomnia; I get up half-dead in the morning. And last night I suddenly heard footsteps. I got out of bed and cautiously went out into the corridor. There was no one there. The steps now resounded outside the window, from the street. But I did not notice anyone outside. Yet as soon as I stepped away from the window, the steps began to resound again. Sometimes they were drowned out by the roar of a passing car. But when it subsided, the shuffling of someone's cautious feet again became audible. And the heart began to quietly die of some obscure, dark fear. 'Do I hear or not hear?' I thought with great sorrow, standing alone in the dimly lit corridor of the hospital. I wanted immediately to go to the street... But the doors of the offices on each floor were locked for the night.

I went back to the ward and went to bed again. But I could not sleep. Whenever some steps began to approach, I woke up immediately.

10

7 April

In the morning I awoke with vague anxiety, as if I had missed a very important matter, or was late either for a plane or a train. The first thing I saw, lifting my head from the pillow, was a letter on the nightstand. My heart jumped.

Fear ran with an ominous flame through my body. I twisted the sheet with convulsive movements. I wanted to see if it was the same handwriting. Yes, the same. When I started reading, I caught myself thinking that, in addition to fear, I was curious about the content of the letter.

Loving stranger!
I am very grateful to you for your reply. I once again became convinced that you are a man of traditional humanistic convictions.

But life is like a great, unimaginative bazaar where everyone can find everything he needs. But have you ever had to buy a completely useless thing? This is where the main intrigue lies. After all, you agree with me: if we do not need to change the everlasting canons and representations, why do we strive for something new? But do not deny that any development, any progress, is impossible without innovation. Covering the entire history of our civilisation at a glance, it is impossible to conclude that humanity has ever been happy. The main characteristics of this story are endless war, famine, terrible epidemics, natural disasters, poverty and violence. To all this, in our day, purely technological disasters have been added: poisoning of water, soil and air.

But let us digress from global generalisations and turn to the fate of the individual. Take us, at least – you and me. Are we happy? I personally do not assert this. How can I be happy, seeing so much violence and injustice around me, and being powerless to resist it all? For how many centuries have we believed in good and justice? And yet we are always persuaded that our faith, confronted with real life, is shattered like a clay toy. And all the same, stupidly and recklessly, we keep our old beliefs. They say that the blind man desperately clings to what is in his hands. Maybe we are blind, and our blindness is spiritual…

We need faith. We believed in the mystical power of fire and water – there was no element left that we did not worship. And how many gods have there been for mankind! And the prophets! Great leaders and speakers! And we all believed. So what? Has our sad fate been made any easier? Believe in the triumph of goodness, humanists appeal to us. When, in what century, will this doomed good celebrate its victory? In all probability, never. And you know, my friend: there are desires that do not come true, no matter how much we feel them.

There is a quite legitimate question to ask: why is this impossible? Because within its intellectual space, humanity has long been lost. Our temples of good and evil have been erected in violation of building codes. And now there is only one thing: to build new ideas about humanity, conscience, justice… completely from scratch. 'The greatest epochs come when we have the courage to rename all our evil as our best', Nietzsche once remarked.[8] Stereotypes of former days, habits and ideas do not allow us to peer into the face of truth. Many names are known, the bearers of which were once condemned and executed through burning, hanging, or betrayed, or expelled to foreign lands – and later recognised as geniuses and titans of mankind. Some even ranked as saints. How many works of artists and writers in the most highly civilised countries were declared immoral, as destroying the foundations of the existing society – and later, with the arrival of new generations, recognised as the best creations of human culture? All this is due to the fact that we are captives of prejudice and conservatism. It is time we got rid of them, and then immediately our consciousness will be illuminated by a flash of high intelligence, and the clear, visible space of a new life will open before us. So our consciousness needs liberation. Spiritual freedom is necessary. There should be no obstacle in its path. Only boundless spiritual freedom can bring true happiness to man!

Sincerely,
Your unfamiliar friend

Any grain of good or evil arises on the ground first as an idea. Then it sprouts as things that contain faith in the world. The ideas in the letter of the 'stranger' are comparable to a nuclear bomb dropped into the world of our spirituality. God knows what the consequences of such an explosion, and the radiation, would be.

I could not calmly reflect. My nerves tensed like drawn strings and were about to burst. A new breakdown was coming. Losing control over myself, I jumped out into the corridor with a cry: 'This is an outrage! Damn it! Who lets him into the ward?'

A nurse came running. She had only recently been hired.

'Where are you looking at?' I yelled at her rudely, unable to restrain myself. 'Who is he, and why do you allow outsiders to enter my room?'

The nurse, as best she could, calmed me down. She asked what had happened. Shivering with indignation, I could not explain my claim to her intelligibly, and only waved the letter in front of her nose, repeating endlessly: 'Here you are... Here! What other proof do you need?'

Eventually, she began to understand everything. 'Nobody came to see you on my shift', she said, looking at me in surprise.

'Where did this come from, then?' Incensed, I shook the letter.

'Well, all right', said the nurse in a conciliatory tone, 'but you need to calm down first. Get a little rest. And then we'll figure it out.' She took me back to the ward and gave me a pill.

---

[8] In *Thus Spake Zarathustra*; in English also as 'The greatest epochs of our lives come when we gain the courage to rebaptise our evil as our best'. [Tr.]

'You'd better not go out for a walk today', she advised. 'And in the evening, if anything bothers you, ask the doctor on duty to give you an injection before going to bed.'

'Please, excuse me', I said in a calmer tone, taking the nurse's hand in a friendly way. 'I was angry, I yelled at you. But believe me, this is all happening. I'm not delirious. I feel like a wounded beast. Recently I have been receiving letters from some unknown person. He plays hide-and-seek with me: he tosses the letters into my room, but does not announce himself. Look, this is the last letter. I have long wanted to catch him, but all my efforts are in vain. This is what drives me crazy.'

She looked at me carefully and became thoughtful.

'When did you find this letter?' she asked.

'Just now.'

'Just now?' exclaimed the nurse in fright. 'You know, I've only begun working here... I don't understand how everything works yet... But I shall bear in mind your complaint. For now, lie down... rest.' She closed the door quietly and tightly behind her.

I could not calm down for a long time. At eleven o'clock I went to the autogenic training session. However, my state of alarm had so mastered me that neither the cute lips and pearly teeth of a young doctor, nor her hypnotic spell calling for spiritual bliss, nor the lulling music, could distract me out of my depression.

In the evening, I sat down to write a reply:

Dear distinguished stranger!
We have been playing blind man's buff for quite some time. We debate, not seeing each other. We jump inconsistently from one topic to another. We pile all that we know into one heap, for the sole purpose of proving our rightness. If we do not determine the parameters of our discussions, and if we do not establish rules for their correct conduct, we are at risk of arguing fruitlessly for the rest of our lives.

So you say that the path traversed by man is in tragic error, as the guiding star, which calls for virtue, was initially chosen incorrectly. And from here, they say, the notions of good and evil, love and hatred, honour and dishonour have all been defined in a distorted way, the priorities set arbitrarily. We need to give up our lofty ideals and spiritual aspirations. Of course, you do not speak out openly, and do not use the word 'refuse', but all you have is this.

But people are unhappy in their world, not because they diligently observe all moral laws, but quite the contrary – because they violate them. They are not unhappy because the sanctuaries of the spirit were built according to wrong calculations, but because we have defiled them ourselves, and have not kept them in proper purity. Every living creature in the world strives for freedom. Freedom, in your opinion, is the deliverance from any restriction: do whatever you want; no one should disturb you. But the sense of duty to other people, charity, honesty, conscientiousness, should limit our actions, restraining them in the framework of the moral law. You would like to convince me that freedom does not recognise any framework, even honour and dignity. So, it turns out, human actions that do not know the boundaries – all lawlessness and fraud, prostitution, robbery and so on – are nothing but the manifestations of unlimited freedom. According to this logic, the ancient Roman Caesars, Nero, Caligula and others, who permitted themselves any depravity or debauchery, extreme cruelty, bloodthirstiness, shamelessness and treachery, will be the freest people in human history. They did not recognise any moral limitations: they cohabited with their own mothers, brought their favourite horses into the Senate and the like. But there is a saying: a dog has a master, and a wolf has Tengri.[9] All who have transgressed the boundaries of God's will, sooner or later, face the trial of History.

Perhaps mankind has been saved from destructive debauchery and spiritual decay precisely by religion. And if it did not succeed in finally defeating Iblis, then at least the demon would be convicted. The fear of God separated man from animal – do you agree with this? And shari'ah law, not the law of unlimited, unbridled freedom of personal tyranny, forbade the people to copulate with their own daughters. But if, in your opinion, we separate freedom from real life and worship it as an idol, it is very possible that we shall return to that crazy debauchery.

Locked in the dungeons of our subconscious, condemned by moral law, all low-lying lusts, the animal insatiability of vice, cruelty and meanness, ingratitude and betrayal, this black host of the evil spirit, are eager for freedom and await the hour when we faint, lose confidence, lose our vigilance. And if this happens, what terrible monsters, serial killers and robbers we shall release from the *zyndans* – the prisons – of our inner world!

When you see a beautiful woman on the street, you are tempted. Man is not an angel. But you should calm yourself! It is possible she is a faithful wife, such as you are a respectable person, and a caring mother of lovely children such as your own. Here you are obliged, having shown firmness, to give yourself a command: 'Stop!' Because freedom means the ability to do everything that does not harm other people. If you cannot stop, then you will simply be a slave to your animal instincts.

When the great Socrates was asked, 'What is the difference between you and the kings?', he replied: 'They are slaves of their passions, and I

---

[9] This proverb harks to the Kazakhs' mythic Turkic origins – specifically, the tradition that they are the descendants of wolves – and refers to Tengri (Tắŋir), the chief deity of the ancient Turkic peoples.

am their master.'[10] Socrates was a hundred times freer than these slave-kings.

The meaning and content of life are made up of simple truths. Our trouble is that we do not perceive this simplicity. We, on our own whims, like to choose the most intricate paths, to perform various unthinkable, unnecessary exploits and overcome all sorts of difficulties. Everyone knows how harmful the habit of smoking is: lung cancer kills more people than any other disease, causing not 'direct death' as destined in old age, but 'side death' caused by our stupidity, vices or bad habits. And here, in order to defeat cancer, huge national resources in many countries are being spent; world industry is working on the side of oncology, to combat cancer, while the problem is very simple. Well, it's harmful and dangerous to smoke – so do not smoke! If you smoke, quit smoking. However, in the fight against man-made problems, humankind always loses. Statistics show that 41.4 per cent of all people who died, except the victims of earthquakes, fires, floods and other natural disasters, traffic accidents and criminal acts, are victims of smoking. That is, about half of the whole world suffers from consuming tobacco.

A trivial problem, solved by a simple effort of will, turns into an insurmountable number-one problem for humanity! Well, is it not monstrous? A small bug in front of us turns into a huge, apocalyptic Beast! ('The people give themselves the greatest suffering because they ignore simple truths': the words of your beloved F. Nietzsche.[11]) You probably think that to solve this problem it is necessary to introduce universal mandatory smoking by law – this is based on your reasoning about free choice. Man must give up any attempt to fight his bad habits. You therefore secretly seek only one thing: that the little man should remain a miserable slave to his desires.

Freedom is within a person, in his mind. How many declared freedoms would be left external to a person – but if he is a scoundrel and a sycophant, all freedoms are useless for him, since he was originally a branded slave and will remain a slave forever.

'Freedom is a clear conscience!' said Periander of Corinth, a wise man who lived seven centuries before our own era. Admit it: it's beautiful! This means that freedom is achieved only through spiritual perfection! Before such freedom, we should take off our hats and bow to the ground.

When, in which age, will the victory of good come? Not without malice, you ask this question. It would be foolish and naive to assume that it would mean the complete eradication of evil on Earth. The triumph of good is where people are firmly aware of the need to generate good

---

[10] We were unable to locate this quote and believe it is the character's interpretation. [Ed.]

[11] As before, no reliable source or attribution of this quote exists. We believe this to be the character's interpretation. [Ed.]

constantly. It is necessary to define clearly what victory and defeat are in this constant, enduring struggle. We have not talked about this yet. In our minds, victory is represented as the successful, powerful blow of a boxer who dispatches his opponent with a knockout, or by the dexterity of a gangster in an action movie, who manages to draw a gun first and shoot an enemy. That is, the deceased are considered defeated. However, the defeat of Jesus Christ, killed by his enemies with incredible cruelty, was also the greatest victory for humanity. Yes, there are losses in this life that are more valuable than victory.

What can be more noble than the act of a sparrow, who, wishing to protect her chicks in the nest, rushes into the mouth of a huge snake? Is not her death a great victory? And she is worthy of our admiration.

'What is "courage"?' Abaj[12] remarked with indignation. 'Why are all the evil villains tend to be desperate, brave men?'[13] Are those cruellest, capable of bloodshed, recognised by us as brave, and their ability to kill as a feat? Is that so? But in that case, what is left for those who are capable of spiritual feats? For example, being unafraid to admit your mistake, not being reflexively harsh to others but being harsh to yourself, punishing yourself first of all, exercising self-control: are these not all remarkable feats? After all, the most formidable lion is not able to repeat the heroic deed of the sparrow, who has the determination to rush to the obviously stronger, mortally dangerous enemy. Probably, some of these concepts need to be revised.

Your considerations are based on the fact that the ideals of good are not compatible with the imperfections of people, and do not correspond to earthly reality itself, in which there is nothing absolutely perfect. I agree with you on the latter, because the imperfection of the world is the impetus for its development. The continuity of life is subject to the laws of constant development. If something were to reach full perfection, it would fall out of the endless chain of development and lose vitality. So, artists – striving for perfection in their work – clearly realise that it is unattainable. However, thanks to their fierce aspirations to perfection, they manage to create beautiful works of art.

Only by seeking ways to cure the most terrible diseases, to capture the most impregnable fortresses and by suffering defeats worthy of great victories, setting themselves unattainable goals of spiritual perfection, is humanity able to expand the horizons of its capabilities. Consequently,

---

[12] Abaj Ķûnanbajûly (Abai Kunanbayev; 1845–1904) – the most influential of all Kazakh poets, also a composer and philosopher. He is considered to be a reformer of Kazakh literature on the basis of enlightened Islam; his works also reflected the European and Russian cultures.

[13] 'Ķara sôzder' (Book of words); 40th Word. Translated from the Kazakh by the National Bureau of Translations. [Ed.]

this discrepancy with the higher ideals of earthly reality is not a shortcoming of theirs, but, on the contrary, an advantage.

God bestowed all of us with kind feelings, good inclinations and wonderful living conditions, so that we could improve this world. But we did not use these good gifts of the Lord. Now, instead of looking for the causes of mistakes in our sinful lack of will, in our weakness and impermanence, we are trying to destroy all that has been created by the soul and by conscience; we want to nullify the entire spirituality of mankind.

The laws of human existence are established by people themselves; therefore, their fulfilment depends on them. True, the laws of Nature are much more severe than those made by humans, and many of them directly injure our higher sentiments, our sacred institutions, our morality. However, we cannot obey those laws of bestial existence, we are not animals. They do not and cannot have any moral norms, such as self-sacrifice in the name of God, in the name of love. There is no aspiration for spiritual purification through suffering. The idea of holiness can only be in man and in no other earthly creatures. If this is so, then why should we assert that the laws of Nature are superior to human laws, and that only they are true, and that the spirituality that is given is directed by God only to identify, reveal and underscore our hopeless sinfulness? Then it turns out that we give up moral principles, obey animal instincts and, following our nature, justify all our vices. And morality itself is questioned, and we believe that we should correct it, but not our sinful souls.

So, we are establishing a new order of values: what was considered bad is now considered good. To kill a man is quite normal, because it corresponds to the law of Nature, according to which no murder is subject to any court.

And now we have unlimited freedom! Do whatever you want. All moral bonds are thrown off. If you wish, indulge in debauchery, sell your wife, trade your conscience, sneer at everything pure, lie and cheat... because this is the natural right of everyone. You're like a robber who has escaped from prison: cut, kill, rob. (This is, apparently, your 'bird of happiness', which has fallen on an outstretched hand!)

Oh, no, my unknown peer! The rules of this great life were not set by you and me. And they have been broken not by the strong, but by the weak; they are unbearable for the latter, and not for the former.

Farewell!
Unknown friend

P.S. All the persecuted heroes, burned at the stake, hanged as heretics, the righteous and the prophets, were condemned to death not by people, but by governments. People saved them from oblivion and forever retained the names of the martyrs in their memory.

Hiding the letter in the appointed place, I returned to the ward and, under the impression that composing my message had left, I lay awake for a long time.

I recalled the stranger's first letter, in which he spoke about the meaning of *yin* and *yang*, the key concepts of Chinese philosophy. The transition of the first kind of phenomenon to the second, and vice versa, the unity of the two opposite components: all this seems clear to me. But why should these two principles merge and form one single thing? Why should white necessarily mix with black, useful with harmful, good with evil? Discarding any crafty game of the mind, it is impossible to call, as things of the same order, a fire kindled for cooking and the fatal flames of a fire in which all acquired human goods burn – although both cases require a combustion process. No, these are different phenomena, although the common primary element is fire. But who seeks to pile so many different concepts on one frying pan?

And it's profitable, damn them, for all moral monsters, spiritual hermaphrodites, slippery moral amphibians, ready to grovel and serve two masters right away: lies and truth. Oh, the freaks of this world always look at life with unkind eyes; they would like to take revenge on the whole world for their ugliness. I find these properties in my secret correspondent. Like a ruthless, fanatical terrorist, he is planning how he would blow up a universal spiritual temple – in the construction of which people have expended so much moral effort. He wants to destroy the results of works of the human spirit across the millennia – in an instant. After that, we would have to, whether we wished to or not, return to an animal, un-spiritual existence.

Spiritual terrorism must be resisted.

11

8 April

Loneliness – what is it? It seems possible to endure all life's hardships, any slander, even violence; but to resist constant loneliness is beyond anyone's power. I have heard that suicide is committed much more often in the most prosperous, developed countries, and not in countries with low standards of living. The reasons for suicide are very different: incurable disease, unhappy love, broken dreams... But the main reason is loneliness. Of course, not every hopelessly sick person decides to commit suicide. When you have people close to you who love you, it is hard for anyone to commit suicide. Other struggles fraught with frustration cannot shock you, but when a person cannot endure suffering it is because he does not have a close friend who shares his pain. So if you suffer grief, and you have no one to share it with, then loneliness becomes your lord. From now on, like a beloved, it takes possession of all your attention, accompanies you through all the nooks of your twilight existence.

Loneliness is your destiny. In the end, you grab it by the skirt and follow it obediently to the very end, and you go to the misty country of the other world.

Scientists have discovered, beyond the distant galaxies, so-called 'black holes', which absorb everything that draws near to them – even light. Irretrievably. Loneliness is a black hole. It absorbs all the light of your soul, all your strength, all the joy of living. The spiritual energy devoured by your loneliness would enable you to accomplish many great feats. Lonely people do not even dream about great feats, however.

It has now approached me. It's very close. I feel his touch with my heart, which suddenly became painful, cramped, uncomfortable. And I'm running in fear, looking for someone to talk to. I stop the nurses in the corridors and ask questions about their lives. I listen to their answers, as if all this is very interesting to me, and I pray that they can talk to me for as long as possible. Many of them, looking at me, make big eyes, believing that I'm crazy, and some simply do not reply and pass by, smiling with mockery.

Finally, I went to the autogenic training session. Rather, I ran to the place where, again, I could look at the pretty doctor with slightly parted lips like a child's, always ready to chirp something comforting. I sat down in an armchair, but my soul was anxious. Throughout the whole session I pretended to be asleep; I sat with my eyes closed and did not open them even when it was all over. At last, I pretended to wake up – and, oh, a miracle! Directly in front of me I saw the doctor, who gazed at me silently and studiously, and there was such a glorious smile on her face! The eyes were kind; their radiant light warmed my soul instantly. How little a man needs! One kind look, and you can be almost happy.

However, I was thrown off by what she said: 'But you did not sleep?'

I was sure that I could convince everyone that I had fallen into a sweet, deep sleep. She said this in a friendly, playful tone, and my embarrassment immediately passed. Ah, I do not need anything: just to be looked at with such a sweet look. Suddenly she took my hand and asked a completely unexpected question: 'Could you tell me those thoughts that are tormenting you?'

Again, I was thrown off. How to give her what she was asking for? How?

My hand began to sweat with excitement, and I released it gently. The young doctor looked at me with sympathy, as if to say: 'Be calm. I did not say anything that might offend you'. Her eyes, as bottomless as the sea, shining like morning on the steppe, poured warm bliss into my chilly heart. Those eyes calmed, comforted, lulled me.

'I'm sorry if something offended you', said her kind eyes. 'I did not mean to hurt you. I just wanted to ease your suffering. The soul of a person can be helped only by another soul. Look, look into my eyes. They do not deceive, they speak only the truth.'

'You are warm: a light breeze of warmth emanates from you', I answered. 'I noticed this the very first time. But I did not understand to whom your warmth was directed. Yes, my thoughts torment me. But there are so many of them…

many restless thoughts. And I'm afraid of giving them to you. I'm afraid of causing you irreparable harm.'

'To save you from painful contemplation is happiness for me, too.'

I had the sudden impression that she had spoken the last sentence aloud.

'What?' I asked, wanting to make sure I had heard correctly.

'To save you from painful contemplation is happiness for me', she repeated quietly.

The inner, silent conversation turned into an external, audible one, and this did not suit me. The conversation with the eyes was more sincere and more understandable. The spoken word often sounds ambiguous or indistinct. I preferred to speak with my eyes.

'To tell you the thoughts that oppress me would mean... to give you my fate', I continued in silence, realising clearly that to say such words aloud only once in my life would have been a much more difficult problem for me.

'I'm ready to take on everything', her eyes answered, full of determination. My heart began to beat loudly.

'Really?' I did not notice that again, I had spoken aloud.

'Really', she said, calmly and firmly.

A powerful stream of life-giving feeling, like water bursting through a dam, flowed into my half-withered spiritual world. This unprepossessing desert turned into a blossoming oasis instantly, drowning in greenery. Yes, there is great power in the world, which can raise up a person and fill his life with a higher purpose! It takes only a little luck to meet her...

With a dry, burning hand, I gently grasped both of hers. She looked down helplessly, submissive and somehow sad. She tried to free herself with a weak movement, but I held her, because my heart was filled with confidence, my spirit was filled with unprecedented courage and strength. I felt a sense of self-triumph.

But this, of course, is obvious frivolity. After all, just a minute earlier, I, poor fellow, exhausted by universal loneliness, was spared from this terrible fear by this gentle girl. Now, it turned out, having acquired unprecedented strength, I wanted to direct them against my dear benefactress.

I pulled her to me. The gentle fragrance of her perfume wafted over me. Her palms swayed and flinched. And, oh, God, the more she trembled, the more confident and aggressive became my impudent desire. I was like a shark, smelling blood. I did not recognise myself; it was as though I had been replaced. Finally, I became conscious of the truth: yes, it's me all the same, but in my glorious animal form. The beast of my instincts took advantage of a good moment and crawled out of the deep prison of my subconscious.

'No! No!' I half-whimpered, half-whispered. 'Never! Never!'

After fighting with my beast, I finally drove him back into his dungeon and, raising my head with a sigh of relief, I saw... I saw the doctor's young, confused, pink face.

'I did not mean you. I said this to myself. To myself...' I explained it like a child, pointing my finger at my fragile chest.

She smiled shyly. The pink dawn on the pure face of a man is a sure sign of spiritual purity and tenderness. From people who have not yet forgotten how to blush, we can expect that they are endowed with inner beauty, a primordial conscience and a love of the truth.

She sat down next to me in a chair and wanted to say something, but I covered her mouth gently with my hand. Marvellous, soft lips touched my palm.

'You do not need to say anything!' I whispered. 'After the conversations between our souls, nothing needs to be said... Everything else would be superfluous.'

She giggled, and, as if putting the last exclamation point in our silent, sincere conversation, looked at me so tenderly, with, oh, those radiant eyes! And again, it seemed to me that in my soul a magical oasis had blossomed.

Sometimes reality is like the most wonderful fairy tale.

12

9 April
I rejoice as a man who was, for a long time, confined to a dark, stuffy room, and has suddenly emerged into the sunshine and the expanses of active life, into the multitude.

The obsession at all costs to track down the author of the anonymous letters has gradually let go of me. If you do not count one thin, young man with long bangs falling on his eyes, who always tried to hide in his room upon seeing me, I no longer suspected any of the patients. And that little fellow, as I soon learnt, suffered a rare phobia of directly looking at himself, and hid not only from me.

However, some time passed, and thoughts of the 'unfamiliar peer' again began to return to me. I began to think about new plans, new ways to discover him. Who knows, maybe I shall meet him today... With this thought, I went out into the courtyard for a walk. For several days, I had not ventured out there. During that time, it turns out, some changes had been made in the composition of our group. The big, bearded man was gone – he was a fighter – and there was no sign of his shaggy enemy, either. The red-haired talker who liked to list all his famous ancestors had disappeared. From old acquaintances, only one swarthy 'Jesus' was sitting on a corner bench, preaching quietly and profoundly to himself. The rest were newcomers, and most of them preferred to walk with dull expressions down the paths, not communicating with anyone. All my attempts to enter into contact with them were unsuccessful, and soon I felt embarrassed to even look into the faces of the poor creatures.

Vainly staying out until the evening, I went back to my room, tired, and fell asleep.

13

13 April
I was filled with indifference to everything. For the past few days my head has been hurting, my brain aching. I cannot even work on my diary. And my unfamiliar peer has disappeared. He threw his insidious thoughts into my head and *disappeared*. I'm not worried that he died – I do not even care that he is still alive. However, the evil thoughts that he shared with me do not give rest to my soul.

The desert approaches the fertile lands, sweeping them with sand, like the expansion of evil, increasingly making an oasis of human morality. The more vulgar and immoral are works of art, books and films, the more money they earn in the market. No one listens to Beethoven anymore, but, like ants on honey, amateurs run for the roughest, noisiest, most primitive music. A great director cannot, for decades, find the means to make a new picture, while the pornographer bathes in gold as part of the global cultural elite. What does this say? Immorality is the most in-demand product of our day.

If a famous film star in a highly developed country has her photograph taken naked for magazines, and gives an interview in which she shares with the reader how many orgasms she can have during one sex act; if the parliament of that country passes a law permitting same-sex marriage; and if all this is served as an achievement of democracy, then can we talk about the victory of good over evil? Rather, we have here the defeat of good.

But the customs in this era of the decline of empires are not a reflection of the laws of the existence of all mankind. These laws contain the mathematical logic inherent in the creation of life, and in the total debauchery of our time there is no such logic. There is only disastrousness in it, and direct aspirations to self-destruction. Just as a drug addict or an alcoholic who realises he will never be cured can commit suicide, mankind can get rid of spiritual disintegration only at the cost of global suicide. If, in the war for the soul and the mind, good will actually be defeated, then there cannot be any other prediction about its consequences.

Yes, yes, it is not easy to destroy modern mankind by external factors – neither a nuclear catastrophe nor an asteroid crashing from the sky. Mankind will die as a result of its own debauchery. But should there be some main cause of universal spiritual disintegration? Undoubtedly, it lurks in a disease of selfishness, in our almighty, irresistible, unbridled 'I'. But does man consider it necessary to curb this monstrous 'I'? Is there something genuinely exalted in him that can allow him to overcome himself?

Take a cheetah. This carnivorous beast takes from her cubs pieces of meat – snatches them straight from their mouths, not because she shows animal egoism, as biologists believed at first, but because of the need to protect them from death: greedy cubs can die from overeating.

In all spheres of life – during eating and drinking, in rivalry, in sex – we resemble the cheetah's cubs. Nature saves animals from wild egoism and greed, but does not think about man, with his high intelligence. Yet no one can save people from disastrous greed, only they themselves can...

Blind feelings are necessary for survival. However, they cannot be the dominant force in a world of high-quality intelligence, and, more importantly, they do not need to be. However, it seems that human beings still cannot come out of their own 'I' and from that blindness. If all those 'Is' were to unite into a wholesome 'We', then the implementation of humanistic principles would certainly be easier.

The most terrible feelings and wrongdoings, such as cruelty, jealousy, pride, greed, lust, alcoholism, sexual compulsion and miserliness, which serve as barriers to spiritual growth, evolved from 'I' – and it's not a secret to anyone. As we know from history, disagreement among leaders was the main cause of the fall of the major states. Any disagreement begins with an 'I' that does not want to be controlled by anyone. The reason for disagreement among family members, as well as the reason for most divorces, is selfishness and unwillingness to compromise.

Without words, it is clear that relatives and friends quarrel precisely because of this lustful egoism. Where the 'I' rules, and where 'We' is absent, there can be no love, no brotherhood, no mutual consent. 'I' is always immoral, like a shameless person who wants power over everything and ruins everything. Those who live under her power are always unhappy, although at times, they seem quite happy. 'I' cannot defeat the rest of the world – and is, in turn, defeated.

'Life is always a shipwreck', said Ortega y Gasset.[14] The RMS *Titanic* sank on 14 April 1912. Everybody knows about this. Faced with an iceberg, a huge, newly built luxury liner heading to New York quickly sank to the bottom of the Atlantic Ocean. On board this most prominent ship were many intellectuals and wealthy people. The ship crashed into the iceberg and began to sink, but before that, more than two thousand people – the richest and happiest – fled in dread over the decks.

How can 'I' be saved, each of them thought, each of these 'I' lost in fear. There was no time or opportunity to think differently. This was a natural phenomenon. But a wise person always wants to live according to the highest principles of the spiritual world. That's why you should first think of others before caring about yourself. This is a war against 'I'.

Millionaires promised untold sums of money for a place in one of the lifeboats. But the captain gave the order to place only children and women in the boats first. Helping those who could be saved, the ship's crew – led by the captain and 1,500 passengers – remained aboard the sinking ship. The ship's orchestra played until the last minute, when the musicians were already knee-deep in the water. And they perished, performing the majestic hymn of the

---

[14] The character's paraphrase of a quote from *The Revolt of the Masses*. Translation into English from the Kazakh by the National Bureau of Translations.

triumphant 'We', which on the wings of eternity flew over the cold ocean abyss. The captain of the ship died with the crew, and with all the doomed passengers.

Thus, thanks to this system of 'We', the ship's captain demonstrated the great potential of humanity through the realisation of its noblest principles. If, at that moment, all the crew members and passengers had been driven by 'I', they would have died as animals.

14

19 April
I became entangled in this web, being of sound mind and clear memory, and, it seems, I began to get used to my condition. When I found another letter in the drawer of the table, I took it out without any fear in my soul, opened the envelope and began to read it, as if it was a message from an old friend.

Dear friend!
For some time I could not write to you, because I was seriously ill. [Here I smiled involuntarily; like a twin, he is sick at the same time as me.] Your last letter pleased me, although, as you know, I do not agree with you at all. You present as absolute the meaning of good, although the concept of the Absolute is applicable only to God. And then, any law that does not correspond to the truth of things is unenforceable. The laws of good, in your opinion, are unrealisable; therefore, they are stillborn. If the laws of good are impracticable, they only provoke society, deepen its contradictions and cause people to feel the sadness of unattainable desires, dissatisfaction with life, confusion and anxiety, senseless rivalry with each other. To overcome all these negative things there must be a compromise between good and evil, the recognition of both as equal and necessary for humanity. The ideas about good and evil that were formed in ancient times are no longer relevant today. Instead of these philosophical, archetypal relics, we must use the concepts of Negative and Positive – equally necessary for life, as well as charges with the symbols '+' and '–' electricity. Only when we accept the equivalence of these forces will our world be no more divided into two different parts, two irreconcilable camps.

Long before us, my friend, there were intelligent people who correctly determined the inner content of evil. The French poet Baudelaire sang it in a book called *The Flowers of Evil*. He sings of love and evil as secret things. Now I am devouring this book. The Japanese writer Akutagawa Ryūnosuke wrote: 'Human life is not worth one line of Baudelaire.'[15] If we all became as frank and consistent in our conclusions, the concept of 'humanism' would change significantly...

---

[15] In a short story, 'The Life of a Fool'. Translated from the Kazakh by the National Bureau of Translations. [Ed.]

Do you remember Picasso's drawing *Dying Minotaur in Arena*? In this print, in the middle of a bullfighting arena, the wounded Minotaur howls like a wolf, looking at the sky. And someone from behind the barrier holds out his hand to him – apparently a young man not yet intimidated by the generally accepted concept of the evil – and strokes the monster's bull head, showing pity and mercy to him. This young man stands a step closer than the whole cruel crowd of spectators to the ideals of true good.

From this, it follows that only by not dividing people into good and evil is it possible to have compassion for everyone, and not just for loved ones. Homosexuals, so despised by you that you do not even consider them as people, are still people. And the laws that are written for them are adopted not just by parliaments of democratic countries, but by life itself. (I think you already noticed that I was reading your fresh entries in the diary. You used to hide your notebooks for fear that people would look inadvertently. I could not resist again; I read your letters – look, my letters were copied there, and now I can say that this is our common diary, is not it, my dear friend?) You should love humankind.

But the physician ought not to treat the sick with disgust. Do you not think that it's indecent for people such as moralists, apologists of good and morality, to show disgust? Let's not forget, my friend, that there were many homosexuals among the geniuses who worked so hard for the glory of mankind.

Oh, it would be nice to meet you at last!

Waiting for your reply,
Your unfamiliar friend

God only knows what this unfortunate man wants from me.

Returning to the ward, gathering my thoughts, I quickly wrote a letter back:

Dear stranger!

There are feelings and concepts that require cleanliness unto themselves. They are love, honour, justice, conscience. They should be in pure form. There is no loyalty with betrayal, honesty with a dash of deception, love with a bit of treason. It's either yes or no. I provided my arguments in full, in my previous letter about the grace of God. I am not going to repeat it. The ideal of good is not a law, which can be amended depending on the circumstances. The ideal is a guiding star, pointing not at the place where you need to arrive, but giving the direction you need to follow. Therefore, one should not blame the guiding star in the sky when one is lost.

In order to improve life, you do not need to change ideals, you have to correct yourself. Revision of the laws of good and evil are only useful to sinners and villains. Only this can save them from that shameful stigma, that mark on their foreheads. 'You can justify them, do not punish them, but please call evil by its name', Dostoevsky said.[16] And is he wrong?

I agree that it is necessary to love all people, without dividing them into 'worthy' and 'unworthy'. But the Minotaur of whom you spoke is not a symbol of evil itself. And the young man who took pity on him, did he stroke his head and feel sorry for evil and not for the suffering, dying creature, the victim of evil itself? Probably the true meaning of the picture is the latter. Such a love for everything living – dying – is quite understandable. You want to erase the line between good and evil in your reasoning. To take pity on a hopelessly sick person is not to feel sorry for the disease itself. It's pity for someone who dies from a disease. 'We should not fight with a sinner, but with sin', Mahatma Gandhi said.[17] Those who are not afraid to sin do not fight against sin. The fact that the notion of human consciousness is not recognised by people plunged me into thought. Finally, I found an answer…

Theft is considered a disgrace and a crime by all peoples. However, for someone who is used to stealing, this is not a disgrace. For a woman who has tasted the sweetness of betrayal of her husband, this is not a sin or shameful debauchery. She is not ashamed of adultery itself; she is ashamed of being convicted of adultery. There is no rule that prohibits something after entering into sin. That is, when you cross a certain threshold, you will have an animal freedom, you will be free from disgust. Yes, it all depends on the habit. And smoking, and drunkenness, and drug addiction, and debauchery. Once you step over your conscience, then there is nothing shameful for a man. He is already under another sky, in another country, where everything is already possible. And he regrets only that he did not do all this much earlier.

You should remember one thing. To cross the threshold is a hundred times easier than to not do it. Here, not much effort is required, only giving vent to the animal instincts. And to not cross, you need will, and the power of morality. You need to have a will similar to that of an alcoholic who quits drinking or a drug addict who stops using. If you do not have such will, then you deceive yourself and say that there is nothing wrong with crossing the threshold.

But morality is not an empty, abandoned house that you can enter without permission at any time. No, it is more like a monastery with a strict charter, in which there are only those who accept this charter with humility and goodwill. And there it is impossible for anyone to enter who believes that there is nothing terrible in crossing the threshold of conscience. He does not know that, having done this, he has lost conscience forever.

---

[16] In *A Writer's Diary*. Translated by the National Bureau of Translations. [Ed.]

[17] A paraphrase of a quote from *My Life* by M. Gandhi. Translated from the Kazakh by the National Bureau of Translations. [Ed.]

You say that you do not have to be squeamish. Are you telling me this? It's indecent. So, dear friend, the feeling of disgust is a category of ethics. In this sense, a doctor can be squeamish. A person who knows purity cannot help but feel disgust for dirt. I would very much like to wish you to feel this feeling.

Your stranger

Had I written the reply correctly? I decided to read the stranger's last letter again. Then I noticed that I had lost sight of his main idea. Homosexuality, in his opinion, has the right to exist, because it is quite human and should not be despised. 'Oh, it would be nice to meet you at last!' struck my eye. Wait... wait... suddenly, a suspicion from nowhere burned me like an electric current: is he a homosexual? Then everything is clear. It turns out that all his cunning arguments are aimed only at justifying his disgusting inclinations. That's why he had to mix good and evil in one frying pan, and stubbornly tried to prove that dirt is not dirt.

I remembered some of his previous letters. It is necessary to expend so much mental energy to justify your vice. My guess was quite unexpected for me. I had tried so hard, straining my brain to adequately answer him! What a shame...

How insulting, his attention! I am sick of him. I have never experienced such abomination of the soul. Well, you want to meet me? Come on, I don't mind. You will see what a beast you have awakened in me with your insults. I have nothing to fear – it's people who have uneasy conscience who should be scared!

And then I wrote at the end of my message: 'I shall wait for you tomorrow at 20.30 in the resources department, in the basement.' I placed the letter in the agreed place.

Now I look forward to the meeting with impatience. I want to see him. There is no more dangerous enemy than one you do not know in person.

15

20 April

The attending physician had prescribed injections. The nurse preparing them was a talker: 'Be patient', she said, 'do not be afraid of anything. Now, you're going to feel a hot wave all over your body... It's not scary... It will pass quickly... Now, now...'

Her chatter did not calm me, but thoroughly frightened me. My whole body was seized with trembling, and my blood pressure shot up. 'I'm dying', I croaked, without recognising my voice. The nurse ran out of the procedure without a word, leaving me alone, but returned very soon with some woman in a white coat. Together they thrust a couple more pricks into me, and put me on stools arranged in a row.

Only after half an hour did I begin to recover. I felt much happier, and even tried to joke with the women, telling them how I had been frightened by the words of the nurse and then, in turn, had frightened her with sudden fainting.

But the nurses did not really trust my cheerful state and took me to the ward to put me to bed.

Before lunch, a doctor came to me – straight as a hammered nail, a boy in glasses. He took my pulse and then, as if doing me a great favour, touched my forehead with a sticky palm, stood up and went away. His demeanour seemed to say: I knew how everything would be in advance, and everything will be as I expected.

After lunch, I managed to fall asleep, and I dreamt:

Some huge building with high ceilings. There is a crowd here. Everyone is standing in a queue. I, too, need to stand in that queue, but I cannot find the end of it. I go out into the street, and see that the queue is huge: it continues beyond the edge of the city. Wanting to look from above to see where it ends, I climb up a skyscraper. From the roof, shaken to the very depths of my soul, I see that the black chain of the queue stretches to the foggy edge of the Earth, and is lost beyond the horizon.

With a feeling of deep melancholy and heaviness in my heart, I go down and ask someone: 'How do I get into this queue?' He replies: 'My dear man! No one has managed to get to the end of it. Many people bequeath their place in line to their grandchildren and great-grandchildren.' The man's face seems familiar, but I cannot remember where I met him. 'Listen, brother, forget all this and come with me', he says. The voice is soft, benevolent.

I squeeze through the crowd after him. It seems that the queue has been divided into several streams, in different offices. We arrive somewhere. 'My place is here', says the man. 'Sit down and wait.' He leaves. I sit in a chair, and my soul is filled with the joy of unexpected luck. Wow – I do not have to stand in this lifelong queue! But then I think: what do I need here, in this office? I'll go in there, and then what? What will they ask me about? After all, in fact, I do not even know why I am in this queue. It is awkward, somehow…

Then I see a sign on the door of the office I have to enter – and read my name on it. 'My word, but it's me!' I say to the secretary, pointing to the sign.

'I don't care', she answers, with unconcealed boredom in her voice. 'If it's you, then go to yourself!' I stand in confusion before the door. From behind it, there are encouraging voices: 'Come on, man! Come in, whoever it is!' But I hear someone else whispering: 'Be careful! Do not hurt yourself!'

Finally, I decide to enter… Oh, God! Coming… coming out from behind a table… I see myself. My own self, walking in my direction. He is tense, pale, angry. Fearfully, I back away. He walks towards me. He's already very close. I feel his breath on me. He stretches out his hand, hard and cold, like a dead man's. I scream and wake up from my own cry.

The first thing I see when I wake up is the face of the nurse standing by my bunk. It turns out that she had touched me with her hand to wake me up, and her palm was icy; apparently, she had just washed her hands under the cold tap.

'Sorry', she said, embarrassed. 'I scared you. I brought you tea. Drink it until it is cold.'

'Thank you', I said, not letting go of her cold hand.

It's good to wake up after a nightmare and find yourself again in the real world, in which everything is so clear: a nurse comes and brings tea on a tray.

By evening, the weather had deteriorated. Rain was falling on the street. Suddenly a gust of wind blew up and began to tear around the hospital yard. I was sitting on the ward at that time, worried and waiting for the appointed hour of the meeting.

I barely touched dinner; I tried to eat, but nothing doing. I walked back and forth in a small room, then went out into a long corridor. I went out into the street and wandered around the yard. No one was there. Alone, I whispered to myself: 'Come on, get your strength! Keep your head higher!'

I did not know how much time had passed, but gradually I managed to put my feelings in order and shore up my confidence – and soon I was finally ready for the encounter. At 20.30 I went down to the basement of the household block. But there was no light in the part where the mattresses, clothes, furniture and other equipment were stored. It may have been turned off, or perhaps the bulbs had burned out. The darkness was solid: somewhere there had to be an old chair, but it would be impossible to find. I had chosen a meeting place poorly. Or perhaps it was he who had deliberately turned off the lights – the suspicion occurred to me.

Suddenly it seemed to me that I heard a rustle of someone's footsteps. I froze in my place. Yes, it's him! Pressing my back against the wall, I listened attentively. I tried to determine the direction of the sounds, but now they were heard from the opposite side. My stranger was making fun of me! The sounds now began to come from all sides!

Then my patience came to an end and I spoke, trying to lend my voice as much calm and firmness as possible: 'Well, that's enough. I am aware of what's going on. Are you here?'

My voice in the basement silence sounded frighteningly loud. 'You wanted a meeting, here I am...' I wanted to add, 'I have come', but I could not – I did not have enough breath. Finally, gathering all my strength, I said it. I could not imagine that my voice would sound so loud. I myself was horrified by it. Then there was a grave silence.

I spread my arms wide and moved forward, touching the walls along the corridor, in complete darkness. Something shone in front of me as I turned the corner, and suddenly a ghostly shadow flashed past. A wild cry escaped from me involuntarily, and I swung my fist into this shadow. My hand encountered something dense, fragile; I heard the ringing of broken glass.

There I was, squatting in complete darkness, in the basement of the hospital. I was lost, unhappy. I had entered into a fight with my own reflection in a mirror. Tears that were invisible to the world poured from my eyes. Oh my God! What is my problem?

The hand hurt badly. With difficulty, I got up and wandered to the exit. Fragments of glass crunched underfoot. Staggering, now and then bumping into walls, somehow I managed to get to my room. As soon as I got there, a nurse ran in after me. Apparently, she had been waiting for my return.

'You look terrible! Where have you been, what's with you!'

'I slipped and fell in the street', I answered, almost inaudibly. My voice was unfamiliar.

'You're so pale! I'll call the doctor.'

'Do not...' I wheezed. I was so tired that it seemed as though the last of my energy was leaving me. 'Do not call the doctor...' I took a deep breath to collect myself and said: 'Bandage my hand...'

The nurse scurried away from the ward and soon appeared again with the doctor on duty. While she was washing the wound and bandaging my hand, he took my blood pressure, listened to my heart and asked some questions. I paid no attention to them, I was silent, because my soul was infinitely far from all this fuss. It seemed that the doctor prescribed an injection, as the nurse slapped me on the buttock and pierced it with a needle. But I looked at all their actions with the eyes of an outsider, as if what was happening did not concern me. As soon as they left the ward, I fell asleep.

I woke up at midnight after a dream that was short but fathomless. Waking up, I did not realise where I was at first. Gradually, I came to myself, and again began to think. Recent events were restored to my memory. The first thought that came to mind was: 'And yet, why did he not come to the appointment?' Although... 'Yes, did he receive my last letter?' suddenly came to my head. I jumped from my bed and flew out into the corridor. I ran to the table, put my hand into the box. Fumbled there a folded piece of paper... So it is! It turned out to be my letter! So, he did not get it. For some reason I couldn't take it. With a pounding heart, I fell on a chair next to me. So that's it... 'He did not get... He did not get it', I muttered to myself. Now everything is clear. And I was exhausted, like the madman who fought the windmill...

16

21 April

Today, examining yesterday's events from all sides, I find a number of incongruities. First, is it reasonable to rush headlong into a meeting with an unknown person at a designated place without even having obtained their agreement? It's awkward for me to admit this, but I really did not think about it.

Second, I did not even bother to ask where the stranger is from – this hospital? Perhaps not at all from the hospital, but from somewhere outside? So is it not stupid then, to set a meeting point in the hospital's basement, where the Devil himself would get lost? Apparently, I got it so much into my head that he is an omniscient, omnipresent bugger, and that finding himself anywhere, anyplace, at any time would not pose a problem for him.

Third, why did I need such a meeting at all? What direct effect would it have to this war of ideas between us? Although, who knows... because the psychological side of the fight is also important. All this time, only he dictated the rules of the game; I followed them without a murmur. Communication in the form of correspondence, a cache in the corridor, intrusion into my inner world, causing me anxiety and spiritual trauma – all these were his initiatives. It's time for me to go on the counter-offensive, to dictate my conditions and force him to fulfil them.

At 12.00 I had an appointment with the doctor. As always, he sat silently at first, scrutinising me. I was silent. We looked at each other, and were silent.

Then he said: 'How do you feel?' in a formal manner, similar to a 'Hello', which did not require 'Thank you, I feel well' as an answer. I did not reply. The doctor sat directly in front of me without stirring, as if nailed to the chair.

After a while he said: 'Go, have a rest.'

I got up and left. Back on the ward, I took out the stranger's letters and read them again, in order. It seemed as though an entire lifetime had passed between his first and last letters. I feel that, during this time, there have been some profound changes in me. No, it's not about my views – they're still the same. But a kind of grief continuously gnaws at me. I never suspected, before these letters, that the roots of the dark forces hostile to the good go so deep.

There are two paths in the spiritual world: one consists of human frailty; the other, of the highest reason and humanism. The lower path is the realm of the worldly, the carnivorous, the consuming. The masses walk along it. The higher path is spiritual and moral, accessible to the few. The elected. But we have now, everywhere, deployed propaganda for worldly values. It seems we have resigned ourselves to the fact that this is the hour of the masses.

Worldly interests are based on everyday pleasures. Satisfaction is like wine: who would refuse a taste of good, aromatic wine? It cheers you up, gives you a feeling of warmth and light. What else is needed in this short life, of which we have only one? Sometimes this idea seems legitimate and natural. But many hidden threats and dangers are concealed in that same sweet wine. The most common of these is the miserable fate of alcoholics. Pleasure without limits leads, sooner or later, to 'spiritual alcoholism' and moral debauchery. Similarly, other vehicles for an unrestrained 'buzz' – the thirst for profit, the craving for power without regard for casualties, adultery and fornication, setting fire to your neighbour's house in order to cook scrambled eggs: this is a rogues' gallery of moral degradation. It is sad that many people do not notice the sprawl of such evil, or do not want to notice. There is not even any desire to resist it. Therefore, the dangerous enemy is never named; its habitat has not been defined.

Defying one's basic conscience; heedless of proportion whether of food, sleep, desire or envy; drugged by selfishness: insatiable, crazy life! Yes, crazy life! You cannot call it by another name. My unfamiliar contemporary has crossed all conceivable and unimaginable boundaries. Disbelief in good, indifference to it, is a lighter version of indulgence in evil; with this, you can still somehow live, somehow seek and find a common language. Open abetting of evil, being its accomplice, is a more severe form of opposition. The possibility of reconciliation is zero. But my stranger not only supports evil, he actively propagandises for it and idealises it, worships it. What challenge, what threat could be more dangerous?

He boasts that he reads Baudelaire, who poeticised evil, death and dark forces. But whatever kind of genius that man may have been, it is impossible to claim that human life is not worth one of Baudelaire's lines. However, I have not read his works myself, though I have had heard different opinions about them.

During a stroll after dinner, I stopped at the hospital library. I entered a spacious room, lined with bookshelves from floor to ceiling. The windows were on the sunny side, so it was especially hot and stuffy; it also smelled of varnish and paints there. Apparently, they were doing repairs in the next room. The librarian was a Korean woman stultified by all the stuffiness. She seemed angry and spoke to visitors with a scowl. She did not even want to look in anyone's direction, and answered all queries in a curt and extremely irritated tone of voice.

I sat down at the table and flipped through the newspaper broadsheets, examining only the photos and reading the headlines. According to them, one could understand that the state was flourishing, that great success has been achieved in different spheres, that there are temporary difficulties... reports from abroad... I did not so much as glance at the columns with spicy advertisements or sensational articles: I was afraid I would vomit from disgust. So often, one finds some nasty thing there.

After a while, I raised my head over the newspapers and asked the librarian: 'Do you have a collection of Baudelaire's poems?'

The infuriated Korean woman, pausing only for a second, gave a reply like a robot: 'Yes, but someone has checked it out.' She fumbled in the drawer of the file cabinet and added softly, as if speaking to herself: 'The due date has expired... The book is in Room 10.'

I flinched. 'In which room?' I stammered.

'Room 10', she said, and looked at me in surprise.

I gasped, and began to suffocate with anxiety. 'How? Room 10... this is my room! I'm alone there. And I did not take such a book. I have not even seen it!'

'See for yourself, here.' She held out the card with an offended air. 'Read that, if you don't believe me.'

I rushed to her desk, grabbed the card and peered carefully at it. But I could not see anything. 'It's impossible, it's impossible', I muttered to myself. 'I don't see anything...' Then I began to understand: trouble had arrived. I was in real trouble.

'What's the matter with you?' I heard alarm in the librarian's voice. 'Do you feel unwell? I'll call a doctor. Sit down, don't move...'

'Why shouldn't I move? What happens if I move?'

I raised my head and looked around: people had gathered nearby. I recognised my nurse among them. She asked: 'Is your head spinning? Does your chest hurt?'

I could not reply with anything, except 'No… no…' because I really did not feel anything. Holding me by the shoulders, the nurse guided me to the ward and put me to bed. The doctor on duty arrived and began to ask what had happened. Reluctantly, confusing my words, with long pauses, I told him.

'I did not take this book, I swear – I did not even see it', I repeated insistently, as if trying to prove my innocence. The doctor seemed to understand something. He started giving instructions to the nurse. Then he left quickly.

I was given medicine and began to calm down. But a small, unpleasant tremor continued to pulse through my body. After dinner – which I did not touch – I was given an injection, and I fell asleep like a dead man.

17

22 April

It seems that they decided not to wake me, and I arose only for dinner, when they brought food to the ward. I washed my face, dressed and ate. I began to remember yesterday's events. I was in a secret state of uncertainty. Despite my efforts, I could not calm down.

The nurse took me to the doctor. I followed her obediently. He sat completely alone and with a serious look that read as though he had no other business but to meet with me. I sat in front of him for a long time. He drummed on the table and was silent.

'I want to speak seriously with you', he said sullenly, as if preparing to announce the death of a person close to me. 'That is, if you are ready for a conversation.'

'What should I do to be ready?' I asked in bewilderment.

The doctor did not seem to expect my question. He lowered his eyes and pondered.

'You start the conversation', he said at last. 'Talk to me. Do you have anything to tell me?' He looked at me expectantly over his glasses.

· 'Yes, I have', I suddenly blurted out, determined. 'Ever since I entered your hospital, I've been receiving letters from some unknown person.'

'Do not worry. Tell me everything from the very beginning, and do not rush. Do you want to smoke?' He pulled out a pack of cigarettes.

I shook my head. 'No thank you, I do not smoke.' Then I continued: 'So, no matter how hard I tried to discover the author of these anonymous letters, it was all useless. He is hiding from me. He is so insolent that he dumps them directly into the ward. But that's not the point. He is very dangerous, with his disastrous ideas, like a terrorist armed with an explosive device. These ideas, like epidemics, can spread very quickly. Because their principles are based not on moral responsibility, but on the basest instincts, and correspond as much as possible to the motivations of the masses. After all, an epidemic capable of devouring the lives of millions of people also begins in the body of one particular person. No one can guarantee that this idea in one head will not turn into a tragedy for all mankind tomorrow. That's why I had to meet him. And for its poison, I have quite an antidote. But he avoids meeting me. The most monstrous thing is that in one of his letters he reports that he is reading a collection of poems by the French poet Baudelaire, who was called 'the poet of evil'. Yesterday I asked the librarian, and she told me that the book is supposedly in Room 10. But 10 is my room number! And I did not take out such book... I am going to become a madman soon...'

I became agitated again and fell silent, taking a breath before continuing: '...So that's what I want to say. Despite his boldness, he could not manage all these tricks alone, without someone's help.' I looked into the doctor's eyes. 'Tell me, Doctor, do *you* know him?'

In the office, there was a deathly silence. The doctor lowered his head, staring at the countertop, and tapped softly on it.

'Yes', he answered shortly.

I jumped out of my chair. I could say nothing, as if my tongue had been cut. Thoughts were tangled in my head. I just opened and closed my mouth noiselessly. But this bespectacled doctor only smiled mysteriously and gestured for me to sit back down. I obeyed involuntarily, but did not take my eyes off him.

'I've known everything about you for a long time', he said calmly. 'Now listen to me carefully. I'll explain the context. In medicine, the sphere of the human psyche is the most mysterious one. Therefore, within this sphere, there is as much mysticism as real science. Take, let us say, the phenomenon of a split personality. I once told you about this. Science has not figured it out yet. For some reason, in one and the same person, there appear to be two subjects who contradict each other in everything.'

He shot me a sharp, attentive look through his glasses.

'Sometimes one personality actually replaces the other. This is not a fairy tale, but a real psychological phenomenon. Here are some examples, which have long been described in the history of psychiatry. In early 1887, an elderly man arrived in the American city of Norristown, in the state of Pennsylvania. He introduced himself to everyone under the surname "Brown". He was engaged in trade; his business was selling office accessories. He always attended church. From time to time, he went on buying trips to Philadelphia. An open and friendly man, Mr Brown soon gained the trust and respect of the people of the town.

'But one day, on 14 March, the townsfolk heard from him that he was not Brown, a seller of stationery, but a certain "Reverend Bourne", a preacher from the state of Rhode Island. He begged everyone to believe him, which led to great embarrassment among the townsfolk. Of course, they did not believe him. But soon, Bourne's wife came to Norristown – she had somehow found her unhappy, missing husband. He was, as it turned out, in fact a preacher, and she took him home.

'This story continues, but for us it does not really matter anymore. What is important is that this can happen to a person.' The doctor lit a cigarette, leant back in his chair and, with the air of a man who has divulged a dissenting opinion in a committee, continued his speech thoughtfully: 'Apparently, the social roots of these phenomena are hidden very deeply. After all, despite the fact that medicine usually refers them to the category of pathologies, similar things are quite observable in the behaviour of an absolutely healthy person. Having committed a mistake or an unseemly act contrary to one's nature, a person, condemning himself, would repent: "the Devil made me", "the Devil beguiled me", "the evil spirit prevailed…"

'This is indeed a temporary transfer of power from your hands to your second "I". Honestly speaking, we all have split personalities. Changes in our "I" happen, however, at every step. Well, let's say we say "no" when it is clear to us that we should be saying "yes". We say what we are supposed to, for example, we "love" the one we really hate. We support dubious initiatives when we do not believe they can succeed. All this, is it not evidence of our duality? Or a humble, amiable person, having become rich or attained power, becomes completely different: rude, swaggering; but towards those above him, he again turns into a timid fellow. Call it "double-dealing" or "split personality", the essence of the matter will not change.'

Then the doctor's face took on a contemptuous expression. He tapped the ashes off the cigarette, looked at me as if he had just remembered my presence, and continued:

'Remember "After the Ball" by Tolstoy? The Colonel, in the evening at the ball, shines like the most gallant of gentlemen, charming all the ladies with his excellent manners – and the following morning, presiding over the execution of a soldier, he shows himself to be a bloodthirsty beast, a cruel killer. Is this not an example of a split personality?'

I could not stand it any longer, and interrupted the doctor: 'All right, I agree with all your reasoning. But what does our case have to do with it, and what does all this have to do with my question?'

'Just do not think that I began this long discursion for fun. This is not true… The "stranger" with whom you corresponded for more than a month does not hide anywhere. He is inside you. He is you.'

'What does this mean?' I asked, not quite understanding the doctor's words.

'Every three, sometimes four days, you wake up in the morning as another person: your nemesis, the mysterious "stranger". Compared with you, who are now sitting in front of me, your twin is much more open and sociable. He has long since realised his condition, and knows his diagnosis. And he took it upon himself to correspond with you. But you do not remember your other self, and so you wrote all these letters back. And we did not say anything; we were afraid to traumatise you and make the possibility of treatment completely hopeless. All this time we have chosen not to interfere, but only observed from the outside. But now everything has reached the edge. Only you can help us – with your mind and your will.'

A horrible avalanche flooded my heart. It seemed as though everything had been crushed by stones, covered with mud. As soon as I realised that these disastrous ideas were in me, I could not stand it any longer. I lost consciousness, which I discovered only when I woke up. A stinging, burning stink in my nostrils made me shake my head. They had shoved ammonia under my nose.

'Open the window!' commanded the doctor, who slapped me on the cheek.

Finally, I came to myself. The nurse took me to my room. Everything that happened after that was like a vague dream. A doctor appeared, told me how difficult it was for him to inform me of my diagnosis, that the critical moment had passed, that he wanted to try hypnotherapy and so on. I did not interrupt; it was as if he was telling all this to someone else. Only when he began to describe some of the features of my 'stranger', with which he usually wakes up in me in the morning, I began to choke with fear.

'When... will he appear?' I asked, holding my breath.

'Today seems to be the fourth day', said the doctor, raising his eyebrows 'Yes, the fourth. So, tomorrow morning.'

I was very scared. I wanted to yell, to scream at the whole world, but I had no breath; I could not cry out. It did not fully register in my mind that tomorrow someone else, not me, would wake up in my place, in this bed – someone cynical, yet more communicative than my own sullen self... a disgusting 'unfamiliar fellow'. No, it was impossible.

In the evening, I had no appetite. At night, after lights-out, my beautiful doctor from the autogenic training sessions came to my room. She was on night duty. Were she to have come at another time, I would have been sincerely delighted. But I had no strength, no desire just then. I noticed, though, that her manner was less that of a tender, charming girl; it was as though she were a more mature woman with a stern, remote expression.

'We all knew what was happening to you', she began guiltily. 'In order to fully examine your condition, we had to become acquainted with your diary...'

'Who is this "all of us"?' I asked cautiously.

'All of us. Of course, we who work here. After all, everyone should be informed', she replied, justifying herself.

I imagined how amusing it was to watch the convulsions of the experimental rabbit.

'I sincerely sympathise with you', she continued in a sad voice. 'What happened to you is a great sorrow. But I must admit that getting to know your diary has been one of the brightest and most significant events of my life. All the best and noblest things on Earth have long become dilapidated, like the ruins of an ancient palace, ready to collapse to the ground. Only thanks to people like you, I still manage to see the beauty and nobility of our spiritual world. I believe you. You are a holy man. In this world, holiness is considered an anomaly, as when two-headed mutants are born. But this is not just! The sanctity of man is not ugliness. It is, of course, more natural than the appearance of mutants...'

I did not particularly listen to her words. I kept thinking about that long-standing silent conversation between us. 'I like you', I said with some resentment, 'but not the present version; I prefer the one who looked like a young, white-toothed fairy. With silent conversation, you came to rescue me at a difficult moment. Now you are too sharp, educated and efficient. For you, I am just an object of scientific interest. You hurt me... You're not the one. That is why –'

'But she's in me! Here!' she whispered hotly, pressing her hand to her heart.

Again I longed to speak with her wordlessly, as on the previous occasion, and with my gaze I asked her a question: 'When will I see her?'

She did not understand the 'question', as if she had forever forgotten our common language.

'I shall long for her forever!' I cried silently. She did not 'hear'. With a heavy heart, I bowed my head and fell silent.

'We all have turned into other people.' Suddenly her slightly hoarse, unrecognisable voice reached me. 'We are werewolves, and none of us has retained in ourselves the original angelic purity. Like Faust, we have sold our honour and wisdom to the Devil. Only occasionally can the bitter weeping of infant purity be heard in our souls. Sometimes even we miss that infant. But with a pain in my heart, I shall have to admit that there is no place for her in this dirty, perverse life.'

'Oh my God...'

'Yes, my dear...'

I shivered, noticing how her voice trembled. Raising my head, I saw tears streaking her cheeks.

'Oh, my God...' Everything around me clouded over, as if covered in a shroud of rain.

She rose from her place and stood there in confusion. Then she ran out of the room.

The most difficult moments began when she left. I paced back and forth in the narrow room, finding no place to myself. In the mirror near the door, I saw my unhappy face. For a long time, I did not look again at myself. Under the swollen eyes were heavy bags; a wrinkled frown sat between my eyebrows. Suddenly I flinched; it seemed like someone was staring back at me from the other side. My heart contracted into a ball, and I felt an incredible, endless pain... I turned the mirror around to face the wall.

I was afraid to switch off the light. It seemed to me that once I found myself in the dark, someone in me would mutter: 'Well! Now it's my turn... Get out of here!'

'Tomorrow you will wake up as another person', the doctor had said. In the morning, and in my body, will be the one who endlessly disgraces and humiliates me.

'No. No! No! Never!' I repeated, with bitterness. 'Never!'

I took a breath and calmed down a bit. I took out a washcloth, a clean towel and soap from the bedside table, and went into the bathroom at the very end of the corridor. It was empty at night. I washed myself thoroughly. I needed to wash the tub clean, and filled it with hot water to make it as scalding as possible.

Having returned to the ward, I took the blade I used for shaving. There was no regret, no anger, no resentment. There was only one thing in mind: to complete the plan. What great simplicity! To sit in the tub and gently cut the vein in the wrist. Further – even easier. It's good that the water is hot. The hotter, the better. You do not feel the pain at all. Gently sailing offshore, you float off somewhere in the unknown. I just need to close my eyes tightly, so that I cannot see the blood... and suffer a little. After that, you – my fatal brother, who planned to muck the whole world with mud – you'll find yourself stained with scarlet blood and you'll slide into a world where you'll be comfortable, and sleep, and never wake up, forever and ever.

Well, I shall die in order to kill you. You cannot abandon your fate.

I have a cherished dream:
If one day a worldwide flood of
good should come upon our land,
I shall embrace all the evil in the world
in my arms, and
I'll take it with me to the grave.

Yes, I shall be happy
to become a nameless victim,
who takes the guilt of human vice
upon himself with a jubilant soul
and will save the world from the severity of its sins.

Well, bring me your misfortunes,
and put them in my luggage,
load your evil junk!
And if they all die with me
I shall be glad to die, even today!
...Send me on my last journey,
and do not look for evil in the world.
Live without it!

And just do not knock at all

at my closed coffin with evil.[18]

Thus the diary ends, with one of the darkest poems by the famous poet Múḳaġali Maḳataev.

I do not know the fate of this defenceless, uncompromising person for whom moral purity had become synonymous with God. If by some miracle he survived, remained alive, then from the bottom of my heart I wish him happiness; may he never lose his faith in good. Good health to this holy person, who is trying to preserve the dying ghost of hope to save his soul. And if he is no longer among the living, then... all the will of God. May he rest in peace! Amen!

Translated by Mitchell Albert

---

[18] Múḳaġali Maḳataev (Mukagali Makatayev) 'Ojym bar meniṇ' (I have a cherished dream); translated by the National Bureau of Translations. [Ed.]

KAZHYGALI MUKHANBETKALIULY
(b. 8.12.1942)

Kazhygali Mukhanbetkaliuly is a Kazakh writer and literary translator. He graduated from the Faculty of Philology at Kirov Kazakh State University (now Ăl-Farabi Kazakh National University; 1965), and was head editor of Aķtôbe Regional Television and Radio Committee and editor-in-chief of the *Kommunizm žoly* regional newspaper; senior editor of Ķazaķstan publishing house and the *Žùldyz* journal; executive secretary of *Ķazaķ ădebieti* newspaper; and editor-in-chief of *Žaņa fil'm* journal.

His first short story, 'Žùke ataj', was published in 1964 in *Leninšil žas* newspaper (now *Žas alaš*), followed by short story collections: *Žùldyzdy tùnder* (Starry Nights, 1972), *Toģaj sybdyry* (The Whisper of Forests, 1974), *Žaņģyryķ* (Echo, 1981), *Ķajdasyņ sen, mahabbat?* (Where Are You, Love?, 1981), *Synyķ tereze* (The Broken Window, 2003) and others. In these works, which framed him as a realist writer, Mukhanbetkaliuly predominantly describes the life of his contemporaries during the 1970s and 1980s. He has been a long-time researcher of a hero of the eighteenth-century Kazakh struggle against colonialism, Syrym Datùly. This led to a non-fiction work, *Syrym Datùly*, published in 2004, and a historical novel about the same figure, *Tar kezeņ* (Hard Times), in 2012. A selection of his works numbering twenty-three volumes was published in 2014, completed by another four volumes in 2016. He has translated a number of foreign writers, including Ryūnosuke Akutagawa, William Somerset Maugham, Prosper Mérimée, Guy de Maupassant, Leo Tolstoy and others.

He is a laureate of the State Prize of the Republic of Kazakhstan (2014) and an Honoured Worker of the Republic of Kazakhstan (2003).

Old Friends

Nùralhan, the young director of a large construction project in a remote district, had been called to the head office of the building trust in the capital. It was the first time he had come back to the city since he had graduated from the institute there.

He flew in late in the evening and settled into his accommodation – a double room in a new hotel. In the morning, he quickly dealt with his business affairs and went back to the hotel. Standing in the middle of the spacious room, he wondered what to do next.

'Hmm…' he said. At that moment, his gaze fell on the full-length mirror. He stepped briskly up to it and began making faces at himself in the glass, twitching his lips, eyes and cheeks, and pulling his eyebrows into a frown. But no matter what he did, the expression on his dark-complexioned face stayed almost exactly the same – only his big brown eyes shone more merrily.

'You need to look sharp here, my boy', he instructed himself playfully. 'You're not in the backwoods anymore! Folk here might take one look at you and say "O-ho! Look at this one – as scruffy as a stray calf!"', he smiled at his own joke. What he wouldn't give for one of the dearest friends he missed so much to turn up in the hotel room right now! All right, all right! 'What are you looking so pleased about?' Nùralhan demanded sternly of his reflection. 'Your face looks tired, by the way.'

He straightened out his broad shoulders, took off his light-blue crimplene jacket, and hung it in the wardrobe. Then he undid his tie, rolled up the sleeves of his white nylon shirt, and went into the bathroom. He turned on the taps and began running a warm bath.

No sooner had he undressed, than the telephone buzzed on the desk, as if in alarm at the sight of a naked man.

He jumped to the phone and grabbed the receiver.

'Hello' he said, a little too loudly.

'Is that Room 213?'

'That's right.'

'Hello, Yurik' said a pleasant female voice on the end of the line.

That was odd, Nùralhan thought. Could there really be another man with the same rich baritone voice as his? Perhaps the caller wasn't very good with voices.

'Hello! Can you hear me?' asked the girl. 'Hello? Yurik?'

'Young lady, if you're looking for "Nurik" you're speaking to him. But there's no Yurik here.'

'Really? Are you sure? And who are you?'

'Why do you need to know?'

'Because I'd like to know.'

'Wh...? But... Well, I'm very happy that a beautiful girl like you is taking an interest in me!'

'How did you know I was beautiful? Be careful I don't disappoint you', laughed the voice on the end of the line. 'So are you all on your own, then?'

'Yes – all alone without a friend in the world, my dear. Like our forefather Adam.'

'Perhaps you're waiting for Eve to turn up?' the girl said with a laugh 'Only joking', she added, hastily. 'But you wouldn't mind if I made quite sure that Yuri Seleznev isn't with you?

'When would you like to come up?'

'I'm right here – downstairs in the foyer.'

'O-ho! I see! Well, I was just getting ready to have a bath. I'm standing here without a stitch on. Actually, I was just wondering who was going to scrub my back.'

'It sounds to me as if you're just lonely. Maybe I could ring again in half an hour?'

'Why bother? I have to tell you, I'm...' here Nùralhan twirled a finger at the side of his head. 'Well – I'm not exactly normal.'

'Crazy people never actually admit to being crazy', the girl interrupted him. 'But you'll need to give me a more precise answer than that.'

'Hmm. Well, young lady, if you want me to be more precise, I can hear my bath is running over. Excuse me!'

Nùralhan flung down the receiver.

'You got off to a good start there, comrade director', he said to himself. 'Keep that up, and you'll soon be asking for a transfer to the capital. But now look sharp, if you flood the bathroom, or you'll turn the bed on the floor below into a wet sponge!' He dashed to the bathroom and pulled open the door. Thanks be to Allah, he was on time, but only just. He put his hand into the water up to the elbow and pulled out the plug.

'Good grief!' he muttered. 'Still, what do you expect, blabbing on the phone like that.'

A minute or so later, he was sitting in the bathtub, covered in soapsuds and singing happily to himself:

Water, water,
Water all around.[1]

---

[1] Lines from a song titled 'Seeing off ships', made popular by the singer Eduard Khil.

After his bath, feeling refreshed and invigorated, he put on the suit he wore at weekends, knotted his tie, and looked himself over carefully in the mirror, checking that there was nothing untoward in his appearance. Everything was fine: the suit sat well on him and he was happy with the way he looked. So a young *argymak* stallion,[2] passing through an *auyl*,[3] will step sideways, squinting about him until, confident that all is well and he is making a good impression, he straightens up proudly and walks on, calm and majestic.

'Well', he quipped, 'You've spent quite long enough galloping the world! It wouldn't hurt to fill your belly with oats before they saddle you up!'

He didn't like the idea of going down to the restaurant on his own, and for a moment, he felt a little sorry for himself. 'Maybe I should give those rascals a call?' he thought. 'But will they even be at home? They may not have got back from work yet. That girl hasn't called again, either. Our friend Don Juan was right when he used to say, Never let go of a bird in the hand, or you'll be sorry!' Regretfully, Nùralhan looked at the silent telephone, paced to and fro for a moment, and then left the room.

He didn't feel like eating alone. He ordered a number of small dishes, and poked at them half-heartedly with a fork, before pushing them aside.

'Just my luck. Not one familiar face', he said, looking around him. 'Well, you can't expect your enemies to turn up just when you want to see them most! Never mind, just you wait! Tomorrow I'll show the lot of you!'

He beckoned the waitress over.

'Another drink, please!'

'I can't sir. It's not allowed. I'll get into trouble.' The girl was looking intently into his face, as if trying to tell how the last drink had affected him.

'But I've barely had a chance to try it! I haven't even had a proper taste!' said Nùralhan cheerfully.

'All right. I'll bring you one. But mind—!' she put her finger to her lips.

Nùralhan nodded. 'I get it.'

He downed his drink, settled the bill, and presented the waitress with a box of 'Pigeon's Milk' sweets to thank her for her kindness. He took another box up to his hotel room.

'So you don't want to come and meet me?' he muttered as he climbed the stairs. 'Well then, never mind. But I'll show you! Tomorrow I'll put you through your paces!'

---

[2] *Argymak* – purebred horse highly estimated for its speed, beauty, strength and endurance.

[3] *Auyl* – socio-economic formation considered to constitute the heartland of the nation and a basis for an ethnic and cultural union of the nomadic community. Consisting of 50–70 yurts in the eighteenth century, it developed into its current permanent state of 'rural settlement' (of a minimum of 100 dwellers) when Kazakhs adopted a settled mode of life in the nineteenth and twentieth centuries. *Auyl* can also be used as a synonym for 'native land' and 'homeland', concepts revered by the Kazakhs.

As he went to collect the key to his room from the duty attendant in the corridor, he had an idea.

'This is for you, *apaj*,[4] he said, putting the box of sweets on the attendant's desk. 'Please accept it from a visitor grateful for his rest, which you have guarded now for one whole night and a day.'

'*Ojbaj*,[5] my dear sir, what's all this? After all, it's our job to do everything we can to ensure you get a good night's sleep. If anyone…'

'Take them, please', said Nùralhan, seeing that the attendant wanted to accept the sweets. 'I can hardly take them back now, can I?'

'But it looks bad – almost as if I'd helped you to get a room.'

'That doesn't matter. Especially as you did nothing of the sort.'

'Well thank you! That's very kind of you…'

Nùralhan walked away a couple of paces, then stopped and turned back to the attendant.

'By the way, *apaj*, you couldn't tell me who was in Room 213 before me, could you?' he said nonchalantly.

The attendant began to look through her records.

'Let's have a look. So, in room 213 there was… a Mùsaḳùlov Terlikbaj. From the seventeenth to the twenty-fourth. Until last night, that is. Have a look for yourself.' She pushed the ledger towards him.

Nùralhan had no reason to doubt the attendant, but for the sake of politeness, he studied the entries in the ledger carefully.

'I suppose it's possible a "Terlikbaj" could become a "Terentii"', he thought. 'But I can't see how he could turn into a "Yurik".'

***

On one page of Nùralhan's red address book, there were only three names – each followed by a nickname, and each with its own address and telephone number. While he scribbled all over the rest of the book, he left this page alone. To do otherwise would have seemed an act of disloyalty to his dearest friends. If these names were ever to become muddled up with all the others, Nùralhan would have felt quite at sea – as if he had forgotten the most precious and wonderful times in his life. That would be unthinkable!

Now he took off his jacket, pulled the telephone towards him, and settled into an armchair.

'Whom should I call first?'

For four years, the friends had lived in complete harmony, and it is only later, in their fifth year of study, that Bejsek had changed things by moving out of their room, leaving one of the four beds empty for the first time. He had been 'taken in marriage' (as they had joked at the time) by their fellow student,

---

[4] *Apaj* – respectful form of address used when talking to an older woman.

[5] *Oj-baj* – an exclamation approximating 'oh, my!'; used to express surprise or joy.

Kùlajša. Perhaps, thought Nùralhan now, he should call Bejsek first. 'Yes – I think I will. Say what you like, Kùlajša is one of us. We introduced them to one another.'

He read the name aloud from his notebook: 'Bejsek Ķùlymbetov ('D'Artagnan'). Telephone…' Nervously, he dialled the six-digit number. As the dial turned around with a muffled rasp, his heart began to hammer in his chest.

'Hello? Is that the Ķùlymbetov household? Is that you, Kùlajša? My dearest daughter! How are you!' Nùralhan had suddenly remembered a funny story he had heard, and decided to play a joke on his friends.

'Hello', answered Kùlajša. 'Who's calling?'

Instead of replying, Nùralhan began to shower her with meaningless questions.

'How are your children? Is your family well? And how are the old folk? All hale and hearty, I hope?'

'Fine. But, I'm sorry, I don't recognise your voice…' Kùlajša was clearly starting to feel uneasy.

'And your parents here in the city – are they still in good health? Have you had any news from your in-laws? How's your work? And how are your friends and colleagues?'

'Fine, fine. I'm sorry, but I still don't understand who's calling. Would you be so good as to tell me your name?' There was a touch of irritation in Kùlajša's voice. It sounded as if she might hang up at any moment.

'Oh, goodness gracious! I completely forgot to introduce myself! I'm your neighbour from the *auyl*, I've only just arrived in town. I want to arrange for my son to study in the capital. There's no hope of him getting a decent education out in the provinces! We've only just arrived at the station. So you see how it is. Of course, we have your address – we got it from the *auyl* – but we weren't sure we'd be able to find your house. We'll probably get something mixed up. So perhaps it's best we wait for you here, at the station. Could you come and collect us? Otherwise we'll get lost…'

There was silence on the other end of the phone. Evidently, Kùlajša was lost for words. Nùralhan thought he could hear her talking to someone, with her hand over the receiver.

'Hallo! Hallo!' he shouted, loudly and anxiously, still disguising his voice. 'Could you tell me, my dear – is Bejsek there? Could I talk to him?'

'Just a moment', came the polite, hurried reply. There was a muffled rustling sound but despite that, the sound of Kùlajša's voice could be heard clearly at the other end of the line.

'*You* speak to him. Now they'll give us no peace! The whole pack of them will descend on us!'

Nùralhan grinned to himself. He could just picture Kùlajša's thin, dark face, and the way she always frowned when she was perturbed.

At that moment, he heard his friend saying,

348

'Hello, this is Bejsek!'

And at the sound of that familiar voice, Nùralhan couldn't resist shouting out – as if on parade:

'Hail, D'Artagnan!'

This was clearly not what Bejsek had been expecting. There was a moment's pause before he spoke.

'Gunner – Is that you?!' He asked slowly, in joyful amazement. 'Hello! Well I never – where did you spring from? Where are you?'

'I'm right here, in the Alma-Ata Hotel. I've got myself a room here.'

'What on earth is that supposed to mean? You never said a word... you didn't even call! And now you're staying in a hotel?'

'Now just wait a minute! We always used to think that people from the capital set a good example by staying in hotels. Have you changed your mind about that?'

'Spoken like a true bureaucrat! And a true provincial! You go jumping on the bandwagon and before you know it, it's run away with you! You need to keep a sense of proportion!

Nùralhan laughed.

'All right, you win! I surrender! My hands are in the air – and so are my feet! Now I have to pay a forfeit! What penance do you require?'

'Never mind that. But I hope you realise you can't escape us now? So-o...' Bejsek stopped for a minute to whisper something, then spoke into the phone again – 'So get yourself down here – this instant! If not, you're in big trouble! Kùlajša's going to give you a piece of her mind... do you hear?'

'What do you mean by that? Doesn't custom dictate that it is the hosts who should come to greet a visitor, if he comes from far away?'

These last words were lost on Bejsek, however. Kùlajša had evidently grabbed the receiver.

'Ooh! You clown!' she said to Nùralhan. 'What was the point of that charade?'

'Surely we're not guilty of anything in the eyes of Allah, *bájbiše*?'[6] Nùralhan replied innocently, and began to laugh.

'Just you wait! You've got it coming! So anyway, how are things with you? How's your family? And the children?'

'They're fine, thanks. '

'So you're persisting with your nonsense, and not coming to our house?'

'Ah, I'm afraid to disturb you. You know what it's like, when "the whole pack of them descends on you at once..."' Nùralhan laughed as he imitated Kùlajša's words.

---

6 *Bájbiše* – first wife in the traditional polygamous family, also elderly wife, respected woman, as well as form of address to a hostess.

'Oh, you numbskull! Now you'll never let me live that down! Do you realise, there's no meat to be had *anywhere* in town?[7] You gave me such a fright just now – how am I supposed to entertain strangers? People who live out near the *auyls* are lucky. You can't imagine what we poor city dwellers have to put up with. In any case, you men haven't a clue about hospitality. What do you know about home fires and cooking pots?'

'So if I was to turn up now, there'd be nothing to eat? You're inviting a guest to your house, and planning to starve him?'

'You're impossible!' retorted Kùlajša high-handedly. Evidently, she was reliving the days when she used to boss all the young bachelors about. 'So you won't come and visit us unless I cook you some meat? I'll give you a mug of black tea and a piece of black bread and you'll be grateful for it! Have you forgotten how we used to live as students? You're coming, and that's that.'

'O-ho-ho! Now that's the Kùlajša I remember! The wrathful *hanša*,[8] protector of her hearth, her husband, and her impoverished fellow students! Now I'm quaking in fear! A thousand apologies! Punish me as you see fit. But wrathful *hanša* – isn't it a little late to come to visit you now? I suggest you all come out together tomorrow morning and sample some treats I've brought from the *auyl*. And if you like, we could go downstairs and partake of the delights of the public dining hall. What do you say?'

Rather than answering right away Kùlajša began to speak in a low voice to her husband.

Then Bejsek took the phone and said, in slightly guilty tones:

'So, what's this, Gunner – you can't come out and see us? Are you getting ready for bed? You know we'd come out to you, but we don't have a babysitter.'

'No no, don't you worry. It's late anyway. Why don't we meet in the morning? Bring your wife and get over here! I'll tell Don Juan and Chicken, too', said Nùralhan.

'Hmm. Well, yes, I suppose that would be better. So you're about to call Erġazy and Ḳanat, are you?'

'Yes, I'd like to get you here all together, then I can put myself entirely at your service!'

'All right – so we'll see you in the morning. What time would you like us to come? Oh, and by the way, what's your room number?'

'Room 213. But don't you dare come before eleven! I can't wait to see you! Do you hear?'

'Good. All right, then. We'll see…'

'Good night!' Nùralhan put down the receiver. All of a sudden, he registered what Bejsek had said on parting: 'All right, then. We'll see…' What did that

---

[7] Traditionally, when receiving guests Kazakhs would slaughter a sheep and make a dish called *bešbarmaḳ* with the fresh meat. Nowadays it is still considered essential to serve a meat dish as a sign of respect to guests, even more so in the case of elders.

[8] *Hanša* – the wife of a khan (a ruler).

remark mean? Should he ring back and find out? But no – Bejsek was probably just confused from the lengthy conversation, and had let slip something he didn't mean. Nùralhan told himself there was no point in disturbing him.

He decided to call Erġazy.

Either the first wave of affection towards his old friends had passed, or he was simply tired after the conversation with Bejsek, but suddenly, Nùralhan felt it would be embarrassing to make a song and dance over the phone, as if he had not grown any wiser with the years. He also recalled that Erġazy had gone back to the *auyl* to get married, just before he completed his diploma, and that he had never met his friend's wife. (Incidentally, both Kùlajša and Erġazy were from the same *auyl*, and Erġazy had actually married Kùlajša's sister.) If Nùralhan was too free-and-easy over the phone with this woman he had never met, she would get the wrong impression. Of course, in the old days, he and Don Juan were always winding each other up and playing tricks on one another. They would usually end up getting overexcited, and Nùralhan could never resist teasing his friend about the antics that had given him his nickname. Though when you came to think of it, what antics had there been exactly? They had called Erġazy 'Don Juan' more as a joke than anything else. All the same, his wife would be unlikely to appreciate the nickname, so it was best to avoid using it in her presence. All these thoughts went through Nùralhan's mind in a flash as he dialled his friend's number.

Several long ring-tones sounded before there was an answer. A hoarse, sleepy voice answered:

'Hello?'

'Is this the Äuesbekovs' house?' asked Nùralhan, puzzled. He thought he had dialled the wrong number.

'Yes.'

'Is that Erġazy?'

'Yes.'

'Well, well! Have your antics cost you your voice now? Or maybe you've just got too big for your boots?'

'Huh? I was just dozing. Who is this?'

'A simple man, up in the capital from the provinces. Does that sound familiar? A man by the name of Nùralhan.'

'Gunner – is that you?! Hello and welcome! What wind blows you here?'

'A fair wind, brother, a fair wind! How are you?'

'Very well. And you?'

'Likewise. The fellows from the trust asked me to come and see them. Just for a few days.'

'What trust are you talking about? Have you got a new job?'

'I've just been given an assignment by the Promstroi Industrial Building Trust.'

'Good for you! Congratulations! So you've just been made a director? Why didn't you say anything? Too modest, is that it? I know you! Afraid to offend the honour of your comrades still languishing in the ranks of "ordinary Soviet engineers". You cunning rascal!'

'I'm beginning to regret I woke you up, you *šajtan*![9] But wait! Where's your better half? Would you let me say hello to her, at least?'

'She's lying down. Shall I call her? All right, just a second...'

'No, wait! Why are you in bed at this time? The Sun has barely set! It's not like the countryside here – you have light all day long and all night in the capital, don't you?'

'You keep talking about "the capital", but you don't know what it's like here! We spend all day running around. By evening we're dead on our feet. I've forgotten what it feels like to have peace and quiet!'

'Well, never mind that just now. Tomorrow's the weekend – why don't you and your wife come to see me at the Alma-Ata Hotel, room 213? You can have a break from it all.'

'Have you spoken to the others? When did you get here, by the way?'

'Not long ago... Your brother-in-law has already promised to come at eleven.'

'Ah, did he now? Well, a lot of water has flowed under the bridge since we last saw you. I know it's the done thing, but I won't invite you to visit us now – after all, it's the middle of the night. We need to do these things properly! You're here for a while, aren't you? There's no hurry. So, you want to give the poor folk of Almaty a taste of your hospitality first, do you? I get it! After all, you're a big boss now! Lord Muck from the town of Ensk showing us how to do things in style!'

'Give it a rest won't you?! I just miss you all. I can't wait to see my old friends. So don't be late tomorrow, all right?'

'You bet we won't.'

'See you then! I'll ring off now then. I don't want to disturb your children's sleep any longer.'

'See you.'

'All the best!'

Nùralhan looked at his watch. It was already half past ten. Half past eleven by local time. He looked at his watch again in amazement and pulled the telephone towards him.

'Is this the Bajbolov household?' he asked. A softly spoken woman's voice replied that yes, it was. Nùralhan told her he was sorry to call at such a late hour, and asked to speak to Ķanat.

'He's not back yet', said the woman. She spoke gently, as if apologising for the fact that her husband had been held up.

'Where on earth is he?' asked Nùralhan. It was on the tip of his tongue to add 'Off out at this hour!' but he stopped himself just in time. 'Is he in town, or away on business?'

---

[9] *Šajtan* – Devil, evil spirit in Islamic theology and mythology, chief among *jinns*.

'Oh no, he hasn't left town. He's with his friends somewhere. As soon as he comes in, I'll let him know you called. What would you like me to pass on to him?'

'I'm a friend of Ķanat's. We studied together. I've just arrived from out of town. I'm contacting all my old friends.'

'You wouldn't be Nùralhan, by any chance?'

'Yes, that's right! You mean to say you knew who I was, even though you've never seen me?' Nùralhan felt a rush of affection for this unknown woman. At the same time, he felt angry at Ķanat for running around goodness knew where.

'I'm sorry', he said. 'I didn't think you knew about me, so I didn't introduce myself. I do apologise!'

'It's fine. After all, we've never met – and we can't know what we've never been told.' Her voice quavered slightly as she spoke, 'Why haven't you come to see us? Ķanat talks about you all the time… Surely a true friend deserves more than just a phone call?'

'*Apyraj*,[10] now you've made me feel ashamed. I've only just arrived, you see. I didn't want to come bursting in on my friends unannounced and disturb them.' Nùralhan was feeling so nervous now he had broken out in a light sweat. 'And in any case, Ķanat isn't at home', he added, doubtfully.

'Maybe not, but we're here. Do come!' she spoke warmly. 'Ķanat will be so delighted to see you, I can't tell you. He was only talking about you yesterday!'

'But then I'll be in trouble with the others!' cried Nùralhan. 'Please don't hold it against me, but I thought I'd get everyone together here at the hotel first, and then go round visiting. I've just rung Bejsek and Erġazy and invited them and their wives to come here tomorrow at eleven, and I wanted to ask you and Ķanat along, too.'

'Well, if you've already told your friends, then I suppose it might be awkward.' It was evident from her high, tremulous voice that she forgave him. 'Don't be offended, though', she said, her voice stronger now, 'But I'm on duty in the hospital tomorrow. I don't think I'll be able to get away. So I'm afraid I won't be able to come.'

'Oh dear!' Nùralhan was put out. 'So what should I do, then?'

'Don't worry!' Again, her voice trembled. 'Ķanat will definitely be there. I hope one of us will be enough? And he'll be so pleased to see his old friend. It's so marvellous that you're here!'

'Well, that's decided then…' Nùralhan didn't know what else to say. Nothing came into his head. His mind was a blank, as if all possible words had simply evaporated.

Ķanat's wife sensed his difficulty immediately.

'I'll tell Ķanat all about our conversation. And don't worry!' Her voice became suddenly bright – 'He'll be so happy! I just know it.'

'Well, good night', Nùralhan said. 'Sweet dreams.'

---

[10] *Apyraj* – exclamation of interest, surprise or doubt (sarcastic); also *apyrmaj*.

'Thank you. Good bye.'

Nùralhan slumped back into the armchair. 'Well', he thought, 'They do say that "Fools rush in where angels fear to tread." But at least I've managed to get hold of my band of brothers and invite them over for lunch.' The thought comforted him. His sharp features softened slightly and his face brightened.

He slept the sound, easy sleep of the young and healthy and woke up just as easily, all at once. He rubbed his eyes and took a look at his watch. It was exactly nine o'clock. Although he had adjusted his watch to local time the night before, he had still woken at his accustomed hour. 'How about that?' he said to himself. 'Soon our brains will be as good as clocks. Well, it's true what they say – old habits die hard. Cockerels will sometimes crow at midnight to show us they come from India. Well, who's the cockerel now?'

Heels clacked on the parquet floor overhead, and the sound of heavy coughing came from the other side of the wall. Nùralhan put a pillow over his head, hoping to sleep a little while longer, but the next minute, the whine of a vacuum cleaner started up outside his door.

'If your aim in life is to stop me from dozing – I congratulate you on your success!' Nùralhan flung off the blanket and jumped out of bed.

He walked up to the window of his hotel room which took up almost the entire wall, and opened it as wide as it would go. He felt well-rested, as a matter of fact. His strong, muscular body felt invigorated by the fresh morning air.

'Well, time to get moving. Let's see if it's true what they say: that the early bird catches the worm' he exclaimed and began making the bed. He caught sight of the blue telephone out of the corner of his eye.

'Perhaps the girl from yesterday will call again?' he mused. 'She wouldn't be such a fool as to disturb you at this time in the morning, would she? But then again, who knows what ideas will come into a young woman's mind when she's just woken up?'

'Pah! Just look at you! Daydreaming!' he said to himself, and snorted. Then he flung the towel over one shoulder and went into the bathroom.

Tum-ta-ra-tum!
Don't dream, like a *zigit*,[11] of revels at dawn—
Or you'll find all your power and influence gone!
Tum-ta-ra-tum![12]

He was singing to himself and rubbing himself energetically with a towel when a knock came at the door.

---

[11] *Žigit* – generally denoting a 25- to 40-year-old male, the term can also be used as an honorific indicating bravery, endurance, fortitude and being true to one's word.

[12] From the poem 'Žigitter, ojyn arzan, kùlki ķymbat' ('*Žigits*, it is easy to entertain, but not easy to make laugh') by Abaj Ķùnanbajùly, translated by the National Bureau of Translations.

354

'Who is it?' He shuffled to the door in his slippers. Opening it, he saw Ķanat.
'Chicken!'
'Gunner!'
Ķanat threw himself on Nùralhan and the two friends clasped each other in a heartfelt embrace. Still hugging, they moved into the middle of the room, with many friendly claps on the back and digs in the ribs, before pulling apart and gazing happily at one another.

Then each man took a few steps aside and looked the other affectionately up and down, and each was, in all likelihood, thinking exactly the same thing: 'He hasn't changed a bit!' Nùralhan had always been tall and strong, but he was now heavier, and his large, full face had weathered, so his cheekbones now stood out more sharply. Ķanat's face, once childishly round, had matured, and his mischievous gaze was now firmer and calmer. These slight changes did not go unremarked, but at first, the two were too happy to see one another again to pay them much attention. In their joy they had become students again: the seven years that had passed since those days simply vanished.

'We-ell – as I live and breathe – the man himself! Large as life and twice as natural!' said Ķanat, speaking in his usual florid manner, 'And here was I, thinking you were joined at the hip to your building site.'

'That's work for you, Chicken! Some of us have to toil away, until the kiddies are grown up – isn't that so?' said Nùralhan, looking at his friend with a teasing grin.

'If you mean *me*, you'll have to wait a while yet for me to grow up', said Ķanat. 'You'll be toiling away in the provinces for some time to come.'

'Why do you say that? It's a crying shame for someone with a brain like yours to sell himself short. You can solve scientific problems in your sleep, and you've always been full of daring ideas... Some of us are made for menial work – it's all we're good for, plodders like us!' Nùralhan let out a loud laugh. 'How long are you going to hide your light under a bushel, Mr Scientist, and pretend to be no better than a puddle on the *taķyr*?'[13]

They both laughed.

This had been a favourite expression of Ķanat's when they had been students. If ever he discovered a flaw in somebody else's idea, or a variation on some well-worn but now half-forgotten scientific theory passed off as a new discovery, he delighted in scathing remarks about this supposed 'innovation' and its author. 'You're as shallow as a puddle on the taķyr', he would say. 'Chasing after clichés, parroting the same old stuff – you haven't an original thought in your head.' The best thing about Ķanat's expression was that it could be applied in equal measure to an inventor and to his invention. Nowadays, all that youthful hot-headedness – when they had shouted themselves hoarse, defending their arguments and opinions – was no more than a distant memory, and in fact seemed rather childish.

---

[13] *Taķyr* – type of desert or dried mud flat found in Central Asia.

'Those were good times, though, weren't they?' Ķanat smiled, recalling their student debates. 'We were full of ideas, our heads were clear and our hearts were pure. And the energy we had in those days! It gave us no peace – it felt as if it would consume us. If we'd been shown a mountain and told to level it, we'd have agreed without batting an eyelid...'

'That's enough, Chicken. "What's gone can never be returned" – remember the Yesenin poem?[14] The truth may be as simple and harsh as life itself – but is that any reason to be downhearted? Come on – wake up! You're starting to sound like someone who's jealous of what others have, and forgets he has to find a way to earn a living himself. But enough of this idle speculation. It's time we thought of our bread and butter – in the most literal sense. Let's go down and have a bite to eat while we wait for the others to arrive. Was it a Frenchman who said, "The radiant path of intellectual ascent begins on a full stomach"? Let's go to the snack bar! We can set the world to rights later.'

***

'As Abaj[15] said, "Can an empty stomach ever be silenced until it has taken in good food?"' said Nùralhan, when he and Ķanat returned to the hotel room after a light meal. 'Now, tell me. I'm all ears.'

'What is there to tell?' was Ķanat's rapid reply. In the past, he had always been quick to react. There was doubt and embarrassment in his voice. 'What exactly do you want to know?'

'What do you mean – what is there to tell? Has our Chicken spread his wings so far and reached such heights that he has nothing left to say? All right – if you want me to be more precise, tell me this: has our dear friend Chicken – the only student on our course who graduated with distinction – has he become a leader? Could he head a great camp of nomads en route from south to north? Etcetera, etcetera...'

'A great camp of nomads, you say? So that's your idea of a joke nowadays? Well, perhaps you're right. You lot all stayed in construction work, you just kept on steadily forging ahead in your fields. So any one of you...' Ķanat stopped mid-sentence, gave an artificial laugh and fell silent.

'Why talk about us? What is there to say?' Nùralhan had failed to notice that his friend was hurt, and had shrunk in on himself, like a bird with ruffled feathers. 'You know, my friend, I don't deal in complicated notions these days. I plod along like an ox, thinking of nothing beyond district and town plans. I don't think I'd be capable of anything more. My only source of pleasure is the fact that I work my fingers to the bone and put my back into everything I do. I've no time for any other delights. As they say – one man's lot in life is to be

---

[14] In Russian, 'Chto proshlo – ne vernut'. Translated by Rose France.

[15] A reference to the famous Kazakh poet Abaj Ķùnanbajùly (Abai Kunanbayev).

a *tamada*;[16] another's to be a shepherd. I'm not the sort to swot over science books or chase after honorary degrees. I only do what's within my capabilities. And *you* compare yourself to me! I was one of those students who spent five whole years at the institute trying to get my marks up from "satisfactory" to "good". There's no comparison between us! I, of all people, should know – I made quite a study of your system – that system that brought together (here Nùralhan switched to Russian for the sake of accuracy) "iron logic, accurate calculation and bold imagination". So, my friend, I don't want to talk about me. I want to hear about *you*.'

Nùralhan spoke with such sincerity that Ķanat realised his friend knew nothing of his life, and was genuinely expecting to hear something extraordinary.

'There's nothing to tell, old man', he said tersely. 'Word of honour. At first, I put together a few projects. I outlined some fundamental changes in the use of reinforced concrete in construction work, and calculating some potential economic advantages. And now, all these projects are locked away in ministerial safes. That's all there is to say. It's no big deal. The way I see it, if you don't give young men the support they need at the outset, they'll become lazy and apathetic. I've lost all the drive I once had.'

'Really? But why?'

'You know, Gunner, I still regret transferring to the design institute. If I'd stayed where I was, I'd be sitting pretty now – a specialist in my field. But what am I now? I'm always being told "Draw this up please", "Have a look at this plan". It's the same pointless stuff day after day. I'm drowning in a sea of papers. Sometimes I just want to chew them to shreds, stick my nose in the air and howl! When that happens, I think of you, ploughing straight on through every obstacle that stands in your way with that big chest of yours. Day in, day out, doggedly pulling your load, staggering home after your shift so tired you can barely stand. How I envy you then! What could be better than wearing yourself out working steadily towards a goal! It must be wonderful!'

'Well how about that?! I thought no one could ever envy me my lot in life. You should see us all out on the building site, shouting and cursing, yelling ourselves hoarse! Ha! Well it's the first time I've seen a man who is sorry he doesn't feel the weight of a yoke on his neck!'

'Don't laugh', said Ķanat. He was blushing slightly and trying to force a smile. 'I'm telling it like it is. Honest to God, Gunner, if I don't get out of here soon, I'll suffocate from this rotten life. What hope is there for me here? To become a "decent bureaucrat"? What use is that to the people? Think about it. All day you mess about with papers, and that's it – day after day, until you collect your pension. Your whole life is measured out to the minute. When you get up, when you go to work; when you go home again. After work, you're tired – and then there are other temptations – anything to stop you thinking

---

[16] *Tamada* – toastmaster at a Kazakh *toj* (feast) or a wedding. The *tamada* introduces each toast, orchestrates any singing or dancing, and generally acts as a master of ceremonies.

about what really matters. The latest curse is card games! There are card parties that go on for nights on end. Games of Preferans[17] wherever you turn… And while you play, you drink. It makes me sick just to think of it. And I'm such a hothead, I never know when to stop. It's all just sordid, old man.'

Nùralhan wanted to object, but he had lost the thread of his own thoughts. He was still gazing adoringly at his beloved friend. What Ķanat had said had not yet got through to him enough to seriously upset him.

'Where were you last night, by the way? I rang at about midnight and you weren't home. You weren't playing cards were you?' he asked, with a note of disappointment in his voice.

'Well? What did you think?'

'And you're in a bad mood today, too. Did you lose?' Nùralhan gave a wry smile.

'To hell with the damn cards! When you start feeling angry at everything around you, it's not just your money you're throwing away, it's your life!' Ķanat laughed bitterly. 'And then someone like you comes along and asks "did you lose?" It's true what they say, You've got to laugh, or else you cry!'

'Woah, Chicken – you've got no self-restraint! Maybe the city air is bad for passionate *žigits* like you, eh?' Nùralhan smiled expressively. 'As long as you don't go off the boil completely, and end up just a cog in the machine.'

'Actually, it's quite possible I will. In fact, it's already close to the truth. A great many tasks in life require a steady hand, but we're told nowadays that we need to "keep a steady mind".'

'Ah, is that so? Well I'm glad you've understood that, at least.'

'As far as I'm concerned, there's nothing good about it. Hang it all! Think about it. Thousands of young people like us. They receive their diplomas, and at the same time, they receive an awareness of the latest scientific achievements. They have everything at their disposal: ideas, energy, strength, knowledge. But when it comes to putting any of these ideas into practice, they find their road blocked by host – a veritable host – of bureaucrats who are experts at "keeping a steady mind". Honestly, there are more of them than you can count! And these worldly-wise officials laugh up their sleeves and repeat the same thing over and over: Right then, lad – get to work! Gain some experience and then we'll see… So the young specialist does his best, works himself into the ground – until one day he decides he's had enough. What do I need all this for? he asks himself. And he chucks the whole thing in. It's as if he's been doing time. Why did he study? Why did he gain all that knowledge? That's not how we should treat young people with innovative, creative ideas, Nùralhan. But on the other hand, we shouldn't allow them to grow up too fast, as then they'll turn into hard-nosed careerists just out for themselves. Nobody ever created anything by "keeping a steady mind". All that happens is they grow old before their time. It's soul destroying for young people. That's why there are more and more

---

[17] Preferans – card game similar to Boston or whist.

people on the make nowadays. I feel sorry for those quick-witted *žigits* who succumb to the idea of keeping a cool mind while they're still young. They'll never recover the fire of their youth.'

'I see! Well, you have a point, even if you've maybe laid it on a bit thick. But why are you getting so worked up about it all?'

'Me? I stand by what I've said, and I always will. I don't see what my getting worked up has to do with it.'

'All right, all right. I know you: once you've an idea in your head, it's almost impossible to get you to think differently. Never mind. Why not tell me instead about our "rationalist" friends, Bejsek and Erġazy, and how they're getting on?'

'What can I tell you? They'll be here themselves soon and they'll fill you in on everything.'

'Just look at the time. It's already half eleven! Two hours have passed while you and I have been philosophising!' exclaimed Nùralhan. 'So why are our friends late?'

'It's half eleven, is it?' said Ķanat. 'They'll be here soon... Did you tell them who you'd invited?'

'Of course!'

'You told them yourself? Or did they try to find out who else was coming?'

'What do you mean, "try to find out"?' Nùralhan looked up at his friend, and, seeing a wry smile on his face, almost choked in amazement.

'Have I surprised you? Nothing to be surprised about, old man. That's something else that's become fashionable these days.' said Ķanat. It was impossible to tell if he was joking or being serious.

Nùralhan wondered if his friend was hinting something about Bejsek and Erġazy, or whether, as had often been the case in the past, he was merely making a mountain out of a molehill.

'You're being a bit too mysterious for my liking, Chicken', he said. 'But let's hope things turn out all right in the end.'

'Well said, old man. But whether things turn out all right depends directly on us – on the purity of our intentions and desires.'

'I see – hmm. But why do you think our friends are taking so long?' Nùralhan decided to change the subject. 'I told them yesterday not to be late on any account.'

'What's the hurry? We can wait.' Ķanat flung himself down into the armchair and closed his eyes.

***

At first, Nùralhan thought that his friends must be about to arrive. Then he decided that they had surely left the house by now and would be at the door at any minute. And so it went on – until two o'clock in the afternoon.

'Where have they got to?' he burst out at last, angrily, letting out an oath. He felt somehow that he had to justify himself in Ķanat's presence. 'Perhaps

359

I should call?' he thought. 'Maybe something has happened?' But he quickly dismissed the thought. They would have told him long ago if that was the case. Eventually, his patience snapped and he turned to his friend, who had long since been sitting in silence.

'Well Chicken, I don't know what's going on, but there's a reason for everything. I suppose something has come up. We can do without them, can't we? Shall we go?' He stood and headed for the door.

Truth be told, Nûralhan had never for a moment imagined such a turn of events. He was distressed that after such a long absence his friends had not responded to his invitation to *dastarhan*.[18] But he did not want to show Ķanat how bitterly disappointed he was. As soon as their table had been laid for them, he said merrily:

'Well, Chicken – here's to us. To our meeting. Let's give thanks that we're both alive and well!'

'...And now let's drink to all the good things that have happened these past seven years.'

'...To the good health of our wives and children!'

The toasts came thick and fast; soon both of them were pleasantly mellow from the drink. Ķanat, guessing what his friend must be feeling, was happy to keep him company. Imperceptibly, Nûralhan's sense of hurt began to recede and his spirits were eased. He suddenly felt a desire to talk about what was closest to his heart.

'As soon as they told me I had to come to Almaty, I forgot about everything except seeing you all again. All these memories kept coming back to me. All the quirks of your characters, your habits, the things you used to say.' His face became flushed and his eyes shone. 'I miss you all so much, I just can't tell you!'

'Well, that's often the case for folk who live out in the sticks.' Ķanat said, with a wry smile. 'Time moves slowly out there – that's what's so good about it. So you feel closer to us, to the capital and to days gone by. The past feels more alive to you than it does to us. That's just the way it is!'

'What crazy theories you have!' Nûralhan gave a hearty laugh.

'I don't know what you're so surprised about. You should just try living in this city! It's like being sucked into a time machine. Never in a million years will you find yourself saying I miss so and so, or I'm homesick.'

'But haven't you thought of me at least once in a while – in all these years? Not even once? What a hard-hearted lot you are!'

'Memories are something else altogether. We just don't talk about them. Still waters run deep, as they say. We keep everything hidden.'

'But you do understand what I'm talking about? *Ojbaj-au*', he exclaimed, expressing indignation, 'when I think of my old friends, I get so sad I lose my

---

[18] *Dastarhan* – traditional concept concerning all the dining- and hosting- related practices and etiquette norms. Inviting someone to a dastarhan is hosting according to all the norms of hospitality. More specifically, *dastarhan* is a synonym for dining table or table cloth.

appetite! If you forgot all about me, I don't know what would happen. As for me – I'll never forget you. I just can't!'

'It's a wonderful thing to be so sure of your feelings, old man. Only strong people can have such conviction these days.' Ķanat looked his friend over with appreciation. 'People who are tough and honest and don't give in to anyone.'

'How nice of you to say so! I'm feeling ten feet tall now!

'Hah! I think we should drink to that, don't you?'

'No, I'm not joking, I mean it. I've seen a lot of people in this city and most of them are slippery as eels – in word and deed. I wouldn't trust them as far as I could throw them. But I do trust you. I trust you to rise to any challenge and take any burden on your shoulders, because you're the type who's more likely to keep quiet about his successes and misfortunes than to say too much. Don't you see old man? We always want what we can't have – so people say. I think that's true. Lately I've started to doubt myself and others, but when I set eyes on you again, I started to feel more confident. Remember how just a minute ago I said you hadn't changed at all? It's true. The most important thing is – you're still capable of *feeling* and of *wanting*. We lost all that long ago. Let's raise a toast to having confidence in our friends – let it be our guiding principle in life!'

'Well said! An excellent toast. But where did you get this habit of praising people to their faces?' Nùralhan mused. 'It's a bit embarrassing. Yes, just a minute – I'll finish this one' – he emptied his glass – 'There! You know, my friend, I've lost the habit of speaking so frankly. You see, my life is just work, work, work, from morning till night. I reckon you have more time on your hands to think about other things. That's why you seem to have acquired this disease – you keep touching raw nerves in conversation. You talk like someone on edge. It must be the effect of all these constant stresses... and of all the other benefits of so-called civilisation.'

'Well, you certainly don't mince your words! I wish you were wrong, but actually, there's a lot of truth in what you say. I've noticed this "disease" – it comes of being tired. But have you thought about why everyone's so tired? *I* think...' Ķanat fell silent again, deep in thought.

'Well, I don't know what you think', Nùralhan gave a happy laugh, and his eyes, which were now rather red, shone happily. 'But out in the provinces, we have no spare minute to devote to any of this.'

'Hey! Stop trying to turn it all into a joke. You haven't answered my question. I think you hit the nail on the head just now when you talked about a "disease". And if you haven't considered what causes it, at least hear me out.'

'All right, I'm listening. '

'This disease – this tiredness we see all around us – is the result of hostile relations between people. Where does this hostility come from?' Ķanat scratched his head. 'Well, from a lack of ideas or goals. Imagine a man is ready to start work on some grand scheme – something that will be of service to society – but he encounters an obstacle, so he chucks it all in and occupies himself with something trivial and short-term. He throws himself into all the distractions and entertainments life has to offer (Good God, what I wouldn't give for some grand scheme to take the place of at least part of all that nonsense!) And gradually he begins to feel a growing discontent with himself. And before he knows it, he's angry and bitter, and that's all. He starts to feel like a *mangurt*, a dull creature without a brain or any thoughts of its own. His life is pointless – without any meaning. That's how it is! It's what Russians call "spiritual discontent"… I'd like to see how you'd cope with that sort of life – a life spent doing nothing, conscious all the time that you're achieving nothing worthwhile. You'd feel exhausted in no time. You'd be howling with boredom. And it's not like being tired out from hard work – work that you love. That brings a sense of satisfaction, joy and a heart full of emotion. No – this is something else altogether – a feeling of emptiness, irritation, hostility. It's like an affliction. Well, it's a disease, actually. The disease of tiredness. You're quite right that just about everyone is affected by it. In the city I mean…'

'Well in that case, what we need to do is find an outlet for your incredible mental energy, which could bring a pot of water to boil with no more than a cold stone.' Nůralhan smiled at his friend. 'It's no use sitting around complaining that you've no willpower and you're being eaten up by idleness!'

'I agree. In fact, I've decided that I need to change everything in my life. You know old man, I made up my mind long ago that I'd go and work on any construction site that would have me. Science can wait.'

'Really? And you've really made up your mind?' Nůralhan spoke lightly, but he looked closely at his friend nevertheless, trying to gauge whether or not he was being serious. Although he had only recently been promoted to director, he has already noticed that he had a self-serving tendency to be always on the lookout for good employees.

'Really, truly and definitely!' said Ḳanat, shaking his head from side to side for emphasis. And although he spoke in his usual passionate and decisive manner, his voice was quite serious, as if he really had given the matter some thought.

'Perhaps he's already come to some arrangement', thought Nůralhan, looking quizzically at Ḳanat. 'He'll be snapped up in an instant. Where else could you find an engineer with a mind like his, who is still artless as a child – someone who can be trusted implicitly?'

'What sort of post are you looking for? I suppose you'd like to be in charge of a big government construction site, at the very least?' he asked, not wishing to insult his friend's dignity.

'What are you talking about?! How would I get a job like that? There are no jobs like that going, anyway. A throne never stays vacant for long, as they say. Add to that the situation in the capital, and you'll have some idea of what I'm up against. If I can find a position as an engineer, that's fine. If not, I'd be happy working as a site manager – at the level I reached two years after I graduated. But you know I'm not afraid of challenges. In fact, I'm actively seeking them. I've put up with worse. After all, I was shift manager once upon a time, and that was fine. I wouldn't even mind doing that again. As long as I'm not watching my life slip through my fingers. I don't mind getting my knuckles rapped from time to time, so long as I can see the fruits of my labour. I just want to be able to answer to myself every day for what I've done.'

'Well, I second that. When you work in industry, there's no hiding anything from anyone. It's quite clear what has and hasn't been done.'

'And you can't hide from yourself, either! If a man can't answer to his own conscience, how can he talk about integrity?'

'Ah-ha! Say no more! I see you've developed a social conscience. Our chicken has grown up and taken wing.' Nùralhan began teasing his friend again.

'Oh, forget it.' said Ḳanat with a pained expression. 'I try telling you the truth, but you're just like those other two – Bejsek and Erġazy. You just laugh everything off.'

Nùralhan looked at his friend in amazement. Ḳanat was poking miserably at his plate with a fork and did not even lift his head. It dawned on Nùralhan that he had unwittingly touched on a sore spot. He fell silent, unwilling to probe his friend any further or, still worse, try to console him. Anything he said now would merely be an attempt to justify himself – though he was not sure exactly what he had done wrong.

However, Ḳanat himself soon realised that by staying silent, he was leaving his friend with an undeserved burden of guilt. All of a sudden, he spoke up so vehemently that it seemed all the emotions he had long kept hidden had come bubbling to the surface.

'No, Nùralhan. It's not right. When a man trusts you and wants to open his heart to you, it's wrong to turn it into a joke. There've been times when I've talked about my fears with Bejsek and Erġazy, and they just nudge each other, laugh and make sarcastic comments. It's their arrogant, lazy way of thinking that infuriates me the most. "Oh, you're still thinking like a student" they say, or "You're still wet behind the ears. When will you finally grow up and understand the complexities of real life?" "Never mind – when you've grown up and experienced a thing or two, you'll understand what's what." But weren't we all at university together? They talk as if they've reached some dizzy heights of perfection, while I've been frittering away my time! As if they always think and act like paragons of public spiritedness. Of course, as far as their rank and authority is concerned, they're up there with the best of the competition. And they're good at their jobs. When I'm not actually with them, I feel proud of them. But whenever I try to have a serious conversation it all starts up again – the teasing, the sneers, the cheap digs…'

'But what do they actually say?' asked Nùralhan. He didn't really want to know the details, but he was doing what he could to keep up his end of the conversation, which had started out so carefree and happy, and had now become rather dispiriting.

'They always say the same thing. "Still setting the world to rights, eh, Chicken! What's the point? You're a very eloquent speaker, but we're not at a political rally now".'

'Hmm', Núralhan's response was non-committal.

They fell silent again.

'That reminds me, Ķanat. Tell me about our friends.'

'What do you want to know?' Ķanat asked listlessly, picking up a piece of cold meat with his fork. 'Can you believe they haven't even turned up?!' he said suddenly, sounding as if he had only now realised that neither Bejsek nor Erġazy was dining with them.

'What are they up to?' asked Núralhan, glancing at the door despite himself.

'Actually, I knew they wouldn't come. Then I thought they might, out of respect to you. After all, it's been seven years since we saw one another. But my first instinct was correct.'

'You knew they wouldn't come? How? Did they warn you?'

'Of course not. It's just…'

'Just what?' Núralhan frowned.

'Do you remember how I asked you what you'd told them about this meeting?' asked Ķanat. His voice was self-important and not entirely sincere.

'Well, what about it?'

'And I guessed they'd ask you something like, Who else will be there? Remember?'

'Yes.'

'Well, now do you see? I don't know why, old man, but recently, not everybody accepts invitations to gatherings where there will be other people present. I think that's why Bejsek and Erġazy haven't turned up. Recently, I asked them over to mine and they didn't come then either. It was annoying, but what could I do about it?'

'What's happened to them?'

Ķanat shrugged his shoulders and said nothing.

Núralhan frowned. For some time, he sat in silence.

'Even if you three have fallen out, is that any reason to disdain my *dastarhan*?' he said, hotly. 'That's no way to act. A friend is a friend – no matter what. For five years, we'd have done anything for one another – we'd have shared our last crust of bread. And now, what – we're not on speaking terms, just because of some trivial matter?'

'You're a funny one, Núralhan', said Ķanat, frowning for a moment. 'Do you think everybody feels as strongly about all this as you do? They don't! It's all to do with character – and that's set in stone. The main thing is, don't let anything surprise you. If an old friend starts to drift away – if he's found a friend who suits him better, or if he thinks he has – there's no point thrusting your old friendship in his face and arguing with him about it. Who cares if we all studied together for five years and shared "our last crust" with each other, as you put it? And anyway, is it even decent to talk about our closest and most precious feelings? If we all decided to do that, what would be left of our friendship? Deep down in every one of us, after all, there are truths that can't be spoken aloud. And don't keep harping on about how friends should be sincere and honest. It's the things we can't say aloud that are most important of all. Judge for yourself. A friend is pulling away and you want to keep talking to him about your feelings, like some lovesick calf?!'

'You've started talking in riddles now. Why do you keep beating about the bush? Come out with it. Who's pulling away from whom?'

'Why are you asking me?'

'Enough of all these hints and half-truths!'

'Don't think I'm trying to hide anything from you, old man. On the contrary. But aren't you just a little bit too sure about our university friendship and how it will forever stand the test of time?'

'Am I wrong to think that?'

'To be brutally honest, those of us who live here in the capital have long since become like strangers. When we see each other, we greet each other and go on our way – no more. Why bring up the fact that we used to eat from the same dish? Nowadays, we can't even manage to get together properly for a single evening. I keep trying to work out – what's the matter with all of us now? What's missing? We're none of us badly off these days, so why is it we think only of our own well-being, and toil away only for the sake of moving up in the world and live more comfortably? Bejsek has made friends with a fellow from the regional Trade Union Council. The two of them are inseparable. By the way, you might remember him – he was in the year below us at the institute: an activist, always talking about the Trade Union Council. A cheeky fellow: short and squat, with a round face and bug-eyes.'

'Ah yes, I think I remember him. What was his name though? I remember, he always gave a speech at every meeting.'

'That's the one. Well, now this former activist is in charge of giving out vouchers for holiday homes on the Black Sea. And our Bejsek really wants a piece of the pie – do you see? And this official is delighted to have a friend like Bejsek – who, after all, is director of the Building and Construction Department. If you want to build a *dacha*[19] in the mountains, you need red brick. It's a case of "you scratch my back, and I'll scratch yours"! Of course, no one knows how long a friendship like that will last. But anyway, my point is – these days, Bejsek is friends with people like that, not with you or me. You might protest, "But we studied together for five years; we shared our last crust together!" – But it doesn't matter. Now he and his Trade-Union friend go out every Sunday to the mountains in their private cars. To tell you the truth, I was even a bit jealous of this fellow at first. I racked my brains, trying to work out what it was Bejsek saw in him. Then I realised. It made me feel

---

[19] *Dacha* – country house or cottage, typically used as a second/holiday home by city dwellers. *Dachas* were popular during the Soviet time.

funny: I had nothing to offer my old friend but my own best intentions, but it seemed that wasn't enough anymore. Still, what's the use of raking all this up? What I want to say is, things between us aren't what they used to be. We've lost the selflessness we once had, the generosity and integrity. Where has it all gone? When did the crystal-clear spring of our friendship become muddied? I couldn't tell you – I can't understand it. The worst of it is that when we meet now, it's like paying a social call. You have to watch what you drink, and there's all this fake politeness. Now and again, very rarely, we let our hair down a bit and reminisce about our times as students. We get a bit rowdy, but then we pull ourselves together. After all, we're family men now. We need to behave ourselves. Tell me, how on earth can we hope to be sincere with one another? If you can't feel at ease as an honoured guest in the house of your friend, you're in trouble!'

The longer Ḳanat went on, the gloomier Nùralhan's expression became.

'Stop! That's enough!' He said at last, quietly and firmly. 'It's wrong to rake over trivial grievances in this way, Chicken. We're friends! Friends, I tell you! Didn't you say just now that everything depends on what kind of a person a man is, and on the purity of his feelings? Enough of this conversation. Let's drink to our friends instead. That's the right thing to do.'

Ḳanat chinked his glass against Nùralhan's without enthusiasm. He looked at his friend, who had knocked back his drink in one gulp, and said, pensively:

'You're wrong. I'm not raking over grievances. That's not why I've been saying all this. In the first place, you wanted to know yourself why there was bad feeling between us. In the second place, I won't hide it from you—' his voice was rather aggrieved. 'Whatever may have happened between us now, we were true friends once upon a time, and that's something you never forget. We were thick as thieves back then. And if I can't talk about all this to you, who can I tell? All this is tough for me. My feelings haven't changed! Sometimes I think, why don't my friends feel the same towards me as they used to? We ought to be close. Actually, it feels like a betrayal, their drifting away from me. I know I've said a lot of things today, but don't judge me too harshly. I had to speak up – to do otherwise would have felt dishonest.'

Nùralhan felt an ache in his chest. He was reminded of the howl of a puppy abandoned on a *žurt*.[20]

'Perhaps you and I should stop making ourselves feel miserable', he said sadly. 'Would you like to order something else?

'No – let's go outside.'

***

The heat of the day had abated and the cool of twilight had set in. A cool breeze blew in from the mountains. The fountains, silent by day, had come to

---

[20] *Žurt* – an abandoned nomad encampment or *auyl*.

life, sending up thick white spouts of snow-white foam that sprayed fine mist of water into the air.

'This is more like it', said Nùralhan, turning his broad chest towards the refreshing spray. 'Come here and try it! You'll feel more human in an instant!'

'Do you think I've never seen that fountain before?' Ķanat looked at his friend with a smile and set off into the lobby of the hotel. A moment later he returned.

'Well, old man, my wife is back from work and she's been expecting us for ages.'

'Fancy that! Why didn't you tell me? But how can we go like this, we've had quite a few drinks, after all...'

'It's not as if you're going to a stranger's house!' Giving Nùralhan no time to think, Ķanat grabbed his arm energetically and dragged him off in his wake.

'Wait a minute!' said Nùralhan, confused.

'What for? Sorry, I completely forgot to tell you this morning that my wife had invited you. But on the phone just now she said, Don't come without your friend! Come on!'

'You rascal! You're probably afraid to go back home on your own!' Nùralhan joked, playing for time and trying to gather his thoughts somehow. Then he remembered the woman with the gentle voice who had answered the phone. She had spoken to him as if they had known each other for years. Her manner had been trusting and heartfelt and she had even seemed offended, asking him, 'Why didn't you come straight to us? Is that how friends behave?' No – thought Nùralhan, it would be awkward to refuse her invitation.

'Well, come on then!' Ķanat urged him. 'Look – that taxi has stopped for us – let's get it, quick!'

'All right!'

Nùralhan settled himself into the back seat next to his friend. 'But I warn you – if you ever end up in my part of the world when you're so tired you can barely walk, I'll drag you home with me. That way I'll get my own back!'

'As Allah is my witness, it would be a sin to refuse', said Ķanat, with a merry laugh.

They both threw back their heads and laughed heartily.

Soon the taxi stopped in front of a five-storey, grey building in the Kôktem district.

The door was unlocked. As soon as he crossed the threshold, Ķanat called out in a loud, friendly voice:

'Žanna, come and meet our guest!'

A slim young woman ran out from one of the rooms off the corridor and held out her hand to Nùralhan with a bashful air.

He bowed.

'Pleased to meet you!'

'Welcome!' she replied. 'How are you?' Her voice, which trembled slightly, sounded just as pleasant as it had yesterday on the phone. 'Do come on through!'

Ķanat nudged Nüralhan excitedly. 'So you see how we live! Make yourself at home!' he walked through to the living room ahead of Nüralhan.

A small boy with black curly hair peered into the corridor. 'What's your name, *žigit*?' asked Nüralhan kindly, but the child immediately disappeared. Ķanat, who had noticed a scene out of the corner of his eye, smiled: 'Samat, son, this is our guest, run on out here and say hello this minute!' But the boy had no intention of coming back out, so Ķanat set off after him and carried him back into the corridor, wriggling.

'Now then – say hello to your Uncle Nurik. You rascal, why aren't you saying anything?' The boy stood to one side, panting and frowning stubbornly, then dashed off to his room.

'There you are. That's our little rascal Samat. He's a mummy's boy. And the oldest, Bolat, has gone to stay with his grandmother', remarked Ķanat amicably.

Nüralhan peered into the brightly lit living room, which was clean and tidy and in which every object knew in its place, mysteriously creating an atmosphere of comfort. He listened to his friend's voice, calm one minute, happy and excited the next, and felt suddenly that this was a place of joy and peace. He had been worried his visit might be an inconvenience, but now he was relieved. 'No, I think everything's fine. Thank goodness!' he thought. He felt as happy here as he did in his own home.

Quickly and quietly, Žanna laid the table.

'Would you like to eat straight away or would you prefer to drink tea first?' she asked.

'Žanna, my dear, why are you plaguing our guest with questions? There's wisdom in the old folk saying "A guest is as quiet as a sheep. Put a plate of butter in front of him and he will enjoy it". All the same, old man, what would you like?' He turned to Nüralhan.

'Make up your mind! You say one thing and then another! Apparently, a guest is like a sheep and will eat anything you put in front of him!' Nüralhan laughed heartily. 'Don't mind me, I'm only joking. I think I'd like some tea.'

'Did you hear that, Žanna?' said Ķanat, sitting down next to his friend on the divan. 'Pour us each a *kese* of tea.'[21]

It looked as if other guests were expected besides Nüralhan – the dining table had been pulled out to its full extent. Žanna deftly placed small dishes of food on the table, glancing at Ķanat with a smile.

'Sorry, Nurik' she said, 'But when he's with his dearest friends, my husband acts terribly spoilt – very high and mighty. Look at him, not lifting a finger to help his wife. He's been so delighted since yesterday that he's forgotten about everything else!'

'*Ojbaj*, Žanna, darling, I didn't think. Wait, I'm coming!' Ķanat jumped to his feet and rushed to the kitchen.

---

[21] *Kese* – traditional Kazakh bowl used for serving tea.

Nûralhan knew his friend to be an obliging man and had actually been a little surprised that he had sat down on the divan without thinking to help his wife. Now he laughed, in spite of himself. 'That's just like Chicken. One minute he's away in a dream, the next he's flying off somewhere at top speed. Well, I know what it's like. I often have to run around like that these days!'

Ķanat did not have much work to do in the end. He brought in some fruit bowls, and then Žanna said to him.

'It's all right. You sit down and relax. I'll do it myself.'

'That's right! After all, my friend is here, and we haven't seen one another for seven years. I'm afraid I might not have enough time to catch up!' Ķanat gave Nûralhan a mischievous wink and sat down beside him.

'I don't know why you're letting him off so easily, Žanna. Look how happy he is, the idler!' said Nûralhan, allowing himself to speak in an easier, more playful tone.

Žanna was clearly pleased that her guest was no longer standing on ceremony. '*Au*, Nurik! I've been spoiling this fellow ever since we first moved in together. Still, I have to say, it makes me uneasy when men get involved in the kitchen!'

'Spoken like a true housewife!' said Nûralhan.

At first he had thought that Ķanat's wife would not be happy to speak in such a free and easy way, but Žanna had once again surprised him. 'She really is a very perceptive, insightful young woman', he thought to himself.

'Just you wait!' exclaimed his friend. My *bájbiše* may sound as quiet as a lamb, but don't let that fool you! She grew up in the city, you know, and she didn't speak Kazakh very well at first, so I decided to teach her. Little did I know what I was letting myself in for. Now she's so quick with her folk sayings, I don't know if I'm coming or going.'

'That's just what you need. I remember how nobody could get the better of you in an argument, because nobody could get a word in edgeways. All that teaching paid off' teased Nûralhan.

'My wife has taken over from me very successfully these days when it comes to talking' said Ķanat, nodding towards the kitchen. 'I leave it all to her!'

'That's the only thing you can do!' put in Žanna. 'You see, Nûralhan, this old friend of yours—' here she looked carefully from one man to the other, as if unsure whether to continue. 'This friend of yours is up all hours running about town – first to one set of companions, then to another. And all they think about is cards, billiards and chess! Allah only knows where he goes. And if I ask him, there's always some excuse. So there's no one left in the house to do the talking but me! Isn't that right, Ķanat?'

Ķanat only laughed. It was clear that he had nothing to say in reply. Nûralhan, who was concerned that this playful sparring might develop into something more serious, joked hurriedly:

'Well my friend, when I'm leaving town, I'll clap you in leg irons. Understand?'

But Ķanat was smiling from ear to ear and didn't seem put out in the slightest. And in any case, Žanna had spoken without rancour, and made no hint or gesture to suggest that she was complaining of her husband's behaviour. She seemed to have got used to the fact that he was always out of the house, and made nothing of it.

Well, how about that? thought Nùralhan. Look at Chicken – teaching his wife to put up with his gallivanting! If I stayed out late like that day after day, I'd have long since been plucked and eaten!

Nùralhan remembered how, back in the *auyl*, there were legendary stories of wives who didn't bat an eyelid at their husbands' drunken exploits. Perhaps these women were the heroines of folktales, he thought. Who knew? Nowadays, women would not let their husbands out of their sight. Nùralhan's own wife, at least, always went everywhere with him.

Not bad, Chicken! he thought. You've made it clear where you stand, so now you're free to do as you please. Not bad at all!

His thoughts were interrupted by Žanna's quiet voice inviting them to sit down at the table.

Nùralhan knew from his own experience that the way drink affected him depended on his mood. Alcohol only intensified whatever emotions were there in the first place. Although he and Ķanat had left the restaurant already the worse for wear, tired from their conversation, here, at Ķanat's *dastarhan*, the drink did nothing to alter his calm and amiable state of mind.

***

Before they went to bed, they went outside to get a breath of fresh air, walked along the tree-lined street and then sat in the kitchen for a while and drank a couple of glasses of brandy.

'So what shall we do tomorrow?' asked Nùralhan. 'What are your plans?'

'What do you mean, What shall we do? We'll relax, of course', said Ķanat.

'Wait a minute, I'm not asking you! I'm asking Žanna', said Nùralhan, his eyes twinkling at Ķanat. 'Tell us what you think, Žanna.'

'I don't know', Žanna was washing up at the sink. 'What have you decided?'

'Ķanat and I haven't thought of anything to do – so we're asking your advice.'

Žanna found nothing to say for a moment, and Ķanat began to hum to himself:

If you ask a woman's advice
And do everything she says
Ah, me![22]

'Stop that, you rascal!' Nùralhan made as if to hit Ķanat.

---

[22] A quotation from the epic poem *Ķobylandy batyr*. Translated by the National Bureau of Translations.

'Ah-ha! So now you get it? See what it's like when you're being deadly serious, and somebody else turns it all into a joke!' Ķanat laughed.

'All right. You win. One point to you.'

'That's more like it. After all, if I let my guest pay court to my dearly beloved, it won't be long before she's dancing a jig on my long-suffering head, isn't that right, Žanna, darling?'

Ķanat only allowed himself to engage in this sort of banter in the presence of a beloved friend. Žanna understood this perfectly, and paid no attention to her husband's witticisms. It was a long time since Ķanat behaved so freely and uninhibited, and she had been quietly delighted all evening.

'You're right, we have to entertain our guest tomorrow, what do you think, Ķanat? But we need to discuss it seriously, jokes aside. Nùralhan doesn't often have the chance to visit Almaty. I think we should go to Kôk Tôbe, to the Auyl,[23] and then to Medeu.[24] It's the first time you've been to the capital since you studied here, isn't it, Nùralhan? Everything in that part of the city has been completely rebuilt hasn't it, Ķanat?'

'Why are you asking me? Speak to our guest!'

'Now wait a minute!' Nùralhan said angrily, afraid that Ķanat was going to start making everything into a joke again.

'I don't know how you feel about my suggestion. Think it over with Ķanat', said Žanna and fell silent.

'Ķanat, Ķanat – all she thinks about is her husband', thought Nùralhan, gazing admiringly at Žanna. He looked over at Ķanat, who was beaming from ear to ear, and suddenly felt that his friend was the most fortunate man on Earth. He even felt a twinge of envy.

'Žanna, you've read my mind. That's exactly what I wanted to do tomorrow' said Nùralhan.

'My Žanna always knows what other people are thinking. That's why I never dare contradict her', said Ķanat. 'Well, I'm in favour of that plan, too!' he said, throwing both hands into the air.

Nùralhan smiled, glad to see that his friend was in such a magnanimous mood.

Where there's respect, there's no room for quarrels, he thought, as he looked from Žanna to her husband. It was an age-old piece of wisdom, but he had not often had occasion to see its truth revealed afresh.

***

---

[23] Kôk Tôbe – a mountain outside Almaty. The Auyl is a popular recreation area on top of the mountain.

[24] Medeu – an outdoor ice rink located in Medeu Valley, it sits 1691 metres above sea level.

They left the house early the next morning, visited all the places they had planned, and, after riding down from Kôk Tôbe in a cable car, they came back into town early in the evening.

Nùralhan said goodbye to Ķanat and Žanna outside the hotel. As he went back to his room, he breathed deeply and freely, feeling that he had done his duty. Now there was only one thought in his mind: to stretch out in his hotel bed and get some sleep.

On his way up to his room on the first floor, he heard shouting and some sort of angry commotion. He went up to investigate, but it turned out to be no more than a football match on television, between the Ķajrat and Pahtakor teams.[25] The lounge was crammed with people and the television had been turned up to top volume. The shouts and hubbub of thousands of spectators watching in the stadium merged with the excited yells of the hotel crowd.

'*Apyraj* – maybe I should watch a bit of the match, too?' he thought. He kept his eyes on the television while the duty attendant was handing him his key. All of a sudden, a familiar voice nearby called out.

'*Ojbaj*, look at our football fan!' He turned round and saw Kùlajša, with Bejsek standing beside her.

'*Au* – what are you doing here?' Nùralhan asked, bewildered. He didn't know what to do, squeezed in among the crowds of people in the lounge. It seemed awkward to embrace his friends in front of everyone, but it wouldn't be right either to greet them too coolly, if he wasn't pleased to see them. Hastily, he grasped Bejsek's hand in a firm handshake and just said 'Why are we standing here? Let's go to my room.'

'Lead on', said Bejsek, amiably.

'Welcome to Almaty, Nurik. O-ho! What lovely living quarters you have here! And I was wondering why you didn't come to see us. I see you're keeping house here yourself in a fancy hotel room.'

'All mine of course – it's inherited from my grandfather', joked Nùralhan.

'So you've come at last, then?' Bejsek took off his felt hat and tossed it onto the bed with a characteristically confident, elegant gesture. Then he began to clear his throat, as if he were about to begin a long, important speech.

'So you see, old man – so you see.' Nùralhan was surprised to hear how calmly and coolly he spoke. He still sensed a distance between himself and his friend – either because they had met in the crowd in the hall, or because of something else besides. The thought of hugging Bejsek like a long-lost brother now seemed out of place. 'So, how are you? Both well, I hope?' he asked, in the same calm voice, with barely a trace of excitement. 'How are you, Kùlajša? I swear, you look completely different. *Paj-paj*[26] – evidently our Bejsek is treating you like a princess – keeping you wrapped in cotton wool and feeding you sugar lumps!'

---

[25] Kazakh and Uzbek football teams.

[26] *Paj-paj* – exclamation of delight and appreciation.

372

'Away with you and your nonsense! You'll be giving me the evil eye next. I hear your wife's a beauty. How is she? And your children?'

'Fine, thanks. And your little one is probably running about by now? You haven't added to your brood since I last heard?' asked Nùralhan, smiling at his friends.

'We've got the regulation one son and one daughter – that's the way here in the capital. But we want to hear about your successes on that front!'

'Ooh – I've lost count. There must be four or five of them at least.'

Bejsek smiled coolly, with the dignity that befitted a husband and father.

'Quiet, you big fibber!' said Kùlajša, unsure whether Nùralhan was joking or not. 'You've been married less than seven years. How could you have four or five children?! Or have you found yourself a woman who keeps having twins?'

'Well, it's all up to us in that area.' Nùralhan straightened out his shoulders proudly. 'With the right man, anything's possible!'

'O-ho-ho – you're still playing the fool – just like in the old days. Well watch out!' Kùlajša went behind Nùralhan's back and gripped him in a stranglehold. 'Tell me – are you going to stop talking rubbish, or not? Will you give it a rest?!'

'All right, all right! You win!' said Nùralhan, laughing. 'What strange creatures women are, eh, Bejsek? All they care about is mangling the truth!'

'What can I say?' said Bejsek with a cool smirk. 'The only way you can hope to escape is to keep saying, You're absolutely right, my dear! Otherwise they'll eat you alive!'

The friends glanced at each other in solidarity, then, an instant later, looked at Kùlajša, as if waiting for a reaction.

'Hey, what's got into you?' Kùlajša shook her small, strong fist at her husband. 'You wait till I get you home, I'll give you a piece of my mind! Feeling bolder because you think Nùralhan will back you up? Is that it?'

'Well, when there are more of us men, I can take a few liberties. There are times where you won't even let me open my mouth!'

'Exactly!'

After mollifying Kùlajša with a flattering compliment, the two men glanced at one another, lips twitching in a conspiratorial smile. It was only then Kùlajša realised that the men were laughing at her. Afraid of making another blunder, she quickly changed the subject.

'So', she turned to Nùralhan. 'Have you got something else to offer us besides words? You were boasting before that you had brought some treats from the *auyl*. Where are they? Can we try them?'

'*Ojbaj*, what was I thinking of?' Nùralhan blushed and for some reason, looked at his watch. He jumped up from his chair. 'Let's go down to the restaurant', he proposed.

Bejsek cleared his throat. 'There's no need', he said. 'Seeing as we didn't come yesterday – I hope you don't mind, by the way; some visitors dropped by unexpectedly. But don't think of dragging us off to the restaurant. It's hardly respectable at our age, is it?'

Nùralhan looked at his friend's pale face, which had grown fuller with the years, at his wry smile, and his dark hair which, though touched with grey, was still thick and wavy (not for nothing had he nicknamed Bejsek 'D'Artagnan'!). His friend was even more handsome now than he used to be, thought Nùralhan. He had always held himself nobly, but he had now grown still more stately and aloof. With his proud demeanour, imposing appearance and grave manner of speaking, he was probably an intimidating figure to strangers. However, even here, Bejsek had not lost his condescending manner: he spoke in a peremptory tone, as if he were with one of his subordinates, rather than with his friend. This high-handedness grated on Nùralhan.

'You're a funny one. Who told you that restaurants are only for youngsters?' said Nùralhan with a laugh. However, in all likelihood, his friends sensed that he was offended.

'*Aj*', fussed Kùlajša, 'Who needs restaurants! Treats from the *auyl* are much better! Ever since you told me yesterday you'd brought food from home, my mouth has been watering!'

'In that case, I hold my peace. If it's what Kùlajša wants, who am I to object?' said Nùralhan with a small bow. 'Only please don't be offended if it's not quite what you expect.' He got up, opened the sideboard and quickly set two bottles of brandy, some sliced *ķazy*,[27] a jar of caviar and a boiled chicken.

'This is what I've been dreaming of ever since I left the house!' cried Kùlajša gaily, getting up to help.

'Well, you were created by Allah to enjoy all the sweets of the world. What can I say – you were born lucky!' Bejsek told his wife.

Nùralhan recalled something Ķanat had said long ago, when they had first heard that Bejsek was planning to marry. '*Apyraj* – this girl is born lucky. You'll see – she'll get her claws into our D'Artagnan. She's the type of woman who will be treated like a queen.' At the time, they had been amazed by Kùlajša's bold, decisive character. She had brought a poor student back to her private apartment. They had come back one evening from visiting the young married couple in Tastaķ district and lain down on their iron bedsteads in the dark room of the student hostel.

'To be honest, I can't see what our D'Artagnan sees in that clever scamp of a girl', Ķanat had said.

'Beauty is found in what is dear to our heart, not in what is fair to the eye', Erġazy had lectured him.

'Yes, beauty is in the eye of the beholder. Mark it, my friend Horatio.'

'All right, that's enough from you two. No sooner do I say something than you start giving me sermons', said Ķanat, annoyed. 'But isn't that just what I'm talking about? If Kùlajša was beautiful and charismatic, then I would understand. Or if there was something about her appearance that was absolutely unique... Still, maybe there's something in what you just said,

---

[27] *Ķazy* – traditional Kazakh sausage made from horsemeat.

Nùralhan. Maybe that's where the truth lies. But that phrase, "Beauty is found in what is dear to the heart, not in what is fair to the eye", is just empty words. A lie, made up by men like me, who could never attract a beautiful woman. What's left for us, after all, except to rage at the world because the beautiful women look straight through us, and fool ourselves with sayings of that sort? Well, never mind all that! The point is, this young lady who has managed to lasso D'Artagnan was born under a lucky star. She's a fortunate girl indeed, if life lays such treasures at her feet.'

Erġazy had, for some reason, said nothing. But at the time, Nùralhan had found himself turning Ķanat's words over in his mind…

And now, seven years later, Bejsek himself had said that his wife was 'born lucky'.

Kùlajša reacted to his comment as quick as a flash:

'Isn't that just what I keep telling you?'

The girl Nùralhan remembered as a fellow student had changed indeed. She had put on weight and had the beginnings of a double chin. She had always had a very open nature, but now her speech was frank and uninhibited and even her movements and gestures were bold and free. Maybe it was because she was well provided for, and her husband enjoyed respect as director of the Building and Construction Department. Wouldn't any woman in her position wish to show herself off in all her splendour? Yes, indeed, Kùlajša was a real *bàjbiše*. That was probably why, whenever she spoke, you could hear the same thing in her voice: 'No matter what I say, I'm always right.'

And moreover, Bejsek kept indulging her, encouraging her in her new role.

'Just give my wife the chance to show off, and she'll never stop', he joked.

'Why not? Everything comes from Allah, and I'm happy he's been so generous. And today he's given me yet another gift. Look at the good things at this *dastarhan*!' Kùlajša laughed again.

Nùralhan, feeling he ought to say something, spoke up:

'Well, if our womenfolk are happy, we're happy. Or is that a problem, my friend?' Now it was his turn to make a playful attack on Bejsek.

'Hear, hear!' Kùlajša was gleeful. 'After all, I studied with you – I'm an old university friend, too. Sometimes I need some moral support!'

'And you shall have it' said Nùralhan. 'Guar-an-teed!' He said the last word in Russian, speaking with mock gravity. 'If we don't stick up for the only woman in our company, how could we ever live with ourselves? Certain young ladies abandoned us' – here he winked mischievously at Bejsek – 'And went off with *žigits* from the agricultural institute and the vet school. But you, Kùlajša, stayed loyal to our university. You are our queen!' Nùralhan switched to Russian again. 'And now, my queen, perhaps you would deign to sit down at this modest *dastarhan*?'

'Deign? You'll have trouble getting her out of this hotel room now!' said Bejsek, with a hearty laugh. 'I think we should all sit down at table.'

Still joking happily, they took their places.

***

'What a lovely time we've had tonight – marvellous!'

After he had walked his guests home, Nùralhan returned to the hotel through the streets, which now blazed with light. He kept recalling the words Bejsek had said on parting. 'I can't understand what was so marvellous about it...' he thought. He went over Bejsek's words in his mind, trying to capture the intonation his friend had used, and yet he was unable to divine in them any hidden meaning.

Back in the provinces, there was simply no time to devote to such trifling concerns. In any case, he would never dream of mulling over every word and searching for hidden meanings in every utterance. He had hoped that this trip would be a chance to relax and unwind, but instead... The business side had been simple enough – he had simply had to report on the present state of construction and on any problems and requirements, and to hear their comments and recommendations. The remainder of the trip was to have been devoted to his old friends. But now here he was, trailing back to the hotel as if he had lead weights tied to his legs, with an uneasy feeling in his heart and all sorts of odd thoughts in his head.

What could Bejsek have enjoyed about our meeting? What was good about it? We weren't honest with one another, we didn't have a heart-to-heart conversation. Or was he just trying to make up for the fact they didn't come yesterday? If he had really wanted to catch up properly, he would have agreed to come to the restaurant. But they were in a rush to leave. Odd... And after that, to say 'What a lovely time we had! Marvellous.' I just don't understand it!

On the surface, everything had been as it should be. They had laughed and joked together. After a drink, the conversation had become livelier. But who had spoken? Only the guests, and mainly to praise the foodstuffs from the *auyl*. 'Oh, this home-made *ḳazy* is so good! What flavour! They don't know how to smoke meat like that in the city!' They had discussed the caviar too, which could only be bought for gold. 'Well, you're a dark horse! You must have some high-up connections back home? This costs fifty roubles a kilo.' 'And in any case', Kùlajša added, 'You can't find it in the shops.' Both conceded that rural directors must have a lot of influence, getting hold of any products they chose, even when there was a shortage. They had kept on in this fashion. Nùralhan had said nothing. He didn't feel like eating, but Bejsek and Kùlajša had assailed him: 'You've just been praising the good things you've brought from the country, and you haven't even touched them! Come on, try something!' And once again, friendly laughter had rung out around the table.

He kept hoping that all the witty banter and ironic remarks would end and they would have a more serious, heartfelt talk. But the snacks had all been eaten, the brandy drunk, the conversation had flagged, and still not a word had been said about their friends. As they left, Bejsek and Kùlajša had invited him to visit them.

Actually, at one point he had been on the verge of having a conversation with Bejsek. '*Astapyralla*[28] – how could I forget? The subject did come up, but then the moment passed...'

Now, every detail of this unpleasant scene came back to Nùralhan.

Bejsek had wanted to have a cigarette, and, despite his friend's protests, he had gone out on the balcony. Nùralhan was left with Kùlajša, who kept glancing at her husband before whispering,

'By the way, who came to see you yesterday in the end? Did Erġazy and Ķanat come?'

'Well, you never turned up, so what's it to you?' Nùralhan retorted.

He shouldn't have spoken so harshly, of course, but the words were out before he could think. Then, in an attempt to compensate for his lack of tact he had smiled, thinking as he did so, Idiot! Blurting out the truth, and then trying to make up for it by grinning like a fool.

Thankfully, Kùlajša seemed oblivious.

'Don't judge Bejsek too harshly' – she nodded towards her husband. 'He has his reasons, Nùralhan.' She lowered her voice to a whisper, still stealing surreptitious glances towards the balcony. 'You see, if they meet up these days, it always ends up in a row. They start arguing and shouting at one another. You know what men are like once they have a drink inside them. And that Ķanat especially – he flies into a rage and loses his head completely. He won't see reason, and he stops at nothing. He says things he'd never dare think, let alone say, if he were sober. He has no tact, and no caution. What kind of friendship can survive that? We don't enjoy meeting up at all any more...'

As the saying goes, a rider knows the foibles of his own horse: Nùralhan had come to know Ķanat's character very well. But though he had witnessed his friend's quick temper, he felt that this abuse was unmerited.

'I wouldn't say he was like that', he said with a dry smile. He was starting to feel uncomfortable, and had a sudden desire to laugh unkindly in Kùlajša's face.

'Oh, stop it!' she said. 'Don't pretend – Ķanat's always been like that.'

'It's the first I've heard of it.'

'Never mind him! Let him take care of it himself. But that's not all. We don't get on with Erġazy and his family, either.'

'Why ever not? He's your brother-in-law twice over!'

'Ooh, you fool! Here I am opening my heart to you, and look at you...' Kùlajša pouted and fell silent.

'Sorry, I didn't mean it. Tell me.' said Nùralhan amicably.

'What was I saying? Ah, yes. Well, last year, a neighbour from Erġazy's *auyl* came to try to get into the institute. So we fixed him up to study with a good friend of Bejsek's. As you know, you don't get something for nothing, so we

---

[28] *Astapyralla* – exclamation of indignation, fear.

asked them to get a present for the teacher to thank him. And Erġazy made a terrible fuss. Of course, Bejsek can help a few postgraduate students get taken on at the institute – thanks be to Allah, we do have some influence. But that Erġazy's got some cheek! He seemed to think it was up to us to pay for his favour! There's no pleasing a fool, as they say. They really messed us around. They didn't give a thing, needless to say, and the boy failed his exams. And now they won't forgive us, and they've all but stopped speaking to us. What it's got to do with us, I'd like to know? Some people!'

'Hmm. I see...'

'So, to cut a long story short, we're not friends any more. That's the way it is, now, we keep our distance, and none of us is prepared to make the first move. Erġazy's not so bad, but his wife! She was so offended she broke off all relations with us. Tell me, how can we sit at a table with that ungrateful pair?'

'So that's how it is with you.' Nùralhan had only just realised that Kùlajša was talking about her own sister. Now he was starting to understand why nobody had turned up to see him the day before except Ķanat. 'Well, look at you. You're becoming a real *bájbiše*! I think you fulfil all the requirements to be considered a woman *bi*.'[29]

'Stop it, you fool!'

'I mean it!

'Shh' Kùlajša rolled her eyes towards the balcony. Nùralhan turned and saw Bejsek coming back into the room. That was the end of their conversation.

And this meeting was what Bejsek had called 'marvellous'. Only now did he realise that he was wandering like a lost soul outside the hotel, unable to think of anything but his meeting with his friends. He was even tottering a little.

'So they want me to take sides with them and not to be friends with Erġazy and Ķanat any more? Or maybe they want me to help them restore good relations between them and the others.' It made his head ache to try to work it all out. 'No matter how badly you've quarrelled, it's never easy to part with old friends. I expect I got here at the painful moment when their friendship was breaking down, and they were all wanting to give me their side of the story?'

Nùralhan sighed deeply. His heart began to ache horribly. He felt trapped.

Apyrmaj, what should I do? Good grief! Yesterday, when Ķanat told me, I acted so calm and reasonable – but now? No – this won't do at all! I'll go to see them tomorrow and tell them to their faces – all of them. I have to say something...

***

---

[29] *Bi* – an influential figure in the power structure of traditional Kazakh society, elected from among the most distinguished, eloquent members of the community as one who proved his or her knowledge of the law. A *bi* would pass judgments on petty crimes, whereas serious crimes would be heard in the court comprising multiple *bies*. *Bies* also functioned as counsellors to khans and diplomats.

But neither on the following day, nor after did Nùralhan do as he had planned.

He went to see Bejsek first. As he thought about what he would say, he felt seriously worried. Should he tell him everything that was on his mind, in a tone of mild reproach? Or just drop a friendly hint and hope he would understand? But as it turned out, Bejsek had invited a whole crowd of people over to his house. Nùralhan could hardly say anything in front of a group of strangers. 'This *žigit* is from the Ministry, this is the Chief of the Building Administration in the neighbouring district, this fellow here is a representative from the Trade Union. These are my very best and closest friends', Bejsek explained, as he introduced his guests. 'Well', Nùralhan thought, 'I was hoping to have it out with Bejsek and Kùlajša, but now they're surrounded by new friends.' He didn't know anyone in Bejsek's circle. There was no question of a frank conversation. He had to sit politely at the table. All evening he was reserved and polite, and he left having achieved nothing.

Then he hoped to meet with Erġazy, but it turned out that he had left town because he had some urgent business in a neighbouring district. They had not even managed to see each other.

Only Ķanat did not desert his friend. He would call Nùralhan in the afternoon and look in on him every evening at the hotel. Nùralhan saw no point in talking to him about what had happened. After all, Ķanat had told him everything on the very first day.

And so, his few days in the capital passed, and with every day his distress increased. Unable to do anything, he felt more upset every day, and in the end, all he wanted was to be left alone. Just before he left, Ķanat managed to persuade his friend to come and visit him again, and saw him off to the airport.

At the airport, they wandered about talking of this and that, deliberately avoiding the subject that was tormenting them both. Nùralhan felt subdued. He did not want to reminisce any more about those wonderful times of youthful struggle and adversity when they had all been students together – he had no desire to bring up the subject. It was as if he was afraid that he might violate the sacred memory with a careless word. As for Ķanat, he did not enquire why his friend had become so silent. In all likelihood, he sensed the reason without having to be told. What sense was there in raking up the past?

So one left, while the other stayed. But for some reason, deep inside, they both were howling. Howling!

Translated by Rose France

DULAT ISABEKOV
(b. 20.12.1942)

Dulat Isabekov is a writer and playwright. He graduated from the philological faculty of Kirov Kazakh State University (now Äl-Farabi Kazakh National University). He worked as a senior editor of the State Committee for Television and Radio Broadcasting (1967–68), senior scientific editor for the Kazakh edition of the *Great Soviet Encyclopaedia* (1968–70), head of department at *Žŭldyz* literary journal (1971–76), editor at Žalyn publishing house (1976–80), editor-in-chief of the Repertoire-Editorial Board of the Ministry of Culture of the Kazakh SSR (1980–88) and director of Žazušy publishing house (1992–95). Currently, he is editor-in-chief of *Mädniet* journal.

Isabekov had his first short story, 'Žolda' (On the Road), published in 1963 in a collection of works by young Kazakh writers, *Zamandastar* (Contemporaries). He has authored dozens of prose collections and more than twenty plays, the majority of which have been staged in several countries, including Kazakhstan, Russia, Tajikistan, Turkey and Bulgaria. His most significant prose works include the novels *Beket* (The Stop, 1966), *Ašy bal* (Bitter Honey, 1969), *Mazasyz kùnder* (Restless Days, 1970), *Ķara šaṇyraķ* (Native Home, 1973), *Dermene* (Wormwood, 1966), *Tiršilik* (Life, 1975) and *Ķarġyn* (Whirl, 1980). His short stories have been translated into German, Czech, Hungarian, Bulgarian, Chinese, Turkish and Uzbek. Several of his works have come out in English: *The Little Pearl and Other Stories* (2014), *Song of the Swans* (2017) and *Short Stories Dedicated to the 25th Anniversary of Kazakhstan Independence* (2017). His first screenplay, for the 1975 film *Khrani Svoyu Zvezdu* (Cherish Your Star), was based on his short story 'Gauhartas'; it has been followed by a dozen other screenplays over the years.

He is a laureate of the State Prize of the Republic of Kazakhstan (1992), the International PEN Club Prize (2006) and the Platinum Tarlan Award (2006).

Growing Pains

By mid-afternoon, the heavy grey clouds of November pervaded the sky, yet appeared indecisive about what kind of rage to spew upon the bare earth below. At first, they released blankets of snow, but then followed with rain so relentless that the coal-black soil of the road turned instantly to slush.

This dark storm coincided with the seventh-day funeral gathering for Ķūrmaš and his wife Ajsùlu, who had recently died tragic deaths. The superstitious country folk whispered throughout the gathering – 'The sky is bewailing the sudden death of the young couple!'... 'The sky is shedding tears, thinking of the orphan they leave behind...' – as they interpreted the events of Nature in a such a way as to emphasise its inherent goodness.

It was a long time before the tears of mourning had dried from the eyes of those gathered, except the blood relatives of the deceased. When they began the final ritual of covering the grave with soil, Taṇat wept so ferociously that everyone began to weep again themselves, as they recalled shared experiences with the dead couple. Taṇat's lamentation also appeared to embody the definition and feeling of true, precious friendship.

He had spent a few days with Ķūrmaš's boy, Ǎulet. Ķūrmaš had many relatives in the *auyl*.[1] Taṇat was not family, and yet he shared the burden of the funeral and the seventh-day gathering.

After the gathering, only relatives came together, and still, he and his wife were welcomed among them. The family showed their appreciation to them.

'*Raķmet!*' said Tùrsyn, Ķūrmaš's close relative. 'Thank you!' He spoke on behalf of the core group of kinfolk: 'You have done our family a great service... one that many of us could not perform. Now, return to your work. Do not worry about us. When the fortieth-day funeral gathering is to be held, we shall let you know.'

A question had been playing on Taṇat's mind, which he did not feel brave enough to let pass through his lips. He had hesitated, but suddenly felt that the moment was favourable, and addressed the family.

---

[1] *Auyl* – socio-economic formation considered to constitute the heartland of the nation and a basis for an ethnic and cultural union of the nomadic community. Consisting of 50–70 yurts in the eighteenth century, it developed into its current permanent state of 'rural settlement' (of a minimum of 100 dwellers) when Kazakhs adopted a settled mode of life in the nineteenth and twentieth centuries. *Auyl* can also be used as a synonym for 'native land' and 'homeland', concepts revered by the Kazakhs.

'If you don't mind', he began, 'may I ask you a favour? In fact, this is the reason I have lingered here; it is preventing me from leaving... You know that Ķùrmaš and I became friends not gradually, but from birth and by the grace of God. We were born on the same day, at the same hour, in the same maternity ward. At school, we shared a single desk. We graduated our driving course together. We married on the same day, and we celebrated our weddings together. You all know this.

'But the truth is also that, even though two people may be born together and grow up together, it is not Nature's way that we should always live together. Therefore, after our marriages, we went our separate paths. Even so, our hearts never detached. I have two children, and Ķùrmaš and his wife have – *they had* – only one child.' Taņat cast a glance at Äulet. 'Had they not been taken away like this, they would have had two children, too. May you rest in peace... Ajsùlu...'

Taņat became so filled with emotion that he momentarily lost his ability to speak, and his words became indistinct. He wiped his watery eyes with a handkerchief. Members of the family tried to console him: 'Stop, Taņat, take hold of yourself.'

But he continued: 'Yes... Ajsùlu... may she rest in peace... she died bearing a child in her womb... how heartbreaking!'

Hearing these words, Tùrsyn's wife Safura dropped a tea bowl from her hands and exclaimed: 'Good heavens! What are you saying? Was our *kelin*, sister-in-law, pregnant?!'

She was not alone in hearing for the first time that Ķùrmaš's wife had died with child. The assembled relatives, their hearts already heavy, began to wail anew over the deaths. Embarrassed and ashamed that they had heard such news not from family, but from a friend, even a lifelong friend, Tùrsyn apologised: 'We get so caught up in our daily lives that we can forget to care for each other... Ķùrmaš's parents, *šal-kempir*, those elders who were once with us and are now committed to the earth, said: "When we die, each of you will go your own way." They were right. That we did not confide the news of the pregnancy of our *kelin*' – here he cast a look at his wife, as though blaming her – 'seems to be the start of us going our own ways. One day, we shall not even know which of us perishes where.' He took a deep breath.

At this point, Taņat returned to his speech: 'I have been thinking', he said, 'of adopting my old friend's son... Äulet has many relatives who can support him, of course, but if I can play my part in raising the only child my friend left behind, I would be carrying out my responsibility to him.'

Everyone in the family was stunned. Many among them looked down in silence, which lasted a long time. Taņat's proposal was clearly heartfelt and sincere, and spoke to the quality of his friendship with Ķùrmaš – a quality that was becoming rare among Kazakhs. But to let one of their own – Äulet – be adopted, as if there was no one else the boy could rely upon in the midst of such a large family... No; pride and honour would not permit them to accept Taņat's proposal.

Taṇat took great care neither to protest their final word, nor to say, 'you have taken the right decision'. He simply rose from his place, quietly, in surrender, and walked away.

'Should we have allowed Taṇat to take him?' wondered Älibek, Ķurmaš and Türsyn's relative, when the roar of Taṇat's truck outside grew fainter in the distance and faded to silence. 'Was he angry?'

'Nonsense', said a cousin. 'What are you saying! Is our kinsman like a lamb, to be tied up and given away because someone went off in a huff?'

'Stop', said Türsyn, calming them. 'There is nothing wrong with expressing one's wish to help, and we did not agree – so there is no need for further discussion, is there?' Indeed, the conversation was over; peace was restored to the house.

But Äulet felt lonely among his many relatives. He did not, in fact, know many of them well.

**

Six months passed. Ķurmaš's affluent relatives had stood firm as a matter of pride in not relinquishing Äulet to the care of an outsider, yet their initial enthusiasm – and the kindness they showed their young kinsman – gradually diminished. Indeed, it flowed away as drainage water from an irrigation ditch, as everyone resumed their greyish-brown, day-to-day lives.

Äulet had resettled in Türsyn's house, accompanied by some of Ķurmaš's and Ajsùlu's belongings. Türsyn, as his eldest uncle, was his nearest relative. In the ensuing half-year since he had moved in, deep-seated feelings that had never been spoken aloud began to find expression on the parts of both Äulet and the other members of the family. They grew as surely and as invisibly as a chick inside its egg, until one day they began to hatch.

Life is difficult, thought Äulet, if you have not been born into the family you live with.

Äulet had never accustomed himself to being one of the children in Türsyn's house, and as he tried to blend in, he felt himself drifting further apart from his adoptive family. Often, he would find excuses, after school was over, to return home at a late hour. He enjoyed playing with schoolmates, or walking alone in the garden or along the riverbank, full of thoughts. Generally, he preferred to remain outside until the noise of the other children, happy at home, subsided.

Türsyn, and his wife and children, noticed this behaviour and behaved toward Äulet with great kindness and sympathy; but this approach only awakened a youthful, rebellious anger in the boy, who did not wish to be pitied. Although sullen, he was, in some ways, older than his years. An invisible rift formed between Äulet and Türsyn's family, and widened steadily.

One day, Äulet returned late from school again. The family had had their meal and cleared the dishes, and were now busy with their own activities. No one paid any attention to Äulet, who went to his room, removed his day clothes and lay on his bed, adjusting his pillow. Suddenly his whole body shuddered, as though someone had stuck a needle into his heart. He was used to sleeping on the bed that had belonged to his father and mother, but now, he realised, his bed was different. Áulet opened the door to the room opposite his, and saw that Tùrsyn and his wife had replaced his parents' bed with their own, and vice versa.

He switched off the light and lay down to sleep, tearfully.

In his dream, he came across his father and mother, who were rising from their beds. Áulet burst into tears of joy upon seeing them again.

'You were dead', he said, 'and now you are alive again!'

His father smiled and replied: 'How could we leave you alone in this vast world? We have come a long way.' He continued: 'Do you remember, when I was alive, that I searched for my father, who was lost during the war? How I could not find any information about him? And then we received a letter from him. He wrote: "If I do not contact you, you appear not to search for me! Visit me, together with the daughter-in-law." We have visited him now; we shall soon go back.'

'Father, why doesn't he visit us himself?' Áulet asked.

'He cannot come here. The bomb that exploded next to him buried him under the soil. Only his head is sticking out.'

'Can't you dig him out, then?'

'No, we cannot. The soil has become solid.'

'Father, Mother, how peculiar you are – it is possible to dig up even stone, too!'

'No. My father will not allow us to do that. When the bomb exploded, his body was shattered. He has barely pieced it together. If you were to remove the soil, his body would fall apart again. So, we have not touched him. But we shall have to glue the body parts together again. We were about to start doing so when we received this telegram from you.' He passed a crumpled telegraph office form to Áulet. The following words were printed on it:

They have taken away your beds. Come quickly. Áulet.

'I did not send such a telegram, said Áulet, looking at his father in astonishment. But it was nice that you came here. I have missed you so much. I beg you, please do not leave anymore. Is that right? You won't go? Why do you keep silent, Mother? Why do you not smile now, why do you not cuddle me? You won't leave me anymore, will you?'

'We must', said Ajsùlu, suddenly pale. 'We shall leave. Look, just now we have received a telegram from your grandfather. Here it is!'

She placed a sheet of paper in his hand, exactly like the telegraph office form. On it, in the same typeface, the following words were printed:

My body is falling apart. Come quickly. Your father.

Äulet felt himself begin to panic. But his father, smiling as he used to, said:

'This is it. There is nothing for it; we must leave. Do not distress yourself. If they take your bed again, send another telegram.'

'No, no!' shouted Äulet. 'You won't go! You won't go anywhere! I miss our old home; I want to go home. I won't let you go – I won't let you go!'

Sobbing, he woke up and did not fall back asleep for a while, looking up instead at the pale ceiling. He felt sad that this encounter with his parents had been only a dream.

He remained awake. It had become his habit to awaken in the middle of the night or very early in the morning. He tried to fall asleep again as he had been able to do before, closing his eyes and lying still for a long time – but sleep would not come.

When he was four or five, he would lie next to his father and ask him to tell a fairy tale. Ķùrmaš would tell one, two, three: Äulet would never say, 'Alright, that's enough.' His father would begin to run out of tales to tell, and urge Äulet to sleep instead. But the tales would leave a deep impression on the boy, and instead of falling asleep, he would stay awake and travel to the faraway lands and underground kingdoms of the tales.

'Äulet... sleep. I must go to work early in the morning', his father would say.

'I can't!' Äulet would reply.

'Then count to one hundred.'

Äulet would then begin to count – aloud, at first.

'Äulet', Ajsùlu would say from the next bed, feeling both annoyed and on the verge of laughter, 'count silently'.

He then would start to count silently, up to one hundred, then two hundred, then three hundred... Then: 'Dad, I've counted to one hundred five times.'

Ķùrmaš, barely awake, would roll over onto his other side. Concealing his exasperation, he would say: 'Do not count the numbers themselves; enclose a thousand geese in a barn, and then let them go out, counting each of them. And be careful! Do not miscount.' Fascinated by this new form of entertainment, Äulet would construct a barn in his imagination, round up a thousand geese and then begin to count them, setting them free one by one. 'It really is much more fun to count the geese than to just say the numbers!'

Äulet strove to keep the correct count, carefully monitoring the geese as they departed through the small barn door, honking and waddling; but he would suddenly find himself miscounting and repeating numbers, so he would restart the count from the beginning. He would begin to feel dim, and could rarely exceed two or three hundred geese before sleep claimed him.

This method was failing Äulet now. He could count up to six hundred geese without slowing down. As morning approached, he decided to go outside, where a dozen hens picked lethargically at some rubbish in the yard. The November cold seemed to carry a touch of frost; the water in the yard from yesterday, in small potholes, was frozen. Äulet came to the side of the ditch at the front of the yard, pushed away the mint and reeds and dipped his hand into the clear, icy water. Deprived of its swift summer current, the water nevertheless flowed steadily and noiselessly. Within hailing distance, on the edges of the slope where carts passed, ice sheets appeared as white shells.

Áulet cupped some water with both hands and washed his mouth, enjoying the delicious flavour of mint. He repeated the action again and again, until his fingers lost sensation. He sat upright. His body felt frozen: he had left the house wearing only light clothes.

Suddenly, he felt warm breath on his neck and turned to look over his shoulder. But it was only Aḳtôs, his dog, who had accompanied him to Tùrsyn's house. Aḳtôs stretched and looked at his master, as if enquiring why he was sat by a ditch and washing in the dawn. Áulet hugged the dog's neck, patted his forehead and rubbed his cold nose. Aḳtôs had no objection, and stood silently, touching his nose to Áulet's temple and blinking. He was wondering, Áulet thought, why he had been moved from his family home and now sheltered in another house; why they had abandoned their former home; where his adult masters had gone. He was, Áulet believed, expressing his disapproval of this situation clearly. Aḳtôs licked his lips once and turned his head away.

Poor dog, thought Áulet, how can he know that in two or three days, he will long even for this life, once his only remaining loyal master departs for the city to go to boarding school?

For Tùrsyn had consulted with his relatives, and together they had decided to send Áulet to boarding school, the better to spare him from being a constant topic of idle gossip in the *auyl*. A new life – an absolutely mysterious, new life – awaited Áulet.

At first, members of his family visited him often in the city, one after another, demonstrating a determination to stay in touch. As it turned out, however, that was only in the beginning. Their visits later became rare, until soon no one visited him at all. The kindness shown by his relatives (who were preoccupied with their own lives) gradually dissipated, as heat in wintertime.

***

His life in the *auyl* now a thing of the past, Áulet sometimes thought about his family; but only one person had not forgotten him yet, and would not allow him to feel lonely: Taṇat, his father's steadfast friend.

Holidays were most painfully lonely for Áulet, and he looked forward impatiently to their end. Vacations were like boundless prison sentences. But human beings are born to adapt, and Áulet, too, mastered that law instinctively and became used to those times of year. After a week or two, he would begin to avoid people. His soul craved peace, solitude, privacy. He would borrow enough books from the school library to fill a bag, and would plough through them one by one. Sometimes he would even miss lunch.

He read from early morning until late in the evening. When he wasn't buried under a heap of books, his mind would soar beyond the pages and travel across many horizons. He often thought of his mother, or of his father's huge truck, and Ķürmaš's big teeth when he smiled. He reflected on the sad, colourless moments in his life after his parents' deaths, and thought of the sad eyes and unhappy circumstances of his orphaned dog.

Äulet would lie this way for a while before turning to the next page of the book he was reading, and would not pay attention to the passing of time. His thoughts were like an endlessly long, knotted rope.

Meanwhile, Taṇat had promised Äulet that he would come during the winter holidays and take him somewhere. But he was meant to arrive in the evening, and Äulet began to lose hope: something has happened, he thought. Other kids, who had been appearing on and off in the yard, finally disappeared altogether. Like Äulet, they were, perhaps, alone in their rooms; when family was late to arrive, the children often locked themselves into their little worlds and avoided being seen as waiting, again and again.

The headmaster of the boarding school, Mansürov, came twice to chat with Äulet. He mentioned the city's skating rink and told Äulet he would take him there. His smiling face reflected the same kindness, year after year.

Anger overwhelmed Äulet. His pride was injured. He wanted to stand and run outside.

Half an hour later, he did indeed go to the front gate, and sat on the small, wooden bench beneath the inscription Boarding School No. 4. It was late morning. The cold had not yet lessened in sharpness, and Äulet had sat on the shady side of the bench; he began to shiver.

A while after that, a red Zhiguli stopped and a tall, moustachioed man in a new sheepskin coat got out of the car. He came up to Äulet and asked, in a cheerful voice: 'Are you waiting for your father?' Äulet nodded instinctively, without knowing why. He didn't like the question.

'Yes, I am', he said quietly.

Just then, a boy, older by one grade, ran out of the yard and hugged the big man.

'Why were you late, Papa?' he asked, smiling, yet on the verge of tears. 'It's been two days since holidays began!'

The man clapped his son on the back, leaned forward to his head and inhaled. 'I was late because I had to collect your grandfather and grandmother and take them home. They are waiting for you there, too... and I bought a new bicycle for you...' Then he added, in a whisper and holding up his finger as though about to tell a great secret: 'I shovelled the snow on our land with a bulldozer, so that you can test the new bicycle: three hundred metres by fifty metres!'

'Hurrah!' said the boy. 'Well done, Papa!'

Father and son hugged each other again and laughed loudly. Then they noted that Äulet had left, and looked at each other.

'His father might be busy, too', said the man, answering his own question. The boy did not say anything, being familiar with Äulet's situation. 'Now, go get ready', said the man.

'I'm ready', said the boy. 'I was ready two days ago.' He then dashed into the main campus building.

I have to leave, Äulet thought, as he sat at his usual place in front of the window. I have to go... but where to? Anywhere. It doesn't matter. I just have to leave this place. I can't bear the headmaster's pitying looks.

His thoughts turned to the perennial flowers that grew across the gate to the *auyl* where he had lived before coming to the city, near the bridge a little higher up that road: his parents' graves.

'I have to go', he said aloud.

As he rose from his place, the other boy's head popped through the doorway.

'Come along with us if you like', he said tentatively, trying not to offend Äulet's dignity. 'We can go skating... make the dogs fight...'

'No, my uncle should come.' Äulet replied confidently. Hearing this, the other boy smiled brightly.

'Goodbye, then! See you soon!' he said.

The boy shut the door and left. A hush fell over the room. When Äulet looked out the window he saw Mansürov and the man in the sheepskin coat talking. They lingered there awhile, then bid each other goodbye. Immediately after the headmaster returned to his office, the groundskeeper came outside and began shovelling snow. The man was in the habit of doing his job with singular focus: he never took breaks or even raised his head until he finished clearing the yard. Thus, Äulet was able to sneak out the gate unnoticed. The groundskeeper did not notice him pass even when he was mere steps away.

***

The bus ran twice a day from the city to the *auyl*. Äulet caught the first one, took a seat at the back and looked out the window. He decided he would return on the next bus back. If anyone at the school enquired later, he could tell them he had gone for a walk around the city.

Every vacation, every holiday, made it clearer and clearer to him that he, as an orphan, had no one who would stand with him – not only when he was alone, but even if he faced death. The care shown him by teachers and the headmaster, for Äulet, was not *love* as such, but duty. They showed the same care for all the children; it was their job. Once free of such responsibility, they would not give a toss. All in all, he reckoned, no one would care if he lived or died.

Although he couldn't say quite why, in recent days he had found himself liking or trusting others less and less. His carefree, once-sincere smile had been pushed off his face gradually by a heavy countenance, like a dull day in autumn. He had begun to prefer solitude to communicating with others as he had once done: going for walks alone until fatigue set in, then curling up in his bed in the corner.

Having spent several years at the boarding school, Áulet was, by now, well acquainted with his fellow students and the teachers. Some had become good friends; others, distant rivals. His scholastic aptitude, open-mindedness and discipline had all been noted and praised. He had been especially cheerful, and listened attentively to his teachers' talks about justice, morality, kindness and intelligence; he had believed what they said as he had trusted in God.

Suddenly, all this trust had vanished.

He asked himself honestly: was this sudden? Or did it start when he was living with Túrsyn and his family, sleeping in the bed that had belonged to his parents? It wasn't the only item that had been taken: he would not soon forget how his parents' property had been divided among his relatives, who had squabbled over the belongings; or that he, the rightful heir, had not been taken into account. Even Aḳtôs, his dog, only ate the food that remained after Túrsyn's own dog had finished.

His parents' graves, two small mounds among many other graves at the top of a rise, had not been tended to. A crescent-moon symbol made of blue iron had been placed between the two mounds; but it had lost its colour, and was now faded and sad.

Áulet had been to his parents' graves for the first time, with Aḳtôs for company, during the first year he was away at boarding school – when he still visited his relatives every holiday. Whenever Aḳtôs heard his voice, he came running to him, barking and swinging his tail; as if that were not enough to express his affection, Aḳtôs would leap up onto Áulet's chest and make every attempt to nestle into his arms. Then he would gallop to the house and run back, barking and leaping. Áulet would let his dog lean against his chest, and he would pat his head and stroke his snout and neck. They would rub noses; Aḳtôs's nose remained ice-cold even in the July heat. The two were inseparable during these visits, parting only when Áulet needed to study.

When Áulet left again for the city, Aḳtôs would see him off right to the bus, unable to believe that his master was leaving him yet again, even when the bus shut its doors and drove off. Happiness is an illusion: experience proves that life is made up of cruel moments. Aḳtôs would remain there, lying down at the feet of strangers awaiting the next bus, comprehending his beloved master's intentions less and less with each bus roaring away.

When Áulet grew up, he learned an old Kazakh saying: If you want to torture a dog, separate it from its master.

**

A bird's-eye view of the *auyl* would reveal a settlement tucked neatly against a mountain slope, which looked as if it had been placed inside a straight, four-square frame. A thick layer of snow covered its houses and streets, rhyming them with the white steppe. Only the smoke that writhed from the chimneys provided confirmation of the presence of inhabitants below.

Entirely white houses built in the latest style flanked both sides of the main street. Cars drove back and forth down it continuously, flattening the snow on the road and turning it a brownish colour. Well to the east of the *auyl*, in front of a big, one-storied house, a large truck was running its engine and emitting clouds of smoke from its exhaust pipe. The smoke was unusual; because of the severe frost, it poured forth as if a tank had exploded.

Inside the house, a man in his forties was trimming his moustache and beard in front of a mirror. Taṇat was 'fixing himself up' in preparation for a visit to the city. He had to collect Áulet and bring him home. But it was late: he had not been able to leave work earlier. Through the open door of the kitchen, he could see his wife's silhouette. She was clearly angry about something, and was clattering the dishes. The mirror reflected this clearly.

'We don't have the time to take our own children to their grandmothers. Will they have to spend their holidays locked at home?' she demanded.

'I told you: I shall take them. Why must you repeat the same thing, again and again?' he replied calmly, addressing his wife's reflection.

'*When* will you take them?'

'Tomorrow. Or the day after tomorrow.'

Taṇat's wife grew angrier and said: 'Then I'll take them by bus myself! You can't resist not seeing that boy. You have two sons of your own, but your heart is pierced over someone else's son!'

'*Someone else's* son?' Taṇat shot his wife a spiky look. She saw that anger now sparked in his eyes, but held her position.

'Yes, your *friends'* son!' she said in an exaggerated tone, placing a skillet with *ḳujmaḳ* pancakes on the table. 'Maybe he's *your* son!'

Taṇat stared at her with fury for a long while. Feeling that perhaps she had gone too far, she remained silent. When Taṇat gathered his coat and was preparing to leave the house, his wife's conciliatory tone sounded from the kitchen, implicitly admitting her mistake: 'Won't you have your meal?'

Instead of a reply, the door slammed shut.

***

When Taṇat's truck stopped in front of the boarding school, he jumped out of the cab and hurried to the entrance, where he was greeted by Mansúrov, wearing eyeglasses and a serious expression. The headmaster had discovered earlier that Áulet was missing. The men greeted each other warmly; they were long acquainted now.

'Is Áulet here?' asked Taṇat, noting the worry on the headmaster's face.

'I hoped that you might have information!' he sighed. 'He was here in the morning. Now he is not in his room. What to do?'

'The fault is mine', said Taṇat after a brief silence. 'I promised the boy I would come yesterday. He might have gone to his family's home in the *auyl*, perhaps?'

'No', Mansůrov said, shaking his head. 'He would not go to them...' He elaborated: 'None of his relatives visit him any more. Have people become so heartless, even to their kin? Normally it would not be an issue, but the holiday period makes it difficult. Usually, he stays alone on campus. Poor boy... He is a sensitive child. I hope nothing bad has happened to him. And this beastly cold... Tomorrow we were supposed to go on an excursion together with children from another boarding school – but he disappeared suddenly.'

The groundskeeper approached them.

'Yes, *aḳsaḳal*?' said Mansůrov, using the respectful address for an older man. 'Do you want to say something?'

'Yes, I do. I will tell you something. Recently I found four cigarette stubs when I was cleaning the toilet. What a shame!'

'Only?' said Mansůrov, smiling. 'Maybe you can find more.'

'Do not make fun of me. It means the children smoke! They must be properly brought up!'

'Well', sighed the headmaster. 'Everybody uses the toilet. Moreover, we do not carry out educational work out there. If you see a child smoking, bring him to me.'

Mansůrov ushered Taṇat in and shut the door.

***

Äulet stood at the gravesite, contemplating the memorial marker that read:

The names of these two cherished people,
who sacrificed their lives to save children from fire,
shall never be forgotten.

Äulet had been in the habit of visiting his parents' graves when he felt lonesome. There was no grief or despair in his eyes, however; only the spark of decency. He was a reserved boy, with an expanding consciousness. It was dawning on him that his parents had lived very different lives from those around them, that they had lived *for other people*.

With his sleeve, he wiped snow off the gravestone portrait of his parents together and stepped back, looking at their smiling faces looking back at him.

'Don't worry', he said confidently. 'I am grown-up now.' Then he waved at them, smiling, and headed towards the bus stop.

He would make every effort to fulfil this reassurance to his parents, he thought, and walked along cheerfully. A storm had just begun to gather some momentum; and although the locals knew of his parents and of Äulet himself, no one was aware of the boy's presence.

A bus stopped, and people carrying suitcases, buckets and bags disembarked. Some carried fir trees for the New Year's Eve celebration. As Äulet boarded the bus, he felt someone's hand on his shoulder. He glanced back and looked right into the face of a man of average height, with an impressive black moustache.

'Äulet! Is that you?' said the man, smiling. He, too, carried a suitcase.

'Either get on, or get off!' muttered one of the passengers jammed at the front of the bus. 'Don't block the entrance!'

Perhaps it was the impending New Year's Eve that made the man a little cheerful; he gripped the boy's shoulders enthusiastically and ushered him off the bus, leaning forward to kiss him on the forehead. 'What are you doing here on such a stormy day? Why are you going back to the city without stopping at our home?' The man spoke non-stop. 'Why are you so serious? Do you not know me? I'm Türsyn! Your father's brother!'

'I know', replied Äulet formally. 'Greetings!'

Türsyn was taken aback by his nephew's cool expression and reserved words. But he persevered: 'Come on, let's go home. I'm glad that you have come to greet your elder uncle. Look at you, ready to depart so soon! The younger generation is growing up shallow-hearted, I suppose!'

With great reluctance, the boy followed the older man, who led him by the hand. On the way, Türsyn continued chattering. 'I am sorry we could not call in and see you! Work followed by more work. Goddamn work, it never ends! Don't be upset! You have become a grown-up boy, and you do not think to visit us yourself. How are your studies?'

'Not bad.'

'Our children also finished the term well. Today we are circumcising our youngest son; yesterday we slaughtered a two-year old horse. We are making a *sùndet toj*, a party to celebrate the rites. Your visit is excellent timing. Everyone in the family will be there.'

Suddenly he shouted at a person walking in the distance: 'Hey, Otaš! Stop! Äulet is visiting us!'

The man stopped, turned toward them and shouted back: 'Who?'

'I am telling you: Äulet. The son of Ķùrmaš!'

'Ahh! Walk faster, I'm freezing!'

Türsyn turned to Äulet and said: 'He is no distant relative to you; our fathers were siblings. He works at the poultry farm, a farmer who knows the business well.'

They drew nearer to Otaš, who said: 'Hey, is this the son of Ķùrmaš? Oh! He has grown up! Which year are you in at school?'

'First year of secondary school', Äulet replied, in measured tones.

'Good boy! I'll kiss you when I come to Tùrsyn's house in the evening – my hands are not free now…' The older man smiled at Tùrsyn. 'I am bringing car parts from the shipper in the next *auyl*. How many cases of vodka have you bought?'

'One for you, two for the rest.'

'If that's not enough, we can get more!' Otaš laughed. 'Well, see you in the evening.'

'OK. Good luck!'

They parted in different directions.

***

That evening, warming himself by the fire in Tùrsyn's home, with the extended family gathered for the *sùndet toj*, Otaš perked up and addressed Äulet: 'A boarding school! What is a boarding school for? As if you didn't have family! After the holidays, bring your papers and books – you will live in our house and study there.'

Many of the relatives sitting at the table murmured in agreement.

'Tùrsyn is right', Otaš continued. 'The younger generation is growing up with shallow hearts.' He turned back to Äulet: 'When you have children of your own, they will not know us at all. Even now, you do not know each other. Tell me, how many children do I have?'

Äulet looked on silently.

'You see', said Otaš, now indignant. 'You don't know! You don't even know my name…'

Otaš's wife intervened: 'Enough, do not shame the boy. When you drink vodka, you become sentimental! Most days, you deny knowing anyone, so who are you lecturing! Where were you, if you are so involved? If our young people do not know each other, it is your fault.'

'Ah, I'm only speaking my mind; what I know is—' But Otaš had no chance to finish his sentence, as his wife thrust a chicken drumstick into his open mouth. She continued to drink her tea, unconcerned.

The assembled relatives burst into laughter. When it subsided, Tùrsyn's brother Älibek took the floor. Äulet did not like how the man had sat at the table all night, puffed up, aloof with a superior air. He was short, with mischievous eyes, and his hair was slicked back as though licked by a giant tongue.

'It is a *toj* – celebration – today', said Älibek grandly, as if he had just made an important discovery. 'Yes… a celebration! A big celebration. I congratulate you on this occasion. However, there are good traditions and bad traditions. To circumcise a child… in this day and age, comrades…'

'Not *comrades*, but *kinsmen*', corrected Otaš, becoming heated.

'Our kinsmen are also our comrades', Älibek replied firmly. 'In modern times, this tradition does not sit well. It is old-fashioned. First of all, it poses a danger to the life of the child; second, he wastes time in bed, recovering. The thing about tradition is—'

'To the point!' cried Otaš, pouring more vodka.

'From the perspective of modern medicine—'

'Come, brother-in-law, put the medicine aside', Türsyn's wife Safura said, interrupting the speech. 'Add your good wishes to the occasion.' Several other of the women nodded and made approving noises.

'And what about your sons?'

'Leave his children, ask only about him.'

Ălibek pressed on: 'In short, I am against the circumcision...'

The women began to giggle among themselves. 'Well, considering his height', one of them whispered, 'do you think the rest is... all right?'

'What is there to be cut...?' laughed another.

Ălibek stammered, becoming angry now. 'In short', he repeated, 'for the celebration...'

'Yes, speak about this, rather!' someone remarked.

Otaš raised his shot glass. 'Yes, why not give it a rest, instead of blabbing on.'

'What are you blabbing about?' retorted Ălibek, who had not yet taken his seat.

'Why protest now, at the celebration table?' Otaš said. 'Why not speak your piece before the celebration? Where were you then? Was your mouth stuffed with millet powder?'

'Do not insult my honour!' Ălibek said, raising his voice. 'What else do you do but drink vodka? That's your thing, isn't it!'

'Oh, so you don't touch vodka? Do you mean to say you bought a Mercedes by saving your money in dribs and drabs?'

'Dear relatives!' Türsyn broke in. 'Let's not start. We each own a vehicle. In two days, the New Year will be here. Let's put our anger aside and raise a toast to it!'

'Indeed!' roared Otaš, delighted. 'And let me add that we all do well enough. The times have been good to us. Let's be kind to each other. To family!'

***

By the New Year tree, which glittered above the toys and gifts under it, Türsyn and Safura were now speaking privately with each other.

'Ăulet will go back tomorrow', said Türsyn. 'Should we give him some money?'

Safura was indifferent. 'What will he do with it?' she said. 'Aren't his clothes and food free there?'

'Yes... they are, but...'

'Wasn't Otaš boasting that the boy would come and live in his house and go to school? Where is he now? Let *him* give him money!'

Türsyn frowned and looked away before replying: 'Are we to send him away without money, that someone else should give him some? He's my brother's son! If he does not need money, let's buy clothes for him, at least.'

'We'll buy clothes during the summer holiday. He might lose them, anyway.'

Türsyn sighed and blew on his hands. 'You're a dark one', he said. 'Fine, let him go without a coin!'

'He's found family closer than we are. He is an outsider, anyway. Moreover, we have no money to give right now!'

'Right. It's difficult to talk to you. You have an answer for everything. I give up.' Türsyn turned and went outside.

***

Äulet made his way back to the bus stop the following morning, saddened by this contact with his family. Again, he felt his loneliness keenly.

As he waited, the bus appearing in the distance, he suddenly heard a voice call out: 'Hey, žigit!'[2]

Äulet turned his head quickly to the source of the voice, and saw Taṇat looking at him, smiling. He ran and clung to his neck.

'Greetings', Taṇat said, as the boy kept him in an embrace a while longer. 'This time you seem to have missed me more! I learned you were returning to the city, so I came to take you back... What is the matter? You look unhappy...'

'Taṇat aġa,[3] do you have many relatives?'

'I am not blessed enough with family. But I have some.'

'Well, I have many...'

'Right. Come, let's go to the car.'

As they were driving, Äulet suddenly asked: 'Taṇat aġa, tell me please – how did my father and mother die?'

Taṇat looked at him in surprise. 'But... you know the story well.'

'One more time', said the boy. 'I want to listen to it again.'

Taṇat shook his head. 'Well', he said, 'your father and I went to school together. We sat at the same desk. Up to graduation, we were inseparable. We graduated the driving course together as well. To our surprise, we were also in the same barracks during our military service. People laughed at us, joking that we were dating... We did not even have dinner without each other... We were married on the same day, too. But after that, life seemed different. As friends, we became a little farther apart than previously.'

'At first, it was you who was in love with my mother, wasn't it?'

---

[2] *Žigit* – generally denoting a 25- to 40-year-old male, the term can also be used as an honorific indicating bravery, endurance, fortitude and being true to one's word.

[3] *Aġa* – respectful form of address to an older man, which can be translated as 'brother', 'uncle'.

Taṇat braked hard, and his truck skidded to the edge of the road. He fastened his eyes on Äulet. 'Who told you that!'

'I heard.'

Taṇat exhaled. 'Someone from the *auyl*, probably', he muttered. 'Look, you're not a kid anymore, Äulet. Maybe it is good for you to know. I became acquainted with your future mother first, yes. Later, your father got to know her as well. I saw that he fell in love with her. I also knew she had the same feelings for him. It was a foregone conclusion. I did not get in the way of their relationship.

'Anyway, we married at the same time, as I've said, and celebrated our wedding party together. After she graduated, your mother came to the *auyl* as a kindergarten teacher. It was an old, wooden carcass of a building. When the children had their lunchtime nap, a fire broke out. Even now, no one knows the cause. In a flash, it spread rapidly. Ḳùrmaš realised that the kindergarten was on fire by the smoke; he drove there as quickly as he could and burst into the building. There were other people, of course, but the two *auyl* firefighters were not to be found at their station at that moment; perhaps they had been sent elsewhere on business. These things happen.

'The flames were spreading everywhere; the others were afraid to enter. Almost everyone had got out in time, but there were two or three children still inside, suffocating from the smoke. Your parents ran for them. A moment later, the building collapsed. They were able to throw two of the kids out the window in time. The last one was a girl. The boy wasn't injured, but the girl was hospitalised with a broken leg. She later recovered.'

Moved by the retelling, Taṇat was silent. Neither he nor Äulet spoke for a while.

Then Taṇat said: 'By the way, the girl is in the same city as you now. If I remember correctly, she is your age. Same year at school. Her surname is... Serikbaeva. Yes, Serikbaeva. Her father was a mechanic. Later, he moved to the city.'

Äulet stared at Taṇat for some time, and stayed still. Taṇat, somewhat discomfited, averted his eyes.

'So. You love me... only because you loved my mother.'

Taṇat was taken aback, and then became enraged and slapped Äulet's face. Äulet did not cry. He sat there, still staring. Not knowing what else to do, Taṇat also sat, unmoving. The boy opened the door and slowly began to exit the cab. 'Goodbye', he said.

Taṇat pulled Äulet back into his seat. 'No!' he shouted. 'You will go with me!' But he leaned his head on the steering wheel, and whispered: 'I'm sorry, Äulet...'

Äulet looked at him and said: 'Well, let's move on.'

Taṇat started up the truck and they began to drive again.

***

Áulet walked down a very long school corridor. Everyone was in class but him. He stopped before a door marked '5-A'.

When the bell rang, students began bustling out of their classes for recess. The door to 5-A opened and more young people spilled out, followed by their teacher. Vigilantly, Áulet watched them emerge. Four or five girls stopped in front of a window and began chatting. Áulet walked towards them slowly, and they stared with some apprehension at the strange boy approaching them.

'Are you from 5-A?' he addressed them, even though he knew they were.

'Yes', smiled one of them.

'Will you tell me... Is there, in your class, a... a girl with the surname Serikbaeva?'

'Yes. She is an excellent student!' replied one of the girls.

'Can you point her out?'

'Sure', replied the second girl, and ran to the door. 'Dana!' she called. 'Someone wants to see you!'

Dana came out of the classroom. She was a pretty girl, above average in height, and wore white bows in her hair like big butterflies. She smiled half-warily. Áulet was astonished when he saw her, and became tongue-tied.

'Are you looking for me?' she asked Áulet sweetly.

'Yes... it's me...'

'I don't know you.'

'Me neither...'

The other girls, watching this scene, began to laugh all at once, embarrassing Áulet terribly. But he recovered enough to ask: 'Your father used to work as a mechanic in our *auyl*, didn't he?'

'Yes', Dana replied, smiling quizzically.

'My father was a driver. And my mother... was a kindergarten teacher.'

The smile disappeared from Dana's face, and she raised her eyebrows. She was disconcerted, and not a little impatient. 'So, then?'

'After, then... they... I am – I am Áulet...'

'Áulet! You're Áulet?' The girl exclaimed, barely able to control herself; she embraced him, then stepped back and ran into the classroom, covering her face with her palms.

The other boys and girls had no idea what had transpired, and some of them ran after her. Dana was sat at her desk with her head in her arms, weeping. Two boys, fancying themselves the defenders of Dana's honour, confronted Áulet.

'What did you do to her?' demanded one of them aggressively.

Áulet said nothing.

'I'm speaking to you! Answer me!' The boy took hold of Áulet's shirt collar.

'You wouldn't understand', said Áulet calmly.

'*What*! Look at this genius! Marat, will you knock some sense into him? I don't want to dirty my fists!'

The second boy, Marat, threw a punch at Áulet's chin; Áulet recoiled, and before Marat could strike him a second time, he advanced, grabbed the boy's arms and twisted them behind his back. Neatly, confidently, he flipped the boy face-down.

Marat, on the floor, his pride extinguished, asked in bewilderment: 'Are you a wrestler?'

'None of your business. Go, now!'

The two boys scrambled and were about to run away when Äulet shouted after them: 'Hey, not there! Go to Dana!'

The two boys stopped and went into the classroom. Äulet remained standing in the corridor, unsure what to do. A teacher poked his head around the end of the corridor and called him: 'Hey! Boy! Come here!'

**

Taŋat and Äulet sat in the cab of the truck, in front of the boarding school.

'So, you have become a *žigit*', Taŋat said, ironically. 'Fighting doesn't make you a man, though. How did you find that girl?'

'There are only a few schools in the city', Äulet replied. Then, coolly, maturely, he added: 'And it's not "fighting" if it's self-defence.'

Taŋat shook his head. 'I feel responsible. I am failing to give you my best efforts. Forgive me for that. I hope you do understand everything.'

'Last Sunday, I was at Dana's house. Her parents turned out to be nice people. In summertime, they will take me to Antalya with them.'

'I see...' Taŋat threw a look at Äulet unsmilingly and said, in quiet tone that betrayed a little jealousy: 'Yes, Antalya is far better.'

Both of them sat silently for a while.

'Taŋat *aġa*', said Äulet. 'May I ask... Do you love your wife?'

Taŋat looked at him, rattled again by yet another surprise question from the boy.

'Äulet', he said, as pleasantly as possible in his deep voice. 'Please, do not ask such questions.'

'All right', said Äulet, his own voice deepening.

Two boys approached the truck and knocked on the fogged window of the cab. It was difficult to make them out, so Äulet wiped away the mist with his palm. It was the two boys with whom he had fought.

'What are you doing here?' asked Äulet.

'Hey, Äulet!' Marat called. Äulet opened the door. 'Good day', said the boy, looking at Taŋat.

'We came to you', said the other boy, 'to tell you that this coming Sunday is Dana's birthday. Shall we go see her?'

'We shall!' said Äulet cheerfully. 'What kind of gifts shall we give?'

'I don't know', said the other boy.

'What's not to know!' said Marat. 'My cat gave birth to five kittens. We can take her three kittens, one from each of us.'

'And I have three lottery tickets', said Áulet. 'My relatives gave them to me as gifts when I went to the *auyl*.'

'Excellent! Three kittens, three lottery tickets!' Marat clapped his hands. 'Well, we're off. See you tomorrow!'

When they had gone, Taṇat asked: 'Do you study together?'

'No, we don't', replied Áulet smiling. 'We fight together…'

***

Álibek's house was austere, with nothing superfluous in it. He was a meticulous, competent man; the rooms were compact, like his personality. He rarely committed a misstep.

His wife was eating soup in the kitchen, alone, when the door opened slowly and Álibek entered. He looked perplexed.

'What's going on?' she said. 'Why are you so late?'

'Žamal, I don't know what to do' he replied.

'Your face has turned pale! What's happened to you?'

Álibek looked around, as if checking whether or not anyone was listening. 'Come here!' he said.

'But there's no one around… what is it?'

He looked around again, and whispered in her ear. Žamal's eyes went wide. She sat there, immobile, then rose up as though resurrected. 'Get ready, put your coat on!' she said to her husband.

'*You* put your coat on. I have not taken mine off.'

***

Tùrsyn and his family were watching television when Álibek and Žamal entered. They were nonplussed by the couple's sudden visit.

'Is everything OK?' asked Tùrsyn, concerned. 'Come sit at the head of the table. Children, please lower the television volume. What is going on?'

'All is well', said Álibek, casting a glance at his wife.

'But you look so alarmed… Your faces…'

'Our faces? No, no… Perhaps it is the influence of the spring harvest', said Žamal, smiling tightly.

'The spring harvest?' wondered Tùrsyn aloud. 'Can it have such an impact on office workers…?' Then, to his wife in the kitchen, he called: 'Safura, cook some meat!'

From the kitchen, Safura called back: 'Just a moment!' The clatter of dishes was heard.

'Oh! Do not trouble yourselves', said Álibek and Žamal, chiming in together. 'We'll be leaving shortly…'

'No, you will not!' Tùrsyn turned to his son. 'Máden, run to the shop, please.'

'Father, in ten minutes, the hockey starts', protested the boy. 'Ask Serik, he doesn't understand hockey anyway…'

'You ought to be ashamed of yourself! You are in secondary school; he's in primary school, and too young to go to the shop by himself! Come on, run, you'll be back in time.'

'*You'll be back in time*', said little Serik, taunting his brother joyfully. 'I'll turn off the television until you return. Then hockey will start later.'

Măden rubbed his forehead and stood up.

'Ah, we are in a hurry', Ălibek said, but Žamal kicked him under the table, and he added quickly: 'But, er, we can go by car, then you'll be sure to be back in time.'

The boy looked at them and said, logically: 'Then why not go yourselves?'

'Hmm, yes, I suppose I can—'

Tùrsyn interrupted and scolded his son: 'You would send a guest to the shop?! Get going this very instant!'

But Ălibek insisted, and, driving back from the shop, he stopped the car and spoke to the boy: 'Do you remember, Măden, some time ago, I gave you something…'

'When?' asked Măden, straining to recall.

'In wintertime. At the *sùndet toj.*'

The boy shrugged his shoulders noncommittally.

'Perhaps you forgot…? Lottery tickets.'

'Ah, I do remember', said the boy, laughing.

'Good lad!' He patted Măden on the back, relieved. 'Clever boy! Well, tell me – where are they now?'

'Who?'

'What, "who"? Those – what I am telling you, the lottery tickets!'

'Ah. I gave them away.'

'Gave them…?' Ălibek began sweating, and his voice took on an imploring tone: 'Tell me… please… who did you give them to?'

'*Aġa…* What is the problem?'

'*Who did you give them to?*'

'To Ăulet! On the same day you mentioned. I gave them as a present, because I did not have any money to give…'

'Oh…' Ălibek was greatly alarmed, but smiled artificially, trying not to show the boy his feelings.

'Why, do you have regrets?'

'Me? No. Why would I regret it? There was a whole pack of lottery tickets; I regret that I did not give them all away!'

'Ah, OK… Let's go, I'll miss the hockey. Russia and Canada are playing. Are you a hockey fan?'

'Yes, I am! Very much! I'm an avid fan!' Ălibek raised his voice to convey an enthusiasm he hardly felt, his mind preoccupied with other thoughts.

Măden stared at him strangely.

***

Tùrsyn swept his arms upward, baffled, and replied to his wife: 'I don't have a clue why they came... or why they left!'

'They didn't even stay for a meal', Safura remarked.

'They didn't even let us open the vodka', added Tùrsyn, looking at the three bottles on the table.

'Măden, what did he say to you?'

Măden was stationed in front of the television, absorbed. He seemed on the verge of passing through the screen. The hockey game was heating up.

'Măden', Safura called again, going over to tap her son on the shoulder, 'did he say anything to you?'

'Yes', Măden replied without taking his eyes away from the screen.

'What did he say?'

'He asked about a lottery ticket... Mother, please, step aside!... Come on, come on... GOAL! Well played!'

'Lottery...?' Safura repeated. Husband and wife looked at each other.

'What kind of lottery...?' Tùrsyn began.

But Safura appeared to have understood something. 'A-ha!' she said. 'There is always a reason. He is not someone who takes a single step without a reason. Wait... Măden, what did you reply to him?'

'Mother, please, the game...'

'No. What did you say to him?'

'I said that I had given the lottery tickets to Ăulet.'

'To Ăulet?! Is that true?'

'Yes, yes... Come on, come on... pass!... Oh, what a pity!'

Safura motioned to Tùrsyn, and they went to another room.

'Do you see?' she asked, when they were alone.

'Not at all', Tùrsyn replied.

'I know what this is about.'

***

Outside the shop, two or three men chatted noisily.

'They say they do not have the ticket!'

'They gave it to their nephew, who is studying in the city.'

'Ah! They must have been too stingy to give him money instead. Serves them right!'

'How are they going to get it back?'

'They are always lucky! They have a Mercedes that they won. As for me, I have never found even a coin in my life. Amazing, isn't it...?'

They spotted Otaš in the distance, drawing nearer, carrying an inner tube on his shoulder.

'Hey, Otaš!' one of them called. 'Why are you not celebrating?'

'Celebrating what?' he replied.

'Your tyre...'

He passed his hand gently over the rubber of the inner tube. 'Yes, it's been well mended', he said, delightedly.

'Yes, it was, it was mended very well!' the other man said, without actually looking at the tube.

'So, what is the reason for standing here?' Otaš asked, immediately realising something else was on their minds.

'Well, when are you going to celebrate the Mercedes you won?'

'It is not ours. It is Áulet's. The lottery ticket was gifted to him, and he won it. He shall have it. But I can celebrate *that* with you.'

'So you say. But what does the person say who *gave away* the ticket? Here is the heart of the matter!'

'Amazing', repeated the man who had never won anything. 'I have never found a coin on the road or on a bus. Why is that so?'

'It means you've never lost anything, either!' said Otaš, entering the shop. 'You have to lose to find, my brother! To lose!' The group followed him in.

The man contemplating his luck did indeed look lost. 'Interesting', he mused to himself. 'What should I lose? What if I have nothing to lose...?'

***

Mansůrov greeted Álibek and Žamal with good cheer, and brought them into his office. He was pleased that Áulet's family had come to visit the boy. He nodded in acknowledgment of the time they were spending, and said: 'I understand how busy you are; we live in an age governed by time pressures. So much work. Thank you for coming. It is difficult to expect kindness from a child who has not been loved.'

'Certainly', smiled Álibek. 'We are not distant relatives of the boy! Our fathers were siblings; if we do not visit him, then who will? It is just a matter of being work-bound, as you say.'

'His parents were closer to us during their lifetimes, more than to others', Žamal added. 'We always had meals together. They passed away too young, poor souls. They were noble. And Áulet is also growing up brave, like his father.'

'You are right', Mansůrov agreed happily. 'He is devoted to his friends. He is intolerant of injustice. Why, recently he ended up fighting to protect a girl's dignity.'

'A fight!' Álibek and Žamal exclaimed together. 'Why fight?'

'Do not worry', the headmaster reassured them with a smile. 'We discovered that the other boys initiated the fight. In general, he is the most disciplined boy in his class.'

'Yes, this is evident. Last time, on his holiday, he stayed at our house', said Álibek, shooting his wife a sly look.

She played along: 'He taught our children new things. He is very sensitive, addressing us as *aġa* and *apaj*.[4] You know, he is always offering to help: "What help do you need, what would you like me to do?" This school clearly provides an excellent example.'

'Thank you!' Mansùrov could not resist showing his pride. 'All our parents appear to be as appreciative. Do come during the next holiday, would you? Don't let Äulet stay alone in school.'

'Oh, what are you saying!' Älibek spread his hands and drew back as if he'd taken offence. Žamal also feigned resentment, and pursed her lips. 'Even *before* the holiday, we shall visit him many times. Not like before, thank God; now things are going well.'

'I apologise', said Mansùrov, embarrassed. 'Sometimes the educators are the ones who make mistakes!' He laughed loudly to defuse the tension.

'You're right', Žamal said, also trying to lighten the mood. 'They do make mistakes. There is one teacher in our *auyl*. In the middle of the lesson he often asks to be reminded what grade he is teaching, and if the children say, "the seventh grade", he might say, "What! Why didn't you tell me that at the beginning of the lesson?"'

She laughed heartily, thinking that the men would join in, but saw immediately that the headmaster was smiling only faintly. Älibek glanced at her angrily. Her smile faded, and she became embarrassed herself.

'Hmm', said Älibek, redirecting the conversation. 'May we see Äulet today?'

'Of course, of course', replied Mansùrov, looking at his watch. 'Their classes finish in an hour. Let me show you to his room.'

***

With the inner tube around his neck, Otaš walked unsteadily down a muddy slope, singing a song that evidently consisted of only two lines, repeated with the same melody.

Oh, my love… oh, my dear…
Oh, my love… oh, my dear…

Suddenly his wife appeared in front of him, very animated. She had clearly been searching for him.

'Shame on you!' she said, upon seeing that Otaš was drunk. 'What on earth were you "celebrating" tonight?'

Startled, her husband regained some self-control and grew serious. That he was indeed drunk was never going to be anything but plain as daylight, anyway.

'No special reason', he said. 'We ourselves' – he tried to reply standing straight – celebrated.'

---

[4] *Apaj* – respectful form of address used when talking to an older woman.

'What?'

'This! An inner tube…'

'Ah, why don't you jump in the river and drown together with your inner tube!'

'It won't sink in water.'

'I'll *make* it sink!' retorted his wife angrily. 'You've run out of reasons!'

'Well, there was another reason. We celebrated Áulet's new car…'

His wife stared silently at him for a while, then asked: 'Can you drive now?'

'Of course! I'll show you what real driving is! Where is the car?'

'Sit', she said when they arrived at the car, which had been parked at the edge of the road. Then, changing her mind, she said: 'No, I'll drive. You'll make a mess of it.' She took the driver's seat and started the engine.

'Why are you staring at me? Look back… back! Tell me if there are any cars behind us.'

'No, there aren't.'

She reversed the car, but immediately they felt a great thump, followed by the sound of someone cursing. A spray of hay covered the windows and darkness permeated the interior of the car.

They got out and saw that they had reversed into a wagon loaded with hay. The rear left fender of their car was damaged.

'You drunken rascal!' Otaš's wife cried. 'What did I say? I asked if there were any cars behind us!'

'True', Otaš conceded, adding: 'But that's a *cart*, not a *car*…'

His wife's eyes widened in fury; she was lost for words.

The thin and enraged cart-man, who had also tumbled over the car and into his hay, stood up. Straw clung to him. 'I'll take you to court!' he raved.

'Take *him* to court – *him*!' she said, pointing at Otaš. 'He said there were no cars when I asked… Troublemaker!'

'He was right!' the cart-man said. 'It is not a car, but a cart! And your husband wasn't driving, you were! You will bear the responsibility!'

He continued his tirade: 'Yes, you! And last year, you drove over my only tupping ram! It's true! You did it right with this very car! The only tupping ram in this *auyl*! I brought it from Türkistan; now you can't find one anywhere. That time I forgave you, but now I won't!'

'It's true, there are no tupping rams anywhere', Otaš agreed.

'Why are you blathering!' his wife said, glaring at him 'You want to see me convicted? OK, let me be convicted, then!' She turned to the cart-man. 'Go to your court!'

The cart-man unfastened his horse from the cart and climbed up on the animal, bareback.

'If… well, if you pay a fine, I won't go to the police', he said, turning back after a short distance.

'How much?'

'Five thousand tenge.'

'Up yours!' The woman gestured rudely at him with her thumb in between two fingers. 'One thousand tenge.'

'Five thousand', said the cart-man stubbornly.

'One thousand five hundred...'

'If you make me even angrier, I'll increase it to *ten* thousand tenge', he replied.

'Hey, come here, please', Otaš said to him, beckoning. The cart-man climbed down from his horse and walked over.

'Here', said Otaš. 'Here.' He walked with the man over to the other side of the cart, behind the scattered bales. When the pair returned to where Otaš's wife was standing, the cart-man was in good humour.

'Well', he said to her. 'Two thousand, then.'

She counted out the notes and gave them to him.

The couple returned to the car, and the wife resumed driving. Soon they pulled onto the asphalt road that led to the city.

'What did you say to him?' she asked Otaš. 'He became so cheerful.'

'One must know how to find a common language!' Otaš boasted. His wife looked at him suspiciously. Feeling more himself, he looked around and added: 'Hey, where are we driving to?'

'To see Äulet.'

'Why?'

'Quiet; I'll explain later. You'll get us into an accident.'

Otaš saw then that the speedometer indicated a hundred and forty kilometres per hour. He shut his eyes and whispered, *Audhu billahi minash shaytan ir rajeem...*[5] and wiped his face with his palms.

***

'Today you will stay with us here', said Žamal to Äulet in her most caring voice, gesturing to the hotel suite. 'We obtained permission from the headmaster. In the morning, we'll show you the city properly, and then take you back to school.'

'Thank you very much', said Äulet, delighted.

'For you, we ordered the best suite in the best hotel in town.'

'Are you on holiday?'

'No. To visit you, we got a day off. Älibek, will you go to the snack bar and bring something for Äulet?'

'Oh, I don't need anything, *apaj*', Äulet said. 'We've just had dinner...'

'No, no', said Älibek, 'there is still time before going to bed. You will get hungry – I'll be back soon.' He went out into the corridor.

'*Apaj*, will we go to the park tomorrow?'

---

[5] A rendition of the verse of the Qur'an: 'I seek protection in Allah from the accursed satan'. [Ed.]

'Yes, any place you wish.'

'There's a girl in another school. Her name is Dana. You probably do not remember, but my father and mother rescued her...'

'Yes, yes... I do remember.'

'Can we take her with us?'

'Certainly! Why would that be a problem? We'll pull out all the stops for Äulet's friends! Let's go to her house tomorrow and collect her. How are your studies?'

'Good.'

'Well done. The headmaster also praises you.'

Älibek returned to the suite with a number of food parcels, wrapped in paper.

'Oh, you're fast', said Žamal. Show us what you brought... Fried chicken, red caviar, mango juice... even kiwis! Where did you find them?'

'When there's a will, there's a way!' Älibek laughed in his squeaky voice.

'Äuletžan[6] has a friend he likes', said Žamal, 'a nice girlfriend. We have decided to take her around with us tomorrow.'

'Excellent!'

'Älibek *aġa*', asked Äulet after some time had passed. 'Why did you not visit me before? Sometimes... I was homesick for the *auyl*.'

'Forgive us, Äuletžan', said Älibek, softening his voice. 'It will not happen again. You have the right to resent us.'

'No, I am not resentful', said the boy, speaking in a very adult manner.

'From now on we shall visit you regularly. Would you like to go to Ystyķkôl this summer?'

'Certainly! For real?'

Älibek drummed his fingers on the table. 'We shall go to Ystyķkôl together.'

'What will your brother say?' asked Žamal.

'I give my consent!' Älibek replied, and they slapped their palms together.

They remained silent for a while. Älibek walked to the television and turned it on, and then moved to the other room, where Žamal joined him.

'I don't think he won anything', she said.

'Impossible! Look here' – he produced a notepad, in which a series of numbers had been taken down – 'everything is written here. Maybe he doesn't know about it yet?'

'Possibly. Let's ask him casually.'

'How should we ask?'

'You ask', she said.

'No, you ask', Älibek insisted.

'Fine', she replied. 'You have your heart palpitations; I'll ask.' With that, she rejoined Äulet in front of the television.

'Oho! Roza Rymbaeva is singing', Žamal said, sitting next to him.

---

6   *Žan* – lit. 'soul', appended as a suffix to express affection.

Äulet did not say anything, but kept watching. When the song ended, Žamal turned to him and asked, in a mild voice: 'Äulet, if you suddenly' – and here she laughed insincerely – 'won a Mercedes in the lottery, what would you do?'

Äulet laughed in turn, genuinely, and replied: 'Then I would give it to you.'

Žamal put her hands on her chest – and fainted.

'Älibek *aġa*! Älibek *aġa*!' cried the frightened boy, holding Žamal and preventing her from falling.

Älibek, who had been listening to their conversation behind the door, leapt into the room. 'She has a heart problem', he said calmly. 'Don't be afraid, don't be afraid... Just a moment, just a moment!' Together they set Žamal on the bed.

'Älibek *aġa*, shall I call for a doctor?'

'No need. I'll give her the medicine now. Bring me some water.'

When Äulet left to fetch water, Älibek leaned over his wife and whispered crossly into her ear: 'Ah, so this is how you show your strength? I would have asked him myself! Come to your senses, quickly!'

Äulet returned with the water; Älibek took a big sip for himself, and sprinkled the remainder onto his wife's face.

Žamal's eyelashes began to flutter.

***

Otaš and his wife had booked a similar suite right below the one currently occupied by Älibek, Žamal and Äulet, and were entering it when the wife took note of her husband's baggage: 'Put the *tyre* away!' she said. 'Is it glued to your neck?'

But Otaš was now completely sober. 'There is a hole in it', he said. I'll mend it now... Look, I have glue with me...'

'Yes, what you don't do at home, you're doing best here! Because of you, we were late for everything!'

They began to settle in.

'How much do we all need?' said Otaš, considering everything. 'It is absolutely shameful.'

'Why? Is he family? Yes, he is. What is there to be ashamed of?' She paused. 'I wonder where they took the boy... all of this because of your carelessness! Anyway, I won't give them anything.'

'Let's go to the snack bar. I'm hungry.'

'Sit here. I'll bring food up. Otherwise, you'll just drink vodka again.'

Otaš took the inner tube from around his neck and sealed the cap tightly again before stashing it under the bed.

His wife was about to make her exit when they heard a voice say: 'Good evening!' They turned to see Türsyn and Safura entering the room. Otaš jumped up.

'Where are you two coming from?' said Otaš's wife.

'We wanted to buy clothes for the children', Safura said. 'What about you?'

'We came here to fix the car. Someone hit it last night and damaged it.'

'While it was parked?'

'Yes. Just at the place where it was parked.'

'What's happening to people?' Safura sighed.

The two women proceeded to the snack bar together, leaving their men in the suite. After a moment's pause, Otaš's wife said to Safura: 'Tell me honestly: are you really only visiting the city to buy clothes for the children?'

The other woman stared at her. 'Yes', she replied, unwilling to reveal the real reasons.

But Otaš's wife noted the lie in her face and eyes. 'It seems that Älibek and his wife are also here', she said. 'They took Äulet! Speculator hucksters! What terrible people!'

'I know', Safura said at last.

'What?'

'That Älibek and Žamal took Äulet... and why you have come here, too.'

'To be honest', Otaš's wife said, looking at her intensely, 'he has no closer relatives than us.'

'Oh, sure!' Safura said ironically. 'That's why he came and stayed in your home every holiday! You came here regularly seeking Äulet, and knocking on the door of his school!'

'And you? What about you?'

'Last holiday, he stayed with us, in our house. You didn't even invite him for a meal! And now you claim you are closest. Shame on you! It was we who arranged for him to attend the boarding school!'

'We were planning to take him to live with us. From this September, he will live in our home and go to school!'

'Why didn't you take him last September?'

'... We didn't have time.'

'You didn't have time? You didn't have the *intention*! Here is the hidden motive!'

There was a long silence. Then Safura said: 'Now, everything is clear. But while we are arguing, Žamal has brainwashed the boy by now. Oh, how could she have known first?'

'They are both ruthless, with their secrets! I didn't even see their car in the car park. They must have taken him where no one will find them. They do everything to serve their own interests.'

'We know what we're here for', Safura said. 'Now we must outstrip Žamal!'

'Agreed!'

They returned to the suite, where they had locked their husbands in. Otaš's wife handed the food parcels to Safura while she inserted the key and turned it.

'Squeeze more! Squeeze it more vigorously!'

Otaš's voice could be heard in the far room as the women entered, but the two husbands noticed immediately that their wives had come in, and became quiet. They ambled into the room one after the other. The women could not believe their eyes: Tŭrsyn and Otaš were *drunk*, both swaying as they attempted to appear casual.

Otaš's wife looked around, checking whether or not there was, in fact, another door to the suite. She walked to the window and looked out. Third floor! They could not have exited from the balcony.

'Where did you get...?' she began.

'What?' asked Otaš.

'What do you think! How did you become drunk?'

'No, we did not drink', said Otaš, swallowing hard.

'We did not drink!' declared Tŭrsyn, backing him up.

Otaš's wife walked into the other room and returned with the inner tube – now considerably deflated – and two glasses.

'This!' she hissed. '"I'll mend it! I'll mend it!" *This* is your big secret? No wonder you keep it around your neck all the time! And stupid me, I believed you: I'll mend it...' Safura!' She handed the glasses to Safura, who placed them on the table. Otaš's wife squeezed the inner tube and began to pour vodka from the nozzle: two full shots.

'"You have to know how to find a common language!" I wondered how you had become the kind of person who can find a "common language" so easily with everybody! Now try to be good at finding a common language!' She poured the two glasses of vodka out the window.

Tŭrsyn shut his eyes; Otaš craned his neck slightly and looked wistfully at the wasted vodka.

***

Taṇat had his truck up on a jack in front of his house and was changing the tyre, with his thirteen-year-old son helping him. His wife came out of the house and stood by them.

'What's on your mind?' Taṇat asked her a moment later.

'No, nothing', she said, smiling. 'It's just that... you've stopped visiting the boy at his boarding school in the city...'

Taṇat looked at her in surprise, and said: 'What happened; did you have some kind of dream?'

'Yesterday, I went to the *auyl* where Äulet's family lives. I called in at my old schoolmate's house...'

'Yes. And?'

'I'm worried that the boy could be damaged: you see, Äulet has won a Mercedes in the lottery.'

Taṇat stared at her. 'Why "damaged"?'

'He is still young. He does not know the value of such things.'

'What are you talking about?'

'Well, he did win a Mercedes...'

'Good heavens! Is that true?' asked the boy, widening his eyes.

'Yes', said the woman, pityingly. 'In my opinion, you should visit him as soon as possible, to be next to him during this time. Or bring him home. Who knows, someone might target him...'

'You may be right', Taṇat said, reflecting on the situation. 'It's not as though his family ever visits him. But I haven't got the time today.'

'Good on you, Áulet!' said the boy, happily. 'I'll ride in his car with him – *vroom*! We'll drive around all day!'

Taṇat looked at him disapprovingly, and the boy's smile vanished.

'Make the time, go to him today', said the wife. 'He is a young boy; you don't want him to be defrauded...'

Taṇat looked at his wife with some suspicion, but decided she was sincere and sympathetic: her features were gentle, her eyes like a lamb's.

***

'I see Áulet has many relatives after all!' exclaimed Mansùrov in wonder at the two couples in his office. 'I had the opposite impression. But people can be mistaken sometimes.'

'Certainly, people can be mistaken', Otaš's wife said.

Recalling Žamal's words, he interrupted her. 'Ah, but this is not an educator's mistake, this is a mistake common to people in general. And you are now making up for lost time.'

'Yes', said Tùrsyn. 'We bear responsibility for that.'

'*Apyraj*,[7] is it Áulet's birthday today?' asked Mansùrov in wonder. 'All of you, arriving since yesterday...'

'The spring sowing will start soon. We intended to visit him before it', Safura said.

'How are you related to Áulet, then?'

I am the cousin of Áulet's father', Tùrsyn said.

'We are his closest relatives', said Safura.

'This man is his relative too – our grandfathers were brothers' said Tùrsyn, referring to Otaš. 'Next to him is his wife.'

'Right', the headmaster said, after a pause. 'What about the people from yesterday?'

'They are just kinsmen', Otaš's wife said. 'They are not closer to him than we are.'

Mansùrov nodded and said: 'I was not here when you arrived late yesterday, but do see him now that you are here. His kinsmen who are with him will return him to school. Maybe you can meet him during the break.'

---

[7] *Apyraj* – exclamation of interest, surprise or doubt (sarcastic); also *apyrmaj*.

'No, we wanted to show him around the city for the day', Otaš's wife said.
'Well... tomorrow is Sunday. Go around the city then.'
'Goodbye for now', she said. 'We'll meet again.'
They bid farewell to the headmaster and left.
'I can't stand this anymore', said Otaš, when they reached the yard. 'Let's go back; we can return later.'
'Agreed', said Tùrsyn.
'It's clear what *you* have in mind!' Otaš's wife said to her husband. 'A restaurant! Be patient!'
The women walked behind the men as they advanced. Safura said: 'The headmaster doesn't know anything. If Äulet had won a Mercedes, surely he would have heard about it! Wouldn't the entire boarding school be talking about it?'
'But it is indeed true', Otaš's wife said, surprised. 'Maybe he lost the ticket?'
'It was Älibek who gave him the ticket. That huckster wouldn't do the slightest thing without a motive. You're right: that means it is true.'
'If it was Älibek who gave him the ticket, shame on him for trying to claim it back!'
'Just so. People today have forgotten about ethics. He gifted it to our boy. Legally, it must be ours as well!'
Otaš's wife threw a sidelong glance at Safura. 'The ticket is with Äulet', she said. 'Your son gave it to him. Äulet is closer to us rather than you.'
'Where is this law written?'
'It's been so since ancient times!'
'No, thank you! You know, I was thinking we should share the prize with you if we get the ticket into our hands – but you seem to have only bad intentions!'
'What spite! You, share it? I would share it!'
They continued arguing, until they realised that Tùrsyn and Otaš were nowhere to be seen.
'Hey... those two have disappeared', Otaš's wife said.
'Good riddance!' Safura was angry now.
'You see?' said the other woman. 'You are cruel. You don't even have compassion for your own husband!'
Otaš called out from behind a clump of trees: 'We're here! Let's go back. I need to fix the car.'
His wife stared at him coldly as she joined him. Otaš got into the car and leaned back in the passenger seat.

***

Älibek, Žamal and their two young guests had been sightseeing in Älibek's car, and had stopped at a shop selling clothing for young people to buy some clothes for Äulet before going on to enjoy a meal at a restaurant in the city park. Spring sunbeams glowed weakly through rows of trees, and everyone had a smile on their lips.

Žamal admired Äulet's new jacket. 'It fits you well', she said. 'Dana, do you like it?'

'I like it very much', the girl nodded.

Älibek decided to probe for more information. 'So, Äulet', he said, 'what news have you got to share?'

'No news', Äulet replied. 'Soon we shall go on an excursion to Ḳazyġŭrt.'

'Hmm', Älibek rejoined indifferently. 'Nothing else has... changed?'

'No, no changes', said Äulet sincerely.

'Žamal *apaj*', smiled Dana, displaying her white teeth. 'There is a funny boy in our class. One day, he told us, when he came home from school, his father asked: "What mark did you obtain on your work?" He said, without trying to hide it: "I got a 'two'." "Why did you get a 'two'?" his father shouted at him. He replied: "It was not me who got a 'two', but you – because you did my sums for me yesterday!"'

Äulet guffawed with relish; Älibek and Žamal gave short laughs.

'Isn't that funny?' Dana asked, looking at them.

'Funny! *Absolutely* funny!' Älibek said, nodding emphatically.

Dana continued chatting happily: 'When Taṇat *aġa* took Äulet and me to the mountains, we went skiing. Äulet was always falling down!' She laughed in a melodic voice.

'I fell down only four times', Äulet said, pursing his lips.

'No, seven!'

'I won't fall next winter.'

'Of course not; you'll have grown up by then...'

Everyone went back to their meals. Älibek, bringing a drumstick to his mouth, said: 'Back in the *auyl*, a pupil won a moped in the lottery.'

The children did not say anything; they barely even paid attention. Älibek and Žamal looked at each other and shrugged their shoulders.

Dana, noticing the time, said suddenly: 'Ah, I must go. My mother allowed me out only for two hours!'

Glancing at his watch, Älibek said: 'OK, then, let's go back.'

Driving in the car after dropping off Dana, Älibek broke the silence by asking Äulet quietly: 'Äulet, do you remember... you... have you got a lottery ticket?'

'A lottery ticket!' Äulet looked at him, confused, then at Žamal.

'Yes, a lottery ticket', she said. 'When you visited the *auyl*, Mäden gave you some...'

'Oh, yes... yes.' Äulet said, smiling.

'He remembers! Good boy!' Älibek said heartily. 'Where is it?'

Äulet sat there, thinking, hesitant.

'What, have you lost it?' Žamal said, fearing the worst.

'No. I have not lost it.'

She smiled. 'Oh, my clever boy. Of course, Äulet would not lose it!'

'Why are you asking?'

'You know…' Älibek said, calmer now. 'I made a big mistake. Those tickets belong to a firm, and I – by accident – gave them to Mäden, who gave them to you.'

Äulet was silent.

'Please, try and remember', Älibek continued. 'If you wish, I'll give you a hundred more tickets.'

'Why not give *those* to the firm?'

'It is impossible, Äulet. There are certain numbers written on them.'

'Yes, it is impossible', Žamal chimed in. 'Your *aġa* will be taken to court.'

'Taken to court?!' At this, Äulet became afraid.

Taking advantage of the boy's fear, Žamal added: 'Yes, he will be taken to court. Otherwise we would not ask for these three tickets.'

'But I… I gave them to Dana, as a gift for her birthday.' Äulet spoke in a hoarse whisper.

'To Dana?' Žamal said, and tapped Älibek's shoulder: 'Let's go.'

'Žamal *apaj*', said Äulet. 'Let's not! How can I possibly ask for them back?'

***

Älibek pulled his car up to the boarding school, only to see Tùrsyn's and Otaš's cars stop next to it. Älibek and Žamal screwed up their faces at them, and their eyes narrowed with disdain.

'Ah, there you are', Tùrsyn said, getting out of his car and walking up to them. The others got out, too.

'We have been looking for you everywhere', said Otaš's wife. 'Where did you take Äulet and disappear to?'

Älibek and Žamal also got out. 'What are you doing here, one after another?' Žamal asked.

'What about *you*?' remarked Safura.

'We were showing Äulet around the city.'

'Do not play the fox', Otaš's wife said. 'We know the real reason.'

'If you don't believe us, ask him!' Älibek said.

'What's with you, arguing in front of the boy?' Otaš said. 'Come over here.' They walked some ways off from their cars.

'Frankly', Safura said, 'the lottery ticket belongs to us.'

'Well, it's ours now', Žamal said. 'You want to claim it for yourselves? Where is your shame?'

'Äulet is closer to us than to any of you!' Otaš's wife said. 'The law is on our side.'

'Sure, you'll just grab them like that!' Safura said, becoming angrier. 'Has Äulet ever even seen your house?'

'Hey, my kinsmen', Otaš said. 'What is wrong with you all? Are you not ashamed?'

414

'If you're ashamed, then keep quiet!' said his wife, interrupting him. 'They're not ashamed – why should we feel any shame?'

'Tùrsyn, say something', Otaš pleaded. But Tùrsyn was unsure of what to say. Finally, he mumbled, unconvincingly: 'I agree with Otaš.'

At that moment, Äulet came up to them. 'Greetings, Tùrsyn *aġaj*', he said, smiling innocently.

'Äulet! So you have become a big *žigit*!' Tùrsyn said. 'Let me kiss you on your cheek.'

'And both my hands are free, not like in the wintertime', Otaš said, recalling their meeting some months earlier. 'I can kiss you properly now.'

'Ah, my dear, we were miserable when we didn't find you', Otaš's wife said, hugging Äulet. 'Now you can come with us for a drive around the city. Is that OK?'

'I have to go to school', Äulet said, surprised by this sudden gathering of his relatives and growing more suspicious by the minute.

Älibek and his wife looked at each other, and took the opportunity to slip further away from the group.

'Missing one day won't make a difference', Safura said, embracing him, too. 'And it's not every day your family visits you! Tomorrow is Sunday—'

'Why did you all come together?' interrupted Äulet, becoming extremely unsettled.

'Well, the spring sowing is coming, and we'll be busy. That's why we came now', replied Tùrsyn.

The boy turned his head to the roadside, and suddenly shouted loudly.

'Tùrsyn *aġaj*! Tùrsyn *aġaj*! Where are they going? Stop them, please! Please…!' Äulet broke into a run after Älibek's receding car.

'What happened? Where have they gone?' asked Otaš's wife and Safura uncomprehendingly.

'Äulet! Äulet! What happened?' Tùrsyn and Otaš ran after the boy.

When they reached him, Äulet said: 'They are going to Dana's! I gave her the lottery tickets! For her birthday!'

It dawned on everyone what was taking place, and they grew alarmed.

'Äulet! Get a hold of yourself!' Tùrsyn said. 'We'll catch up with them!' They got into their cars and drove after Älibek and Žamal. Tùrsyn, Safura and Äulet took the lead car.

The boy was crying from apprehension and frustration.

'What filth they are', Safura said. 'Can you direct us to Dana's house?'

'Of course! Faster, Tùrsyn *aġaj*! Faster!'

The two cars roared to a stop, one after the other, in front of the gate to Dana's house. Äulet got out of the car and rushed inside. Älibek and Žamal were speaking with Dana's mother.

'… It's inconvenient, certainly, from our side', said Žamal. 'Very embarrassing… but we need to take the lottery tickets back. Please, do forgive us.'

415

Äulet burst into the room. Everyone looked at him, unnerved.

'Where is Dana?' he asked, his eyes filling with tears.

'Äulet!' Dana's mother exclaimed. 'You... what's happened?'

Dana, preparing for school and wearing beautiful bows in her hair, came out of her room, smiling; but she halted in astonishment on seeing Äulet, whose face was pale, and Älibek and Žamal – to whom, of course, she had just said goodbye after their excursions around the city.

Now another group of people, led by Türsyn, entered. Dana and her mother began to feel afraid.

'Äulet!' Dana cried out, beginning to tremble. 'What has happened?'

'Dana! Give me the tickets back! Get them back to me! Quickly!'

'Tickets...? The *lottery* tickets you gave me for my birthday?'

'Yes... yes! Quickly!'

Dana stood there, looking at Äulet with wide eyes. Suddenly she began to cry. She removed a book from her schoolbag and flipped the pages. Älibek and Žamal took sharp intakes of breath as they watched.

'Here', Dana said upon locating the tickets, which she had safeguarded between the pages. 'Here!' She threw the tickets at Äulet, and ran back to her room in tears.

'What a shame', Dana's mother whispered repeatedly, clutching her collar in bewilderment and displeasure. 'What a shame.'

Äulet picked up the tickets off the floor, ripped them viciously into four pieces and threw them at Älibek and Žamal; then he, too, began to weep.

Älibek collected the ticket shreds with shaking hands and shoved them into his pocket.

'Go away... get out!' shouted Äulet at the couple. 'Here, take these, too!' – he tore off the new jacket and trousers Älibek and Žamal had bought him – 'I don't need them! I don't need them!'

When Älibek and Žamal prepared to leave, Türsyn and Otaš blocked their way.

Dana's mother began to realise what was happening, and tears came to her eyes.

'Such a 'family'!' she said contemptuously to them. 'I wondered why you were so overly concerned about him! You thought there was a winning ticket there? The tickets didn't win anything! Dana kept them only because Äulet had given them to her as a gift!'

No one spoke. They all stood dead in their places.

Älibek's cheeks twitched. He dipped his fingers into his pocket again and again, nervously. Žamal's eyes bulged as she stared at her husband.

'Here! Check for yourselves if you don't believe it.' Dana's mother took a newspaper out of a desk drawer and tossed it to Älibek. 'Check it!'

Älibek and Žamal compared the ticket numbers with the numbers in the newspaper. The others, overtaken by curiosity, crowded around them. Älibek checked the three tickets repeatedly. Then he looked closely in his notebook, and lifted his head slowly. He was sweating intensely.

'I… I wrote down the numbers incorrectly', he croaked.

Tears formed in Žamal's eyes.

Otaš walked up to Äulet. 'Äulet!' he said. 'Stand up, please.' He patted the boy's back, but Äulet shook him off.

'Get away!' the boy shouted. 'I don't need any of you!' He raised his head to look at them all. 'Tùrsyn *aġa*… all of you… just go away!' Tears of fury and grief overwhelmed him, and he sobbed loudly.

Now tears began to well up in the eyes of Safura and Otaš's wife, too.

***

In Mansùrov's office, one of the school's teachers sat in an armchair. The headmaster, his arms crossed behind his back, paced the floor.

'If I had simply been told of it', he said, 'I would not have believed it. I saw it with my own eyes… What a shame!' He shook his head.

'Did they apologise?'

'Well, they came. But what was the point of that? We simply do not know what kind of people are among us. The children we bring up will grow into tomorrow's adults, and what kind of people will they become? Does everything depend on upbringing?'

'If it is not innate in human nature, upbringing can only attempt to point the way', offered the teacher.

'No', Mansùrov said emphatically. 'Upbringing is not only in school, but everywhere: at home, outside, at the train station, in a plane. Not in words, but in deeds. Every adult is a teacher. They should set an example for their children, and strive for honesty.'

Just then the door opened, and the old groundskeeper appeared. 'Mr Director!' he said, addressing Mansùrov in a low, gruff tone, as though confiding a big secret. 'I found three new cigarette ends in the toilet.'

'Put them in your pocket!' shouted Mansùrov in anger and exasperation. 'Now close the door, please!'

The groundskeeper vanished.

He concluded his speech: 'I believe this sincerely… How is Äulet?'

'He has not lifted his head from the bed.'

'Do not disturb him. Let him rest well. I can barely tolerate all this, let alone him.'

'The two relatives who came here afterward do not appear to be totally senseless…'

The headmaster did not reply. He only shrugged his shoulders.

***

Äulet sat alone at the end of a bench at the long table in the middle of the yard, where the students worked on their lessons in the summertime. He had stopped weeping over the recent events, but was continuously deep in thought. The bitter truths he had been forced to confront had siphoned his strength.

It was after dusk. A truck stopped in front of the yard, and Taṇat emerged from it. He walked into the yard, then straight ahead to Äulet's dormitory; a short while later, he came back outside. There were lights arrayed on wires across the length of the table, but there was no need at this time to have them all lit; only one of them, at the end, was on. It swung in the cold spring wind, and occasionally illuminated Äulet's silhouette.

Taṇat noticed the boy sitting there forlornly, and slowly walked in that direction.

'There he is... hey, Äulet!' he called, with good cheer in his voice. Then again, more quietly: 'Äulet!'

Äulet did not raise or turn his head. Taṇat was confused, and not a little taken aback; he did not understand Äulet's unresponsiveness.

'Äulet?' he said again, more tentatively. 'Didn't you recognise me? Why didn't you reply?'

'I knew it was you', Äulet replied coldly. 'Why did you come?'

'What do you mean, why did I come? Äulet, are you OK?'

'Why did you come? Tell me!'

Taṇat raised his head slightly and leaned back, now apprehensive.

'I won a Mercedes in the lottery', Äulet said, heavily.

'So I heard', Taṇat said. 'It's true, then?'

'Yes, it's true!' He continued, in an acerbic tone of voice: 'So here I am, waiting for *you*, to give it to *you*.'

'Stop, Äulet, what is this about?'

'Why aren't you happy?'

'Happy? I am almost offended.'

'Liar!' said the boy, turning his head to look squarely at Taṇat. 'That's a lie! All of you, pretending to love... what liars!'

Taṇat was perplexed. 'But I don't need anything at all – has something happened? I suppose I am late, I admit that; I could not leave work earlier. I'm sorry, Äulet...' Taṇat leaned forward to embrace the boy, but Äulet flinched and moved away.

'Go away! Just get out! I don't need anyone anymore! No one!'

'Äulet!' Taṇat raised his voice and drew nearer. But the boy recoiled.

'Do not come close! Do not come close to me!'

'If you keep this up, not only will I come close, I'll also clip you on the jaw!' Taṇat snapped. Äulet rose and bounded away, and Taṇat got up to follow. The boy tripped on a piece of wood and fell. Taṇat caught up with him and hoisted him up, dragging him to the illuminated spot in the yard. 'What happened, tell me now!' he demanded when they came face-to-face under the light, shaking Äulet's coat collar.

Two or three boys, still up and about, were passing by at that moment. When they saw the stranger shaking their schoolmate aggressively, they whistled sharply. A second group of boys rushed outside. Moments later, they were surrounding Taṇat, and without further ado they rushed at him and began assailing him with their fists. The young men jumped on Taṇat as though he were a thief; Äulet could not hold them back once they had begun, however hard he tried.

From the corner, the old groundskeeper ran out, brandishing his mop. At the other end of the yard, the door to the headmaster's office flung open. 'They smoke, they fight!' shouted the groundskeeper, admonishing the teachers who were now sprinting into the yard. 'This is their upbringing!'

'Look out!' one of the boys shouted, and they all dispersed quickly.

Taṇat sat on the ground, clutching his head.

***

In one corner of a small restaurant, Tùrsyn and Safura sat with Otaš and his wife. They were each contemplative in their own way.

'Well, from our side, it was a mean trick to play!' Otaš said guiltily.

'We've left a scar on his heart', Tùrsyn sighed.

'What devil made us do it?' Otaš's wife wondered, wiping her tears with a handkerchief.

'This whole ordeal may never be undone', Safura said, her eyes moist.

The four of them went silent again.

Otaš said: 'I would never have believed that we could be responsible for such an experience. During peaceful times, when we enjoy lives free from conflict, it is so easy to be "good"; but when temptation arises, we are like dogs from different packs, chasing greedily after whatever feeds our secret hungers. If this lottery had never happened, perhaps we wouldn't have realised what we are truly capable of. But there's no use feeling sorry now. To the day we die, we won't forget it. Nor will Äulet.'

'What shall we do now?' asked Safura, crying now. 'How can we heal this scar on his heart? We all have children. If they were orphans like Äulet, and their relatives did something like this…' She could not speak any further, and simply began sobbing. Otaš's wife joined her.

'Stop', Tùrsyn said. 'Not in front of people; they won't know why you are crying!'

'Never mind – if they want to look, let them look', Otaš's wife said, sniffling.

***

Älibek and Žamal sat in their car at the edge of a road on the outskirts of the city, leading away from it.

'You started this whole mess', Žamal said. 'Do you have eyes or bumps on your forehead?'

'Well, what would you be doing if we had actually won the lottery?'

'I don't know. Maybe we would think it over. Now, how can we look people in the eye?'

'Maybe we should move somewhere else?'

'Oh, I don't think we can escape so easily…'

***

Taṇat drove fast, Äulet beside him in the truck. Taṇat's head was bandaged: the blows he had endured had not been light.

'So, I won a head covering in the lottery', said Taṇat, smiling.

Äulet looked at him and laughed.

'But does it hurt?'

'My right ear is ringing.'

'When my mates land punches, you can be sure the ears will ring…'

Taṇat glanced at him and smiled again. 'We're building a big reservoir', he said. 'When the construction is finished, you won't need the Black Sea or the Baltic Sea. Several types of fish will be bred there. Together with your boys, you'll be able to fish all summer long. On Sundays, I can drive you there myself…'

Äulet was dozing off. He could not follow Taṇat's words any longer.

At the moment his eyelids joined in sleep, a radiant white light filled his field of vision. The light resolved itself into two white bows like the wings of a butterfly. Then came a vision of Dana, the bows in her hair, running through a field of red flowers. She had tears in her eyes, but it was not clear why. From behind her, Aķtôs appeared, running alongside her and looking up eagerly.

Translated by Mitchell Albert

ORALKHAN BOKEY

(28.09.1943 – 17.05.1993)

Oralkhan Bokey was a writer, playwright and journalist. He studied journalism at Kirov Kazakh State University (now Ăl-Farabi Kazakh National University; (grad. 1968). He worked for regional newspapers, *Eŋbek tuy* and *Kommunizm tuy* (1965–68), before joining the editorial office of the then-influential newspaper, *Leninšil žas* (now *Žas alaš*). He then became manager of the prose section of *Žuldyz*, the literary journal (1974–83) and editor-in-chief of *Ḳazaḳ ădebieti* (1983–91). His first collection of short stories, *Ḳamšyger* (The Whip Fighter), published in 1970, brought him recognition as a unique writer who successfully combines the literary devices of prose and poetry. His style was polished over the years in the following books: *Ùrker* (Pleiades, 1971), *Ḳajdasyŋ, ḳasḳa ḳulynym?* (Where Are You, My Little Foal? 1973), *Mùztau* (1975), *Ắn salady šaġyldar* (The Dunes Are Singing, 1978), *Ùrker auyp barady* (The Pleiades are Dying Out, 1981) and *Bizdiŋ žaḳta ḳys ùzaḳ* (Winters Last Long in My Homeland, 1984). His final trilogy, *Aldanġan ùrpaḳ* (The Deceived Generation), has remained unfinished.

Bokey is well known as a playwright. *Ḳulynym meniŋ* (My Foal, 1974), *Teketires* (The Clash, 1976), *Ḳar ḳyzy* (The Snow Girl, 1982), *Zymyrajdy poezdar* (The Trains Are Speeding By, 1984), *Žau tylyndaġy bala* (The Boy Behind Enemy Lines, 1985) and *Men sizden ḳorḳamyn* (I Am Afraid of You, 1987) have been staged at the theatres in Kazakhstan and across the former Soviet Union. His works have been published in German, Slovak, Bulgarian, English, Hungarian, Arabic, Chinese and Japanese, among others. He received the Ostrovsky Literary Award (1978), the Lenin Komsomol Prize of the Kazakh SSR (1976) and the State Prize of the Kazakh SSR in Literature (1986).

Kerbúġy

A mighty bellow rang out.

The grey deer Kerbúġy[1] had not drunk or eaten at all that day. He had really wanted to drink, but no sooner would his lips touch the cold water of the spring and its banks, covered with thin ice, patterned like lace, than he would come over in a shiver and his legs would shake, as if he might collapse onto his antlers at any moment.

He stepped back but his thirst proved stronger than he was. It burned his insides, forcing him forward. Three times he approached the spring and three times he stepped away. He could not understand what the matter was: he wanted to drink and there was a spring of water, bubbling merrily away at his feet, and yet he was quite unable to bring himself to lower his muzzle.

He had clearly become older and weaker and this was a woe more bitter than anything he could think of. And yet he had been standing there for several minutes, thinking quite the opposite. No, he had not settled into old age and there were sure to be many days of frolicking ahead for Kerbúġy. He had grown weak, but not from old age. It had simply been that over the rutting season, his legs and antlers had known no rest for three whole days.

He had not been this exhausted during the rut the year before, while the year before that he had seen to every last doe in the herd. So, what had happened? Perhaps the early autumn that year had been particularly cold and windy, freezing him to the bone? However, the autumn would be followed by a six-month-long winter, a savage dragon in these parts, and yet he had always survived it as if it was nothing more than a mosquito bite. This autumn had come early, it was true, and the Sun was now constantly shrouded in dense, heavy clouds, drifting like ice floes on flood water. The sky would hang low and grey and rain would fall from morning till night. This fine, cold rain fell at a slant, making the very earth itself groan wistfully.

The wind, too, equally cold and piercing, moaned as it carried the incessant bands of rain. It was the groaning of the forest, though, that was the saddest sound of all. Its voice would merge with the wind and rain, and it would seem to be not so much a groan as a plaintive lament about dashed hopes. The grey deer Kerbúġy let out a protracted bellow.

His voice was no longer what it had once been, but he still managed to produce an echo of the might he had once commanded. But an echo was all it was! Previously, his mighty call had reverberated over a considerable distance

---

[1] The name given to leaders of the deer herds in these parts.

and his trumpet-like voice had echoed a hundred times over through the snowy mountains and ravines that harboured terror and death. Now, though, no one heard him. The old stag just stood above the stream, swelling with the rain, and his roar sounded like nothing more than a whine or a cry for help. However, not a soul responded to his belated call. Where had his great speed, his strength and courage all gone? He had always been ready to sacrifice all for their sake. He had recalled every moment in his life with a shudder of delight but now everything had deserted him, he had grown old and tears rolled down his face.

And yet the deer would not give up. No, he was far from old. It had simply been the restless, young deer and the harsh autumn that had eaten away at his energy. As it was, he was not doing badly. He was still holding himself together. Stepping away from the stream, he cried out again, calling to his herd, but this was not the victorious bellow of the mighty stag Kerbůgy, rather the call of a poor, deserted deer. There had been no reply and, having waited a little while longer, he set off into the mountains. However, as luck would have it, even the mountains were not their usual selves. It seemed they had grown taller and, however far he climbed, the ledges and passes appeared never-ending. He scrambled over the rocks, lost for breath, his throat sore. Something was weighing him down and blocking his progress. He stopped to rest, his head hanging low. It seemed that, if he had not reached the end, he had certainly submitted to fate. His proud head now drooped, his chest, once mighty and heaving, was now devoid of strength and he felt as empty and voiceless as the grave. This headstrong, wild animal, growing new antlers every year and never permitting a single tender caress, had now become meek and mild and there was surely no greater humiliation. He had been struck hard in the side during his last battle and the unbearable pain reared its head once more, almost dragging him down to his knees.

He had thought back then that he would now only dream about the dance of a young doe and that he would never be able to nestle up close to the side or back of a mother doe, who had walked proudly before him, that he would become lost in a thick fog, sink in the depth of the rushing river and never make it out alive. All these thoughts had rushed past him and he raised his head, wincing from the pain and stress of it all and bellowed with every muscle.

Early the previous morning, Kerbůgy had gathered his herd and led them into the mountains. The bucks had surrounded him, looking like they would rather die than let the does go with him. Kerbůgy, though, had not been head of the herd so long for nothing; he had always come out on top in combat. He had driven off the young bucks and bellowed with nostrils flaring. The herd had been split in an instant. The does had scattered and the bucks had raised their antlers high in the air and, churning the earth with their hooves, they had closed in, preparing for battle. They stood facing one another, snorting and looking askance at Kerbůgy, each hoping to come out on top.

A strong, young buck stood opposite Kerbůgy but averted his gaze; he was shaking all over. And how! Entering the rut with the leader of the herd was no easy matter. Kerbùġy, though, felt little better. He already knew that this year would be particularly difficult for him, which was why he had wanted to drive the herd out bright and early. However, the young stags had stood in his way. Kerbùġy looked over at his opponent: he was young, with just fifteen soft branches on his antlers. And Kerbùġy was shy of him?! What would happen when he would be the last one standing to face the strongest of them all? The opponents stood there; they hesitated, overcoming a moment of timidity, and then suddenly rushed at one another with everything they had.

Antlers clashed and battle commenced, mighty blows followed one after the other. Strong antlers, already showing their first branches, cut through the air with a whistle. It seemed the ground was being showered by sparks flying from heads and antlers. This was a battle to the death, for the right to be the leader. The heads of the stags, beautifully pointed, as if honed by the hand of a master craftsman, reared up and crashed furiously into one another. Only silhouettes could be seen in the all-encompassing, thick fog, the likes of which one only encounters in the Altaj mountains. Then, the mist crept into the hollow, dragging its tail behind it and everything became clear; after a three-hour battle, only Kerbùġy and his opponent, the young stag Žasbùġy,[2] were left in the yellow-green clearing. The others, having suffered defeat, had dissolved into the mist.

This was to be a real tussle. Kerbùġy knew well the laws of courage and strength in the mighty tribe of deer. But what he didn't know was that this law also existed among the sons of Adam, who regarded themselves as the most intelligent creatures, and that they were even crueller and more bloodthirsty. People were not like deer, who but lock horns once a year and then live peacefully side by side. Kerbùġy knew nothing of this, although he had occasionally wondered why people kept wild animals in enclosures and had a passion for hollow deer horn.

Where there is combat there is justice! The reverie came to an end. Žasbùġy stood, clawing the earth before the old leader. Kerbùġy's gaze clouded over, he found it hard to raise his head, ringing from the heavy blows he had suffered, and it was then that he realised how genuinely exhausted he was. Žasbùġy, though, continued to look askance at him and claw the ground. His enormous frame was completely tense, ready to rush into battle at any moment. In these mere seconds, Kerbùġy suddenly saw Žasbùġy not as an enemy or an opponent in battle; rather he saw himself in his youth. He closed his eyes from this clear realisation of his end and his head felt heavy. He perhaps would have fallen to the ground in this stance and remained there had it not been for the powerful call to the rut that rang out. The young stag had seen that the leader had weakened; he could have overcome him with a single blow to the side, but he was a deer of honour. Kerbùġy felt ashamed. He summoned all his pride, the legacy of his wild ancestors, which had never betrayed him, he raised his

---

[2] Lit. young deer.

head and dropped his antlers. His wide, wet eyes simultaneously destroyed his opponent and pleaded for mercy: 'Concede your turn this once. You have your whole life ahead of you. Concede. Who knows, I may no longer be here when next autumn comes around.'

Žasbùġy took a step back and prepared for the rut, his eyes blood-red. For a moment, it appeared to Kerbùġy it was not a deer standing before him but a cruel, bearded old man with a hacksaw, preparing to cut off his precious, eighteen-branch antlers. It seemed that this old man had started greedily to drink the blood that gushed from where his majestic antlers had once stood. The man, his beard a deep red from Kerbùġy's blood, then appeared to kick him cruelly in his sides before letting him go. He felt a burning affront, like frozen steel, and he shook with anger. There he was, his mortal enemy! While the two stood, squaring up to one another, the other deer peacefully tugged at the grass, indifferent to who would fall and who would become the leader. Kerbùġy clawed at the ground, bringing up a clod of earth with his hairy hoof, and stepped back. Suddenly, lightning flashed down onto his enemy with a bang.

He lost consciousness for a moment and, when he came to his senses, he saw Žasbùġy walking away, rocking and reeling. Tears sprayed from his eyes and he trumpeted a loud bellow, just as he had done in his youth. It was his last call and it was unlike any call a deer had ever made.

… Kerbùġy raised his head picked at a yellow birch leaf and began chewing for the first time that morning. The mist had not yet dissipated. Lone raindrops broke through, here and there. The air was heavy and damp. Water ran along the ground and in the sky; touching the birch tree likewise brought forth a torrent of droplets. Tears fell from whatever he touched. Žasbùġy's call could not be heard either; he must have drifted further away from these parts. There was not a soul in the forest. Not even his call could be heard. He was alone and the herd had gone.

In any case, he would not have had the strength to sort out all the hungry, young does. Sensing his lack of strength, they had instantly rushed away. It would be most irregular for an old, decrepit deer to drive away so many young does. But Kerbùġy moved them along with his antlers and they ran off in the direction he had determined. The young stag who had lost today's rut was among them, barely dragging his legs behind him and looking most unlike himself.

Kerbùġy turned back several times, lowering his antlers threateningly, and his beaten opponent instantly recoiled and dashed away, to stumble along in the safety of the herd. All it took was for Kerbùġy to turn around and all the young does galloped over to Žasbùġy and began sniffing him. Žasbùġy kept his wits about him. Having achieved with such effort what had probably been his last victory, Kerbùġy understood that he had neither the strength nor the desire to do anything more. Nevertheless, with nostrils flaring, he wooed a fragrant, mischievous young doe with a blue-black coat, from which the stink of strong, deer flesh was emanating. His bones ached and all his joints had seemed full of a heavy, yellow liquid. The pain was unbearable. After all, the battle had lasted the entire day. Where had his strength and his fury gone? Where had the days gone when he would get a dozen young does together and make sure they all got what was coming to them?

He stumbled around the young doe with that self-indulgent feeling that every male creature possesses, not just human beings, a feeling that can destroy everything in the world. He rubbed up against her side, nuzzled up and jumped about, but he felt as if a heavy, black rock lay in his chest and he was incapable of doing anything at all. The tormented doe, also unsettled, simply directed her beautiful eyes pitifully and silently over to the young Žasbûġy, who held himself at a distance, not risking an approach. The doe's head began to spin and she shook all over. Finally flagging and bleating pitifully and meekly, she looked submissively at her tormentor. But to no avail! Kerbûġy had no strength left. He had nothing left in his once powerful body, other than a desire to remain standing. At this moment, Žasbûġy could bear it no longer; he had been tormented by this horseplay, by the haughty old stag's infirmity and inability to even shake his antlers properly. He leapt at the old Kerbûġy like a snow leopard, bringing him crashing to his knees by the doe. Then, Žasbûġy, with a roar and a whistle, rushed at him, as if saying, 'You're dying, you old dog and there you go doing the same as always!' and struck such a terrible blow to his side that the old warrior, who had known no defeat in ten years, fell right onto his back, his legs waving weakly in the air in a pitiful fashion. Seeing all this, the does ran to the victor, circling around him and licking his muzzle. The next moment, Žasbûġy was already leading the entire herd over the pass. Kerbûġy might still have been capable of jumping to his feet and catching up with the herd. If it hadn't been for the young doe, then none of the strong and powerful females would have rejected him. However, every last desire had been extinguished within him. It made no sense why he had rushed into that battle or what he had hoped to prove, when he knew perfectly well how it would all end. Old age, oh, why are you incapable of seeing yourself?! A day spent in the arms of a young lover is sure to bring you a thousand days of torment and suffering.

Kerbûġy lay there for a long time, gathering his strength. At first, he had felt no pain, but that had probably been down to his fever. Now, all of his insides ached terribly. His legs had a mind of their own and he barely made it to the edge of the forest. Once there, he lay down in a deep thicket and remained there until morning, without moving a muscle. He made his way slowly to the stream only after dawn had emerged. Three times he approached the stream, and yet was quite unable to bring himself to lower his muzzle.

... He began to climb the hill again. The dried birch leaf Kerbûġy had recently swallowed must have become stuck on the roof of his mouth, for it caused him great discomfort and he could not get rid of it. His stomach rumbled; he had not eaten a single blade of grass since before the rut. His sides were sunken and his insides seemed to have become all matted together. The shoots of newly emerging antlers ached in dull torment. These antlers had brought him so much pain and unhappiness that he had lost all faith in the whole, wide world. He had decided to now find himself some thick cedar underbrush and curl up there until the end of his life – it was but a crow's foot away – to lay there, think and remember. However, the first thing he heard was the jubilant cry of his conqueror Žasbùġy. The sound had carried from the distant ridges. He knew this jubilant roar very well. There had been a time when he, too, having cut open the head of the old leader and taking over the herd, had sung this booming victory song. But the world is not immutable and everything must come to an end at some point.

It was possible that Žasbùġy was his own flesh and blood, his own son. The only thing was that his antlers did not have eighteen branches, but fifteen. Perhaps Kerbùġy was the last of that breed with eighteen-branch antlers. It could perhaps come to pass that this young fool, whose bellow now deafened the foothills, would sire a deer with thirteen branches, that the next would sire one with eleven branches and, in the end, the young would be sired with no antlers at all, and these timid creatures could no longer be called deer. All this was possible. Žasbùġy should have held the wide-spreading, eighteen-branch antlers of the old stag in high esteem, for he would never have anything of the like. But he had acted differently; he had engaged in battle and had taken the herd away. What intelligence could there be in the barefaced does? The ruler is the one with the greatest strength and it is he they shall follow. The does have no brains and no antlers; it was no surprise they were so timid.

Once, a doe had given birth to Kerbùġy in a thick caragana thicket all alone, a place where no people and no beast would venture. She had waited until he had made it to his feet and only then had she led him to the herd. The things he had seen since that time. He had seen good and bad, known great joy and great sadness. However, he had never been able to forget his first suffering.

… The deer had been grazing peacefully on the hillsides and hollows when cries and hoots had suddenly rung out. Horsemen had emerged from the bushes, ķiryķs[3] in hand. Kerbùġy had stood dumbstruck, not knowing what was happening. Suddenly he had caught sight of a bearded man on a black horse with a star on its forelock, rushing straight at him. He had been unable to come to his senses when a ķiryķ had been thrown around his antlers. He had seen the deer rushing to the low land and he had sped after them. However, the people on their fast steeds, crying out and closing in from all sides, had forced him first into a large enclosure and then into another, smaller one. And so, he had moved from one enclosure to the next, each one smaller than the last, until he had walked through a small gate, which had slammed shut behind him.

Someone had poked him with a stick, forcing him along the fence and onto a wooden walkway, blocked off at one end. Kerbùġy had stood there, frightened,

---

[3] *Ķiryķ* – light pole with a rope and a lasso or a loop at the end used for catching horses.

427

shifting from one leg to the other. He had not understood how and for what purpose he had found himself in this small, enclosed space. He had wanted to save himself, but had ended up in a trap. Suddenly, something had clamped the sides of his head in a vice-like grip. His heart had missed a beat as the walkway had collapsed into the depths below. The clamp had squeezed all the harder, the sky had fallen to Earth, the forest and the mountains had drooped their peaks to the ground and the entire universe had been turned upside down in the deer's tear-filled eyes. The master of this universe had walked about with a hacksaw at the ready, and the deer could see his own reflection in the man's insatiably greedy eyes. The crooked teeth of the saw had bitten into the furry base of the antlers and Kerbùġy had thought that a million ants had invaded his skull to feast on his brain; how his even, pearl-white teeth had ached back then. His huge, frightened and pleading eyes had filled with blood and almost jumped from their sockets. That was how this proud, free deer, racing the wind from hilltop to hilltop and from hollow to hollow, had first come to behold the bitter-sweet start to life.

And all this had been because of humans. He had concluded that people hold all the power, all the wealth and all the freedom. Kerbùġy had indeed always loved these two-legged creatures, but now he had come to realise just how greedy and insatiable they could be. It was people themselves who generate such overwhelming hatred to their kind. Kerbùġy's current situation was just as pitiful as that of an infant whose foot has been caught on a giant nail. Kerbùġy had regretted not having been born without antlers. Oh, the violence! People were prepared to trample over all that is beautiful, smash down all that has been erected, sully all that is pure and innocent, injure all that is healthy and full of energy and desecrate all that is sacred. At the same time, they always have a 'justification' for their deeds: 'No pain, no gain' or 'There is no such thing as coincidence. Everything in life is either a trial or a punishment.' And how would they justify the torment that Kerbùġy had endured? It was, after all, because Kerbùġy had been unable to stand up for himself and ask them, 'For what?' that they had made him a victim of their own passions. Then they would even philosophise, saying that 'Everything in this life is both a risk and something sacred'.

He had been released from the clamp and galloped away, jumping in an attempt to shake his antlers, but his hornless head had appeared as empty and dry as an old keg. Then he had been filled with anger, like lava from a volcano. In a single bound, Kerbùġy had jumped over the tethered black horse with the white star and bolted like the wind, in any direction, just to get as far away as possible from people. He had run without rest until he had no strength to run any longer but then he had reached a mighty barrier – a wooden palisade fence. Kerbùġy had run along this fence in the hope of reaching its end, but the fence had proved endless. Once he had run over all the hills and hollows, he returned to the place from where he had started and it was then that he had realised that all the deer were living in an enclosure. A space, surrounded by stakes. In summer, the enclosure was spacious and they would walk to the waterhole or out to graze. In winter, they would be herded into a narrow space. In winter, they would drink from the stream that never froze and eat strong-smelling silage. In spring, no soon had they broken free of this enclosure, than they would be herded back in and their antlers removed. Clearly, the deer knew no genuine freedom and nor would they ever know it.

Kerbüġy lay there under the thick cedar thicket and recalled how he had pined for his freedom after his antlers had first been hacked off. How many winters had passed since then, how many springs and how many times he had been deprived of his horns. Throughout his life, there had never been an instance when he had shed his antlers with their eighteen branches of his own accord. Eighteen branches were the blessing that nature had bestowed upon Kerbüġy but also his bitter misfortune, too. It was no wonder that the people had pounced on him like crows to carrion, forcing him into the holding pen before all the rest.

He lay there for a long time, shivering like a downtrodden dog. No one came to him. Even the people had disappeared, who, at the height of the season would throng here like bees round a honeypot. Not a single one of the bucks who had surrounded him and blocked his way approached. And where had his deer friends all gone, who in early spring would let him through first to break the ice, submissively following in his wake? Everyone had gone and left this old stag behind. The most terrible thing of all, the bitterest pill to swallow, was to die alone, forgotten and unwanted. Once again, he remembered the time when he had been at the peak of his powers, when he had made sure not even a bird's wing would flap in his vicinity. He had always been the centre of attention. During the days of the black frost and at any other time of danger, the herd had made sure he was not out in front and not at the rear, but in the centre of the herd, where it was safer. The best grass and the clearest, purest water had been reserved for him. And here he was, their former leader, lying weak in the dust. No one came to him. Nothing in this life was permanent. Kerbüġy was overcome with despondency and desperation. Where, oh where had his kind all gone? Could they really have all followed the blind rutting call, without even sparing him a single glance back?

If only there had been but a mouthful of water! The leaden fog dissipated and the Sun finally emerged through the trees. It appeared to ask Kerbüġy tenderly, 'So, how are you feeling?' Down below, the alpine stream thundered over the rocks. Only Mother Nature had not forgotten him. Kerbüġy rose from the thicket and turned his heavy muzzle towards the Sun's rays. With a strained and hoarse voice that even he found frightening, he gave a short bellow.

With that, his voice faded altogether. He looked up at the snowy peaks of the small mountains, glimmering white through the haze.

In his childhood, when he had been a small fawn, this peak had appeared impossibly high, but once he had become an adult, it was as if it had grown smaller. Now, though, it rose up high to the heavens and appeared unattainable once more. Kerbùġy saw this snow-capped peak as some magical dream. He pined for it and looked up with hope, believing that one day his hooves would walk its pure white cover. During the difficult moments in his life, he only had to close his eyes to see Mount Akšoķy[4] through the haze, rising up in all its majesty, beckoning to him with the reverberations of his bellowing. Sometimes, that pale white ghost would suddenly transform into a wolf or a bearded old man. Kerbùġy would be frightened half to death and would be quite unable to close his eyes.

He didn't know that his distant ancestors had once lived in the foothills of this ridge of Mount Akšoķy. The free deer herds hadn't known the *ķùryķ* and had chosen the lushest, most verdant meadows with their fragrant grasses and walked to the watering holes where the tastiest, purest spring water would be found. They would cross slowly from hill to hill, from valley to valley, and sleep through velvet summer nights wherever tiredness overcame them. On other nights, when the full moon bathed the Earth in its ruby light, the thousand-strong herds, grazing here and there, seemed like carefree hordes of some mysterious army. With each passing year, the tribe of deer had slowly begun to fade away. Later, the deer had been deprived of their native land and they could find no joy at all in the alien grass and water.

Only then had the deer realised that they had lost not only their native land but, with it, the freedom they had enjoyed since birth. When the sharp teeth of the hacksaw had touched the base of their antlers, their most precious and most sacred possession, they had felt a premonition that these strangers had cut off their freedom and would never give it back. And so it was: when the outsiders deprived the deer of their native land and imprisoned them in this small patch of land, they went on to harm the horses that were the pride and joy of the local peoples. Those strangers had simply written a declaration in the name of the Tsar, seized the pasture land and evicted the people who had tended the horses out into the naked steppe.

Having rested for some time, Kerbùġy got up and slowly made his way to the fence. The wooden staircase in the distance, which had swollen from rain and damp, was as pale and grey as it had always been. It had been the same the year before, that was how it was now and that's how it would be always. Always.

Kerbùġy timidly stretched his neck and rubbed his muzzle up against the fence. The slightly sour aroma of carrion reached his nostrils. Kerbùġy clawed at the ground and shook his head. Then he took a step back. He looked up at Akšoķy once more and, again, it shone white through the blue haze, like the white seagull of his dreams. A light breeze drifted down from the peak. It was fresh and warm, like new-drawn milk and, just like milk, it instilled new strength and vigour. He imagined that he could hear the call of his ancestors from Akšoķy, calling him to battle and to an unending, unyielding pride for

---

[4] Akšoķy – lit. 'White Mountains'.

this indescribable beauty. Oh, that carefree life! It was only possible here, by Aķšoķy. And yet access to Aķšoķy was obscured by this fence of stakes, deathly still, but still impregnable. If it weren't for this fence, Kerbùġy would not have been here. He would have galloped away to Aķšoķy to plunge his muzzle into the snow, munch and crunch it until he had cooled his blazing insides and his mighty heart, so burnt by sadness, dreaming and aspiration. He would wail with every last ounce of strength: 'Oh, sacred Mother Nature, sacred freedom, sacred beauty, I would sacrifice myself for your sake', and he would weep bitter tears. Then, he would leap up and stretch himself high, towards the moon, to fall down dead on his back. And he would not regret his death.

He stood there behind that cursed fence and looked up at Aķšoķy for so long and so intently that the peak began to waver and swim about like a mirage. The wounded Kerbùġy gulped in the air, to emit a furious roar that would cause the snow to slide from the mountain and his chest, withered and dry as a keg, to break into pieces. It was a faltering, strained and, frankly, rather pitiful cry.

The desolate, grey rocks, however, would not even dignify the old stag with a response; they continued to stand as they always had and not a soul replied.

The Sun waxed stronger and stronger and the dew, which had glistened on the bluish leaves like beads, now fell and disappeared. The Earth was insatiable and greedily lapped up every drop.

Birds had once sung here but now, not one was left and only their distant farewell cry could be heard from up on high.

From a hollow far away, the mating cry of a young deer was heard, followed by a sudden gunshot and then silence.

That is how things go in life: the young come together, the old depart, the weak are killed off and life goes on, regardless.

A helicopter came down to land somewhere nearby. People are always lacking something and now they had found a way to climb up into the skies.

Kerbùġy no longer believed in anything; he expected nothing but found disappointment wherever he looked. He had exchanged all the joys of life for his present old age, his wounded and embittered soul, his intolerable torment. He had come to hate everything in this world, everything that lived and moved. He had forgotten forever that he had once adored all of this in his youth. He decided to take a risk.

Suddenly, a great fearlessness and determination entered him. He had to get beyond this cursed fence and win himself freedom. He decided to leave his body, covered with wounds, on the other side of the fence. He wanted to taste freedom for the first and last time in his life and set out on that joyous journey, that limitless freedom that is called *death*. He prepared himself with positive impulses and an open heart.

His body was broken and shattered; his chest ached and his heart strained, but he still tensed every muscle and charged his every fibre with hope. He wanted to sacrifice his tormented soul for this heroic mission, which he had never had the courage to face throughout his life. He had been born a bold

431

creature, and this is how he would die. He would strive for the hills, like his ancestors before him and would thus demonstrate an example of eternal bravery. He would not die unhappy or deserted. He would follow the example set by his ancestors, those proud, defiant children of the mountains. This was how he would bury his daring heart, which had always striven for courage and devilry. This deed would be his last. He would free himself of every thought that had troubled him – people and their grabbing hands, the shameless young doe, the humiliation in the face of his young opponents, his old age and, finally, this fence. He would demand his freedom back, his freedom that nature had gifted him and which had been encircled by this accursed wall.

His eyes were burning and he rushed forward with every last ounce of strength. And there it was – freedom. He stood quite still for several seconds, unable to understand what had happened, but then he realised that the fence was behind him and that he was standing on free ground; that no one was his master any longer. He rushed off in the direction of Aḳšoḳy.

He ran, afraid to look back and see that cursed fence! There it was: his dream that was Aḳšoḳy! There was a post in front of it. Kerbŭġy sniffed at it, rubbed his muzzle against it and then his side. He looked around, a shudder ran throughout his body and he suddenly bellowed loudly.

At that moment, he was young and strong once more; there was not a deer in the herd stronger than him. The mountains must have realised this, for they echoed his trumpet call and it resonated at length over the mountains, for his whole life came to an end with this call.

And indeed, that was probably the case. He stood there and looked out; he was suddenly young and strong, and ready for any deed. But at that very moment, two bullets sank between his horns and the two burning, pulsating points of pain that had remained from his antlers. The old deer crashed to the ground.

Not a hair moved on his body; he was dead and that was that.

Submitting to death, his body, which had tasted freedom for only a moment, turned cold and finally became truly free. It was unclear how it had happened, but he had been shot from two different sides. No one came to him and no one claimed the shot that had killed this free deer on this free land. And so Kerbŭġy the powerful, still undefeated leader was left to lie there under the green post on a clearing no one owned.

In the meantime, a jubilant bellow could be heard from the enclosure beyond the wooden fences.

Some say that Kerbŭġy, in his striving for freedom, never really died at all. Others believe that deer acquire their freedom only in the next world, in the afterlife.

Translated by Simon Hollingsworth, edited by Simon Geoghegan

MARHABAT BAIGUT
(b. 25.05.1945)

Marhabat Baigut is a writer, journalist and translator. He graduated from the Faculty of Philology at Kirov Kazakh State University (now Ăl-Farabi Kazakh National University) and for many years worked at regional Šymkent newspapers, *Šamšyraķ* and *Oņtùstik Ķazaķstan*, as well as for the Regional Party Committee. He subsequently occupied significant administrative positions in the region (1985–2008) and was the head of the regional branch of the Kazakhstan Writers' Union. Currently, he is editor-in-chief of *Qazyġurt.kz* magazine.

Baigut is considered a master of the short story genre, and has published around two dozen collections of short stories, including *Šilde* (July, 1978), *Syrbùlaķ* (1980), *Internattyņ balasy* (The Boy from the Boarding School, 1985), *Năuirzek* (Roller Bird, 1988), *Ķorġansyz žùrek* (Unprotected Heart, 1993), *Dauystyņ tùsi* (The Colour of Voice, 1993), *Mašattaġy mahabbat* (A Love Story in Mašat, 1995), *Sert pen senim* (Vow and Faith, 1997), *Ădebiet păniniņ perištesi* (An Angel of Literature Classes, 1999), *Aķpandaġy mysyķtar* (Cats in February, 2000), *Kiikoty* (Oregano, 2005) and *Ištarlyķ pen ķuštarlyķ* (Envy and Passion, 2018). A number of his works have been translated into Russian, Ukrainian, Uzbek, Turkish, Karakalpak and Sahka. Baigut has also translated books by Vasily Shukshin, Chinghis Aitmatov, Yuri Pokalchuk and Washington Irving into Kazakh. His essays have been collected into two volumes titled *Saġynyš sazdary* (Melodies of Longing, 2002) and *Kùngej kôņil* (Cheerful Soul, 2014).

He was awarded the Ķùrmet (1996) and Parasat (2010) Orders, the Alaš International Literary Award (1996) and the title of an Honoured Worker of the Republic of Kazakhstan (2004).

The Kazakhs of Hamburg

The winter of 1995 turned out to be as soft as a tender-hearted woman. After several light blizzards, the first signs of a dry spring began to appear. Residents of the *auyl*[1] of Kôkterek left the hay untended. The sheep and cows in the barn seemed to rush with appetite to the abounding hay at first, but soon they, too, began to neglect it, and the hay piled up.

The distance between the *auyls* of Kôkterek and Hamburg is six kilometres and six hundred and fifty metres. A few years ago, when a canal was being dug along the asphalt road, Nătibek Nesipbajůly, who lived in Kôkterek's best house, personally obtained this figure, measuring German-style. The news that a few more German families were moving from Hamburg now reached him from his own wife, Pătima.

At the end of a warm April, Nătibek and Pătima sat and drank tea, having done all the morning chores. Suddenly, the tea became thin. Nătibek, who had suspected something wrong because Pătima had set out the lump sugar, not the crystallised sugar, glanced at his wife. He noticed that she sat crookedly, and was looking in the direction of her father's native *auyl*.

'Nemerebaj and Šôberebaj each bought a house in Šymkent', Pătima said. (Before relating this bit of information came her announcement of the impending move by several German families from Hamburg, in reply to which he had said nothing.)

'So what's the big deal?' Nătibek could not remain silent this time. 'Perhaps they put enough money aside when one was a secretary of the Party committee, and the other an accountant.'

'People say they want to buy Hans's house in Hamburg', said Pătima.

At this, Nătibek nearly dropped the blue bowl with the small cotton-flower pattern. Instead, he brought it to his lips and swallowed heavily. He burned his tongue, but did not want his wife to notice. The accursed tea burned everything in its path. Tears formed in his eyes.

Pătima fixed her stare at a single point, as though she could see her father's native *auyl* clearly, behind Mount Tùrkitau.

---

[1] *Auyl* – socio-economic formation considered to constitute the heartland of the nation and a basis for an ethnic and cultural union of the nomadic community. Consisting of 50–70 yurts in the eighteenth century, it developed into its current permanent state of 'rural settlement' (of a minimum of 100 dwellers) when Kazakhs adopted a settled mode of life in the nineteenth and twentieth centuries. *Auyl* can also be used as a synonym for 'native land' and 'homeland', concepts revered by the Kazakhs.

Soon after Kazakhstan's independence, history teachers at the local middle school proved that Nătibek's *auyl* had been called Kôkterek fifteen hundred years earlier. After 1942, however, it became widely known by its nickname, 'Hamburg': Germans had come to dwell there in the cold autumn of 1941. They were called 'settlers' then, though in fact they were being forcibly *resettled* in the area. The Germans arrived by train on one of those cold autumn afternoons, and the railway station was packed with carts and wagons that were soon filled with German adults and children alike, as well as their belongings. Judging by what the Kazakhs in the district told each other, clicking their tongues in surprise, the Germans – despite their large numbers, and although they had many children – remained calm and quiet, making no noise either when disembarking from the trains or loading up the carts awaiting them in rows.

There had not been a single sound.

It's true that Kazakhs like to embellish and exaggerate, of course. But one of those carts had belonged to Nesipbaj, Nătibek's father, who had been one of those surprised observers. According to the stories he told his son many years later, when the train stopped and the Germans began to load the carts, only the orders of the commanding authorities and the snorting of the thin horses could be heard; when they were departing for the *auyls*, the only audible sound was the creaking of carts.

As everywhere, the 'settlers' were to join Kazakh families. Kôkterek was notable for its agriculture, so more Germans were sent there. By the spring of 1942, they had been squeezed onto Kazakh land, nevertheless living in harmony with their neighbours. In 1942, they requested allocations of plots in the lowlands, on the upper side of Kôkterek, and began to settle there as well.

At a time when death notifications were being delivered by the dozen to the homes of Kôkterek, and even after the end of the war, the weakened inhabitants of the *auyls* mourning the dead could not collect themselves; they did not notice that the German *auyl* (the official name of which was 'Birlik') became 'Hamburg', and had blossomed and evolved.

It's a sin to complain. Kôkterek only benefited from the Germans of Hamburg. Problems with equipment, marketable milk, pigs and chickens and other agricultural dilemmas were completely solved by the Germans. The Germans of Hamburg did not gossip, lie or brag like everyone else, and did not know the meaning of arrogance. Cleanliness and order ruled the day, both at the collective farm and at home.

Kôkterek also changed. No one today can deny that it improved significantly compared with other *auyls*. People try not to show it, but they have striven to imitate the Germans. The previous year a few families had moved from Hamburg to distant Almanïya, and their homes were purchased by other Germans. Nătibek recently learned that Germany is indeed called 'Almanïya'. Some still confuse it with Albania, and many do not even understand that Almanïya and Albania are two different countries.

All these thoughts ran quickly through Nătibek's mind, and his tongue – which could barely cope and which had been burned by the tea – had to work hard so he could ask: 'Is it true? Is Hans Weissler really moving? To Almanïya?'

'True, true. Your friend Weissler is moving. To Germany or to Albania, how should I know?' replied Pătima, without altering her gloomy expression.

Hans Weissler lived in an even lower part of already fabulous Hamburg, situated in the lowlands. Everyone knows that the lowlands in the mountainous areas bloom in a special way, in all colours. On a cool evening the previous summer, on a drive in their eldest son's newly purchased car (he worked in the district seat and was already familiar to everyone), he and his son had turned off the road to say hello to Hans and his wife Kilda[2] – who was a little unattractive, according to Nătibek, but with a strong physique and as straight a posture as a poplar. The couple met them with open arms.

How not to rejoice, given that two of the Germans who had arrived in Nesipbaj akṣakal's[3] cart on that cold autumn of 1941 had been Kilda's parents? They had even lived with them one winter. Later, the late Nesipbaj and Kilda's parents discussed the possibility of engaging Kilda to Nătibek – who had not been entirely against it, although Kilda's nose was too sharp and long, and was always red and peeling, and this sometimes gave him pause. In any case, at the same time, while on a stroll, he had noticed Pătima – who had come from Kyrgyzstan to visit his sister, over the Tùrkitau Mountains. At that time, his now-wife had seemed, to him, a beauty. She was talkative and seemed so housewifely and nimble that he did not even look at her feet. The girl Kilda was also not against a possible marriage, but after the dances that evening she chose Hans irrevocably. For how could she forgive Nătibek for dancing all through the night, but staring madly at Pătima?

When Nătibek arrived with his son, Hans and Kilda were sitting and drinking tea at a handsome table by the wolfberry bush, on beautiful chairs, as in a film. Seeing them, they rose from their seats and began to greet the guests joyfully. Tea was served all round, with sugar, of course. Nătibek drank his tea, sipping and sweating; his son, slightly embarrassed, had stopped earlier. Nătibek paused at that moment and thought, What would my eldest son look like if Kilda had taken the place of my Pătima...?

'We bought a new car', said Nătibek, now sated with tea. 'Bring the kôrimdik[4] here, Kildažan!'[5]

---

[2] Kilda's original name would, in fact, be Hilda; its rendering reflects local Kazakh pronunciation, and perhaps affectionate adoption of Hans and her by the community.

[3] Akṣakal – traditionally, a well-respected and powerful elder in charge of the community. Nowadays, a reverential form of address to elderly men in general.

[4] Kôrimdik – gift presented to the owner of a newly acquired asset as an expression of good wishes.

[5] Žan – lit. 'soul', appended as a suffix to express affection; Kilda thus becomes Kildažan.

436

'Well, come on then, tell me what you would like for yourself!' Kilda said, wiping her hands on her apron. 'Take anything you want.'

'I would like Hans's hands!' Nătibek said. 'Let this be your *kôrimdik*; it would be enough for me if your husband will occasionally inspect the heart and other insides of our car, our Zhiguli...'

'Why did you suddenly become so meek? Say it to Hans himself – why tell me?' Kilda replied in Kazakh.

'But Hans obeys you, doesn't he? Has he really changed?'

'Oh, this friend of yours wants a *toķal* – a second wife – these days...'

'Our Pătima has two younger sisters who are still unmarried. Let's become in-laws, *ojbaj*![6]' said Nătibek.

'Do you care about your car, or are you speaking from your heart?' retorted Kilda.

'In our times, one must be calculating...'

Hans interjected, shaking from laughter. 'Is it true that Nătibek nearly married you?' he asked.

'It's not just in our times that one must be calculating', said Kilda, 'but in those times, too! Nătibek calculated, and married Pătima.'

Nătibek said: 'We've presumed on Hans's kindness and gone quite far; let's finish this.'

But Kilda did not stop. 'Why, are you really afraid that Pătima will hear you, you bastard?' she joked.

Everyone went from the yard into the street to look at the car. Hans and Kilda were very taken with it, and inhaled repeatedly, taking in the scent of the new car with pleasure.

'Now, this is worth celebrating – it would be a sin not to drink a hundred ounces!' Hans said.

They all went back into the yard. Nătibek marvelled that, at first glance, the grounds were nothing special; but look again, and it was amazing. The doors and patterned windows were as beautiful as in a fairy tale. There was a dream of a bathhouse there, too, and a cellar, a pantry and some other room, plus a mechanised cattle room. Even the leaves of the grapes planted evenly between the house and the cowshed lined up in rows and grew upwards. The number of fruit trees, too, grew as if by command, no more and no less. According to everyone, and certainly according to Nătibek's own observations, the Germans built their cowsheds and other outbuildings to be much stronger than even their houses. They were legendary among all the inhabitants of Kôkterek. It was impossible not to be surprised at the cleanliness of the stalls, where the cows, goats, sheep, pigs and other animals lived – but especially the cowsheds, which had water, chopped hay and combined feed, all in separate compartments, distributed through pipes and troughs in just the right amounts, at certain times down to the minute and second.

---

[6] *Ojbaj* – an exclamation approximating 'oh, my!'; used to express surprise or joy.

For example, pressing a brown button lightly resulted in food being poured for the cattle without any noise – without even any rumbling or knocking. Pressing a bluish button had clear, pure and tasty water pouring out from an elongated, cast-iron bowl. Pressing a third button saw recently dropped, still-smoking manure immediately swept and cleaned. All the cows, white or black, gleamed from head to hooves; even a little dust did not stick, let alone manure. All the animals were thoroughbred.

All the Germans in Hamburg were orderly and expert in matters of households and farms, but Weissler had a special talent, and stood out among them.

Back at the table, they drank fine wine. The Germans, and especially the Germans from Hamburg, did not drink vodka. They drank wine, only wine that they had tried and tested themselves, which they themselves fermented. Even this wine was brought out very rarely, and in small measures. Nătibek did not hesitate to ask for a full pour, and drank it at once. He looked at everything around him with desire.

'You are looking around so enthusiastically, as if you are seeing all this for the first time!' remarked Kilda, as watchful as ever. 'Well, spit it out or you'll jinx us inadvertently.'

'What was your cow's name?' asked Nătibek.

'Era.'

'Yes, Era… people say that your Era knows language… is this true?'

'Of course she knows! Our Era has calved three times and knows three languages', Kilda replied.

'Oh, you nasty woman!' said Nătibek jokingly, and rose from the table. 'It is impossible to talk to you normally!'

'Well, you yourself asked. I just answered, and here you are, sulking', Kilda said. 'Era's genealogy is the Kazakh white-headed, black-and-white cow, right? Hence she knows Kazakh. We bought her mother from some Russian brothers. How could she not know Russian? Am I right? Right… And since birth, her upbringing is German… Now you can count up all the languages yourself. You're good at calculating, aren't you? If you cannot calculate it yourself, you can go and ask Pătima…'

'You mean to say you would like me to return to Pătima?'

'Hell, no! You can stay here until you are blue in the face. I just need to tell your friend that it's time to feed the cattle.'

'All right, then, we'll go', said Nătibek. 'Let's get out of here before this old witch of yours has eaten us… Thank you, my friend Hans!'

'Let's go say hello to Era first, otherwise it will be awkward', said Kilda. 'We'll remove your evil eye – spitting will be enough.'[7]

'OK, let us look, then', said Nătibek. They headed for the cowshed along a bright concrete path. When they approached, Nătibek wiped his feet several

---

[7] Traditional belief holds that spitting three times prevents the evil eye.

times at Kilda's insistence. Hans gave him a white coat to put on. After that, he was allowed to enter the room where the cow stood.

Nătibek glanced at it and froze, unable to avert his narrowed eyes. It was not a cow – it was an *oil painting*. It was a picture-perfect cow. Such a precious animal, with such shiny hair could only exist in television adverts or in the pages of a glossy magazine. Well, there's no such thing anymore in Kôkterek, no.

'Era, this is our friend Nătibek – we tell you about him constantly', Kilda said. 'He lives in Kôkterek. Come on, get acquainted!'

Era turned and nodded her head. What's more, it seemed she also mooed happily.

'Got it? She greeted you in Kazakh', said Kilda, gloating. Nătibek was already embarrassed. Then Kilda tidied up the table and went to attend to some chores outside.

'What's wrong with my friend Hans?' Nătibek muttered to himself. 'Why did Nemerebaj and Šôberebaj know that they are moving before we did?' He wanted to say this aloud, but he didn't – first, because he was a little afraid of Pătima; second, because his tongue had still not ceased burning.

Thinking back, Nătibek realised that he had not seen Hans and Kilda for a long time. Nor had they been seen at the dairy farm, either. The *sovkhoz* – the state farm – was now being run by others. The former secretary of the Party committee, Nemerebaj, and the former chief accountant, Šôberebaj, had left the business and travelled a lot to the city. As the former chief economist, Nătibek only occasionally involved himself in such farms. The new bosses – that is, the new team – did not permit him to participate in the affairs of the *sovkhoz* or of the office. It was a mess: chaos everywhere.

In any case, Nătibek, Nemerebaj and Šôberebaj were among those who had managed to find a way out in this turmoil and organise functioning businesses. They were more or less wealthy people now. Of course, if the other two had really purchased homes in Šymkent, as Pătima had said so gloomily, it meant that Nătibek had been left behind. That was acceptable to him – but he could not idle around now and watch Nemerebaj and Šôberebaj bargain for Hans Weissler's farmstead. This fear is what underlay Pătima's anger. She was a proud woman, of course; her maternal line was Kyrgyz. Mumbling all this to himself, Nătibek fell deep into thought, curing his burned tongue with saliva.

The same evening Nătibek learned from Pătima of his friends' impending move, he returned to Hamburg. It was two days after Hans had come back from a long trip. Kilda was a little ill.

'Yes, it's true, we're moving', Hans sighed. 'You know that my eldest daughter works in a big position in Moscow? So she persuaded us. I'm moving, my brother Nătibek. And without delay: we want to move to the end of this week. It's good that you came. Let's have a heart-to-heart talk for a few hours. From tomorrow, there will not be a minute of time to spare.'

Nătibek felt sore and sad in his soul. 'Hamburg without Hans will lose its beauty,' he thought. 'And can it be true, that I will never see Kilda again? What can you do… they are closer than family.'

Behind the sadness in his soul, of course, a more mercenary side of Nătibek was already making certain calculations. 'And what will happen to the dairy farm without them?' He reflected that, a year earlier, when several German families had moved, many harvesters were left without jobs.

But he dismissed these thoughts for a while, and asked Hans: 'Tell me honestly… do all the Germans want to move?'

'Well', said Hans, 'have I ever been dishonest with you? Let me think… The family of Franz and Erich will move after us. Andreas and David may move next year. Both the Zieglers will move together with us. It is possible that those who live in the short street will stay here. Do you want me to count you those who will *not* move?'

'No, no, I was just asking', Nătibek replied. 'Last year, when only a few German families moved, so many harvesters were out of work. God, it's a sad story with those harvesters.'

Hans sighed again. The wind had died down, and evening closed in. The sky had been clear, but now a few clouds appeared. The two men looked upward, hoping for rain. In the Ķazyģürt area, or a little nearer, a darkish cloud loomed.

'I need to sell the farm and the house as soon as possible', Hans said.

'Ah!' Nătibek flinched. Slightly dumbfounded, he quickly recovered himself and smiled.

'Nemerebaj came', Hans added, and Nătibek flinched once again. 'And Sôberebaj.'

Nătibek was confused, like a fish caught in a net. He gulped the clean air of the windless evening, but it seemed to him that there was not quite enough air. His back was sweating and then freezing.

Hans Weissler always spoke frankly, so it was clear that, when he mentioned Nemerebaj and Sôberebaj, he had no intention of overstating the price of his land. 'Ah, what to say about the intelligence and accuracy of the Germans', thought Nătibek. 'They are also good friends. They do not display hypocrisy or sycophancy.' Still, his friend Hans, showing him kindness, told him everything as it was, and hinted that Nătibek could find an opportunity to become the new owner of this flawless household.

However Kilda might have tried to hide her sadness on her gentle, welcoming face, she still moved much more slowly than usual before bringing tea. She also put something else on the table: those delicious wines. Hans did not wait long to pour it. Needless to say, Nătibek also drank his without hesitation or need of much cajoling.

'My brother Hans!' Nătibek said, noting how decisively a high-quality wine can spread throughout the whole body, making one warm and jolly. 'You understand me as nobody else, and I understand you. Now, I have never encountered such a household, such an operation, as yours – not anywhere.

Nor do I begrudge it! You know, I'm not jealous of anyone. But it's true that I do not want it to go to people such as Nemerebaj or Šôberebaj. Do you understand? I would grieve if such a fairy tale of a farmstead were to go to such greedy people...'

Hans smiled. Slightly abashed, he scratched the back of his head.

'Do you know what I mean?' Nătibek continued. 'Do you understand me? I believe you have understood, judging by how you just scratched your head in the Kazakh manner...'

'But you three are of the same clan', Hans said 'In general, I do not like to slander anyone...'

'I do not like it either; I'm just telling you because you are my friend.'

'On the one hand, I should treat the three of you equally. But, on the other hand, of course, I would be more pleased if you and Pătima would become the owners of my home. It would bring me peace wherever I go.'

'My dear man, let me...' said Nătibek Nesipbajůly, and stood and pecked Hans Weissler's cheeks several times. 'Come, come Kildažan, let me rain kisses on you, too! You will leave soon...'

'My summer cold is very contagious', Kilda said, backing away. 'Can't you see I have the flu? Otherwise, I would not mind... In the fifty years of our acquaintance, I've never seen you so excited!'

'It's more trouble than it's worth to argue with this woman', said Nătibek. 'OK, my friend Hans, tell me – how much are you asking for your house and land?'

'You know that we do not like to dissemble', said Hans, chewing green onions. 'Thinking about ourselves, our needs, our future... having thought through everything, we arrived at the sum of seven thousand dollars.'

The top of Nătibek's head pulsated. He quickly calculated the figure in tenge, and reckoned that for such a property, it was hardly an expensive asking price.

Hans continued: 'My Kazakhs do not have bad proverbs. I especially like this one: *Nysap sajyn bereke* – "Moderation is the key to lasting welfare". Time is short, of course, or it would have been possible to ask for more.'

Nătibek knew very well that Hans did not speak aimlessly. He sat in silent contemplation for a long time. The flowers on the wolfberry bush began to fade. He thought of his eldest son, and of his youngest son, who had his own small business. Looking toward Tùrkitau, he remembered his wife's relatives. Still more thoughts carried him toward Taškent. In order to avoid regret later, he decided to act firmly. Courage had not yet left him, and he was not one for retreat, in any case. Hans became uncomfortable with silence and began to hum the song 'Anama' – 'To My Mother' by Šămši Ḳaldaâḳov.

Suddenly, Nătibek returned to reality: 'Hans!' He said loudly. 'Can you wait three days and three nights? Will you wait?'

'I'll wait. If you really intend to buy, what can I do? I'll wait.'

441

'Nätibek!' Kilda added, coughing from afar. 'If you really plan to buy our home, then I shall not sell Era to anyone. I'll present her to Pätima.'

'I am very grateful to you, my dear! If I cannot find the money and close the purchase with you in three days, I shall blame only myself on the fourth! If Nemerebaj or Šôberebaj offer you more, and you change your minds, it will be your fault!'

Having spoken thus, Nätibek vanished in the darkness.

That night, there was little rain. Still, expectations of the moonless night were not justified. At the same time, on the other side of Mount Tùrkitau, in Kyrgyzstan, it rained buckets. Having prepared since early morning, Pätima took to the road to ask for help from her younger brother, who worked at a mine in a small section of the Talas River in Kyrgyzstan. Nätibek and Pätima's eldest son, who worked in the district seat, went to Uzbekistan to his own son-in-law, who ran a plant in the town of Šynaz, in the Syr Dariâ province.

In a nutshell, by the fourth day Nätibek had collected almost exactly seven thousand dollars, and was hurrying to Hans Weissler.

It was hard to say goodbye to the Germans. Not a single person present at the farewell was unmoved; no one resisted shedding tears. Whereas, in that cold autumn in 1941, hundreds of Germans were loaded onto the wagons that flooded the station and did not even squeak, now, when just a few families were moving, Germans and Kazakhs alike began to clamour and weep, making considerable noise.

'You see', said Nätibek, sobbing. 'You have also received something from us Kazakhs... you see?' Pätima and Kilda, embracing each other, could barely part.

A few days passed. Nätibek and Pätima, along with several of their grandchildren, moved from Kôkterek to Hamburg. Afterward, both Nemerebaj and Šôberebaj moved to Hamburg, one after the other. Nemerebaj bought the house of the older Ziegler brother, which did not lag far behind the Weissler farmstead in terms of splendour, and Šôberebaj bought the younger Ziegler's house.

There were Germans, Kazakhs, Russians, and even Turks who had pleaded for the opportunity to purchase the beautiful Era, but Kilda kept her word: Pätima received the animal as a gift: she was as valuable as a precious stone, and her milk flowed in a stream. Era probably understood more than most people that Kilda was moving; she seemed to weep, blinking her long, black and white eyelashes, and even Pätima – who could seem cold-hearted – sobbed.

After moving to Hamburg, Nemerebaj and Šôberebaj began to visit Nätibek, which had not been the case in earlier times.

'Hello, to Nätibek Weissler, from the elder Ziegler!' said Nemerebaj, entering the gate. '*Guten Abend*, Herr Naty-Beck Weissler!' said Šôberebaj. '*Ich bin* Šôberebaj Ziegler!'

Pätima, in imitation of her close, dear friend Kilda, did not invite Nemerebaj and Šôberebaj into the house; instead, she laid the table in the yard and brought tea and wine. All three owners, as if exhibiting German restraint, did not conduct themselves too freely at the table, and ate and drank unhurriedly.

During their first get-together, they discussed the care and maintenance of the farms and houses they had acquired, as well as partial or full cowshed mechanisation, and shared their views.

On the following occasion, Nemerebaj and Šôberebaj entered the yard each with an air of confusion and distress. Nemerebaj related that his three apple trees had withered; Šôberebaj told of his grapevines, built in rows, which had begun to fade. Nătibek, too, sighed heavily, as if to indicate that his yard, too, was evidently losing its former pristine state.

'Yesterday, my younger son broke one of the cowshed mechanisms', said Šôberebaj anxiously. 'When the television was jamming, he used to hit it with his fist, and when the hay cutter stopped working, he hit it with the blunt end of an axe and broke it completely. That accursed bastard... children do not appreciate things earned by their parents' hard work!'

'I remember one conversation, which happened about ten years ago...' Nemerebaj began.

'Well, Germans speak briefly and do things efficiently, so do not go on for a long time', Šôberebaj said.

'Go ahead, continue', said Nătibek.

'It's already short – you're making me prolong it with your protest', Nemerebaj complained, before starting again: 'If I am not mistaken, exactly ten years ago one of the best writers today, Dulat Isabekov, came to the *auyl* of Nŭrlysu, where he was born. During the war, his family had moved there, and soon after Dulat's birth they moved back to Montajtas. And this very writer was staying at the Commissar Ķasymbek's house. The heads of the districts came, and I also helped to receive the distinguished guest.'

'Who came, you say?' asked Šôberebaj.

'Dulat Isabekov, he says', said Nătibek. 'Writer-playwright. One of the best men of letters of our time... Did not you know that?'

'Of course, I know that!' Šôberebaj said. 'The journalist Dăulet Isabekŭly, I know him very well.'

'Well, no. Dulat Isabekov and Dăulet Isabekŭly are very different people', Nemerebaj replied angrily.

'It's not the same person?'

'You know, you amaze me – you don't read, do you? How can you confuse Dulat Isabekov with God knows who!'

'Wait, wait! Do not downgrade him, saying "God knows who". What do you mean, God knows who? He is also one of the best. He is not just any journalist, he is a *hajji*![8] A *hajji*! Got that?'

---

[8] *Hajji* – a person who completed a mandatory pilgrimage to Mecca; a *hajji* would be revered as a devoted Muslim among Kazakhs until recently.

'Yes, yes, I know of him. He writes "Dăulet Hajji Isabekŭly" anywhere he can; how many wall calendars has he published and signed now? He never stops. Maybe he's a good person, maybe he is a *hajji*. But the story is not about this man, but about our wonderful writer, Dulat Isabekov!'

This argument between Nemerebaj and Šôberebaj did not abate. Nătibek could bear it no longer, and finally said: 'Nemerebaj, what did you want to talk about in the beginning?'

'I wanted to tell you about an amusing story that Dulat Isabekov told when he came to Nŭrlysu, and you're not letting me tell it...'

'Well, tell it now, come on! Šôberebaj has stopped. Do not speak ill of the *hajji* behind his back, speak about your Dulat.'

'All right', said Nemerebaj, 'Dulat Isabekov, in that summer of 1985, sitting in the house of Commissar Ķasymbek, said: "The Germans are an amazing people. A few years ago, in the upper part of Almaty, we bought a *dacha*[9] from a German; after three more years of neglecting it completely, we barely made a Kazakh *dacha* out of it." That's what he said. That's what I wanted to tell you about.'

Šôberebaj roared with laughter. Nătibek also laughed.

'Three years of neglect and he barely made a Kazakh *dacha*!' Šôberebaj did not stop laughing. 'I really have not read this writer. Ha! Now I shall have to read his work. You see where everything comes from!'

At the end of the third week, Pătima invited the women of Kôkterek for tea, dividing them into three groups for three separate occasions. Only afterward could she feel freer, as if removing a weight from her shoulders. In each group, approximately fifteen or twenty women walked around, touching, tapping and admiring everything. Everyone was pleased and impressed.

When they met Era, several women almost fainted from delight. Nătibek's order that no one be allowed to approach the fully mechanised cowshed was contravened slightly, and of course it was not possible to find so many white coats for fifty or sixty women. The long and the short of it was that the tripartite arrival of the guests greatly transformed the yard now owned by Nătibek Nesipbajŭly and formerly owned by Hans Weissler.

The fourth week was quiet and passed without incident. But trouble came during the fifth week. Era, for no reason at all, suddenly fell ill. She was constipated, and no matter how many doctors were called or how many drugs were injected, nothing helped. The beautiful cow stood up, as stiff as a pikestaff. Gradually, she began to look dusty and dishevelled, like the cows of Kôkterek. 'Perhaps she was cursed', said people from the region. 'Perhaps she is yearning for her former owners and became sick', said others. 'Or maybe she ate something she wasn't supposed to...'

'You are to blame for everything!' said Nătibek to Pătima.

---

[9] *Dacha* – country house or cottage, typically used as a second/holiday home by city dwellers. *Dachas* were popular during the Soviet time.

'You're no better!' cried Pătima. 'You could not take care of it like Hans did!' said Pătima, and added, showing the harsh extremes of her character: 'Oh, God! Better to take me, than Era!... Do not make a mockery of us in front of our friends and enemies, oh Lord!'

On the fifth day of that week, in the afternoon, Era ceased blinking her long, black and white eyelashes and died.

A message was sent to Kôkterek, and a crowd of women came and expressed condolences. Pătima grieved heavily. Sitting in the reception room, she suddenly composed a memorial song and began singing it:

Oh, woe, woe to me!
Oh! A piercing wind blew,
and my strength gave out,
an animal with gem-like wool,
whose evil eye dispatched you?
Hamburg as the Garden of Eden
covered in green, all over.
My dear Era, given by Kilda,
which enemy hexed you?
The stones of Sajramsu are sharp;
the milk of my cow is rich.
My dear Era knew three languages.
What enemy brought you down?
Woe, woe to me!

Hearing this song, the women who had come from Kôkterek became uncomfortable.

'What a shame! *Žeņeše*[10] sings a *žoķtau*,[11] and we did not even signal our arrival!'

'You don't say!'

'I suppose we are becoming heartless', said a representative of the delegation.

Nătibek, passing through the courtyard, said in astonishment: 'What is she jabbering about?' He wanted to say: 'Let an animal die rather than a man, and take all our troubles with it.' However, he could not.

Era's body spent one night in the fully mechanised cowshed; the following day, it was given to the ground by a grove on a hill.

---

[10] *Žeņeše* – form of address to a sister-in-law or, generally, an older married woman.

[11] *Žoķtau* – memorial song performed by the closest female relatives of a deceased person; it typically describes the best qualities of the deceased and expresses lament and the performer's sense of loss. The women are referring to the practice of *dauys šyġaru*, or ritual wailing, performed by females arriving at the threshold when coming to pay their last respects to the deceased.

***

Neither Pătima, who sang her memorial song dedicated to Era, the beautiful cow, in 1995, nor her husband – who was so surprised by her conduct – could have predicted that the Kazakhs of Hamburg would enter the new millennium as citizens of a new, independent state.

Within two years, the sons of Nătibek and Pătima would privatise almost all of the former socialist farm's combines and tractors, along with half its land. Within five years, their own sons and daughters would, together, launch a farm that could boast of thoroughbred cows and automobile-tractor stations. They became wealthy people who employed the descendants of Nemerebaj and Sôberebaj.

Unfortunately, Nătibek died too soon to see all this. Now, Madame Pătima visits her relatives on the other side of Tùrkitau frequently, driving her white Jeep. On the road, she whispers: 'Eh, Nătibek… why did you abandon me so soon?' Then she sighs with regret.

From time to time.

Translated by Mitchell Albert

SMAGUL YELUBAY

(b. 9.03.1947)

Smagul Yelubay is a Kazakh writer, journalist and screenwriter. He moved to Kazakhstan from Turkmen SSR in 1961 and graduated from Kirov Kazakh State University (now Ăl-Farabi Kazakh National University) in 1971, before going on to study screenwriting in Moscow (1974–75). He was first deputy managing editor and then managing editor at Ķazaķfil'm (Kazakhfilm) studios (1976–92 and 2008–10 respectively); editor-in-chief of *Parasat*, a literary journal (1992–95); a journalist at Radio Liberty in Prague (1995–2004); and vice-president of the Kazakh PEN Club (2004–8). Since 2010, he has been a professor at the Žùrgenov (Zhurgenov) Kazakh National Academy of Arts.

His major work is the trilogy *Aķboz ùj* (Lonely Yurt), about the famine and repressions in Kazakhstan during the 1930s; it has been translated into English, Turkish and Spanish, and was published in the USA and Turkey in 2016, and in Spain in 2018. He has also authored several short story collections: *Ojsylķara* (1972), *Sattar soķpaģy* (Sattar's Path, 1974), *Žaryķ dùnie* (The Bright World, 1978), *Bilte šamnyṇ žaryģy* (The Light of the Wick-Fed Lamp, 1989), as well as novels: *Minăžat* (The Prayer, 1994), *Žalģan dùnie* (The Mortal World, 2001) and an essay collection, *Ķiâmet-ķajym ģasyry* (The Age of the Last Judgement, 2011). He wrote scripts for a number of feature films, including *Ķyzyl otau* (dir. Ķanybek Ķasymbekov, 1989), *Ôtelmegen paryz* (Atonement, dir. Serik Žarmùhamedov, 1983), *Batyr Baân* (dir. Slambek Tăuekel, 1992), and a TV show about the early years of the Kazakh Khanate, *Almas ķylyš* (Diamond Sword, dir. Rùstem Ăbdirăšev, 2016).

He has been awarded the Orders of Ķùrmet (2005), Parasat (2018) and the title of an Honoured Worker of the Republic of Kazakhstan (2013).

Gift for the Grandson

Šonaj began to feel restless even before the train was past the station at Otar. He gathered his belongings into his *ķoržyn*[1], draped his *šapan*[2] over his shoulders, and settled himself by the window. Craning his skinny neck, he peered intently at the landscape as it flashed by him.

Šonaj's travelling companion Ajymžan, the daughter of Úlman *aķsaķal*[3] a student in Almaty, was lying on the upper bunk. Thanks to her, Šonaj had suffered no lack of tea. She turned out to be a calm, good-natured girl.

Šonaj was a tall man, gaunt and stooped. He wore a long stripped *šapan* robe and belted it with a towel, as did all *aķsaķals*, the older men among his neighbours – Kara-Kalpakians, Uzbeks and Turkmens. Šonaj had been born in Kazakhstan, but ever since he could remember, he had lived in Kara-Kalpakia.

He was going to Almaty because he had a son there. But it was not his son that his heart yearned and ached for, it was his grandson, seven-year-old Edige. Šonaj kept watching out the window and craning his neck as if Edige were waving and calling to him from afar. Last summer, when Šonaj was leaving Almaty for the *auyl*[4], his grandson had run to him and thrust something into his side pocket.

'What's this, Edige?'

'It's a bag, Grandpa. Bring me back some *asyķ* from the *auyl*, will you?'

Well, how can you refuse your grandson?

Over the summer, Šonaj had visited close and distant relatives in Ķoŋyrat, Hoželi, Šomanaj, Nôkis. Mindful of his grandson's commission, after each feast of mutton he had put the *asyķ*-knucklebones in the little bag. Now, filled to the brim, it lay at the bottom of his *ķoržyn*, his colourful carpetbag.

---

[1] *Ķoržyn* – a saddlebag, bag or a container primarily used to store food.

[2] *Šapan* – traditional quilted coat, typically worn by men; it comes in different forms depending on the social status of the wearer and which region of Kazakhstan he comes from.

[3] *Aķsaķal* – traditionally, a well-respected and powerful elder in charge of the community. Nowadays, a reverential form of address to elderly men in general.

[4] *Auyl* – socio-economic formation considered to constitute the heartland of the nation and a basis for an ethnic and cultural union of the nomadic community. Consisting of 50–70 yurts in the eighteenth century, it developed into its current permanent state of 'rural settlement' (of a minimum of 100 dwellers) when Kazakhs adopted a settled mode of life in the nineteenth and twentieth centuries. *Auyl* can also be used as a synonym for 'native land' and 'homeland', concepts revered by the Kazakhs.

The closer they got to Almaty, the more slowly the old man felt the train was moving. Endless autumnal steppe, bleak distances, still stretched on both sides of the tracks.

Šonaj had moved in with his son in Almaty only recently. Before, he and his old wife had lived in Kara-Kalpakia. Two years ago his wife had died, and he had been left alone in a large, spacious house. All the farm work fell on his shoulders, but he had no intention of giving up and stubbornly toiled away.

His son and daughter-in-law kept saying they were going to move him to Almaty, they were not going to leave him here alone. But the old man would have none of it.

'Why go wandering in my old age?' he said. 'And what would happen to the farm we built up little by little, my late Rǎuiš and I? How can you leave your own hearth, when you've lived beside it all your life? No, I'm not going anywhere.'

Šonaj firmly stood his ground. Only when his son and daughter-in-law made up their minds to move away from the *auyl* with little Edige did he break down, his eyes welling with involuntary tears. He and his wife had raised the grandson. This parting was bitter for Šonaj.

Three days in a row he lay in bed with his face buried in his pillow. But it is truly said that to live in the *auyl* is to live in a golden cradle. When they learned of Šonaj's distress, his friends, neighbours and relatives began coming around. Some made tea, others stoked the stove, swept the house.

When anyone boiled meat in honour of a visitor, Šonaj was sure to be the first invited. But as they say, while it's nice to be a guest, home cooking is best. Šonaj often thought about Rǎuiš, who had left him too soon, she wasn't even sixty-four, he thought about Edige, whom he loved very much, and at length he began wasting away with sorrow.

One day a friend suggested, 'Marry some old woman. Two together have an easier time of it.'

'At my age I won't find one better than Rǎuiš. I'm seventy-seven, after all. And no, I haven't outlived my wits.'

But now, as luck would have it, his blood pressure began spiking up. One morning, when he was getting out of bed, he collapsed on the floor. His whole farm, the horse, the ten sheep, the cows and calf were left with no one to look after them. Besides, winter was coming. Šonaj accepted the hopelessness of his situation and urgently summoned his son by telegram. The son came. They sold the livestock, the house.

'Take me where you wish', Šonaj said.

That was how he ended up with Toḳtasyn in Almaty. The apartment was on the sixth floor, no elevator, the old man had trouble climbing the stairs. His one comfort was Edige, who kept him busy from morning to night telling fairy tales and playing games. The son and daughter-in-law were gone at work all day. At times Šonaj felt that he had shut himself up within the four walls as if in a prison. He barely lived till spring. When a bright Sun began to shine and

449

the earth dried out a little, he left for his *auyl*. There, he received a boisterous welcome, the old women even burst into tears...

In the evening the train reached the outskirts of Almaty.

'We're here, aren't we, daughter?' Šonaj asked joyfully.

'We're here, we're here.' Ajymžan laughed, her eyes sparkling.

At the station they got into a cab, and Šonaj thrust a piece of paper in the driver's hand.

'What's this, *aḳsaḳal*?' the cabbie asked.

'My address. A new one.'

A telegram had come while Šonaj was staying in the *auyl*. The son and daughter-in-law had announced that they were planning to move to a new apartment, they wanted to live in a quieter neighbourhood. The move had apparently taken place, since the telegram had the new address.

Šonaj was elated. In every little boy carrying a schoolbag he imagined he saw his grandson, who had also started school this year. Not knowing how to express his delight – today he was going to meet his favourite! – Šonaj turned to Ajymžan.

'Daughter, why not come in with me. You can get to the dormitory later. Have a cup of tea with us, you'll rest up from the trip.'

'Thank you *ata*,[5] but I can't.'

It occurred to Šonaj that she might feel uncomfortable with Toḳtasyn, who was her teacher. There had been quite an incident last year: for a long time Toḳtasyn hadn't given her any grades. Let her study a bit harder, he said.

Šonaj had found out about it from the girl's father, Ülman, with whom she lived in a neighbouring *auyl*. He had immediately telephoned his son in Almaty and bawled him out. Why be so harsh with the girl, when she's taking correspondence courses and comes to the city only once a year?

'Here we are!' the driver said, slowing down beside a multi-storey building.

Šonaj tried again to persuade the girl. 'Come now, daughter. Since you're here at the house, it's awkward if you don't come in.'

'No, no', Ajymžan protested resolutely. 'I'll keep this cab and go on to the dormitory. Please excuse me. But thank you very much for the invitation.'

When the cab drove off, Šonaj straightened his belt and looked around. Old women and old men were sitting on benches near the entrances, kids were racketing in the courtyard. He hoped to catch sight of his grandson among them, but the boy wasn't there.

Hoisting his *ḳoržyn* to his shoulder, he went over to some old women and addressed one of them.

'Does Šonaev live here?'

'Yes.'

'Which apartment?'

'Forty-seven. On the fourth floor', the old woman said.

---

[5] *Ata* – lit. 'grandfather'; respectful form of address to an older man.

Šonaj started slowly up the stairs and made it to the apartment with difficulty. He thought he heard a shrill childish voice from behind the door, and his heart leapt: Edige, my little grandson!

The door was unlocked. Šonaj walked in and threw his *ķoržyn* on the floor of the hallway.

'Who's there?' came Toķtasyn's voice.

'Halloo!'

'*Kôke!*'[6] His son came running from the room.

'It's me. But where's Edige? Edige-e! Come here, rascal!'

He looked into the room and stepped back in fright. The apartment was practically empty, no familiar things, none of his grandson's toys.

'Father', Toķtasyn began, but Šonaj interrupted him.

'Where's Edige? Where's my daughter-in-law?'

'You might come inside first', his son grumbled, and dragged the heavy *ķoržyn* to the kitchen.

Šonaj's old heart sensed something wrong. He took off his shoes and halted in the middle of the room, which stank of tobacco. He looked around. Truly, there was nothing in the room but one bed, a table and a chair. This was an uncalled-for insult.

Šonaj bellowed at the top of his voice, 'Who emptied this house?! Answer me!'

Toķtasyn came out of the kitchen carrying a teapot. He was just as tall as his father and just as stooped. After a silence, he scratched the back of his head in puzzlement and let himself down on the chair.

'But Father, you see it all yourself. Why ask?'

'What do I see? Not a thing, not one damn thing. Make yourself clearer, don't mumble.'

'How could it be clearer… We're divorced.'

'You degenerate dog!' Šonaj all but wept. 'Where's Edige?! I ask you, where's my Edige?!'

'With his mother. That's the law.'

'I'll show you the law!'

Šonaj's first whistled near Toķtasyn's ear. Toķtasyn ducked.

'Calm down, Father.'

'I'll show you calm down! I've lived to old age – never have I seen such disgrace!'

Šonaj still wanted to get at his son, give him a good whack, but the son, knowing his father's heavy hand, spun around him like a top.

Out of breath, the old man dropped on the bed.

'Find me Edige, or else—!'

'But I'm not even allowed near him.'

'Take me there, I'll do the talking.'

---

6   *Kôke* – respectful form of address to an older patron or protector; it can be applied to both males and females.

'You won't get anywhere.'

'You degenerate dog, what have I come to,' the old man grieved. 'So it'll just be us alone? Edige must be waiting for me, he's worn his eyes out watching: "Where's my Grandpa?" and all you have to say is, "We're divorced." You can shoot each other for all I care, but get me Edige!'

The old man lay down on the bed, turned his face to the wall, and pulled his *šapan* over his head. In the middle of the night his blood pressure spiked, his temperature soared, and they had to call an ambulance. Only after an injection did he fall calmly asleep. He did not wake up until noontime. It was light, Toḳtasyn had long since left for work.

Šonaj sat up in bed and suddenly heard a high-pitched female voice from the entry: 'Peek-a-boo!'

Šonaj scrambled to his feet in bewilderment, thinking, Who can this be? God save us, have they come to rob us?

'Who's there?' he called.

A young woman he did not know walked in wearing slacks. She stared at Šonaj in surprise.

Šonaj relaxed. 'Hello, daughter! Come in!'

'Hello', the girl said uneasily. 'Toḳtasyn's not home?'

'He's at work, obviously', Šonaj growled.

'Have a good day, then!' the girl blurted, and rushed to the door as if someone were chasing her. Mystified, Šonaj shrugged his shoulders.

His son showed up for lunch, made tea and fried two thin slices of meat. They ate in silence. When Šonaj said that some girl had come, Toḳtasyn mumbled something unintelligible. When he went back to work, he left the key to the apartment, in case his father took it into his head to go somewhere.

Šonaj untied his *ḳoržyn*, pulled out the little bag of knucklebones, put it in his pocket and went down to the street. He knew that for money a taxi would take him anywhere, so he headed straight for the taxi stand, which wasn't far from the building. He had decided that he could easily find Edige at school.

'Where to?' the cabbie asked, yawning.

'Son, take me to the Kazakh school.'

'There are several Kazakh schools in the city.'

'Take me where they teach first-graders, son.' Šonaj answered simply.

'Hm-m.' The driver pondered. 'Not an easy problem. But all right, let's go.'

After driving in a circle around the city, they stopped near a school. The yard was full of dark-complexioned youngsters. Several found time to greet Šonaj as they ran past.

'Hello, *ata*!'

'Hello, sonny.'

He asked one youngster whether he knew the first-grader Edige Šonaev. The boy shook his head and ran after his friends. A teacher came over to Šonaj and after hearing his question said that they didn't have, and hadn't had, anyone by that name.

'But is there another Kazakh school hereabouts?' the old man asked.

'There's a boarding school nearby, on Kirov Street.'

Šonaj soon found this school too, but Edige wasn't there either. He did learn that there were six Kazakh schools in all in the district, so he had another four left to visit.

By evening he had been to all of them. Not one of them had a pupil named Šonaev Edige.

The old man returned home very late and deeply weary. His son, fearing a fresh outburst of anger from his father, did not ask where he had been all day.

The next day Šonaj hired a taxi and began driving around to schools again. It developed that there was one more Kazakh school somewhere in precinct six. The cabbie turned out to be a nice, friendly person. Privately Šonaj decided that if his grandson was in the city, he would find him despite all, no matter what it cost.

He reached the school at last. Instead of fifteen roubles, he thrust a whole twenty at the cabbie; the man found himself obeying Šonaj. Classes were in progress; there wasn't a soul in the corridor. The cabbie opened the door of the first classroom a crack, then turned to Šonaj and whispered, 'There's a lesson going on.'

At this point the door opened, and a stout, solidly built woman, a teacher, appeared.

'Excuse me', the cabbie said. 'This *aksakal* is looking for his grandson. Šonaev Edige. He started first grade this year. Would you know anyone by that name?'

'Šonaev Edige?' the teacher repeated. 'Yes, we did have a boy by that name.'

Šonaj felt his heart had stopped beating. He thrust his head forward, all attention. 'You *did* have you, you say?'

'Yes, but the boy's mother took him out of school, probably a month ago.'

'Oh, Allah!' Šonaj groaned, shrinking into himself and all but sitting down on the floor. His hands dropped helplessly.

'*Aksakal*, are you ill?' the cabbie said in alarm. 'What should we do? He's ill.'

But now the bell rang. Šonaj gradually came to himself. The cabbie told the old man's story; the teacher frowned and nodded her head. The children spilled noisily out of the classrooms into the corridor. Supporting Šonaj, the teacher led him to the exit, telling him along the way, 'You needn't have gone to the trouble of looking for your grandson in Kazakh schools. His mother said she wanted to send him to a Russian school. The boy was very bright, we hated to part with him. I tried to get his mother to change her mind, but she wouldn't budge.'

'Oh, Allah! Oh, Allah!' the old man keened, shaking his head in sorrow. 'Well, how can I find him? What do you advise?'

'I just don't know', the teacher said uncertainly. There are a lot of Russian schools in the city. If you want to find him, I think you need to look in the schools in our district. She'd have to put the boy in one of the closer schools, you know, not far from home. They live somewhere near here, I think. Edige used to come to school on foot.'

Despite all, the cabbie really was a nice person.

'*Ata*, get in, I'll take you to one more school', he offered. 'The Russian schools are full of Kazakh kids. Maybe this time you'll be lucky.'

At this school, the cabbie ran in by himself. Soon he returned crestfallen. The boy wasn't here either.

Šonaj came home that evening totally exhausted, with a headache, and went straight to bed.

His son asked, 'Father, where have you been all day?'

Šonaj did not answer. He lay as if dead, with his *šapan* pulled over his head. After he had rested a while, he explained to his son, 'I looked for Edige all day. Ransacked all the schools.'

'It was silly to go to the trouble', Toḳtasyn frowned. 'You should have asked me. After the divorce, you know, she changed Edige's last name. I often looked in on him while he was at his first school. But it didn't seem to make me feel any better – or him either. It was especially hard on him. I thought about it and decided not to show my face at all. Why torment myself and the boy.'

'Worthless, all of you!' Šonaj raged. 'Think of it, he's given up seeing his boy! His very own son, his own flesh and blood! No, nothing will stop me. I'll find him, he's waiting for me.'

After this conversation, Šonaj completely stopped talking to his son about what he was doing. He must have visited every single school, every single street. Sometimes he went by taxi, sometimes on foot. Distances did not frighten him – in his day he had travelled on foot from the Embi to Horezm. More than a few times he stopped passers-by and asked how to get to this place or that. Many abandoned their own errands to escort him, for there are more than a few kind hearts.

And when he went by taxi, he did not begrudge the money, because then the cabbies did not begrudge their time. He had enough money from the sale of his house and property in the *auyl*, six thousand or so. Three he had given to his son and daughter-in-law to buy a set of furniture, the rest he had put in the bank against a rainy day.

When he arrived at his destination, he would abandon the taxi and make the rounds of the street on foot. Every time, he was filled with excitement – any minute now he would meet his Edige. He stopped and questioned every boy with a schoolbag. And wandered like that until evening…

Today a wet snow was falling, it was slippery and unpleasant. Yet the streets were full of people, especially around the bus stops.

Šonaj hurried along with the rest of the crowd, cane in hand. The skirts of his long sheepskin coat hampered his stride, but still, his eyes darted in all directions – though what could he see when the crowd was so thick?

As he walked, he pictured Edige asking him reproachfully, '*Ata*, why don't you come to me?' and himself answering, 'But sonny, why are you keeping out of my sight?'

At length, the old man began to lose heart. Twice he was almost hit by a car. 'Oh, Allah! Did I ever think I'd come to this?' he sighed heavily.

The dusk was thickening rapidly. I have to get home before dark, Šonaj thought.

He stood at the edge of the sidewalk and raised his hand in the hope of flagging a taxi. He was near a bus stop, where a lot of people were waiting.

The bus finally came, but it didn't have room for everyone who wanted to get on. Again, the thought of a taxi flashed across his mind, but there were no free cabs to be seen.

Just then, as the bus started up, a loud cry rang out from the window.

'*Ata*! *Ata*!'

Šonaj turned toward the voice and saw Edige pounding his hands on the glass.

Šonaj lunged for the bus, but it was rapidly moving away.

'Stop! Hey, Edige! Stop!' Šonaj shouted. He ran after the bus, and the skirts of his sheepskin coat flapped in the wind. 'Oh, Allah! *Stop*, you devilish hunk of steel! Damn you to hell!'

If he had managed to overtake the bus, he would have clung to it with a death grip.

But suddenly Šonaj slipped on the snow and sprawled flat. He felt himself land hard.

Summoning his last strength, he got up and flung himself after the bus again, but immediately fell. His body would not obey at all, his legs had turned to cotton.

'What a pity', he grunted, pushing himself up with both hands and watching the bus go. Perhaps he might have gotten to his feet somehow, but his cane had flown off to one side. Never in his life had he felt so helpless. A young fellow picked up his cane from the street and handed it to him.

'*Aksakal*, can you stand?' he asked. Šonaj shook his head no. It hurt him to make the slightest movement.

'Don't touch him', came someone's voice. 'I think he broke his hip. I saw him fall. We have to call an ambulance.'

A crowd quickly gathered. Šonaj lay on the snow with his eyes closed, and his lips moved.

'He's saying something', said one of the passers-by. 'Quiet!'

The youth who had picked up the cane bent over the old man, listened, and shook his head. 'I can't understand anything.'

But Šonaj was thinking, If I live, my boy, my Edige, you and I will not fail to meet.

From the distance they heard the siren of the ambulance.

Translated by Susan Brownsberger

DIDAKHMET ASHIMKHANULY
(10.06.1950 – 23.05.2015)

Didakhmet Ashimkhanuly was a Kazakh writer and journalist. After graduating from high school in 1968, he worked as head of an automobile club, served in the Soviet Army (1969–71) and was a stonemason at the Almaty House Construction Plant. He then enrolled into Kirov Kazakh State University (now Ăl-Farabi Kazakh National University) to study journalism (1972–78). He worked as a journalist for a number of years, first at the East Kazakhstan regional newspaper *Kommunizm tuy* (1975–76) and then at *Leninšil žas* (now *Žas alaš*; 1978), later occupying senior positions at several newspapers: *Ķazaķstan pioneri* (now *Ůlan*; 1978–80), *Ķazaķ ădebieti* (1980–92), *Zaman Ķazaķstan* (1992–93) and *Tùrkistan* (1993–2015). While serving as president of the El-Šežire public fund and publishing house, Ashimkhanuly published nearly 100 volumes of works by early twentieth-century intelligentsia, banned in the Soviet Union, collecting them into the 'Alaš mùrasy' (Heritage of Alaš [Alash]) series.

His own collections of short stories and novellas include *Aķbaķannyņ tolķyndary* (The Waves of Aķbaķan, 1981), *On birinši kùz* (The Eleventh Autumn, 1987), *Samyrsyn sazy* (The Melody of the Fir Tree, 2000), *Ăņgime emes ăņgimeler* (The Stories Which Are Not, 2011) and three volumes of selected works. His books have been translated into German, Chinese, Mongolian, Ukrainian, Tatar and Kyrgyz. He translated the works of Jack London, John Galsworthy, Anatoly Kurchatkin, Andrei Lupan, Timur Pulatov and others into Kazakh.

He was awarded the Alaš International Literary Award (2005) and the title of an Honoured Worker of the Republic of Kazakhstan.

Grandmother's Samovar

Two months had already passed since little Ajžan's parents had brought her here from the *auyl*.[1] This should have been enough time to thaw the heart of this completely estranged child, not to mention thoughts of her native hearth and home, and yet, despite her parents' desperate endeavours, with their affectionate terms of *ajnalajyn*[2] and 'our little foal', the stubborn girl's little heart remained impregnable. Life at home had changed beyond recognition over these past two months. Before, everyone had been quite happy with a couple of sandwiches and a cup of tea for breakfast, but the little girl had grown up in the remote *auyl* and had grown accustomed to fresh milk, so there was nothing for it but to get up at the crack of dawn and trawl all the shops until some was found. It was Telžan who took on this task, although Gùlsan did not have it any easier either. From early morning, from the moment she opened her eyes, she would begin rushing about the apartment, washing and dressing the child, putting on her shoes, ceaselessly worrying and beside herself until her husband would appear at the door with the milk. Then, having thrown together a quick breakfast, she would take her daughter by the hand and rush off to work.

The same scene would play out every evening, only in reverse order: with the silent, taciturn child in tow, she would do the shopping on the way before returning home with her bag so fully loaded with groceries that her legs could barely carry her.

'Oh, Lord, what kind of a person are you? You can't get a place at the kindergarten or even find a nanny; do you understand the torment I have to go through?!' she would blurt out, unable to restrain herself. Telžan was the reason for all these problems. 'This is all because of your whim; it's you and no one else who insisted on getting your mother to raise the child. And now you can pick up the pieces.'

---

[1] *Auyl* – socio-economic formation considered to constitute the heartland of the nation and a basis for an ethnic and cultural union of the nomadic community. Consisting of 50–70 yurts in the eighteenth century, it developed into its current permanent state of 'rural settlement' (of a minimum of 100 dwellers) when Kazakhs adopted a settled mode of life in the nineteenth and twentieth centuries. *Auyl* can also be used as a synonym for 'native land' and 'homeland', concepts revered by the Kazakhs.

[2] *Ajnalajyn* – used to show affection for a child or a youth; it can be translated as 'my dear' or 'my little one'.

In such moments, Telžan would remain silent because he knew only too well why Gùlsan was so upset. She would fly off the handle not because she had grown tired waiting for a place at the kindergarten to appear, far from it. After all, this was a matter of a few months and all they needed was to be patient. It was something else that distressed and tormented her: her own child still had no wish to accept her as her mother and, moreover, she would shy away from her more and more with each passing day. Telžan knew his wife's feelings well, for the same thoughts had been gnawing away at him, too. At first, they had consoled themselves, thinking that this was how things were supposed to be: the child was in a new place; she would soon find her feet and become accustomed to life. Only, there would be no sign that Ajžan was growing accustomed or that she would respond to her parents' affection. A long time went by and she would still greet them with a shy, cautious look, frowning and forever bothered about something. It would be a rare occasion when the parents saw their daughter distracted by anything, playing or even walking from room to room. They could not get a word out of her at the table either; she would take a pinch of bread, go through the motions of poking her fork at her plate a couple of times and then, without a word and without raising her eyes, she would quietly get down from the table. She seemed prepared to spend the entire day on her own, without moving from the settee in the sitting room. What was surprising was that she would never utter a word of her own accord. If they asked her something, she would reply; if they asked her to move, she would comply. In the mornings, Telžan would quite often notice her reddened eyes. Evidently, when she was on her own at night, she would secretly cry. Only recently, Telžan had witnessed her sobbing.

That evening, he had stayed on a little later at work. The moment he crossed the threshold, he had heard his daughter's sobbing voice. He threw off his shoes and rushed into the sitting room as fast as he could. Ajžan was lying face down on the settee and quietly sniffling, her little shoulders shaking from time to time.

'What is the matter, sweetheart? Why are you upset?' he asked in confusion and stroked the girl's hair. Ajžan, however, pushed him away in offence and, her little nose sniffing, she wept even more loudly.

Telžan was at a loss; for the first time, he sensed how helpless he was before his own daughter. He wanted to calm her but she wouldn't stop, she had rolled up into a ball and wouldn't even let him near. As luck would have it, Gùlsan had disappeared somewhere, too. He ran from room to room but, unable to locate his wife, he found himself forced to pace helplessly around the settee like a moth over a fire, quite out of its wits. The worst thing of all was that he didn't have the faintest idea why Ajžan was crying. Soon, though, he was able to discern a solitary word through the quiet sobs: 'comb!' and then 'my comb?!' Telžan stood perplexed in the middle of the room, trying to work out what this could mean but, at that moment, the front door slammed and Gùlsan rushed into the room with a frightened look on her face.

'Did you do this to her?' he asked her from the threshold. 'Why is she crying?'

His wife, though, walked silently, passed him and, pulling a new, green comb from her bag, she thrust it into her sobbing daughter's hand.

'Sweetheart, there's nothing to be crying over. Here's a comb for you. It's a new one. Have a look, it's straight from the shop. Only you stop crying now, there's a good girl.'

For a moment Ajžan calmed down and studied the comb closely. Then, she thrust it away.

'My comb...' she began to repeat through sobs once more. 'Mine is black!'

Only then did it dawn on Telžan. He recalled that his daughter had indeed had an old black comb that she had brought with her all the way from the *auyl*. The only thing it had in common with a real comb was its name. It had been made from ox horn a long time ago; it was completely wizened and its teeth eroded away. He remembered well how she had never let it out of her sight and had taken it everywhere with her. What was strange was that Ajžan had almost never combed her hair with it; sometimes, she would bring it to her nose and breathe in its smell. At such times, Gùlsan would invariably wince squeamishly. So, it transpired that the child had been crying over this old comb.

'Where is it?' he asked, turning to his wife. 'Where is her black comb?'

'I threw it out', Gùlsan replied, her face darkening. 'It's so awkward at work, in front of other people. It was so dirty and she sticks it up her nose.'

'Find it! I don't care where, but find it, even if you have to dig for it!'

Gùlsan was seriously frightened, for she had never heard her husband talk like that. She slid out like a shadow and soon returned, silently throwing the familiar old, chipped and broken comb onto the armchair next to her husband.

That night, the couple slept in separate beds for the first time. It seemed that he had sensed for the first time how dear this tiny living creature, their own child, was to him.

Sensing the living, hot little body of his daughter, gently sniffling as she slept next to him, he felt something strange welling up inside him, which he had never experienced before. Carefully reaching over, Telžan sniffed the old, wizened horn comb that Ajžan clutched in her hand, and he thought he could smell something strangely familiar and reminiscent of childhood. Indeed, the smell was incredibly reminiscent of *ajran*[3] or newly drawn milk, mixed with the fragrant aroma of dried hay. He breathed in the smell once more with pleasure, fearing it might disappear at any moment. Something tickled his throat.

He only had to turn away from the comb and an unknown fear suddenly overcame him and he sensed the transience of something that he really didn't want to lose. It occurred to him that something, which he sensed was extremely important and dear in his life, had indeed been lost forever. But what was it?

---

[3] *Ajran* – sour drink made of cow, sheep or goat milk fermented with lactic bacteria, often thick and used both as food and as a beverage.

What had he lost? Tormented by his thoughts and conjectures, he had fallen asleep without realising it. That night, he dreamt of the big black *saba*, the leather vessel for *ķymyz*[4] that had always stood at the door to their home. This *saba* was a miraculous thing. The *ķymyz* had never ceased to flow from its neck, even when the entire *auyl* had come visiting. He dreamt of his mother pouring him a large bowl of *saumal* – fresh mare's milk. He had been about to bring the full bowl to his lips when someone rudely snatched it from his hands, spilling the cool liquid onto his clothes, saying, 'That's enough! You'll drink the rest when you're at boarding school.'

'Oh, please let me drink just a little more!' he snivelled and, with that, he woke up. He was tormented by a terrible thirst. His mouth was parched and he licked his dry lips. Lying there motionless in the room, flooded with the moon's blue light, he could clearly smell the aroma of *saumal*. So strong was the sensation that it tickled his nostrils. So that was what it was! To make sure, he leaned over and sniffed the hair of his daughter, who was sniffling peacefully in her sleep. That was where the smell was coming from. Afraid of waking the sleeping Ajžan, Telžan carefully climbed off the settee and went to the kitchen. Turning the tap, a jet of water shot straight out, spattering him with a sharp smell of chlorine. He caught his breath, either from the sharp chlorine smell or from the cold water. Shaking the water from his face, he raised his head to see Gùlsan, standing dishevelled in the doorway. He could see from her expression that she still bore the grudge from the previous day.

'Right then!' she said after a short pause. 'I may be the child's mother, but you are her father. I will not be the only one to suffer here. From tomorrow, it'll be your turn; you try and take her with you!' With that, she turned abruptly and walked out of the kitchen.

Perhaps this was for the best, he thought. The next morning, father and daughter left the house early. On that day, he saw that Ajžan was smiling and laughing and was as uninhibited as all children of her age. Telžan couldn't get enough of it and kept looking at her. What a wonderful smile she had! What could have caused it?! There were indeed reasons.

An almost complete portrait was already hanging in Telžan's studio; he had been thinking of exhibiting it. It was called *Áže*.[5] It was a portrait of Ajžan's grandmother, and it had been from her hands that Telžan had drunk the *saumal* from the black *saba* in his dream that night. No sooner had they entered the workshop, when his daughter caught sight of this portrait.

'Grandma!' she cried, spellbound. 'My grandma!' She looked radiant and ran up to the portrait, stroked it and repeated, 'Grandma! That's my grandma!'

---

[4] *Ķymyz* – beverage of fermented mare's milk highly esteemed for its refreshing qualities; it is the main drink for special occasions.

[5] *Áže* – lit. 'grandmother', used as a term of endearment towards elderly women.

How pretty she was when she was genuinely happy. Telžan took his daughter under his arm and, lifting her up, he instinctively sniffed her tar-black hair that smelled of *saumal*, kissed her forehead and put her down again.

'That's right', he said emotionally after a silence. 'That is indeed your grandmother. Only she is a long way from us now. She is looking for a deer with golden antlers for you, my dear.'

'No, Papa, not a deer', said Ajžan, pouting. 'She's not looking for a deer over the mountains, but a saiga with little golden horns. She told me that herself.'

Telžan bit his tongue from the unexpected response. How could he have forgotten? After all, he had heard this tale a thousand times himself in childhood. It was hurtful that his small child still didn't know that her grandmother was not walking beyond the mountains but was resting in the damp soil under a small hill, not far from her native *auyl*. The poor, naive child, how could she know that her grandmother had left on an eternal search for a saiga with little golden horns?

After this episode, it was as if a new Ajžan had appeared. Each morning, she would wake up earlier than everyone else, as if afraid of being late to meet her grandmother. What was surprising was that she ate up all her porridge at breakfast. And so, it continued every day.

After breakfast, they would leave the house together and take the bus to the studio on the outskirts of the city. The girl's haste was understandable: she was hurrying to meet her beloved grandma. She would spend days on end by the portrait. She would drag it, puffing and panting, to the window, she would fall into silent thought, gazing at her grandmother's face, or she would have long conversations with her. At times, when she became overcome with yearning, she would say impatiently:

'Papa, when will we go to the *auyl*?'

'In the autumn', he replied.

'And when will it be autumn?'

'When the leaves on the trees turn yellow.'

The girl immediately looked at the lush-green tall poplars growing outside the window and, guessing that their leaves would not turn yellow any time soon, she fell silent and sighed sadly.

In such moments, joyful that his daughter had finally spoken, Telžan eagerly awaited further questions from her. There were times when they would have a long heart-to-heart. It seemed that Ajžan was beginning to grow accustomed to her parents and to her new surroundings. Soon, however, the girl dug her heels in once more.

It happened one Sunday when the entire family was drinking tea in the kitchen. Ajžan customarily broke off a piece of bread but did not eat it, rather she suddenly asked, looking strangely at the round kettle standing before her,

'*Aġa*,[6] when will we drink tea from a real samovar?'

The daughter's question caught Telžan unawares and he even shuddered from the unexpectedness. The word *samovar* evoked in him something distant and familiar from his early childhood, something warm and close to his heart that reminded him of his father's house. He was about to turn to his wife, to share this intimate memory with her that his daughter had unexpectedly aroused but, seeing Gùlsan's displeased expression, he hesitated.

'Don't you like tea from a kettle?' she asked, making a clumsy attempt at a joke.

'People don't drink tea from kettles like that', Ajžan said, pouting. 'A kettle is only used to heat the water to wash with.'

'What nonsense are you talking about? Where did you see such a thing?' Gùlsan blurted out, frightened.

'At grandma's, in the *auyl*. Grandma told me herself that it is *haram*[7] if a person goes into the yard without a kettle.

'You heard what you wanted to hear', said Telžan. He silently got up and left the table.

Although little Ajžan's words had disconcerted both her parents, by the evening the matter had somehow been forgotten and things continued much as they had been before. But the little girl remembered everything. At breakfast the next morning, she nodded towards the kettle, this time with a certain distaste, and asked again:

'So, *aġa*, when are we going to drink tea from a samovar?'

'But sweetheart, why do you think a kettle is any worse than a samovar? What difference does it make where you boil your water?' Telžan replied, unable to find another response.

'No, it's better to drink tea from a samovar. Grandma also said that guests come round to drink tea from the samovar and having guests round means you find happiness and good fortune.'

'Telžan, find that samovar, would you? Even if you have to dig for it. Perhaps we'll see more visitors and we'll be all the merrier for it', Gùlsan said.

That same day, having visited almost half the shops in the city, Telžan did eventually get hold of an ill-fated samovar. Seeing her father triumphantly placing the shiny-new, nickel-plated samovar on the table, Ajžan clapped her hands with joy. However, this joy did not last for long. Barely had the girl opened the lid of the samovar than she fell silent and raised her surprised eyes in her father's direction.

'*Aġa*, but where is the pipe, you know, where they stoke the samovar?'

'Sweetheart, but this is an electric samovar and the water in it is heated by electricity', Telžan said and began hastily to unwind the speckled cable and

---

[6] *Aġa* – a form of address to an older man, which can be translated as 'brother', 'uncle'.

[7] *Haram* – 'forbidden' in Islam. (In this context, 'if a person goes into the yard without a kettle' means 'if a person doesn't perform ablution'.)

dust the outside of the samovar. 'We pour the water in here and plug it in. You'll see: the samovar will come to the boil in under five minutes. Then we'll brew the tea and will enjoy some lovely fragrant tea, all three of us!'

Just as predicted, water was poured into the samovar, the cable was unwound and plugged into the socket. Happy that he had appeared to have calmed his daughter down, Telžan turned to Ajžan. The little girl was sitting with an expression as if she had been deprived of her very last hope. She rushed into her father's arms, weeping.

'Grandma! Our samovar!' she repeated over and over through her tears.

That night, no one could sleep, everyone deep in their own thoughts. And these thoughts all centred around the grandmother's old copper samovar.

***

Ajžan had never actually stopped thinking about her grandmother from the first day she had arrived in the city. She would only have to close her eyes to see her grandma, running towards her with arms open wide. She thought she could hear her grandmother whispering quietly and tenderly in her ear, 'My dear, you have run yourself into the ground, you have. Let's go and have some tea.' Ajžan felt tickled by her grandmother's warm breath. She would only have to remember the tea and she would become incredibly thirsty. However, how could that chubby little kettle ever satisfy her thirst? 'Call that tea? Now, grandma, she made real tea. What a pleasure it was! You could drink as much as you liked and you'd never get full. That's because tea from a samovar is always hot and fragrant.' Whenever she drank tea from her grandmother's samovar, her nose would perspire and she would get really hot. What was most important, though, was the echo of her grandmother's stories that she told when they drank tea. Her grandmother wasn't like that *aunt* Gùlsan, who would just sit there like a statue, simply knowing when it was time to pour the tea. She didn't have the patience. Her grandmother was different: she would always talk with her as if she was an adult. 'Listen to you, old woman, what are you talking about with this six-year-old girl as if she was a sixty-year-old woman?' her grandfather would say with a laugh.

'Who else do I have to talk with if not my granddaughter? She's all I have left; everyone else has gone their separate ways, like ships that pass in the night. I don't think my conversations will be in vain; perhaps she'll hold onto something in her heart and remember a thing or two. Who knows who she'll have to listen to after we've gone', her grandmother had once said pensively and, removing the smoke pipe, she had brought the chubby, steaming samovar into the house. The old yellow samovar, with its handles sticking out like a pair of ears and its intricate tap, always stood at her grandmother's right hand. It never stopped humming like a bee, much like the atmosphere in the house. Sometimes, it would wheeze and emit such big puffs of steam that it seemed it might stamp its little feet and blow off its rattling lid at any moment. As was her habit, the grandmother would turn off the tap and, adding a spoon of thick milk, she would begin pouring the fragrant tea into the bowls. Oh, what bliss it was to drink tea from grandma's samovar!

'That's what I call keeping up family tradition, old girl, just look at her drinking her tea!' the grandfather would exclaim at such times, with genuine surprise on his face. 'That's who we'll leave the samovar to.'

'Yes, who said we'd never find someone to leave the samovar to?' the grandmother had replied with a melancholy sigh. 'I thought I'd be able to pass it onto reliable hands, such as one of the daughters-in-law in the family, but my hopes were not fated to come to pass, you see. It's hard to look at all these modern types: they only want what is new. A samovar is too cumbersome for them. That's old hat! they say, screwing up their noses and they don't want anything to do with it. They fail to see that a time will come when the old-fashioned things will come in handy. But what am I talking about? I've seen for myself how my daughter-in-law milks the mares with that contraption of hers. And what an awful name it has! She turns it on and it sucks the milk until it draws blood. It's one thing for the cows; they've somehow become used to it, but it's the mares I feel sorry for. Stupid me, I even gave away my *saba*. Why on earth did I do that? Do you think they know its true value?! They say they threw it out because it had no use but, instead, they use aluminium pots and pans. But who'd drink *ķymyz* if it smells of metal? So, I ask them: "What are you doing, my dears? Who on earth prepares the sacred drink that way?" But they simply laugh at me and explain to me as if I were a daft little child: "Granny, the *saba* is a thing of the past. We'd be happy to use it but how can we fulfil the plan by collecting milk in thimbles?!" I am afraid to leave the samovar to them. Do you think they'll look after it? There's fat chance of that!'

Despite all her sighing and groaning, the grandmother took good care of her samovar and cherished it fondly. 'The samovar is the centrepiece of any *dastarhan*',[8] she would say. She would scrub it every day, wiping the gleaming copper with a clean white cloth. On numerous occasions, visitors to the house would identify with the five gold medals, embossed on the round side of the samovar and it would be a real honour for them to drink from this legendary piece. However, no one in the house, not even the grandmother, knew when and how it had come into their possession. That said, the grandmother and little Ajžan both knew there wasn't a single samovar in the *auyl* that sported such medals. Ajžan was quite sure that a samovar without medals was a bad samovar and that tea from a bad samovar was not worth drinking. Perhaps it was because of this that their house was always full of visitors, come to drink tea from their samovar.

---

[8] *Dastarhan* – traditional concept concerning all the dining- and hosting- related practices and etiquette norms. Inviting someone to a *dastarhan* is hosting according to all the norms of hospitality. More specifically, *dastarhan* is a synonym for dining table or table cloth.

It was indeed true that their home was always full of visitors. They never seemed to go anywhere else. Those who lived in the *auyl* came on foot, those from farther away came on horseback. Some would come, some would go and others might even stay the night. Everyone would be welcome at this house, young or old. Sometimes, the grandmother's yellow samovar would steam away in the yard from morning till late in the evening. 'A guest in the home is an honoured person and should be shown respect, never shown the door. That was the custom of our ancestors', the grandmother would say. There were occasions when Ajžan's aunts and uncles would all congregate to visit the senior members of the family. Before even crossing the threshold, they would cry out how they had missed the grandmother's tea from her yellow samovar.

'Drink up, my dears, you are most welcome', the grandmother would say, happy and contented, pouring the fragrant tea into her guests' bowls, into which she would never forget to add a pinch of cloves, supposedly to improve the flavour. 'When I'm gone, who will be left to serve you tea? You'll be left all alone.'

After a couple of bowls and woozy from the grandmother's tea, the guests would start up a leisurely conversation, joke and laugh. As always, the conversations would be steered by aunt Kùlzipa and there would be nothing strange in this, for she was, after all, the oldest of the daughters-in-law. She would sometimes forget herself in the thick of the conversation, occasionally even jokingly launching into the grandmother herself:

'I'll leave, I will! Why are you suddenly trying to frighten us all, you old bird?' she would chuckle, infecting everyone else with her laughter. 'Just take a look at all these people who'll be left behind after you: an entire forest of them! And if you don't want them all to become parched, you'd better hand over your samovar to me without a second thought.'

'Oh, you want the samovar, do you?!' the grandmother pulled her up. 'You ought to be ashamed of yourself, talking like that! You live like some lone wolf and not a single person comes to visit your home all the livelong day. And if anyone were to cross your threshold, well, your hair would stand on end. Why I wonder, do you need such a big samovar; it'd be far too much for you. You, my dear, would make do perfectly well with tea from a simple kettle.'

'Oh, come on, Mama, we can't even joke with you. Why kick up a fuss over some old bucket, anyway?' aunt Kùlzipa would usually respond in a conciliatory fashion. 'One thing I still can't understand is why this samovar keeps such a hold over you!'

'Oh, my pretty, sweet thing! You have never known cold or hunger from the turbulent times; who are you to judge?' the grandmother fumed. 'The things we have seen and suffered in our time! There were times, and you should thank the samovar for that, when we would have perished for sure if its fire had ever gone out. I remember how my mother, bless her soul, was forced to sell everything in the house for a handful of wheat; the samovar was the only thing she didn't touch. Guests come because of the samovar and guests in the home ensure prosperity and well-being, that's what my mother used to say. My mother's words reminded me of one instance.

'It was spring out in the yard. The house was completely empty; all that was left were the walls. All our hopes were pinned on father returning from the city, where he had gone in the middle of winter. There we were, three hungry little children, just sitting from morning till late at night, looking out at the road for him to return. Mother set up the samovar without a word and came to join us. All we did was sit and look. From time to time, mother would throw wood into the samovar. She didn't do this to make tea but so that the samovar would give out as much smoke as possible. You see, the smoke would be visible from a long way off. One day, we caught sight of a lone traveller out on the road. We only thought of one thing: whoever this person was, if only they would turn in our direction and come to visit us! For some reason, I was convinced that this traveller would be carrying hot bread in his coat and that it would be a great shame if he didn't turn our way. The man had evidently noticed the smoke from our samovar. He stopped and stood there for a while, leaning his chest on his stick as if in two minds, but then he strode forward in our direction. He was terribly thin and he had a thick beard. His sunken sockets with bright eyes that shone as if from craters, spoke of one thing only – extreme hunger. Seeing him face to face, mother silently wiped her tears on the back of her hand and, getting up, went to prepare supper. Supper consisted of two small ribs and some old, meatless bones that she had been saving from the winter. Mother placed all this into the cooking pot. While supper was being prepared, our guest uttered not a single word, just sat there in silence with a vacant look on his face. Only when he was passed a bowl of broth did he stir and a faint blush of colour appeared on his sunken cheeks. After that, he drank a couple of bowls of tea, which was actually nothing more than hot water, and, leaning on his stick, he departed. He left, leaving us without a single hope for tomorrow. Having given the last of what we had in the house, our mother just sat motionlessly where she was, staring strangely at the silent samovar. When we had completely lost all hope and had got ready to go to sleep, under an old, short fur coat, a man unexpectedly appeared in the doorway. Tripping over the threshold in the dark, he noisily entered the house and dropped something onto the floor with a bang. It was the same traveller who had visited us earlier. "Sister, if only everyone had a heart like yours. You have a kind heart, for sure. Go on, sister, put the pot on, would you?" he muttered as if he had quite lost his mind. Then, with tears in his eyes, he embraced each one of us children with arms shaking and kissed each of us on the forehead. It turns out that our guest had hit upon some good fortune. He had come across a snared deer out in the steppe and he had brought it to us as a sign of his gratitude.

'So, you see, my dears, this samovar has seen a good deal in its time. Then times got better for us. We honoured our ancestors as was fit, here under this *šaṇyraḳ*,[9] we welcomed many guests and, in a word, we saw plenty of joy and merriment. However, as folk say, life has its ups and downs, and we also had our fair share of sadness and grief: we laid our nearest and dearest to rest and our home was full of tears. And yet there were many happy moments, too; our daughters-in-law entered our home over this threshold. We celebrated the coming of grandsons and granddaughters. And this samovar here has witnessed it all. It is the dearest thing in the whole world for me, because it has heard the voice of my grandfather and my grandmother poured tea for her guests from its tap. So why shouldn't I value it as a sacred relic? If you can learn to handle it fittingly, it will serve you well for just as long!'

'But the time of the samovar is behind us now. There are things for every time', aunt Kùlzipa said, refusing to give in.

'Oh, there'll come a time when silver will lose its value, I don't dispute that. It's not a good idea to laugh at old things that are past their time. You might just fail to notice that something will be lost with them that may not come back again. Why do I say this, my children? It is so that you learn to distinguish good from bad, before worrying yourself over what is old and what is new. That's what I'd like to wish for you all!' said the grandmother, concluding her parable and, as if blessing each of us, she expressively ran her palm over her face. 'And, please, don't go thinking I am trying to lecture you. I am not some crow, who'll live for three hundred years. The time will come when I will have to go the way of all the Earth. In old age, a person becomes simple-minded in the eyes of a child and prattles on, much as I do. So, please don't judge me if I have said something untoward', the grandmother added.

Ajžan was particularly fond of the times when her grandmother would hold her and say, 'Let's go'. This was because her grandmother would only have to say these magic words and they would hop on the little blue bus that would stop once a day in their *auyl* and go visiting relatives. It was nice to go visiting and even better to leave for home, as her relatives would give her presents. Someone would give her a dress, another, some toys. And there would be so many sweets in pretty wrappers! An embarrassment of riches, what could you say? Going visiting with grandma was a true delight. The only trouble was that her grandmother, for some reason, had departed the last time without even warning her. Her father had said she had gone to find her a saiga with little golden horns. Ajžan would become sad and wistful when she recalled her last conversation with her grandmother. It had been just a few days before her grandmother had departed over the mountains to find her a deer.

They had been sitting on a hill just beyond the *auyl*. The sky above was a deep blue. The roofs of the houses down in the hollow where the *auyl* stood could be seen through the blue-grey haze. The sound of the river could be heard in the distance. The grandmother had been holding a spindle and a ball

---

[9] *Šaṇyraḳ* – upper dome of the yurt; its image is considered to be a symbol of unity. Here it is synonymous with 'house'.

of snow-white goat's wool. Ajžan sat close by her side and cleaned the coarse hairs out of the wool, while her grandmother span. Close by, their favourite white goat was grazing on the slope; Ajžan and her grandmother would bring it out to pasture here each morning from early spring.

'Oh dear, will he not be coming this year too? No, no, he simply must! He'll come for sure.'

'Who are you talking about, grandma?'

'About your father, my little darling', she replied sadly.

Her grandmother was a remarkable person: before, she would berate uncle Telžan, saying he was a drip, a ditherer and that he was weak-willed; now, though, she seemed to think of him every day and really look forward to his return. Little Ajžan would fall out of sorts when her grandmother spoke of uncle Telžan as 'your father' or 'your Papa'. She had only ever seen this *Papa* of hers twice. One winter he had come alone. He had been in a terrible hurry to get somewhere. He had spent the night at their house and departed for his distant city the next morning on the blue bus. The second time, he had brought some auntie Gùlsan with him. She remembered it well: it had been the year before last and they had stayed a whole week with her grandmother. The guests had spent every day cooing around Ajžan and they had put her to bed with them every evening. She had agreed but, in the middle of the night, she had woken up, burst into tears and gone looking for her grandmother.

'What a silly old woman I was to take you... It was all to no purpose, it seems...' the grandmother had muttered.

Who had she had been talking to? Ajžan had looked around, but there wasn't another living soul out there on the hill.

'Grandma, who are you talking about? Is it me?'

But her grandmother had continued to spin her spindle as if she hadn't heard her bewildered granddaughter's question. After that, she had begun to talk to herself again:

'Poor child, what will become of you when my eyes finally close? How will you see your mother and father as your own? You have never really known their parental affection.

'Your destiny, you see, is to suffer until your heart understands everything for what it is. Poor child.'

'Grandma, who are you feeling sorry for?' The confused little Ajžan had asked and embraced her grandmother tightly.

'No reason, sweetheart, no reason. I just happened to be thinking about your father... Oh, just look at you, all dishevelled! Come here, my little calf, and I'll plait your hair', the grandmother had said, deep in thought and, sitting the girl on her lap, she had slowly unwound the loose plaits and begun combing her hair with her old, horn comb. She couldn't remember how long her grandmother had busied herself with this favourite pastime of hers, but she had then felt the old woman's hand stop and the comb slide down.

'What's the matter, grandma?' Ajžan had said, turning around, frightened that her grandmother had fallen ill. She had sat there, one hand supporting herself on the earth and the other resting on her chest. Her face had broken into a strange, guilty smile. Soon, though, having caught her breath, she shook her head a little, calming her granddaughter, as if to say she shouldn't fear, that it would pass and she just needed a moment to get her breath back.

'Don't you fret, sweetheart, it's just my old heart making itself known', she had said, inhaling deeply. 'The poor thing's seventy-five and it must be exhausted. It, too, is feeling its age and it beats so hard, I sometimes think it'll leap right out of my chest. And not for nothing, I bet. It won't be long now… It seems the time has come to prepare for my long journey ahead…'

'Where is that to, grandma?'

The grandmother had not really noticed this question before, but on that occasion, she had placed her hands on Ajžan's little shoulders and pulled her close.

'Do you remember the tale of the saiga with the golden horns?'

'Yes, grandma, I do.'

'Well then, sooner or later, I will probably be going to look for that saiga for you. Your mother and father will come from the city and bring you some treats; lots and lots of sweets, I don't doubt. And don't you go crying or come looking for me, alright?'

'I don't want anyone but you and I don't need any sweets!' the frightened Ajžan had replied, in tears. Her grandmother had smiled a guilty smile and squeezed the girl tightly to her chest.

The next morning, Ajžan had been woken by a clamour and a din. Voices were coming from the street and the doors inside the house banged continually. A woman could be heard crying. She had jumped in fright from her bed and run to the door to learn what had happened, when strong hands picked her off the floor. The stranger had only managed to say, 'The child, get the child out of here!' when their neighbour, a short, fat woman, had appeared in the doorway and led her out onto the street. The last thing she had managed to see from behind the neighbour's wide skirt was the yellow samovar, lying on its side by the threshold.

…A round moon had appeared in the window, gleaming like her grandmother's samovar after a polish. Ajžan couldn't sleep. She lay nestled into her moist pillow near her father with her eyes open. It appeared that he wasn't sleeping either. What thoughts had overcome him, she mused.

***

What must be, will be, as the saying goes. Evidently for good reason. Who would have thought that their mother would leave them on this of all summers? She hadn't been ill, and no one could actually remember her ever complaining about her health.

He remembered everything vividly. When he and his wife had finally made it to their native *auyl*, the house had been in full mourning. People filled both small rooms: the old *aksakal* elders, including a number of the younger *karasakal*,[10] were seated; the women and the young people all stood. When they had appeared in the door, the throng of people seemed to be split in two by a whip and a narrow corridor formed in the crowd. The father, seated in the place of honour, surrounded by the *aksakals*, rose with some difficulty and, nestling his head on his son's chest, he wept hard. Having had a good cry, he nodded to his son to take a seat beside him.

'The Almighty has failed to fulfil my request', the old man said after a silence and failing to notice his tears, which had trickled over his beard. 'I asked Him for only one thing and that was not to be left alone in my later years. But he paid my prayers no heed and now I am left all alone. We lived forty years side by side, the old woman and I, and yet she never once called me by my name, such was her respect. And now she has gone forever.'

The people sighed heavily. Kùlzipa, who had been sitting at the end of the *dastarhan* near the yellow samovar, began whining and weeping. Telžan also sensed his eyes were misting up. His mother had often said: 'People only appreciate the value of things when they are lost.' Had anyone paid heed back then to his mother's words or stopped to think about the wisdom they imparted? Oh, how wise his mother had been! Her every deed, her every step had had a profound meaning. Even the fact that she had addressed her husband not by name, preferring instead the affectionate 'old man' or 'father of Telžan', had been a genuine, sincere sign of respect for his father. But was this the only thing that had distinguished his mother from others? Had anyone ever seen her with her head uncovered? And no guest had ever left their home with a heavy heart! Had she ever raised her voice when passing a home in mourning? Yes, his mother had lived a commendable life! The only thing was that for some these were just old customs while, for others, they represented recollections that pained the heart.

'Death, my son, is a heavy burden of grief, but everyone has their own form of sadness', said Nùrġali *aksakal*, sitting by his side, breaking the weighty silence in the house. 'There are times when a young person perishes in their prime, having never known the joys and trials of life. Of course, that is terrible. However, there can be no anguish when a person lives out their allotted number of years. These are the laws governing life and death. Death, however, does not simply take a treasured person away from us; it also brings sadness and grief. But what can we do? It would appear this is the lot of us mortals. We may weep and we may wail, but we cannot bring back the dead. In any case, the loss of a tree that has blossomed, having brought forth its fruit, is not such a sad thing; the same can be said for a person who has lived a decent life. Your mother left this world with a light heart. After all, she witnessed her sons finding their

---

[10] *Karasakal* – lit. 'black beard', a term for a middle-aged man.

feet and making a home, and she saw her daughters flying the nest. She even managed to nurse grandsons and granddaughters. So, there you go, my son! Don't be sad. That is how the cards lay; the Almighty takes people away, but their good deeds and their memory remain with us forever. Your mother led a decent life. She enjoyed the love and respect of all around her. Everyone here in the *auyl*, both old and young, addressed her with the respectful *apa*.[11] Therefore, let the good that remains after she has gone bring joy to the people.'

'The *aksakal* is right in what he says', came the cries.

'May all your wishes come true, my son.' Kùlzipa set about pouring the tea and soon the bowls were passed around. Noisily slurping his tea from his latest bowl, Nùrgali continued:

'Oh my, who would have thought that in a matter of half an hour, a person might close their eyes for all eternity. On that same day, bright and early, I was about to go up onto the hill behind the *auyl* to look for my grey mare when I saw an old woman sitting there. I took a closer look and it was her, my old stablemate, the mistress of this house. "Hey, what are you doing out so early on that hill? You must be waiting for your old man, the way you're looking out at the road", I said to her as a joke.

"What do you mean, my old man? I've lost my goat. My son's supposed to be coming from the city this summer, and I have been fattening this goat to mark the occasion. But this morning, the goat disappeared somewhere." She was finding it heavy-going and kept taking breathers. "We're not getting any younger, you and I, Nùreke.[12] It gets harder and harder each day, making it up this hill. Right now, I can't seem to get my breath back and my heart nearly leapt from my chest while I was climbing up here." Not half an hour had gone by and I was returning, in the saddle, when I saw her in the very same place, only this time she seemed to be lying there helplessly, with her hand clutching at her chest. She was so pale, you could barely make out her face. I don't remember how I managed to climb down from my horse, but I ran to her; all she could do was move her lips a little: "Get the... old man..." was all she said. There's life for you...'

'And she never got to voice her final request. Oh, *apa*...' Kùlzipa sobbed, wiping her tears with the end of her black headscarf, which had slid down to the back of her head.

A deathly silence reigned in the house.

'She had obviously guessed that death was close at hand', the father of the house interjected. 'Yes, she had a final request: to be buried in the graveyard at the top of Ķaratùmsyķ, alongside the remains of our ancestors.

---

[11] *Apa* – depending on the region, aunt, sister, mother or grandmother; it is also a common respectful form of address for older women in general. In the given context it refers to 'mother'.

[12] An affectionate term for 'Nùrgali'.

'That won't be hard', *aksakal* Nûrġali said, stroking his grey beard. 'Incidentally, the manager is sitting here with us. Those five kilometres would be no distance at all if he gives us a car, right? Am I right, Sùltan?'

Telżan stole a sideways glance at this pockmarked *żigit*,[13] overly plump for his age, who sat in the most honoured seat among the *aksakal*. He and this Sùltan had once studied together. Now, though, it was hard to recognise him, and he had become so terribly overweight that he looked like a round pot full of butter.

'Ķaratùmsyķ, you say?' Sùltan double-checked expressively, with a deep furrow appearing on his forehead. 'Ķaratùmsyķ... Hmm... It'd be hard to get there by car.'

'So then, not a car but a tractor, say? We'll secure a trailer on the back. Nothing doing...'

'Well, tomorrow is a working day. You've set me no easy task, let me tell you.'

'Hey, I know what you're thinking, my dear man', Nûrġali interrupted his deliberation for all to hear. 'You're thinking, why drag the old woman up the mountain, when we could bury her in the graveyard next to the *auyl*. On the one hand, of course, you are right; after all, the dead aren't really bothered where they lay – the earth's the same wherever they lie. Only don't forget that we are children of the people, people who, since time immemorial, know how to honour their dead, respect their mothers and pay heed to their elders. This woman, rest her soul in peace, piously honoured and preserved the customs of her ancestors. Therefore, we who remain among the living have a simple obligation to fulfil her last request. This is not a religious ceremony, don't worry. This is a matter of respecting the memory of the dead and her ancestors. It's our sacred duty.'

'And what do you want from me?'

'Give us a tractor and trailer by noon tomorrow and two or three fine men to dig the grave. That's all.'

'Alright, we'll see. Things always look better in the morning', Sùltan muttered.

By the time they had finished the meat, read the prayer and cleared away the *dastarhan*, dusk had come down thick. Only the closest relatives remained along with five or six *aksakal* elders. The deceased mother of the house lay behind a red, silk curtain in the right corner. Settling down more comfortably a little way away, the elders engaged in unhurried conversation. The house was quiet, with only the kerosene lamp on the stove crackling from time to time. The *aksakals*' conversation was as sad and quiet as the dark night itself, touching on old age, infirmity, death and about how the young were all forgetting the customs of their ancestors. Everyone listened respectfully to Nûrġali. The

---

[13] *Żigit* – generally denoting a 25- to 40-year-old male, the term can also be used as an honorific indicating bravery, endurance, fortitude and being true to one's word.

aḳsaḳal, mentioning the sad event that had occurred here, suddenly began talking about the distant past, about the time when the Khan Abylaj ruled the people:

'This story took place a long time ago when our land was black with dust and the Sun stood as high in the sky as it does now. It happened that the famous *bi*[14] Ḳazybek had passed away. He was known among his people as the Eloquent, thanks to his talent for fine oratory', the *aḳsaḳal* began. 'As was the custom at that time, our ancestors would bury their famous khans and bies way out in Tùrkistan, by the mausoleum of the holy Ḳoža Ahmet Âssaui.[15] It was decided to take the remains of Ḳazybek the *bi* to this blessed place. But how? This all happened in the middle of summer, the hottest, most torrid of seasons. It would take a caravan half a month to cover the distance from the endless steppes of Saryarḳa, where the revered Ḳazybek had died, to Tùrkistan. How could they keep the dead man's remains intact for all this time? But these people, who had wandered the vast expanses of the steppes for centuries, had their secrets. The body of the deceased was wrapped in a fresh hide, covered in snow-white felt, set upon a stretcher and, at dusk, when it was cooler, the funeral procession, headed by the *batyr*[16] Bôlek, set off on its long journey. They walked all night and only the next morning, with the first signs of dawn, did they make a stop. A deep pit was dug and it was here that they interred the dead man's body until evening.

'The caravan rested during the day, building up its energy for the night-time crossing, and all the while they poured cold water over the felt. Then they dug a deep pit and preserved the body of the deceased there until the night-time. I bet no one knows about the properties of felt nowadays. I recall how, in my youth, they would send us out to graze the horses all day long in the Sun. We would wrap our *torsyḳ* canteens[17] in pieces of white felt doused in water and the water inside would remain ice-cold right up into the evening... Anyway, the caravan, headed by *batyr* Bôlek, finally reached the foothills of Ḳaratau, having crossed the yellow steppes of Saryarḳa and the parched *taḳyr*[18] soil of Betpaḳdala. As always, a pit was dug and the dead man's body lowered inside. No sooner had

---

[14] *Bi* – an influential figure in the power structure of the traditional Kazakh society, elected from among the most distinguished, eloquent members of the community as one who had proved his or her knowledge of the law. A *bi* would pass judgments on petty crimes, whereas serious crimes would be heard in the court comprising multiple *bies*. *Bies* also functioned as counsellors to khans and diplomats.

[15] Ḳoža Ahmet Âssaui (Kozha Akhmet Yasawi; 1093–1166) – poet and religious figure, who influenced on Turkic peoples in adopting Sufism.

[16] *Batyr* – originally term for 'hero' or 'valiant warrior', roughly equivalent to the European knight; nowadays the term signifies military or masculine prowess.

[17] *Torsyḳ* – container for liquid made from the neck leather of a camel, bull or deer.

[18] *Taḳyr* – meaning smooth, even or bare, is a type of relief occurring in the deserts of Central Asia.

the people settled down to rest, weary from their long, night-time crossing, when the watchman cried out:

"We're under attack!"

'Indeed, some hundred horsemen could be seen over the crest of the nearest hilltop, charging straight for the caravan. The people began to panic: some rushed for their horses, others, for their spears. Then, amidst this chaos, a booming voice rang out:

"Stop!" It was the *batyr* Bôlek. "There is nothing to fear, so pull yourselves together! I have seen much in my time. Even if these are insatiable bandits, come to plunder our caravan, I don't recall ever hearing that even they would trespass against the body of a deceased man. Remain calm, sit still and don't move."

'The calmness of the people, you see, bewildered the attackers, who had galloped up, reined in their horses and huddled together. One of the uninvited guests soon stepped forward. He was evidently their leader and, pulling up his horse on its haunches, he cried out menacingly:

"Who might you be? Where have you come from and where are you going?" Only then did the *batyr* Bôlek rise, calmly and with dignity, and responded:

"We are accompanying the remains of the *bi* Ķazybek the Eloquent to his final resting place."

"Well, you wretch, no need to mince your words with me! You don't need to hide behind a bi's title. We don't care who you have lying there, be it Ķazybek or anyone else. All that you needed to tell me was that you were burying a man..." And, turning his restless steed sharply round, the horseman lashed at the poor creature with all his might. The other riders all raced after him with a whoop...

'Those were the days! Even bandits honoured the dead. Nothing was sacred for them and yet they were unwilling to trespass against the body of a dead man...' *aķsaķal* Nùrġali concluded his enlightening tale.

The first cockerels were crowing and it was getting light. Telžan's uncle, who had left to ask for a tractor at the farm office, only returned at noon. He had returned with nothing. It turned out that Sùltan had been called away urgently to the district and, without him, no one had wanted to take the responsibility of allocating a tractor. Not only that, but they had barely managed to find the people to dig the grave! Everyone had been at work, busy trying to meet the plan.

This turn of events had been most unexpected. The father of the house, with profound sadness in his eyes, looked over at the peak of Ķaratùmsyķ as if it were inaccessible to them.

It was there, at the peak of Ķaratùmsyķ that the remains of their ancestors were buried.

It had only been five kilometres to Ķaratùmsyķ.

The dead woman was buried in the graveyard nearest to the *auyl*. However, everyone came to the funeral, apart from the women and children, because the graveyard was close by.

The old copper samovar remained, smoking in the empty yard, with its lonely handles protruding in different directions like a pair of ears.

***

Gùlsan hadn't realised that the samovar had boiled itself dry. Instead of checking and adding more water, she had lit it up again. Then, remembering something important, she had gone indoors to tidy herself up. She had been unable to resist the temptation and was applying shade to her eyes, puffy from the tears and lack of sleep, when Kùlzipa's blood-curdling cry interrupted her, seemingly cutting right through her:

'Oh, my! Oh, my! It's gone and melted!' she screamed, waving her arms about, running around the samovar. 'We've lost grandmother's samovar. We failed to watch over it. Where is that drip from the city? What a fool she is; does she realise what she's done? Oh, how dense can you be? What does she know?!'

'You're the fool!' Gùlsan blurted out without thinking, still looking out from the crack in the door, 'Acting the know-it-all! What do you know beyond a full udder?! Fool!'

***

The large Sun began to rise on the horizon, glimmering gold like the old yellow samovar after a polish. Telžan hurried to the dairy, which stood just around the corner. Still sleepy, Gùlsan shuffled barefoot to the kitchen and stood there a moment, intending to plug the samovar into the socket. Then, however, she placed the little, chubby kettle onto the gas stove. 'That'll do!', she said, not wishing to waste electricity on heating the samovar.

Translated by Simon Hollingsworth, edited by Simon Geoghegan

JUMABAY SHASHTAIULY

(b. 10.10.1950)

Jumabay Shashtayuly is a Kazakh writer and journalist. Having completed his high school education at 18, he was employed as an assistant shepherd, served in the Soviet Army (1969–71) and worked for regional newspapers (1972–76). He then studied philology at Kirov Kazakh State University (now Äl-Farabi Kazakh National University; (grad. 1979) and worked as a newspaper correspondent for *Leninšil žas* and *Socialistik Ķazaķstan* (now *Žas alaš* and *Egemen Ķazaķstan*). He later moved on to senior positions at the journal *Žalyn, Ķazaķ ădebieti* and *Zaman Ķazaķstan* newspapers and at Ķazaķ (Qazaq) Radiosy.

His debut short story, 'Ķiâda' (A Long Way Off; later renamed 'Aspan ķora' – Celestial Office), was published in 1982 in a collection of works by young writers, titled *Taņ nùry*. His own short story collection, *Ķyzyl ķar* (Red Snow) came out in 1984, followed by *Žala men nala* (Slander and Grief, 1987). Two novels followed, *Bizdiņ zamannyņ Aâz bii* (Aâz bi of Our Times, 1997) and *Žaņġyryķ* (Echo, 2004). Shashtaiuly is famous for his harsh realist style. In *Ķyzyl ķar*, in particular, he portrayed the hardships endured by shepherds in remote *auyls*, which earned him the criticism of the Soviet authorities. Undeterred, in the novel *Bizdiņ zamannyņ Aâz bii*, Shashtaiuly depicted the Kazakh SSR Communist Party leaders on the verge of the 1986 Želtoķsan (86' December) revolt of Kazakh youth against the Soviet system. His literary essays were collected in two volumes: *Žyr-žolbarys* (Tiger Song, 1996) and *Sarġajġan paraķtardaġy saġynyš* (Longing in the Yellow Pages, 2016).

He is the recipient of the Award of the President of the Republic of Kazakhstan (2000) and a laureate of the Alaš International Literary Award (2012), as well as an Honoured Worker of the Republic of Kazakhstan (2012).

Waking Dream

The black-market millionaire named after Abylaj Khan awoke with a start from his deep sleep in the dense night, gasping. His heart coursed wildly, his nerves were aflutter and sweat dampened his whole body. He reached over to switch on the bedside lamp with the silken cover. Like an arrow, the light shot through the darkness and blinded him. He jerked upright, and the explosion of light rang in his ears with a fierce vibrancy.

He looked around fearfully, as though seeking an emergency button to press and end this horrid experience. In the blurry residue of the light, he saw a figure like a demon suspended in front of him, staring down its nose. Instead of eyes it had two silvery gashes, as if the fur around its eyes was affected by salty corrosion. Having never had such a vision, the millionaire named after Abylaj Khan remained still for a while, in his bed, alarmed. He considered the image before him. Now it seemed that the face of this demon held a look of peaceful contentment. But its eyes were still pinned on him, and this made it look even more frightening. He shivered at the thought that he would meet with a rage of red flame if this devil so decided. He was overcome by an oppressive loneliness, along with a cold frustration that sprang from a deep recess within his chest.

He turned his head. A sleeping figure lay next to him on the bed: a woman, unmoving, the sheet covering her only below the waist. Her nakedness made her appear as if she had just been born, he thought. The whitish skin that could be seen through the tangle of black hair was attractive – but he looked at her indifferently, without emotion. He thought of his wife. She would not have ignored even his slightest stirring. This fond notion, however, could not calm him. He changed his focus to other objects in the room, gazing at them as if he were not in his own home, but an overnight guest in some strange hotel.

A line of small, triangular beads hung downward from the bedside lamp stand, as if they were growing like that and would eventually freeze into elongated icicles. The image of his wife's soft, round face appeared, her lustrous eyes staring at him from a distance, and he shivered. Her expression was serene, but with a hint of sadness. This woman – who had endured all the hardship life could inflict – had graced him with care and benevolence. He felt discomfited. The figure sleeping quietly beside him suddenly seemed to him to be another form of demon, and he averted his eyes from her. Instead, a wolfskin hanging on the wall entered his line of sight. He stared at it. Had it come from the alpha? Or a she-wolf? 'Oh, you blind, two-legged fool, what does it matter to you if I – a dead wolf – was female, or the head of my pack!'

478

He stared at the ghostly talking pelt on the wall as it transformed from wolf to fox and back again, and wondered if he had gone completely mad.

His weariness was such that he hadn't the energy or will to look out the window. Out there, in the spacious yard below, in an expensive foreign car, his short, square-built bodyguard was surely asleep and snoring like a buzz saw. The man's shoulders and neck looked as if they had been forged from a single piece of cast iron; when he clenched the jaw undergirding his pale face, he looked like a panther standing his ground, face-to-face with a mortal enemy. His small, brown eyes were set in an abundant whiteness. They could throw the most savage, terrifying look at an adversary. Here was a godless devil who could focus his fearsome power on a single point with the slightest glance when receiving his orders. At first, the millionaire named after Abylaj Khan believed it to be an expression of the man's instinct for self-protection; later, he understood that it emanated from a deep well of anger in a man who was ready to mete out any violence to achieve his ends, whenever the situation so required.

But why was he ruminating about his bodyguard? Was he simply trying to escape from the nightmare in which he found himself? A bodyguard is just a large, heavy sack. This thought apparently satisfied the millionaire named after Abylaj Khan, and he turned his attention elsewhere. He picked up the remote control from the night table, switched on the Japanese-made television and began flipping from one channel to another. He paused on one channel, where, on-screen, a line of barely clothed young women enacted a sinuous, swinging, rhythmic dance of lust. Their gleaming eyes, smiling faces and salacious movements might have stirred some viewers, but for the millionaire named after Abylaj Khan the scene had no special attraction, aroused no desire; he persisted in his dour mood.

He lifted himself out of bed and cautiously made his way, with catlike steps, toward the large mirror by the side of the bed where the woman was sleeping. He pushed a button and a dim light shone, allowing him to see the reflection in the mirror of a man he did not recognise. His coal-black hair was streaked with grey lines, and the tips of his moustache were white. His ovoid face showed signs of tiredness. He looked into the man's eyes, searching for some sign of kindness or compassion, but all he could discern in those dark, deep-set orbs was a cold and aloof being. He had a snub nose that appeared to thrust upward, as if from a life filled with violence. His face appeared to have a healthy complexion – light brown skin with no blemishes – but it was spoiled by gelatinous bags hanging beneath his eyes. Worst of all were the wretched wrinkles at the edges of the eyes. Damn it! They shouted out like a crier of ill omens, a pitiless herald of old age. An extra shiver of anxiety crawled over him.

He could not bear standing like this a second more, and pushed the button again. The light switched off, and, in a flash, the figure appeared again, this time as its negative image: a dark black shadow that reflected dimly and mysteriously at the centre of the mirror. He turned away and tried to console himself by watching the movements of the nearly naked women still dancing on the television screen, as if they would beam a light or some solace into the darkness that was overcoming his soul. Their movements were now, for some reason, more solemn compared with the wild shaking he had seen earlier; they looked as if they were spent of their passion, and he could not make sense of their slow-moving dance.

He picked up the remote and switched to another channel. Now a scene appeared on-screen that seemed to reflect the world of the strange room he was in. A woman lay in bed in a prone position, with no apparent concern for anything at all. A man who was about to leave the room stopped and turned away from the door. He walked back and grabbed the handle, but halted once again. Then he turned his head back sharply, stared at the woman and walked over to her. The millionaire named after Abylaj Khan was amused by the behaviour of this swag-bellied, fat-necked man, and observed him motionless, unblinking. The man went up close to the bed and spread his feet wide, allowing him to lean forward and plant a kiss directly in the middle of the woman's behind. Then he left at last, with a satisfied countenance.

'Devil be damned, what is this pig doing!' muttered the millionaire. Disgusted, he clenched his teeth and pressed the 'off' button on the remote control. His heart raced, and its restless reverberations sounded to him like the ticking of a clock that cut through the silence of the dreamlike space. That stupid pig who had kissed the woman's bottom resembled his bodyguard. 'Ah,' he thought, 'so perhaps he, too…'

Suspicion ran through his mind. Was there a secret pleasure that had eluded him? A strong curiosity was aroused in him, an impulse to be beastly. He pulled away the sheet half-covering the body on the bed in front of him and marvelled at its huge, domed buttocks. 'This is a place where shame and conscience do not exist', he thought. But suddenly they appeared to him as grotesquely obese humps, monstrous to his sight. What could he do? A sense of fury came over the millionaire named after Abylaj Khan. He felt sleazy, and became furious with himself. Though men may find success and amass fortunes, they are prey to their basest inclinations.

'Oh, God', he thought. How enveloped in loneliness he was. An abundance of alluring, fatty flesh beckoned in front of his eyes, yet he was at a loss as to what it meant to him. The *auyl*,[1] the district, the city – he owned a house in each. With a simple call to his personal bulldogs, a fresh, new concubine could be placed in any of them – in *all* of them – without the slightest delay. Had he

---

[1] *Auyl* – socio-economic formation considered to constitute the heartland of the nation and a basis for an ethnic and cultural union of the nomadic community. Consisting of 50–70 yurts in the eighteenth century, it developed into its current permanent state of 'rural settlement' (of a minimum of 100 dwellers) when Kazakhs adopted a settled mode of life in the nineteenth and twentieth centuries. *Auyl* can also be used as a synonym for 'native land' and 'homeland', concepts revered by the Kazakhs.

reached the point where things of the flesh disgusted him? Was he empty of all desire? He was repulsed even by the gestures of kindness a woman might make. Was this a strange disease he had contracted? What would satisfy the hole at the core of his being?

As he rejected earthly pleasures and tried to escape from desire, thoughts from his past began to consume his mind. Events unravelled before his eyes like an antique silhouetted animation, which he stared at with a puzzled frown. He lay back on the bed and concentrated his gaze on the ornamental mouldings of the ceiling, focusing on a single point and hunting for hidden thoughts. One thought stung him: had he not short-changed the craftsman who had made these intricate carvings, a man he had known since childhood? It was only now that he had even bothered to look at this fine handiwork, with its artfully placed geometrical reliefs at the edges of a squared design. Money made easily is money blindly spent. The imaginative embroidery on the ceiling would endure for longer, he thought, and in greater peace, than the life of a wealthy businessman. That poor artisan, who would cast fearful glances at his powerful patron, left behind something solid and worthy. He did not know why he was troubling his mind with thoughts of this humble craftsman. With just a glance, his barking blackguards would demolish a mountain for him, crush stones with a simple 'Yes, sir!' But this poor church mouse of a mason was diehard and uncompromising in his dedication to his craft.

The millionaire took a deep breath, growing tired of this line of thought.

It was ten years since he had turned up in Almaty, having abandoned his wife and children because of bad luck and, worse, alcohol. He had arrived during the 'era of plans'. He became a taxi driver, and had worked for a square-built taxi company director who was so greedy, he might as well have had a throat shaped like a piggy bank. It was never enough for him to be satisfied with normal profits from his business operation. He would ring in the middle of the night: 'I shall be somewhere. Call me at the appointed time; you will give me a lift home.'

This was infuriating. Damn it to hell, we are from the same clan! he had thought. But there was nothing to do but simply play the game and get used to it. 'If you prove to be handy and loyal, you might be rewarded; even a new car is nothing for me. It is like *'kak pit'to dat'* – easy', the boss bragged in Russian, with a threatening undertone. But he tried to ignore the director's rants and focused his eyes on the steering wheel and the road ahead of him during his long shifts. 'Hey, don't you get it?' the boss called out in a mocking tone. 'They say that your ancestors were humiliated by the Great Ones of our clan. Are you not some scoundrel bearing a grudge?' In fact, he hardly remembered his own father's face, let alone anything about his ancestors. Had they been inferior to those of the square-built boss? Well, they had not begotten a successful heir in him, so perhaps the boss was right to mock him and smirk.

Why, the millionaire named after Abylaj Khan thought, am I lying next to this young woman in this house that I'd had built, after so many years, and still harbouring a grievance against a taxi company director from the city who had joked at my expense and treated me like dirt?

From his present vantage point, it seemed inconceivable that he had ever allowed the boss to get away with his vile taunts. 'Why are you people from the Ekej clan such useless devils?' he had said one time, staring in his face as if he were really about to pick a fight. These rude words had made the driver lose himself, as if someone had levelled a sharp blow to his head. 'All the *viruchka*, all your earnings from today – you'll give them all to me, your tribal brother. I'll take it and put a smile on the face of one of your *ženge* – one of your "sisters-in-law" – who I keep for pleasure.'

He had turned to reply to his vicious, square-headed boss; but when he looked at the coarse, snorting man, he felt only shame for the existence of such a creature lacking the smallest spark of humanity. 'Keep your eyes on the road, or you'll smash the car', the man blurted.

'No clients today, *kôkesi*[2], the driver muttered, using the respectful term for 'older brother'. 'It seems I won't even cover the cost of petrol.'

'Stop your whining and show your tribal skill! Later, you will remember that when you were facing desperate times, the person who gave you this job was me. Almaty is awash with Kazakh vagabonds like you.'

The insults burned hot inside him, but he realised that they would not ignite into flames: he had become a dead man walking. 'Stop!' the square-built boss shouted at him. 'Any driver from our company, when they see my shadow approaching, immediately looks for the slightest chance to find my favour. I felt sympathy for you, considering our common roots. But you know no respect – so slink away… get out of my sight, get gone!'

The millionaire named after Abylaj Khan shook as if the taxi company director's shouting from so many years ago still echoed loudly in his ears. Back then, he had just taken it all in silence, not only the personal insults but – worse – those directed at his clan. But now he knew that the boss had been of a lower sort than even the crude bodyguards he now kept in his employ. Perhaps the man had been cunning enough to satisfy his gluttonous ambitions; but what would he do in a confrontation with those same bodyguards, who, with only a hint of their menacing presence, could silence the cries of a wailing baby faster than any lullaby? He could imagine him begging for forgiveness before the inevitable, final punishment. Or would he be cold and resistant to the end, like the crooked yet hardy branch of a strong tree before it, too, must break? It's hard to meet such a Kazakh these days, though.

His thoughts turned to his associates. They were like horses whipped so many times as to be frightened of everything – worthless beings, never in stable jobs, divorced, untrustworthy. Their highest accomplishment was to land in prison. No wonder he often felt pangs of embarrassment, thinking how the

---

[2] *Kôke* – a respectful form of address to a patron, supporter and protector; it can be applied to both males and females.

482

world must judge him by the company he kept. His man in the expensive foreign car outside was a mere swindler, a lowly horse thief. If anything should happen to him that would expose some weakness, those hangers-on would be ready to tear him to pieces. He had struggled through poverty for years, and survived; now that he had attained wealth, he thought, what good was it? Wealth did not relieve him of the worries in his soul; instead, these worries only increased. The fragility of success in such an unfaithful world made him dream of disappearing to a distant place where he could find true freedom. Was this the affliction of all men in the world? Or were there some who truly did not care? He remembered Žorabaj, who had had similar ambitions for wealth and power. His own mother used to prick him with comparisons: 'You cannot compete with Žorabaj', she would say. 'You will never overcome him. His fathers and great-grandfathers would eat even cattle that had died naturally and were *haram* – unclean and forbidden – claiming that it was all from honest labour. Greed is in their blood.'

Such remarks caused him to stare at his mother as if she was someone he didn't know. The cooling of his countenance would send her into a depressed state, so that she could no longer look him in the eye. Both mother and wife would each find something wrong, even as they were provided for, with orderly lives, ample wealth and little work. What kind of resentment was this, that their hearts should turn into frozen lumps that would never melt? If he could only find a glimmer of cheer in the thin, wrinkled face of his mother, he thought, he could find a cure for the sorrow that ached at the centre of his soul. Maybe it was in her nature, from her years teaching in primary school: she would look at her own son with the same stern, condescending glare she gave to her most underachieving pupil.

The freckles on her face looked like reddish pockmarks on a bed of pale skin. But his father, people would say, had been a handsome man with striking good looks. How was it that he, may his memory be blessed, chose this woman? Although he was no infidel, he could not suppress the unholy thoughts that came to his mind, and burst out laughing. Oh, you wretched man, what about your own wife's looks...?

His mood turned dark again as he was reminded that he was terminally cut off from the possibility of normal, warm, familial relationships. But he remained impassive, envisioning the eyes of his mother, full of grief, as she let out a burst of disappointment and regret: 'My son, the spirit of your ancestor Šikil looks over you. You must free your soul from your arrogance and pride. Šikil *kisi* – here she used a respectful form of address – 'may he rest in peace, was a man who remained humble even though his opinions commanded the respect and obedience of his clan and all those around him.'

Because she had been a schoolteacher during an era antithetical to religious sentiment and all forms of superstition and tradition, it seemed strange that she referred to this ancestor, whose name was Sarybaj, as 'Šikil' (which was a secondary adjective for *sary*, or yellow). Because the clan women refused to pronounce his proper name at all – an ancient custom when referring to the elders – he had always imagined Sarybaj as larger than life, a strong, towering man with a red-yellowish complexion whose veins pulsed bluish when he made some momentous declaration, instilling fear and admiration among the inhabitants of the *auyl*.

The elders called Sarybaj 'Sareke', a respectful formulation of the name, which thus demonstrated their humility before his *aruaķ* – his spirit. Is everyone who has become a big man considered a saint? What, then, of Žorabaj's great-grandfathers, who had herds of horses and sheep? Yet if anyone had ever sung their praises, those songs had never reached his ears. On the contrary, when a respectable guest arrived at their door and the daughters-in-law of the household started hanging the big kettle on the tripod to prepare tea, the Žorabaj elder would return a haughty look as if to warn against showing too much generosity to a visitor. These rumours of such ungodly and un-Kazakh meanness were difficult for the millionaire to believe. As for Žorabaj himself, he could not say whether or not the man had inherited good or ill manners from his ancestors: their dealings with each other were always conducted with casual respect.

Žorabaj had small eyes like a badger, and always pursed his lips tightly when he became inquisitive. Short and stocky, he would turn his thick neck to one side and then the other, inspecting the lay of the land and assessing a situation. His brown eyes would hint at nothing that would reveal his inner thoughts. His eyes might start to shine as if he were about to make an illuminating observation; but they could change in a moment and become pensive as he relaxed his muddy-coloured, pudgy face.

He liked to bring a cigarette gently to his lips as if it were a dear friend, inhaling strongly and blowing out the smoke in a steady stream, and his whole face would become purple with energy. The smoke emboldened his conversation. 'Mark my words, I'll stake a claim to our government for compensation for the thousands of horses that the damned Bolsheviks confiscated from my grandfather. They surely plan to start selling the land, but first I'll privatise my grandfathers' pastures.' Žorabaj spoke with confidence and never betrayed a sense of worry or concern. He was not the kind to lose sleep over everyday problems or even business matters. 'Žorabaj is a tough young man, hardy as stone', he recalled his mother's lament. 'He looks out for himself first. You need no excuse to gather backstabbing friends of the bottle around you, always ready to plunge into a sea of vodka. Not one of them is truly well-disposed towards you; not one of them serves you wholeheartedly.'

This thought of drink and bad company made him feel ashamed again, he considered the misadventure of leaving his wife and children in the *auyl* for Almaty and a squalid life as a poor taxi driver, driving mindlessly with a herd of other lost souls... and for what? To be abused by square-built bosses who would spit on your forehead, sweet swans in the morning and raging bulls by afternoon... by the little, red-faced evil one who crushed him with the look of an alpha horse blocking any competitor from his mares. He had prayed that no one from his *auyl* was nearby to hear the boss when he spewed abuse with his unholy words in Kazakh and Russian.

'Hey, collective farmer', he would bark, his nose protruding in your face. 'Your place is over there, at the edge. As a *toḵal*,[3] you don't rule the kitchen.' He would look at you as if you were a stray dog, with a cold rage in his eyes, enough to make a weak man tremble. If he had caught the boss alone, he might have killed him with his bare hands, but he was always surrounded by his gang, and any act would be met with a fourfold reply. There was no solution other than to keep quiet and in one's place... at the edge. It was only at this point in his life that he became overwhelmed with a sense of powerlessness. He could not even muster enough willpower to clench his teeth. That damned square-built man knew how to make you feel that you were under his stirrups. He was also as swift as an arrow to grab one's daily earnings, and performed such tasks flawlessly.

The millionaire named after Abylaj Khan, lying in bed with his illicit companion, reflected on these difficult times and struggled to suppress the well of emotion gathering in his heart. He recalled his missteps with his wife, how she became suspicious by the way he touched her. Kǎmila, how heavy were you with sadness; I can still see your eyes glistening with tears. Song lyrics from the folk love lament 'Kǎmila' echoed in his memory: 'Ah! That I drank the poison of love / It would have been better to die young than to suffer such torture.'[4]The soaring wings of song that carried these words made him feel again that he was one with his beloved, and his eyes became wet as if with morning dew.

'The wife you have chosen has a body that is full and rich; she will surely give you strong and healthy progeny. Let God keep her under His protection.' Who had said these words? His mother? No, no, she would know that being complacent would only bring bad fortune. Maybe it was some idle comment blurted out unthinkingly by some random guest? Because he was young and inexperienced, these words went to his head. How silly, to evaluate a woman's worth through obsolete preconceptions. Shame. Nevertheless, such preconceptions caused him to say something, the memory of which still made him red with regret: a few years later, he recalled this comment, and, in a poor attempt at a joke, said to his wife: 'What a shame I am already married, when – look around – there are so many beautiful girls around!'

His wife had taken immediate offence. '*Bǎse*',[5] she said, 'you are looking at other women? As for me, what is my advantage over those younger and more slender unmarried women? My children's shoes are torn, and our debt is up to our ears. My status is lower than that of a widow.' He had sat still,

---

3 *Toḵal* – in a traditional polygamous family *toḵal* was a second, subordinate wife.

4 From a folk song 'Kǎmila', translated by the National Bureau of Translations.

5 *Bǎse* – an expression of assurance, approval, or anger and annoyance (sarcastic); in this context the latter is the case.

head drooping, struck not so much by the harshness of her words but by how alienated the two of them so clearly were from each other. Does my wife pray to God for my well-being or my destruction? he wondered.

And what about the good deeds of their poor friend Beregen, who had helped her and their children in a dark hour? Beregen was a childhood friend; they had grown up together. Later, when they had money, Beregen and his wife became slave and servant to his family. They entered as wood and left as ash. Beregen tried to avoid him, saying a quick 'hello' and always acting as if he were in a hurry with business. Kămila would deliberately seize the moment to issue instructions: 'Fetch the children from school.'

'Hey, Băke', the millionaire would say, using an affectionate nickname for 'Beregen', 'come, let's have tea together. If my boy Mŭrat has to wait for you a bit, it's of no consequence!'

But Kămila would not have this, and, sending a disdainful glance in her husband's direction, would say instead: 'Mind that our daughter must not be late for her classes. Beregen can have a meal when he returns. There is no shortage of food in this house.'

'Ăbeke', Beregen would say, using the affectionate form for 'Abylaj', it is better that I go now.'

Kămila would keep her eyes trained on him until he was out the door, and then complain: 'All their food and clothes are from this house. They take from this house and never say that they are full, the ungrateful beggars.'

Such words! It was clear that she must have completely forgotten how Beregen had helped during that long period in her life when she was the hungry and needy one. 'His brainless goat of a wife does not even clean the house properly', she once said, moving her finger across the table as if drawing a line through a layer of dust. The millionaire named after Abylaj Khan shuddered at the memory of his wife's arrogance. Even if he had any sensible comment to make to her, she would end the conversation with: 'First, go deal with your harem.'

It had become no better with his mother: 'Hey, don't get too big for your britches, you only became rich yesterday!' Her snapping voice would sting the corners of his ears. The more she cursed him and complained, the more it made him feel that he was the last person in the world. If he happened to come home drunk, after a long absence, her words could be even worse: 'It would have been better to be childless than to have gotten into such a mess with this herd.' Unsatisfied with the force of her words, she even disturbed the peace of his dead father, complaining to his spirit: 'You made me give birth to too many children. And then you abandoned me by dying! The indignities I've suffered in order to raise these vultures. To give them opportunities, the effort I made! I became powerless in front of snub-nosed Žaķan, forced to obey his commands.'

The millionaire named after Abylaj Khan was startled when he heard this. 'What did that mean? Did that snub-nosed Žaķan take advantage of my mother, then?' He felt his chest; it did not seem to be his chest at all but rather some dark, dense material that was alien to him. He sighed heavily and wondered again whether he was asleep or in a waking dream.

The night was so black; there was such a grave darkness, it seemed that morning and light would never return. He felt himself sinking into drowsiness. The amount of drinking and smoking he did had given him reason, on occasion, to knock on the doors of doctors. Even though he had been able to say farewell to vodka, he could not do the same with cigarettes. He wondered how he had been managing to cope without a cigarette for some time now, in fact, and surprised himself. He switched on the lamp again. The glasses on the coffee table, filled with yellowish and dark, mahogany-coloured orange and pomegranate juices, caught his eyes in the light. He pulled out a cigarette from his box of Camels, illustrated with a picture of a camel slowly plodding in the desert. He lit up with the lighter next to the woman and took in a long drag of smoke.

As he exhaled, he savoured the bitter taste of the smoke as if its harsh flavour could pull him from the void in which he found himself. Though he was skin-to-skin, cheek-to-cheek, with the naked figure next to him, he could not penetrate the cloak of coldness he felt between them. He had once desired such beautiful, svelte, swan-necked young women, although he was bothered by the thought that they knew life too soon. It seemed to him that he had been attracted to the rotten scent they carried, and feared that because of his weakness, he might have lost what remnants of sincerity and true feeling he had ever had. This fear ground at his heart and made him feel defensive. Even so, he had felt himself in heaven upon meeting this fair-complexioned woman with sad, penetrating black eyes and an affectionate nature.

In the beginning, she presented herself to him as shy, embarrassed, tinged with shame, twitching nervously and even nearly fainting. In such situations, he fell into the grip of mad and uncontrollable emotions, as if he wanted to subordinate everything to feeling and forget the rest of the world, all of existence. He recalled holding her tight against him with the fervent desire to let loose all his kindness and benevolence on this waif, who seemed as innocent as a fawn.

The trembling vibration of a moaned '*žanym*' – 'darling' – echoed into every corner of the room. The flames of passion continued blazing until finally all went quiet, as if a tiny spot on his forehead had cooled down. He sank back into womblike comfort. His companion's eyes rolled up and down, flaming, sparkling, an expression of satisfaction on her face. He was approaching fifty and wondered what he was doing, giving himself over to these feelings, thinking he was just a fool. The thought ran, blurry, through his mind that to fulfil such a woman one needs to muster brute physical force. The fawn, as if dying for the sake of lust, broke the embrace and moaned as she moved, touching and kissing him in lower places. He was revolted – even more so because he could not resist these gifts of passion – and he glanced around fearfully with the look of a person losing all of his senses.

He tried to force himself to stop, so that he would not veer off the cliff dividing a man's higher and lower impulses. But he lacked the will, and felt that he was falling into a whirling abyss. Finally, he gave in and collapsed. He observed the woman. She was still breathing heavily, and her desirable breasts moved up and down. She wrinkled her small nose and her flaming eyes came to rest and became bleary. He whispered to her through clenched teeth: 'Are you a prostitute?' She pretended not to hear his words. He only noticed that her eyelashes moved. Whether or not she regretted that she had accidentally revealed her secret, he did not know. She lay still and quietly on the bed, almost as if she were dead or imprisoned by the magic spell of a hot sweep of lust that overstepped all boundaries of custom and propriety.

He managed to resist seeing her for a few days. But soon he felt his animal urges rise up, and after three days he longed for her madly. Yet the disgust he was beginning to feel was also creeping deeper into him, and he felt as if both his body and his soul were becoming heavy with filth. It was as if unclean elements, small particles, were being wedged in his throat and his mind. Maybe he had contracted a sickness from his unholy lifestyle. He told himself, I shall never allow myself to approach this evil again, and he felt satisfied with his firm decision. Then the process would repeat: evil temptations would stir up within him, and those devilish bacteria would tickle his nerves and disturb his peace.

'You are bewitched, and you will bring me down with you. If you wish to be cured, you only need go to the mullah', his wife implored him. At that moment, he felt that his inner world was completely ridden through with crawling insects and worms, and that if he were to be cut open, they would fall out and scramble noisily to the ground.

When his square-built boss dismissed him that night, he had let out his anger by speeding down the roads of Almaty in his car. He'd paid no attention to the people trying, with their arms and hands, to flag down the taxi; they were like illusions flashing and disappearing at the periphery of his vision. When he reached the city's outskirts, he suddenly longed for vodka, and without thinking, he stepped on the brakes. If only he could find a place, he thought, where he could be alone, drink to his heart's content and then fall into a long, long sleep. He was still on his shift, however, and decided to stay in the taxi, continuing to vent his angry thoughts against the square-built boss. How did that man become a person of such importance? He gripped the steering wheel and imagined that his hands held the boss's collar and then his throat, which he seized with all his fingers and choked to his satisfaction. He noticed, in the rear-view mirror, that his temples were flaring, and his eyes looked as though they were burning, casting flames, and this caused him to calm down a bit: he was shocked by the power he found within himself. He wondered if he could harness the power of his gaze. The oval brown face he saw in the mirror was intelligent – that of a man capable of many things.

The depth of anger inspired by the bullying, square-built boss made him see a part of himself he had not recognised before. He, too, could summon a cold, austere gaze that would instil fear in his enemies. But that admirable face in the mirror – was it that of a man who had left his wife and children, who was repeatedly cursed by his own mother and who let himself be stepped on by others? This thought worried him. His mother's warnings about his vanity came to his mind.

The millionaire named after Abylaj Khan shuddered. What was it that he had admired in his face in the car mirror? A bitter smile formed on his lips.

'Hope springs eternal.' For who was he at that time? No one but a struggling taxi driver. Of course, there are few who can overcome the adversity of poverty and find a path to wealth and success. Fortune is a distant dream to a man making his living gathering pennies. He lit another Camel. It burned as quickly as horse dung, and soon he was puffing on a small stub.

For some reason, his thoughts turned to his old hunting hounds, his borzois. He could see their faces in front of him. The one with glistening brown eyes stood vividly in the millionaire's imagination. That dog had captivated him with his capacity for kindness, and for this reason he had no patience for people who cannot follow the simplest instructions of care for a dog. A good dog needs to be fed beef; if only Beregen's wife could have done just that. Instead, she threw him measly leftovers and bare bones. How many times must an adult be told the same thing? His speckled, short-coated borzoi had become gaunt. During his last visit, the dog had shown his soulful devotion, attending affectionately to his master. But he was subdued, and did not jump as was his habit; the radiance the millionaire had once seen in his eyes was gone. His heart seemed to have withered in his master's absence.

When he'd awoken from these musings, he still felt the need for vodka – but he had to continue driving. He picked up a couple of passengers who needed a short ride. One of them was a stingy Kazakh of the sort that counted not just stones but grains of sand. He cursed himself that he had to look badly on one of his people, because the man's meanness reflected poorly on all. Turning down a street that was less travelled, the miser immediately complained: 'Hey, driver, I see you are trying to make the route deliberately longer, but be warned, I am smart; I won't pay more than two roubles.' He stayed calm and ignored the passenger's carping, but the man would not keep quiet. 'I know every corner of the city. Do you think I studied for four years at the technological school and five years at the institute for nothing?' He glanced in the mirror sullenly and observed the braggart's face. Even if this man had studied for twenty years, he still looked like a coarse beast of burden. His hair was brushed back, with the sides cut very short and a shaggy tangle at the top. It seemed cheaply done, but perhaps he thought it made him look sharp. It reminded the driver of his youth, when a number of his cohorts had had such haircuts. With this memory, a warm current passed through his heart; but he shuddered as the passenger continued to rant with increasing madness in his whitening eyes.

The man's tone of voice seemed heartless and severe, but the driver also perceived an element of slackness and weak will in it.

'Brother, drive to the left – drop me by that car with the red stripe across the middle', the passenger said. But the driver sped up, as if intending to shoot past the appointed destination. 'Hey, stop!' the passenger cried anxiously, and the driver stepped hard on the brakes. The man in the back jerked forward, nearly hitting his nose against the front seat, and bounced back to his original position with his entire weight. He stared at the driver, perplexed; the driver remained impassive, gazing out the windshield.

'Here you are...' Hesitantly, the man held out two roubles in coins between his fingers.

But the driver remained still, and said calmly: 'My boss warned me that if ever I happened to give a lift to anyone who had studied in Almaty for ten years, to never take even one rouble from that person.'

The passenger did not know whether to be amused or angry. 'Is your boss a good man, or is something going on here?' he asked.

The driver continued: 'He warned me to be careful, that if I met a person who had studied for ten years, they were very likely to be madmen.' The passenger immediately took offence, but was barely able to blurt out, 'Hey...!' before the taxi driver cut him off coldly: 'Get the hell out of my sight – right now!' Meekly, the man began to get out of the cab, stepping carefully, but no sooner had he exited than the driver gunned the accelerator and sped off, leaving the passenger almost tottering over onto the ground.

Once again, a sinking feeling of loneliness and disappointment overtook the driver. He had given his trust to the square-built man, and to honest work in the city. What was happening with this world? He had wandered away from his family and *auyl* only to be caught between that devil of a boss and ungrateful bastards such as the ten-years-of-study passenger. He must simply have the ill luck of the poor. He recalled his mother's complaint to a neighbour on a morning of one of his visits: 'A bad child may come from a good parent, the elders have told us. His father died not from vodka, but from a natural death, at the time appointed by God. He was a strong man with a strong will; he was not led by the nose, by others. My ancestors were also of good stock.' Did she think he was sleeping, or did she want him to hear these words? She spoke loudly, but in a tremulous voice. He wanted both to hear the words and to block them out. He laughed that he had seemed so thick-skinned, for her words did not, at that moment, inspire worry or shame.

The neighbour replied in a sympathetic tone: 'Dear Bătima, he is still young. It is not easy for men to find their path to manhood. In their youth, it is normal that they wander; later, these wanderers settle down and become good men.'

'Damn his youth! The place he belongs is six feet under!' his mother whipped out, as if she had not even heard the neighbour's comforting advice.

He lost his good humour and froze as if someone had poured ice water over him. It now seemed that there was no place for him to call home; even the ground of his own *auyl* was not his country. His arteries pulsed; his vision blurred. Each new utterance in his mother's voice hit him like an electric bolt.

The four walls of the room were narrowing, and the words resounded in its shrinking air.

'A long time ago, when his father Asķar died, that snub-nose Žaķan chased me, offering marriage. What a silly woman I was, thinking only of their future. The old women in earlier times were right to say that it is better to have an old fart of a husband than to have thirty children. What a pity, that I did not at least accept someone like Žaķan.'

She then imitated Žaķan's snuffling voice, said something in a whisper and guffawed heartily. His mother's absurd laugh was humiliating. It compounded the ill effects of her sour words. When she continued, she resumed an austere tone: 'When children grow up, it is good if they become self-sustaining. It is a disgrace that neither the elder one nor the younger has the least spark of intelligence. How can I bear it, that his children are fed like beggars without any meat? I was forced to implore Beregen, Nùrlybek's son, the one who works as a guard at the grain warehouse, saying that his friend was alienated from his wife and children and that they had to go without flour and meat. He agreed to help, without hesitation. The next day he brought a sheep carcass. He even refused any payment.'

It is difficult for you to regain your good name, once you stumble, he thought now. How could she not consider the tens, the hundreds of roubles he had brought every time he visited the *auyl*? But she kept praising the sheep carcass Beregen had given once, as if she had never received anything from her own son. He had lost entire nights of sleep, not blinking up to sunrise, thinking over and over about this preposterousness. Was there any place in the world where he could be free of such thinking?

He looked at the naked woman lying next to him, who was covered with a duvet below the waist. It seemed to him that the world had become a place devoid of either honour or shame, in which anyone might simply walk outside with no clothing whatsoever. He was tormented by the notion that the meaning of *shame* had been irrecoverably lost – that if the woman turned to lie on her back, she would not even bother to raise her hands to cover herself.

The words of his wife, which she had spoken to him just before he had left for Almaty, came to his mind: 'There is no difference between a man who chases after every woman and a dog that urinates under every tree.' Then he thought of her lament during their first quarrel: 'Why did God cause our paths to cross? I would have been better matched with a shepherd or a tractor driver.'

The image of Kămila appeared suddenly to him as that of an angry Kalmyk, as the elders would have described her. Had she been wise, she would have learnt to accept life as it was and to find joy. She had become cold and stale – not a wife, but an adversary. She was arrogant and prideful, as if she had been born like that. He wondered why the men of olden times muttered, when they were irritated, 'Oh, my dear *kôzelim.*' It seemed to him that the hidden meaning of this expression referred not to the Turkish word for 'beauty', but to *kozel* – 'goat' in Russian: 'Oh, my dear *kozel!*' He found himself saying these words

aloud, and again glanced at the woman lying next to him, naked, prone and motionless. He laughed at the incongruity, though once again a disturbing rage grew inside him – yet this, too, subsided, and he returned to his original apathy.

'Damn you!' he said to himself, as his attention turned elsewhere. His thoughts now turned to the friend who had presented the wolfskin as a gift, one of the drinking buddies his mother so detested. When he presented the gift, he had said, in seeming kindness: 'Äbeke, let this wolfskin hang proudly on a wall of your newly built house.' The millionaire named after Abylaj Khan had interpreted it as a gesture of goodwill – traditional belief held that a wolfskin hung on the wall offered spiritual protection. He had even rewarded the man by assigning him to a position in one of his firms, later promoting him to head of the warehouse. When the friend reported a break-in at the warehouse, the millionaire did not pay much attention – but later, when he reported a fire, he ran there in a hurry. One side of the long warehouse was a smoking husk of black charcoal, and a red-green inferno was consuming its centre.

The bitterness he suffered over the loss of his enterprise accumulated, bit by bit. It seemed worse than death itself. Among the people scurrying around in the mayhem was this stupid man who had given him the wolfskin. Upon seeing the millionaire, his head shrank into his shoulders. The blood of the millionaire named after Abylaj Khan boiled. When the man approached him, it became clear that he was totally drunk. 'Äbeke', he had murmured in a weak, pathetic voice. The millionaire looked him over and wondered why he had not noticed his obvious character flaws before then. He had only himself to blame. His whole face was red, as if he had just emerged from a boiling bath. What could he say to someone so entirely inebriated? Why hadn't he asked this miscreant whether the skin was of a male or female wolf?

Apparently, he had forgotten to turn off the lamp in the corner of the room when pacing back and forth earlier: it now lit the room feebly. The wolfskin on the wall seemed animated, crawling upward with its ears flattened. Alert, attentive, he envisioned his own familiar face smiling bitterly and noting every tiny movement in that place, every nuance of feeling. Slowly, he began falling asleep.

In a dream vision, his borzoi gave birth to puppies. Oh, God, was it a *tôbet*, a Kazakh mountain dog? The small heads of newborn pups were attached to the teats of the mother, who was stretched out and asleep. There seemed to be at least five or six of them. It was said that a good dog would not give birth to more than four puppies. If they were well cared-for and fed only beef, they might grow healthily and be tamed easily. That dunderheaded wife of Beregen! If she could only follow instructions! Perhaps he should speak to Beregen instead.

The one with black spots must have been the male. The poor puppies' eyes were tightly shut, and they sought the teats hungrily. Didn't their faces conceal an enormous grief? Sorrow and pity melted his heart, and he could not look at them for an instant longer.

He found himself sitting in his car. He was speeding through blocks of many-storied houses before emerging onto a wide street, where he continued driving uphill. The image of the puppies' pitiful, blind faces nuzzling up against the teats was projected before his eyes.

Suddenly, he saw a child of about five years old running along the side of the road, crying out and shaking his fist. What could this be about? he wondered. He looked ahead and saw a man walking quickly, his posture upright. He strained his ears to hear what the child was shouting, and then caught it – a plaintive, high-pitched cry for his father: '*Kôke... Kôke!*'

Why is that man not paying attention to the child, damn him! thought the millionaire named after Abylaj Khan, trying to observe the situation more carefully. The child fell to the ground as he tried to jump across a ditch that had appeared in front of him, and even then, he stretched out his arms, calling to the mysterious figure ahead of him. The agony on the face of the innocent child struck the millionaire as being the result of a history of deep depression and utter hopelessness, and his heart pained. The tall figure disappeared into the dense blocks of houses across the street. The child remained where he had fallen. The millionaire, understanding nothing, drove on.

The millionaire named after Abylaj Khan woke up in a dreary state of confusion. He felt that once he put his face against the cold autumn air and took a large gulp of it, he would surely feel refreshed. He had just returned from a two-week business trip abroad. The directors of his firms were looking forward to his return, in order to hold a joint meeting in one of the cities in the south. He had felt like shouting: 'You cannot decide things without me?' Soon he would set off to the assigned destination, where there would be important issues to resolve.

On the way, he was persuaded to visit a sacred site prior to the start of the meeting. He and his men stopped in front of a huge, greyish, domed building built around a thousand years earlier. The entrance was on the eastern side of the building; the paint on the doors was peeling. Inside stood a large stone in the shape of a Kazakh cradle, covered by a white cloth. The shrine guardian was kneeling in front of the stone with his eyes tightly shut, swaying rhythmically as he gently recited words from the Qur'an. A young woman dressed head to toe in white, like a devoted student, was observing one of the five daily prayer rituals – the *namaz* – and quietly reciting the *surahs* in a murmur becoming of a female worshipper.

The millionaire named after Abylaj Khan discerned something attractive in the praying woman, her figure set in a holy posture and her dark eyes shining. She stirred something within him that he recognised as a kind of unreasonable hope. He felt a tinge of embarrassment at the devilish thoughts that tickled him – that he could be in the thrall of temptation even in the most consecrated of places. The shrine guardian's round, thickset face did not seem befitting of his position: he looked more like a common trader in the market. The millionaire wondered why a person with a slim, strong build had not been chosen instead;

but at that moment, the shrine guardian finished reading the Qur'an and cast a tired look at the group of men. Silently, they exchanged greetings. The shrine guardian remained in his kneeling pose.

The timid young woman placed a donation on a plate covered with white cloth, and slipped away. Again, and in a ringing voice, the shrine guardian read from the Qur'an. The colleagues of the millionaire named after Abylaj Khan also started placing donations on the plate. He felt as if he had come there with pure intentions, and that an act of worship here could absolve him of his sins. He put his hand into his pocket, pulled out a hundred-dollar bill and placed it respectfully at the edge of the plate. He could not help but notice that the eyes of the shrine guardian seemed to focus intently on the green bill, and his mood sank with the suspicion that there might be greedy intentions afoot. When the shrine guardian finished his reading with prayers for the departed, he paused and turned his attention to the congregants: 'Dear guests, thank you not for your gifts, but for the honour of your visit. Please, be at ease in the sainted home of our holy ancestor. When you go out, please turn to the right.'

The millionaire named after Abylaj Khan greeted the woman, who had prepared tea, and proceeded to the far end of the table. His colleagues joined him. As they settled, the shrine guardian came and sat in the manner of a tailor, with his legs folded beneath him. 'We are the servants of God, followers of Muhammad', he said. 'It takes thousands of days to become a king; to become a poor man takes only a single day.' Why are people in sainted places so fearful? wondered the millionaire. What is it to be a poor man, if one does not know the taste of being a king?

'Please, have some tea.' The cold voice of the woman made the millionaire shiver. She had a longish face and seemed to keep her eyes fixed on him. Were she not middle-aged – her only apparent imperfection – she might have been a fashion model parading on a red carpet, the equal of other beautifully built models. But her face was as pale as a white sheet of paper, as if she harboured suspicions about something. She placed a hand on her temple. He wondered about the meaning of this, and suddenly he reckoned that one of his colleagues must have come to this place without performing ablutions.

'Ah, I did not give you tea at all', she said, somewhat confused. The men rustled in their seats: 'We've finished, we've finished.' They got up and passed their hands gently over their faces while saying the customary '*Amin*'. As they walked out of the room, the woman stood at the door and beckoned to the millionaire. '*Ḳaraǵym*',[6] she addressed him gently – will you pause for a moment?' His heart thumped, and his head began ringing.

'I have special gifts, for which I have suffered a lot', she confided in him. 'Your presence here stirred some anxiety within me. I can see that you are not an ordinary man. You are also generous. But four months ago, you committed

---

[6] *Ḳaraǵym* – affectionate form of address to one's juniors; here it means 'my dear young man'.

a sin: you were so content when your dog gave birth… but you kept moving forward, and did not turn to look back at your son, who was running after you, calling, *kôke*!'

'Oh, God!' he replied, 'wasn't that just in my dreams!?'

'I do not know, *ķaraġym*', she said. 'But that is what I have seen.'

Translated by Mitchell Albert

ALIBEK ASKAROV
(b. 21.01.1951)

Alibek Askarov is a writer. He is an alumnus of both the Institute of Fine Arts and the Faculty of Journalism at Kirov Kazakh State University (now Ăl-Farabi Kazakh National University). He worked at various periodicals as a correspondent. Since 1986, he has been the managing editor of Ôner publishing house. He was a Deputy Minister of Communications of the Republic of Kazakhstan (1993–98), served in the presidential administration (2005–12) and was general director of the National Academic Library in Nur-Sultan (formerly, Astana) and Almaty (2012–16). Since 2016, he has been director of the National Book Chamber.

Askarov published his debut short story, 'Tùlki aulaj barġanda' (When Hunting Foxes), in 1967 in a regional newspaper. His first book, titled *Ķùtmeken* (Land of Prosperity), came out in 1979, followed by *Tajga tolġauy* (Thoughts of Taiga, 1981), *Erte tùsken bozķyrau* (Premature Dew, 1989), *Socializm áŋgimeleri* (Stories of Socialism, 2006), *Socializm hikaâty* (The Tale of Socialism, 2007), *Kešegi kùnniŋ hikaâsy* (The Story of Yesterday, 2008), *Batar kùnniŋ boâuy* (The Colour of the Setting Sun, 2012) and *Altajda atķan kùz edi* (It Was Autumn in Altay, 2009), among others. He has authored more than forty works of prose, some collected in a six-volume edition of his selected works (2016). Askarov is well known for his travels; twice he ascended Mùztau, the highest peak of Altaj (Altay) mountains, which led to an essay 'Mùztau nemese žerdiŋ kindigine saâhat' (Mùztau or Journey to the Centre of the Earth, 2016). Likewise, his 'Ķajyrymdy ùmit mùjisi nemese žer šetine saâhat' (Cape of Good Hope or Journey to the Ends of the Earth, 2017) came out following his trip to South Africa. His novels and short stories have been published in Beijing and Moscow.

He is an Honoured Worker of the Republic of Kazakhstan (2006), a laureate of the State Prize of the Republic of Kazakhstan (2001) and a recipient of the Parasat Order (2014).

Mona Lisa

In the mid-1960s, after their fourth year, the students from the journalism faculty were sent on a six-month work placement.

Tôleužan was assigned a position at the regional newspaper in Ķaraġandy. Once he had arrived and reported to the editorial office, he immediately set about finding himself a hostel, as he could not afford to live in a hotel for six months. He phoned every number that the editorial staff had given him and he finally found a tiny room in a three-storey, dried-clay house on the very outskirts of the town, which housed mostly construction workers. Carrying his belongings on his back and grabbing a bag of books he had brought with him, Tôleužan set off to his new digs without delay.

He cleared away the rubbish, dusted and tidied the room, set up his bed as comfortably as he could and, according to his now established custom, he hung on the wall a portrait of the *Mona Lisa*, which he always carried with him.

Yes, this was the famous portrait by Leonardo da Vinci, in a glass-fronted and gold-coloured frame. It was not the original, of course, and not even a specially printed reproduction, but just a large plate he had ripped from a fine art book he had found. Tôleužan himself had made a white mount for the picture and carefully placed it in an attractive frame.

For Tôleužan, who had grown up in the backwater *auyl*[1] of Betpaķdala, university was like an entirely new world, and he had devoted himself to his studies with considerable fervour. Like a traveller, irrepressibly thirsty after emerging from an endless desert, he had immersed himself in his studies; he never missed a lecture, seminar or extra lesson and spent day and night with his head in books. Other students found it hard to master the curriculum, but not Tôleužan; he studied not only from the textbooks, but also from a host of other sources, discovering completely new literature in the process. He studied the works of many prominent European writers, from antiquity to the present day. He may not have read everything out there, but he had certainly covered everything that might prove useful to him in later life. Where possible, he strove to study not only works of literature, but also social sciences and history, and

---

[1] *Auyl* – socio-economic formation considered to constitute the heartland of the nation and a basis for an ethnic and cultural union of the nomadic community. Consisting of 50–70 yurts in the eighteenth century, it developed into its current permanent state of 'rural settlement' (of a minimum of 100 dwellers) when Kazakhs adopted a settled mode of life in the nineteenth and twentieth centuries. *Auyl* can also be used as a synonym for 'native land' and 'homeland', concepts revered by the Kazakhs.

he discovered much of interest in the field of philosophical thought. He did his best to delve as deeply as possible into the much-vaunted European culture, for he knew that to become a true intellectual, he would need to work hard, for he would never have the time in future to educate himself.

Tôleužan knew no rest. When his hostel chums would invite girls out to have fun in the park or the dance hall, he too would dress up, even donning a tie, but he would head to listen to a symphony orchestra instead. This he would follow with the ballet or the opera. To be honest, he didn't really understand all these symphonies, the ballet or the opera, and his rather wild nature, moulded far away from the sophisticated cultural fads of city life, didn't really embrace them, but he went along all the same. He believed that Europe was the pinnacle of world culture and no matter how serious the book he perused, this unwavering belief would always remain unchanged. With time, Tôleužan's convictions had become more and more steadfast and he worked like a man possessed on what he saw as his self-improvement.

He regularly visited art galleries and on one occasion had caught sight of a large book of the works of Leonardo da Vinci. He had been desperate to buy it, but it had been unattainably expensive for him. Nevertheless, Tôleužan went to see everyone he knew, borrowed the amount he needed and bought the book. Leafing through the pages, he learned that the brilliant Leonardo had favoured his *Giaconda*, the mysterious portrait of a young woman with an enigmatic smile, above all his countless other works. Her name, he discovered, was Mona Lisa. The great artist took his *Mona Lisa* with him wherever his destiny took him. Of course, not the young woman herself, but the portrait he himself had painted. It had come to Tôleužan in a flash: if that is what Leonardo da Vinci had done, why should he not do the same?! And so, he had decided to follow the example of this genius. Tôleužan had carefully cut out the *Mona Lisa* from his book, placed it in a beautiful frame and hung it on the wall above his bed. He had frequented many a room in these last four years but had never once parted with his *Mona Lisa*. The first thing he would do the moment he arrived at a new place would be to hang his favourite picture over his bed. Only when he had to join the student construction brigade for the summer holidays would he be forced to leave it behind in storage at the hostel.

This current work placement was set to stretch over an entire six-month period, so Tôleužan had brought his *Mona Lisa* with him to Ķaraġandy. When he entered his tiny room at the construction workers' hostel, he hung it over his bed as usual.

Ten days passed.

Once, having sat over his books until two in the morning, Tôleužan overslept and, when he arrived late at the editorial office, the head of department was already waiting on tenterhooks for him.

'How am I to understand this?' he growled, shaking his head. 'I was ready to trust you with an urgent job. I thought you were a quick and keen young journalist and this is what you do!'

Tôleužan apologised and made it clear he was prepared to fulfil any assignment.

'Alright', replied the manager amicably and immediately calmed down. 'The Kùzembaev Mine is set to break a new record today. I want you to go there and write it up on the spot so that the article is on my desk first thing tomorrow, alright?'

Tôleužan had no choice but to agree. He took a photographer with him and rushed off to the mine in the office car. He went down a deep shaft and spent most of the day underground. This was the first time Tôleužan had ever been at a mine face and he found everything genuinely interesting. Having gleaned the information he needed and full of new impressions, he made it home by the evening.

The moment he entered his room, he discovered his mother, sitting huddled in the corner, so small and thin that she had seemed to have shrunk. What a turn up that was; their *auyl* was right back next to Betpaḳdala! How on earth had his mother Gùlajym *šeše*[2] made it all the way to Ḳaraġandy, he wondered. And how had she possibly found this godforsaken hostel in the big city?

Suspecting something was wrong, Tôleužan looked anxiously at his mother.

'I went looking for you at the newspaper. They gave me your address', she admitted. Her voice was unusually cold, as if she were talking to a stranger and not her own son.

'Mother, what are you doing here?' asked Tôleužan, unable to conceal his concern.

'Rumour reached the *auyl* that you'd been given an apartment in Ḳaraġandy. The news was false, it turns out. There had been some mix up, your friends at the newspaper told me.'

'Clearly, someone had heard I was going to Ḳaraġandy and decided that I'd been given an apartment. Perhaps they were just jealous.'

'I'm damned if I know. I thought you were having a housewarming party. So, I came straight here to see with my own eyes, and then...'

Only then did Tôleužan notice that his mother's eyes were puffy and red as if she had been crying all this time. Now, tired from her weeping, she was sitting, completely worn out. It seemed that more wrinkles had appeared on her forehead and they had become more pronounced. Swollen veins had appeared on her long, gnarled fingers. And her complexion was not what it had been the summer before; she had grown paler, dried by the Sun, as if she had been scorched by the heat of the feather-grass steppe.

'Mama, what is the matter? Is everything alright at home?'

'Everything's fine, my dear.'

'So why have you been crying? How is grandfather? Is he well?'

'He's quite well, yes.'

---

[2] *Šeše* – lit. 'mother', also a form of address to older women – *šešej*.

'So, tell me, what is it? How's Ajša *apa*?'[3]

'She's fine as well, my dear.'

Unsure quite what to do, Tôleužan paced around his mother at a loss. He eventually set about making some tea. He boiled the water and laid a modest spread on the table.

'Right', he said, extending a tea bowl to his mother with both hands, 'Spit it out! What on earth has happened? Enough of the suspense!'

Gùlajym *šeše* took a couple of sips of the tea and her eyes welled up once more.

'Oh, Tôleužan, my one and only!' she said at last, straightening up. 'I was widowed at seventeen. I didn't ever wish to offend you unintentionally and I devoted myself to your upbringing and never married again. What's there to hide now: so many worthy men made me proposals. However, I never gave any of them a second glance, although my heart really pined. I did everything I could, and I managed to bring you up and set you on your path in the world. The things I have suffered and the torment I have endured, my little foal. This life has turned me into an old woman and yet I am only forty, you see.'

'Mama, do you really think I don't know that?! I do, I really do. I will be alright and I will not disappoint you!'

'My little one, I am not reproaching you for a moment or begrudging what I have given. I'm not trying to show I'm anything special. In fact, I didn't want to say anything, but you have asked me to speak.'

'Mother...'

'Your father was the best of all *žigit*.[4] If it wasn't for that damned war, he would have become a prominent man and the pride of his people. But what can you do? These hopes have been dashed and they have melted away as if in a dream. Come what may, but at least I still had you after I lost him, and I found my support in you. Your father and I lived only three months together, but I have spent my entire life honouring his memory. I have praised the Almighty and I will be grateful to Him in this life and the next for giving me such a noble husband as your father. I nursed and pampered you and I worshipped the ground you walked on, and all so that you would grow to become as strong-minded, resilient and proud as your father.'

'Mother, I know. Thank you for everything you have done. But what have you got so steamed up about? Just tell me what has happened.'

'I was still carrying you when your father left for the war. Before he left, he told me firmly that if I were to bear a son, I should name him Tôleužan; if a

---

[3] *Apa* – depending on the region, aunt, sister, mother or grandmother; it is also a common respectful form of address for older women in general. In the given context it refers to 'mother'.

[4] *Žigit* – generally a 25-40-year-old male, it can be used as an honorific term indicating bravery, endurance, fortitude and being true to one's word.

daughter, then I was to choose the name myself. I kept my vow and gave you the name Tôleužan. When you went down with typhoid, I prayed to Allah day and night that you would recover. I even prayed at the grave of a saint, which was a day's journey from us, and I spent the night there alone. You are our only heir and the last to bear the family name, after all. God heard my prayers and you recovered. I fostered a new dream: that the Creator would not forget my only son and that you would grow to become a decent man. Glory to the Almighty, for this dream came true as well. You turned out as good as the next man and got into college with no difficulty. It won't be long until you graduate, either.'

'Mama, please stop beating about the bush and spit it out: is there something I have done? What is going on?'

'Could I have ever expected this of you, my son?!'

'*Ojbaj-aj*,[5] Mama, what is it?!'

'You can forget about me, but how am I to understand your lack of respect for your father's memory?'

'Mother!'

'All my life, I dreamed that my only son would bring me heirs, that he would continue his father's life and that my husband, lost at the age of twenty, would be reborn a thousand times over. That, after so much suffering, I would be able to enjoy the sweet scent of long-awaited grandchildren and finally find peace and happiness...'

'Mother...'

'No, just wait! It now seems that your father's dreams and your mother's hopes have been dashed forever!'

Gùlajym *šeše*'s sullen eyes suddenly flashed and she looked sternly at her son.

'It turns out that you don't give a damn about anything and plan to marry this... Not just someone of a different faith but a girl with a pot belly!' She spoke in an icy voice and nodded in the direction of the *Mona Lisa*.

'Mother...'

Tôleužan sat, completely lost for words.

'And a girl with freckles all over her face... What on earth do you need a woman like that for? She must be a good five years older than you, perhaps even ten!'

Tôleužan turned his entire body to face the picture on the wall. Perhaps because he had dragged the portrait here, there and everywhere that the young woman's face had indeed become covered with barely noticeable marks, similar to freckles on the skin, or maybe it was because he hadn't got round to cleaning the glass for a while and it had become fly blown. Yes, and her stomach did indeed appear round. Would you believe it?! His mother really wasn't one to

---

[5] *Ojbaj-aj* – exclamation of indignation.

miss a trick! Completely perplexed and not knowing whether to laugh or cry, he stared once again at the *Mona Lisa* in surprise, as if it was first time he'd clapped eyes on her.

What a turn up for the books!

Alright, but why has this image, which has created such a stir all over the world, not affected my mother in a positive way? he thought. I worship this picture, yet all its magic has failed to rouse the soul of the one person who brought me into this world and raised me in such suffering.

Gùlajym *šeše* wiped the tears from her face and continued lecturing her son, only this time, Tôleužan was not listening to her; it was as if his ears were blocked. Rising ponderously, he took the picture from the wall, carefully removed the image of the Mona Lisa from the frame, folded it in half twice and then turned to his mother.

'Mother, it's all because of this?!' and he extended the folded paper to her.

He looked jovially at Gùlajym *šeše*'s pale, wrinkled face and it appeared to soften a little.

'There's plenty more I wanted to say, but my throat is dry. Give me your tea!' his mother uttered contentedly, hiding the picture unnoticed but securely in the pocket of her large, multicoloured flannel dress.

Translated by Simon Hollingsworth, edited by Simon Geoghegan

TALASBEK ASEMKULOV
(1.08.1955 – 23.09.2014)

Talasbek Asemkulov was a *kùjši* (traditional musician and composer), writer, screenwriter, journalist and a scholar of mythology, ethnography and history, as well as a literary and music critic and literary translator. He was adopted and brought up by his maternal grandfather, the famous *kùjši* Žùnisbaj Stambaev. He received his traditional musical education from his grandfather and his friends, including the renowned singer Kărim Bajmùratov, the *kùjši* Ġaziz Nùrpejisov, the shaman and astronomer Myrzahan Oŋġarov, the blacksmith Ahmetžan and the master musician Tôleutaj.

Asemkulov was regarded a virtuoso performer of *kùjs*, many of which have been preserved and popularised thanks to his work. At the age of seventeen, he released a solo album, *Kùj Bajžigit*; another solo album, *Taltùs* (Noon), came out posthumously in 2016. The latter contains seventy-three rarely performed *kùjs* and features archival recordings of his grandfather.

Asemkulov's debut short story was published in 1985 in *Žalyn*, a literary journal. His major literary work is an autobiographical novel about his childhood, *Taltùs* (*A Life at Noon*, 2003), which won a prize awarded by the Soros Foundation – Kazakhstan and has been translated into English, French, Spanish, Arabic, Chinese and Russian. His other works include the novel *Tăttimbet Seri* (2012; about a political figure and virtuoso *kùjši*) and screenplays: *Biržan Sal* (dir. by Doshan Žolžaķsynov and Rymbek Ălpiev 2008; about a legendary poet, singer and composer), *Ķùnanbaj* (dir. by Doshan Žolžaķsynov 2015; about a famous political figure Ķùnanbaj [Kunanbay Oskenbaiuly]) and *Tomiris* (about a Skyrthian queen; it has not been made into a film). A five-volume collection of his selected works appeared in 2016. As a musician, writer and researcher, Asemkulov devoted his life to the rehabilitation of traditional Kazakh music.

The Old Kùjši

He studied the military service card presented to him, as if he had never seen one before.

'Have you come for long?'

'I'll be here about a month', Ăžigerej replied.

The enlistment officer leaned back in his chair and laughed.

'This is the first time I've ever seen such a thing and I have been chief enlistment officer in Baršatas for twenty years now. When I first came here, I was a young man just like you. I held the rank of lieutenant then but now I'm a captain', he said, casually nodding at one of his epaulettes. 'This is the first time in twenty years I have seen a man arriving for a month's leave, and a common soldier to boot, registering for service. Now that's discipline for you.

'You were probably a decent soldier. Thank you, brother.'

He pulled open the drawer in his desk, taking out a square stamp. He dabbed it lightly on his ink pad and then slapped it onto the document.

'There, go home and get some rest. Before leaving, you'll spend another day here. If I'm not in, the secretary will strike you off the register.'

Having emerged into the open, Ăžigerej looked at his watch. It was half past nine. He still had an hour and a half before his bus was due. He headed into the *auyl* centre,[1] as his *žeŋge*[2] had asked him to get a certain something. The shop was open and its heavy door wore a thick coat of green paint. When he threw open the weighty door, he saw a fair-faced, burly woman behind the counter. She had been waving away a man who had been pleading with her for a certain something for himself when her attention turned to Ăžigerej.

'What'll you have, young man?'

Ăžigerej looked over the shelves.

'Do you have any pepper?'

'We do', the woman said and placed several bags onto the scales. 'Take your pick. There's Ukrainian. There's Uzbek.'

---

[1] *Auyl* – socio-economic formation considered to constitute the heartland of the nation and a basis for an ethnic and cultural union of the nomadic community. Consisting of 50–70 yurts in the eighteenth century, it developed into its current permanent state of 'rural settlement' (of a minimum of 100 dwellers) when Kazakhs adopted a settled mode of life in the nineteenth and twentieth centuries. *Auyl* can also be used as a synonym for 'native land' and 'homeland', concepts revered by the Kazakhs.

[2] *Žeŋge* – sister-in-law, an older brother's wife or older relative; also, a reverential term for an older, married woman.

'Garmdori', the man next to her read from the packet and asked ingratiatingly, 'What does that word mean?'

'It means red herb', replied Äžigerej. 'That's what the Uzbeks call pepper. Some Kazakhs, too.'

'Well I never', the saleswoman said, 'I've been working here all these years, and I never could understand what that word meant. And you, young man, explained it to me in a minute.'

Sensing that the woman had dropped her guard a little, the man blurted out,

'Hanšajym, pour us half a litre, would you?'

'No, I won't', replied the woman, instantly changing her tone.

With his head in his hands, the man said dolefully,

'My head is about to burst.'

'It can drop off, for all I care', the woman said, turning to Äžigerej. 'Well, will you have any? How much?'

Äžigerej took a closer look at the man, who had managed to get himself into such a state, so early in the morning. He was of medium height and lean, with a thin, pale face. He was speckled with grey stubble and his eyes appeared faded. He was wearing a shabby blue jacket and dirty black trousers that sagged at the knees. His hands were shaking. Äžigerej felt a sense of pity he could not quite fathom.

'Do you have any on draught? I'll pay.'

'What on earth for, young man?' the woman said, looking at Äžigerej in annoyance.

'Hey, Hanšajym, this young man wants to stand me a drink, so what business is it of yours?' the man said, brightening up. 'It's your job to sell it.'

'This is not a restaurant for pouring drinks', the woman said, taking the weights from the scales and laughing maliciously in the man's face. 'I'd be doing nothing wrong if I clipped you round the ear with one of these.'

'Alright, then give me a bottle of red wine', Äžigerej said, placing a three-rouble note on the counter. 'It's on me.'

'Well, aren't you the insistent one', the saleswoman said. In one motion she took a bottle from a crate and banged it onto the counter. 'There, drink your last drop.'

'Thank you, brother', the man said, weighing the bottle in his hand and he headed to the window. It fell silent in the shop. The man opened the bottle and glugged the wine. Then he grunted, 'Ahh.'

'Get it down you, my good man', Äžigerej said in a barely audible whisper.

'Rascal!' the woman said, shaking her burly frame with laughter. 'He's incorrigible.'

Another *ahh* could be heard from the window.

'He doesn't hang about', Äžigerej said, aching from laughter.

'That rascal and I went to school together', the woman said. 'He was a sultan among *žigits*³ then. But look at him now. The poor wretch. His wife comes here every day and pleads with us not to sell him any vodka. But can you really fight fate? If a man is destined to lose his dignity, lose it he will.'

She weighed out Ăžigerej's purchase and wrapped it up.

'That'll be six roubles fifty-two kopecks.'

Ăžigerej threw seven roubles onto the counter.

'Where does he work?'

The saleswoman gave a wave of the hand.

'Nowhere. This is his job. He used to run the cultural centre. He was a musician, a *kùjši*.⁴

Ăžigerej's interest was piqued.

'A *kùjši*, you say? What's his name?'

'Žùman.'

Ăžigerej was taken aback.

'Wait a minute... Žùman? You mean, *that* Žùman? Good gracious!' and he turned to the window in awe. The man, it turned out, was looking at him, his head bowed. Their eyes met.

'That's right, sunshine. I'm *that* Žùman', and he approached, limping on his right leg. 'And you are Ăžigerej. I recognised you immediately.'

'Are you well?' asked Ăžigerej, a little flustered.

'Oh, you beggar', the man said. He blushed and his eyes filled with tears. 'Is that really how fellow *kùjši* greet each other?' He leaned back a little and his arms flew out in an embrace. 'We are hardly strangers, now are we? I worshipped your grandfather and I worship those talented fingers of yours.'

When Ăžigerej embraced the *kùjši*, whose vertebrae protruded from his skinny back, he felt a great tenderness and sympathy well up inside. Then he shuddered, as if from a sudden chill.

'Don't you worry, sunshine', Žùman said, slapping him on the shoulder. 'That's how things turned out, that's all. You've just come across your older brother in hard times.'

'These things do happen', the saleswoman said.

'Come with me', Žùman said. 'We can have a good old chat. After all, when am I likely to see you again?'

---

³ *Žigit* – generally denoting a 25- to 40-year-old male, the term can also be used as an honorific indicating bravery, endurance, fortitude and being true to one's word.

⁴ *Kùjši* – composer and talented performer of a *kùj*, a musical piece for traditional instruments. Asemkulov himself was a renowned *kùjši* and this tale is partly autobiographic, set in the early 1980s, when very few musicians of this traditional genre had remained.

By the time they had emerged from the shop, the Sun had already risen a spear's height above the horizon.[5] I've never been so surprised in my life, Äžigerej thought, walking the winding streets with Žùman.

'Sorry, old man', Žùman said, looking at him in supplication. 'I'm in a wretched state and I can't even invite you to my place. I don't want you to see the disgrace that is my home. Don't be angry, alright?'

'There's no need to belittle yourself like this, big brother', Äžigerej said. 'I understand, I really do.'

'This is the cultural centre', Žùman said, once they had approached a large building with a blue roof. 'We'll sit in here.'

They went down a corridor and Žùman opened a side door. Musical instruments were heaped in a pile in the centre of this spacious room. Äžigerej picked up a *dombyra*[6] and began to look it over.

'These belong to the district orchestra', Žùman explained, placing two chairs opposite each other. 'There are only two people in this *auyl* who can spare me the time of day. Tynyštyķ, the orchestra's director and Hanšajym, who you know.'

Äžigerej picked up another *dombyra*.

'They're all good for nothing', Žùman said. 'Leave them be. There's a *dombyra* here that I selected myself', and he turned the key in a cupboard in the corner. He took out a *dombyra* wrapped in cloth and extended it to Äžigerej.

'Here, this one's better.'

It was clear that the instrument, although factory-made, had been well cared for and was in excellent condition. It had been treated with a thin coat of supple varnish and the large, long pegs had been made of hardwood. Äžigerej touched the strings. The *dombyra* had been tuned in fourths. He grasped the strings in his hand, slid over them, pulling them back until they creaked, and then let them go. Then he touched them again. The tuning remained unchanged.

'It won't go out of tune', Žùman said, watching his every move. 'It's tuned to "Alķoņyr",[7] or what you would call *in fourths*.'

'Äbiken's tuning was higher than fourths',[8] Äžigerej said.

'Äbiken didn't play on thin strings made out of goat gut, but on thick, sheep gut strings', Žùman said, 'which is why he tuned his *dombyra* higher. To be honest, I am pleased with you. I've only seen the old masters apply this manner of re-jigging the strings by grasping them in the hand.'

---

[5] An ancient measure of time that equates to the Sun rising about 5–6 metres above the horizon or 7.00–7.30 am in summer.

[6] *Dombyra* – the most popular musical instrument among the Kazakhs, made of wood and stringed with animal's intestines. It can be of different shapes, with 2–4 strings and 8–24 frets, the most typical one being of oval shape, two-stringed and with 12 frets.

[7] A Kazakh folk song played in a particular key.

[8] Refers to the renowned *kùjši* Äbiken Hasenov (1897–1958).

'Well, that's how they check to see if they're ready', Äžigerej said and plucked at the strings once more. 'The strings are still tight.'

'Well', Žùman said, breathing in deeply, 'it was a dream of mine to hear you play. It looks like this dream will come true today. Play!'

Äžigerej fell into thought, unable to select a *kùj* off the cuff. What *kùj* could he play for this *kùjšī*? He barely noticeably raised the pitch of the *dombyra*. He removed the *ḳašaġan*[9] quartertone fret and the *orphan* fret. He moved the *tender* fret a finger's breadth.

'Bravo!' Žùman said contentedly. 'You haven't touched the strings, but I can already hear the *kùj*.'

Well, here goes, Äžigerej said to himself nervously. He placed his fingers on the *dombyra* sound plate.

Žùman froze, unable to take the tear-filled eyes on his long face from the *dombyra*. It was as if he could hear the melody, not just with his ears, but with his eyes and body as well. The *kùj* came to an end.

'What can I say?' croaked Žùman. 'Turns out, you can imbibe suffering as if it was water. Thank you. You've given me wings, my dear man.'

He rose and paced up and down the room. Then he sat down again. He turned his brightened face to Äžigerej.

'"The Ḳosbasar[10] of the Plaintive Lament". The melody that Tǎttimbet played to comfort Kùšikbaj after he had lost his only son. Play another.'

He played three 'Frenzied Ḳosbasars', one after the other. He had seldom encountered such an expressive instrument that was so comfortable to play. After a while, the strings settled, as if they had become as one and the melody emerged not from the strings but seemingly from the ends of his fingers.

He had planned to conclude with the 'Ḳyrmyzy Ḳosbasar',[11] but he couldn't pluck up the courage. Instead, he began to play 'From the Heart'. Žùman stood up, went up to the window and sat down with his back to Äžigerej. The melody ended but Žùman continued to look out the window, without stirring. He finally cleared his throat and spoke in a somehow voiceless manner.

'Play the "Ḳyrmyzy Ḳosbasar".'

Äžigerej moved the loosened frets, tightening them more firmly. He played the melody that Žùman had requested, putting all his skill into the piece and not omitting a single inflexion.

Total silence filled the room. The two men, who had only just met, sat in silence as if they had known one another all their lives. They had understood

---

[9] *Ḳašaġan* – lit. 'an unbroken horse that constantly runs away'. It is the traditional term given to the quartertone fret on a *dombyra*.

[10] *Ḳosbasar* – cycle of 62 philosophical *kùj* about the life and death of the nineteenth-century composer and performer, Tǎttimbet. According to legend, Tǎttimbet performed the cycle to calm his father, who entertained suicidal thoughts after the death of his beloved son.

[11] *Ḳyrmyzy* – red-orange steppe flower that blooms only a few days in a year.

one another without words during this conversation that had lasted a lifetime and which had only just ended or, rather, which had run and run.

Later, Žùman walked Ãžigerej to the bus and embraced him tightly.

'I was wrong. Oh, how wrong I was', he said with a sigh. 'It turns out that the *kùj* melody lives on… It's not for me to tell you what to do, but I will tell you this. Ãžigerej, my dear brother, don't stray from your true path. Don't ever part with the *dombyra*.'

Ãžigerej was abashed and didn't know what to say. After all, a man bruised by life can be sensitive and easily take offence.

'I never thought I'd meet with you… in such circumstances', he said finally.

'Don't trouble yourself', Žùman said. 'I understand what you want to say.'

He lit up a cigarette and stood there in silent contemplation.

After a pause, he said, 'There is one more thing I want to ask of you. Not for my sake but for yours. Not even for your sake but for the sake of the *kùj* that exists for all of us. On your way home, stop off in Sarykamys. Atyġaj the *kùjši* lives in that *auyl*. I have heard that he is still alive. He is an exceptional player. Get to know him and treasure what he knows. Please don't be angry that I didn't play for you', he said, extending his hand. 'I wouldn't have the courage to touch the *dombyra* now. Later, if fate dictates and I see better days ahead, then maybe. If we meet again, I will show you my art.'

The driver signalled it was time to leave.

'All the best to you!' Žùman said.

'You look after yourself', Ãžigerej said. 'We'll meet again in better times.'

Once the bus had reached the end of the street, Ãžigerej looked back. Žùman was standing dejectedly, his shoulders slumped. Ãžigerej shivered inside. He did not look back again.

***

The bus had almost reached Sarykamys, exposed to the sultry wind, when a dark cloud shrouded the sky and fine rain began to fall.

'It'll feel better at last', said an elderly woman who had been continually tormented by the stuffy atmosphere.

She wiped profuse perspiration from her face and buttoned her green dress up to her neck.

'It's incredible. Is autumn supposed to be so hot? The heat is worse than in July.'

'They said on the radio that we'd have 38 degrees', a young lad said.

'The blessed day has begun to get worse too', said an old man sitting next to Ãžigerej. 'Once, things seemed to run their course. They used to call this season "summer without the flies". Autumn used to be a blessing for the soul and it would last until the first frosts in November.'

The bus stopped at a circular common in the centre of the *auyl*, the people headed for the door and torrential rain began to fall to the earth. It instantly fell dark. Soon afterwards, the bus departed. Left all alone and unable to withstand the rain that came hurtling down like stair rods, Äžigerej hunched over, his head pressed into his shoulders, and looked around. In the flashes of lightning, the houses of the little *auyl* could just about be seen. Muddy water bubbled and foamed all around. The latest lightning flash illuminated a house standing right beside him. Äžigerej decided to seek shelter there, no matter who lived inside. However, the door to the building, which bore a tin sign reading *Canteen*, had been locked.

He heard someone calling to him. When the world was once again filled with the green flashes of lightning, he caught sight of a man waving to him from under the awning of a shed or dilapidated house. Slipping and tripping, Äžigerej rushed over to him.

'Come inside, son', a middle-aged man said, shepherding him past. 'Well now, you really are soaked through! They say that any man who makes forty steps away from home is a stranger in need of help. Let's wait for the rain to pass together and have a chat, eh? It'll probably pass soon.'

A lad was sitting on his haunches and smoking inside the little shed. He flicked ash and addressed Äžigerej with a grin:

'You were wasting your time trying the canteen door. I don't think it's been working since the Second World War.'

'Where have you come from?'[12] asked the middle-aged man.

'I went to Baršatas to register for military service', Äžigerej replied. 'And now I am on my way back to Ajġyz.'

His soaked shirt had begun to stick to his body and he began to shiver.

'So why did you get off here then?'

'I have business in Saryḵamys. By the way, you're from this *auyl*, right? Would you point me to the home of the *aḵsaḵal*[13] Atyġaj?'

'Atyġaj, you say?' The man lowered his eyes in thought. 'I don't know. I live on the farm, but Ḵadyržan here – he's from Saryḵamys itself. He must know.'

'What does this old man do?' the young lad said, stubbing out his cigarette and getting to his feet.

'I've no idea.'

'Well, if that's the case, I can't help you', the young lad said with a smile. 'I only know one Atyġaj. He got old ahead of his time. But he's not an old man as such. He's the *auyl* mechanic.'

'Does he play the *dombyra*?' Äžigerej asked and immediately realised how out of place his question must have sounded.

The man spluttered.

---

[12] It is deemed bad luck to ask where someone is going, so the accepted approach is to ask from where they are coming.

[13] *Aḵsaḵal* – traditionally, a well-respected and powerful elder in charge of the community. Nowadays, a reverential form of address to elderly men in general.

'I'll go and demand *sùjinši*[14] from my brother-in-law. He's so unlucky he'd get bitten by a dog even if he was up in the saddle, and here someone has come looking for him', the lad Ķadyržan said in fits of laughter.

He calmed down and took another cigarette from the pack.

'If you're looking for that Atyġaj, then you have strayed off course. I'm joking about him because he is my brother-in-law. But he's never held a *dombyra* in his life. And that's the truth.'

'Maybe he has a namesake', the man said.

'No idea', Ķadyržan said. 'I know only one Atyġaj.'

The sheeting rain had begun to let up. The Sun had appeared in the chaotically vagrant clouds, the grey fog receded and the world was once more bathed in light.

An old woman pulling a cow on a rope appeared from the other side of the shed.

'That's auntie Bătiķan', Ķadyržan said. 'If anyone knows, she does.'

'Hello, granny', Ăžigerej said.

'What is it, love?' asked the old woman, looking at him, quizzically. 'I don't recognise you; whose son are you?'

'You don't know him. He's from Ajġyz', Ķadyržan said, raising his voice. 'He wanted to say hello.'

'Oh, so he's come from Ajġyz to say hello to me?' the old woman said. 'May your family grow and grow, my son.'

'Everyone in this *auyl* likes a joke', the man said.

'Granny, this lad has come looking for a man named Ajġyz', shouted Ķadyržan. 'He says this old bloke is a *kùjši*. Do you know him? A *kùjši* called Atyġaj?'

The old woman cupped her ear to Ķadyržan. 'What's that you say? Say that again. What's he saying, are they keeping all the crazies in Ajġyz now? And what are they going to do with them?'

Ăžigerej couldn't contain himself and laughed out loud at the old woman's barbed joke.

'They're probably *ķurdas*'[15], the man said. 'Only *ķurdases* could joke about one another like that.'

'Who doesn't know that old card', the old woman said. 'You've come on a good day, son. Please take your Atyġaj and all the other crackpots away with you. God will grant your every wish if you do.'

'Where can I find him?' Ăžigerej asked.

At last, the old woman gave him a serious answer.

---

[14] *Sùjinši* – Kazakh tradition whereby the person who brings good news is given a gift.

[15] *Ķurdas* – term for people of the same age or contemporaries. In Kazakh culture, relations between *ķurdases* are affectionate, allowing the taking of liberties and undue familiarity, and often accompanied with poking fun at each other.

'I was joking, son, don't you fret. Your old man Atyġaj lives outside the *auyl*, in his father's old house. Cut diagonally across the *auyl*', she indicated, pointing to the west, 'and walk about a kilometre. You'll come straight to Atyġaj's house. Godspeed, son. And say hello from me.'

It was a long, sun-dried wattle-and-daub house with a flat roof. There were many outbuildings and sheds for livestock. It was completely open, without a fence in sight. The fire pit dug out in front of the entrance was full to the brim with water. Before entering the house, Ăžigerej looked out at the steppe once more. It was still overcast. The peaceful steppe, spreading out as far as the eye could see, was breathing moisture. It'll probably rain again, he thought.

Ăžigerej entered and shut the door behind him. He stood a while in the corridor, while his eyes grew accustomed to the dark. Then he followed the long wall. A loud conversation came into earshot. He felt for the doorknob with his hand. He pulled at it twice and the heavy door eventually squeaked open. There were two people in the half-lit room. At the back of the room, on the *tôr* – seat of honour, sat a red-haired old man on thick fur bedding. He was as thickset as the door Ăžigerej had just entered through. An old woman poured tea with her back to Ăžigerej. The two of them looked at their guest in surprise.

'*Assalamualaikum*', Ăžigerej said.

'And unto you peace, my son', the old man replied. 'Come and join me on the *tôr*.'

Ăžigerej took off his shoes and sat down on his knees before the old man, extending both hands in greeting.

'How are you, grandfather? I trust you are well?' he asked and then turned to the crooked old woman: 'And are you well, grandmother?'

'Very well', the old man said with a contented look and stroked his beard. 'Make some fresh tea, old woman. It seems our guest could do with warming up.'

He sipped from the bowl in front of him.

'Tell me about yourself, son. Where have you come from?'

They lingered for some time over their tea. The old man obligingly and repeatedly offered Ăžigerej a small dish of *ķuyrdaķ* offal stew, a plate of butter, *ķürt* dried cheese and *bauyrsaķ* dough buns, laid out on the tablecloth, pleased with his guest's healthy appetite. He simply drank tea and continually extended his empty bowl to his wife for more. Once Ăžigerej had eaten his fill, wiped his face and sat back from the table, the host downed several bowls of tea, as if there was nothing untoward in his thirst. Then he retrieved a handkerchief the size of a blanket from the pocket of his plush, brown jacket and proceeded to slowly wipe the sweat from his brow.

'Well, son, you've probably come all this way to see Atyġaj for a reason. What is it you want to ask?'

Ăžigerej remained silent for a while, looking at the old man, who was calmly awaiting an answer. Then he decided to get straight to the point and said,

'Grandfather, I've heard that you are a *kùjši* and I've come to learn from you.'

'Who told you that? How does he know that I'm a *kùjšī*?'

'A man called Žùman told me.'

The old man's eyebrows gave a jolt. In the next moment, he looked over at Äžigerej with a scoff.

'Oh, my dear fellow. I parted with the *dombyra* many moons ago. Žùman was right: there was a time when I plucked the strings. I roamed the entire steppe, performing to the people. But that was back then. Now... now, my strength is not what it was. Let me tell you: I haven't held a *dombyra* in twenty years.'

'So, you're too mean to share your craft with a child?' said the old woman, who had been silently pouring the tea up to that point. 'He has come to you with a request, after all.'

'Oh, my old woman', the old man said, shifting in his seat, 'to pick up the *dombyra* again will be as hard as calling up the spirits of ancestors long gone. I have one foot in the grave and the dogs have long since left after gnawing the bones from the feast, so to speak, and you want me to go out and entertain the folks?'

Äžigerej felt sick on hearing the old man's words and he looked out the window. It had already turned dark. He returned his gaze to the old man. Atyġaj, stroking his whiskers, had been pensively looking at his guest the whole time. Äžigerej lowered his head.

'I don't know', he said breathlessly. 'I don't know. The Kazakh people are a boundless, lifeless, burnt-out steppe. I am forever walking and I have no idea if I will ever reach my goal. There is no end of the road in sight. God created me, filled my heart with *kùj* and perhaps this is why hope has not deserted me. It is this hope that leads me forward. I believed my elder brother, who so loves the *kùj* and that is why I came to you. He spoke of a tall aspen tree with its leaves rustling in the wind, but all I have found is a withered, old stump that is good for nothing but firewood. The *kùj* has deserted the Kazakhs. I was an idiot to believe otherwise. The melodies exist only in my mind, then.'

He looked out the window once more. Out in the dark there was not a thing to be seen.

'Enough', he said, getting up and heading for the door. 'I have wasted my time and I have to be getting home.'

'Wait a minute, son', the old man said, when Äžigerej already had his hand on the doorknob. 'Just a minute.'

Äžigerej turned round. His bones creaking, Atyġaj rose from his seat and walked over to him laboriously.

'Just a minute, son', he said, grasping Äžigerej by the wrist. 'Sit down. Let's talk.'

Äžigerej sat down.

'Oh, Lord, you were pretty scathing just now', Atyġaj said, returning to his seat. 'Alright. For you and because of what you've said, I will try once more to gallop out bareback on a yearling, just like I did in my childhood.'

He turned to the old woman.

'Salikha, where is that *dombyra* of mine? Bring it to me, would you? And turn on the light; it's dark in here.'

Soon, the room was filled with light. Atyġaj unwrapped his *dombyra* from a cloth and looked it over closely. There were no strings. The sound bar had eight frets.

'Turn up the light.'

The host picked up something the size of a block of wood from a corner. It was a whetstone.

'I travelled to the banks of the Baḳanas for this', boasted Atyġaj, opening his folding knife. 'A genuine, soft stone, this is. The knife blade simply glides over it.'

He took a long time sharpening his knife, wetting the stone with water from the kettle. From time to time, he tested the blade by cutting a sheet of paper.

'There, it's ready', he said, bringing the blade to the lamp. 'Come over here, son. Now we need to clean the soundboard under the frets.'

He asked the old woman to lay a white cloth on the table. He placed the *dombyra* on it.

'Son, I can't wield my fingers as I once could. Cut away all the frets for me.'

Removing the frets from the soundboard, Ăžigerej marvelled at the craftsmanship in the instrument. The resin from the wood had been rendered. There was not a trace of glue to be seen between the body of the *dombyra* and the upper string plate. Ăžigerej took a closer look. The string plate had been cut from the same piece of wood as the sides, in one piece.

'Grandfather, there is no join here', he said, unable to restrain himself.

'Yes, the usual practice is to hollow out the body from a piece of wood and then stick the string plate to it. The body of this *dombyra* was cut not from the front, but from the back', the old man explained, pleased with Ăžigerej's powers of observation. 'The top has been glued to the body from behind.'

Ăžigerej was amazed at the craftsman's ingenious idea; he had found how best to relay the vibration of the strings, through the upper plate, to the entire body.

'That's all of them', Ăžigerej said, returning the *dombyra* to the old man.

Running his hand over the soundboard, Atyġaj used his knife to cut off all the uneven bits. Then he gave Ăžigerej a sly look. 'Take a look at this. Have you ever seen anything like this?'

He began to pour cold water from a large, yellow kettle into the hole in the *dombyra*'s soundboard. The water soon began to pour from the hole.

'What on earth are you doing?' Ăžigerej asked in astonishment. 'The glue will surely soften, won't it?'

'Oh, little one, you still have much to learn', the old man boasted. 'Nothing will happen. Let me explain. This is no ordinary glue that you can buy in the shop. It is Kazakh glue made in the old way and it holds permanently.

'I could boil this *dombyra* in a pot and the seams wouldn't come apart. That's one thing. I poured water in because the *dombyra* had dried out. There's one thing you failed to notice. Try to remember it in future. A genuine *dombyra* resonates even without strings; it emits a mournful hum. You didn't try flicking the body when you were holding it just now. That was a mistake. I did.

'The *dombyra* doesn't hum, rather it chirps. And you didn't notice it. Wood, and especially wood soaked in rendered resin, will never absorb surplus water. It will drink only just as much as it needs. That is your first lesson.'

'How long will it remain with water inside?' Äžigerej asked.

'As long as you like', Atyġaj replied. 'Now we need to find it some strings.'

'Will these do?' Äžigerej retrieved a reel of kapron line.

Atyġaj looked carefully at the string, wrapped it around his fists about three feet apart and tried to stretch it. His eyes fell on the picture of a fish on the wrapping.

'This is a fishing line from a shop', he said, returning the reel to Äžigerej. 'You can throw it on the fire. It's totally worthless.'

He looked at his wife.

'Saliha, is there nothing left of those strings you were braiding on the spindle?'

He admiringly looked over the string his wife had found him and gave it to Äžigerej.

'That's what real strings look like, son. This is a string from the gut of a six-year farrow goat. It's really eloquent. It speaks like a human.'

'It looks like everything is ready', Äžigerej said, measuring the string the old man had given him against the length of the *dombyra*. 'So, when will the lesson begin?'

Atyġaj didn't answer. It was only when a dish with a mountain of meat had been placed on the table and he had begun to cut it with his penknife, that he slowly began to speak.

'I have heard you out. And now it is my turn. Return to your *auyl* tomorrow. I will be ready in about two weeks. Come back then.'

The autumnal heavy rain fell all night. The old man tossed and turned and sighed all night.

***

The day was overcast, but it was still hot and stuffy in the small wood. Walking slowly over the soft cover of bird droppings, dry leaves and twigs, Äžigerej emerged into a clearing. The Saġa Mountains were pensively shimmering blue in the east, a fragrant, cool breeze wafted down from the distant peaks to caress the land and Äžigerej welcomed it with open arms. There was a mountain spur on one side, which melted into endless steppe; on the other was a thick forest, interspersed with birch, aspen, hawthorn, silverberry and honeysuckle. Between the two was the wide valley of the River Ajġyz. Red clover, a flower that looks like a small child with shaggy hair on a thin neck, the bluegrass with its vitriolic colour, thermopsis, which is also known as Kalmyk pea, and thousands of other grasses whose names Äžigerej didn't know, all fluttered in the unseen autumn wind. He approached a single hawthorn bush, the top of which he had seen amidst the tall grasses. He had remembered this tree since childhood, with its ever-so-sweet berries. He took one and bit into it. The taste was just the same. He placed a dry leaf on his palm.

It looked as if it had been cut from fine brass. A sweet leaf, burnt on the wind, he said to himself. Tomorrow... No, in two days, I will finally find the happiness I've been seeking so many years. I will learn the craft of a true *kùjši*. Just two days. He glanced once more at the hawthorn and then headed off to the *auyl*.

Why does the smoke from the hearth rise vertically in autumn? Äžigerej galloped on his horse from up in the mountains. He pulled at the reins when he had reached a small graveyard and then he began to descend down the hillside. The dust that the horse's hooves had kicked up remained in the air as if speared into the ground. It was a pretty sight. He thought that the old *aḵsaḵal* Ġaziz kept his bee garden in these parts. The hives were where they had always stood, in a clearing amidst some silverberry trees.

The beekeeper in his mesh hat was fumigating the hives. Hearing a noise, he turned and removed his hat. It was Ġaziz himself.

'*Assalamualaikum*', Äžigerej said, taking the shovel-sized hand of the old man in both of his.

'And unto you peace, my son', Ġaziz said with a smile. 'I saw you just now from afar and I thought you might pop in on your way back. Have you been gathering silverberries?'

'Well, I wanted to, but the bees wouldn't let me close. One almost stung me', Äžigerej replied.

Ġaziz laughed out loud.

'True, they can be right wicked if you provoke them. They're not ones for jokes. Not long ago, some rascals came by to take some honey and pulled down one of the hives. The bees chased after them and the kids jumped into the river. The bees stung the poor blighters badly and a couple of them even ended up in hospital. I was barely able to calm the bees down and had to spray them with water.'

The old man waved a hand in the direction of the road.

'What are we standing about here for? Come and be my guest in my little hut.'

They had sat down in the small hut on the edge of the bee garden. Ġaziz picked up a black, soot-covered teapot from a tripod over the fire and gave Äžigerej a large bowl with some deep-red, fragrant honey.

'This is fresh honey from this autumn', he said.

He cut large slices of cold meat, broke baked flatbread from the fire and placed the pieces on a tablecloth.

'There you go. We'll have some tea and a chat. The wife left this morning to the *auyl* with a tub of honey on the cart.'

'When I was a child, I remember you taking the apiary on a cart to the summer pasture. Do you still do that?'

'No. We've grown too old and tired for all that. It seems the children have no interest in keeping the business going. I haven't moved from here at all in recent years. It turns out you can collect honey under the silverberries while living here. The honey you're eating is from those same berries.'

They sat until late, sipping their tea in silence.

'Your late grandfather didn't share my love of the bee garden', Ġaziz said, interrupting the silence. 'He used to tease me, calling me a *kùjši* tending flies. A couple of times he tore me off a strip for performing *kùj* wrongly. A quick-tempered sort was that unforgettable old grandfather of yours.'

'Incidentally, I wanted to ask you', Ăžigerej said, looking hopefully at the old man. 'Do you know a *dombyra* player called Atyġaj?'

'Atyġaj?' Ġaziz thought for a while. 'Ahh, yes. Yes, now I remember. A long time ago, the Abraly district had been broken up and we were merged with the Aâgôz district. That was the autumn of '49. There was a festival of sorts in Aâgôz. A stage had been set up on the back of a truck and musicians performed for us. Atyġaj was one of them. Oh, he was the genuine article. He was in his forties back then. Although he was getting on a bit, he flickered away like the flames in a fire. He was incredibly tall, too. Him holding a *dombyra* would be like you holding a spoon. Yes, that's right. He was a virtuoso player. A virtuoso.'

Ġaziz shook his head, as if still amazed at the event.

'He was a blacksmith in Saryḳamys. Once, he had to travel to Ajġyz and he stayed at our house. Seeing our axe, he laughed and said, "You might know about beekeeping but you have no idea how to handle metal". He took the axe from its handle, went to the *auyl* blacksmith and tempered it for us. I swear to God, there were times I would chop metal with that axe and yet there would be not a scratch on it. I would even chop bone and the axe would get stuck in the stone underneath. I never did understand how he had done that. It was a regular old axe from common-or-garden steel.'

'So, he had formulated a special tempering solution', Ăžigerej said.

'Why are you asking about him? Is he still with us?' Ġaziz asked.

'Yes, he is well.'

'May he see many more years', Ġaziz responded.

He took a jar of honey from a shelf and placed it in front of Ăžigerej. 'Here take this for your *žeŋge.*'

'You shouldn't go to so much trouble!' Ăžigerej said.

'No trouble at all', the old man frowned. 'Tell her that old uncle Ġaziz said hello. What about you? Are you here for long?'

'For a month.'

'When you were a boy, you were black as the ace of spades, but you've become paler since then. They say the air is no good in Almaty. You should come to the *auyl* at least once a year, recite a prayer at the graves of your ancestors, relax a while and drink *ķymyz*,[16] he said pensively. 'I saw you once, playing the *dombyra* on the *tilibizion*, or whatever they call it. You have reached a level when you can bring tears to people's eyes when they listen to your craft. But don't stop there. Keep studying. We... I am like a wizened, legless, old horse which will never gallop again. Your generation has left us behind. You've made it in the world. Go and conquer the heights we never managed to.'

'I think the heights are right up ahead', Äžigerej said.

'But don't you go forgetting about me, now', Ġaziz said with a playful grin. 'I'm your teacher, too, you know. Perhaps only two or three, but I taught you some *kùjs*. Mention my name, too, alright?'

'Of course', Äžigerej said, extending his hand to the old man. 'How could I forget a teacher like you?'

'Farewell.' Ġaziz embraced Äžigerej and kissed him on the cheek. 'When you come next time, who knows whether I'll be alive and well or under a mound of earth over there', he said, pointing over to the graveyard on the hill. Be well and may Saint Ķydyr[17] bless you.

***

'Alright then, son, listen up.'

Atyġaj had picked up the *dombyra* and made himself more comfortable.

A long, long time ago, before the Straight Path and the Ancient Path, there lived a khan whose name was Genghis. He had a hero warrior called Ket-Bùġa. One day, sitting in his chambers, Genghis fell into thought and he said to his confidants, 'It appears I have conquered all four corners of the globe and all seven continents.' One of his viziers then said, 'No, sire, there is one enemy you have not yet overcome.' 'Speak!' Genghis Khan ordered. 'My Lord, the country you have yet to conquer is called Misr. Send your forces there and the King of Egypt will cede his throne personally, or you will have him executed. Only when you conquer Misr

---

[16] *Ķymyz* – beverage made from fermented mare's milk, valued in Kazakhstan for its refreshing qualities; it is a main drink for many special occasions.

[17] *Ķydyr* – legendary saint who brings luck, happiness and prosperity; he also grants people's wishes and helps those in distress. In Kazakh mythology, *Ķydyr* can appear in different guises, hence the saying 'One of the forty is *Ķydyr*' (that is, every person should be treated with respect).

will all four corners of the world be entirely yours.' Genghis sent for
Ket-Bùġa there and then, and gave him the order. A large detachment of
troops, their pennants and flags flying in the wind, set out at sunset.

Atyġaj drummed the strings. The sound he produced was like a wave against a
cliff face.

The troops rode for a very long time and when the steeds had become
exhausted, they had reached Egypt. However, the King of Egypt was
recalcitrant. 'Genghis wishes to battle with me? I will see what he is made
of', he said. With these words, he called for his military commander.
'The warrior Ket-Bùġa stands at our gates. Go and tell him to return
home while he is still in one piece, or else I will set my bold warriors on
elephants upon him.' The Egyptian commander, on hearing this order,
emerged from the gates and announced, 'Ket-Bùġa, you are a fine warrior,
but let us not shed blood here. Return to your homeland.'

The old man played a brief melody from a single theme. It was incredible! It
was as if a noble word, uttered only the once, had sounded. The melody, akin
to a swan's cry, reflected the whole essence of the commander. Äžigerej was
amazed at the wisdom of the kùj, investing so much meaning into a matter of
seven or eight sounds.

But Ket-Bùġa would not agree. 'The spear hand of my khan is mighty and
his lasso will catch anyone it wishes. Tell your king to vacate his throne
voluntarily and throw his crown at the feet of my khan.'

A titanic, frightful melody was played in the Kalmyk kùj.
Who could have withstood such a sound?

The gates opened and the Misr troops came out of the city to the sound
of enormous trumpets and drums. A battle commenced, which blackened
the Sun.

This time, an entire kùj was played. The kùjšï's fingers, which had appeared
clumsy at first, now rained over the dombyra plate like a deluge. Äžigerej caught
his breath.

Genghis Khan's experienced warriors would not retreat. They defeated
the enemy and threw the king's head, still wearing its crown, at Ket-Bùġa's
feet.
Back in the steppe. Ket-Bùġa had an only son, Batyl. He, too, was a
mighty hero. Once, a caravan had arrived from China and began trading.
There was a girl on the caravan who radiated beauty like the Sun and the

Moon. The young man saw her, fire engulfed his heart and he fell in love with her. They made an arrangement. 'If you are bold enough, come to the reeds this evening and we will meet', she had said. When dusk had fallen, Batyl arrived with his friend Arġynsejit, both completely unarmed, at the agreed spot. However, the beauty with whom he had fallen in love was actually a water nymph-*peri* and she tried to drag the *žigit* deep under water. They battled long and hard. When Batyl thought he was done for, he suddenly managed to escape from her iron claws and he somehow made it to the shore. The *peri* cried out, 'If I am not destined to be with you, then die!' and shot an arrow into his back.

Atyġaj sipped his tea and continued.

The things that happen in life. The father was away and his son dies like that. The following day, Genghis gathered his confidants. 'My warrior's son has perished. Find the murderer and bring them to me.'

The khan's chief vizier was a man called Mùḵaly. He interrogated Arġynsejit, sent soldiers off in pursuit of the Chinese caravan and brought it back. The khan ordered the execution of every member of the group. Hearing this, the head of the caravan fell at Genghis's feet and said, 'Sire, you might cut off my head, but you cannot cut off my tongue.'

'Speak!' Genghis responded.

'My Lord, we are people of an underwater nation. Our king's son came out onto the land and we have lost all trace of him. We had been sent to find him', the head of the caravan explained.

'If that is so, why did you kill the only son of my hero-warrior?' the khan asked. 'Sire', the man replied, 'the king's daughter was travelling with our caravan. A king's daughter is hardly going to heed my words, is she? When my back was turned, she managed to seduce the poor lad. What could I have done?'

'If that is so, then send one of your people for her', said Genghis. The head of the caravan had no option but to send a messenger for the girl.

'This is the plea of the girl when she had been thrown at the feet of Genghis Khan.' A sorrowful *kùj* then played, reminiscent of an old *ḵobyz*[18] theme.

But Genghis Khan showed no pity and he ordered the girl's execution. Ket-Bùġa, meanwhile, had captured Misr, placed his governors and was basking in his victory. Then, one day, news reached him that a caravan was nearing from his homeland, with forty people dressed in mourning.

---

[18] *Ḵobyz* – traditional Kazakh musical instrument with a wooden body, two to four strings and a bow made of a horse's mane. It is the main attribute of the *baqḵsy* rituals when healing people and is considered sacred.

'Oh, Lord, what has happened? Allah, protect us from evil!' the hero said with worry. The caravan arrived in the city and Ket-Bùġa emerged to meet it. The forty people in the caravan removed their belts, threw them around their necks as a symbol of their submission to his will and fell at Ket-Bùġa's feet. Weeping and tearing at their beards, they informed Ket-Bùġa of the death of his son. Ket-Bùġa wept with the words, 'Oh, my poor Batyl, the apple of my eye, why, oh why did you get involved with a *peri* daughter?! Now I am all alone!' He played this *kùj*.

A quite unfamiliar *kùj* then played, swaying, sobbing and weeping. Atyġaj played for a long time, rocking from side to side. It seemed that the only son of this ancient warrior ancestor had only now perished and that this *kùj* had only just brought the news of the death of his son, with the sad ring of a bronze bell. The ancient, long-forgotten voice of courage and pride seemed to have come alive; it had played out once more in the fearsome sound of a wave crashing against a cliff face.

The *kùj* came to an end. Ăžigerej, Atyġaj and the crooked old woman, who had been sitting near the door, sat completely still, not making a sound. It seemed that the ghosts of an age-old life, having returned from another world before dissipating once more into the past, were passing by before them in a solemn procession.

The old woman broke the silence.

'Oh, oh, old man', she croaked. 'You have become your old self again, as if you've been reborn.'

Atyġaj gave a laugh and made himself more comfortable.

'And you thought it would be easy for this Atyġaj in his eighties to get back in the saddle?'

The old woman stoked up the fire with more cakes of dried sheep dung, boiled the kettle again and poured out fresh tea.

'Grandfather, what was that *kùj*?'

'That, my son, was the "Broken Bùġa *kùj* of Ket-Buga"', Atyġaj replied. He stretched out his numbed legs and drew himself closer to the table. He drank down several bowls of tea, hurriedly, one after the other.

'Wife', he said, looking contentedly over at her, 'you make really tasty tea, you do!'

Ăžigerej nodded in agreement.

'I've heard excerpts from this *kùj* from different *kùjšis* in the past. But I have never seen a person perform it in its entirety and with such expression.'

That evening, Atyġaj played more than thirty *kùjs*, each one better than the last. Ăžigerej was only further convinced of the limitless richness of the *kùj*. His confidence that he knew and had heard sufficient now appeared rather arrogant. In fact, he was unaware of many secrets, for there were many melodies he had not yet heard.

Now inspired and with the bit between his teeth, the old man kept hold of his *dombyra* for a long time. Only when it had become completely dark did he lean it against the wall.

'Well, my son, I think that's where we will stop.'

He lay down on the blanket by the side of the table, leaning on his elbow and stretching out his legs with pleasure.

'I'm tired', he said and lay there for a while, cracking his fingers as he bent them this way and that. 'I played for you. For your sake. The Kazakh people haven't asked after old Atyġaj for twenty or thirty years now. No one bothers to know if he is still alive or not. There was only the one time, when a group of people came here from Almaty. They spoke with me in haste, while their engines were warming up. You are hardly going to play *kùjs* for people who come at dusk without even unsaddling their horses, now are you? They began questioning me like the NKVD officers used to. They asked in what year I had been born. What my parents were called. Who my teacher was. I kicked them out.'

Ăžigerej burst out laughing.

'That's grandfather for you', the old woman added with a laugh. 'If he doesn't take a liking to a conversation, he'll give you what for and send you packing.'

Late that night, Ăžigerej felt tired after all the impressions of the day. He had had his fill of fresh meat and had drunk his fill of tea, but he was in high spirits and he ventured outside.

Why do the stars seem so large in autumn? That's one of the secrets of nature, he thought, looking up at the night sky. It can get so cold out in the steppe on a summer's night that butter might freeze. In autumn, the water freezes over, too. He breathed in the air with relish, his face and chest facing the icy cold breeze that was flowing over the steppe.

'Take care you don't catch a cold', Atyġaj said from the door.

He switched on the radio that he was holding.

'This has been a habit of mine since the war. I listen to what is going on in the world.'

This agreement is a major political success for the Soviet government. The world's press sees it as the most important event of recent years.

Atyġaj pricked his ears.

'What are they talking about?'

'They say we've achieved yet another political victory', Ăžigerej said, stretching contentedly. 'But they are seriously mistaken. The most important event of recent years occurred right here, in Arḳa.[19] Nothing more important than this has taken place in the world today.'

Translated by Simon Hollingsworth, edited by Simon Geoghegan

---

[19] Arḳa, or Sary Arḳa – steppe of central, eastern and northern Kazakhstan.

RAKHIMZHAN OTARBAYEV
(19.10.1956 – 17.02.2018)

Rakhimzhan Otarbayev was a writer and playwright. He graduated from the Pushkin Oral Pedagogical Institute in 1977, and subsequently served as the attaché of the Kazakh Embassy in the Kyrgyz Republic. Otarbayev held senior positions at Maṇġystau Regional Broadcasting Company, Atyrau Kazakh Drama Theatre, the administration of the President of the Republic of Kazakhstan and the National Academic Library in Astana.

His debut short story collection, *Ķupiâ tùn* (The Mysterious Night), came out in 1987. In the coming years, a number of other collections followed, namely *Šer* (Sadness, 2006), *Žuldyzdar ķulaġan žer* (The Place the Stars Fell Into, 2002), *Žajyķ žyry* (Song of Žajyķ, 2003), *Ķaraša ķazdar ķajtķanda* (When Geese Return, 2006), *Aspandaġy aķ kôbelekter* (Heavenly White Butterflies, 2009), *Bizdiṇ auyldyṇ amazonkalary* (Amazons of Our *Auyl*, 2012), as well as two volumes of selected works. His works have been translated into Turkish, Arabic, English, French, Italian, Bulgarian, Russian and Kyrgyz, and two volumes of his works have been published in China.

Otarbayev was a renowned playwright; his plays, including *Bejbarys sùltan* (about a thirteenth-century Egyptian ruler descending from an ancient Kazakh tribe), *Bas* (The Head), *Našaķorlar novellasy* (Novella of a Drug Abuser), *Syrym Batyr*, *Mùstafa Šoķaj*, *Ámire*, *Narkom Žùrgenov* (Žùrgenov, the People's Commissar) and *Ġabit* are dedicated to historical figures and events from the Kazakh past. Many have been staged at Kazakhstani as well as foreign theatres. A number of theatre festivals dedicated to Otarbayev's plays had taken place in Atyrau, Šymkent and Taraz.

Otarbayev was the recipient of the International Aitmatov Award and of the Parasat Order (2013). He was also titled an Honoured Worker of the Republic of Kazakhstan (2006).

Heavenly White Butterflies

Pity the ants that toil beneath your feet –
They have their souls; to them their souls are sweet.

Shahnameh[1]

Having chased white butterflies again, he woke up, quite exhausted and with a parched mouth.

***

He walked along the right side of the street for a long time, vanishing from view then reappearing, emerging then melting away amidst the hurrying passers-by, all brushing past one another. He was walking towards the bazaar. It was the same every day. And every night his thirst would give him no peace.

The morning Sun, already as intense as the noonday heat, would burn his temples. Cocking his white cap aslant to cover his itching head and opening his eyes wide, he looked up at the vast sky. A lone cloud grazed aimlessly across the blue expanse, like a shabby, orphaned camel with clumps of fur hanging from its sides.

The lazy sparrows, refreshing their beaks with the morning dew, would fly up and then come down to land again, fussing restlessly around the people. It was as if these unfortunate creatures were seeking their destiny at the bazaar that August.

'Oh, the times we live in!' someone said nearby, and the young man turned to face the voice. However, he didn't see anyone addressing him by name. An old granny was passing by, treading gingerly on her right leg, evidently tortured by rheumatism. She seemed to be handing out advice to the young girl accompanying her or maybe they were aspirations:

'And I used to be just like you.'

Her companion grimaced as though something was bothering her and yet, in spite of this, cast a playful eye over everything around her. Perhaps she was looking for someone. Her belly button peeped out between her blouse and belt, like a third eye, invasively ogling those who walked before her. Its gaze even appeared to capture the other side of the street, viewing the passers-by most attentively.

---

[1] Abolqasem Ferdowsi. *Shahnameh: The Persian Book of Kings* (transl. Dick Davis, foreword Azar Nafisi). Penguin Random House, 2018.

'And you will end up just like me...'

He was only able to gather his thoughts when the old woman and the girl had disappeared from view. Was he really the only one drowning in sad thoughts and bearing the burden of grief for all eternity? Everyone was the same, it seemed.

The young man, who went by the name of Dǎuren, sold trousers at the vast bazaar in the big city. The bazaar may have been vast, but his pitch was small, just big enough for a meagre tomato seller to set down a bowl. He would lay out his trousers in white, blue and black piles that caused one's eyes to ripple.

'Žǎke, they really suit you' or 'Lady, they could have been tailored for you!' he would say, praising his wares. He always had all kinds of customers hovering around him: young fellas as fleet as fireflies, 'silver beards' as skewed as sickles, sky-high giants, bandy-legged short-arses, hurry-scurriers and the rotund with waists the size of thighs, the generously ungrudging and the penny-pinchers... Not bad, you might say, but the pennies accrued by the end of each day were indeed enough for the curly topped, good-looking lad to pay his rent, put food on the table, occasionally lay on a spread or support his mother who lived on her own in the *auyl*[2] of Žarbaj.

How his mother – who had resolved to preserve the family home of her deceased husband – would rejoice at his monthly visits and the gifts he would bring. The poor woman would see him off all the way to the end of the *auyl* in her wide, swaying dress, the golden rays dancing in her skirt as if she were carrying the sunshine in its pleats, and she would continually call him her young foal. On parting, he would leave in a calm and even kindly frame of mind.

Returning to town, he would throw himself straight back into the impetuous, chaotic and ragged rhythm of his city life. This was a place where even souls were traded, but the young man never wilfully fell into the mire. But this was where Ǎlima stood. The girl who sold water by the entrance to the bazaar. A birthmark the size of a millet grain was hidden right in the middle of her brows. Yes, she was the one! Whenever he sold some trousers, he would drink several glasses of her water in a row.

'So, you've come from the salt marshes of Kerbala, have you?' she had once asked him with a bashful smile.

'No, I've come straight from a pile of trousers', he had replied eliciting a peal of ringing laughter. Not simply laughter, but something which elicited the lucid, tinkling resonance of a smashed glass had filled the air. From that time on, it was no longer water he sought but that tinkling, resonant sound which

---

[2] *Auyl* – socio-economic formation considered to constitute the heartland of the nation and a basis for an ethnic and cultural union of the nomadic community. Consisting of 50–70 yurts in the eighteenth century, it developed into its current permanent state of 'rural settlement' (of a minimum of 100 dwellers) when Kazakhs adopted a settled mode of life in the nineteenth and twentieth centuries. *Auyl* can also be used as a synonym for 'native land' and 'homeland', concepts revered by the Kazakhs.

brought joy to his ears. Oh, that ringing! Even now, when invisible to the eye, he could still hear its echo.

The girl was an orphan and she had grown up with her brother and his wife. There was always a certain hope peeping out from behind her childishly innocent demeanour, shining through her timid nature. It was probably this hope that kept her charismatic laughter alive.

They agreed to marry in the autumn, to bring his mother over from Žarbaj and to live together. There was just one unfortunate thing…

'They built the Palace of Marriages on the ancient graveyard, which they first razed from the Earth. Oh, Allah, a curse upon them!' Hearing this, he turned once again to face a familiar voice. It was the old woman, treading gingerly on her right leg, afflicted with rheumatism, but who was now freely perspiring. She was walking, moving her slender shoulders continuously.

'There are an awful lot of weddings taking place today', the girl said, stretching the word *aw-ful* like chewing gum, her satisfaction evident while revealing to all and sundry her one-eyed belly button.

'Well, the cattle are fat and the harvest is ripe. How could there not be plenty to go around?' the old woman let slip. The girl walking with her fell silent and lost heart for some reason. 'Alas, the youth of today just can't keep their promises', the old woman continued her sermon. 'By the morning, the agreement made the night before will have already been forgotten… Oh, where is that damned bazaar, hang it all? It can only be a stone's throw from here, but we never seem to be getting any closer.'

And it was hardly surprising: seeing as she would stop at any shop along the way, flitting forwards and backwards, not letting anyone past her.

There was just one unfortunate thing…

At Dãuren's busiest time of day for trading in trousers, someone called loudly to him:

'The bazaar manager is asking after you! You'd better get over there, quick!'

He froze. What could this mean? He had seen the red-faced, green-eyed boss only once before. The women at the bazaar would drool over his incredible riches, quite unable to satisfy their insatiable gossip about him.

'What's there to say: he changes his suit twice a day!'

'What are you going on about his rags for, you fool?!! He takes to the wheel of a new car every week! He bought his wife a villa in Paris. And they say she now only bathes in *Chanel*.'

'He only has the one daughter and she never gets out of his Jeep. I hear she wants to get married; at least she's found something to try her hand at.'

'Oh my, if she is not married, that means she certainly has her eyes out for a future husband. She's not going to have to run around in circles like you or me to find a husband?'

'I'll say. You should have seen her that time when she married that black guy and then, having fallen out with their tribal leader, she was chucked out of his African country. Why would she want to move after that? Oh, she'll be in no rush to get married, all right!'

And so, on they hummed like bees in a hive.

What did the bazaar manager, a man who had everything, need Däuren for and what services could he possibly require? The young man was seriously alarmed. There were many people from out of town and he didn't want to lose his pitch. What's more, his mother would always wail whenever he came to see her that he shouldn't rely on those in elevated positions. It was as if her son, a trouser seller, was making it his custom to befriend the rich and powerful.

When he nervously entered the spacious office, his knees shaking treacherously, the red-faced, green-eyed man stood up with a smile.

'Come in, my son, come in. I've long had my eye on you and I wanted to get to know you better.'

The young man blinked, completely at a loss. The boss looked over his slender shoulders and then at the rest of him, much as a tailor might.

'Peace be upon you!' he greeted the boss, becoming all the more confused.

'And peace be upon you too. Have a seat. And rest easy. The hell with those trousers. Get rid of them! From today, you'll be my assistant. Together with my daughter...'

'But I still have a lot of items unsold.'

The boss burst out laughing.

'Oh, my son, no one will go without trousers, don't you worry; others will sell them instead.'

It took Däuren a long time to come to his senses.

***

He walked a long time, vanishing from view then reappearing, emerging then melting away. He walked towards the bazaar. It would be the same every day. His unquenchable thirst would give him no peace. He would eavesdrop on the mindless conversations of the people on the streets. One little old man, walking amidst the hustle, vented his anger on his long-legged, spotty-faced son with a nasal, whistling lisp.

'*Las-st* year you *s-sold* the neutered red bull and planned to get down to s-study. Your teachers-s are all complaining that you *s-still* can't read. That really is-s s-something! Your mother *is-s* convinced that her pride and joy will become a judge. Back in our time, we devoured *as-s* many *books-s as-s* we could get our hands-s on. You've *bes-smirched* my name, S-sylķybaj, you mangy little dog!'

'Give us a break, will you, Papa.'

***

It turned out both of the bazaar manager's assistants were of approximately the same age. Syrġaly, the daughter, as the women at the bazaar (good-for-nothings that they were) had said, was the same girl who had fallen out with the tribal leader; she was rosy-cheeked and spoilt. Her conduct was licentious. Her eyes were not of the same green as her father's, rather the colour of the sky. When she would stop when meeting someone, her hot, heaving pomegranates would thrust right at him. Like it or not, you couldn't miss them.

On the day of his appointment, Älima joked with a grin:

'It'd be good if our big-shot assistant would come and patronise our water.'

'Whatever happens, I will always stop by your watering hole!' he replied and proceeded to empty a full glass. 'Oh, and by the way, let's go to the theatre tomorrow. I hear there's an interesting play on at the moment.'

'Let's go. But will you take me in your Mercedes?' she asked cautiously, in a whisper.

'Of course.'

The tinkling sound of smashed glasses rang out, filling the air.

Later, he went into the boss's office. The boss was sitting silently, his head hanging low. His daughter, flushed, stood next to him, as motionless as a stake in the ground. She looked menacing, like a shorn, gelded billy goat. Her eyes, the colour of the sky, were spitting bolts of lightning.

'What are you playing at?!' she fired at Däuren straight from the off. 'What do you think you're doing?! You're a senior manager. Second-in-command to Papa. And yet there you are at the gates, drinking water the colour of cow's piss. Name me a single trader who'd respect you after that! Eh?!'

With his head drawn into his shoulders, he began to sag guiltily.

'Your fridge is so full, it's fit to burst. What are you playing at?'

'Alright, alright', her father said in an attempt to calm her down, raising his drooping head a little. 'That's enough. Däuren, my dear lad, you still need to speak to people. But don't let those people get too familiar with you. If they get a hold of a trouser leg, that will be it. Before you know it, you'll be under their thumb. The devils. Syrġaly is concerned about your name. You and my daughter need to back each other up and watch over one another. While I admire and take pride in you from the sidelines.'

'I'm sorry... It was an accident...'

'What are you playing at?!'

'Syrġaly, that's enough! Listen, Däuren, these are my plans. We're not going to sit here stewing in our own juice, happy with owning just this bazaar. The neighbouring regions, plus Almaty and Astana, have a great many new shopping centres. We need to look at their achievements and, if we have the experience, we must make use of it. The market's wild out there today, but it won't be there tomorrow. What we have to do is serve the people impeccably. And this is something I want to entrust the two of you with.'

'Very good, sir', he replied obediently.

'Well, that's excellent! Then you'll fly out today. Here are your tickets.'

'How long will we be gone?' the daughter said, the pink flush returning to her face and the bright-sky colour to her eyes. 'Can we take our time? Say, about a month, two or three?'

'As you wish', her father replied.

***

He walked a long time, vanishing from view then reappearing, emerging then melting away. He walked towards the bazaar. It was the same every day. His thirst, his unquenchable thirst, would give him no peace…

The puny, nasal-voiced old man continued to hammer away at his long-legged, spotty-faced son in his lisping voice:

'When I was your age, I never got down from my *hors-se*. My unhappy youth was *s-sacrificed* for your *s-sake*. I *s-said* to you: if you can't *s-study*, you *s-should* marry. I wanted to go to our neighbour Ḳůdajbergen and pop the *ques-stion* to *his-s* daughter. But you dug your *heels-s* in, though, *s-saying* she was chubby. *What's-s* wrong with that? You don't know *what's-s* good for you, you dog. *S-she'd* give you warmth in winter and shade in *s-summer…*'

'Give us a break will you, Papa', the man's son defended himself in the same way as ever.

'Oh, the poor thing! *He's-s* pouting like a *s-small* child!'

***

They stopped over in every city and town and woke up in the same bed. During the first days, when he tremulously kept his distance from her, he would hear her now customary outburst:

'What are you playing at?! All this manna from heaven would probably never have fallen upon us if it hadn't been for me. I love you to death, I do. What are you playing at?'

'Alright, alright. I love you too', he mumbled.

His mane of hair sagged.

'If that's true, then get rid of that water seller. As soon as we get back!'

'Erm…'

'What are you playing at?!'

'Alright, I've already said I would, okay?'

After that he got to thinking: what had he become? A man pinned down by the soft limbs of a woman, nestling in between them, rather than a *žigit*[3] who could tame a wild horse? Or a tireless blacksmith, forever working the bellows to keep the coals white hot? Instead of a man who thriftily worked the bazaars, had he become a milksop in a state of honied bliss? No, something was stopping this lone native of Žarbaj from behaving like a real man.

As soon as he returned from his trip, he rushed straight to see Älima. He could hardly wait for the unruly queue to her pitch to dissipate.

---

[3] *Žigit* – generally denoting a 25- to 40-year-old male, the term can also be used as an honorific indicating bravery, endurance, fortitude and being true to one's word.

'You in one piece?' she said, greeting him with a smile. She smiled, but there was no tinkling of glass this time. She had surrounded herself with an invisible sorrow. The birthmark between her eyebrows, which had been reminiscent of a grain of millet, appeared to have multiplied. A network of barely discernible ant trails had begun to spread over her face.

'Your mother came over from Žarbaj, looking for you. She said her arms and legs were aching and lamented that she could hardly hold back her son now he's become such a big boss. She could hardly hold back her son', she repeated, either mirroring the mother's words or uttering her own. 'Hm... So, when will we bring her over?' she muttered after a pause. 'We never went to the theatre either, Dắuren.'

'All the interesting shows have finished...'

***

He walked a long time, vanishing from view then reappearing, emerging then melting away. He walked towards the bazaar. It was the same every day. His thirst, his intolerable thirst, would give him no peace.

'Get lost!' the old woman brushed off the nasal-voiced old man. They both continued to give Dắuren no peace with their tittle-tattle, day in, day out. 'Look at him, says he's decided to find himself a second wife in the city. No woman would give herself to you, even an old lame one like me, wouldn't let you catch her!'

'Don't you joke like that! I'll force you out to eat the *grass-s*. I still drink the *kymyz-z*,[4] I can *s-still* walk and eat *hors-se* meat. Go on... Give me your *address-s*, won't you?'

'Get out of here, you old scoundrel! You should be ashamed of yourself in front of the children.'

And the long-legged, spotty-faced youth and the girl with the one-eyed belly button also gave him no peace devouring each other with their eyes and giggling as they ate their ice cream.

***

That day, the young man and the radiant Syrġaly visited the Palace of Marriages and submitted a marriage application.

'The sooner this month passes, the sooner we'll have the wedding and go abroad', Syrġaly dreamed.

'What? To Africa, you mean?'

'Oh, Allah forbid! Who in their right mind would say such a thing?!' The budding bride blushed crimson as if she had been dipped in pomegranate juice.

---

[4] *Kymyz* – beverage of fermented mare's milk highly esteemed for its refreshing qualities; it is the main drink for special occasions.

'No, to Žarbaj. I've heard they're really quite close.'

They both suddenly burst out laughing, anticipating one another, and the tension lifted.

After lunch, still ill at ease and having hurried off to work, he heard someone say:

'Ălima was picked up in an ambulance!'

'They say she drank some water and collapsed.'

'That wasn't water, that was poison! They made her drink it, oh lord, they surely did!'

'She was seven months' pregnant, too!' screeched the women, shaking the Earth that had been turned on its head as it was.

His head span and he turned on his heel there and then. By the hospital entrance, he almost walked straight into Syrġaly. What was she doing there?

'What are you playing at?!' she exclaimed, coming to an abrupt halt. The morning colour in her cheeks had darkened and her sky-coloured eyes had turned white again.

'Let me through!'

'What are you playing at?!'

He muscled his way through to the operating table. An elderly surgeon, dressed all in white, looked at him with grey eyes. Two nurses standing next to him screamed, as if they had seen the Angel of Death in the flesh:

'Stop right there!'

'Be strong.'

'We've done everything we could.'

'Please accept our condolences...'

Suddenly, a light rose from the body that had only just been covered with a white shroud. It was his true Ălima! Floating up, like an apparition over water, it stopped next to Dăuren, who was frightened to death. Having looked at him for a short while with both yearning and reproach, she began to evaporate into the air like steam. Butterflies, like spring apple blossom, fluttered around her, taking this apparition away with them.

***

He was walking a long time, vanishing from view then reappearing, emerging then melting away. He walked towards the bazaar. It was the same every day. His intolerable thirst had completely done for him.

People disregarded him like one disregards a shadow. How rude they were, pushing and shoving and blocking his way! There was no old woman, her legs had succumbed to her rheumatism, and there was no trace of the short old man either. The long-legged, spotty-faced youth embraced his girl so tightly around her bare waist that she was in danger of turning into an amphora, as if someone was trying to prise her away from him.

'I could eat you up', the young man ventured to his flighty girlfriend, stroking her one-eyed belly button, intending to go a step further.

'But would you get your fill?' she whispered playfully, shooting glances from side to side.

'I'd come back for more.'

It was a shame the castrated red bull had been butchered the year before for the sake of this hungry dog. He still had no great gift for his letters, but nevertheless, he had left his father by the wayside.

The bright apparition, unnoticed by everyone except Dàuren during the marriage ceremony, floated up and came to a halt between him and Syrġaly. This time it looked down without yearning or reproach. In place of the previous, timid hope, which had now been extinguished, the sad image was now awash with anxiety and worry.

'No-o, I beg you', it said, biting its lip and shaking its head. 'No-o!'

A cloud of white butterflies, like apple blossom in spring, fluttered and fluttered between Dàuren and the bright apparition from the other world. His eyes flickered as if his eyelids too had become coated in apple blossom. The music boomed out. Bekbolat howled the song 'My people'[5] in full voice.

Dàuren fell unconscious…

From that moment on, forever chasing white butterflies in his dreams, he would wake up exhausted, his mouth parched. The doctors said he had diabetes, brought on by his nervous disposition.

At the entrance to the bazaar, he heard an admonitory voice, saying, 'A child born out of wedlock in search of its father, will never find a place for itself in either this world or the next.' He looked around attentively but not a soul in the packed crowd cared less about the voice or about him; they simply drifted on with their bags like sheep through water. Well, he had remembered, and that was something: it had been the voice of his mother, who had been at the wedding of her only son, only to return in tears back to her native Žarbaj.

The words she had spoken about his and Älima's child came to life in his ears. Or was it that he had heard them once, a long time ago, back in his childhood?

Arriving at the spot where Älima had once sold her water and that the bazaar manager had long since covered in asphalt, he sat down, like a beggar child.

'Give me water. Water! Water!'

This was a plea that he was to repeat forever at this spot, but it was never clear who he was making it to. Whatever the case, he didn't expect a response. He would sit there, rooted to the spot, deep into the night. His silent vigil had become a custom for him, a daily routine. He would return to the same spot the following day as well.

White butterflies… Fluttering white butterflies…

Translated by Simon Hollingsworth, edited by Simon Geoghegan

---

[5] 'Elim meniṇ', a song performed by Bekbolat Tileuhan.

TURSYNZHAN SHAPAY
(b. 1.02.1957)

Tursynzhan Shapay is a Kazakh writer, journalist, literary scholar and literary critic. After graduating from the Kazakh State Pedagogical University (now Abaj [Abai] Kazakh National Pedagogical University) in 1979, he went on to teach at a secondary school in the Almaty region (1979–84). His subsequent career spanned head of department at Kazakh Television (1984–85); managing editor of Žazušy publishing house (1985–86); head of literary criticism department at *Žuldyz* journal (1986–90); senior research fellow at the Äuezov Institute of Literature and Art (1990–98); and production editor at Kazakhstan TV and Radio Corporation (2001–6). In 1994, he completed his thesis, 'Ķazaķ poèziâsyndaġy lirikalyķ tùlġa problemasy (1980-žyldar)' (The Problem of Lyrical Personality in Kazakh Poetry in the 1980s).

Shapay authored more than a hundred literary studies articles, the majority of which are devoted to issues in contemporary Kazakh literature and to studies of the work of Abaj (Abai). His debut volume on Kazakh literature, *Oj tùbinde žatķan sôz: ădebi syn maķalalar* (The Hidden Word: Literary Criticism) came out in 1998. His other scholarly works include *Šyn žùrek – bir žùrek* (True Heart – One Heart, 1999), *Ķazaķtyŋ žany* (The Soul of the Kazakh People, 2001) and *Kùlki ẑăne kôz žasy* (Laughter and Tears, 2015). A two-volume edition of his selected works was published in 2017. Shapay translated novels, short stories and non-fiction by German, Japanese and Georgian writers into Kazakh. He is the recipient of the Lenin Komsomol Prize of the Kazakh SSR (1990), the Tôlegen Ajbergenov Literary Prize (1986) and the Alaš International Literary Award (2000). He was also titled an Honoured Worker of the Republic of Kazakhstan.

The Mirror Shrine

So many ages had gone by since that Old Man led me away with him, that I had forgotten where he came from, when he came and who he was. We had walked through mountain passes and over mountain crests, we had trudged through waterless deserts where the Sun blazed down mercilessly. We had sailed across blue seas and seen many countries. One day, in the midst of a vast, unfathomable, blossoming steppe blanketed by silvery heat haze, in which the rays of the Sun were reflected, we descried a marvellous, tremulous fortress or palace, which appeared to be dancing, so that it seemed like an apparition.

As we approached closer, with every moment the glittering, mysterious palace in the haze changed in incessant movement, sometimes expanding, sometimes flickering and shrinking...

On my last legs, I was barely able to keep plodding after the Old Man without falling behind. The sole of my foot had been burned intolerably by the parched and singed earth of the region before the blossoming steppe, the Sun had broiled my head unendurably, there was a pounding in my temples from the appalling heat and my eyes had gone dim. My throat had dried out, the roof of my mouth seemed to have been cured in the Sun, my parched tongue didn't fit in my mouth and I had no voice to say anything... The Old Man walked quickly, almost running, as if everything were quite normal, with the flaps of his threadbare robe fluttering. The black-as-black callouses on his toughened, bare feet looked like shoes that he had put on. The soles of the 'shoes' were like thick, tawed ox leather. His swarthy legs, themselves almost as black as scorched leather, fused into a single, unified whole with the black earth, so that I could not see the Old Man walking along. And since he held himself upright and the hem of his dirty, white robe fluttered, he seemed to be gliding across a smooth, dark, watery surface. The form of his head, familiar to me since time immemorial, and the forward-striving Greek profile of his swarthy face were frozen like the features of a bronze statue. He was gliding... or flowing along...

The silvery mirage was reflected in his eyes as a whitish glimmer.

Around the mysterious Mirror Palace, with the rays of the Sun reflected on its domes and all the colours of the universe glinting and shimmering on its walls, an emerald paradise appeared, with rich meadows of luscious, green grass; it was cool there. When at last I reached the lovely trees with their branches bowed down by an abundance of fruit, I collapsed in their shade and I fancied I had found what I had been seeking...

...I thought it was a small piece of a broken mirror, about the size of my palm. After picking it up off the ground and wiping the dust off its surface, I peered into it intently. And the more intently I peered, the more powerfully I was transfixed by a shudder of incomprehensible terror. Darkening, the surface of the mirror transformed itself into a gaping, bottomless well shaft. My faint, nebulous image, reflected in the black sheen and staring up at me from the bottom of the abyss with the eyes of a serpent, was like a phantom that had found its way into the mirror from the world beyond. I know that this frightened me... It seemed to me that if the appalling vision were to become more clearly discernible, at that moment my heart would burst... The longer I gazed into the gradually deepening abyss... the more clearly I felt it stealthily pulling me in, drawing closer to me. I did not want to look, but I had no strength, no willpower. I was spellbound by the black well shaft. Unable to tear my eyes away from this mysterious, silent spectre that had frightened me so, I was flowing out, drop by drop, into the bottomless darkness, I would soon be totally depleted. In a little while the monster in that abyss would leave nothing of me behind, it was going to suck me in and swallow me... It intended to remain here in my place! Shuddering and trembling, I clutched the edge of that small shard of the abyss, the size of my palm, in an even tighter grip.

Suddenly, in my sleep, I realised that this was a vision in a dream. The very instant I realised this, out of old habit I cried out desperately, as loudly as I could, in a strident voice, trying to wake up, hoping in this way to rid myself of this terrible dream.

The mirror fell from my hands.

I thought I had cried out... When I awoke with a suffocating sensation, exhausted by the oppressive dream, I just barely discerned the sound of my own weak voice, seeming to come from a distance. I discovered that the Old Man was peering intently at me, wide-eyed. As soon as I opened my own eyes, the roguish glint of his eyes, aged by the wisdom of a thousand years, so faded and colourless that they looked like accumulated pools of standing water, started flowing deep inside me, spreading rapidly, coursing through all my veins and gradually being absorbed. A silvery haze covered over the Old Man's eyes once again and they began shimmering as blindingly bright as a mirror. I lay there as if naked under that pitiless mirror hanging over me, presenting both my soul and my heart to general inspection... Those dully glinting eyes, enveloped in wispy, silvery vapour, pouring their invisible, colourless impulses into my own eyes, for them to go wandering through my veins, and then draining them again in a single gulp, read me unhurriedly, like an open book.

Like someone who is naked, hastily placing his hand over his private parts out of a sense of shame, I squeezed my eyes tight shut and put my hands over my face.

'That's enough, now get up!' the Old Man ordered me. The muffled, thousand-year-old voice seemed to come from under the ground... When I looked at him again through my slightly parted eyelids, he was standing not far away, massaging his calves by turns with his black, calloused feet that looked like crow's feet, and looking at the Mirror Palace, covered in shifting patterns of light and shade that moved across it like clouds. Lifting up my head, I looked around... A snow-white tablecloth had been laid out only an arm's length away from me. Set out on it was an abundance of all manner of fruits and sweet things. A goblet of baked clay held transparent spring water... Water... I reached out my hand for it, licking my cracked lips with my dry, swollen tongue. 'Stop!' the Old Man shouted harshly. Badly though I wanted to drink, and despite my half-swooning condition, I obeyed that stern, imperious voice and stopped instantly. The Old Man pointed to the mirror gates of the Mirror Palace. I got up, dragging my feet untidily, and plodded with slovenly steps over to the Old Man. My figure was reflected vaguely in the mirror gates. No matter how hard I peered at it, I could not see my face clearly. But that was not what concerned and astounded me. I was amazed that the Old Man, who was standing beside me, was not there beside my figure in the mirror gates! 'Where are you?' I asked. 'I am beside God'... 'You are where?'... 'The countenance of a saint is not reflected in this mirror', the Old Man replied. And immediately he took me by the hand and led me towards the mirror gates.

As we approached, my reflection shifted in the direction of the far corner of the mirror, moving away from us. Only now did I notice that the walls, dome and gates of the Mirror Palace made up a kind of boundless, unlimited space that revealed itself gradually, expanding inward, deepening and receding. When we came close, the blinding sheen of the mirror-walls, flickering like a mirage, began fading gradually, like the footlights in a theatre, and it started getting darker... On reaching the gates, the Old Man wiped his perspiring forehead with his sleeve, and in that instant I suddenly realised why the form of his head had seemed so familiar to me since time out of mind – it was the forehead of Socrates, so familiar to everyone.

Standing facing the mirror gates, which had already been transformed into black marble, the Old Man swept his hand through the air like a sword, and the gates opened as if they had been cloven in twain. Staggering back from the fearsomely daunting light that blazed up like the sudden glare of a lightning flash, I squeezed my eyes shut, and when I opened them again, we were standing in pitch darkness... The curving, semicircular arc of an amphitheatre was revealed before us. Thousands of glittering, sparkling mirrors were arrayed, set close together, on the audience seats of the gradually ascending tiers that were carved out of the solid rock. As soon as we walked out onto the illuminated stage... I shattered into fragments as I was reflected in those countless mirrors, and in being reflected I seemed to go rushing along those rows, curved like a tautly drawn bow, in the way that cards are cut, shuffled and fanned out in the hands of a conjuror... The entire amphitheatre was filled with my image. I was like an actor facing his own images.

'Everyone who knows you in this world is here', said the Old Man, indicating the mirrors around us with his hands. 'Now try to find yourself!'

Having said this, the Old Man took me by the hand and led me up to the rows carved out of the solid rock, moving back and stepping in behind me, so that he was standing immediately behind the nape of my neck. I do not know myself how I realised that the members of this 'audience' were my own astonished and good-natured image, as imprinted on the consciousness of those who knew me. Various versions of my own 'self'. In the assessments that could be glimpsed in those familiar eyes, I saw Myself... There, for instance, looking at me in amazement as they twinkled in the mirrors at the very end of the row, were various representations of the long-ago me of my childhood years... Perhaps they were friends of my childhood, whom I had not met since I grew up, or my teachers... Or they could even have been my parents, who were sometimes distressed by the present-day me and pined sadly for my time of angelic innocence. I saw myself in the mirrors of girls with whom I was in love at school. I did not look very distinctive... And look, there was a mirror clouded over with a dense mist that rendered it murky, almost dark. I could not see anything in it.

'She forgot you a long time ago!' said a Voice standing over my very soul. I could hear a note of mockery in it.

I lingered for a long time in front of the murky mirror... She was my first love...

I walked on, passing along the rows. And I saw myself in every possible kind of guise! I was good-natured, I was hard-hearted, I was an idler, I was greedy, I was cunning, I was spiteful, I was a scoundrel, I was a moron, I was stubborn and capricious, I was an ignoramus, I was... It was hard to believe it, but there were very many such versions of my image.

'Many see you precisely like this!' The Old Man kept pace with me, chattering like a magpie. 'If you seek the truth, you must acknowledge this too.'

I did not know why, but I did not wish to glance behind me... The Old Man's breath was cold.

Having reviewed the glittering rows, we walked higher. We moved up to the halfway point. That repulsive individual in those dismally dark mirrors, blackened and obscured by either dirt or soot... As Allah was my judge, I had never been as utterly repulsive as that, and I probably never would be!

'Your enemies... Examine them thoroughly!' the Old Man said in a stern, peremptory tone of voice. His icy breath scorched the nape of my neck. I shuddered...

'???'

'Did you think you had no enemies? Hah! You have relatives who find it abhorrent that you can even walk this Earth... You know nothing... you know nothing at all!'

Everything the Old Man had said proved true – I lost count of the black mirrors. My heart grew heavy and I sighed bitterly: 'This temporal world!'

One mirror especially surprised me – as I walked closer, I saw that the reflection in it changed constantly, sometimes flaring up angrily, sometimes blushing... it was ashamed of me! When my reflection in the mirror saw me, it was unable to look straight at me and lowered its eyes guiltily. I could not tell how, but it was quite amazing, perhaps the clairvoyant Old Man standing behind me and observing me so closely was projecting into my mind some mysterious, invisible waves of suggestion, but I realised that this was a genuine mirror... I recalled all my sins in this temporal world, committed knowingly or unknowingly.

At some point those who were weaker than me, and had therefore suffered from my actions, would see me in the image of this self-same wretch in the mirror... Or rather, they wished to see me thus. And I... I understood everything, I saw it all... but I did not feel any pangs of conscience at all. I understood it, I saw it... but I regretted nothing. Oh, this temporal world! I pitied these naive mirrors...

'Yes... It is all lies!' The Vile Mockery that was following me with its chilly gaze, missing nothing, scanning my thoughts, sending shivers down my spine, that self-same spiteful Mockery chuckled: 'In this world there is neither fairness nor truth. This world is like sand that slips through your fingers, a nebulous phantom, a deceptive mirage. And nothing more!'

It seemed that the Old Man wished to disabuse me of something, to disenchant me. Or to humiliate me and mock me... I could not understand the Old Man. I was afraid to say anything in reply.

Finally, we reached the rows where I was seen in an attractive form. I lingered here for a long time, forgetting my weariness and hunger, forgetting the Old Man's mockery, and how tormented I was by thirst. I peered into the deceptive mirrors, at a multitude of various pleasant images, admiring my own darling reflection... I knew that all the mirrors here lied. Both the bad ones and the good ones. But despite that, in front of the 'good' mirrors, I involuntarily drew myself erect and my mood was uplifted. Especially in front of that mirror at the end of the row. Here I looked very much like myself... no, this was how I should have looked... how I would have wished to look... no... it was me, myself. It was not an image. It was Me! Because love was reflected in that mirror... Who does not love himself? Who...

'This is your very best friend', said the detestable Old Man, laughing behind my back. 'He beholds you with the eyes of his yearning for perfection and the ideal. He is nothing at all like you!'

'Perhaps so!' I replied, giving way and almost exploding in indignation. 'But a friend is a man's second self!'

'Hmm... hm. I believe it was Xenon who said that... but do you really believe those words? You know, I once also had many friends. And I had even more sheep. The interesting thing is that people knew exactly how many sheep I had, but... ha-ha... no one knew how many friends I had... See how worthless my friends were...'

'That does not apply to my friends', I said, keeping my gaze fixed on the mirror. 'My friend...'

'... is not worth a single sheep', the Old Man said in a confident tone of voice. 'Two and a half thousand years have passed while I have been journeying between the two worlds... Two and a half thousand years! You can trust me.'

My back shuddered, chilled by his cold breath. When the Old Man mentioned two and a half thousand years, I almost surrendered, but I clung on stubbornly to my resolution nonetheless.

'In the final analysis', I said, raising my voice in anger, 'this world, this person... the mirrors, in the final analysis, and you... you too, you are all no more than derivatives of my independent free will! I am all there is in the world! All the rest is lies... You also are a lie...'

'Heh-heh-heh... I see you also have a few hazy ideas from those wretched little philosophers. Do you have any words of your own at all? Well then, now go over to that mirror standing on its own.'

Cherishing a vague hope in my heart, I hurried towards the mirror indicated by the Old Man. It was the absolutely genuine Me, no more and no less, with no embellishments, because no sooner did I look at my reflection in that mirror than I was overcome by anguish. Yes, it was me, the everyday, habitual me... who had become such a sickening bore to me!

'It's me...'

'No, it is not you', the Old Man replied again. 'It is only your own idea of yourself... Look in the mirror, which side is your right ear on?'

'On the right.'

'Which side is your right hand on? Come on, lift your hand up!'

'On the right.'

The Old Man laughed.

'In the mirror you stand contrariwise to yourself, reversed. Is that not right? That is, the right side of your body ought to be reflected on the opposite side, on the left. Is that not right, what do you think?'

I could not think of any objections to that. In my helpless fury I said nothing.

'Everything is deception', the Old Man said in an indistinct voice redolent of the damp on the bottom of a grave, a voice from a distance of two and a half thousand years. 'Not to mention all the rest of it, your idea of yourself is also a deception. You are not here!'

'Then why did you bring me here?' I exclaimed, gasping for breath. 'After all, you led me away, promising that you would "help me to comprehend myself", didn't you?'

No sooner did I say that, than the Old Man's voice rang out stridently, like an echo reflected from a cliff.

'Then look at me!'

The Old Man's unexpectedly strident shout set all the mirrors in the amphitheatre rattling and swaying. They turned cloudy and their gleam began to fade.

I did not stir a muscle. I was afraid...

'Turn round this way! Look at me!'

And suddenly... at that precise moment I sensed that it was not an Old Man standing behind me, but a cold, pitiless mirror. Neither a friend, nor an enemy, looking at me from behind with the eyes of a gaping grave, from out of a darkness of two and a half thousand years, was an indifferent, unfeeling mirror, the impassive and lifeless gleam of which seemed to shine right through my very insides, presenting the entirety of me to general observation, leaving nothing hidden! A pitiless mirror! Appalling and dead! Precisely at that moment my image hung down over me, behind the nape of my neck. It was not bad, and it was not good. It was meaningless, hovering over my soul, just like the sombre, mystical, spectral vision from the bottom of the abyss, with its cold eyes glistening dully, like mercury. How compassionate my enemies were! The unflattering images in my enemies' mirrors were not lifeless. How just my friends were! The beautiful deception in their eyes was nonetheless alive. No! The dead man in the dead mirror was not me. I was a living deception, who had found his reflection in the multitudinous mirrors of the amphitheatre.

'All this is falsehood!' said the Old Man, reading my thoughts (I had no doubt about that now). 'The truth is right here behind you, only a step or two away. You only need to turn your head.'

I still could not bring myself to look at the Old Man, I became flustered and started trembling in fear.

'I do not wish to meet Myself. It is a bad omen...' I said in a trembling voice. 'This falsehood is my home, my refuge!'

'Then why did you need to seek the truth?'

I do not know why, but when the Old Man asked that, I recalled his mirror-eyes, veiled with silvery haze, the sight of which had made me shudder on awakening...

'The truth in this world is these mirrors', I said, imparting conviction to my voice. 'I am what they say. And what they say is lies... But all of it is me. I do not need any other truth.'

'You have started speaking your own words...' the Old Man said in a surprised voice. 'But you are mistaken. Greatly mistaken! In this world there is only one truth. The only truth, which you are seeking in this world, is the very first truth and the very last – you Yourself. On the day when you finally understand yourself, you will find yourself alongside the Absolute... If you do not believe me, turn around. Look at me!'

'I do not believe you', I said. 'I will not look!'

'Why do you not believe me?' the Old Man asked in an impatient, whispering, rustling voice... 'Remember those trees in paradise, hung with fruit, the fruits on the spread tablecloth, the *zam-zam* water[1] in the goblet of baked clay. All of that has been made ready for you!'

Especially when he mentioned the water, the cold, transparent water...

---

[1] *Zam-zam* – holy water in Islam.

'I don't believe you!' I cried out, alarmed that I had very nearly glanced back. How difficult it was to withstand the temptation of the devil... 'I know that behind you is a waterless, dried out land, and there people burn in hell... I know there is no one who can free me from that hell. Once you have achieved your goal, you will abandon me... disappear...'

'Look at me, I tell you!' the Old Man hissed like a serpent, scorching the nape of my neck with his poisonous breath, so that chilly shudders ran over my entire body. 'Turn around and look into my eyes, wretched one!'

I was shuddering. I clenched my teeth and did not move.

Suddenly the Old Man started weeping. A strange kind of sound, a sound of hopelessness, like the howl of a wounded wolf, echoed around the amphitheatre, and I felt afraid.

'Why-y-y-y?' he wailed, straining to force out the doleful word in a voice ringing with despair. 'Why... For two and a half thousand years I have been wandering in vain between the two worlds. Two and half thousand years! Why does no one wish to see his true Self, why does no one wish to learn, why, oh Lord! You are my final hope... Look this way, for God's sake, turn towards me! Save me from this torment. You will remain in my place, you will wander between the two worlds... for eternity... I am weary... Wea-ea-eary...'

Only now convinced of the correctness of my misgivings concerning the Old Man's mission, I stood frozen to the spot...

'I shall remain with them', I replied resolutely, pointing to the mirrors of my friends and enemies that surrounded me...

We were standing at the very centre of the amphitheatre. Suddenly rays of light started sparkling and glittering on the surfaces of the mirrors. Everything around me blossomed in all the colours of the world and came alive.

'Be gone from my sight!' I cried out loudly in the same manner, still not turning around, to Death hanging over me and quietly, pitifully weeping.

'You fool!' the Old Man muttered in weak voice bereft of hope...

Fool? Did the Old Man say 'Fool'? The Old Man was mistaken! That was not true. There was no truth behind my back at that moment! Truth has no tongue. Truth does not give such an explanation – 'fool'. It is dispassionate. One can only experience it, read it in one's heart. Or, having seen it, die.

I sensed that the Old Man's mirror had come alive, and now it was powerless, dismayed, because it had given free rein to its feelings, failed to withstand its grief and suffering, deviated from the truth...

Sensing this, I swung round abruptly and looked behind me!

The Old Man-mirror jangled and collapsed in front of me with a crash, shattering into small pieces, turning into a heap of trash.

And then the amphitheatre began sparkling and thousands of mirrors – all of my acquaintances in this world – got up off their seats and started applauding. My relatives and friends wiped away their tears. My enemies threw armfuls of bouquets...

The Old Man disappeared without a trace, as if he had never existed...

It turned out that my wife had come and sat down at the foot of my bed and turned on the television. A festive assembly to celebrate the Day of Independence... People who had risen from their seats applauded, clapping their hands, and then one by one sat down again. Taking a sip of water from a glass standing in front of him, a large man prepared to continue his speech. It seemed to me that behind the orator, immediately behind the nape of his neck, a ray of light glinted in a cold mirror. While I rubbed my sleepy eyes and then raised my head to take a closer look, the camera switched into a close-up shot.

Translated by Andrew Bromfield

NURGALI ORAZ
(b. 25.08.1960)

Nurgali Oraz is a writer and playwright. He graduated from the Faculty of Journalism at Kirov Kazakh State University (now Ǎl-Farabi Kazakh National University). His debut short story was published in *Leninšil žas* (now *Žas alaš*) newspaper in 1979. Six years later, his first short story collection, titled *Sokpak žol* (Footpath, 1998), came out, followed by *Bakyršanyŋ balalary* (Children of Bakyrša, 1988), *Kazyġürt okiġalary* (Events in Kazyġürt, 1995), *Tùngi žalġyzdyk* (Loneliness in the Night-Time, 2008), *Aâktalmaġan ertegi* (An Unfinished Fairy Tale, 2002), Biiktegi sùlulyk (Unattainable Beauty, 2008) and *Sikyrly kôl* (The Magic Lake, 2011). His prose works are highly regarded by the literary community of Kazakhstan.

Oraz's selected essays are collected in two volumes: *Daladan kalaġa kelgender* (Arrivals in the City, 2006) and *Žylkynyŋ kôz žasy* (A Horse's Tears, 2012). He is a notable playwright, author of *Taudaġy tùn* (A Night in the Mountains, 2011), *Dôp-dôŋgelek dùnie* (The Whole Wide World, 2017) and *Adaskan žùldyz* (The Wandering Star). The last play won the International Independence Contest (2017). His works inspired a feature film, *Ǎureleŋ* (Bustle, dir. by Sǎbit Kùrmenbek; 2007), and his prose works have been translated into Russian, Turkish, Uzbek and Sakha. His short story 'Kulyk' (Craftiness, 2010) has been included in the primary school curriculum in Kazakhstan.

He is a laureate of the Alaš International Literary Award (2003) and Mahmùt Kaškari (Mahmud Kashgari) International Literary Prize (2014).

545

The Nest of the White Cranes

Everyone in the small Kazakh *auyl*[1] was discussing the good news that Aķmyrza had quit drinking. There would be no more payday bingeing; he'd now take responsibility for his family and live a proper life. Although many of the village gossips doubted that Aķmyrza would keep his pledge, there were none who wished him to fail, if for no other reason than for the sake of his wife and children.

Even Mother Nature herself seemed happy about the news, bringing an early spring with mild weather and clear, blue skies. The snow-covered steppe showed signs of fresh, green patches of grass on its endless blanket of white.

Upon returning from work, Aķmyrza would sit on the old wooden bench in his front yard, smoking strong Russian cigarettes and contemplating his sad, sober destiny. From time to time, one of his sons would come and sit beside him, watching his face from the corners of his eyes and pitying him.

Aķmyrza was short and slim, with the bandy legs of a Kazakh horseman. No one had ever described his face as handsome. His physical appearance was in no way impressive: it comprised an odd assortment of poorly developed limbs and parts assembled in a strange, if not comical, way. Even in sadness, he looked out of place.

Looking skyward, Aķmyrza saw an exaltation of cranes flying so high that he couldn't see their long, stork-like legs or the broad expanses of their huge wings. They seemed so proud in flight, and so free from the Earth, as if to signal to all those land-bound souls that there was so much more to living than merely survival.

These thoughts filled Aķmyrza's eyes with tears. Where are you flying from, sainted birds? he wondered. I don't remember the last time I saw you. The sight of the free, flying cranes thrilled Aķmyrza, and imbued him with feelings of wonderment and delight.

His son Kelesbaj interrupted his thoughts: 'Why are you crying, *kôke*?'[2]

---

[1] *Auyl* – socio-economic formation considered to constitute the heartland of the nation and a basis for an ethnic and cultural union of the nomadic community. Consisting of 50–70 yurts in the eighteenth century, it developed into its current permanent state of 'rural settlement' (of a minimum of 100 dwellers) when Kazakhs adopted a settled mode of life in the nineteenth and twentieth centuries. *Auyl* can also be used as a synonym for 'native land' and 'homeland', concepts revered by the Kazakhs.

[2] *Kôke* – respectful form of address to an older patron or protector; it can be applied to both males and females.

'My eyes are tired', he answered.

'My eyes are never tired', said the boy. 'I can look long into the distance as much as I want.' He looked upward, as if to prove his words.

'Stop it, your eyes will get tired'.

'My eyes are *never* tired', insisted the boy.

'He is a stubborn one', said his brother, Tăškenbaj, who was repairing his bicycle nearby. 'Now he'll be looking at the sky for the rest of the day.'

Aķmyrza was both surprised and disturbed; it occurred to him how little he knew about his sons.

'I saw the cranes yesterday', said Kelesbaj. '*Kôke*, have you ever seen white cranes?'

'No, son, but I know they exist. In my life, I've only seen the greys and browns.'

'Where do they live, the white ones?'

'I don't know, perhaps in distant lands...'

Cranes stirred something in his soul: memories from long ago. His barefoot childhood, the soft steppe grass gently tickling his feet. He glanced at Kelesbaj's feet and noticed that his shoes had holes in them.

'Your shoes want to eat, son. Are you wearing them to school?'

The boy said nothing. Embarrassed and annoyed, he turned away to watch Tăškenbaj ride his bicycle away from the house, toward the nearby shed. Then the boy looked back at his father and whispered: '*Kôke*, Tăškenbaj has *no* shoes. That's why he's wearing galoshes.'

Aķmyrza couldn't think of anything to say, so he patted the boy on the head. What is Ķamar doing? he thought. Our boys need new clothes. He decided he would take all his sons shopping on his next payday. In making this decision, he felt better.

As a mechanic at the local garage, he was paid well. But he could never remember how much money he'd given to Ķamar, and how much he spent on vodka. Each payday he'd come home drunk, and usually pass out in the yard. But at least he always made it to the yard before the vodka took complete control of his senses. Then Ķamar would threaten to leave him. He pitied her. She could not care for their five children, and she had an alcoholic husband as well.

Her face still looked sad, he had noticed. While doing housework, she had been trying not to look at Aķmyrza sitting in the front yard, alone. Perhaps she had guessed that he was thinking about alcohol again. It meant she was still suspicious of him.

***

Ķamar had spent the day cleaning the house, and it seemed brighter now. Every day was a long series of chores, attending to the family's needs and trying to make the most of the little money her husband allowed her – the bulk of his pay, of course, being spent on vodka. Her nerves were frayed, and she often beat the children to make them quiet down and give her some peace. The little ones, she sent to bed. Kelesbaj watched television until the eleventh hour. Tăškenbaj was trying to assemble some pieces of metal he'd found in the street and brought home.

Arysbek was the only one who was doing his school homework. Aķmyrza was curious to see what his eldest son was reading. He went up to him and saw a thick book on the table in front of the boy: it was not a textbook. Arysbek looked very embarrassed. He closed the pages and looked at his father as if asking, How may I help you? Aķmyrza couldn't do anything but walk away, to bed. Then Ķamar went to her bed, too, tired from her chores.

'Ķamar', Aķmyrza called to his wife in a low voice. 'I've quit drinking... Do you hear me? Forever... I won't take another drop of that stuff.' Ķamar was silent. 'Don't you believe me?'

'I'm not sure', she replied.

'I promise you.'

She sighed. 'We would live better if you didn't waste so much money on that poison.'

'I promise you', Aķmyrza repeated.

'If you gave up drinking, it would be better for all of us', she said, softly. 'Come closer.'

'Quiet, Aķan... The children will wake up. I'll come...'

'Come here.' He slipped under the duvet, filled with guilt, and hugged her still-trim body to his. He had registered her use of the affectionate nickname – 'Aķan' – that she'd given him after their wedding, so many years earlier. Then, a year later, Arysbek was born. Aķmyrza got drunk with his friends to celebrate his son's birth... then his second son's birth... then the third son... up to the point where he began to drink regularly, complaining that he hadn't had any daughters. He continued to get drunk with his friends, and Ķamar stopped calling him 'Aķan'.

Poor thing, he thought, she deserves such a better life than I've given her.

'Ķamaš',[3] he asked, 'what did you think about all day long?' He looked at her face and added: 'Tell me the truth.'

She was silent again. Then she sighed, and said: 'Do you think I have time for thinking?'

She pulled away from him. 'I am as busy as a hamster in a wheel, from morning until bedtime. I want our boys to have what other children have: proper clothing... shoes... enough to eat... even toys. Do you know I walk to town and wash floors in the government offices? That I do knitting and sewing for other women? That I do all this in addition to taking care of our family?'

A tear ran down her cheek. 'I've been dreaming of the day our eldest son will marry. Arysbek can bring his bride here to share the work with me.'

---

[3] Ķamaš – diminutive form of Ķamar.

'Oh, he is too young for that.'

'He has grown up. After finishing eighth grade this year, he wants to enter college.'

'Is he in the eighth grade? I thought he was in the seventh', Aķmyrza said. Suddenly he remembered Tăškenbaj's galoshes. 'Ķamar', he added after a while, 'let's buy new clothes for our children on my next payday. Make a list of what each of them needs.'

But she was already asleep.

Aķmyrza couldn't sleep. He lay in the dark with his eyes open, thinking of something Ķamar had told him about Arysbek spending time with a girl from his class at school. The girl had a lovely, pleasant mother, and he remembered the proverb: 'If you want to marry a girl, look first at her mother'. Then, smiling, he fell asleep.

***

When the apple trees are blooming, it's hard to take your eyes off the elegant white flowers that cover their gnarled limbs. The yard of the small Kazakh home contained many apple trees.

Aķmyrza came home from work and began clearing the winter's collection of animal dung from the shed near the house. The boys came to help their father with this annual spring cleaning.

'Kôke', said Tăškenbaj, 'Arysbek dreams of having velvet trousers.'

'I'll buy him trousers.'

'But they are very expensive!'

'I'll buy the trousers, full stop!'

'If you don't have enough money, I'll be wearing Arysbek's old boots for the rest of the year.'

Aķmyrza dropped his spade and turned to look at the boy in surprise. Tăškenbaj's words had affected him strongly.

'I shall have enough money', he replied. 'Enough for everyone. I shall buy *everything* you all need.'

As if waiting for such a reply, Zadariâ and Montaj began to plead for toys:

'A car for me!'

'For me, too!'

Their father having acknowledged their requests cheerfully, both boys ran away happily, shouting, 'Hurrah!' Once they had disappeared, Tăškenbaj seemed to want to speak, but something was holding him back.

'Kôke', he said at last, 'we have to return the flour to the baker.' Embarrassed, he averted his eyes.

'What flour? Did he ask for it?'

'No, but his son is always teasing me at school. He says you're a thief.'

'No, that's not true. We didn't steal the flour. I only borrowed it. We'll soon return the sack or give him some money.'

Aķmyrza recalled the incident. One evening during the winter gone by, drunk on his way home, he had passed the bakery and noticed that the baker needed help unloading a truckload of flour sacks. The man had asked him to lend a hand. Mindful that Ķamar had been complaining about a lack of flour at home, Aķmyrza decided to borrow a sack... No, wait, this idea came later. At first, hoping to get some vodka from the baker, Aķmyrza worked hard to help him. After setting down some sacks, he looked at the baker and asked: 'How's this?'

'Great!' replied the baker. 'May you live a thousand years!'

But that wasn't what Aķmyrza had hoped for. Instead of a 'thousand years', he wanted a 'hundred ounces' now. Setting down the next sack, he asked again: 'How's this?'

The reply was the same.

At last, losing patience, he took a direct approach: 'Let's drink up!'

'Oh, Aķmyrza', replied the baker, 'the shops are already closed. And there is no vodka in the house.'

'If you want it enough, you'll find it. Go to the "Ķalmentorg" and get it.' (There was a man named Ķalmen who sold vodka covertly from his home, for fifteen roubles.)

'But I have no money!' said the baker sadly.

'In that case', said Aķmyrza annoyed, 'I'll take a sack of flour.' He hadn't used the word 'borrow' on purpose.

Stunned, the baker didn't know what to do. 'Impossible', he said.

'Possible!' replied Aķmyrza, lifting up a sack and making his way home.

'Oh, Aķmyrza, stop! Stop it!' shouted the baker, shaking his head.

Ķamar learned the truth about the flour too late to return it; by then it was almost gone. She felt embarrassed and was upset with Aķmyrza.

***

For spring, it was a hot day. The air was full of dust from the cars passing in the road, and Kelesbaj was sweeping the yard. Aķmyrza's sons waited impatiently for their father's payday.

That evening, they would discuss the purchases each of them required. Kelesbaj wrote in big letters on a sheet of paper:

1. For Arysbek – velvet trousers (imported)
2. For Tăškenbaj – boots (size 39)
3. For me – slippers and shirts
4. For Zadariâ – a toy car
5. For Montaj – a toy car (the cars should be identical, otherwise they will fight over them)
6. For Mama...

'Oh, leave me until the next payday', Ķamar laughed. Thus everyone agreed on the list as it was.

At last, the long wait came to an end. From morning, the boys took turns riding the bicycle to the road to see if Aķmyrza was coming. But there was no sign of him.

Tǎškenbaj, tired of waiting, went off to play football. The Sun set below the horizon of the steppe. Arysbek found a book to occupy his interest while the little ones went into the house, sad. Only Kelesbaj remained, standing by the front gate, waiting for his father.

Then he saw Tǎškenbaj running in the direction of home. Kelesbaj was so happy that he couldn't even call his mother to tell her the good news. Something caught in his throat, and he lost his voice – which occurs when, after waiting so long and so excitedly for an event, the hour finally arrives. He rushed towards his brother, and although he ran out of breath, he managed to shout: '*Kôke*? You've seen *kôke*? He's coming, isn't he?'

His brother didn't answer, and at once Kelesbaj noticed that he was crying. Kelesbaj stared at him, confused. 'Why are you crying?' he asked. 'Did you have a fight with somebody? What's the matter? Where is *kôke*?'

Tǎškenbaj wiped his tears with his sleeve and said: 'He's drunk, as usual. Over there, near the fence.'

Kelesbaj felt deflated, as if all the joy in his life had been stolen at once; the happiness he had felt for so many days was gone, as his world crashed around him.

'How can this be? Why does he cheat us so?' Kelesbaj whispered, with trembling lips. Tears came to his eyes and made tracks down his dusty cheeks. Suddenly he felt a strong wish to run away from this house, from this *auyl*, from the father who caused such embarrassment. Forever!

Aķmyrza straggled along the edge of the road, supporting himself by clutching at the fence posts along the way. Eventually, he reached his own front gate.

The little ones had come from the house along with Arysbek, so all five sons now stood just inside the gate. They stared at him. He swayed back and forth on rubbery legs; then, using all his willpower, he straightened up and stepped carefully toward the boys. The stink of vodka permeated him. To Aķmyrza, in his drunken state, his sons were lined up as cranes before taking flight. His mind was in turmoil.

'I'll be a son of a bitch', he exclaimed, for suddenly the boys transformed into white cranes, poised to fly away. No... no, they couldn't fly, however much they attempted the feat. They struggled upward, and fell down...

'Where are you flying to?' Aķmyrza whispered. 'Your nest is here.'

He reached out for them and fell on his face, his arms extended like the legs of a crane before leaving the ground.

Translated by Mitchell Albert

ZHUSSIPBEK KORGASBEK
(b. 6.02.1961)

Zhussipbek Korgasbek is a prose writer, essayist, screenwriter and journalist. He graduated from the journalism faculty at Kirov Kazakh State University (now Ăl-Farabi Kazakh National University) in 1984, and was first employed at the newspaper *Žas alaš* as a correspondent, subsequently rising to the position of editor-in-chief, which he also held at the major literary newspaper *Ķazaķ ădebieti*. He is general director of Žas órken, a children's publishing house.

Korgasbek's debut short stories emerged in the literary papers of the Kazakh SSR in the mid-1980s. His first book, *Kôgildir keruen* (The Blue Caravan), a collection of poems, was published in 1985 by Žalyn publishing house, to be followed by a collection of short stories, *Žansebil* (The Desperate), ten years later. Two more collections soon appeared, *Žyndy ķajyņ* (The Raging Birch Tree, 2009) and *Kôkžaldar* (Wolves, 2003), as well as a novel, *Ùlpildek* (Young and Tender, 2012) and two feature films based on his short stories: *Žansebil* (dir. by Aâĝan Šăžimbaj, 1992) and *Talan* (dir. by Bolat Ķalymbetov, 2018), the latter based on the story 'Ķasķyr adam' (The Wolf-Man).

Zhussipbek Korgasbek has made a series of TV programmes about the literary figures of Kazakhstan, and written a number of well-received essays: 'Aņyz adam' (A Legendary Man), 'Mùķaĝali men Fariza' (about the Kazakh poets Maķataev and Ongarsynova), 'Aņyz Oralkhan' (Legendary Oralkhan [Bokey]), 'Aņyz Beksultan' (Legendary Beksultan [Nurzhekeyev]) and 'Toraņĝy men Tùrsynžan' (Blue Poplar and Tursynzhan [Shapay]).

Korgasbek was awarded the Žalyn publishing house prize (1987), the title of an Honoured Worker of the Republic of Kazakhstan (1998) and the Tarlan Hope Award (2001).

Art

It is not every day a man has the fortune to encounter such a wondrous vision – as beautiful as a rainbow spreading all its colours across the horizon. This vision walked into his large, bright office of its own accord, shapely calves showing dazzling white beneath the hem of a shortish, sea-green dress. It walked in through the door and advanced towards him with small steps, moving so regally that it could have balanced a brimming jug of water on its head without spilling a drop. With each movement it seemed the wrapping had begun to slip to the floor – but no: it was the vision itself stepping towards him, until, not allowing him a moment to gather his thoughts, it sat down defiantly to face him.

'Why would anyone with your looks come trailing in here like some wretched scribbler?!'

He spoke these words with anger and a sense of insult. He was yet to attain serious fame – and the constant, unceasing rush of life filled him with bitterness. Face to face with this fair-skinned girl, who seemed to give off a faint breath of virgin soil in early spring, he felt wounded to the core of his soul, almost humiliated, because he was as gloomy as an old, angry bird of prey. But he had noted already that the girl's hair was as rich and dense as the new grass that springs up after a fire on the steppe, as black as coal, and long enough to wrap several times around her neck.

A shadow seemed to fall on the hollows around the girl's eyes, and her face became sombre below the arcs of her brows, darkening like a meadow that has been watered. The upward sweep of her eyelashes, the thick hair that sprung from her parting, and the heavy, glossy black eyebrows lent her beautiful face a slightly stern expression. He had never had success as a poet, but now he recalled a poem he had composed in his youth:

> You said your love tore you asunder,
> My love for you was like a hunger.
> But must I now be forced to suffer?
> Shall we be strangers to each other?
> The days flow past as fast as ever –
> Your heart, from this hurt will recover,
> And you will find – and wed – another,
> Then weep – to know your youth is over.

The fair-skinned girl's entire body seemed to respond perfectly to her every whim. Was all this to begin again now? Why was his flesh so quick to succumb? He had never looked at a young girl in this way since he had been a young man. Everything he had at his disposal was simple – a warm house, a good wife, black tea and black ink – but in his manners and habits he was as scrupulous and demanding as a true aristocrat – and always would be. And time, was precious to him now – more precious than pigeon's milk![1]

'So why have you come to see me then?'

'I grew up reading and rereading your books, *aġa*.'[2]

Her voice was like the chime of glass goblets. But no matter how it caressed his ears, he refused to succumb to its enchantment, suspecting at once that her attempt to speak was an ambush, concealing a deep and treacherous subtext. Then, suddenly, his soul flared with indignation. Always at the mercy of his emotions, he now exploded in fury as if he had glimpsed of a mortal enemy.

'Everyone in Kazakhstan reads and rereads my books. You consider this a worthwhile topic for discussion?'

No sooner had he brought the conversation back to familiar ground, than other words altogether threatened to come spilling out of his mouth: 'Ah, but how beautiful you are, though!' And indeed, from her head to her toes, the girl seemed to give off a breath of *saumal*.[3] If he were to reach out and touch her fingers, or her elbow, they would be as soft as featherdown. Her sleeveless dress allowed his reluctant gaze to caress her shoulders, which shone like freshly shelled eggs. His gaze travelled hastily down to assail the shapely calves of her legs, which showed beneath the hem of her sea-green dress.

'I esteem you as a mentor, *aġa*', said the girl. 'I have chosen to follow a literary path, and I dream of becoming a writer. But I have not come to plague you with requests. I can see your gracious character for myself, and that is enough.'

In his mind's eye, he saw those slightly plump pursed red lips, which seemed to be waiting for something. He had studied the anger of women closely, for he had depicted it in many of his books, in his portraits of the consorts of khans and sultans. He sensed that this girl felt his disregard for her beauty as an insult to her honour and dignity. Strange to say, he felt exhilarated at the thought. He was about to let fly another comment, to put an end to any thought of a further meeting, when the door to his office creaked open. The fat, dark-faced man who now entered let out an exclamation of delight, as if he had stumbled upon a gold nugget as big as a horse's head.

'Oh-ho – is this a picture, or is it real? Am I awake or am I dreaming? Who is this glorious creature? What talented hand created her?'

---

[1] 'Pigeon's milk' is an expression used to refer to something precious and rare; also, a name of a sweet delicacy.

[2] *Aġa* – form of address to an older man, which can be translated as 'brother', 'uncle'.

[3] *Saumal* – fresh mare's milk, considered to have healing properties.

The fat man's clumsy intrusion aroused disgust in him, like an unclean hand dipped into a fine meal. Seeing a blush spreading over the cheeks of the fair-faced girl, he almost exploded with fury. His fixed and glassy stare now showed undisguised hostility, and his pale face twisted into a furious scowl. Anyone transfixed by that stare was forced to surrender. The sabre of his tongue, once unsheathed, never spared its victim. He made mincemeat now of this poor, fat wretch.

'Well', he said to the girl. 'There's no point in you asking favours of hacks like him!'

He was panting, overwhelmed by emotion, unable to control the sudden flame of jealousy that had sprung up inside him. This fat man had called in at his office several times in the past, hoping to strike up a friendship with him; now he had hurled an unthinkable insult straight into the man's face. The man was a nonentity, but he was most furious with himself, as he was unable to understand why the man aroused such jealousy in him over the fair-faced girl. Were it not for this upstart, this girl, though she had travelled specially to see him, would have been of less than no importance to him. He had been on the point of showing her politely out of his office, but now he had changed his mind.

Perhaps the fat man's earthbound nature came to his aid at this point. When he heard that terrible word – a deadly affront, if truth be told – he did not lose his head or writhe in indignation, but deftly deflected it towards a less personal target.

'Talented writers may make our literature, but hacks make our literary community.'

He knew the fat man had many books to his name, but who would have the fellow capable of such a clever comeback? He generally took delight in witty rejoinders, but now he was furious. Every work *he* produced was a small event in his native land, inspiring glowing reviews and inducing a dizzy fever with its intoxicating vapours. When he was held in its spell, he felt head and shoulders above everything and everyone. As one who bore the name of Mataj,[4] he should let no man utter an insulting word in his presence. He had already made mincemeat of the man, but safe in the knowledge the blood would not stain him, he drew the sabre of his tongue once again, and plunged it into living flesh.

---

[4] Mataj – the writer's name is actually an invention. It is the name of a group of mountain ridges on the southern edge of the Žetisu (Dzungarian) Alatau, as well as a clan of Najman tribe.

'I beg you, Šyŋdauyl, stay silent. Do not defile your lips. Normally I would not beg anything of one so lowly. But even the *jinns*[5] have their righteous. And you, after all, are more than just a hack. You are a talented hack.'

Then he saw a grey-blue shadow creep over the dark face of the fat man – an amazing sight. Just like soil turned by the plough, it did not even shimmer, it *shone* bluish grey. 'Why on earth do women act so compliant around him?' he wondered. The fat man rushed to the door in a rage, his feet thundering on the floor as if his body weighed twice its weight. He slammed it shut with such force it almost brought the wall crashing down.

It felt like a slap in the face. He shuddered, then quickly composed himself.

'My dear *aġa*, why must you behave like this?' asked the girl.

'Because I have no empathy.'

'What do you mean?'

'I mean I am not capable of love. And yet I am quite distracted with jealousy.'

'I don't understand at all, my dear *aġa*.'

'I don't know how to explain it. *You* for instance – I've never seen you before, and yet I'm seized by jealousy.'

'What are you jealous of? And who's making you feel so jealous?'

'It's not that I'm jealous of you as such… It's beauty. I feel jealous of beauty, faced by thick-skinned imbeciles like that one. They worm their way in everywhere, they take everything. They've spoiled everything.'

At a certain point he felt that it must be some other people altogether sitting there, talking together in low voices in that spacious office, just after the fat man's stormy departure. After all, it was impossible that a modest girl, fresh from the *auyl*,[6] could speak to him so frankly and assertively from the start. And neither was he the frivolous sort who could open his heart to the first stranger he met, like a watermelon split open. It dawned on him dimly, somewhere at the edge of his consciousness, that his coolly detached writer's mind was entering deeper and deeper into the experience of a man of emotion.

His face was round, like the face of a snow leopard; it was cruel when it tensed, and, even when it softened, and he smiled, there was something terrible in that smile. When he went through to the darkened restroom behind the

---

[5] *Jinn* – an intelligent spirit created from fire (as opposed to angels created from light and humans created from earth), invisible to humans. *Jinns* can be male or female, Muslim and *kaffir*; they can be born, marry and die. They appear in different forms and move at great speeds. It is believed that non-Muslim *jinns* can possess human beings and do harm, whereas Muslim *jinns* serve a *baḳsy* to heal people and fight evil *jinns*.

[6] *Auyl* – socio-economic formation considered to constitute the heartland of the nation and a basis for an ethnic and cultural union of the nomadic community. Consisting of 50–70 yurts in the eighteenth century, it developed into its current permanent state of 'rural settlement' (of a minimum of 100 dwellers) when Kazakhs adopted a settled mode of life in the nineteenth and twentieth centuries. *Auyl* can also be used as a synonym for 'native land' and 'homeland', concepts revered by the Kazakhs.

office, only his round face glimmered in the dark. On entering the dimly lit room, his first action was to cast an appraising look at the elongated features of the girl's face, and at her tall, thin form. In poor lighting, figures seem taller and faces longer. When he switched on the light, the girl vanished, and he saw only a lifeless painting, wrapped in a dust sheet. Grabbing it with both hands and holding it as far away from him as he could, he peered closely at it once more. Goodness knows, if he had come across this radiant girl in everyday life, he would not have given her a second look. In fact, he might even have squinted at her in distaste, imagining her defiled by Šyṇdauyl's impure hands, and for one simple reason: it was only his own pen that could produce angels entirely without sin, and without the slightest resemblance to a living soul.

Half-disdainful, half-caressing, he ran the outer edge of a curled finger over the beautiful girl on the picture. He looked at her this way and that. Taken as a whole, there was something about her that was flawed, something missing, and yet he could not work out precisely where it was. He leaned the picture against the wall, tilting it slightly backwards, and looked carefully at it again. Everything seemed to be there, but still, something was wrong. If he were to sit at his desk now and try to describe the girl, this shortcoming he sensed would naturally come to light somehow in one place or another. 'Why not try?' he thought, and the idea fired him briefly with enthusiasm, but he quickly rejected it. He had more than enough writing to do without that. With this thought, he turned the picture face to the wall, to prevent it from distracting him further.

As he was going back into his office, he noticed that the oil paint on the canvas had run, and was trickling to the floor. He was too late to snatch his foot away and, as ill luck would have it, stepped in the edge of the stain. He wiped his foot clean on the floor, as if he had stepped in dirt, and left the room. The pool of reddish-brown paint did not soak into the parquet floor but lay glistening on the surface. Suddenly, the paint seemed to come to life, gathering itself into a ball and stretching upwards. A moment later, the young girl appeared on the spot where the stain had been, adjusting her hair and her sea-green dress. Without the boldness she had shown so recently, shamefaced and blushing, she made her way into the office. With a light movement, she tossed back her loosened, tousled braids, walked to the chair she had been sitting in, and sat down, timidly, but with an air of familiarity. Apart from a few drops of reddish-brown paint which had splashed onto the side of her face, he saw no particular change in her.

'Being a writer is unimaginable torture.' said Mataj now. 'It's like walking across a bridge a hair's breadth across: with the fires of Gehenna on one side and the cataracts of Jannah on the other. Many have perished there – some have choked in the water, others have been burned to ashes. The wails of the soul's torment are more terrible than that of the flesh. And I hear those wails every day.' He spoke as if he were drawing some lengthy conversation to a close.

And though his face – round as the face of a snow leopard – looked dissatisfied, still he looked more than ever like a great predator licking its chops. As she sat there, the fair-skinned girl seemed to be listening with him to the anguished wails of suffering souls. Her chest was thrust forward and every inch of her body expressed compassion and the hope of salvation.

Mataj spoke again:

'Once, when I was a child, a circus came to the *auyl*. One of the circus boys showed us his trick – he walked barefoot on burning coals. Everybody was in awe, except me. I suppose I never had a childhood; even then, I sensed that my whole life would be a long walk over hot coals. My feet were swollen and covered in bloody sores from the constant burns. And there were always any number of "friends" who would lie down on their sides or stand on all fours, and happily blow on the coals beneath my feet.' His words revealed just a fraction of the grievances and bitter memories shored up in his heart.

To the fair-skinned girl, it seemed that the writer could not take his eyes off her. In fact, although his gaze was turned towards her, he did not see her at all. The boundless mist that rose up from the ocean of his life dimmed his view, and the fair-skinned girl vanished amidst the white-capped waves, invisible as a slender twig coated in sea foam.

'There is no nation like mine anywhere else in the world. But those ill-wishers who are trying to make our nation stray from the true path have almost achieved their goal. And those authors who write books about the whole of humankind are also doing us a disservice. They patronise their own nation; they look down their noses at her, as if she were not a part of the wider world. Our nation seems to me at times like a child, pouncing on glittering baubles. I am afraid, too, that she is often misled by people. She races off here and there, like a child flying red and green kites.'[7] He spoke pompously, with a sort of malicious glee.

His face, round as the face of a snow leopard, had now shrunk to the size of a fist, contorted into a tight grimace. The fair-skinned girl, now habituated to his anger and observing it calmly, sat in a submissive pose with a docile expression in her face. She even seemed to take pleasure in his angry outbursts.

'A nation that fails to cherish its genius makes a catastrophic error. The most terrible affliction in this life is the inability to distinguish what is first-rate from what is bad. There are people among us who will try to trip us up or stab us in the back. Our nation is plagued by *shaitans*[8] who turn our people first against one and then against the other. Now all that's left is to leave the country, and I have the chance to do so', said the writer. His eyes were wide with excitement and full of angry tears, which he had not stopped to wipe away.

The fair-faced girl was about to wipe away his tears and even reached out, as if to demonstrate that she had every right to do so. But the writer seemed to take back his tears; it was as if he had drawn them back into himself, and this alarmed the girl.

---

[7] The colours red and green in Kazakh culture indicate something beautiful and elusive.

[8] *Shaitan* – Devil, evil spirit in Islamic theology and mythology, chief among *jinns*.

'Well, if this crowd don't appreciate me, coming generations will. What do you all know anyway? Your souls are choked with such a heap of rubbish... it will take an age to rid yourselves of it. That story you told me, about dreaming of becoming a writer and coming here to find me, is no more than an empty pretext. But you're on the true path. May fortune smile on you', he said. 'In short, thank Allah that you haven't fallen into the clutches of a hack like *that one*' – he added, stressing the last sentence as if this were the crux of the matter.

His face, round as the face of a snow leopard, seemed to relax, break into a sweat, and soften ever so slightly. The fair-faced girl, meanwhile, had lost all hope; she shrank in on herself like some useless piece of carrion disgorged from the maw of a beast, her head drooping lower and lower. At that moment, just as the conversation was coming to an end, an artist came stumbling hurriedly into the bright office. There was a sensation of something rushing past at high speed – then a loud crack rang out nearby. The vision was transfigured so fast that no one noticed a thing. A few more minutes passed and then, with loud exertions and a great deal of fuss, the artist picked up the oil painting he had completed the day before and, holding it in front of him, left the room.

Translated by Rose France

ROZA MUKANOVA
(b. 14.10.1964,)

Roza Mukanova is a writer and playwright. She studied journalism at Kirov Kazakh State University (now Ăl-Farabi Kazakh National University; (grad. 1987) and began her career at the Department of Literature and Art at the State Central Museum in Almaty. She has held senior positions at the Kazakhstan Writers' Union, the Ministry of Information and the Senate of the Parliament of the Republic of Kazakhstan. Since 2011, she has been a drama professor at the Kazakh National University of Arts in Astana.

Mukanova has published several collections of short stories and plays, including *Žaryķ dùnie* (A Bright World, 1994), *Dùnie kezek* (The Unstable World, 1997), *Ķŭdiret-kie* (Sanctity, 2001), *Šatyr astyndaġy men* (Me Under the Shelter, 2008), and two volumes of selected works (2007 and 2014). She translated *Kısasü'l enbiya* by Rabguzi into Kazakh (2001). A short story that earned her renown is 'Măŋgilik bala bejne' (The Image of the Eternal Child), adapted for stage (1996) and made into a film titled *Ķyzžylaġan* (Leila's Prayer, 2001; dir. by Satybaldy Narymbetov). Her adaptation of Ăuezov's novel *Ķaraly sŭlu* (Beauty in Mourning, 1997) and her play *Sarra* (2016) have both been performed on stage.

Mukanova is a laureate of the Kazakhstan Youth Union Prize, *Žalyn* journal's Tôlegen Ajbergenov Literary Prize (1989) and the Alaš International Literary Award (2002). She is an Honoured Worker of the Republic of Kazakhstan.

The Image of the Eternal Child

Note from translator: From 1949 to 1989, the former Kazakh Soviet
Socialist Republic oblast of Semipalatinsk (Semej, now part of the
East Kazakhstan region) was subjected to several hundred nuclear test
detonations, both in the atmosphere and underground. Over 200,000
villagers in the region were thus exposed to radiation – often deliberately,
so Soviet scientists could determine its effects – and over half that number
continues to be affected. Soil, water and air remain highly contaminated,
and serious physical deformities in children were and are a common
occurrence.

A gloomy, black-shrouded figure fled before the quiet girl Leila, who was
hurrying to the ravine on an otherwise still and peaceful night. Who might be
wandering at this hour? she wondered.

'I am the spirit of humans', replied a terrible and unfamiliar voice in the
distance. But the girl Leila trusted no human – and certainly no so-called 'spirit
of humans'. Her sole consolation, her only close friend, was the wonderfully
full moon, which soothed the silent night. She would whisper to the moon
of her misfortunes, and of the grief her soul had been suffering. The moon
graced the bereaved *auyl*[1] of Ķarauyl, which had been ripped into fragments,
and almost beautified it with her divine, milky whiteness. Sometimes she would
glance with pity at Ķarauyl, and then at the little girl Leila, gazing up at her.
The moon would recline, stretching to her full roundness and scrutinising the
hollows and cavities on the surface of its larger neighbour.

Perhaps, at a time like this, she addressed the earth: 'Goodness, have you
been left without any pride? What have they done to you? You are as worn out
as an old duster! Who is this lonely person hiding in the ravine? Does a sixteen-
year-old look like this? What a place, that a young woman can look as if she is
the age of a child! Who is to blame for these torments? Who has created such
a scene?'

---

[1] *Auyl* – socio-economic formation considered to constitute the heartland of the nation
and a basis for an ethnic and cultural union of the nomadic community. Consisting of
50–70 yurts in the eighteenth century, it developed into its current permanent state of
'rural settlement' (of a minimum of 100 dwellers) when Kazakhs adopted a settled mode
of life in the nineteenth and twentieth centuries. *Auyl* can also be used as a synonym for
'native land' and 'homeland', concepts revered by the Kazakhs.

The moon would speak such words, blaming unknown forces, or the people who had been living in this place, for their weaknesses. It seemed that she knew of the notorious devastation that had taken place, watching every deed from the sky and cursing the guilty parties, rolling onto the thin clouds and weeping. Meanwhile, Leila had dozed off; suddenly, she shivered, and awoke. A tear dropped from her eye and fell onto her chin.

'Oh, shining moon!' she said. 'Do not pity me. I'm an innocent girl. I am every human being's equal: I feel the same way as they do, I am not brainsick. However, my little soul is full of distress and bitterness. I'm an ordinary person – but for the others, I'm just a cripple who forces people to appreciate their lives. When the villagers of Ķarauyl see me, they say: "God created this girl to make people grateful for having all their limbs, for keeping all parts of their bodies intact." Is that true, shining moon? I believe in you, and trust only you! What do these people say about me? Who am I? Am I an eternal child who will never grow up?'

Leila was talking to herself now: the silent moon had travelled further on. But she calmed Leila, calmed the land. 'I wish to be someone normal for my age', Leila continued. 'Yes, I want to be a beautiful, slender girl, I *want...*'

She climbed out of the deep ravine in which she had been hiding in the dark. Through her tearful eyes, she watched the round, white moon, which seemed to be fleeing. Still trapped in a child's body that she had inhabited since the age of eight, Leila rose her veined, wrinkled hands up and waved.

She called out: 'Uh-uh! Do not escape from me! I'll find you anywhere. Are you scared of me? Are you afraid, or do you also hate me...?'

The moon shifted further away from the disfigured girl, leaving this cracked, pockmarked land behind and taking the dark night by the hand. The girl Leila shouted after it, still waving her arms.

'Come again tomorrow', she said. 'Let's meet here. I'll be waiting for you. I'll be waiting in this ravine, bright moon!' When she had uttered those words, Leila shuddered, now cold. Her chin trembled, and her heart beat quickly and sank.

To Leila, walking back to Ķarauyl, the summit of the Šyņġystau – once wide and vast – looked low, as if it had diminished. Hills like upright deltas looked spooky in the darkness, and she felt afraid. She was also fearful of the 'spirit of humans' following her – one of those dark hosts of the night, which might only have been seeking shelter in the mountains.

Leila was unable to see anything clearly. Everything dimmed before her eyes. She had been living with her aunt Ķatira, and now became short of breath while approaching her house. Leila stretched her arm out towards the door, then immediately retracted it. She didn't want to encounter those hostile eyes, whom she knew would stare at her. I shall wait until they go to bed, she thought, and stayed outside the door for a while. Suddenly, she was startled by aunt Ķatira's unexpected voice.

'Where did you go at this hour, as if possessed by a devil? What the hell are you doing!'

Leila looked down. She didn't want her aunt to notice her swollen eyes, red from sweat, or to see how exhausted she was. Will Ķatira ever understand my sadness? I'd better stay silent and calm, thought Leila.

'Where were you, I asked!'

Leila didn't reply. No, no. I shouldn't tell anyone that I go to the ravine to see the moon and tell her my secrets. I go there when there is nobody on Earth who could understand my soul. Only the moon. Please, do not look for me anywhere, do not ask me anything and leave me to my grief!

'Ah! So now, you've become mute. Now you want to be dumb. Is that what you wish to be called? We'll see. People will call you "dumb" after this!'

Leila gave her aunt a sharp look. Ķatira sneered, casting a glance at Leila's arms and legs. The girl began to shiver again, now from anger and sorrow, unable to bring any calm to her wretched body. Whenever someone looked at her deformed arms and legs, she felt awkward and ashamed, and began shuddering. She did not want anyone to gawk at her large, veined hands, which looked like the hands of an elderly woman, and her very small legs. Yet Ķatira stood before her and looked her up and down with loathing and deliberate mockery. How Leila suffered during such moments. Alas, there was no place to hide.

'Where were you?' Ķatira demanded again. 'Where do you go, at exactly the time we need someone to give a hand with the cattle in the shed? Tell me, damn it!'

Leila, her eyes downcast, replied quietly: 'I am a human being, am I not?'

Ķatira exploded. 'Such words! "I am a human being", she says! Why don't you take a good look at your dreadful body, you "human being", eh?'

Ķatira's poisonous tongue could cut Leila's innocent soul to bloody pieces. Leila had heard such horrid remarks before from Ķatira, of course, and she would shed tears and sob; this time, however, she became stiff and didn't turn her pale face and sharp eyes away. She said: 'Cruel, heartless and unfeeling people are always satisfied with themselves. You mock me, aunt. Do you think I've asked God for my "good fortune"? Yes – I prayed to God for my fate! I do everything you ask me to do. Tell me, aunt, have I ever harmed you?'

Leila covered her small, undeveloped face with her wide, clumsy hands, and fell to her knees. Now, in this position, she began sobbing. She let the tears stream from her eyes. No one ever stopped to ask what was wrong, or to comfort her. They thought it was natural for Leila to cry; it was natural for her to be in such a state. 'Poor thing!' they would whisper in passing. 'May God see your tears, but not us! May the Almighty bless you and help you!' Leila knew they were addressing themselves, not her. That's why she escaped to the deep ravine at night, to look up at the round and silent moon.

The moon shone brightly, lighting up the ravine. Travelling above the Earth, tonight it searched relentlessly for the girl Leila. It asked after her, accosting the rivers of Ķarauyl on the plains and in the mountains. 'Where are you?' the moon entreated. 'Why aren't you there, in the ravine?' It asked this tenderly, as a mother would, reaching out with warm hands and flying across the ravine. 'Oh, my baby!' the moon said, her motherly voice extending the length of the ravine.

The motherly voice called out, shattering the silence: 'There were explosions under the mountains of Degeleŋ when you were in my belly. Do they still go on, or have they stopped? You would wake up from those terrible sounds and scream from fright. You were too restless and troubled. You would look at the reddish mushroom clouds flaming and rising from the foothills of the Šyŋġystau; you liked to run in that direction, laughing. Do you still do that?... "Mum, I dreamt about the mushrooms beyond the mountains – they were hanging in the air", you used to say. Then your grandmother, God bless her, would answer: "Oh, apple of my eye! One day, you shall also become like that mushroom, flaming and glowing and attracting people's eyes." And then she would kiss you gently on your forehead ... Where are you now? Where did you go?' The voice in the ravine died away. The moon rose up high, searching for the girl Leila in every sweet meadow. But there was no girl to be found, gazing passionately at the moon.

Leila hated crowds; she fled from any place where people assembled. However, the following day, Ķatira insisted that she participate in an *auyl* gathering: 'Let's go; there is a *toj* – a big, festive party – in Ķarauyl. You'll be refreshed by the change of scenery.'

Leila didn't know what to say. 'People's eyes... Gossips... the talk of the crowd...' she mumbled. She didn't want Ķatira to guess that she was thinking of her abject condition. 'I am too tired', she said at last, hoping the excuse would suffice.

'Oh, stop it. Let's go!' Ķatira said, and began to shake her. When she saw how reluctant Leila was, she began to tickle her. Leila couldn't help but giggle at first; when she began spluttering from laughter, she rose to her feet, lay her big hands on the older woman's chest and pushed her away. Ķatira became pale with anger.

'Fine! If you don't want to go, then don't go!'

'I'll go!' replied Leila abruptly, and repeated herself as though insisting: 'I'll go.'

Everyone is joyful, she thought to herself at the gathering, observing the happy faces of the villagers around her. And that is only right! For the happiest thing in this world is to have all your parts, to be whole. Why am I the most dismal person in the world? Leila felt new tears forming in her eyes, and she concealed them from the others. I know I shall never grow. Oh, God! What other hardships do You have in store for me? I wish You had killed me at birth instead. Why? Why must it be like this? God, You have no need of me; You also want to ridicule me, to make fun of my childlike form, to play with me!

'Leila! Lailek! Snow-white Leila!'

A young man's gentle voice brought her out of her reverie. Someone in the crowd was holding out his hands and approaching her.

Oh! Leila was surprised. It's Ķúmar. How handsome you are now, Ķúmar! Lovely Ķúmar, my old desk-mate at school. You often called me 'White Lailek' – 'White Stork'. You used to say that the white stork is a very tender and elegant bird!

The girl Leila was so taken aback she nearly fainted.

'Did you recognise me?' asked the young man, smiling gently.

'I did. Why wouldn't I? My, how you have changed, though. You've become so handsome. You are happy—' She stopped short. 'Excuse me... do not...'

'You are also a happy person, Lailek.'

Ķúmar behaved naturally, taking no notice of the girl's frozen body. He didn't want to hurt her feelings or her pride. Putting his hand on her shoulder, he said: 'Lailek, let's dance. I invite you to dance with me.' He lifted the girl from her seat and kissed her on her forehead. She felt as if her heart had gone still. The young man walked into the crowd with Leila, and they danced. Soon each forgot about the people around them, whirling to the music. Leila closed her eyes; she felt dizzy, unable to open them. The music and the dance awakened feelings of femininity she had long set aside. She stayed still, her arms around Ķúmar's neck.

The young man whispered quietly: 'Lailek! White Lailek...' Leila opened her eyes at once. 'We were looking forward to this festival', Ķúmar continued. 'So many people have left the *auyl*; it looks so deserted. I was happy to see you...'

Leila's pale face flushed deeply, and she felt confused and shy. She was ashamed and irritated by her short cotton dress and her red band, which her aunt had persuaded her to wear as though she were a schoolgirl.

One of them had grown from a child into a young adult; the other had abandoned hope for the future and remained frozen in time, a child forever – and a disabled one at that. Was this destiny? Leila couldn't listen to Ķúmar's words anymore; his voice now sounded distant, ethereal. She was at once plunged into sadness, and stood there, as immobile as a deaf woman. Leila tried to hide her clumsy hands. She shut her eyes.

As though awakening from a deep sleep, she opened them after some time. She was alone now.

'Ķúmar...' she whispered. 'Ķúmar! Where are you...?'

Leila searched the crowd around her, staring at the villagers suspiciously. 'Where is Ķúmar?' she enquired many times. 'Did you send him away? Where... *where*?' She had, for the first time in her life, dared to believe that a dream could be made real, and had welcomed the opportunity – only to see it vanish instantly. She had felt herself flying, only to be dropped from a great height. The girl Leila cried out: '*Ķúmar!*' The people around her giggled and gossiped.

She wanted to plead with them: People, save me from this suffering! But she knew that only the ravine awaited her, and the kind, merciful, bright moon.

That night, Leila stared at the sky tearfully, watching the bare moon caress it gently.

Ķarauyl was in mourning. The elderly leaned on their sticks and heaved deep sighs. Women in black embraced each other and bewailed their loss. They were hardly able to raise their heads, saying through their tears: 'O, we are wretched! We have no future before us. We are now barren. They destroyed our ancestors' lands!'

The women, exhausted from sorrow, put their heads on each other's shoulders and wept. Leila, horrified, searched for Ķatira – but she couldn't find her. She didn't understand what had just happened in Ķarauyl, why so many people were suffering. She just stared at them with wide eyes.

My goodness, what has happened to these people? Leila trembled and shut her eyes.

The people of Ķarauyl witnessed an enormous crater, and more exploded ground that day. They saw how the rivers had dried, how the moon was obscured.

The despair in Ķarauyl seemed to reach the ears of the authorities far away. That night, unfamiliar people in sterile, white smocks came and selected all the disabled people, all the eternal children, and drove them away from the *auyl* in a black bus. Many parents were overcome with fresh grief – these were their children, after all. Leila had been in the ravine, and nobody had looked or asked for her. As usual, she had been hiding there from people and speaking with the moon. She had related all her young dreams, and her new love for Ķůmar; she whispered all her girlish secrets. The moon seemed to understand, and shed tears for her.

Leila sat there much longer than was her habit, feeling cold and hugging her knees with her long, bulky arms. When she rose, she felt that her body had become heavy. She had no strength. Do I have an autumn cold – perhaps even a high temperature? She felt so weak that she could barely reach her aunt's house and open the door.

Ķatira's furious face and wide, angry eyes only deepened Leila's miserable condition. 'I'm warning you for the last time!' Ķatira shouted. 'If you return again at this hour, I'll kick you out of the house for good, understand?'

Ķatira was agitated. Leila heard a howling wolf from afar.

'Please, do not send me anywhere', she said in a weak voice, her chin quivering and her face pale.

Afterward, Leila became very ill and was confined to her bed. She could not even open her eyes. If something touched her hands or legs, she awakened at once, whispering, 'Ķůmar... is that you, Ķůmar?... where have you been? I have been looking for you since that day... Let's dance as we danced before... you lift me up, and we'll whirl round. Let us... Ķůmar!'

So she lay there, delirious with visions. No one paid any attention to her severe condition, or listened to her ravings; no one was especially concerned.

One day, after the doctor had visited her and departed, Leila raised her head feebly. A group of strangers was gathered around her bed. Two of them were introduced as regional officials.

'We came to see you, Leila', they began, and Leila was glad to hear such words. Her pale face reddened, and she looked down. It seemed to her that these people had brought something good with them, so she waited to hear them out.

'Dear Leila, you have seen many troubles, and suffered much', said one of them, and paused for a moment before continuing: 'We are organising an assembly. You know, some children were taken to the city before, though we haven't heard anything further about them. But you are unique; there is no one else with your condition. We would like to show you to the people.'

At that moment, everything went black for the girl Leila. A loud humming filled her ears. I am a symbol of a disaster... a witness to the day when my people suffered a catastrophe. Right... I do not represent anything good, only evil and horror. Oh, my God!

One of the officials continued: 'So... let's get ready to go...'

For a second, she felt as though she had lost consciousness. Then she opened her eyes. There were none of the usual tears this time, however. She could not cry. Only a woeful sound like a croak squeezed her throat.

'Please', she said to the group. 'I do not want to be a symbol of misfortune. Have mercy on me. Although I appear pathetic and disabled, I desire only goodness, only good things...'

The visitors frowned and remained silent. They could not appreciate the girl's tender soul, or her reluctance.

'See, how high-minded she is!' muttered Ḳatira. 'A real troublemaker!'

Leila stared at everyone around her, then whispered: 'Will Ḳúmar be there? Is he participating?'

The strangers didn't understand, of course. Leila shut her eyes and lay there for some time. Then she addressed everyone: 'I am not going. I shall not go. Please, do not wait for me.'

Ḳatira threw up her arms. 'Thank God, I am happy with the success of my first-born child, at least', she said in an exasperated tone. 'I watched him grow up and make his way in life, and that's enough for me! We shall celebrate his accomplishments at the *toj* tomorrow!'

Life is so cheap for you, thought Leila upon hearing this. How can you sacrifice me just to enjoy yourself for one day at a *toj*? Just stop it! Stop! She wanted to shout, but found herself unable to utter a word.

But now Ḳatira had become lively again, and Leila heard her chatting to another guest who had dropped by: 'I'll leave Ḳarauyl as soon as the *toj* is over...'

Once Ḳarauyl was a sacred place, Leila contemplated. It has lost its distinction now. They say that 'every angel is followed by a devil'. Why does so much misfortune occur on this land, where the great poet Abaj was born and lived? Oh, what has the Almighty in store for us?

That evening, moonlight descended upon the face of this suffering girl. The moon had been searching for her again, peeking through the windows of Ķarauyl; at last, she had found her. Bright and round, her beams touched Leila's face. The ailing girl smiled. The sight of her old acquaintance from the window warmed her. Her eyes became moist; hurt by people, wounded by fate, she held the moon in her gaze as if she were about to lose sight of it. 'Do not forget that you've been the only friend to the most miserable person in the world', she whispered.

Leila and her celestial friend did not part from each other's company for a long while, the moon kissing the girl sweetly. She felt pity for Leila, and claimed her attention from the Earth as Leila, in turn, claimed hers from the night sky. After many hours, they separated, retreating to their very different worlds.

The luminous moon continued on her journey around the Earth, moving further and further away. But Leila didn't want to look away. Although she was in more pain than ever from her illness, she tried hard to train her gaze unceasingly at the moon – but could not, as both her will and strength became depleted. The light from the moon illuminated the paths of tears from her eyes, which pooled at her temples as she finally reclined.

The tears obscured her sight. In agony, she tried to dry her eyes with her ungainly hands, but she could not even move them. Leila closed her eyes for a time.

Her eyes did not open again.

The moon stroked the dead girl's face for as long as she could, but the time soon came to say farewell. They parted at last: one a child of the Earth, the other a child of the night.

In the morning, Ķatira busied herself, preparing the feast for her son, when she suddenly took notice of the fact that Leila, silent, had not stirred once. She rushed to her immediately, and stood at her bedside, staring.

'Damn it, did she die?' Ķatira shouted. 'My God! She died! On such a favourable day! What am I going to do?' Bewildered and distressed, Ķatira paced back and forth, talking to herself. 'How dare she! Just as we are preparing for the feast! What a puny little thing! Am I to announce her death on a day of celebration? Let her lie this way… nobody knows, and nobody will know.' Thus the woman made a decision, covered Leila's face and rushed out of the house.

Yet upon entering the road, she was startled by the sound of wailing. Walking further, she came across Ķarauyl villagers in black mourning dress, weeping and hugging each other, expressing condolences and sorrow. How terrible to her ears were these words of torment, describing hopelessness and horror. People were wailing: 'Gracious God, are they going to destroy us? They did it again yesterday night! More explosions!'

She trembled with fear, and thought of the girl Leila. Could the nuclear explosions have caused her death? she wondered. But now she had more pressing concerns, and became angry: she did not want the wailing people in black to set foot on her property.

'Away!' she shouted at them, 'get out of my sight! You are not going to ruin my son's celebration! For God's sake, leave me these moments of happiness! Leave us to our lives!'

She thought of Leila's stiff body, still in the house. Her face went pale just then, her body weak, and she crumpled onto the ground.

As the crowd in black approached her house, Ķatira became mute, alternately beseeching the crowd with upturned palms and burying her face in both hands. Finally, she fainted at the edge of her land.

When she revived, the moon lit Ķatira's face, despite the fact that it was now a distant crescent and appeared as though it had been halved. Ķatira whispered: 'God Almighty, the moon in Ķarauyl will never be as bright again as in the old days, milky white and chasing the darkness from this land!'

With trembling fingers, she loosened the buttons on her jacket, which were pressing hard into her chest.

Translated by Mitchell Albert

AIGUL KEMELBAYEVA
(b. 21.03.1965)

Aigul Kemelbayeva is a writer, screenwriter and literary critic. She graduated from Kirov Kazakh State University (now Äl-Farabi Kazakh National University, 1987) before going on to study fiction writing at Maxim Gorky Literary Institute in Moscow (1989–94). She worked for newspapers before taking up the position of head of the Literary Department at Ķalibek Ķuanyšbaev (Qalibek Quanyshbayev) Kazakh State Academic Theatre.

Kemelbayeva is the author of a variety of prose works, including a short story for children, 'Žetinši ķŭrlyķķa saâhat' (A Trip to the Seventh Continent, 1986), a collection of short stories, *Tobylġysaj* (2001), and a novel, *Mŭnara* (The Tower, 2003), as well as essay collections: Mǎžnùn žùrek (Majnun-Heart, 2013) and *Sôz-Hikmet* (Words of Wisdom, 2016). She has published more than two hundred literary articles and essays in major Kazakhstani papers, many of which reflect on Kazakh literature in a wider, world literature perspective. Her short stories have been collected in *Nezavisimyy Kazakhstan: Antologiya Sovremennoy Literatury* (Kazakhstan During the Years of Independence: An Anthology of Modern Literature) published in 2013 in Moscow and translated into Turkish, and in a German anthology of international prose, *Glückliche Wirkungen: Eine Literarische Reise in Bessere Welten* (Berlin, 2017). She adapted Maġžan Žùmabaev's (Magzhan Zhumabayev) short story 'Šolpannyŋ kùnäsi' (Šolpan's Sin) into the film *Kùnä* (Sin, 2005; dir. by Bolat Šǎrip).

She is the recipient of the Daryn State Youth Award for Literature (2000), as well as nineteen other literary awards, including the Baubek Bùlķyšev Literary Prize of the Kazakhstan's Union of Journalists (1998). She has been a member of the Kazakhstan Writers' Union since 2001 and won the Soros Foundation – Kazakhstan award for a debut novel with *Mŭnara* (2000).

Kôkenaj and Ḳalḳaman

Dedicated to the bright memory of Ǎnuarbek Isahanùly, the direct descendant of Kôkenaj batyr

Ḳalḳaman escaped his tribe on account of love...[1]

The events narrated in the poem 'Ḳalḳaman-Mamyr' (1912), by the great poet and philosopher Šǎkerim Ḳùdajberdiùly, took place exactly two hundred years earlier by the River Syr.

Polaris, the guiding star of the north, was born on the sky.

In a dream, Ḳalḳaman saw one of his very distant ancestors, from the seventh preceding generation. The old man was walking a wet, straight path through the mountains, towards the smoky horizon. A cloth sack covered his horse's head. A second rider followed, astride one horse and leading another.

Near the banks of the Syrdariâ, Ḳalḳaman had been for a stroll with his friend Itbaḳa. During troubled times, Itbaḳa had lost both his parents; in terms of kinship and community, therefore, this sorrowful son was counted among the dead. Itbaḳa was ready to die without any fear, believing in the old expression: 'After death, there is no humiliation'. In one of the more brutal battles, Itbaḳa had made way for Kôkenaj, giving that great hero his own horse and thereby saving his life.

A messenger arrived with news of a terrible rumour: the forces of the Dzungar Khanate, like melted ice on the ocean, were preparing to raid the peaceful Arġyn and Najman tribes. Kazakhs had enjoyed a calm winter that year; however, with mid-spring, when the cuckoos began singing in the woods, the number of invaders had doubled. The messenger had also alerted the Ùjsin tribe of the Senior *žùz*[2] that the Kyrgyz inhabiting the wide, open mountains and the Žetiôgiz River with their myriad horses were supplying the Dzungar chief Tayiji with weapons and food; they also equipped their horses. The Kyrgyz were sympathetic to the Dzungar and Kalmyk Khanates, and promised to join their war against the Kazakhs.

---

[1] From 'Ḳalḳaman-Mamyr' by Šǎkerim Ḳùdajberdiùly. Translated by the National Bureau of Translations.

[2] The *žùz* are ancient Kazakh tribal divisions. The Senior *žùz* inhabit the southern and south-eastern parts of Kazakhstan; the Middle *žùz* are found in the central, eastern and northern parts of the country; and the Junior *žùz* derive from the west and south-west.

By then, the clans inhabiting Žetisu and Ķaratau were exhausted from moving back and forth, fleeing each invasion. All young Kazakhs, including Ķalķaman and Itbaķa, had become accustomed to sleeping with their scabbards and combat knives. In better days, they would roam the steppe freely, visiting any Kazakh dwellings they came across.

Someone – a warrior? No, a dervish – was walking along the road, hurrying beside the Syrdariâ and scaring the bustards flocked there like ants. The young men lying on the green grass, their horses tied up, raised their heads at once.

'Greetings to you, young men!' the dervish addressed them. 'May God save your souls! Damned, rotten life!'

He settled down on the grass on his back, put his sack on his head and fell asleep immediately, snoring. He dozed a bit, woke up quickly and then stared at the steppe stretching into the distance.

'Our ancients bore witness that this place, the Ķarahan Hills, once was a virgin land ruled by Itbaķa beg!'[3] he said.

Itbaķa flinched, surprised to hear his name spoken by the stranger.

'I do not own a house or a hearth', continued the dervish. 'The leaves are my blanket, the ground is my bed. I'm as meek as a lamb. Dervishes often move to and fro, from one place to another, existing like that. You are always under threat on the battlefield, my lad, annihilator of Kalmyks. Your enemies will curse you, demanding: "A humiliating death for the Kazakh!" By the way, you will live long.'

'I wouldn't say that everywhere I go, I see Ķorķyt's grave',[4] replied Itbaķa. 'Probably, death more resembles a lightning bolt that strikes you suddenly.'

'I'm making my way to our forefather Ķorķyt's grave, in fact', said the dervish. 'Nomads will move from the Syrdariâ soon. You, brave men, have your targets. I know you're mighty combatants, but be cautious – you are not quick to obey the elders, and this will cause you many troubles. You will bear the hard life of a warrior, making the woods your home, abandoning your clan against your will.'

He turned his bronze face to Ķalķaman, and his eyes grew sharp. 'My respectable young man', he said to him, 'you are the honourable son of a famous tribe. It is said that if a girl does not cast the first glance, a man will not see her at all. Your glory will be as bright as Ķorķyt's light, illuminating the years to come. Be careful with your sentiments and emotions!'

---

[3] *Beg* – title for noblemen, more specifically, a lower military-administrative rank after khan.

[4] Ķorķyt was an eighth-/ninth-century philosopher, poet and musician. According to legend, he sought immortality as his life drew to a close. In lonely torment, he hollowed out a precursor to the *ķobyz*, a classical Kazakh stringed instrument associated with shamanic healing. Playing its music, he staved off death – until he fell asleep and was bitten by a venomous snake. Thus the saying: 'Wherever you go, there is Ķorķyt's grave' (i.e. you can't avoid death).

The dervish took out a flute and played a mournful melody, which sounded like a camel calf bewailing the loss of its mother. Then he started to ponder aloud: 'When the mother Syr was named Ķyzyl-Dariâ and flowed across the gigantic Ķaraķùm, its channels never dried, by the power of Almighty; it flowed as if it wept from being thirsty in the wild sands. Since our ancestors dwelled in the Ķarahan Mountains, the Syr flowed to the Kerderi Sea, which was renamed the Ôgiz Sea; I suppose people have forgotten about those years. Ķorķyt was born during that peaceful time. A legend says that once upon a time, a slave from the Syr who was begging for his freedom had a prophetic dream: the Creator of the world, the Almighty, showed the rainbow to his beloved slave. Can you imagine this Absolute Power selecting stars with different colours of flowers, and joining them into a brilliant arc? Green, yellow, red and blue, shining... why was it hard to believe, then, that two great waters should stream into the sea? When the earth and sky merge, the soul of a man rises up. According to our ancestors' premonition, the two waters which flowed into the Khazar Sea – the Syrdariâ and the Âmudariâ – changed direction and streamed towards the Kerderi Sea, a sacred area, enabling the Noġaj, a tribe rich with *batyrs*,[5] to shelter from invasions and wars. Now it is your turn, and you must stand in defence... If you do not mind, let's have our dinner here.'

They hunted for bustards, dug a triangular hearth and started the fire. The flames illuminated the rays of the sunset.

'Since ancient times', continued the dervish, 'when they escaped from their enemies, my people acquired the habit of returning to the Syrdariâ, calling it "Great Mother". The Betpaķdala Desert defends its saiga antelopes, and its Kazakhs, too. A silent desert is a shelter for a person; this truth is familiar only to dervishes and tumbleweeds. When people move from their lands, they lose their consciousness. The folk who are *alive* greet each other. Where are your casks as wide as lakes, full of *ķymyz*[6]? Where is your *tuyrlyķ*[7] made of mink fur? Were they left in the Ertis or Esil or Nùra rivers when we hastily abandoned our lands? A thief will die on the ride, as the saying goes. As the Dzungars' invasions of our lands are wrong, their guts will be eaten by dogs. Before the stars in the sky fade away and the first rays of the day arrive, I pray to the Almighty. Do not forget that Tùrkistan was the centre of spirituality for our prophet predecessors. A human being is mortal. Remember that all your noblemen will be buried there. I witnessed a hundred wild geese in flight, hit by sudden lightning; and I saw how seventy of them fell immediately from the sky, dropping on the ground. I was bewildered by the force of a golden

---

[5] *Batyr* – originally term for 'hero' or 'valiant warrior', roughly equivalent to the European knight; nowadays the term signifies military or masculine prowess.

[6] *Ķymyz* – beverage of fermented mare's milk highly esteemed for its refreshing qualities; it is the main drink for special occasions.

[7] *Tuyrlyķ* – a thick covering for the lower part of a yurt, typically made of felt.

arrow! Dzungars and Kalmyks will still attempt to destroy the Kazakhs. In forty years' time, even peaceful people are likely to see such a disaster.'

The dervish kept silent during dinner. Relaxing afterward, he settled down on the ground. In the morning, there was no sign of him. The two young men remembered only his last words.

Among the peoples who bear the eye-shaped insignia, the Tobyḳty are particularly adept in moving on horseback and camelback; the Arġyn and Noġaj tribes had seen many invasions – generations of their people were brought up in cradles on horseback. The Dzungars and Kalmyks had defeated the Najmans and Kerejs and pushed them away from Altaj and Esil. When these tribes had been expelled from their lands, the legendary sage Ănet Baba was seven years old. Since then, seventy-seven years had passed; by that time, the Dzungars in the east had become powerful. For Kazakhs, it was a matter of survival: the age of peace, food abundance and plentiful horses had long disappeared. The Arġyn-Ḳypšaḳs, Najman- Ḳoŋyrat and Kerej-Uaḳs could not find any rest along the banks of the Esil and Nùra rivers, in the fertile and rich steppes of Saryarḳa. These tribes migrated to the Ùjsin Senior žùz and Junior žùz lands, escaping their enemies and moving nearer to Tùlkibas, Ḳazyġùrt, Židelibajsyn, Ḳozybasy, Šu, Žetisu and Ùš ḳiân in search of territory.

Since the seasonal birds had flown over Tyrnauyz and crossed over Mount Ḳap, reaching the Syrdariâ, Bajġazy's daughter Mamyr had changed. In the lakes, rich in thickets of reeds, swans would not leave their cygnets until the first cold. Beautiful Mamyr, Bajġazy's single daughter – herself like a cygnet (for *mamyr* means 'cygnet', as well as the month of May) – had not been engaged to anyone yet. She was living with her parents, as was said, 'on the right side' – a reference to the traditional place in the yurt where daughters who had not yet been married resided. Although it was high time for her to get married, no one dared to send matchmakers to Bajġazy, a wealthy and respectable man. They did not wish to embarrass him – he who had raised his daughter like a boy – by reminding him, implicitly, that he did not have an heir. The Kazakh tribes had settled and grazed horses in the steppes since the time of Alaša Khan, their common ancestor. Beautiful Mamyr also grazed horses, and carried a bow with arrows. The neighbours pitied Bajġazy for not having an heir – but nobody would say so out loud.

Mamyr gathered the horses, left the mares to the stallion and returned to her *auyl*.[8] On her way home, she met two young men. She recognised Ăjtek's youngest son and Olžaj *batyr*'s brother, Ḳalḳaman. Mamyr had been a rider

---

[8] *Auyl* – socio-economic formation considered to constitute the heartland of the nation and a basis for an ethnic and cultural union of the nomadic community. Consisting of 50–70 yurts in the eighteenth century, it developed into its current permanent state of 'rural settlement' (of a minimum of 100 dwellers) when Kazakhs adopted a settled mode of life in the nineteenth and twentieth centuries. *Auyl* can also be used as a synonym for 'native land' and 'homeland', concepts revered by the Kazakhs.

since birth, and Ḳalḳaman had achieved the same level as she had – he boasted of his speedy horse and proposed a race. The noise from his horses' hooves summoned the other two, and the three riders galloped along the steppe, racing like birds flying in the sky.

When the elders attended a dinner elsewhere, the young people of the *auyl* organised a traditional party for young people – a *bastaṇ̇ġy*. Having exchanged her 'male' clothes for a woman's garments, Mamyr appeared as slender and striking as a falcon. She wore a bird-beak ring on her finger, moon-shaped *šolpy* – ringing pendants – in her braids and chained silver earrings. Thus did everyone observe her wearing such an outfit for the first time, and no one could hide their surprise at registering her beauty. Mamyr had never made use of ornaments, but that night she also wore an embroidered *taḳiâ* cap, to which her mother had affixed owl feathers from her own parents' collection – they had once been famous in the district for collecting them. Ḳalḳaman and Mamyr had splendid matching headgear: hers the feathered *taḳiâ*, his a *bôrik*, a round, fur-trimmed cap.

After midnight, while playing *aḳsùjek*,[9] Ḳalḳaman exclaimed: 'How lovely you are, like a tender duckling, girl in the feathered hat! Alas! You are my clan sister, darling Mamyr, Bajġazy's Mamyr!

Mamyr smiled proudly and replied: 'I'm not the one for you, Ḳalḳaman; we are forbidden to each other…' The young man's heart was set aflame upon hearing this response. Mamyr noticed his look of passion, and a sudden idea struck her. (Its source was the epic poetry of love, and she cast Ḳalḳaman in the role of the prophet Yusuf, who was said to have fallen so in love with Zulaikha.) Consumed with desire, the girl said: 'I would be grateful to the Creator if you were to become mine. We are not the first ones who shall break the law of the steppe, which does not allow us to be engaged to co-descendants until the seventh generation. I won't turn away from you, even if they kill me tomorrow. What do you respond to this, my love?'

When Ḳalḳaman realised the world would be dark without Mamyr, he shivered from the horror of losing his love; however, he understood that he was committing a transgression. The two lovers met each other near the *auyl* at dusk. Although he was sure of his love for Mamyr, Ḳalḳaman confessed his doubts to her.

'Duckling, Mamyržan, Bajġazy's favourite', he said, sitting astride his horse and looking straight into the girl's eyes. 'A stallion – the leader of the herd – will send away the fillies. The leader never touches them, because they all belong to a single herd. One drop of poison infects a whole cauldron of wine. Our ancestors were afraid of mixing the blood of kin. How can we hide the fact that we both belong to the same clan?'

---

[9] *Aḳsùjek* – lit. 'white bone', a game played by adolescents in the summer; participants throw a cow's long shinbone into the woods and run searching for it. The objective is both to exercise attention and have a framework for socialising with the opposite sex.

'Ķalķaman, those words do not mean anything to me. I have made my choice, my darling! I met you with the help of the Almighty. I fell in love with you; I see how noble you are. Though I was born a girl, I took the role of a son for my father. How long shall I reign as Bajġazy's golden falcon? I am fifteen now, and you haven't been engaged yet. We are not able to break the rules governing marriage. In the worst case, we shall wait and see!'

The clouds travelled along the dark sky, and thunder raged with bright flashes of blue lightning, frightening the earth. Hail came down with fury alongside the rain. Yet Mamyr felt nothing but passion for her lover, and would have felt this way even if the lightning had struck her.

At last, the gentle summer season found the Middle *žùz* tribes that settled around the Ķaratau Mountains extending to the Šu River. Cuckoos began their mating calls – the males were relentless. In the lakes overgrown with cattails and marshes were many nests of crows, grey herons, ibises and bitterns. Birds did not cease their noisemaking all night.

The lovers met again in the place called Bôriojnaķ.

It was soft with thick cattails and bulrushes. Mamyr entrusted her horses to the stallion and arrived to see her man.

'I understand you', she said. 'It's true that no one ever heard of a man from the Tobyķty marrying a girl from his own clan.' Her eyes shone brightly. 'My fourth ancestor in the Tobyķty, great-grandfather Sary, had four sons: Mămbetej, Ùmbetej, Mămbetsopy and Kišik. From Mămbetej, my father, Bajġazy, was born. From Kišik, your father, Ăjtek, was born. If they are brothers, we are their grandchildren. Do not blame me for describing the family tree. I suffer much from the fact that both of us are co-descendants. Today a rider from the Najman steppes visited us to make a match and hung his silver-topped whip, unfolding it. My father did not return the whip. This means I'm engaged now. You cannot ask a girl's hand who has been engaged. Do you agree, Ķalķaman?'

'My darling, my swan, I'm ready to sacrifice myself for your sake!' replied Ķalķaman in a halting voice. 'Tell me you are mine; the rest is in vain. The Prophet also never knew his future.'

That day, old Ănet Baba had a nightmare. An attendant flung open the doors of the white yurt, and, without kneeling, entered and announced: '*Tăte*,[10] I have terrible news. Kôkenaj *batyr* has sent me to inform you that two wrongdoers of our tribe have sinned and brought shame on us by breaking the great law that has existed since Žănibek Khan's time. Kôkenaj is outraged and furious. He seeks to kill these two lunatics. The brothers Olžaj and Bajbôri are grief-stricken; they are asking if Ķalķaman should take the girl and escape from the *auyl*...'

'Do not rush, my son; tell me these things without haste.'

---

[10] *Tăte* – depending on the region, a form of address to an older woman, or man, meaning 'aunt', 'sister', 'uncle', may also signify 'mother' or 'father'.

'Ķalķaman and Mamyr have married secretly! Kôkenaj *batyr* is saying that Mǎmbetej and Ùmbetej will punish the wrongdoers by themselves, and if the girl's side consider their honour, they must do as he has ordered. I come to tell you this, *tǎte*. If I am misspeaking, please forgive me!'

In early years – when Tǎuke Khan's grandfather, Esim Khan, the Brave Giant, conquered Tùrsyn Khan in Taškent – one of his daughters, Ķoņyrbike, was given to Sary. Kišik and Mǎmbetsopy were born to her; Mǎmbetej and Ùmbetej were born from Sary's first wife.

Ǎnet Baba, who was eighty years old at this time, sat on the *tekemet*, the ornate felt mat covering the floor of the yurt, with his eyes shut. He swayed from side to side, deeply affected by the news. Hard times had arrived. If Ķalķaman and Mamyr had indeed left the *auyl* hand in hand, this would be a heavy blow for the tribe.

From Ǎjtek's first wife, Olžaj was born; from his second wife, Bajbôri and Ķalķaman. Ķalķaman had now reached his sixteenth year. By that time, Kôkenaj, who descended from Ùmbetej, was about sixty years old and the leading *batyr* of the Arġyn tribe. He considered the Kalmyks his permanent enemies – he could raid them forty times during a night, like a wolf. He was not only famous in Tobyķty, but also among wider Arġyn and the Middle *žùz*. Kôkenaj had lived his entire life waging bloody battles, having his meals on horseback and sleeping with his spear next to him.

He was a powerful man who was used to selecting the best horses, and had a very stubborn, unforgiving character. Ǎnet Baba, leader of the Middle *žùz*, was visited by a young advisor of the Senior *žùz*, Tôle. Tôle *bi*[11] hailed from Ùjsin territory. He had studied religion in Taškent, and had good knowledge of the secrets of the natural world, and of geography. The pale face of the wise old man, once radiant with wisdom, was now sunk in confusion. 'Oh, dear', he said, 'the elders used to say that nobody hears how owls fly, and nobody blames young men for their sins. Ķalķaman, my son, will bear many curses and suffer much! What should I do? Hares may pull dead lions by their beards.'

He wanted to speak with his nephew Kôkenaj face to face and come to an understanding. Yet Kôkenaj did not accept the old man's proposal to give Mǎmbetej a dowry and double the fine for the wrongdoing.

'I'll ask the *bies* to adjudicate Ķalķaman's shameful behaviour at trial', Kôkenaj replied. 'As for Bajġazy's daughter, I'll kill her myself – and no one can stop me, no mercy for her. I'm not going to forgive them, although they are of my own clan. To break the rules of the ancestors is a great sin; it is the beginning of a malady... The cause of any event, any disaster, any crime is a woman! It must be you who takes responsibility for stopping this nonsense... those two have brought shame on us! Our tribes have suffered many losses from the red-headed Kalmyk invasions; it is outrageous when we destroy ourselves

---

[11] Tôle (1663–1756) was the head *bi* (judge) of the Kazakh Senior *žùz*, as well as an orator and poet.

by neglecting the codes of the steppe.' He said all this as if making a vow, gripping his scabbard firmly in his hand.

'Kôkenaj, be patient; the Qur'an and the *shari'ah* permit the marriage of two grandchildren. All human beings emerged from two pairs and a drop of blood. It is regretful that the race of Adam and Eve occasionally make errors. And mixing blood is not a crime for other nations of the Earth, only Kazakhs. However, Kazakhs... I agree completely with the point that our blood is pure because of men's honour', said Ănet Baba, looking down.

'*Tăte*! You are encouraging those jealous kin around us to assume that the Tobyķty are insane. They knew the fact that it is abnormal to marry until the seventh generation! I am not Kôkenaj if I allow anyone to break such a tradition, which has existed from Žănibek Khan's time, or if I am not able to stop the acts of perverts!'

'Do not blame the innocent – and don't make vows! They are not horses to sacrifice... both of them are of your own blood...'

'You are wrong, *tăte*! Marrying his own clan sister is a big crime. This behaviour can't be compared with a childish cousin's tricks. If he wanted to marry, there are many girls about! Ķalķaman has trampled on the traditions of the folk.'

Ănet Baba realised that, for Kôkenaj, Ķalķaman and Mamyr had become severed limbs. He was ready to murder them. Ănet Baba decided to save the young couple, no matter their crime.

'Although Tobyķty is a small community, it isn't degenerating', Kôkenaj continued. '*Tăte*, no one knows the *shari'ah* as well as you do. But the Qur'an teaches us not to marry our mothers, sisters or daughters. If anyone commits this shameful act, he is an unbeliever.'

Kôkenaj's harsh censure forced old Ănet Baba to weep with regret; the fierce words made his old bones ache. Kôkenaj *batyr*'s mother had been a Kalmyk, and people concluded that his strict character was his blood inheritance from her. The Kalmyk beg Ûlaly beheaded the Middle *žùz* leader Ķožabergen in 1647; Ķožabergen's wife, still pregnant, was enslaved by the raiders. His two brothers, Suyrbas's sons Ăli and Sary, were young. Thirteen years later, accompanied by Olžas *batyr*, Sary exacted vengeance for his brother's death, defeating Ûlaly in battle. Ûlaly had had a Kazakh wife, and their beautiful daughter was given to Ûmbetej. Kôkenaj was born from this marriage. His mother named him 'Kuknai' in Kalmyk, which meant 'Green Poppy'. He became the commander of Tăuke Khan's force, and was famed as a courageous warrior, hard as an iron, who knew no mercy for Kalmyks or anyone else. He would go on to cross the thousand bridges of Hell, fighting for months and years on the borders of his land.

A month after his argument with Ănet Baba, a terrible rumour spread among the humble Najman and Kerej tribes that Kôkenaj had murdered Mamyr, shooting her in the heart with an arrow. Thus Mamyr was killed by her brutal clan brother: she had not been able to utter her last word – '*apa*'

– 'mother' before dying, like a swan, blinking her tender eyes. Not long after that, half of the twelve clans of the Arġyn (the Ķarakesek, the Ķanžyġaly, the Bãsentiin, the Atyġaj, the Ķarauyl and the Tobyķty) held a meeting, at which people shared their great grief and marked the event.

The renowned Ķanžyġaly orator Išpek *bi* made a declaration, as loudly and clearly as a wild goose: '*Bies* and *begs*, listen to me! Oh, Ãnet Baba, wise man, righteous man! Ķalķaman is too young, and has shamed Kôkenaj *batyr*. We are noblemen; we have sprung from an honest nation; we were not born from slaves. Rumour, like a downwind, spreads far. Our people are gentle, like lambs. I cannot say that this great tragedy will not pass to the Ķypšaķ, Najman, Ķoŋyrat, Kerej and Noġaj, as well as the Ùjsin, Alban and Dulat, Ķaŋly, Ysty, Šanyšķyly, Ãlim's Kete-Sômekej, Žetiru's Tabyn-Tama, Bajùly – all sons of Alšyn, even to those Adajs who dwell in the sands neighbouring the Turkmen, Karakalpak and Bashkir. This crime, and our shame, will be known to all.

'We've maintained our honourable name and pride, and have been highly respected since the time of Oġyz. A daughter is but a guest in a house. Through marriage, our daughters belong to other tribes, is this not so? We witnessed the shame when a brother married his own clan sister. Our ancestors decreed that no man among us may marry a girl until the seventh generation, because a weak and nondescript thing may be born from them. Our predecessors preached this in order to maintain the purity of the race.

'This great disaster is beyond enduring. I do not blame the kinship. We all descend from Ķanžyġaly and Tobyķty, two related tribes. Wise Ãnet Baba, you are the seed of great nomads, our spiritual guide. Please, give us your answer; do not mystify these people! The nation's power is in its heroes; a hero's power is in the nation. Do not become involved with undesirables. These troublemakers are to blame. What would we do if tiny Tobyķty separated into two because of them? We were born from Kazakhs who had abandoned places when they took offence. Our brother committed a crime – that is why the folk are waiting for the elder's decision. It is intolerable to behave as slaves, and forget the ancestors' blessings. This conflict is not the conflict over widows; it is to avoid future maladies! We grow because our blood is clean. If the clans mix their own blood, we are certain to beget monsters. Say your piece, even if the sinner is of your blood! A bad example is infectious. Say your piece, if you are a faithful *bi*. Think of your folk!'

'Ķalķaman, my dear boy, apple of my eye, how could I blame you?' said the *baba*, his eyes full of tears. 'I shall not kill this child myself!'

'Better a glorious death than a shameful flight!' said Išpek *bi*. 'They say an eagle on the rocks pushes out one of its own eaglets. Kôkenaj killed his clan sister because the pride of his tribe was offended, and the kinship of Mãmbetej and Ùmbetej agreed. Otherwise, they would not want to keep relationship ties. Do you want the family of Sary *bi* to become foes after this? Even if it were so difficult to decide the matter, releasing Ķalķaman without any punishment would be a blow to the clan. Sacrifice the ears, keep the head!'

Although Änet Baba was exhausted from the debates, he insisted on protecting the young man: 'My people's hearts are merciful, and their wills are heavenly strong. They never wish for anyone to die young. Be kind to your kinfolk. The Almighty favours forgiveness and kindness. The resentment of the innocent will cause us many troubles... Do you wish for me to kill this child, stoning him? Who hasn't gone mad from falling in love with a woman? Did you forget that you were once ready to die for them? Are you willing to break my wings and pull off my tail? A man learns everything from Nature. Birds have thick feathers in winter and change in summer, acquiring light ones. Nature is in opposition to cruelty. When birds want babies, they begin to nest. The thick forests bloom with the help of birds; our land thrives with the help of the younger generation. If the young commit errors while young, this is not an enormity... May God the Great Redeemer forgive their sins! A sin is a gate that leads to sincere repentance.'

The crowd listening to the *baba* was against executing Ḳalḳaman, and hoped he would fight out this debate. But the two sides could not come to any concord. In the end, Änet Baba declared that the punishment should be what is called *oḳ bajlau*. According to the ancient tradition, a person sentenced to death would ride through a gauntlet of archers, who would let their arrows fly as he galloped by. Survival meant innocence, and death meant guilt. While Ḳalḳaman rode on a speedy horse, Kôkenaj would be among those drawing their bows at him. Everyone knew well that Kôkenaj was a highly skilled archer. In one battle with the Kalmyk Khoren, warriors witnessed him catch an arrow speeding toward him and return it in kind to his enemy. This time, if the arrow reached the victim, it would be considered just. Ḳalḳaman would be blamed for his true, passionate love. 'Oh, Creator, Almighty, you are the judge of what is white or black, you provide the answer', concluded the old man in grief.

The slope of the Bôriojnaḳ Pass, suffused with the aromatic flavour of wormwood, was crowded with warriors who had arrived to watch the *oḳ bajlau* carried out. Several great warriors were selected to carry out the cruel ritual. Most of them were noted *batyrs* who had been raised on battlefields and ridden hundreds of miles on horseback in darkness, cold or heat, ready to drink their enemies' blood.

When Kôkenaj *batyr*, on his dappled white horse, joined the line of archers, a warrior from the group blocked his way. Kôkenaj remembered this young man, who had saved his life by giving him his horse during one battle. He was a relative of Mamyr's mother.

'Kôkenaj *aġa*,[12] may I have a word?' said the young man. 'I am from the Najman tribe and wish to speak. A wolf cannot eat its pup! To witness two deaths of your own blood will be difficult for you. Your folk is against the young man's death. My ancestor and hero Kišilik fought against Genghis Khan, and was a mighty warrior. I beg you, give your turn to me! I'll aim to

---

[12] *Aġa* – form of address to an older man, which can be translated as 'brother', 'uncle'.

miss Ķalķaman deliberately. *Aġa*, do not let a future warrior be killed because of a girl! Ķalķaman is not your ancient foe. He is not a duck in the woods, to kill him in such a way.'

Ķalķaman did not beg for his life. Ănet Baba opened his hands to give his blessings. The old *baba* pleaded with the deities for mercy for this child; he played his *ķobyz* and entered into a trance, attempting to dispel the excessive negative energy from the spirit world. Ķalķaman reflected on his carefree days, when he was as unimpeded as the wind on the steppe, drinking the water of youth. He decided to wear his hauberk and meet his death on the field as a target. As he prepared, Ănet Baba encouraged him: 'If you are a real man, then be one! If you are to die, you shall; if you are to live, you shall restore your honour.'

The territories of the Ķosaral River, since the time of Ormanbet *bi*'s death and the deaths of many of the Noġaj, had become an eternal, silent tomb. They could be seen from the horizon. Ķalķaman rode through this land as nine arrows were loosed in a single instant, as wild as birds, before failing: the archers had not dared to kill the youth. Kôkenaj became violent; his cruel eyes were fierce, and even his grey beard looked furious. He had called horseback 'home'; now he drew back his bow and shot. The arrow nearly knocked Ķalķaman off his horse, but he proved fortunate. He clung to the animal's head and galloped away.

Ķalķaman's sister had disguised herself as a man, and watched the scene unfold from the crowd. She had had an upsetting dream in recent nights, and had prepared herself for the worst. 'Kôkenaj did not listen to the young warrior of the Najman, whose ancestor had battled the fearsome Genghis Khan. What does he have in his mind?' whispered one of the witnesses to the other. 'See, how bravely that young man claimed. If Kôkenaj gave his turn to this warrior, I was sure this man would shoot a failed arrow. What a man!'

The Tobyķty side roared, '*Aķ žol! Maâboz!*'[13] Then its riders galloped after the injured Ķalķaman. The arrow had broken the silver side of the saddle and hit the young man's leg, nearly breaking the bone. Yet he rode as fast as a wolf. His pursuers could not catch up: he was beyond reach. When he saw he was clear, he stopped and cut the tail off his horse, which signified that he was leaving his clan forever and halted his pursuers. His childhood friends from the Najman and Ķanžyġaly tribes did not stop chasing after him, however, and in the end they reached him.

Kazakh men usually took two horses with them – one for riding, and another tethered to the first, with which to alternate during a long trip. Knowing that, Ķalķaman's sister sent a horse bearing two sacks of provisions after her brother: some *ķurt* – salty cheese; dried horsemeat; two flagons of water; and flint and firewood. Thus, the young man had two horses with him, the second tethered to the first, and he alternated them during the long journey. Itbaķa

---

[13] *Aķ žol!* – Godspeed! *Maâboz!* – battle cry of the Tobyķty.

jumped astride his brown stallion and rode out to Ķalķaman, who was bent double and bandaging his broken leg tightly with the sleeves of his garment. Tears streamed from the eyes of his stallion.

'Don't do this... stop!' said Itbaķa abruptly. For it was he who had asked Kôkenaj *batyr* for permission to aim at Ķalķaman and shoot to miss. 'If you leave, the other tribes will think the Tobyķty are cruel and wicked. Although you harbor a grudge against your people, do not forget that we descend from Alaš!'

'Unfortunately, I'm dead to Tobyķty', replied Ķalķaman. 'I cut my horse's tail. It is a final sign of my departure, Itbaķa. They shall count me among the dead. So please ask them to bury me – ask them to push my spear into the ground and put a black banner on it! I cannot say they are my clan. I am not desperate; however, my soul is burning! How can I forget what torture I endured? Tell them not to look for me after this!'

He fastened his silver belt to his hip and led one of his horses to the shimmering horizon, like the ancient Bashkir and Oġyz. Then he disappeared. As he rode from one slope to another, the road widened. The grass grew green and thick. Tulips bloomed. Summer arrived on the fragrances of numerous flowers.

Back in the *auyl*, one of Ķalķaman's *žeņge*, sisters-in-law, shed tears and recited some burial verses she had composed:

If a horse longs for its herd, it will twitch its head and ears.
If a warrior longs for his tribe, he will saddle his horse and ride!

Have you ever seen a land dearer than the Syrdariâ?
Do you know a tribe closer-knit than the Tobyķty?

Ķalķaman, you were a leader! Ķalķaman, you won't be back; you won't forgive your kin. You won't live with us any more. You'll not see your land any more. We'll not find our noble man, wherever we may search for him, whenever we try to spot his traces, even in the Milky Way!

I am a sorrowful one. I lost my *ķajny*, my brother-in-law. I lost my wings! He will be back during the rains of March; he will be back during April the beautiful!

He will arrive from distant lands. Then the steppe will flower. The dead can't be resurrected, but the living will return!

Ķalķaman headed from the west to the south-east, orienting himself by the Polar Star to the land where his mother, Ķaldyķyz, had been born. Ķaldyķyz was of the Ùjsin, and married into the Tobyķty according to Kazakh tradition when she reached marriageable age. Her brother, Šapyrašty Ajķym, resided in the northern part of the Alatau Mountains.

Ķalķaman passed countless gazelles grazing on the steppe. Then it rained a deluge; the sky thundered, and lightning crashed upon the earth. The young man was now sick, with a high temperature, and found himself losing consciousness. He could barely open his eyes, but when he did, someone in a white turban was turning to him. Is this a dream? Ķalķaman wondered. He remembered his tethered horses and raised his head – and came face-to-face with the old dervish who had once approached him on the banks of the Syrdariâ. The man picked some sorrel with arrow-shaped leaves and applied them to Ķalķaman's wound. Kneeling, he untied his turban, which looked for all the world to Ķalķaman like a burial shroud.

'I swear by the name of the Prophet Muhammad, my white turban is indeed my burial shroud! May God bless you. As they say, among any forty people you meet, one might be Ķydyr, who will bless you. A saint is God's favourite servant. Baba Tùkti Šašty Ắziz, my spiritual guide, gave me the vision. Here, this plant is for treatment of wounds, it will cure you. So... what are you doing alone on the steppe?'

'A dead hero never chooses the ground upon which to die. I am dead; I hope my tomb will not be among my tribe!'

The old man said: 'Are you from the Syr, or Sauran, like an ancient Kete? The wings of a falcon become stronger when it flies.' He noted his tribal insignia. 'Let us wish for good. Food for both the young man and the wolf is on its way, they say. If you cross over that slope, you'll come to an *auyl*; a bonesetter will set your broken leg.'

Ķalķaman still took long to recover his senses, and his feelings were as vague as fog. However, he was ready to see everything on his way, and to trust anyone he met. After sunset, the pair ate some salted, grilled meat and drank some *ķymyz* from a leather dish.

'In the north, in the dense forests, a yellow-headed, unfamiliar tribe dwells', said the dervish. When the Pole Star appears in the sky and falls into the blue eyes of those inhabitants, there is night on that side; however, at this very time you'll find your Senior žùz relatives.' When Ķalķaman recovered, he caught wild animals on the steppe and grilled their meat, preparing further provisions for the long journey. When he was thirsty, he had his *torsyķ* filled with water. The Alatau Mountains had streams, and were full of wild goats and their kids, and wild argali sheep and deer, which frolicked on the rocks. There was no border between land and sky. The air was fresh and cool, fragrant with the scents of different grasses and flowers. The young man hadn't experienced such delights of the senses before. How on the Earth could such a pleasant place exist, like Eve's garden? The flavours and aromas of hundreds of fruits on the trees reached him, like stars in the expanse of night sky.

At last, he entered into a region of thick woods and gardens of apple trees, which covered the slopes like a newborn's swaddling. Here, wild bears foraged and birds picked fruit from the trees until the end of autumn. When the Pole Star reached the horizon, Ķalķaman navigated the millions of stars in the Milky Way and finally came to his maternal uncle's *auyl*.

Twelve years passed. The Tobyķty had sought Ķalķaman, but a great famine interrupted their plans. The following summer, the Tobyķty resolved to try again, but new Dzungar raids saw many of them killed off. The survivors faced one of the most terrible events in Kazakh history, the *Aķtaban Šŭbyryndy* – the 'Years of Great Disaster'. The armies of Galdan Tseren, the eldest son of the Kalmyk Khan Tsewang Rabtan, invaded Kazakh lands like seven-headed dragons, and annihilated two-thirds of the inhabitants. They cut the bellies of pregnant women; they skewered toddlers on spears. In the days when all warriors used spears and swords, Kazakh warriors could face their foes with ease; however, the Dzungars were first to possess firearms, with which their numerous forces unleashed lead bullets as though they were raindrops. The Kazakhs became refugees, fleeing from steppe to steppe and eating dried fruit, grass – anything they found growing on the land. They escaped barefoot, covering themselves with deerskins instead of blankets and living in little shelters formed from spears. For these refugees, camel milk was food and drink alike; to avoid dying from thirst, they drank the sap of birch trees, later giving rise to the expression *Ķajyŋ sauġan* ('milking the birch tree'). The events of this tragic time have been commemorated in the ballad *Elim-aj* ('My People'), sung about the children deprived of their parents, who were as defenceless as orphaned fawns.

During the Great Northern War between Russia and Sweden, the Russian Empire prospected for gold in the east to offset war expenses. Before building military fortifications on the borders inhabited by nomads, Russia deployed spies to the deserted territories by order of Peter the Great. Russia captured the northern lands, and the Dzungar Khanate, the eastern parts. The densely populated khanate began to fight for more land, moving west into Kazakh territories. Hundreds of thousands of Dzungars raided Kazakh lands along the banks of the Ertis and Esil rivers, thus denying even the birds any chance of inhabiting these places. Secret caravans from the khanates of Kokand, Khiva and Bukhara transported armour to the Dzungars; the Russian Empire provided them with guns, and they obtained bullets from the Swedes. Enemies from all parts raided Kazakh territories. There was a real threat to the existence of the tribes descended from Alaš.[14] Galdan Tseren had strengthened his kingdom and military force after his father's death; the seven rivers nourishing the fertile valley of the Blue Sea attracted the Dzungar tribes, and they added to their conquests. Alakôl, Bejne Sea, Keŋ Uaķ and Sasyķkôl were invaded by the Kalmyks. The Black Ertis flowed with blood and bodies.

---

[14] 'Alaš' – another name for the Kazakh people.

'Warriors! Unbelievers have captured your lands!' called an old *žyrau*[15] to his people in the war against the Dzungars. 'The motherland is dearer than gold; when the people stand, they can reach the sky!' The Kazakh armies lifted their clubs, spears and hammers against the invaders, and fired arrows into them. The Dzungar forces, countless though they were, never tended to their wounded or buried their dead: according to their beliefs, the law of the battlefield held that all casualties must be left behind.

In 1723, along the Syrdariâ and its two longest branches, the Aḳtal and Ḳaratal, Kôkenaj confronted the Dzungars with five thousand warriors, attacking them for a month until Kazakh clans moved west to the Ḳaratau Mountains and the Žajyḳ River, nearer to the Russian Empire. During this battle, Kôkenaj lost his six sons and Ӑnet Baba lost five.

The Dzungars' tactics, in response, consisted not of stealing livestock but killing more Kazakhs. Women hid their sons under cauldrons in their hearths, where they had gathered the corpses; in so doing, they saved the next generation. The vengeful Dzungars ordered the extermination of the families of Kôkenaj and Ӑnet Baba. They intended to take Kôkenaj's grandchildren and play with their bodies as if in a game of *kôkpar*.[16] One of Ӑnet Baba's sons, Šaḳabaj, survived, as did his wife, who gave a birth to a son – the last grandson, whom they called Baḳaj. Kôkenaj's six-year-old son, Žӑmeṇke, also survived, and his grandson Tùâḳ would later continue the line.

When the Great Disaster struck, many Kazakhs vowed to die rather than leave their land, and Ӑnet Baba, then ninety-seven years old, was among them. He wept like a baby in the cradle after his clan abandoned the territories. Long-necked cranes migrated in the sky above his head that summer.[17] During a brief interval between wars, Kôkenaj took the *baba*'s bones from Ḳošḳar Ata to the city of Tùrkistan, to inter in the mausoleum of the great Ḳoža Ahmet Âssaui.

The Kazakh refugees from the great war moved near the city of Sauran, on the right side of the Syrdariâ. Many were taken into slavery. In the two hundred years since this calamity, the members of several Kazakh generations joined Dzungar tribes; in turn, some Kalmyk and Dzungar widows, with their children, joined Kazakh families. Many captive women and girls became mothers to both tribes, and did not stop shaking their cradles. Kazakhs and Kalmyks struggled until the collapse of the Dzungar Khanate in 1758. The heaps of bones littering the steppes became tombs. Then the time of Abylaj Khan arrived, and Kazakh power was resurgent.

In the land of Ùjsin, and in the clan of Aḳsiyḳ Elibaj, Ḳalḳaman's uncle Šapyrašty Ajḳym welcomed him warmly and adopted his nephew into the clan.

---

[15] *Žyrau* – poet, performing his topical verses to music, but also an epic storyteller, military commander and counsellor to the rulers.

[16] *Kôkpar* – sport in which a headless goat carcass is advanced by players on horseback towards the opposing team's goal.

[17] This expression signifies the death of a person.

The uncle married Ķalķaman to three wives: the first was his widowed sister-in-law; the second, a widow captured in a battle; and the last, a young girl. The clan elders insisted that they themselves pay the price for Ķalķaman's marriage to the girl, out of respect for his courage in battle.

From then onward, Ķalķaman's descendants adopted the five-pointed insignia of the Šapyrašty Ajķym sub-clan. When asked, 'What's your bone?', referring to their lineage, they would answer: 'Ķalķaman Tobyķty'. The expression also arose, among people, '… as in Ķalķaman and Mamyr's conflict'.

Nor did the Ķanžyġaly, Tobyķty and Kùrleuit forget Ķalķaman. Although the Kùrleuit belonged to the Ķypšaķ tribe, Tobyķty's father Kenžesopy adopted him. During a festive occasion, in fact, when the Senior *žùz* Ķasķarau's horse took first place in a race, the Tobyķty side enquired about Ķalķaman.

The Tobyķty had moved from the Syrdariâ. From Ájtek's first wife, Olžaj was born. Olžaj had three sons, Ajdos, Ķajdos and Žandos. Ajdos's own four sons survived the wars. A Tobyķty clan numbering forty people crossed the Oral Mountains and reached Or, Elek and Ojyl. Further on, they stopped at the Mùġalžar Hills. They searched for better lands in the deltas of the Yrġyz and Torġaj rivers. Ajdos's four sons (Yrġyzbaj, Keŋgirbaj, Torġaj and Topaj) were born from his young wife during the seasonal migrations. In the waters of Kôtimtal, Kôtibaķ was born. During eventful periods of famine or war, Kazakhs would name their children Boķty ('Shitty'), Bitti ('Lousy'), Ķùrtty ('Wormy') or Ķylšyķ ('Tiny'), in order to save them from misfortune and the Evil Eye.

When Kôkenaj died from an arrow in 1728, his thirteen-year-old son Mamaj wept over him, his arms around his neck. He became Mamaj *batyr*, the khan of the Junior *žùz* during the reign of Nùraly Khan, and participated in the wars to defend Edil and Žajyķ, the Altaj and Tarbaġataj Mountains and the Bejne Sea from the invaders. Fifty years later, he led his clan to eight rivers in the mountains: his own ancestors' land. Kindiktau was inhabited by Arġyn-Najmans, who had moved earlier. Keŋgirbaj *bi*, Olžaj's son, strengthened the minor five-*bolys*[18] Tobyķty.

Translated by Mitchell Albert

---

[18] *Bolys* – administrative term adopted in the nineteenth century; it consisted of 10–15 *auyls*, each made up of 50–70 families.

DIDAR AMANTAI

(b. 5.02.1969)

Didar Amantai is a bilingual writer, poet, screenwriter and journalist. He studied philosophy at Kirov Kazakh State University (now Äl-Farabi Kazakh National University) and screenwriting at Žùrgenov (Zhurgenov) Institute of Theatre and Cinema (now Žùrgenov Kazakh National Academy of Arts; (grad. in 1994 and 1997 respectively). He worked for the *Zaman Ķazaķstan* and *Žas alaš* newspapers and for the Khabar television agency (1996–2004), later taking up the positions of director at the *Žas alaš* and *Azamat.kz* newspapers (2005–6), and of general director and editor-in-chief at *Nachnem a ponedelnika* (2004–8). He was the host of TV shows 'Abaj' and 'Zamandastar', broadcast from 2006 to 2008, as well as managing editor of Ķazaķfil′m (Kazakhfilm) studios (2009–15). He also served as inspector in the administration of the President of the Republic of Kazakhstan (2015–16), advisor to the Minister of Culture and Sport and director of the Semej Regional Branch of Ķazaķstan (Qazaqstan) Television and Radio Corporation.

His first collection of short stories, *Post Scriptum*, was published in 1996, followed by *Ķasterle meni* (Cherish Me, 2000), *Gùlder men kitaptar* (Flowers and Books, 2003), *Kùzgi randevu* (Autumn Rendezvous, 2005), *Ķarķaraly basynda* (In Ķarķaraly, 2010) and *Mahambet filosofiâsy* (Mahambet's Philosophy, 2014). His works have been translated into many languages, including English, French, Spanish, German, Italian, Russian, Chinese, Korean, Arabic, Turkish, Mongolian, Georgian, Finnish, Swedish and Uighur. He authored biopics of such well-known Kazakh figures as Nùrġisa Tilendiev, Älžappar Äbišev, Ķasym Amanžolov, Žùsipbek Elebekov, Mukhtar Magauin, and feature films *Găkku* (2011, dir. by Ġaziz Nasyrov) and *A-ġa oralu* (Returning to the Point 'A', 2011, dir. by Egor Konchalovsky).

Amantai has twice won the literary competition of the Soros Foundation – Kazakhstan, the Daryn State Youth Award (1999) and the Tarlan Hope Award (2007). He is also an Honoured Worker of the Republic of Kazakhstan (2013).

Your Cherished Eyes

Tap... tap... The two feet stamping down the pavement stopped suddenly. The gates of the big driveway, usually open, were now shut. Wondering, he waited a bit. *Tap...* He lifted the other foot. *Tap...* Confused, he continued pacing the street. The sound of his shoes on the cobbles could now barely be heard. *Tap...* Suddenly, he stumbled over a bucket made of birch bark and fell to his knees. The smart cap he wore slowly slid off his head.

Stretching as he got up off the ground, he stared at the enormous gates. In front of him stood the painted gate panels, tall and flat. These solid gates had an iron cross-brace belting the middle, and looked as heavy as stone. From not far away, he heard the soft, lively voices of a group of kids predicting the weather for the following day, and advancing cheerfully. They were talking about ancient times and geology. Millennia ago, continuous lightning and thunderstorms attacked the Earth. Hailstorms were ceaseless, the skies roared and land was obscured by the torrents of water flooding permanently over vast areas. The laughter and voices became distant as the kids disappeared. He stopped and looked around attentively.

His cap, embroidered with precious stones, was enlarged in a close-up. Red One, caressing his face, paid particular attention to his clothes; it zoomed in on his old shoes and then retreated swiftly. The steppe was in the frame now; a long shot depicted it in a bright image. Every low voice, bleak rustle, deep sound – everything that could be echoed – was being recorded vividly.

He turned his back. Behind the house, some pine trees, resembling the tails of wolves, stood drowsily in the gentle breeze. It carried their fragrance and tickled one's nose. If the breeze changed direction, this pleasant aroma would travel up to the sky, rising ever further upward, like a bull freed from its pen. The scent of sour pine resin would spread through the air bountifully, like a flock of ducks rushing from a green ravine. The smell would fill slumbering chests with abundance, as though the heavens were scattering pearls and raining dew. The inhabitants of the hot, stifling city delighted in the scent.

People in the street, wandering back and forth while breathing in this air, felt as if an unforgettable summer tune rejoiced in their hearts. The previous evening, the scent had been accompanied by a silver moon floating and exulting in the blues of heaven. The arrival of summer and the fresh scents from the woods cheered every dull and depressed soul. The heat had been intense; it was the end of July, and people were looking past the beginning of August and anticipating a brownish autumn. September, October and then unpleasant November would follow; people awaited them silently.

A door opened and a dog appeared at the threshold; then a little puppy ran past it, up to the gates. The massive, spotted crossbreed followed, attached to a lead and sporting a muzzle and a decorated collar that was made from thick leather and looked as though it had been cut into strips; it had a bright iron buckle. While the dog walked, the beaded knot of chains attached to the lead sparkled like a dagger edge reflecting sunlight.

The floppy-eared puppy with appealing eyes reached him, affectionate and innocent, barked several times and then sat down. Having broken the silence, the puppy barked again and again for a while without stopping. Then, agitated by his own uproar, the puppy howled and followed his peer. The other dog was as enormous as a calf.

He noticed a young man holding a bottle in a remote doorway. The man stopped, poured some cognac into a glass and gulped it down. He stared vacantly into the distance, as though looking for something, and waited like that for a while.

In autumn, the suicide rate in Almaty increases. The previous year, Fuad had crashed his car on the bridge. Witnesses said he was crossing the Sain Street Bridge at the intersection with Shalyapin Street, and smashed the edges of the bridge at such a fast speed that everything in his way collapsed from the impact. He was found stone dead. Ķamariâ had asphyxiated herself. Ãlišer burned all his manuscripts early one morning, and hanged himself before Marfuġa arrived. Delicate Múhtar tied his friend up so that the latter couldn't interfere, then shot himself in a stable in the Medeu Gorge.

He sat on the curb. The plodding boots approached him.

I am tired. Life seems like a one-way bus, and the passengers get off at stops along the way. I don't understand where they have disappeared to, or if they are still waiting at these bus stops – although I do know that the bus won't ever return to those stops. At this moment, I miss them. It is only I who misses them; others miss other people. This is the reason I must stay alive. Otherwise, who will miss them?

He looked at the innocent face.

Why hurry? We'll get off at one of these stops, together or separately; the stops are distant from each other, and do not follow any route. Destiny... the meaning of life... the aim of the life cycle, alas, is death. Yes, this is all God's will. Providence, yes. You know, my dear, that Polti suggests that there are only thirty-six stories in existence? Jorge Luis Borges, in his famous piece, 'The Four Cycles', reduces this figure to four. However, I think a couple of plots are enough to depict this bustling world. Unfortunately, any narrative arc depicting this world comprises two bases, just like infinity. The first is a positive story about God, declaring the existence of the Creator; the second, denying God's existence, suffers from its own assertion. The form changes, but the meaning remains the same.

Silence prevailed.

We build cities for the sake of our future: to live in them. However, they remain behind us, like cemeteries. Cities are unnatural environments. They are artificial, against Nature, a dead phenomenon. Cities are satellites that circle around the culture within a spiritual space. Cities are not genuine. They are never the originals. Houses in cities are the poor copies of primitive human shelters and cave dwellings. Poets celebrate them in vain; what they say in their verses is false praise, unworthy of fame. Above all, cities are the homes of insane desires, sheer greed and insatiable materialism.

The wind blew gently. The soft breeze refreshed his lungs, and he resumed his speech in a raspy voice:

I have two protruding temples. I wear armour as vast as a block of ice. When I walk, I walk as a sultan. I am as speedy as an arrow, a leader of men. When I speak, I do so in a masterly fashion, as an orator. When I seize, my reach is like a long lasso. I am a rock for my people as a buttress to a fort. I am the last judge, the heir to the throne. I am as strong as a mature camel's molar, chewing bushes. I am one among the wheatgrass, shaking the lake. I clear the sky, reveal the Sun on a grey day. I am the one who discerns between the faithful and the *kaffir*.[1] I am Sùjinišùly Ķaztuġan![2]

When he pronounced the name of Ķaztuġan, his voice rose.

I saddled the snow; hail, hail, hail, snow, solid underwater, icy on top, never melted under the Sun, never warmed at night. I was the leader of

---

[1] *Kaffir* – slur referring to non-Muslims, approximating 'infidel'.

[2] The quotation is from *Bùdyrajġan eki šekeli*, a *tolġau* (ode) by the fifteenth-century Kazakh *žyrau* (poet, warrior and councellor to the khans) Sùjinišùly Ķaztuġan. Translated by the National Bureau of Translations.

the vast army; I rushed toward my goal as powerful and relentless as the mighty wind that chills the ice itself.[3]

Then he stopped, and shouted:

I rushed, roaring, to the edge of the Sun![4]

He trembled, so loud was his voice.

Life begins with delight and ends in sorrow. No one lives forever. This mortal world betrays even the Ajmadet hero Dospambet[5] ... Oh, where are you, Rabiu-Sůltan-Begim, Žauḥar-Hanym, Ġajyp-Žamal-Sůltan-Begim, Toḳtar-Begim, Aḳ-ḳozy-Bike, Žaġan-Bike, Hoča-Patšajym, Žaġym-Hanym?[6] Shall I see you just once, Anar, Žanar, Gùlmira, Sắule, Bota, Ajnùr, Ăsem, Maržan, Šynar, Elmira, shall I see you once?[7]

He stepped forward and caught sight of a sharp-beaked sparrow. The humble bird was sitting on a low fence. It flew down quickly and pecked breadcrumbs, then sunflower seeds. Its energetic movements cheered him. Out of the blue, when he met its millet-shaped eye rings and cold stare, his body shivered. The objective lens of Red One filmed this tiny image of the hero in a medium long shot. All of a sudden, a wide-breasted pigeon appeared near the bird. The eyes watching the event switched their attention to this new subject. It was a long-tailed, white-feathered pigeon, like a character from a fairytale, with a turban-like crown and a big belly. The camera retreated and the pigeon was filmed in a full-length shot. The piece of glass, observing the tiny yard carefully, reflected the golden Sun shining from above.

A beautiful, swarthy woman came out of the house, wearing a silk scarf around her neck. She looked depressed, and gave off a feeling of grime and sadness, as though she had lost all hope. He dragged his boots and approached her, slowly at first, then picking up the pace. In a few seconds, he was facing her. She squatted down in front of him and took his hands, searching his pale face curiously, registering his fearful expression.

'Don't be afraid', she said, 'I'm out of sorts, too; I've no luck or happiness.'

Still afraid, he distanced himself from her. A smile played about his lips. 'OK', he said.

---

[3] From *Ajnala bùlaḳ basy teŋ*, a *tolġau* by the sixteenth-century *žyrau* Dospambet. Translated by the National Bureau of Translations.

[4] From *Ajnala bùlaḳ basy teŋ*.

[5] From *Ajnala bùlaḳ basy teŋ*; Dospambet was also a *batyr* (military commander) descending from the Ajmadet tribe.

[6] All these are names of historical figures – the wives and mothers of khans and sultans.

[7] All these are contemporary Kazakh female names.

The woman pulled him closer. He hesitated, not knowing what to say, and tried to remain still. She embraced him, and then kissed him. Now he watched her pretty smile silently. In an instant, he took in her bleak appearance, her big eyes full of tears, her dejected posture. She appeared to grow as cool and low-spirited as a hot iron after being unplugged. She looked miserable, desperate. He felt like weeping aloud. Then he hesitated and stepped back.

'When sorrow and grief invade one's life, existence darkens. The world turns to gloomy night – and a living thing becomes used to this sadness. Suffering develops into a habit. It turns out to be a casual thing; a soul will become addicted to this state.'

The strange and unfamiliar woman began sobbing. It was near evening, a period of uncertainty, a time of distress and anxiety. He felt frustrated and distressed, and stood there with a lump in his throat, his pride burning. He started to breathe fast and heavy, until he pulled himself together.

'Today, Niger fell off a cliff like a bird, and broke her ankle.'

He watched the surroundings with his dark, innocent eyes and then turned his gaze to her. Her large, beautiful eyes sparkled like fire. He smiled, and she did, too. Suddenly, a wooden window on the corner building opened, and a young man could be seen.

'Where are the *zeriza*?' he asked. 'The cherished ones?'

'The diamonds, pearls, agates, emeralds, gems, rubies, corals, amethysts.'

'What about the *bhatia*?'[8]

'The one in the box?'

'Yeah.'

'I don't know.'

'Goodbye, Niger-*Patšajym*.'[9]

'Firdausi, goodbye, don't forget me, remember me.'

'I shall remember you, Niger-*Sültan-Begim*.'[10]

The young man was weeping. The wooden window closed again. The woman approached the gates and opened the secondary door, then stepped out. Standing indoors, she said: 'You may not enter.'

Looking at the woman, now suddenly cheerful, he smiled warmly.

'Stay home', said Niger-*Patšajym*. 'Why should you travel far? Nothing can be found even in the unfamiliar places.'

The hinges slowly moved, and the iron gates closed quietly.

'Only cities have life. Go out into the streets, brave hero', said the woman, clacking her high heels along the street.

He took two steps and turned back. The lens adjusted its focus to different shots: close-up, medium close-up, medium long shot, full shot, long shot.

---

[8] *Zeriza, bhatia* – general terms for precious stones.

[9] *Patšajym* – 'queen'.

[10] *Sültan-Begim* – in the Middle Ages, a Turkic form of address to highly placed women.

The summer was at its height. The hot breath of the season had blown in from gates, pine trees and stones. It was spreading everywhere, pouring from fences, slipping from hedges. Summer was encroaching through doorways and peeking into windows. It ran out of houses like a child with pigtails flying, and went down the avenues and boulevards, soaring through the air like a bird. Heat radiated even from the breezes running through the flowers and plants, and from the tram rails. Summer could be discerned in the fading grass, and in the wooden cottages and tall buildings cracked with heat. It flooded the city with sand, made everyone's throats thirsty, and burned from the inside out.

Almaty would be startled one day, when the heavy rains swam in, appeasing its thirst and bringing cool air and silken rainbows. During the rainy season, the rivers of the city would wear away, carrying stones. As soon as the streams had been pacified, young people would turn over the stones, hoping to find something valuable underneath.

He saw the camera looking at him, and smiled. The sunny, warm days of July, the joyful presence of summer – a happy smile – entered through the lens and appeared in the square frame, depicted in a gorgeous close-up.

Suddenly, a woman's pleasant voice broke the peace between them: 'Kenesary! Nauryzbaj!'[11]

The sequence of shots stopped abruptly. Red One lingered on a child's happy smile.

Translated by Mitchell Albert

---

[11] Kenesary Ķasymŭly (Kasymov; 1802–47) – considered to be the last khan of the Kazakhs and the leader of the struggle for liberation from the Russian Empire; Nauryzbaj (1822–47) was his younger brother and supporter.

DAUREN QUAT
(b. 10.02.1973)

Dauren Quat is a writer and journalist. He is an alumnus of Ăl-Farabi Kazakh National University, where he studied journalism (grad. in 1997). He has worked for regional newspapers in Almaty and Aķtôbe, and for a number of national periodicals, including *Ķazaķ eli, Žas alas, Altyn orda, Žas ķazaķ* and *Ķazaķ ădebieti*, where he was a correspondent, editor, assistant editor and chief editor. Since 2009, he has served as president of the Abaj-Aķparat Public Foundation, and director of the web portal www.abai.kz; since 2018, he has been editor-in-chief of a major literary newspaper, *Ķazaķ ădebieti*.

Quat first started publishing short stories in 1995 and has attracted the attention of the literary community for describing modern issues in conjunction with ancient myths. His major collections of prose works, *Ălķissa* and *Bôri sokpaķ* (The Trace of the Wolf), came out in 2015 and 2018 respectively. A number of his short stories have received wide acclaim, such as 'Mùjiz taraķ' (The Comb Made of Bone), 'Tas monša' (The Stone Bathhouse), 'Begimajdyṇ žyry' (The Song of Begimaj), 'Šahmarannyṇ kitaby' (The Book of Šahmaran), 'Ķyzyl ăulie men Mùsa ġalajsalam' (The Holy Ķyzyr and Moses the Prophet), 'Mysyķ pen Marusya' (The Cat and Marusya). His works have been translated into Japanese, Turkish and Russian.

He was awarded the Makhmut Kashgari Literary Award for Writers of the Turkic World (2013) and Ġabit Mùsirepov Literary Award (2014). He holds state awards for Outstanding Achievements in the Informational Sector and 25 Years of Independence.

Pygmalion in the Backwoods

He was not awkwardly tall, but lanky, and seemed leaner, fitter than everyone else – probably because he was so thin. Friends joked: 'You're nothing but skin and bones!'

In the *auyl*[1] there were almost no girls. After graduating from school, the beauties with brown eyes did not hesitate to leave for the city. This was a sad state; otherwise, life in the *auyl* would be quite a lot more fun. Yet the inhabitants of the *auyl* were busy from early morning till late at night. People managed not only to cheer themselves up, but also to tend their farms. They were friendly; no one had any insidious thoughts.

Of course, they were not isolated from the rest of the world. They were quite well informed about politics, watched movies, read books. The herdsman and the shepherd had old, torn books. They lavished praise on poets and writers, and dreamed that some would one day come to the *auyl*. Once upon a time, in fact, the *auyl* had been visited by the famous poet Mùķaġali Maķataev. A photo taken with him in the middle of a large group could be found in every house. Glancing at that picture with hearts full of love, both the older and younger generations of the *auyl* would exclaim: 'Ah, the great Mùķaġali!' Whether influenced by the poet or because of the natural splendour surrounding the *auyl*, the inhabitants of Tùŝybùlaķ – 'Fresh Spring' – were delighted by everything beautiful. They were all skilful orators and demagogues, and could compose verses spontaneously.

Any poets or writers who remained under the impression that no one in the modern age reads any more should travel to this distant *auyl*, where their talents would be respected and praised. Probably they would be met by a trustworthy stringbean of a man named Ķareke.

'Wait', he would say, stopping the guest for a moment, 'let me take your photograph in order to preserve the memory.' Ķareke did not own a camera, but he posed his hands so artfully, as if he was indeed holding one, and clicked the 'camera' with one stroke: 'Don't worry, your photo will be ready tomorrow'. The following day he would bring your picture, which, in fact, would be a

---

[1] *Auyl* – socio-economic formation considered to constitute the heartland of the nation and a basis for an ethnic and cultural union of the nomadic community. Consisting of 50–70 yurts in the eighteenth century, it developed into its current permanent state of 'rural settlement' (of a minimum of 100 dwellers) when Kazakhs adopted a settled mode of life in the nineteenth and twentieth centuries. *Auyl* can also be used as a synonym for 'native land' and 'homeland', concepts revered by the Kazakhs.

pencil drawing and a perfect resemblance. 'Here you are', he would say. The residents of Tûŝybûlaķ were no longer surprised by this, but, being art lovers, they were always happy and satisfied. They respected and appreciated him.

'Ķareke, tomorrow my son goes to school. Take a picture of him, please, so that he can recall his childhood when he grows up.'

'Ķareke, man, we are celebrating our fortieth wedding anniversary with all our family and friends, but the city is so far, and all the walking wears us out: think up something yourself, we need a picture with our heads close together.'

'Ķareke, my friend, come to our home for Nauryz, the spring festival; our old drawings are out of date.'

Ķareke always had commissions awaiting him. He was always fielding requests; even the elderly people of the *auyl* would come to him and say: 'The government has asked us to update our passport photos.' He never denied or refused anything. 'Come, stand here in front of this white backdrop', he would reply, and then 'click'. The resulting 'photos', formatted in 4×5, 3×4 ravished passport department staff with delight. 'Why doesn't this talented guy leave the *auyl?*' they wondered, shaking their heads.

What can a man do? Ķareke could have travelled far from the *auyl*, but his old mother would not hear of it. 'You are my only child', she would wail, bursting into tears. 'What are you going to do in the city? Please stay.' So he bid farewell to his dream of becoming a famous artist. But his pencils were always in his pocket, along with the torn cover of a student notebook, or a box of candy, or white cloth, or something else. He was always ready to draw, to make a new picture at any point. Residents called the old *auyl* a 'farm', and Ķareke drew everything in it: a broken plough; a harrow lying under the sun; a workshop with a door that did not lock; a bathhouse with an old chimney; tall trees that rushed into the sky; a goose and a duck bustling on the shore of a lake; frolicking stallions; a withered bridge that barely reached the opposite shore; the curving main road; walls; a rider ascending a mountain; iron-roofed sheds. All were depicted in the 'photos' of Ķareke.

He recorded all the seasons, too. The previous winter, he had sketched and painted the thin snow that fell straight from the sky without wind, which was soft and fluffy beneath his feet, and the dull pace of life on the farm. From the Suyķsaj Gorge, a cold wind blew. Pedestrians went down the street, freezing. A calf shivered from the cold, as if trembling in apprehension, and pressed against the cow. Crows hovered in the air, frozen like black holes. The frost resulted in a landscape as striking as a work of art, in which the reddish rays of the Sun embraced the entire steppe. You could see the fine lights of Ùrker – the Pleiades – shining high in the sky. Ķareke drew such scenes. During that year's winter, he had drawn and painted the white snow, a foggy night in the *auyl*, the Milky Way dividing the stars between the north and the south. A wanderer covered in snow approached the *auyl* on horseback, water vapour expelled with his horse's every breath. Ķareke called his work *I Sing about January* and composed a poem, which he wrote below the picture:

The stars appear to keep secrets.
This world has frozen in the arms of a melody.
The moon shines over the sleeping *auyl*,
which is covered with a white blanket.

Other works depicted spring, summer and autumn, and were full of remarkable scenes native to the land, which Ķareke painted with all his love. He was a true master who could produce several shades from a single colour. For example, his painting *Spring Lake* revealed a wide range of blues: dark blue, black-blue, light blue, weak blue, sluggish blue, grey-blue, sparkling blue, deep blue, brown-blue, bluish... 'I used forty-seven blues here', said Ķareke. 'I was fighting time. If I had been able to ramble more, and enjoy the landscape, I would have found ten more shades.'

The residents of Tùŝybúlaķ looked with admiration at Ķareke's visual record of the tiny details of the *auyl* and the surrounding landscape, to which they did not normally pay much attention: 'Look at the broken plough!'... 'Look at the curved bridge!'... 'Look at the workshop!'... 'Is that last winter?'... 'This is spring – how true!'

Ķareke had other drawings and paintings, which he was too embarrassed to show his neighbours. He was a shy man, after all. When his friends talked about women, he would blush deeply; he was thirty years old, but unmarried.

'Hey, Ķareke, you've been alone for long enough, let's get you married', they would say. 'Let's go, Ķareke, we'll pick you a girl, you just get married and that's it.'

'If the girl does not mind, why not?' he replied.

'It's agreed, then, give us your hand. We'll find you a bride, and you'll get married this Friday.'

They all travelled to neighbouring *auyls*. They were introduced to beautiful girls and exceptional women who had not yet married; Ķareke met with them all under the supervision of his friends. But he could not find a common language with anyone. He could not communicate with them because, first, he did not know how to engage with a woman, and second, he used formal, overly literary words and phrases when he spoke. 'Indubitably', he would say. 'Weather permitting.' 'I beg your pardon.' 'What a pity.' 'What can a man do?' 'That's appropriate.' He was not trying to appear polite; in fact, it had been his habit since childhood to speak in such a manner, and when he was alone with a girl, he steeped himself in such language.

'Milady', he told one young woman, 'I shall not present any cause to trouble you. I am but an ordinary man, seeking a kindred soul.' Naturally, this was confusing for a girl who had never heard such poetic words.

'What are you saying? What are you looking for?'

Ķareke replied in simpler language: 'I need a life partner, to be a couple.'

'Where do you work?'

'We do everything possible. The early bird catches the worm, after all; we arise early in the morning, and set to work like ants.'

'Aġa,[2] you speak in such a strange way.'

'I always speak this way, my dear girl.'

'You say "my dear girl"?' The young woman covered her face and laughed loudly, then ran out of the room. She muttered in ear of the thunderous young man who had led Ķareke to her: 'He's a funny one – he talks like a grandfather. What's up with him? Is he a poet or a dreamer?'

Among the girls and his friends, drunk on fizzy wine, Ķareke wanted to sing, and one of his friends – who had not lost hope that Ķareke might yet seduce the runaway girl – asked him to do so. The drunken Ķareke became brazen. He began, at the top of his voice:

> You are not a girl, but red wine
> It is not proper for you to joke with me
> You broke your day promise at night
> I had to caress not you, but my bag[3]

On the way back to the *auyl*, his friend admonished him, laughing: 'You're too much, you! We went to the next *auyl* intentionally for the girls, and you sing "You're not a girl"! Don't you know any other songs? We are returning empty-handed!'

***

But Ķareke was not returning empty-handed; he seemed to be 'photographing' a girl who had spoken with him, and whom he would remember forever. Back home, in order not to wake his elderly mother, he tiptoed into his room and began to sketch this girl. The artist made a series of his most intimate paintings following the trips to the neighbouring *auyls*. He hesitated to show them to his peers – they portrayed the girl in half-clad poses, not quite nudes, but then the silhouette of a woman in silk garments would stir any man, troubling him and awakening his desire. In one picture, it was possible to notice a figure pressing the girl to his breast: indeed, it was Ķareke himself in the image. Sometimes the silhouette moved away, expressing the silent desire of a man for a woman, and an arrogant beauty who does not see a handsome man in love with her – or, if she sees him, pretends not to recognise him. After applying the finishing touches, Ķareke sighed: 'My dear, my ray of sunshine… become my wife.'

---

[2] *Aġa* – respectful form of address to an older man, which can be translated as 'brother', 'uncle'.

[3] From the song 'Ķyzyl asyķ' ('Red *Asyķ*') by a Kazakh composer, poet and singer Ůkili Ybyraj (1860–1930), translated by the National Bureau of Translations.

Ķareke often embraced the image of the girls he depicted and prayed. 'Let's go', he implored, 'do not stay lifeless; burn my flesh with hot breath and fill my world with light; come to me. Arise from the paper. Emerge, and light my candle!' The heartless girl stayed silent, but Ķareke's heart began to beat violently, as if he were stroking the girl's swan neck, her lips that craved kisses, her breasts that wanted affection, her slender waist, her arousing thighs... he experienced an unearthly pleasure.

One night, on TV, he saw a Kazakh girl wrapped in black. She was in a country called Syria, where people were fighting and firing at each other, and told of her cruel fate, choking back tears. The girl had been deceived by her friend into leaving her family and becoming a member of a religious community. The day she graduated from university as an English teacher, her friend introduced her to a group of strange men. Her acquaintance with one of the leaders of the group grew into an intimate relationship; the relationship developed into love, and marriage soon followed.

'Don't expect me to perform any of your wedding rituals. Our traditions are different, and we do not like ignorant people who deviate from God's way with their *haram* customs. Sheikh Omar in Saudi Arabia is pleased with our marriage. It means you are my wife now.' After convincing her of his love and her duties, he told her he had business abroad, and was leaving for a short while; then he disappeared. The girl was, by then, fully accepted as a member of the community. She abandoned all traces of her former life.

Her husband began to send text messages to her mobile phone. One message read: 'My brother will give you some money. Fly to Turkey. Come quickly. I have problems'. She left immediately, and once in Turkey she went to an address according to new instructions. When she arrived, the men there took the money and sent her away. They said: 'Your husband is in Syria – you will find him there.' Meanwhile, Syria had become a terrible battlefield on account of the civil war there. The wife still did not know where her husband was, and in attempting to find him, was brutalised every day by men. Now, telling all this on the broadcast, she wept bitterly and could not speak further.

Ķareke had just fed the cattle in the evening before watching the girl in black on television, and was stunned. 'What beautiful eyes, God!', he murmured. He was upset not by the girl's hard fate, but by the tears that fell from her deep brown eyes. Her outfit covered her completely – even her face. Only her eyes were visible, and they wept from agony. As usual, Ķareke wanted to take the girl out of her black outfit – but it did not work. She was compressed into it, and would not agree to leave it behind.

'I'll pull you out', said the painter. 'Dear girl, do not resist; come out and join my "maidens"...'

First, he drew the black apples of her eyes, dark like night, and then her eyebrows, which were arched in sadness. Next, he needed to draw the woman's face to fit her eyes. 'She probably has high, plump cheekbones', he thought, 'and a bright face.' Yes... but the chin was too elongated. The image turned her beauty into a cold, dispassionate soul. 'Perhaps it was better to draw her with a round face? No... that was a mistake. A round face does not fit the eyes; it spoils everything...'

It was better to consider the image of a woman who had endured terrible torture. She had slightly elongated cheekbones... she was emaciated. On her pale, creased face were the remnants of grief. Such a woman aroused pity in the heart of a person. She had suffered, but her beautiful eyes said: 'Do not sympathise with me, do not pity me, understand me and give me hope.'

He wanted to choose black eyes, dark dresses, black lace... but none of these worked. The black he wanted to match her black eyes with the dress and the lace, to search for inspiration in the colour black – but he was unsuccessful. Meanwhile, those brown eyes shed bitter tears. 'Ah, those eyes! What can I do with you?' said Ķareke. From that night onward, he would whisper continuously: 'Mesmerising eyes... beautiful eyes... contemptuous eyes...' He stopped caring for his old mother; the whole farm was left to God to care for. He dropped everything: even the hungry cattle in the shed scavenged for anything they could eat. He did not cut wood, fetch water, kindle the fire. His elderly mother went limping about and shared her alarm with her neighbours: 'I know my son has been cursed. Day and night, it is as though he is sleepwalking, talking about an "eye". My poor son is jinxed...'

The kind, cheerful and sincere residents of Tûŝybûlaķ were appalled by Ķareke's state. 'Oh, talented man!' they said. 'If God decides to mortify you, He will. It's all in His hands.' After a while, they resolved to do something. 'We need to treat Ķareke', they said, 'no two ways about it. If it continues, he will go crazy.' Yet, soon afterward, terrible gossip began to spread. 'Ķareke has gone mad', people whispered. 'His house is filled with horrible pictures of a woman in a black dress... a monster.... God forbid, if you look at them, you will be shocked.'

These words were not entirely untrue, however. Since seeing the girl in the black outfit with the brown eyes weeping bitter tears on television, Ķareke painted only with black paint. He painted dark night scenes, in which black eyes peered out at the viewer; black mountains, at the peaks of which dark eyes gazed at the heavens in prayer; dark forests, in which black eyes stared from the shadows; dark clouds pouring bitter tears of black eyes; dark eyes staring into a black mirror; dark water flowing, dark waves becoming smooth, black eyes; black dark eyes destroying black stones; a horse with the black eyes of a woman; birch leaves imbued with the magic of female eyes; scattered black-eyed apples near a black pot... an eye hanging on the wall, another near a window, the third on the door. A few eyes lying on the floor. Four or five eyes staring from the ceiling. Eyes, eyes, eyes... It was impossible to get through these eyes. Yet some of the *auyl* residents wished to behave honourably, and did not have the will to step on these 'eyes' of Ķareke's and crush them. They began to raise a ruckus, and decided to visit wise Aġymsaly *aķsaķal*,[4] who was over ninety. Aġymsaly ran his fingers through his white beard, which extended to his chest, and closed his large eyes. He said: 'The *baķsys*[5] of old are gone; were any of them alive, they would have found Ķareke themselves. But there is still one: Ķarakenej. If it is necessary, then call him.' Hearing the words of the *aķsaķal*, several young men left immediately to find Ķarakenej, who lived alone on the Šynžyrly River. Two days later, the *baķsy* arrived in Tûŝybûlaķ, amidst a swirl of rumours in the air:

'We could not find the baķsy, even after searching in Šynžyrly night and day; you won't believe it, but when we decided to return after giving up the search, he came out of a pit surrounded by a black stone. As God is my witness, he was all dry...'

'It is impossible to understand the healer. He was saying, all the way back to the *auyl* that he had swum to the bottom of the lake and seen a mermaid named Ûmme, that he was having fun. He said incomprehensible things. We told him about Ķareke, and he replied, "Stop blowing smoke, I know about him already"...'

'When we told him about Ķareke, that he draws eyes from morning till night, he poked his head out of the car window and began to caw like a crow. A crow then appeared, and accompanied us all the way into the *auyl*...'

The *baķsy* gave instructions to find a black sheep without spots.

'Is it even possible to find one?' the men wondered, and then joked: 'If we do not find one, then Ķareke will paint it black.'

The older people did not approve of such humour, though, and frowned: 'You laugh when someone's soul is in trouble, when it struggles with the Devil? Look for a black sheep, even in the neighbouring *auyls*!' In the end, a black sheep without spots was found, of all places, in Ķareke's own barn. The *auyl* residents were happy about this and considered it a good sign.

The *baķsy* instructed them to milk it and butcher it. Then he heated a tin can by the fire, poured in sheep's milk and covered the can with a blue handkerchief. Then he went into Ķareke's room while everyone waited outside in anticipation. Some time passed, during which the milk boiled and the healer gasped from within the smoke: 'Bring the sheep's liver! I'll heal him with it.' The *baķsy* grabbed the liver, went back into the room and began shouting.

Those who watched what was happening through a crack in the window said: 'It was terrible... Do not ask, it was a real nightmare. Ķarakenej took the

---

[4] *Aķsaķal* – traditionally, a well-respected and powerful elder in charge of the community. Nowadays, a reverential form of address to elderly men in general.

[5] *Baķsy* – shaman, a priest of Tengrism said to possess unique abilities (e.g. clairvoyance, healing powers, access to the spiritual world). *Baķsys* typically treated minor ailments with plant-based or other medicines and entered into trance states to heal more serious diseases. It is believed that they had *jinn* slaves helping them during divination and healing rituals.

liver and turned into a black camel before attacking Ķareke, who transformed into a black dragon...

'When the *baķsy* turned into a spear, Ķareke became a shield. When Ķarakenej prayed in the guise of a black cat, Ķareke became a black snake. The *baķsy* turned into a whip and began to flog the snake; Ķareke became a black club.

'But suddenly, Ķarakenej assumed the form of a girl in a black dress, and began to curl up before Ķareke, who stretched out his hand and collapsed. Then the healer became a crow and flew away.

'He could not cure Ķareke.'

After the healer vanished into to the sky, a great mullah appeared in Tûŝybùlaķ. 'He knows the Qur'an by heart – only he can heal Ķareke', said people in the troubled community. Although the mullah appeared to be an old man whose beard reached his waist, he was, in fact, a forty-year-old man who wore short pants. He was a little quick-tempered. When he was asked to read the Qur'an in the name of Ķareke's late relatives, he reacted fiercely: 'I came here not to heal sick corpses, but to a sick person.'

'You know best', replied the inhabitants of the *auyl*, who were worried about Ķareke. 'Do what you think is necessary.' The mullah pulled Ķareke out of the room; the poor man was still staring at the white paper. He was thin and pale, and had not shaven for ages. His eyes were barely visible; his cheekbones protruded; his nails had sprouted. He was already thin and tall, and now he was even thinner, so he seemed even taller.

The mullah enquired: 'Do you have a headache?' Ķareke shook his head.

The mullah said, 'He's in pain.' Then he read a sura from the Qur'an, intoning beautifully. Ķareke began to laugh at the people who had gathered.

'See, he's laughing', the mullah said. 'A demon has possessed him. I shall chant the *surah* for three days and three nights.' And so he did, and for three days and three nights the inhabitants of the *auyl* of Tûŝybùlaķ listened to the melodic voice of the mullah reading the extraordinary verses. At the end of that period, Ķareke revived: the mullah's ritual had re-energised him. But over the next three days, he painted a sad blue sky that seemed to descend on a pair of big, magical eyes gazing up in horror.

'Please forgive me, people', said the mullah, 'I have no more strength.' The holy man, who had appeared strong and ardent, now seemed timid. 'The demon is very strong. But it seems that I have weakened it. There is still hope. This sick man is madly in love with a woman in a *niqab*. In the name of God, if he marries a religious girl and chooses the right path, he will rid himself of this disease and become a normal person as before. Therefore, give Ķareke into our care. His place is in our community.'

'Mullah', said the compassionate residents of Tûŝybùlaķ, who would not dream of leaving their brothers in distress. 'Thank you very much for your kindness! But it is not necessary. Let Ķareke remain with us.'

'As you wish', said the mullah, secretly delighted to be rid of Ķareke, and departed. Ķareke's friends consulted with each other. The fellow whose idea it had been to drag the artist to neighbouring *auyls* in order to find a wife said: 'We need to get him married soon.' 'What should she be wearing?' asked one of the others.

'It does not matter what she is wearing! He needs a wife.'

'No – she must wear a *niqab*', said a third friend.

Thus the comrades went in search of a girl in a *niqab*. Unfortunately, however, none were found in the vicinity. There were many young women in the city who dressed in dark garments, but Ķareke's keen friends could not find a common language with any of them: not in terms of tradition, or views, or outlook on life. One prospect asked the young men a question about Ķareke: 'Is he on the right path?' These good citizens of Tüŝybúlaķ were thus put in an awkward position when they could not summon a reply.

Then, just when the men were feeling completely desperate, they found a girl who had been abandoned and grown up an orphan, without parental warmth. She had neither home nor family, and did not know where to go. She, too, asked about Ķareke – and gave her consent. She also agreed to wear a *niqab*, and believed the men's promises that Ķareke would treat her with the greatest respect.

The friends immediately sent word to the *auyl*: 'Great news, people, great news! The girl in black is on her way to our *auyl*; Ķareke saw her on TV! The beautiful girl Ķareke has fallen in love with is coming!' Ķareke was exhilarated, and his old mother was ecstatic. The elderly woman was preparing for the arrival. She opened an old trunk containing everything she had kept for years and pulled out all its contents, distributing gifts to everyone who came to her home.

When the bride-seekers returned with the girl, the elderly people were all chattering away happily, recalling many things, and Ķareke embraced the young men, saying, 'Oh, my friends, the sky's the limit for all of you.' But his joy was replaced instantly by sadness when he saw the beautiful woman from the city in her black garb. Ķareke's face fell, and he said: 'It's not her! The girl you brought is not the one I saw...'

'No, it's her', said one of his friends. 'Open your eyes and look carefully!... Do you not see her black eyes? Are you blind?' As he said this, he removed the dark lace veil that covered the face of the girl. She looked shyly at Ķareke.

***

One month passed; then years. The clouds flew over the highest peaks of the Dzungarian Alatau. Rural life was restored. Nothing had changed – only Ķareke was different. Yes, he had ceased talking about the 'eyes'. But he had become sad and withdrawn, and always gazed at the horizon. His friends no longer sought his company; nor was he asked to draw 'photos' anymore. In his presence, the inhabitants of the *auyl* could not talk about *that* picture. They were afraid that his peculiar sickness would arise again.

A rumour began circulating that Ķareke was spending nights in the region of Tamšybùlaķ, which was located near Tùŝybùlaķ. Ķareke later confirmed that he had found what he was looking for there, and disappeared. No one knew where he had gone. His poor mother grieved: 'I have had such trouble late in life. I do not know if it was caused by a demon, but it's been more than a week, more than a month, even, since I have not seen my child. I'm still waiting... Good people, help me. Find at least the bones of my son.'

The unhappiness had fallen on Tùŝybùlaķ. Everyone was afraid for Ķareke, and the residents began sending people out to search for him. They found him quickly, on the outskirts of Tamšybùlaķ.

Tamšybùlaķ was one of God's miracles. It was a huge, rocky cliff that formed part of the Sarytau Mountains. Drops of rock seemed to flow from it, which looked like tears – and these double drops, Lord, looked like beautiful eyes, transparent and magical. The *auyl* residents who witnessed this miracle began to drink and enjoy the waters of Tamšybùlaķ.

***

August was coming to an end, and autumn was near *auyl*. After the story of Ķareke's 'eye' had spread to all the *auyls* and even to distant cities, a young English teacher named Gùltùnyķ came to work at a school in Tùŝybùlaķ...

It was evening in Almaty. In a noisy restaurant, some of the young men of Tùŝybùlaķ gathered around the writer, and after exchanging news about the inhabitants of the *auyl* and discussing other general matters, conversation turned to the 'eyes' of Tamšybùlaķ.

'How is Ķareke?' asked the elderly writer. 'Did he calm down?'

'Oh, Ķareke is excellent', one of the friends said. 'He is a very reliable guy. He works hard to support his children, and is a wonderful family man.'

'He's married? Did he marry the girl you brought him?'

'No, *aġa*. That black-eyed girl's name is Gùlbarŝyn. She's like a sister to Ķareke. You know that he is a heartfelt man; he took care of the orphan, and bestowed her in marriage to another man, after seeing to her every need. And then... he met his beloved, whom he had first seen on TV.'

'She has such a wonderful name', said another of the chatty young man of Tùŝybùlaķ, following up the conversation. 'Gùltùnyķ – "translucent flower". She's a girl who has had some hard luck, but she has come a long way. Despite her experience of a difficult life, she managed to find happiness. And in our *auyl*! And on the farm!

'When Ķareke met Gùltùnyķ, he took her to Tamšybùlaķ, showed her that eye of rock and said: 'This is your eye.' They liked each other, and made a mutual promise never to leave Tamšybùlaķ again. She is now Ķareke's wife and lovely mother of two children. She is a dutiful daughter-in-law who shows great respect to the old woman, and has made her happy.

The writer, listening to these delightful words, smiled kindly. 'Ah, Pygmalion', he said. 'The goddess of love, Aphrodite, took pity on our Pygmalion.'

Translated by Mitchell Albert

YURIY SEREBRYANSKY
(b. 5.08.1975)

Yuriy Serebryansky is a writer and poet. He graduated from Äl-Farabi Kazakh National University in 1997 with a degree in chemistry and ecology. He has worked for the Ministry for Environmental Protection of the Republic of Kazakhstan as well as for the United Nations Development Programme in the field of environmental legislation. Subsequently, he devoted himself to journalism and business. Since 2012, he has been editor-in-chief of *Almatynski Kurier Polonijny*, a journal of the Polish diaspora in Kazakhstan. He lectures at the Open Society School of Literature in Almaty (from 2010) and is editor-in-chief at *Esquire Kazakhstan* (from 2016). He is currently pursuing a degree in cultural studies at the University of Warmia and Mazury in Poland, where he works on his thesis, 'Intercultural connections in Europe'.

He is the author of five volumes of prose and poetry: *Moy Caravaggio* (My Caravaggio, 2006), *Rukopis' naidennaya v zatylke* (The Manuscript Found at the Back of My Head, 2010), *Destination: dorozhnaya pastoral'* (Destination: A Road Pastoral, 2011) and *Kazakhstanskie skazki* (Kazakhstani Fairy Tales, 2017). His book *Altynšaš* (Golden Hair, 2018), written in two parts, fictional and non-fictional, presents the perspective of the Polish diaspora in Kazakhstan, reflecting on the subjects of home, motherland, the steppe and memory. His prose has been translated into Kazakh, Polish and English, and he himself has translated selected poems by Małgorzata Lebda and Gunnar Ekelöf into Russian.

Serebryansky is a two-time winner of the Russian Award for best short prose for his novels *Destination: dorozhnaya pastoral'* (2010) and *Prazhaki* (2014). *Kazakhstanskie skazki* won an award at the 2017 Silk Roads Book Fair and he is also the recipient of the Kazakhstani PEN Club medal (2018).

Riding a Tortoise

To Sergey Kalmykov, an extraordinary artist and a legend of Almaty.

I wanted, perhaps I even *really* wanted, that this story had taken place in August. That's because August is nicer and my birthday falls in August. That's because my birthday always came during the holidays and there was never anyone around. Everyone would always have gone away. But I will talk about the end of March. That's because, at the end of March, I was walking along the pavement toward the Green Bazaar. I walked from tree to tree along the avenue, which was still without its crown of green and with buds barely blossoming, but it seemed that the shadows from the treetops were already covering not only the pavement and part of the asphalt on the road, but the single-storey, carved wooden houses as well.

Of course, they were puddles, not shadows. Puddles that remained after the rain that had eaten up the traces of snow on the grass. I avoided the puddles like a ship, manoeuvring between rocks, only the other way around. I was manoeuvring between seas. My shoes might not have made it to their final destination, if they had become full with water. At least that's how I wanted to imagine it. I am a traveller and my supply of shoes is limited to this trusted pair of mine, although they are rather worn through. I have walked many countries in them, you see. Well, it is as though I have walked those countries in them.

There were very few cars, but the road had been built to take more. That is what I thought about when I stopped to look. Or, more accurately, when I stopped to see.

Coming along the road in the opposite direction to mine rode a man atop an enormous tortoise with a half-round shell. It would have been one thing if it had been any person, for otherwise the tortoise would have been the sole focus of attention, but, as it was, barely anyone even looked in its direction. True, it was pacing its way in a painstaking fashion. Like in a parade of some kind. What is more, before making a step, it brought up its front foot as if making a salute. Placing its foot on the asphalt surface, it froze for a second before lifting the other foot. On the tortoise's back sat a serious-looking man in a beret, with a long nose and a jacket with no sleeves. His trousers were not wide, rather they

610

incredibly flared at the bottom. He looked like a grown-up Buratino,[1] whom Tortilla the Tortoise had for some reason decided to take for a ride.

They moved along at a slow pace. Passers-by, stopping for a minute, continued on their way. What did they think? Probably that a tortoise from the zoo was being taken for a walk. Nothing out of the ordinary in that. It was not a lion, after all.

A car travelled behind them, but did not sound its horn. It carefully overtook the tortoise and only then did it accelerate away. The tortoise couldn't care less. It seemed that it was the tortoise making its way somewhere and that the man up top was simply sitting there and enjoying the ride.

I don't know why, but I stayed where I was. Not only did I stay where I was, but I asked a question. On strange occasions in my life there is something inside that makes me twitch and scratch. My shoulder starts to itch as well. I scratch it and that makes the other shoulder itch too, but then I carry on doing what I am doing. And so, I asked my question.

'Where is it you're going?' I didn't even recognise my own voice. The thing is that it grows faster than I do and there are times I don't recognise myself at first.

'How am I to know? I am riding on a wise old tortoise and it sure knows where it's going. However, either it's a secret or it simply doesn't know how to speak', said the man in the beret with a laugh.

'I see', I said. 'It's a nice tortoise you've got there', I said in the same way someone would say 'That's a nice briefcase you've got there' or 'That's a nice raincoat you've got there'. That was probably why the man in the beret became unexpectedly indignant. 'It's not my tortoise', he flared. 'It's just a tortoise, that's all! And perhaps I am its man!'

'What do you mean?'

'The tortoise invited me to take a ride and I am its guest! So here I am admiring the sights of the city.'

I followed them with short, side steps, taking care to avoid the puddles. Although the tortoise was slow, it had travelled two metres over the course of our conversation, all the while paying me not the slightest attention.

'So how did you learn you were its guest and that it was actually inviting you anywhere?'

The man even half turned towards me, to take part in the conversation more noticeably. He spoke with me as if with an adult which, to be honest, I found rather strange. Only very seldom did people speak with me in this way.

'You probably take me to be an alien. And I can understand that, me being up on a tortoise. Yes. But it's one thing when I am riding on it; it would be quite another if it were walking on its own. Just think about it: would it manage to

---

[1] Buratino – Russian equivalent of Pinocchio, main character of the book *The Golden Key, or the Adventures of Buratino* (1936) by Alexei Tolstoy , based on *The Adventures of Pinocchio* (1883) by Carlo Collodi.

stroll about here on its own? Right here, in the centre of the city and in the height of spring!'

'I think they would take it to the zoo and this would require a large car of some kind', I said.

At that, the man in the beret jumped down from the tortoise, nimbly managing not to get caught in his flared trousers, and stood next to me. What a rotten to-do it was. It turned out that I was only waist-height to the man. However, he paid this no attention whatsoever.

'You see, young man, I am not an alien.'

'But I didn't say you were one, that you were an alien.' He emitted a smell of paint.

'So, who are you?'

We walked along, keeping the tortoise in the corner of our eyes; the creature, it appeared, had not noticed that its passenger had jumped off.

'Please address me using the *tu* form; I am a child, after all. Although I am comfortable with familiarity, I like it when you talk with me as if with an adult.'

'Wow! You know the meaning of the word *familiarity*! I have met an alien child! Peeeeople!' He stretched this last word out so loudly that, if he had not followed this up with fervent laughter, the passers-by would have started asking questions.

'I am a pupil at an Almaty school. I am no A-grade student, mind, just the average.' Suddenly I thought that this man was some sorcerer and that he could help me with my mathematics.

'So, in which subjects are you not an A-grade student, my friend?'

I didn't manage to answer in which, as a policeman's whistle rang out. The tortoise was approaching the crossroads without giving any signals. Naturally, it had no registration plates, either. And so, the policeman had become alarmed at it all.

'It's alright, officer, the tortoise is with us!'

The policeman caught sight of us, looked over the beret, the trousers, my Little Oktyabrists badge and nodded. We crossed the road and watched the tortoise turn to the left. Then we crossed the road again, the same road along which we had been walking, and stood waiting for it under a tree. The tortoise, however, decided not to continue along the road, but walked directly towards us. We turned around. There was a rather big park behind us, with benches and last year's green grass. That was where the tortoise was heading. When it had crossed the pavement, its eyes directed straight ahead, my companion made a gesture to two passers-by, requesting that they let the tortoise through. They let it through without the need for gestures. The two passers-by were a man and a woman, walking arm in arm. They were also out for a stroll. It was a Sunday, a day off.

Once in the middle of the park, the tortoise looked around and set about plucking at the grass.

Then we sat on a bench so that the creature was behind us. We were already we, meaning it was as if we had already made friends.

My companion probably couldn't recall where our conversation had been broken off, and he said:

'I am an artist. I work in the theatre.'

'Are you joking? What is there for an artist to do in the theatre? Do you paint portraits of the actors?' I imagined a line of artists on a staircase, pompously waiting all day for their turn to get their portrait done.

'I dress the stage. Each performance needs its own stage, you see. Decorations, the backdrop and the like.'

'So, you have your own theatre, you have a beret and an enormous tortoise. That reminds me of a story.' For some reason, I reckoned he would not take offence if I made a little joke.

'The tale of Buratino?' he said, and burst out laughing. 'It's not my theatre; I just work there, so that would make me Papa Carlo. I have a lot of work to do there.'

'But do artists actually work? Painting pictures is a sheer pleasure! People like builders do work.'

'If that is the case, what does the theatre pay me money for, do you think?'

I turned to look at the tortoise, because I needed to think for a minute and, at that moment, a strong gust of wind blew last year's leaves and dust from under the bench, sprinkling our trousers, the dust getting in our eyes and nose. Shaking ourselves down, we saw the tortoise leaving the park from the other side. We walked the pavement around the park at a smart pace. An average-sized dog growled at the tortoise, while its mistress tried to pull it back onto the avenue by the lead.

The tortoise made its way along the road and we followed.

My companion told me much about the pictures and the decoration he prepared for the theatre. He told me that when an artist gets an idea for a picture, the inside of his skull starts to itch! He even showed me this in a very amusing way. He portrayed it, you could say. He dropped his beret.

'Perhaps you're tired and you'd prefer to climb back up on the tortoise; I can walk along by the side like before. I am not tired.'

'But we have already arrived', he said. 'Here's the zoo.'

A tram, turning around on its circle, rang out amicably to the tortoise. The creature stepped slowly over each of the rails, with great dignity and considerable concentration.

As we had agreed, I waited by the gates while my companion handed the tortoise over to the zoo staff.

What wonderful gates they were! Quite magical, in fact. The gates of a castle of some kind. They were white, shaped like an arch, with thick walls and sturdy railings. Only it was not a castle beyond the gates, but a tall stairway, leading up to the zoo. The tortoise would have found it very hard to get up there but when I had been to the zoo, I would rush up, running ahead of my parents.

I thought he would take me in, but he only came out to say goodbye.

'You know where the tram stop is, don't you?'

'Of course, I do! I've been here a hundred times!'

'Well then, off you go. It's evening already', he said, walking back through the white gates.

'When will you be out walking with the tortoise next time?' I really wanted to talk with this artist some more, that's why I asked.

'The doctors say I have to check into the hospital and remain there until the end of April, but in May the tortoise will want to go out for a walk again, to see the leaves blossoming and, well, not only to see them', he laughed. 'In May then! On Sunday!'

I was riding the tram with my face pressed up against the glass as I always did. If you blow on the glass, the vapour forms an opaque cloud, which you can draw on. Of course, you already knew that. I love drawing on windows. I tried to design a pattern of some kind but what appeared was the gates of a castle zoo, in which I tried to draw a man in a beret. Generally speaking, I'm not very good at drawing people.

In front of the gates, I drew a large tortoise and myself riding on top.

Translated by Simon Hollingsworth, edited by Simon Geoghegan

The short story is from the collection *Kazakhstanskie skazki* by publishing house Aruna.